LEGEND

of the

CELTIC
STONE

MICHAEL PHILLIPS

CALEDONIA

LEGEND *of the* CELTIC STONE

BETHANY HOUSE PUBLISHERS
MINNEAPOLIS, MINNESOTA 55438

Published by Bethany House Publishers
A Ministry of Bethany Fellowship International
11400 Hampshire Avenue South
Minneapolis, Minnesota 55438
www.bethanyhouse.com

Printed in the United States of America by
Bethany Press International, Minneapolis, Minnesota 55438

Library of Congress Cataloging-in-Publication Data

Phillips, Michael R., 1946–
    Legend of the Celtic stone / by Michael R. Phillips.
        p. cm. – (Caledonia ; 1)
    Includes bibliographical references (p.).
    ISBN 0–7642–2250–3
    ISBN 0–7642–2217–1 (pbk.)
        I. Title. II. Series; Phillips, Michael R., 1946– . Caledonia ; 1.
PS3566.H492   L44   1999
813'.54—dc21

99–6432
CIP

CONTENTS

※ ※ ※

MAPS · CHARTS
ILLUSTRATIONS
DRAWINGS

※   ※   ※

A C K N O W L E D G M E N T S

※ ※ ※

No novelist can write of historical events without great reliance on others—historians mainly—from whom he gleans a multitude of perspectives that find their way into the text. A more thorough acknowledgment of my research sources is included in the Notes and Bibliography at the end of this book.

I commend that appendix to you. I have certainly not written this book in a vacuum, and I would like to recognize those many authors whose works have been helpful to me.

Here I will only comment that this manuscript has been submitted to friends and scholars more knowledgeable than I in certain of the historical eras in which this book is set. I can attest that there are no intentional inaccuracies. I am enough of an historical legalist to spare no reasonable effort to get details precise where it is possible to do so. At the same time, I am as much storyteller as historian. As such I constantly find myself sniffing out intriguing themes and *may-have-beens* and *what-ifs* to which the evidence lends itself, but which the known facts do not positively reveal.

A novelist necessarily offers *interpretive* viewpoints as a result of his storytelling instincts, and it cannot be helped that there are historians who disagree with some of them. Where perhaps greater scholastic expertise reveals errors in the text that follows, I hope those men and women whose erudite authority exceeds mine will forgive whatever unintentional indiscretions I may commit.

The following individuals have been very helpful in various capacities: Bill and Eve Murison (Scots dialect, geography), Donnie Macdonald (Gaelic), Helen Macpherson (fueling the fires), Archie Duncan (history), Joan Grytness (interior maps), Nigel Halliday (Irish issues and for the added richness of his company at Iona, Glencoe, and Edinburgh), Arthur Eedle (British politics and names), Rick Christian (fanning the visionary flames of what *Caledonia* could become), Stephen and Hilary Anderson (for provision of an oasis of hospitality, including an impromptu day in London, and for proofreading), Judith Pella (brainstorming), and Mary Hutchison, Anne

7

Buchanan, and Helen Motter (editorial guidance).

I especially want to thank my father, Denver Phillips, who has now gone to be with the Lord but whose handwritten notes on earlier manuscripts continue as fond reminders of his involvement in the development of *Caledonia*. Thanks also to my mother, Eloise Phillips, for proofreading an earlier draft of the manuscript, to my sons Patrick, Robin, and Gregory, and of course to my wife, Judy, for ten years of encouragement as the vision of *Caledonia* gradually took shape and ultimately became reality.

I would also acknowledge Gary and Carol Johnson, Jeanne Mikkelson, David Horton, Julie Klassen, and others at Bethany House Publishers whose vision for this project has burned, if not *quite* so brightly as mine, certainly in some cases nearly as long, and whose ideas and hard work have been valuable in bringing this ten-year labor, with all its ups and downs, into fruition. Hundreds of thousands of lovers of George MacDonald are deeply indebted to Bethany for its commitment to keeping alive the works of this significant Scottish writer of the last century. Now Bethany adds this epic story of *Caledonia* to its expanding selection of titles about Scotland, for which those interested in Scotland the world over will, I am sure, be profoundly grateful.

Last but foremost, I would use this forum to acknowledge a man whose influence upon me as a writer has been foundational and profound, a name that will be familiar to nearly all who read my words: James A. Michener, the great American novelist and historian, who died in 1997. As George MacDonald has served as my spiritual mentor, James Michener has occupied something of that same capacity in matters historical. Both men have served as literary mentors throughout the years of my own writing. Whenever I write, whatever I write, their styles and perspectives are ever before me.

I have admired Mr. Michener's work now for about half my life and consider him the master at communicating that wonderful, delicate, invisible balance so necessary to turn history into fiction. He has been captivating, educating, and entertaining a vast audience for years in what I can only describe as a wonderfully peculiar art form all his own, masterfully interweaving events and lives from widely varying time periods and multiple story lines—both factual and imaginary—into grand tapestries of vivid color and panoramic scope. I thus acknowledge my debt and thank him posthumously for his contribution to my vision for this effort.

For all these reasons, then, and on behalf of millions of appreciative readers around the globe, I offer not only these brief words, but also the dedication of this present volume.

8

To
the memory of

JAMES A. MICHENER

Master of the
Historical Novel

INTRODUCTION

※ ※ ※

ALL SCOTS TOGETHER

Any book may be enjoyed on a variety of levels. *Caledonia* will be picked up for as many distinctive reasons as there are those now reading these words.

You of Celtic blood will naturally be motivated by love of nation and pride in your ancestry.

Affection for that wild, infinitely diverse, and captivating region north of the Solway and Tweed, however, is by no means limited to those of known Scots extraction. Scotland is a domain of our earth that cannot be visited, the Scots are a people that cannot be known, theirs is a heritage that cannot be discovered without a change occurring inside . . . something mystical, a pinprick into the soul—or it may be the piercing of a razor-tip point of the Highland knife called a *sgian-dubh*—imparting a mysterious sense that a little piece of this place is *yours* too.

Others, perhaps even without Scots blood coursing through their veins and who have not yet been lured into the northern reaches by the magical Caledonian soul-prick, find themselves caught up in Scotland's story for the history it so unforgettably brings to life. It is an ancient and stirring tale full of intrigue, romance, drama, and adventure, whether or not one possesses personal connections to a certain date or place or family name within it.

Noted Scottish author Nigel Tranter writes,

> The Scottish people have always been independent, individualistic . . . and . . . their land is sufficiently dramatic in itself . . . their long and colourful story is bound to be full, over-full, of incident and echoes of that stormy and controversial past. There is scarcely a yard of the country without its story to tell, of heroism and treachery, of warfare or worship, of flourish or folly or heartbreak—for the Scots never did anything by half. This, the most ancient kingdom in Christendom, has more castles, abbeys, battlefields, graveyards, monuments, stone-circles, in-

11

scribed stones and relics of every kind . . . than any other land of its size, in Highlands and Lowlands, mainland and islands.

The ancient land of Caledonia, later known as Scotia and Alba, eventually Scotland, possesses one of the most vivid histories the people who inhabit this globe have ever played out upon it. For Scots the world over, this legacy is no mere bookish chronicle, but rather forms an intrinsic element of who they are. To be a Scot is to possess historically traceable roots that extend backward in time beyond the birth of Christ, back to the very earliest eras when the human creature began to know itself and explore the earth. The heritage of the people who, through the millennia, occupied this particular northern corner of Britain is the legacy, as it were, of a universal tree of the family of man upon the earth. "Remember the men from whence you came" is no mere stale truism, but the very lifeblood by which the Celt lives and breathes.

Scotland's is a story that beckons—of itself—to be told. I approach it not only as a historian and a storyteller here, but almost as a journalist, reporting with marvel the tale I have observed, of a land and its people. As we shall see, it is an ongoing drama whose climax may yet await us!

A passionate love for history—almost *any* history—burns within this heart of mine. The people and events of former times hold a fascination that draws me more powerfully than most of what our modern age has to offer. I happen to believe, as well, in the *significance* of history, that its tales and legends, its facts as well as its myths, are important. They contain lessons and insights and perspectives that can expand our awareness, deepen our knowledge and wisdom of our world, and thus enrich our lives in many diverse ways.

And of pure history—none comes more magnificent than Scotland's!

There will be those who have read one or more of my former books who delve into this chronicle for deeper themes and content than those I have mentioned. I hope you will relish your journey through ancient Caledonia none the less that some of what you may anticipate comes in the more obscure form of historical allegory than you have encountered from my pen upon previous occasions.

There are certain Biblical parallels you may observe as you follow the epic of Scotland through the years. I am certain you will recognize the Caledonian version of Abraham, who went to a land far away to give birth to a nation through his son . . . of Isaac and Ishmael and ongoing strife and treachery between kinsmen . . . of the tribes which gave their names to the various regions of that land . . . of Joshua who crossed the river to do battle and drive out his enemies . . . of Rahab the prostitute, who came into the family of faith and through whom the lineage of promise continued . . . of the aging priest Zechariah, long silent about what had been revealed to him, convinced it would come through the child he had beheld at birth . . . and of course many will know Caledonia's Judas who brought down infamy upon the heads of himself and his clan, as well as see the gospel story in the coming of Columba, the dove.

Whatever additional symbolic parallels may be present, reminiscent of the scriptural narrative, I shall leave for you to discover. The biblical account is, after all, the universal story of the human saga, of all peoples and all lands. Therefore, I hope you enjoy the "parable" of *Caledonia: Legend of the Celtic Stone* for some of its latent spiritual subtleties as well as for its story and history.

I pray, then—however our paths have happened to cross at this moment, and for whatever reasons you personally have chosen to walk these byways of the past with me—that you will be stimulated by our literary and historical adventure together. To all of you I say: *enjoy* the journey . . . and let Caledonia's magnificent history carry you along on its majestic crest.

Let me add the challenge: Be in no hurry to get from the beginning to the end. This is a *long* book. Relish that fact. To help you in that regard, let me quote from Mr. Michener's autobiography, *The World Is My Home, A Memoir*. His thoughts and priorities mirror my own:

> Sometime in the late 1950s an idea struck me . . . and I have been willing to gamble my professional life upon it.
>
> I discovered that television existed within a cruel time constraint . . . the typical hour program was allowed only forty-eight minutes. . . . One evening after I had been well indoctrinated into the mystery and magic of the tube, I had a vision as clear as if the words . . . had been written on the wall: "When people tire of the forty-eight minute television novel, they will yearn for a substantial book within whose covers they can live imaginatively for weeks. The eighteenth-century discursive-type novel will enjoy a vigorous rebirth, because readers will demand it."

This same sense has grown upon me since I began writing, which no doubt explains why my books have become steadily longer through the years. I am delighted now to find myself in such good company in sharing that view.

I hope, therefore, that this first book in the series, *Caledonia: Legend of the Celtic Stone*, as well as the subsequent volumes which continue Caledonia's story, will be ones that you will enjoy "living in" for weeks. Scotland's history is a full course meal—feed upon it as such!

When Scotland's magic begins to weave its spell, you will likely discover that it has infected you with the sense that there may be Scots blood in your *own* veins—or at least that this pilgrimage in search of heritage and roots is one every one of us shares. This, therefore, is *your* quest as well . . . because in a sense, wherever you call home, Scotland is your land as well.

Truly the account of Caledonia *is* every man's and every woman's story . . . for in a mysterious and magical sense—and perhaps more in fact than we are aware—*we are all Scots together.*

—Michael Phillips

CALEDONIA

LEGEND OF THE CELTIC STONE...

In the year 843, Kenneth MacAlpin was crowned king of the Scots and Picts at the small Scottish town of Scone*, uniting for the first time in history the Alban kingdom known thereafter as Scotland. For the ceremony of his coronation, from Dunstaffnage in Argyll, MacAlpin brought the sacred stone of destiny. This stone, upon which centuries of Irish kings were said to have been crowned, was also said to have been transported from Tara in Ireland centuries before by Fergus Mor mac Erc when the Dalriadic dynasty was established on the British mainland.

Upon it MacAlpin took his seat for coronation. Upon it would the kings of Scotland be crowned until the fateful year 1296, when Edward I of England captured the Stone. Edward installed it in Westminster Abbey, beneath a specially constructed chair where England's own monarchs would henceforth be crowned. And there, with only two brief absences, the venerated Stone of Scone, symbol of Scotland's royal links with antiquity, sat, used only for coronations, until 1996. Then, on the seven hundredth anniversary of Edward's theft, the Stone was returned to Edinburgh Castle, there to remain except as required in Westminster Abbey for the coronation of future British monarchs.

This is the story of the origin, and what may well be the destiny, of that historic Celtic stone—hewn not in Ireland as formerly conjectured . . . but in the solitary Highlands of that ancient land known as Caledonia.

---

*Pronounced "skoon," as in "moon."

Cuimhnich có leis a tha thu.

Remember the men from whence you came.

—OLD GAELIC PROVERB

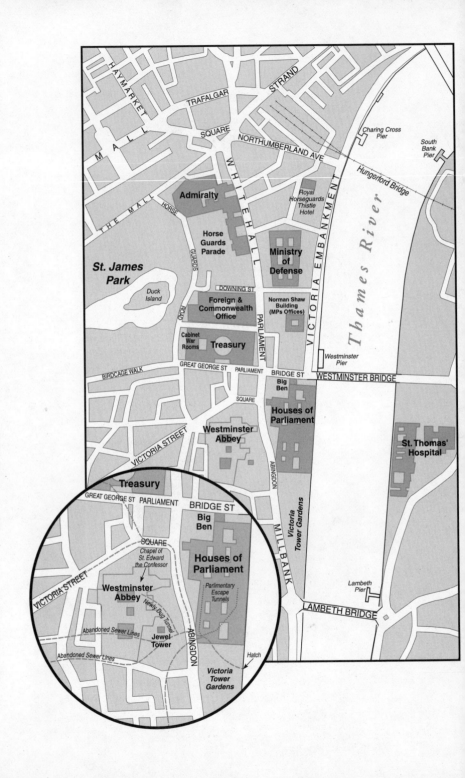

PROLOGUE

This is Kirkham Luddington reporting live from outside Buckingham Palace. . . ."

The well-known BBC journalist had been bringing news to the nation for more than twenty years. But never in his career had he reported a story this huge.

Networks from around the world were scrambling to get to this very spot. Within twelve hours the Mall and both parks would be choked with television crews. Right now, however, the stage was his. As first on the scene, Luddington knew well enough that millions, if not billions, of eyes at this moment were resting on him.

"All the United Kingdom," he went on, "indeed, the entire world, is reeling from the stunning announcement, released by the Palace just one hour ago, that Her Majesty Queen Elizabeth II will abdicate the throne one month from today in favor of her son, His Royal Highness, Charles, Prince of Wales. The Queen issued the following statement, which was included with the press release. I quote: *'It has been my privilege to enjoy a long and fulfilling reign in the service of the British people. However, at this pivotal time in our history, I feel our nation can best be served with leadership provided by fresh blood from the next generation. My son, the Prince of Wales, has served a loyal and dedicated apprenticeship for the role to which history has destined him. The time has come that he be given opportunity to step into that calling. I ask that the support and prayers of every citizen be accorded him as they have me. I thank you each one, my loyal subjects and also my friends and fellow countrymen and women, for the love and support you have shown during my fifty years as your Queen. God bless you all.'"*

Luddington paused to allow the incredible words to sink in. Even outside the Palace in the midst of traffic it was nearly silent.

After a moment the reporter continued. "We will update you with more details as they become available," he said. "Speculation has already begun concerning possible underlying causes for this startling and unexpected development beyond those expressed in the Queen's statement, ranging from health problems to the continuing decline of the royal house of Windsor and the monarchy in general. 'It is possible,' a highly placed Palace official noted to this reporter just minutes after the announcement, 'that the Queen does not want to go down in history as the kingdom's final monarch. What she may be handing Charles,' he went on, 'is not the future of the crown, but its final gasping expiration.'

"A statement from the office of the Prince of Wales is expected later in the day. At this point he has not responded publicly to the Queen's announcement.

"No dates have yet been put forward for the coronation. Early reports indicate that the Palace will likely push plans forward as quickly as possible in order to have the ceremony take place prior to next year's elections. . . .''

1

THE STONE

A thatched stone cottage set between the slopes of two rugged mountains in the Highlands of western Scotland could not have been a more fit symbol of that nation's colorful past. The man and woman seated before the peat fire burning in its hearth, however, were ostensibly discussing the country's future, and their own. They were not as agreed on either topic as one of them supposed.

"The time is nearly at hand, my dear," said the man. "Will he go along?"

"He will agree," she replied. "How can he do otherwise? His career is at stake. We will make sure of that."

"And you, Fiona—you have no doubt led him to believe that you will be part of that future with him?"

The speaker's lips turned up in a cunning smile. But around their edges could be detected a hint of jealousy. In his heart lately he had grown anxious that his suspicion concerning her methods might indeed be correct.

"You do your part in your own way, Baen," the woman replied, "and let me do mine. You handle the politics. I will insure his cooperation. What about the equipment?"

"It is being delivered next week."

"Then we are set for the first week of February?"

"On schedule—three days before the coronation. By then we should be well on our way toward the victory which the Stone will secure. Are you sure you want to be part of the team?"

"Of course. You don't think I would miss the climax of all we have worked for."

"It will be dangerous."

"I've seen danger before."

"I just don't want anything to happen to you," he said, reaching across and attempting to take her hand. She pretended not to notice, however, and kept both hands safely cradling the warm cup between her palms.

"Nothing will happen to me," she said.

"Then let us anticipate that day when our objective has been attained. When we next enjoy tea under this roof, snow will have blanketed the Highlands."

"And we will have our prize," she added.

The man nodded, raising his teacup to acknowledge her words. He thought to himself that two prizes would await him on that day, both the stone they sought and the beautiful woman sitting across from him at this moment. By then he would have eliminated all competitors for her affections.

"To Caledonia," he said.

"To ancient Scotia," she repeated, lifting her cup in answering gesture.

☒   T W O   ☒

The waters of the Thames flowed murky and silent.

From the black, glistening surface a thin mist rose as night descended. Gradually its white wispy fingers crept up past the high banks, extending out beyond the docks to probe London's nearby streets.

With night came February's familiar chill, the damp air easily enough finding the bones. By morning the city would be shrouded in the thick fog for which it was so well known.

A slender, wood-hulled river craft made its way slowly upriver under the Waterloo Bridge and past Charing Cross Pier, slicing through the current almost as noiselessly as it parted the low fog that clung to the west bank about fifty meters from shore. Only one man was aboard, standing in the small cabin at the controls. His speed was no more than two or three knots.

Not all history is written before the eyes of men. The destiny of his oft-forgotten nation would be reshaped during the silent, cold, misty hours of this night. Few would see what they did. But within twenty-four hours the whole world would take notice. He had planned this moment for ten years. His beloved land would soon rise again to rightful global prominence.

As the boat passed under Westminster Bridge and neared the Houses of Parliament, it slowed yet more, then gradually moved shoreward once it was past the bright reflection of the lights lining the terrace of the Palace.* It floated to a standstill just past the wall of the fabled building where it bordered the Victoria Tower Gardens. The pause lasted but a few moments. A dull thud sounded from somewhere below the hull, the signal that his hidden cargo was off.

With the lines he had been dragging now safely disconnected, the boat's pilot throttled forward and continued upriver, faster now in the shadows of the bare maples of the gardens, under Lambeth Bridge and toward Battersea. He would return this way an hour before dawn. And his morning cargo would be heavier by several hundreds of pounds.

Below the surface, four wet-suited figures swam toward the bottom of the black, grimy waters. Now began their phase of this treacherous and momentous mission. When again the light of day rose, they would either be dead, behind bars, retreating in defeat, or safely skimming northward on the open seas with their quarry. The next few hours would determine which. In the meantime, they had work to do.

It was low tide, so they were not as far beneath the surface as they might have liked. But entry now was necessary so that their escape would come when the tide was in, obscuring their movements with several additional feet of black water.

The lead diver switched on the underwater spotlight atop his head. He could see no more than two or three feet before them, but that would be enough. Should anyone above observe the strange underwater light, it would be indistinguishable from the multitude of reflections shimmering off the surface from brightly lit Westminster Bridge and the Houses of Parliament.

They had run test drills with the equipment deep in Loch Ness. No monster had made an appearance, but they had worked the bugs out of this first tricky phase of the operation. Now the leader swam confidently as he led the others toward shore. His job was to find and open the long disused sewer hatch. The other three wriggled behind, keeping close to the light, each

---

*Westminster Palace is the official name for the Houses of Parliament building, and the two terms are used interchangeably.

dragging a heavy watertight container of equipment and supplies.

They reached the upward incline of the river's edge, which sloped up to the perpendicular cement embankment above the surface. The motion of gloved hands and finned feet stirred up a silent storm of mud and grime. Carefully they backed away. The bobbing headlight slowly panned back and forth to help them get their bearings. They had budgeted half an hour to locate the secret door, buried now below six inches or more of silt. For that purpose each of the four now produced three-foot metal rods, with which in orderly pattern they began probing the grid of the bottom with slow up-and-down motion.

Above them onshore, two hundred yards or so south from the point where the river boat had mysteriously slowed, a figure moved leisurely along the sidewalk of Lambeth Bridge. A thick coat hung around his shoulders, and a wool cap shielded eyes and forehead. The only sign of life he showed besides his slow movement across the bridge toward Lambeth Pier on the opposite side, then back again toward Millbank, was an occasional orange flare from the end of the cigarette dangling between his lips. The smoke that followed from nose and mouth was quickly lost in the night.

Next to the cigarette, however, had one been able to probe close enough to see it, a miniature microphone was attached both to a speaker in one ear and a high-powered transmitter in his pocket. In his hands he carried a pair of binoculars. If danger appeared, all except the cigarette would find themselves at the bottom of the Thames in short order. For the moment they kept him in touch with the skipper of the boat, who had disappeared under him and upriver, and the four divers somewhere in the murky flow nearby. Not that the walker could do them much good from here. But if he detected any unfriendly activity from his riverbank vantage point, the others would at least have a few seconds' warning.

No messages passed. The night remained quiet above and below.

All of London seemed quiet, calmly awaiting the coronation of its new king three days hence.

❈   THREE   ❈

A dull clang sounded at the end of one of the probing rods.

Hand motions quickly brought the other three to the site. The light scanned the bottom. Several hands carefully brushed back the accumulated mud so as to avoid rendering further visual search impossible.

They needn't have worried. They had discovered what they sought—a circular hatch about two feet in diameter.

Their leader now set about to open it according to the instructions for which they had paid dearly. Whether an inrush of water would follow, or whether the chamber behind the door was already flooded, he had no way of knowing.

He motioned to the others to back away. If the river poured in, one casualty would be enough.

In less than five minutes, with the equipment brought for that purpose, he had unfrozen the valve. Now he wrenched it counterclockwise with two or three jerking motions of the crowbar. He felt the seal break. No vacuum-rush from the river resulted. If the chamber behind it was full of mud, their mission would be over before it had begun.

He continued to turn the valve till the hatch was free, then pulled open the cover. He sent his light probing inside. The cavity appeared full of water and perhaps remnants of sewer sludge. He signaled to the others, then turned, gave his fins a few quick kicks, and slowly disappeared inside. One at a time his colleagues followed, pulling their bags in behind them.

The moment all were safely inside the decompression chamber and past threat of detection in the river, three more lights burst on. The last now closed the hatch behind them, turning the inner valve tight. At the far end their leader had already located the drain valve, while a third quickly went to work to loosen the large valve-wheel on the hatch leading to the network of tunnels that would take them to their destination.

Almost instantly the thick, sludgy water began to recede. In another five minutes they were able to remove headgear and again breathe air that did not come through rubber tubes. Stale air, to be sure, but now they could get rid of their diving equipment.

Hastily they pulled off oxygen tanks and wetsuits, stashing them for later. One by one they climbed out and into the first of many tunnels they would explore that night.

One minute later, the walker outside on Lambeth heard a single message through his earpiece.

"We're in."

⬚ F O U R ⬚

Far to the north, unaware of the events in progress destined to change his life forever, Andrew Trentham drove through the night toward his home in Cumbria in the north of England. He had spent that same morning in the very building under which these clandestine events were now taking place. For it was in Westminster Palace that Andrew Trentham served his nation and his constituents as a member of Parliament.

At present, however, Trentham was not thinking of his duties in the House of Commons, his role in Tuesday's coronation, nor the election that would follow a month or two afterward.

In his memory loomed the faces of two women.

The one he loved, yet without knowing how to express it. He would see her not long from now, and was not particularly looking forward to the meeting.

The other he *thought* he loved. Only hours before, he had intended to seal that love with lifelong commitment. Her words from today's luncheon date rang over and over in his brain.

"I'm sorry, Andrew," she had said, "but I am going to have to break it off."

He had sat momentarily as one stunned. As he stared across the table, his fingers unconsciously fidgeted inside his coat pocket with a tiny box. It contained the ring he had planned to give her that day.

Had she had some premonition of what he was about to do? How could she possibly have picked that very moment to deliver such a devastating message?

"But . . . but what are you saying, Blair?"

Bewildered, he fumbled for words. "What do you mean?" he went on. "Why . . . why now?"

"I think it's best we do not see each other for a while," she replied coolly, her deep blue eyes not quite meeting his. "I need some time to think."

"*Think*," he repeated. "Think about what?"

"About us, Andrew."

"What about us? I thought—"

"Please, Andrew," she interrupted. "I don't want to argue with you. I've considered this for several days. I'm convinced it's for the best. At least for *my* best," she added.

He had glanced away, shaking his head in disbelief. How could she sound so cold and distant? Suddenly this woman across from him had become a stranger.

Trentham sighed, trying to force himself back to the present. Now the other face returned into his mind's eye—his mother's. She had always approved of Blair, even pushed him subtly toward deeper involvement. He knew well enough that she would not be pleased with news of their breakup.

He did his best to concentrate on the road ahead of him. The memory of today was too painful. He didn't want to think about it.

But he couldn't help it. He *had* to think about it. Never had anything so jolted him. How could he have so misread the signs? The engagement ring still lay at the bottom of his coat pocket.

Had he been a fool all along? Or had something suddenly changed in Blair's life that he was not aware of? If so, why wouldn't she tell him?

He was glad it was the weekend. A day or two in the country might not remove today's sting. But of one thing he was certain—he couldn't face throngs of people just now.

Tomorrow he would go for a long walk in the hills. That might be the tonic to put this unexpected emotional catastrophe behind him . . . *if* he managed to break it to his mother in a way she could accept without conveying by her silence that she blamed *him* for what had happened.

That's the one thing he didn't need—one more aspect of his life for her to disapprove of.

▧   F I V E   ▧

In the tunnels beneath the Palace of Westminster, the four black-clad figures hastened toward their appointment with antiquity.

They needed no map to negotiate the maze. This intricate network of passageways had been drilled into their brains during the year of preparation for tonight's historic theft—the preparation for which had begun a week following the Queen's announcement. That had been the moment they knew the Stone would be brought again to England and thus give them their opportunity.

The equipment they carried was heavy but necessary for what would follow. They had now left that portion of the maze which had formerly been part of London's sewer system and were walking upon a relatively dry, rocky surface.

This portion of the tunnel had been dug almost sixty years before, during the war, as an underground refuge and means of escape should German bombs threaten while Parliament was in session. But it had never been used for such a purpose. Instead, it had been walled up in the early 1950s and since then nearly forgotten. But that had not prevented the Irish Republican Army from learning of its existence and gradually developing elaborate and accurate drawings of the maze with the thought on the part of its more radical element of one day blowing up the entire Palace and the members of Parliament with it.

Cooler heads, however, had prevailed. The plans had eventually come into the hands of other conspirators with their own ideas for changing the political face of the British Isles. That their plan was less violent in nature did not mean that, if successful, it would not have equally widespread repercussions toward the nationalistic ends its people sought.

Arrived at length at the end of the passage, at a point slightly north of the Jewel Tower between it and the Millbank, the four walkers stopped and set down their equipment.

It was ten fifty-three. They had allowed three hours for the task of boring through approximately two hundred twenty-five feet of dirt and rock to a point that would bring them directly under the Abbey. They had already traversed about six hundred feet from the tunnel entrance. Quickly and silently, three sets of hands began assembling the various arms and levers of the borer, while the other two put together the engine and compressor to drive it. Thanks to Chunnel technology and the resources of their financial backer, their equipment was state of the art. They had no doubt they would arrive at their destination under the Abbey ahead of schedule.

Outside, the river-walker crushed one cigarette under his foot and lit another. As he did, a few more words came through his earpiece. He took in the information, then signaled the boat, which was by now docked upriver to wait.

"Ferguson," came the voice over the radio in the galley where the leader of the expedition lay.

He sat up, grabbed the microphone sitting next to the radio, and acknowledged the call.

"They're about to begin drilling," said the watcher.

"Where are you?"

"On the bridge."

"Make your way up Millbank, then. Any activity otherwise?" asked the man called Ferguson.

"Don't see anything."

"How about the river?"

"Only the Fuel and Lubrication Services boats."

"Anyone on them?"

"No one. They're all moored in a row. Otherwise quiet as a tomb."

"Just make sure it stays that way. Let me know if there's a change."

✤ SIX ✤

Outside the Palace of Westminster, Big Ben struck eleven o'clock.

In her residence the Speaker retired to her bed. In those portions of the Palace which concerned them, custodial and security staff went about their business and rounds.

Shortly after the ringing of the half-hour thirty minutes later, a dull sound reverberated through the basement regions of the parliamentary buildings in a direction that seemed to come from underneath the Victoria Tower. Briefly the ground shook. As no one was present in the lower level, however, it was scarcely heard.

A floor above, a uniformed security officer momentarily glanced about.

"What was that?" he said to his colleague.

"What?" asked the other.

"Didn't you feel it?"

"I felt nothing. What are you talking about?"

"I don't know. It almost . . . but that's impossible," he added, shaking his head.

"What's impossible?"

"It almost . . . for a moment I thought I felt an earthquake."

"Now I know you're going loony, mate!"

"You're probably right—don't even know what one feels like. But for just the briefest instant the ground seemed to tremble."

"Probably just the tube rumbling by."

"Why have I never felt it before, then?"

It was silent a moment.

"Maybe I imagined it," he added at length. "Whatever it was, it's gone now."

SEVEN

In his bed in Cumbria, Andrew Trentham lay awake. Blair was still on his mind.

What time was it? he wondered. It must be one or two in the morning.

He had arrived at the estate sometime after eleven. He had spoken briefly with his mother and father, but with some maneuvering had managed to avoid the subject of Blair. He would tell them about her tomorrow. He wasn't up to it tonight.

Besides, what could he tell them? He was still confused about it himself.

What *had* happened? he asked himself for the fiftieth time.

Where had the relationship taken such a wrong turn?

He thought back to the night they had first met three years before. He had been smitten overnight. How could he help it . . . with that hint of a Swedish accent that betrayed her upbringing in Stockholm, where her father had served with the British Foreign Service . . . the long, lively blond hair and deep blue eyes that made her look more Scandinavian than English . . . the serious smile and the rare laugh?

Blair was beautiful, no doubt about that. Blair was intriguing, captivating.

But had Blair ever really loved him?

Maybe he had just deceived himself all along. He knew she saw other men from time to time, but he had assumed that the loyalty of his affections would win out in the end. Had it been wishful thinking from the beginning?

During the long drive north, he had tried to convince himself that he would go back to London next week and patch it up with her. They would talk and resolve whatever was on Blair's mind. Then he would give her the ring.

But as he lay in the silence of the night replaying today's conversation in his mind, Andrew realized he had been naive. Blair was not coming back. There was no mistaking the tone in her voice. As much as he might not want to recognize the fact, she didn't *want* to make it up with him. The relationship was over.

The realization hurt. Not merely that he had lost her, but that he had been so oblivious that it was coming. How could he have been so blind as to be rehearsing words of proposal when his intended fiancée was getting ready to dump him!

He felt like a fool. Here he was a grown man, a member of Parliament, and a popular one at that. The moment the election date was announced, he would probably take a commanding lead in the polls to be returned to his seat in the House of Commons. And yet he felt like a jilted schoolboy.

In the black quiet of night, even the fact that he had a career that would be the envy of any man in Britain didn't seem to matter. All he could think about was the loss of someone he had cared for.

Slowly Andrew Trentham dozed off into a fitful sleep, wondering vaguely to himself what his future held.

EIGHT

In London, another hour passed.

A janitor walked down the stairs into the southwest basement of Westminster Palace beneath the Royal Gallery.

A peculiar sound met his ear. He paused to listen. Whatever it was, he had never heard it before. It sounded almost like underground machinery. He turned and hurried back upstairs to alert security.

Five minutes later, two uniformed officers entered the basement. They cocked their heads and listened, then shrugged. Whatever it was, the sound had disappeared.

"I don't hear anything," said the man in charge. "But we probably ought to notify the Yard."

❂ NINE ❂

I've nearly got this floor stone dislodged," said a man's voice. "—we're almost through. Give me a hand."

At the end of the tunnel they had just completed, the coordinator of the underground team of burglars motioned to the two other men. They squeezed in beside him and with a final effort shoved the ancient tile up and to one side. It slammed down upon its neighbors, sending a dull and stony echo into the blackness. The next instant, with hands busy helping and pushing, the first of them scrambled up into the once-again silent vault, then leaned back down to help up his three comrades.

Beams from four flashlights panned about as the intruders stood and looked around the chamber into which they had just broken. It contained surprisingly modern-looking equipment and racks of linen and priests' robes.

"Where are we, Malloy?"

"In the laundry beneath the Chapter House," answered the man called Malloy. "We're next to the main floor. It won't be long now."

He proceeded to examine the walls and corners and recesses of the room, eventually satisfying himself of his bearings. "This way," he said. "Through one more wall and we're there."

They followed with their equipment, and soon the final few yards of boring had begun. Thirty minutes later, the four stood in the south transept of the main floor of Westminster Abbey, in what was called Poet's Corner.

"Keep quiet," whispered Malloy. "Black Watch guards are stationed outside near all the entrances."

"Where is the Stone?"

"Unless they've already moved it and the chair to the sanctuary, it should be just behind the Chapel of Edward the Confessor, where it was before. This way."

Three figures hurried off, following the speaker. The fourth, however, stood as if in a daze, an uncharacteristic wave of historic nostalgia sweeping over her.

"Fiona, stop gazing about like a tourist," said one of the men.

"But I've never been here before. There's so much . . . history. . . ."

The young woman continued to gaze about. Now Malloy turned.

"Not our history, Fiona," he said. "It's *England's* history. But not ours. This is an English monument, Fiona. Now come, this is no time for sight-seeing. This is a time to make *our* ancestors proud."

Almost reluctantly, she complied. In another few moments they were behind the historic chapel and standing before the coronation chair, under which rested the ancient and sacred Celtic stone.

"All right, lads and lassie," said Malloy, "time for us to get to work so we can get out of here. The night is passing quickly. The tourists have had their two weeks gawking at it. Now it's our turn."

"I still don't see why we didn't just hide inside until the Abbey was closed for the night," whispered one of the men as they set to work.

"That's what the four students did fifty years ago," replied their leader. "Since then they've tightened up security. If we tried that and then broke out through the door, we'd never make it past Parliament Square—especially trying to carry the Stone. We want to get in and out undetected. By the time this night's over, we'll have the Stone, the chair will still be in place, and our entry tunnel will be sealed. They won't have a clue what happened. We'll be down the Thames and those guards out front will still be standing freezing in their kilts."

It took the better part of forty minutes to remove the coronation chair and dislodge the weighty chunk of sandstone from its resting place. At last they had it on the floor, securely wrapped in a thick blanket, and laced about with heavy carrying straps. With each of the four lifting the corners by the two sets of straps, the weight was easily managed.

Slowly they left the Chapel, this time through the North Ambulatory and around past the front of the chancel.

"What's that little red light up there?" whispered Fiona.

The other three looked up.

"It's a motion detector!" exclaimed one.

"Keep your voice down," whispered Malloy angrily. "Everyone stop where you are."

For several tense seconds he stared up at the tiny red spot, which was now flashing on and off rapidly. "How could we have been so careless?" he muttered.

"I don't hear anything."

"It's a silent alarm," he replied. "It's probably already sounding at Scotland Yard. I just hope we didn't set one off when we came in."

"I didn't see anything till we came around this way."

"We might have been lucky. No matter—we've tripped this one now, so we're not doing any good standing here. Let's go—we've got to move fast."

Hurriedly they resumed their escape, retracing their steps to Poet's Corner, where they had gained entry. Malloy and Fiona stepped down. Carefully, the remaining two eased their cargo through the opening after them. Malloy dragged it out of their way. They followed, replacing the grate above them. In another ten minutes, after much laborious pushing and shoving, the Stone and its four thieves stood again in the laundry, where their supplies and equipment still lay.

They set down their blanketed load to take a breather, then began moving toward the darkened tunnel from which they had come earlier.

"Get in . . . careful with the Stone," said Malloy. "I'll mix up the mortar and try to get this floor stone back in place after us. You three start back through the tunnel with the Stone. I'll catch up with you. Even if one of us should happen to get caught, we've got to make sure the Stone is safe."

※   T E N   ※

Inspector Shepley of Scotland Yard glanced about the basement room under the Royal Gallery at the south end of the Palace of Westminster, to which he had been summoned. A half dozen of the Palace's night security guards stood waiting, as if expecting him to see or hear or otherwise detect something suspicious.

All was silent and still.

"You say it felt like a momentary earthquake?" said Shepley, turning toward one of the men.

"I know it sounds a bit daft, sir. But I thought I felt the ground shake, just for a second."

"And then?"

"Nothing more, sir. Been quiet ever since."

"Probably a barge running into the embankment . . . or the tube."

"The tube doesn't run this time of night, sir."

"Hmm, yes—you're right. You checked everything else—all the entries, nothing on the security monitors, no alarms . . . the roof radar?"

"Nothing, sir."

Shepley turned and headed back toward the stairs.

"Well, we'll do a perimeter check," he said, "and get the information from the monitors for all the doors and windows. Better to be safe, you know. In the meantime, station one of your men down here. If he hears anything else, or if he *feels* something, get in touch with me, and we'll install a seismic monitor and get to the bottom of this."

He led the way upstairs and toward the security headquarters for the Palace. Halfway there, however, the inspector's mobile phone rang inside his coat.

Shepley pulled it out and answered it. The message was brief. He turned and headed for the outer exit.

"Sorry, men, you're on your own here!" he said. "Whatever problems you've got will have to wait. It appears that someone's just broken into Westminster Abbey!"

⬚ E L E V E N ⬚

As the river boat approached the rendezvous point, its skipper heard the unmistakable sounds of alarms going off in the city. And too nearby for comfort.

"What's going on, Cruim?" he whispered anxiously into the radio.

"Don't know," said the lookout onshore.

"Have you heard from the others?"

"Ten minutes ago they were in the chamber suiting up. All but Malloy. He was behind them."

"Well, they'd better be there or I'm not waiting around. Look, you've done your job for now. Wander over and see if you can tell what the commotion's about."

"If I get nabbed with this transmitter on me—"

"If you start to get nabbed, ditch it. Just get over there and find out if this has anything to do with us."

At almost the same moment, sounds came from under the boat. Ferguson heard a splash, then a head appeared out of the water.

"Get us out of here, Ferguson," it said.

"All of you attached? Where's Fiona?"

"She's here. We're all here," said Malloy. "—we're ready. But take it slow."

"You got it?"

"We've got it. But it's heavy. We don't want to lose it, or drown our-selves. Just get us past Charing Cross, then we'll load in."

"All right—get back out of sight."

Ferguson throttled gently forward, then turned the wheel slightly and made for the center of the river.

▒   T W E L V E   ▒

The main floor of Westminster Abbey rarely saw so much activity at the height of the tourist season as on this February morning between half past three and four in the morning. Two dozen uniformed policemen and plain-clothes detectives from Scotland Yard moved about, looking for any sign of vandalism or intrusion.

Nothing was found disturbed, nor was a trace of life to be found, al-though admittedly there might easily be a thousand places for someone to hide.

"Search every corner," called out Inspector Shepley, "and all the outer chapels. Whatever's going on, we've got to make sure no one's trying to sabotage the coronation."

It might have taken an hour or more to find anything out of the ordinary had not one of the officers been a Scotsman who had been hoping for an opportunity to see the Stone of Scone during its two-week public display prior to the coronation and now moved as quickly as professionalism would allow in the direction of the Coronation Chair. A minute later his voice was heard throughout the Abbey.

"Back here, Inspector," he cried. "The Stone is gone!"

Running footsteps brought everyone to the scene. There could be no doubt now as to the purpose of the break-in.

"Spread out!" ordered Shepley. "I want every inch of this place searched with a fine-toothed comb. They might still be here. If not, they couldn't possibly have made off with the Stone without being noticed. I want it found!"

Six or seven minutes later Shepley was summoned. He hurried along the stone floor to the Poet's Corner.

"Look, sir," said one of the detectives, "right beside Sir Henry Irving and Sir Laurence Olivier . . . this last grate looks like it's been tampered with."

Shepley knelt down. The metal grate covering a subfloor ventilation shaft did indeed appear to have been recently moved.

"It couldn't be possible. . . ." he mumbled to himself, already mentally assessing the size of the grate in relation to the Stone. The grate appeared about twenty-six inches wide—clearly sufficient for a human body to squeeze through, and probably wider than the Stone as well.

"And if you'll permit me, sir," the detective went on, "where the shaft extends under the wall, just there under the three Brontë sisters, there appears what looks to be a crack, sir."

A half dozen flashlights instantly probed the spot.

The next instant, Shepley had the grate lifted for the second time that night and clanging upon the stone floor. He probed with his light into the tight, dark tunnel which was revealed beneath it.

"Get in there, someone—see where it goes."

Two or three men scrambled and squeezed down into the floor to carry out his order. Moments later they had disappeared. Those clustered about the opening waited. Two minutes later, one of the men crawled back through.

"It's a tunnel all the way to the basement laundry, Inspector."

"Any sign of the Stone?"

"Nothing, sir."

"Let's have a look. Come on, men."

On hands and knees, a dozen of Scotland Yard's finest now made their way until they emerged, standing once again, in the silent and little-known laundry of Westminster Abbey.

"Over here, Inspector," called one of the first three, who had been examining the room as they came. "I think I may have found something."

Shepley hurried to the scene and knelt down where he was pointing. Beams from a dozen or more flashlights illuminated the square of flagstone with a suspicious bead of strange coloration around its perimeter. Shepley probed its edge with a finger.

"The mortar's still soft," he said, rubbing his thumb and forefinger together. "And a rather crude job of it. Whoever's responsible must have been trying to seal this stone from underneath. What's below here?" he said, turning to one of the Abbey guards who had followed.

"Nothing, sir," the man replied. "This is the bottom level. Though they say there's crypts all through the area."

Shepley looked around to some of his men.

"Get it up," he said. "Pry it loose however you can."

Several knives and a screwdriver were produced. One of the edges was lifted slightly, then fingers and hands stooped to grab hold. The stone was lifted back and set aside. Flashlights immediately probed the tunnel below. It was clearly fresh, and larger than that through which they had crawled from the Abbey to the laundry. One of Shepley's men climbed down, finding firm earth about five feet below the level of the floor. He directed his light into the passage leading away.

"What can you see?" Shepley called down.

"It's a tunnel, all right . . . some leftover supplies, a small bag of dry mortar, the container they brought the water to mix it in."

"Which way does it lead?" said Shepley.

"Seems to be east."

"Toward the Parliament buildings!" exclaimed Shepley. "*That's* what they heard over there."

"Aren't there some kind of old sewer drains and tunnels under Westminster Palace?" asked one of the men at his side.

"That's got to be it," said Shepley. He turned to the guard. "You have the keys to this place?"

The man shook his head. Already Shepley was on his way, scrambling on hands and knees back to the main floor of the Abbey. He stood and immediately took out his phone while those who were not involved in the search at the other end of the tunnel climbed out after him.

"Get the river patrol here!" he shouted. "All available units. I want every inch of the Thames lit up like noon. And send me in a chopper. I'm going up top. I'll wait in Parliament Square!"

His men followed him through the Nave toward the door. As they ran, Shepley barked out orders to his assistant, then hurried outside and into the night to await his helicopter.

⊠ T H I R T E E N ⊠

They're on to you, Ferguson!" shouted a frantic voice over the small boat's radio.

"What do you mean, Cruim?" crackled back a voice into the earpiece.

"It's breaking loose, I tell you. There's coppers and blokes from the Yard everywhere! The Abbey's crawling with 'em, and half of 'em are making for the river. I think a helicopter's heading this way."

"Lose the equipment and get out of there!" shouted Ferguson.

He released the steering wheel and jumped briefly out on deck. He glanced from the river up toward the city. Lights from several police boats were moving out from Westminster Pier and beginning to probe the shoreline near where he had just been. Sirens were going off everywhere.

The sounds of helicopter blades sounded in the distance. Once a chopper was up overhead, it would all be over.

He hurried inside to the controls, throttled down slightly, and held the wheel steady straight across the river. He couldn't go much faster, or he would lose the lines underneath. If they could just get close to the other bank . . .

For a long, tense minute he held on, then glanced back. The chopper appeared to be setting down somewhere behind the Parliament buildings. It would be in the air again in another twenty seconds.

Ferguson throttled back and cut the engine.

This would have to do! He ran astern, knelt over the side, and grabbed at the lines, giving each a hard tug. Two heads, now three, at last a fourth all surfaced.

"Get in, Malloy, Fiona . . . all of you," he said urgently. "We can't wait any longer."

"We're not far enough downriver."

"I don't know what you did," replied Ferguson, pulling now one, now a second onboard, "but we've got Scotland Yard and the river police on our tail! I thought you were going to get out of there undetected."

The rest now scrambled aboard, helping one another unload tanks and masks and equipment. Within thirty seconds they were all leaning down to lug aboard the cargo at the end of the final line for which they had labored most of the night.

The instant it was secure, Ferguson accelerated up to as much speed as he dared. Behind him, now the helicopter rose into the air, sending its spotlight probing in a wide arc across the surface of the Thames.

Ferguson veered downriver as he crossed it, now passing beneath Westminster Bridge. If he could just get past Hungerford Bridge, the Festival Pier beyond it would offer them cover. Enough boats were moored on the opposite side of the river that he might be able to sneak in behind one. Behind him the chopper careened about in wide, menacing arcs, its spotlight panning back and forth along the shoreline.

Several unmanned river-tour yachts were moored just ahead. Ferguson spun in behind one of them, throttled back, and cut the engine.

"Get out of sight inside the cabin!" he cried.

Four bodies dove for cover just as the helicopter's beam scanned momentarily past them.

"He'll be back," said Ferguson. "Get the tanks and wetsuits and Stone down below and out of sight. I'll work us through these boats ahead. With any luck we might be able to get downriver far enough that I can get up some speed and get us down to Gravesend."

Again the chopper whirred overhead. When it was again past, all the equipment splashed overboard.

A few moments more they waited. Gradually the sound of the helicopter receded as it banked back across the river and headed in the opposite direction toward Battersea and Chelsea.

Ferguson carefully steered out between yachts and the shoreline for another two hundred yards, then eased out into the channel, turned downriver again, and revved up to fifteen knots.

They passed under Blackfriars Bridge without incident, then London Bridge, now picking up more speed and making for the mouth of the Thames. As they passed under the Dartford Bridge fifty minutes later, they were skimming along at thirty-five knots, and the open sea of the mouth of the Thames lay ahead of them.

Ferguson had a larger craft awaiting them at Southend.

⊠   F O U R T E E N   ⊠

The following afternoon, a private yacht bore northward off the coast of Lincolnshire. Its five passengers, three of whom were asleep in the cabins below, now breathed much easier than six hours earlier. All Scotland Yard and half of London's police force were looking for them and their silent but weighty cargo, but in all the wrong places. The sewer hatch into the river had been found, as well as several well-planted clues pointing in directions the boatsman Ferguson had not been apprised of. Several known London sympathizers with his cause were already being rounded up for questioning.

On deck, one of the divers, an enthusiastic and burly youth by the name of Fogarty, was speaking to their leader.

"Where are we taking the Stone?" he said.

"Where our independence was lost," said the parliamentarian, who thought he had masterminded the symbolic theft. "We are taking it to the spiritual heart of the Highlands. For it is there that the ancient spirit of the Scot will rise again."

A puzzled expression met Ferguson's gaze.

"They were just using us for their own purposes as always," Ferguson continued. "Returning the Stone to Edinburgh in '96 on the eve of an election was just an attempt to curry Scottish favor and win votes. You don't think they really cared about us, do you? The Stone may have been taken to Edinburgh, but it was still *theirs*. Look, the moment they need it to crown their new king, back to London it comes. But now we possess it on *our* terms, not theirs. It doesn't belong in Edinburgh at the whim of the English parliament. It is the property of all true Scots, and it belongs in the Highlands. Our destination is Glencoe," concluded Ferguson. "Study your history, man."

"You mean we're not—"

Behind them the only woman of the select coterie approached. Hearing fragments of their conversation, she quickly caught young Fogarty's eye. He saw the expression, perceived her meaning, and stopped abruptly. He asked no more questions.

"Our battle for independence climaxed at Glencoe," she said as if in answer, but actually to divert his intended meaning. She slipped her hand through Ferguson's arm as she spoke. "Glencoe's treachery must be avenged. We have taken the first step tonight."

"Precisely why it is there that our new quest must begin," added Ferguson.

Fogarty nodded as if considering their words, then turned and walked away. He realized he had been careless and almost said too much.

The two watched him go. When they were alone, the woman spoke.

"You did it," she said softly, smiling up at the Scot.

"I could not have done it without you, Fiona darling," said Ferguson. "Though I suppose we must admit that Malloy, Fogarty, Kerr, and Cruim all did their parts as well."

"We did it together," she rejoined. "Now it is up to your colleagues in the Commons. And you must hasten back to join them."

"I do not like leaving you in Grimsby. I want no danger to come to you in case Scotland Yard does manage to pick up the trail."

"We will be fine. We will put in as weather requires and will be around the coast and safe within days. Malloy is a skilled sailor. But you . . . you are the most important member of the team. You must be back in London and out of suspicion."

Ferguson took her hand. This time she did not pull away. "Just make sure you disappear if there is any danger," he said.

She nodded.

"Then meet me at Glencoe," he added. He brought her hand to his lips and kissed it lightly.

"Don't worry about me," she said. "The Stone will be safe. But take care of yourself as well."

"I shall," he said. "We will meet at the cottage after the election."

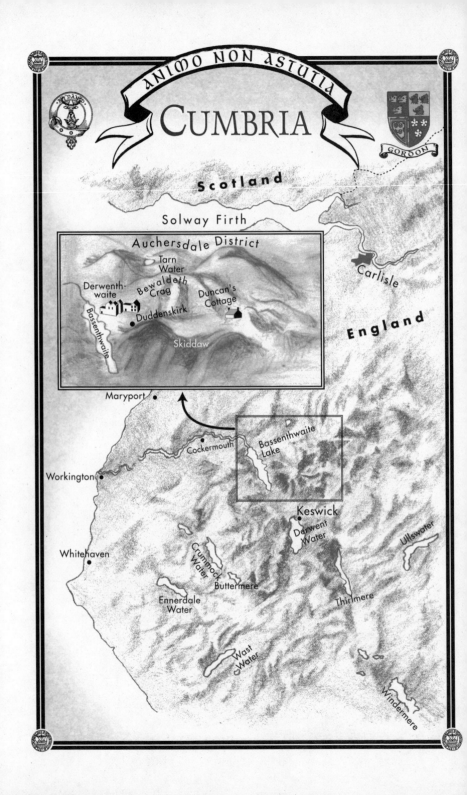

2

HEIR TO A LEGACY

❦ O N E ❦

Mountain winds carry many tales.

Slashing swiftly down from the north, they bore wintry portent of descending arctic storm. In other seasons, from westward across the Irish Channel, offshore drafts brought scents of salt spray and herring, reminders of the coastline less than eight miles distant.

Today's gentle current sweeping across the lonely Cumbrian moor, however, came neither from north nor west, but from the southeast—an unusual heading for February winds in this region. The uncharacteristic origin was indicated by a hint of warmth, along with strange southern fragrances that seemed to accompany it.

The walker who had been upon the open heathland for more than an hour had not explored these fading pathways of his youth for some time—too long, he realized. But the morning's perfume had invaded his nostrils the instant wakefulness came upon him.

In haste, while the house still slept, he had thrown on a plaid shirt, corduroy trousers, and jacket, then grabbed up a favorite walking stick and cap and ventured out into the thin light of the new day. Though the sting of yesterday's luncheon with Blair was still with him, the bright cold morning's air and the sight of his beloved hills quickly invigorated his system with the thought that *perhaps* life might go on in spite of it.

He reacquainted himself with two or three childhood haunts in the morning chill, then returned to the house for breakfast with his mother and father and a look at the early edition of the *Times*. His mother was in good spirits, full of talk about her recent conservation activities. His father was his usual calm self. The subject of Blair did not come up.

The moment he opened the paper, Andrew Trentham's eyes widened in disbelief.

"Did you see this, Father?" he exclaimed.

"Haven't had a chance," answered Harland Trentham. "What is it?"

"Someone broke into the Abbey last night."

"What? Vandalism—anything stolen?"

"Apparently the Stone of Scone," replied Andrew, then spread out the first page again and read through the startling account.

Last night, in one of the most daring raids in recent English history, an unknown number of high-tech bandits tunneled into Westminster Abbey and made off with the historic Stone of Scone, only recently returned to London for the impending coronation. The intruders apparently tunneled through several sealed crypts and into a laundry under the floor of Chapter House—a thirteenth-century monks' meeting room and home of the first English Parliament. They then bored under the floor of that section of the Abbey known as Poet's Corner, removed the historic Stone from beneath the royal chair of coronation, and disappeared—all under the very noses of the contingent of the Black Watch which stands guard around the Abbey.

The Stone of Scone is reportedly the very stone upon which King Kenneth MacAlpin was crowned the first king of Scotland in A.D. 868. It was brought to England in 1296, where it resided in Westminster Abbey until its 1996 transfer to the Crown Room of Scotland's James VI in Edinburgh Castle. During its 700 year tenure in London, the Stone was removed once—in 1657 for Oliver Cromwell's installation as Lord Protector—and stolen once—in 1950, when it was returned after several weeks. Brought back to London two weeks ago in preparation for Tuesday's coronation of King Charles III, the Stone has been on public display in its former home at the Abbey, where it was scheduled to remain for one week following the ceremony.

Scotland Yard is pursuing a number of leads at this time. Evidence has been found pointing to a connection with Scottish nationalists. However, no motive has been suggested, since right of possession of the Stone is no longer under dispute and it was to be returned to Edinburgh Castle well before the elections.

A statement issued by Dagold MacKinnon of the S.N.P. disavows any knowledge of the theft. MacKinnon conjectures that perhaps Irish nationalists are responsible, intending to unite the fabled Blarney Stone of Ireland with the Stone of Scone in a gesture to promote independence of all peoples from the rule of London. Others suggest that the IRA is hopeful of upsetting the coronation and delegitimizing the English crown.

"Why the IRA would be interested in the Stone is a mystery," Scotland Yard's Inspector Allan Shepley is quoted as saying in response. "At present we are ruling out no possibilities." Whether the theft has any connection with upcoming national elections is also unknown.

A statement issued by Buckingham Palace confirms that the coronation will proceed on schedule whether the Stone is recovered by Tuesday or not. The coronation chair, dating from the year 1300, was not damaged in the theft.

Legend connects the Stone of Scone with the Irish coronation stone. Noted Irish druid Amairgen Cooney Dwyer, who was reached for comment at his compound in County Carlow, said: "The *lia fail*, or sacred stone, from Tara in ancient Eire, is considerably larger than the Scottish version and lays claim to the honor of having imbued ancient Irish royalty with power at their crowning. It presently stands on a mound within the earthwork known as Cormac's House in County Meath."

The previous theft of the Stone of Destiny in 1950 was carried out by four Scottish nationalist students who pretended to be tourists, hid in the Abbey after its night closing, then fled with the Stone. They took it back to Arbroath Abbey, where it was laid at the High Altar. It was eventually returned to Westminster Abbey.

Last night's thieves apparently gained entry to former sewer mains through a long-forgotten drain line into the Thames just south of the Houses of Parliament. Sophisticated boring equipment enabled the thieves to dig from these tunnels into several ancient crypts beneath the Abbey, through which entrance to the laundry was gained. Escape was apparently made by the same route, into the Thames. The river's banks and shorelines were combed, but without success.

"The sheer weight of the Stone would make transport difficult," said Shepley. "Motion detectors and alert security staff on hand in the parliamentary buildings brought us to the scene so quickly that in my opinion the thieves were not able to get the Stone far from the tunnel site. I do not consider it unlikely that, in making their own escape, they were forced to abandon the Stone in the Thames. We are dragging the bottom and divers are searching every inch at this time."

The historic Scottish stone, of pinkish-hued sandstone, into which two iron rings are imbedded on opposite ends of the top, measures 26 inches by 16 inches by 10 inches and weighs 336 pounds.

Andrew set down the paper. "I just can't believe it," he said, handing it to his father. "When are these nationalists going to learn . . . and why steal what they already possess?"

"You'll need to return to London immediately," now said Andrew's mother.

"There's probably nothing much I could do if I were there," replied Andrew. "But I'll make a few calls later."

"How will this affect the coronation?"

"I don't know. The paper says it will go on as planned. Perhaps by then the Yard will have recovered the Stone and all will be well. Are you two still taking the train down on Monday?"

"Unless the coronation is changed," replied his mother. "And we're still meeting you and Blair for dinner on Wednesday evening?"

"Unfortunately," sighed Andrew, "we will have to call that off . . . or else it will be just the three of us." The moment had come and there was no use delaying it any longer. He proceeded to tell them what had transpired the day before.

"What happened, Andrew?" his mother said in the familiar tone Andrew had been dreading. "What did you do?"

"I honestly don't know, Mother," he replied, beginning to feel like a child again. "I'm mystified about it, too."

"You must have done *something* to offend her," persisted Lady Trentham, her gray eyes searching his.

Andrew shrugged, then rose and excused himself. He quickly forgot about both Blair and his mother as he found his jacket and left the house. The playful southerly breeze drew him irresistibly toward the hills again. As he walked, he found his mind returning to the *Times* article.

The account of the ancient Stone's theft stirred unaccountable emotions in Andrew's heart. He had seen the Celtic Stone, of course, any number of times when visiting the Abbey, and had been part of the symbolic ceremony in Edinburgh in '96 when it was installed in the castle along with the Scottish crown jewels. He knew the basic facts of its history and its connection with the mystical legends of Scotland's past.

Now all at once the Stone came into the center of his thoughts. Where had it originated? he wondered. What was its significance? Why did the Scots value it so highly? Did it possess some mystical power?

The stone of Arthur's sword was undoubtedly myth. But the Celtic Stone of Scottish lore was a tangible piece of rock, and yet one whose history extended far back into the mists of time. He had heard Scots maintain that the history of Scotland was more ancient and unbroken than England's. If so, what role did the stolen Stone occupy in that history?

As the breezes forecast, an unseasonable warmth quickly began to activate more perspiration than the leisurely pace of Andrew's second outing of the day could account for. He struck out toward the summit of the hill rising not far from the house called Bewaldeth Crag.

With vague thoughts of the Celtic Stone swirling in his brain, and caught up in a general mood of thoughtful reflection brought on by yesterday's incident, he found himself drawn to the past.

Roots, a sense of belonging, he thought, links with the past . . . they *mattered*.

Especially for one in his position. How else could he remain attentive and in touch with his constituency than by maintaining a keen awareness of who *he* was and where *he* had come from? Could he really blame the Scots for wanting to preserve *their* history and the links to *their* roots?

Whatever had happened with Blair, however annoyed his mother might be with him in consequence, it could not be denied that he loved this place, Andrew thought. Perhaps no less than the Scots loved the land from which they had come. Maybe he had needed an emotional jolt to jar him briefly out of the present and remind him of the importance of this land and his roots.

Cumbria held its dark and painful memories for him, it was true. But here was his heritage—this estate known as Derwenthwaite and the tiny village of Duddonskirk about three miles away. The small cluster of houses was situated in one of many twisting and uneven crooks created by the descending flanks of the Saddleback-Skiddaw ridge as it made its three-thousand foot drop from England's third highest peak down through the Auchersdale District to the sea.

This was home—the northwestern Cumbrian Mountains between the

Skiddaw Forest and the Workington Plain. He had grown up under these skies, amongst these hills and lakes and rigorous walking trails, and he loved them.

Andrew paused in his step and gazed out westward.

There lay the sea, outspreading in the distance beyond the rural plain of farmland, crisscrossed by miles and miles of hedgerows, now brown and tidily trimmed for winter. The ocean was as blue as he had remembered it, stretching in its azure glory toward the horizon.

Gradually he turned his vision in a slow quarter-arc until his eyes peered straight in front of him—across the patchy green farmland to the shoreline . . . and beyond, over the sea northward.

There—on the distant side of the firth—Scotland was visible between the blue of the sea and the blue of the sky. Dimly he could make out Southerness Point, the East Stewartry Coast, and a few misty shapes of the Galloway Hills.

Scotland—that mystic northern region whose people, at least some of them, still loved it passionately enough to risk all in the rescue of one of its sacred artifacts.

When clouds lay thick and heavy, it was impossible to descry anything across the expanding width of the firth. But when the sun shone, the ten- to twenty-mile distance was hardly enough to require what old Duncan called the second sight. Today the first would do quite well enough.

Andrew sighed with satisfaction, and went on his way.

▓ T W O ▓

The solitary walker continued his morning's excursion across the Cumbrian hillside overlooking the firth. But now an unexpected wave of melancholy began to creep over him like a chilly London fog. Once more Blair's words attempted to intrude into his memory, and with them the pain and confusion he had felt at hearing them yesterday.

"I'm sorry, Andrew . . . I am going to have to break it off."

Was it her words that had caused this whirlwind of mental activity—these thoughts of Scots and stones, roots and history? What did he have to do with Scotland other than growing up close to her borders and perhaps having a little Scots blood in him from somewhere generations back? His family's faces had long been turned toward London, not Edinburgh. Why had the article about the theft of the Stone given rise to so many new thoughts?

He accelerated his pace in the attempt to shake off the mood.

At thirty-seven, Andrew Gordon Trentham was a man envied by many, widely judged as the prototype of one who had it all. Deep inside, however, he sometimes wondered what exactly he *did* have. What in his life could he look at and honestly say, "I did this, in and of myself . . . not because of my name or what I am expected to do"? Even the estate might not be coming to him had it not been for . . .

He stopped his thoughts in their tracks. He didn't want to go down that road.

From his earliest childhood, others had expected him to do just what he was doing—to succeed, to rise above his peers, to become one of Britain's new generation of elite. He had the sense of being "watched," just as the Prince of Wales, now their new king, had been watched all his life.

Being the son of Lady Waleis Bradburn Trentham insured that all eyes— especially his mother's—were on him.

Working out the conundrums of expectation and conviction in the pressure-filled cauldron of British politics, and within the hierarchical system of a fading aristocracy, was no simple assignment. He was already known as one who would not compromise his conscience, just like his mother, the old-timers said. Nor was he afraid to jump into the fray for a cause he believed in. He would not dirty his hands with questionable practices, but he *was* eager to discard his suit jacket and roll up his sleeves.

Andrew's was a personality still in the process of development. He was *growing*—a good thing to be able to say of any man. The data of his biography were not facts the young Trentham thought much about. The secret at the heart of that biography was almost too painful to recall—and usually he managed to keep it shoved so deep in his memory that he wondered if the incident had really ever happened. One look at the family portrait hanging in the Derwenthwaite entry, however, was sufficient reminder. And its effect in having thrust him inevitably toward a career in politics could certainly not be denied.

He was one of several young and rising members of Parliament, widely recognized as the son of the former Conservative MP* Waleis Bradburn

---

*Member of Parliament, specifically one elected to the House of Commons.

Trentham, and now gaining prominence in his own right. The society columnists and tabloids spoke flatteringly of him as a handsome and articulate graduate of Oxford, the heir to a fortune, with a name that represented one of the last of the country's great landed estates.

None of this meant much to Andrew. He had grown up accustomed to the position that his family, and he in turn, held in the order of things. Thus, he gave little consideration to the honor that was accorded him. It did not seem to him a privilege, but rather an obligation, a requirement that accompanied his particular lot in life, and on a more personal level an obligation within his own family that he could not shed.

Whether his mother put it on him or whether he put it upon himself because of what had happened would have taken Freud himself to figure out. He felt it—that was enough. He had been aware of what he perceived as his mother's expectations almost every day since the accident. Whether these mirrored her actual expectations, she had never confided to him openly. She was a complex woman and did not herself begin to fathom the myriad of ways she subtly pressured him to conform to, yet always fall short of, the vision she held for what her daughter should have become.

Fate had cast the role upon him. He would do his best to steward it wisely and to use what he had been given for the benefit of posterity and whatever good it might do for his nation and fellowman. His parents had trained both him and his sister with a rigid sense of duty and public responsibility along with—for her at least—a very modern view of a woman's parallel duty to rise high in worlds formerly reserved for men.

The political component of their training, therefore, had been focused on his sister, six years his senior. Lindsay had been cut from exactly the same cloth as their mother—ambitious, articulate, and sure to climb into prominence when her moment came. Their mother was a former Thatcherite whose ambitions for her daughter were far greater than had ever been her own.

But those ambitions would never be realized.

Silently as he followed after her on the somber rainy day of the funeral, Andrew had realized that the mantle of family achievement was now upon him, if for no other reason than to demonstrate his own worth in his mother's stoic, teary, black-veiled eyes. As they walked silently back to the car from the graveside—he and his mother, the only ones on earth who knew what really happened—he had determined that he would take Lindsay's place. He would try to give his mother something of what had so suddenly been taken from her. He had been trying ever since.

Yet if he was going to enter politics, Andrew had realized as he grew, he had to be true to his own convictions as well. His mother's initial horror at his party affiliation when he decided to stand as a Liberal Democrat candidate for the Commons had now moderated. She had come almost to admire him for taking a position opposite from hers, though she never said as much to him. Praise was not something that fell easily from her lips.

If Andrew's sister would never reside at Number Ten Downing Street, Lady Trentham had reluctantly come to endorse her son's political influence, if not his specific ideas. Yet to him she continued to convey in a thousand ways she was never aware of that Andrew could not possibly rise so high as Lindsay would have. It was ordinary and expected for a *man* to achieve, she would have said. But Lindsay Bradburn Trentham would have stood high above any and all her peers.

Andrew sighed again and kicked at a pebble in the path. He respected his mother, and probably loved her. But they were not close. Maybe they never would be.

A new odor, borne likewise by the winds but altogether distinctive in character from that which had brought him out earlier, distracted Andrew's thoughts and pulled his eyes from the sea.

He turned his head back inland.

A wisp of white smoke ascended in the distance from a cottage hidden from view, tucked amid the folds of the hills as they rose gradually toward the peak of the Skiddaw some ten or eleven miles to the southeast. The smoke's thin trail had dissipated long before reaching him, but the shoreward arch of its fading visibility left no doubt whence came the invisible aroma that had invaded his senses. It came from over the next ridge, and from the only human abode for miles in that direction.

Old Duncan . . . never without a fire, Andrew thought with a smile. Instantly thoughts of London and his mother began to recede.

And unless his nostrils betrayed him, a few chunks of peat were mingled with the scraps of oak and maple the old crofter was burning. A Scotsman through and through, reflected Andrew. Even if it meant hoarding what peat bricks he could lay his hands on, not so much for the heat they could produce, but to salt his fire with scents from the northern homeland of his ancestry.

Duncan MacRanald, a transplanted sheepherding Scot, had occupied a humble stone cottage on the northeast corner of the Trentham estate, where

Bewaldeth sloped down to the Scawthwaite Fells, for more years than Andrew had himself been alive.

As a youngster Andrew had spent long and pleasurable hours listening to Duncan's tales of the savage lands north of the border. The stories were made all the wilder by the thick Scots dialect MacRanald had made no effort to tame during his years surrounded by the more civilized English tongue.

Though Andrew's father had occasionally shown signs of a distant affection for MacRanald, Andrew had never heard any of his other relations speak of the Scots except with that lofty tone from which Englishmen have created a distinctive form of communication all their own, an inflection conveying unmistakable condescension while employing only the most gracious expression.

There was nothing, on the other hand, that Duncan held in *higher* honor than his Highland heritage. Let the English lift their noses in whatever directions they chose, he was fond of saying—he was a Scot and proud of it.

As the proud Scotsman he was, MacRanald displayed curiously more knowledge concerning the Trentham heritage along such lines than did any other member of the family. By virtue of such knowledge, scattered references to more personal influence of Scottish blood mingled with the stories he had told Andrew as a lad.

The youngster, however, had been more taken with the tales of antiquity. As a lad, Andrew had paid scant heed to the cryptic hints that occasionally fell from the lips of Derwenthwaite's quizzical neighbor.

Nevertheless, Andrew had grown to love the man. And the elder Trenthams had never discouraged their son from associating with the shepherd.

※   T H R E E   ※

Andrew had always considered Duncan little more than a herder of sheep, his scraggly flock comprising his only livelihood. The significance of the fact that his dwelling sat within the grounds of the estate was only one of the mysteries surrounding MacRanald's connections with the Trentham family, whose discovery yet lay ahead for the young parliamentarian.

Thoughts of the old shepherd brought Andrew's reflections to the present. What would old Duncan think of the theft from the Abbey? he wondered. He could not possibly have heard about it, for he owned no radio and took no daily newspaper. Did the old man even realize that his beloved Scotland seemed to be at the forefront of everything these days?

Within very short order after he returned to London, Andrew would face several issues relating to Scotland's future. He wondered what the old man thought about devolution* and the new Scottish parliament. Some Scots were far from satisfied with these recent changes. Devolution, if anything, had only exacerbated the debate. The most strident nationalists continued to call for full and complete independence. Depending on who turned out to be responsible for the theft of the Stone, how would that affect the decisions the Parliament in Westminster would have to make?

Andrew hadn't seen his old friend in two years, and then it had been only a brief encounter across a wild and overgrown hedge in one of the fields of the estate.

How long had it been since he had been inside those stone walls he had loved as a child? How long since he sat staring into the fire of peat and oak, listening to Duncan's voice spin an entrancing tale of brave men whose memories were now lost in the distant folds of history? How long since he had heard that scratchy yet soothing voice hum a few lines and then break into some old Gaelic ballad whose words he could not understand, yet whose meaning he could somehow *feel* through haunting melodies of strange cadence and rhythm?

How long since he took in, half with dread, half with delight, the fanciful descriptions of feral glens and isolated Highland peaks in whose hiding places dwelt valiant clans of kilted swordsmen? How long since his eyes widened as Duncan opened the boards and folded back the yellowed leaves of some tattered volume, there to let the boy behold drawings of warriors and bards, of claymores and harps and scenes of battle? None of the ten thousand volumes in the Derwenthwaite library back at Andrew's own house could compare with the sagas of the mere dozen or so in old Duncan's possession.

---

*A move, instituted by the Labour government of Tony Blair and given impetus by favorable referendums (nonbinding votes of public opinion) among the voters of both regions, to "devolve" more self-governing authority to Scotland and Wales, resulting in new parliaments and First Ministers for both regions. The overall effect is a system perhaps similar to the federal system in the United States, in which power and decision-making authority is divided between the federal government and that of the individual states. The states have significant powers, yet are still ultimately responsible to the authority of the federal government. Such parallels the newly altered regional relationships in the UK. There are those, however, who advocate far greater autonomy, even full independent nationhood and withdrawal from the United Kingdom altogether. For this vocal minority, devolution has been little more than a token gesture.

It had probably been twenty years or more since he had heard one of Duncan's stories. Where did the time go?

And why on this particular day, did the memories come all at once so vividly back?

Renewal of childhood affection for the man rose up within him. He would visit him again—today, in fact!

Andrew turned to face the pleasant breeze that had driven him here, retraced his steps partway down the slope of Bewaldeth, then struck out on a course over the undulating terrain, bearing slightly more northward than the trail he had followed earlier.

There was no path across this hump of the hill toward the Robin Hood and Scawthwaite Fells beyond. Just to the other side of it he would pick up the sheeptrack. Following it northward some three hundred yards would lead him to an eastward trail, which in turn would take him to a wider dirt wagon road leading to the northern edge of his father's property. At least the land itself was not marred with confusing images of his mother. The *land*, if nothing else, belonged solely to his father. After about another mile, along the border to the east, he would arrive at Duncan's cottage. It was the long way round, but the shortest route from where he was now.

The ground beneath his feet felt wet and soggy in places, although the abundance of rocks and thick tufts of grassy clumps kept his boots mostly dry as he made his way down the slope of one ridge and gradually toward the side of the next. Andrew could scarcely make out anything resembling a visible path—another reminder how much time had passed since he had explored these places which had once been so familiar to him. He had left Cumbria for Eton at age thirteen, Oxford at eighteen, and, with the would-be sophistication of youth, had neglected the playful byways of boyhood during every visit back to Derwenthwaite since.

As is nostalgia's habit, though his reflections were filled with pleasant memories, they brought in their wake a return of melancholy. Was memory of his sister partially responsible for his avoidance of these hills and pathways?

He could make out sheep grazing in the distance—whether Duncan's or from one of the flocks to the north, Andrew couldn't tell. The mere sight of their white coats, fluffy in summer but grubby and mud-caked now, combined with the overgrown path beneath his feet, stabbed him with a pang of sudden loneliness, of time slipping uncontrollably away, of longings he could not put words to that neither national reputation nor stature in London could touch or satisfy.

He tried again to shake off the unwelcome doldrums.

He was content with his life, even if he had been sacked yesterday by the woman he was trying to propose to! Someday he would laugh about the whole situation. Maybe not for a while. But he would get over it. Though she had wanted him to marry Blair, his mother would get over it too. He would just avoid the subject around her for a while. And he would meet other women. He just needed a little time to heal, that was all.

In the meantime, he would enjoy a visit with Duncan. That, at least, would get his mind off Blair and his mother!

Andrew sighed, then took a deep, satisfying breath of the air whose breeze still mingled Duncan's peat smoke with the fragrance of southern warmth.

❈ F O U R ❈

As Andrew continued across the fields, the breeze ruffling up his light brown hair as he went, an exuberance began to come over him, like that of a great adventure about to begin.

Twenty minutes later he spied the cottage some hundred yards off. He broke into a run down the slope. Moments later he found himself approaching the worn oak door behind which the old Scotsman made his home.

"Welcome . . . welcome, laddie!" exclaimed Duncan in answer to Andrew's knock. The old man stepped back to look over the panting young man with a great smile radiating on his wrinkled and ruddy face. "What brings ye sae far frae hame?"

The very sight of the old man's worn Shetland wool cardigan—whose shades of red and blue and tan were so overlaid with oil and grime from his flock as to make them nearly indistinguishable, and which contained more holes than a quick glance could count—as well as the brown denim trousers and the black boots that were probably older than Andrew himsef—sent Andrew's thoughts into a tailspin of fond recollection.

"To pay a long overdue visit to a good friend," replied Andrew.

"Then come in, laddie—come in! We'll drink a cup o' tea t'gither."

So saying, MacRanald turned back inside. His guest followed.

Duncan MacRanald had seemed old to Andrew Trentham's young eyes twenty-five years ago. But in the time that had passed since, the weathered lines of the Scotsman's cheeks had not changed much. His healthy crop of hair, however, then only speckled with gray, was now pure white. Altogether untamed, it looked as if the mountain winds were swirling through it, even as they whipped up the snows on the peak of his beloved Ben Nevis itself.

"I'll jist put some fresh peats on the fire," said the Scotsman as they entered, "while you bring the pot, laddie. Ye'll remember, I'm thinkin'."

A minute later Andrew was setting the small iron pot filled with fresh water on the hook above what was now a well-caught fire. Duncan brought a second chair to the hearth, and both men sat down.

"So, how is the life o' an important London man?" asked the host, easing into his chair.

"Busy, challenging . . . sometimes exciting, sometimes frustrating," replied Andrew. "But there is big news, Duncan, about your homeland."

"An' what would that be?"

"The Stone of Scone was stolen last night."

"Ye dinna say!" exclaimed the Scotsman, his face displaying a look of astonished shock. "From atop the grit castle rock o' Edinburgh? How could they hae won int' the place?"

"From Westminster Abbey, Duncan," replied Andrew. "It was taken back to England for the coronation. But now it's gone without a trace."

"Ay, I forgot. Who took it?" said Duncan.

"No one knows. Some say the Scots, some suspect the Irish."

"I doobt it'd be the Irish, laddie. The Stane's got more meanin' t' the Scots."

"But why would the Scots do it? It's already been given to them. It was going back to Edinburgh next week anyway."

Duncan shook his head. He had no answer to that puzzle.

Andrew leaned forward and peeked into the pot. The water inside, however, showed no sign of being yet anywhere near hot enough to produce steam, much less come to a boil.

"Don't you know, Duncan," remarked Andrew in a lighter tone and with a grin as he resumed his seat, "this is the modern age. You should get a microwave oven. You could boil your tea water in seconds."

The very thought sent the old Scotsman into subdued chuckles.

"A microwave in this cottage, laddie—'tis aye a good one, that! Duncan

MacRanald boilin' water wi' a microwave!"

"Not all modern inventions are so bad," laughed Andrew. "The twenty-first century is upon us, you know."

"I'll agree wi' ye there. But a microwave—I canna well fix the twa things in my mind at once: a peat fire in one corner, an' a microwave in the other! Nae, nae, laddie—I'll boil my water slow, an' enjoy the tea the more that it's taken some time an' a wee effort t' bring it t' my lips."

"You're probably right . . . I'm sure water boiled over a peat fire tastes better," replied Andrew, still smiling at the humor of the image he had suggested.

Again they resumed discussing the theft of the Stone.

"What is it about the Stone that makes it so special to the Scots?" asked Andrew. "Why do they call it the Stone of Destiny?"

"Ye might as well ask what makes a Scot a Scot, laddie," replied MacRanald.

"I'm afraid I don't understand you."

"The Scots love their land, the things o' their land, their history, an' their culture. The Stane's part o' them all, as real as if it were alive."

"After all this time . . . in these modern times?"

"The history o' the Scot lives, laddie. The events o' three hundred years ago are as real t' a true Scot as if they'd happened yesterday."

"I remember you telling me the same thing when I was a boy," laughed Andrew.

"Our history's alive, laddie. It lives an' breathes. 'Tis no dead past, but 'tis a *livin'* part o' who we are."

"Every country's got a history. Most people don't feel quite so passionate about theirs."

"No country's got a history like ours. None, that is, but the ancient Hebrews, an' oors isna so unlike theirs gien ye ken whaur t' luik fer the signs o' God's hand in it. Ye can tell," he added with a light chuckle, "that I'm jist a wee prejudiced aboot the matter! But 'tis their history that makes a Hebrew what he is. An' 'tis oor history that makes a Scot a Scot."

"What makes a Scot a Scot, then, Duncan?"

"Ye dinna hae t' look farther back than Glencoe t' find the answer t' that question."

"Glencoe—that's where your ancestors were from?"

"Ay. An' some o' yers, nae doobt as well, an' much o' the MacDonald clan o' which I'm a proud part. If ye want t' find what makes a Scot a Scot, ye'll find yer answer at Glencoe. A piece o' the soul o' every Scot dwells in that wee mountain glen. They tried t' kill the Scots' soul on that evil night. But there's no killing the spirit o' the Highlands.''

"The spirit of the Highlands?"

"Ay . . ." said Duncan as his voice trailed softly away.

A pensive look came over the old Scotsman as the tale he loved replayed in his memory.

" 'Tis a long story, laddie," he said at length. "A sad and bitter story o' freedom lost. We're just comin' up on its anniversary next week."

"Tell it to me, Duncan."

"Noo?"

Andrew nodded.

"Du ye have the time, laddie?"

"I'll make time."

"Then we'll brew this pot o' tea, an' I'll tell ye the tale o' she that might be called the grit-grandmother o' all Scottish lads and lassies since her time, the angel o' the Highlands wi' its spirit in her soul. Then ye'll understand why the blood o' the Scot burns wi' passion fer his land, his history, an' the freedom that was taken frae him. If ye want t' grasp the essence o' Scotland, 'tis t' Glencoe ye must gae first."

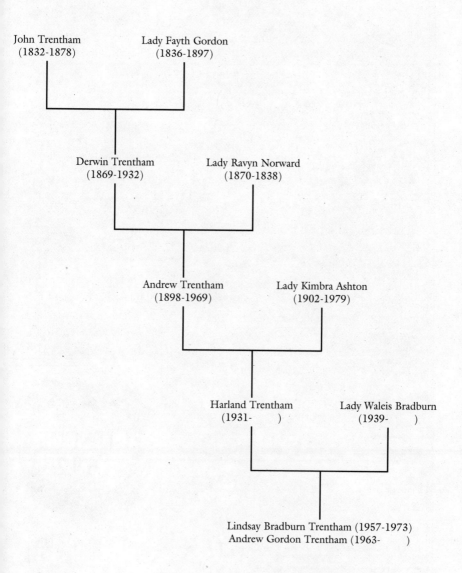

John Trentham
(1832-1878)

Lady Fayth Gordon
(1836-1897)

Derwin Trentham
(1869-1932)

Lady Ravyn Norward
(1870-1838)

Andrew Trentham
(1898-1969)

Lady Kimbra Ashton
(1902-1979)

Harland Trentham
(1931-   )

Lady Waleis Bradburn
(1939-   )

Lindsay Bradburn Trentham (1957-1973)
Andrew Gordon Trentham (1963-   )

Andrew Trentham's Recent Ancestry

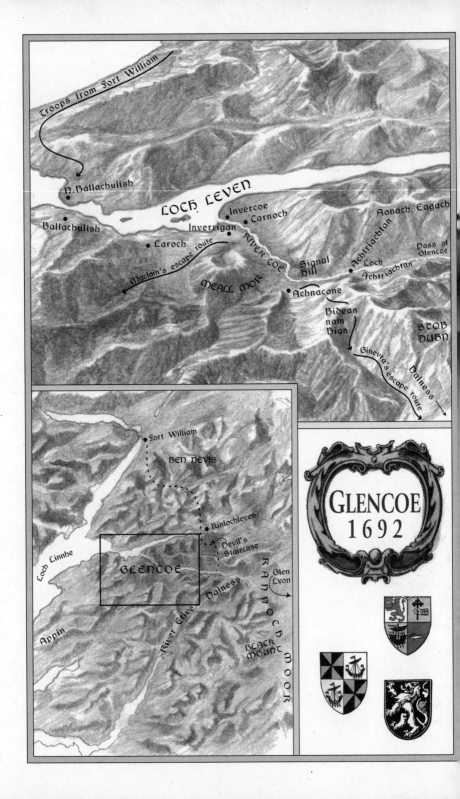

3

The Maiden of Glencoe

February 1692

ONE

It was a rugged, mountainous glen through which tumbled the small river for which it was named, and to which the family called Donald had given its toil and blood from far back in times unknown.

It lay in the debatable lands between the low western forests of Appin, bordering Lochs Linnhe and Leven, and the high inland moor of Rannoch. The narrow valley formed, as it were, a doorway into the central Highlands, and the mountains that flanked it an impassable inland barrier between Strathclyde and the northwest Highlands. And though it lay not many feet above the sea and the nearby lochs, there could be no doubt that it was from the Highlands, rising on three sides around it, that Glencoe derived its soul.

The glen ran east to west, gradually narrowing as it increased in elevation from the shores of Loch Leven, then straightening to no more than a steep passage, climbing up through jagged enclosing heights on each side some twelve miles to the high, desolate watery flats of Rannoch Moor. The western valley itself lay at the base of and between several bare, rugged mountains, some of whose slopes were so steep as to render them impassable to anything but unfriendly Highland goats. North and south, the peaks rose steep and foreboding, leading nowhere but to higher mountains still. These sentinels offered few routes of escape, especially in winter.

The northern wall was called Aonach Eagach, the Notched Ridge, and the only pathway through it was the crooked trail, known as the Devil's Staircase, that ran from Kinlochleven to Rannoch Moor at the eastern door of the glen. To the south, five mountains stood tied to one another by various forbidding ridges. Their lower slopes and glens provided some grass for summer grazing, but they offered few paths out of Glencoe, and only to those who knew them well. The ridges and mountains beyond them simply rose higher and higher, either covered with snow or lost in mists most of the year.

Down the sides of the surrounding hills and in their innumerable crevices and ravines tumbled a thousand small streams, each pouring into the Coe as it flowed from Rannoch Moor downward to empty into Loch Leven at the site of the small village of Invercoe. Boulders and walls of granite created hundreds of waterfalls and chilly crystalline pools. As they cascaded toward the valley floor, gradually the waters slowed and widened into shallow pools, then swelled into the loch of Achtriachtan before narrowing again to continue toward Leven.

For nine or ten months of the year, the upper portion of these streams ran swiftly with the icy water of melted snow. In the dead of winter the smaller ones iced over and ceased flowing altogether. On their banks grew an occasional fir, clumps of stunted pines, with here and there small stands of silver birch, mountain ash, or alder. None grew to any great size, however. Only the overhanging projection of some great boulder, or perhaps the face of a cliff, was capable of giving much shade during the short summer months when it might be needed.

It was a remote region, sparsely peopled in later years. But in those days when Highland life was at its zenith, the valley was fertile and full of life. For the two or three hundred men, women, and children to whom Glencoe was home, clan and earth wove together the fabric of existence.

These inhabitants spoke mostly Gaelic and a little Scots, and were almost entirely of Celtic blood. The cultivated portions of the glen produced little other than oats, kale, barley, and a few potatoes, though in some places sufficient corn ripened during the short summer for the distilling of whisky. Cattle gave milk for butter and cheese. Scrawny sheep also yielded milk and some fleece, and chickens gave eggs and themselves for food. From the nearby lochs, an abundance of fish, mostly herring, saw the people through fierce and punishing winters. Up the surrounding slopes there was much heather and moss, plentiful water and snow, but more rocks than anything.

And there was solitude. Upon leaving one of the half-dozen tiny villages in the glen, one could walk the hills and gaze about in all directions and discover but scant evidence of human abode. The faint perfume of peat fire drifting upward from some unseen chimney might give evidence of habitation. It would still be difficult to discover the cottage it came from, however, so entirely did the houses of that region blend in with the hillsides out of whose stones and turf they had been constructed.

✖ T W O ✖

Near the western edge of the glen, a little more than a mile inland from the mouth of the River Coe, over the cluster of ten or fifteen cottages that made up the village of Carnoch, twilight darkened the sky. Snow would not be far behind.

The girl leaning into the wind as she made her way to the warmth and safety of a nearby dwelling wore a happy smile on her face. Despite the inclement weather and descending dusk, she skipped along merrily, as if it were midsummer. Guests were approaching the glen, and she had particular reason to be hopeful.

They were from a neighboring clan over the hills, and twenty-one-year-old Ginevra Maclain* knew what that could mean. She had not actually seen her Brochan among the uniformed riders. But she *felt* his presence. For one like Ginevra, it was enough, for what she knew came but partially from the sight of her eyes. She depended mostly on unexplained sensations residing quiet and hidden within her soul.

The cottage she approached was of two rooms with an earthen floor, roof of timber and turf with a hole in the center. Stone in this region was plentiful, wood scarce. Thus the timber beams that supported the roof were the most valuable and important part of any home. If the roof went, destruction of the whole cottage was not far behind. The roofs themselves, spread over these timbers, were formed of thick-cut turf or bound heather. Only the largest and most important homes of any community were covered with thatch, a commodity too needful as animal fodder to be commonly used as roofing material.

Barns, or *byres,* of similar construction, sat either adjacent to or as an extension of such structures. The dwelling places of humans and animals might be separated only by hanging skins and hides. During these harsh winter months, cattle had to be kept in and prevented from starvation on what meager provisions could be allotted them, their refuse piled in huge heaps outside.

The girl had seen the soldiers before anyone in Carnoch, though none saw her shadowing their movements. Had any of the horsemen, whom she had spotted approaching thirty minutes before, denoted the wispy figure

---

* *Ginevra* with soft *g,* as in jewel, an Italian form of the French *Genevieve,* meaning "white wave." Maclain, of the clan MacDonald, literally "son of Iain" or "son of John," roughly pronounced M'Kean, or Ma-*Key*-an, with emphasis on "Key."

stalking them, they might have considered her a nymph of these dark, fearsome mountains or perhaps a spirit of some ancient Highland legend. Her wild, flowing hair, however, would have given her away as related, and not distantly, to the current chief. No ghost ever wore such a bright red mane.

Had her own kinsmen spotted her at this moment, none would have paid her much heed. Everyone in the glen knew Ginevra. Most ignored her, though sometimes her peculiar ways unnerved them. She always seemed to turn up in the most unexpected places at the oddest times, watching silently, hearing all. And she always seemed to know what was happening, just as she now knew that the earl's men were coming to seek lodging in Carnoch. The villagers, however, would have to get the news from the chief's two sons, not from Ginevra Maclain MacDonald.

The year was 1692. None of them—not maiden, nor riders, nor the sons of the chief—knew that history was soon to be made. The events about to unfold would immortalize this tiny valley surrounded on three sides by snow-capped and forbidding peaks, and sear this moment of time into the fabric of legend for a nation.

Incredibly, the lass's feet as they hurried over the frozen ground were bare, for she was at home in the elements. Indeed, as well a nymph might, she defied them, daring rain and snow, wind and hail, to do their worst. Her mother was a MacPhail from Laroch, said to be descended from Big Archibald. Her father was nephew to Chief Alasdair. The three, along with her little brother, made their home in Carnoch.

She wore but a plain, thin woolen dress, no coat, no bonnet. Such scant clothing on this night would have worried many a Scottish mother. The days when Ginevra's mother's heart stirred anxiously for her daughter, however, were long past. The girl knew every inch of the glen, every stream, every rock, every sheep path, every peak. She had survived twenty-one harsh Highland winters. Why should she not survive another?

The high regions to the east she had had occasion to traverse many times during recent years as well, for the same reason that her heart had been set stirring with particular hope and eagerness on this evening. For she was a lass in love—that much one look into her eye would reveal in an instant.

That she was one even *capable* of falling in love might have been questioned some years before. For everyone in the glen knew this girl was different from others of human parentage.

❊   T H R E E   ❊

Ginevra's mother had worried for a time. The girl was set apart from the day she was born. Her dark hair, which started out almost black, and the deep blue eyes, which seemed preternaturally aware of her surroundings, immediately attracted the attention of every woman in the village.

"A beautiful baby," the mothers all exclaimed when they first laid eyes on the infant, "and such eyes!"

One among them, however, was not so exuberant in praise of the infant's countenance, a grizzled, ancient woman of wrinkled, leathery skin and more years than anyone in the glen dared speculate on. If she was a witch, no one said it. Yet all feared an evil glance from the old woman as much as they heeded whatever peculiar pronouncements might come from her mouth. Everyone for miles attributed to her the evil eye.

"Aye, she maun hae the second sicht," muttered old Betsy MacDougall upon observing the infant.

A few gasps of mingled wonderment, terror, and awe escaped the lips of the other women. A solemn silence descended over the room.

" 'Tis a blessing an' a curse," the strange woman went on. "An' I be one who ought t' ken, fer I've lived wi' both this many a year."

Ginevra's mother trembled at the words. She knew the danger. She knew that those with the second sight were chosen to walk a lonely path. They beheld what no one else saw, and carried pain no one could take away.

That Ginevra was an unusual child was evident from more than her eyes. As she lay in her cradle, the infant uttered not a peep. Her eyes seemed capable of gathering meaning before the age when most normal children could speak. But as time went on, sounds did not accompany the changes that came to her body. By the time she was two, her mother knew something was amiss.

As the maiden Ginevra grew, her hair gradually changed from black to the bright red of Maclain's himself, while her eyes lightened. The deep color which at first resembled dusk came to reflect the bright blue of midday, eventually transforming into the pale blue of a spring dawn.

Her personality fit both wild hair and pale eyes. A smile usually spread over her lips, but the expression was distant, somehow disconnected from those around her—a smile that came to be accepted as the grin of unknowing simplemindedness. When spoken to, she looked beyond, almost *through*, whoever addressed her, giving no sign that she heard or that the words communicated meaning to her brain. Her face remained as devoid of expression as her eyes were full of strange light, almost an inner luminescence.

Yet by actions and other signs of expression, it was clear her ears functioned properly, that sound, even meaning, registered *something* within her. As much as possible for one so inexplicably severed from the world of speech, she seemed capable of most functions of normality. Even the wisest among the villagers, however, could not tell exactly what she made of what went on around her, or what odd twistings occurred *behind* Ginevra's eyes and ears after words and sounds and sights entered her brain. She absorbed it, that much was clear. But she never gave faintest clue what lay inside.

No one denied that Ginevra was odd in many ways—fixing upon some object and staring at it unmoving for an hour . . . getting down on all fours and imitating a dog, not merely for a few moments but perhaps for days. She took occasionally to wandering the hills alone, at night during the summer months, afraid of nothing. And always was present the blank stare of non-expression. For any indication otherwise, she might have been stone deaf.

Attempts were made to send her to the small school which had recently been established. But the other children treated her cruelly. Ginevra never gave indication whether the goings-on made the slightest sense to her. She would get up from her seat and wander outside and perhaps not be seen for the rest of the day. No discipline, no tongue-lashing, no slap across wrist or any other portion of her anatomy was capable of producing anything but blank stare or sweet smile. As to a change in her peculiar mannerisms, Ginevra was not governed by any rule of conduct or behavior that anyone could gain a clue toward understanding.

One night after the most merciless whipping had produced only a smile in return, even as tears flowed from the innocent eyes, the schoolmaster had been so smitten with guilt over what he had done that he vowed never to touch her again. However odd her behavior, he realized he would never change it by force.

Whether she could read, not even her mother knew. She stared at words on a page with the familiar blank expression that conveyed no hint what she might be thinking.

Even old Chief Alasdair, whose unruly mane, now grown white, had once matched hers in hue, confessed he had never seen the like. Bard Ranald Mac-Donald of the Shield, poet and warrior of more ancient years even than Betsy MacDougall, found himself both charmed and puzzled. Plucking the strings of his small Celtic harp and staring deep into her eyes, softly the bard of

Achtriachtan crooned a melancholy lament to the child whose depths even he could not probe.

> Wee Ginevra oor love, bairn wi' the chieftain's mane,
>   What du ye think, what du ye ken?
> We canna git inside ye, lass—tell us gien ye can.
>   We dinna hear what ye're thinkin', lass—but fain wad we ken. . . .
>   Wha are ye, lass? Tell us gien ye can.
>
> Wha are ye, bairn? What are yer thouchts aboot?
>   We luik . . . we luik but canna see.
> We gaze into yer eyes—only blue looks oot.
>   We see only the twinkle o' stars, the pale o' dawn . . .
>   A vast empty sky. Tell us gien ye can.
>
> O, lass, whaur hae ye come frae? Whaur are ye bound?
>   What is it that hides deep in yer hert?
> Wha are ye, lass? To say, are ye afeart?
>   What du ye think, what du ye ken?
>   Fain wad we ken. Tell us gien ye can. *

The haunting melody in the ancient crackly voice brought tears to the mother's eyes. But from Ginevra herself it elicited but the beginnings of the only sounds anyone ever heard from her mouth—a faint giggle of delight.

The general consensus in the village concerning Ginevra Maclain, great-niece of the chief, was that "she wasna all there."

❊   F O U R   ❊

Ginevra was fifteen when she first met young Brochan Cawdor, of a small sept of Clan Campbell who dwelt near Black Mount on the slopes of Meall a' Bhuiridh at the edge of Rannoch Moor.

She had left the village that morning, wandering upriver about a mile, when the conical hill known as Signal Hill struck her fancy. Immediately she ran toward it, intent to climb the few hundred feet to its peak, stand upon the jagged stone that crowned the hill, and feast her eyes upon the entire glen.

---

* *Wha*—who; *gien*—if; *ken*—know; *afeart*—afraid; *bairn*—child; *oot*—out; *whaur*—where; *wad*—would; *luik*—look; *frae*—from.

A crowd of four or five boys were just then returning from a morning's fishing in Loch Achtriachtan. If she saw them, she gave their presence no more heed than she did that of any human being.

But they saw her.

"Look, it's the idiot Ginevra!" cried one.

They were after her in a flash.

At first the troublemakers were no match for the girl's speed. She was halfway to the top before they reached the hill's lower slopes. But Ginevra's legs were shorter than theirs, and the boys brought to their aid the added resource of sadistic design to sustain their energy.

Ginevra reached the summit as the first two overtook her. She collapsed in a heap at the foot of the stone, breathing heavily. They approached, as exhausted as she, and she gazed up at them with the mysterious smile still on her face.

"Don't smile that way at me!" said the oldest of the boys. He was their obvious ringleader and was by now irritated all the more that it had taken such an effort to catch a mere girl. A box on her ear followed.

She looked up at him with as much expression as she ever displayed, which was a mingling of confusion and pity. She knew him from the neighboring village, but had no idea why he would treat her so. Slowly the smile faded from her face. Catching her breath, she rose to go.

The others by now had gained the summit. Following their leader's mischievous lead, they were not about to lose out on their share of the fun.

"Say something, Ginevra," said one, following after her as she started down the hill.

"What's the matter," taunted another, "cat got yer tongue?"

The others laughed and now scrambled to surround her, preventing her descent.

One of the bolder of the younger boys approached closer and slapped at her face. Ginevra turned away confused, bewildered.

"Be careful," cried the youngest, who hung back nervously. "She'll put a curse on ye!"

"She's just an idiot, Ruadh," the other replied. "She'll not be puttin' a curse on anyone."

"The old witch says she's got the second sicht."

From somewhere on the summit, though no one had seen him approach from the other side of Signal Rock, an elderly man hurried toward them in a feeble run.

"Get away, leave her be, ye nickums!" he cried, giving the two closest a few sharp raps aside the legs with his walking stick.

"What's it to ye, old man!" said the oldest boy, making a few swipes at the stick and trying to grab it from the man's hand.

"Protecting the lass from the cowardly likes o' you, that's what it is t' me."

"Who are ye callin' a coward?" said the boy with imagined courage, spurred on by the knowledge that the others were watching. But behind him their support was quickly vanishing. The youngest, the one named Ruadh, had already turned and bolted back down the way they had come. He feared for his own safety if word of the incident reached his home, for his father was John Maclain, and he himself was grandson to the chief and cousin to the recipient of their torment.

"It's naethin' but a coward who hurts an innocent!" returned the man, giving the oldest boy another deft whack with his cane, this time on the side of the head. The sound of the crack against the thick skull of the troublemaker, followed by the sharp cry of pain from his mouth, was enough to send the remainder of his companions scurrying off after Ruadh Og. The next moment their leader turned and sprinted after them down Signal Hill, shouting meaningless threats behind him.

Her rescuer turned to Ginevra. She stood staring, her eyes more expressive than usual, though it would have been difficult to say what exactly was the expression they contained.

The man approached and laid a tender hand on the head from which red flowed in all directions.

"Dinna pay the nickums mind," he said as he nodded approvingly down. "Ye've got the spirit o' the Highlands in ye, lass. I dinna doobt that the good Lord smiles when he looks doon upon ye. Dinna forget it no matter what men may say."

Ginevra smiled up at him. But it was a sad smile, and she could not hold it for many seconds.

She turned and ran across the top of the hill, continuing down the opposite side from which she had made her ascent.

▦　F I V E　▦

Ginevra ran and ran, reaching the foot of the hill and continuing eastward up the pass along the lower slopes of the Three Sisters overlooking the eastern end of the glen from the south. Steadily the ground rose beneath her feet. Within an hour, walking, climbing, running, stopping every so often for a brief rest, she had covered four or more miles. By now she was far from human habitation, on the northern slopes of Stob Dubh.

After leaving the old man on Signal Hill, uncharacteristic tears rose in her eyes. Running herself to near exhaustion for an hour was not sufficient to stop them. Why she wanted to quell them, Ginevra did not know. She could only tell that when tears came, other strange sensations accompanied them that were confusing and unpleasant, lumps in her throat and aches in her stomach and questions without answers.

Why did the children of the village call her names and throw sticks and rocks at her? Why did the old people try to get her to make noises with her mouth when she had no interest in doing so? She had no need to speak. Hers was a world of feelings, not of words.

But now strange *new* feelings were coming into her. Unknown and fearsome changes had begun in her body. She felt longings she could not express, happinesses that made her cry, sadnesses that made her quiet. When she looked at some of the older boys of the glen—the few who were kind to her— they looked different to her eyes than they had looked before. Sometimes she stared at them, curiously drawn, but did not know why.

This was not the first time tears had risen in her eyes that she could not account for. But never had they lasted so long. Never had she been so unable to make them go away.

She paused to rest on an outcropping of stone and gazed through brimming eyes at the rocky world around her. She was at home here, for the hills were silent as her own soul. The world of men and women was a noisy babbling world. She was a stranger in it. She could find no corner of stillness in the world of men to offer peace. Even in her own home, where she was comfortable and where she knew she was loved—even there no quiet existed that was like the quiet inside her. Even the silences of others were noisy silences.

Here on the hushed slopes, beneath the quiet sky, she was more content than anywhere. The trickling, splashing, tumbling brooks and streams made the kind of music that resonated with the sounds in her heart. The water needed no words to speak, to sing, to tell the world of its travels and adventures and dreams. Why should she need words? Why could not her heart speak like the water spoke, or with the silent meaning of the clouds drifting overhead?

The spirit of the high places was a spirit of calm, of aloneness without loneliness, of solitude and contented seclusion. That same spirit dwelt within her.

Ginevra leapt up from her craggy resting place. Again she ran, yet farther up the glen, up the hill and over a path which in a fateful winter not many years hence would save her life.

Where she ran she did not know. Gradually known landmarks faded behind her. She found herself in a region of the mountains unfamiliar to eyes and feet.

She arrived at length upon a high precipice. She found herself standing at the edge of a grassless boulder overlooking a watery cataract that plunged far below her. She had come to the River Etive, though she did not know its name.

She stood beholding the sight with wonder. But a few moments she stood. Then with sudden abandon she retreated a few paces, turned, and tore off down the slope. A vague notion had arisen within her that if her entire body was wet, the wetness of the tears would go away. She reached a lower rock and without hesitation flew with the grace of an eagle out in the air toward the deep pool of green she had spied from above.

A second of silence followed, then a resounding splash heard by none. Two or three seconds later, Ginevra's head burst out of the pool, cheeks flushed and radiant. The tears were indeed gone. She was bathed from head to foot in the tears shed by the final remnants of the mountain snows.

Her heart pounded, for the pool was icy cold, but new joy swelled within her as well as she climbed from the water on the opposite side and continued on her way.

It was high summer and warm. Ginevra's dress was dry within an hour. When the sun began at last to sink toward the mountains at her back, she did not know where she was. But Ginevra was not afraid. Every hill for miles was her home, whether she had walked their slopes and byways previously or was acquainting herself with them for the first time.

SIX

The lad from Black Mount on the edge of Rannoch Moor was fond of stalking the stag and the hare through the wilds of Meall a' Bhuiridh and Aonach Mor. It was desolate country, dangerous and uninhabitable five or six months of the year, but lonely and inviting for one of Brochan Cawdor's disposition.

He loved to hunt. If he could not find fox, hare, stag or wild boar, one of the ten thousand Highland rabbits that scampered about numerous as insects would do. As he tracked the hills, he dreamed of the day he would ride with the men of his clan into battle against the Danes or the English.

Young Brochan was well acquainted with stories of the Viking invasion of his land centuries before. He knew the legendary accounts of Flodden, and especially the Battle of Sauchieburn, where his ancestor Colin Campbell, first earl of Argyll and chief of Clan Campbell, had risen to prominence, after which the clan's power in Argyll increased greatly. All these stories he had heard from his childhood. They had captivated and filled his brain with romantic fancies of battlefield heroism and images of the glory that one day would rest upon his own shoulders.

At sixteen, with plentiful golden hair and face just beginning to chisel into a man's, his lanky frame was starting to bulge with the muscles of a future soldier. Yet Brochan Cawdor was still too young to ponder the fact that most of the fighting done by the Scots these days was not against invading foreign hordes, but amongst themselves. Well might it be said of his countrymen, "They spend all their time in wars, and when there is no war they fight one another."

The earl's chief man in the region, Robert Campbell of Glenlyon, was Brochan's own great uncle, though in a distant fashion, the intricacies of which he could not trace. That Campbell was considered by many a drunkard who was at the point of financial ruin made the thought of riding behind him into battle none the less romantic in the boy's fancies.

Lost in dreams of adventure, all at once the grayish brown of a rabbit darted like a blur across his path.

The next instant his bow was cocked, a razor-edged arrow strung and ready.

Brochan crept toward the heather thicket into which the animal had disappeared. Carefully the young warrior drew back the wooden shaft and took aim.

Suddenly from behind a rock in front of the thicket sprang a figure. It leapt straight into his line of sight, waving arms and dancing about in wild, frenetic display.

It was a girl! A foolish, stupid girl!

Startled out of his wits, the lad's finger twitched. The arrow loosed and whizzed past her, missing the frantic red head by about three feet. The shaft ricocheted off several rocks and slid harmlessly to a stop twenty or thirty yards beyond.

The rabbit scampered away to safety. The hunter lowered his bow in exasperation and anger, mingled with terror for what he had almost done.

"What did ye du that fer, ye goose?" he cried, running forward. "I might hae killed ye!"

No reply came. The girl relaxed her momentary jig, stood still, and stared at him. He returned the peculiar gaze, not knowing what to make of seeing one so young this far from any habitation or village.

"Whaur are ye frae?" he said after a second or two.

Still she stood staring. His bare, tan, rippling chest was one of the grandest sights the eyes of her dawning womanhood had ever beheld.

"I asked ye whaur ye're frae," he repeated, beginning to lose his patience. "What are ye, deef?"

Now finally did Ginevra answer. A high-pitched musical giggle met Brochan's ears. How could he continue angry with a sound so delightful! He did not exactly smile, but his expression softened. He shuffled back and forth awkwardly on his feet.

"Dinna ye ken I might hae shot ye, lass?" he said, now speaking to her as a child. "An' ye made me miss the cratur."

Ginevra's face fell, but she could not maintain the sad expression for long. Once again the smile broke out across her lips, spreading up into her eyes.

"Why du ye keep smilin' in sic a way?" he asked.

Again came the giggle from the dainty mouth.

"Canna ye du naethin' but smile an' laugh?"

Another laugh, and a shake of the head.

"What's yer name, then?"

No answer followed.

"Whaur are ye frae?" he now repeated.

Still keeping her eyes fixed intently upon her questioner, Ginevra threw her arm back behind her in the general direction of Glencoe. Brochan Cawdor could have no way of knowing that he was quickly becoming the recipient of more communication from Ginevra Maclain than she had ever given to anyone alive.

"Ye're frae the mountains . . . frae Glencoe—whaur, then?"

At the word she began to nod.

"Glencoe . . . ye're a MacDonald, then."

Another nod.

"Weel, I guess I canna hold it against ye, though I'm a Campbell myself. No MacDonald ever hurt a hair on my head. My name's Brochan Cawdor. I wish I kenned yers. What du ye want that I call ye?"

Ginevra giggled.

"Why winna ye speak, lass? *Canna* ye speak?"

A response to that question even Ginevra did not know the answer to. Only another smile met the boy's inquiry.

"Weel, then, I'll jist call ye lassie MacDonald," he said.

The laugh that met his ears this time was pure delight.

"What are ye doin' so far frae home, lassie MacDonald?" Brochan asked.

Ginevra began a little dance, with a waving of her arms, ran a few yards over the heathery hillside, then returned. It was a much different series of motions than that with which she had saved the rabbit from becoming an ingredient in Brochan's mother's stew. The beating of her heart and the explosion of strange sensations erupting somewhere inside her at sight of this boy gave rise to a new desire to express herself. Never before in her life had she *wanted* to say something to another human being. She had never needed to. Now she gave vent to this new feeling the only way she knew how—with animated activity.

She returned and stood before him with an expression that could not have more clearly indicated that he *ought* to understand everything clearly now.

At last he smiled and gave a little laugh.

"Weel, ye're a strange one, lassie," he said. "But ye've a bonnie face an' the bonniest eyes I ever set my sichts on. An' ye got courage, whate'er ye lack in speech."

Unconsciously he glanced up toward the sun. It was just disappearing over one of the high western peaks.

"But 'tis late," he went on. "Ye've got t' get home. I dinna ken whether ye're lost or whether ye ken what ye're aboot as well as any other. An' since ye canna tell me, I'll take ye hame mysel'. Come."

Ginevra obeyed. She followed as Brochan led down the slope in a northwesterly direction, happier than she had ever been in her life.

If Ginevra had known what it meant to be in love, she might have used such words to describe the state of her heart. But she was only fifteen, younger still in the ways of the world, and this handsome, wonderful, friendly boy but sixteen.

It was early to talk of love.

But she knew she had found a friend.

❈   S E V E N   ❈

As the two young people grew, the bond established between them at their first meeting deepened and blossomed.

How they chanced to see each other so often when eleven miles separated the homes of their parents might seem improbable. But where hearts begin to draw close, meetings seem to occur of themselves.

Ginevra hardly slept following her reappearance in the glen after Brochan left her at the point where candles from the first cottages became visible. Not that night, nor the following, nor the night following that. Three days later she was wandering the same solitary moors and slopes and heaths in hopeful thought of catching a distant glimpse of the boy who already occupied her dreams. She did not see him for another week. But when the day finally came that each saw the other on a distant hill, both came running toward the little dell that lay between them. He was as delighted to see her as she was to see him.

"Lassie MacDonald!" he cried.

The mere sound of the name that no one called her but him, in the voice from his lovely lips, sent Ginevra into an ecstasy of dancing gyrations and hand-wavings and skipping about. When at last they again stood before each other, she could do nothing but beam.

"Come, lassie MacDonald," said Brochan, "I'm trackin' a deer—a big one by the looks o' it. But I promise to shoot naethin' while ye're wi' me. We'll jist hae a wee look."

He led the way up the rugged slope, amazed at the girl's stamina and agility as they followed the trail of hoofprint, trampled brush, and musky droppings. She could fly up the rocky ground as quickly as he. Indeed it was *she* who felt the animal's presence long before his eyes detected movement. As they approached, Ginevra made signals and signs with hands and eyes that Brochan was already beginning to grasp. She led the way, making him understand that the creature was near, motioning him into silence that matched her own.

Suddenly he gasped in disbelief. "'Tis the white stag!"

His bow fell to the ground as he gaped in wonder. All thought of attempting a shot immediately left his mind. He had known the tracks he was following had been made by a large animal. But never in his wildest dreams did he anticipate *this*. The great snow-white creature stood drinking at a small pond among the rocks, his expansive rack of antlers riding gracefully as his head bent to the water.

Brochan had heard from his childhood of the great white stag of the Highlands, as had all Highland youngsters. Until this moment, he had only half believed the tales.

The stag apprehended their presence, lifted his noble head, and turned to gaze at them with great, liquid brown eyes. It was an instant that would remain forever etched in both their memories. Only a second more did the magical moment last. Suddenly the stag sprang as if with winged feet over the pond and disappeared among the rocks.

Brochan and Ginevra stood in silence a moment longer, then continued on their way. The encounter left them strangely quiet and peaceful. Gradually Brochan resumed talking. Before long they were on the track of other, more ordinary game. As the afternoon passed, Brochan realized what an asset Ginevra would be to any huntsman. At the same time he knew that whenever they were together, he would not be able to kill so much as a mouse.

For the rest of the summer, as often as they chanced to meet, they hunted together for the sheer joy of tracking and watching and more deeply understanding the ways of the Highlands. With wonder Brochan learned to gaze upon the many wild birds and other creatures of the region with new eyes, not as prey, but as fellow inhabitants of a world that was wider and richer and more beautiful than he had previously known.

In Ginevra's presence he learned to listen to the silence and to hear what the quiet had to teach him. The land and its many creatures became dearer to him because he learned to see all through Ginevra's eyes.

❧ E I G H T ❧

Gradually the air turned, the wind rose, and with it came the smell of snow. Winter descended upon mountains, glens, and moors.

As hearty as was Ginevra Maclain's frame and constitution, no one could now travel in a single day to those high regions where she and Brochan had tracked the stag and the boar and the fox and the elk and hope to return alive.

Ginevra's mother noticed the change in her daughter. Some deeper *knowing*, some keener awareness of life had grown inside her—a yet deeper calm, a more distant expression in her visage, something new in her eyes. All winter the sense deepened that a transformation had come upon Ginevra. It was not until the following summer that the mother discovered its cause.

Late in the spring a lad appeared in Glencoe, a stranger none of the glen had laid eyes on before. None knew him to be a Campbell.

He came asking the whereabouts of a strange girl with wild red hair and a snow cave's eyes of pale blue. A girl who never spoke a word.

It took not long for him to find the one he sought. All in Glencoe knew the lass of pale eyes, flaming hair, and silent tongue.

Immediately the wives began to talk and the children of Achtriachtan, the first village to hear his inquiries, scampered off down the river toward Carnoch with the tidings. Some of the younger children lagged behind and followed the stranger as he went, so that by the time he reached the village where the chief of Clan Maclain dwelt, a multitude of youngsters and barking dogs followed in his train as if he were the piper of Hamelin.

News of his coming had preceded him. From the raucous and varied reports of the children who clamored to her mother's door—that the stranger came from the east, that he was young and strong and handsome—Ginevra well knew who it must be. Ginevra's mother sat rocking as she held her young son, looking at her daughter with question as to what could be the cause of the commotion.

Trembling, Ginevra went to the door and peeped out. In the distance a crowd approached along the village road. At its head strode the tall figure of one who was assuredly a boy no longer. Her heart began beating such that she thought it would explode within her breast.

Slowly she went to the door, opened it, and walked outside. She stood waiting in front of the cottage. He had filled her dreams all through the long winter months. But now she could hardly bring herself to look up. Her eyes sought the ground.

She heard the tumult approach. Gradually it quieted and grew still. Yet a moment more she waited.

"Lassie MacDonald," said a wonderful, familiar voice. "Ye've aye grown into a bonnie maiden since I saw ye last."

Slowly, bashfully, Ginevra lifted her head.

There he stood five feet away, even more magnificent than she had remembered him!

The eyes of the two Highland youths met. Slowly smiles spread over their faces. For a blissful eternal moment nothing else existed in the universe except that both knew they were still one, that they had been all along.

Ginevra's eyes sparkled with light. There was no animated dance now, only a quiet, mysterious happy smile to hear his voice again.

"They tell me yer name's Ginevra," Brochan said.

She closed her eyes for sheer joy. As wonderful as the "lassie" had been, to hear her *own* name on Brochan's lips was rapture indeed.

Both had changed. If Brochan was not much taller, his shoulders were broader and his chest thicker and his voice a note or two deeper. His cheeks were leaner, chin stronger and more angular. He was not yet quite a man. But his hazel eyes bore the dignity of a youth pointed in the right direction, who would be the best kind of man.

As for Ginevra, her body had become the body of a woman. Her face had thinned, her cheekbones grown more prominent, her lips more full, her contours more rounded. Nothing could be done to improve the eyes, the black lashes and brows setting off the pale blue orbs to perfection. Her beauty was indeed radiant, though it took one such as Brochan to see it. Had she not been considered an anomaly, she would have been sought after by every young man in the glen. As it was, none of them paid her the slightest heed, for her strangeness blinded them to the beauty in front of them.

At last, able to contain herself no longer, Ginevra broke into a happy, spontaneous dance of abandon. For a few seconds, her arms flew above her as head bobbed and hair tumbled about.

Brochan laughed with delight.

The spell was broken. Two dozen children and youngsters tore off through the village, each eager to be the first to spread the news of Ginevra's caller from across the mountains.

Now Ginevra was truly in love. She knew it. And her mother knew it.

※ N I N E ※

Whatever might have been the state of her mental faculties—on this question, notwithstanding the visits to Glencoe paid by Brochan Cawdor, the village remained greatly divided—Ginevra was utterly oblivious to the mounting political tensions between England and Scotland. Aware of them or not, however, the collision between the two nations would ultimately destroy the innocence of her silent childhood and youth, and the blissful years of her dawning young womanhood.

In the year 1685, King Charles II of England and Scotland was succeeded by his Catholic brother, James VII. The new king was unpopular throughout both England and Scotland—everywhere but in the Scottish Highlands, where the clan chieftains remained loyal to the ancient Stewart dynasty of the early Jameses and Mary Queen of Scots. James VII might be a Catholic, but he was a Stewart, and that fact was sufficient to resolve the issue in their minds. Highlanders would support him to the death.

The English government, however, adamant that no Catholic could be allowed as head of state, was determined to oust James from rule. So Parliament invited the king's son-in-law, William of Orange, and James' daughter Mary, over from Holland to assume the throne.

William was only too happy to oblige. What man of the times was likely to turn down a kingdom handed him on a silver platter? In November of 1688, therefore, he landed in England with his army, and James VII fled to France. William and Mary were crowned King William III and Queen Mary of England, Ireland, and Scotland.

These events took place in Ginevra's seventeenth year, but she knew nothing of them. Her thoughts were filled with the Campbell lad who dreamed of marching with the earl's men.

Most of southern Scotland supported William's takeover, for the Protestant lowland clans felt little passion for the fading Stewart dynasty and had by then grown gradually comfortable with English rule. But many of the Highland clans obstinately viewed the Dutchman as a usurper to what rightfully should have been a Stewart throne. Eventually hostilities broke out between those who considered James their rightful king, known as Jacobites, and the regime of William and Mary.

In the summer of 1689, King William sent troops north to put down the Jacobite rebels. A force raised from among Highland clans met the government's army at the gorge of Killiecrankie in central Scotland, fell upon it savagely, and nearly annihilated every one of the king's soldiers. In this engagement, MacDonalds were represented more than any other clan, the Campbells the least, for Clan Campbell had little sympathy for the Jacobite cause.

Their victory only deepened the determination of the Jacobites to resist the new order. Fighting continued. King William determined to root out the rebellion against his throne . . . *whatever* measures must be taken. He would *not* let the Highlanders oppose him indefinitely.

※   T E N   ※

Clan Donald, the largest of all Highland clans, stemmed from mixed Norse and Celtic origins. Its name derived from Donald (1207–1249), grandson of Somerled, the shadowy heroic warrior who had conquered much of western Scotland in the mid–1100s. The title "Lord of the Isles," originally applied to Somerled and carried down through the years, reinforced the MacDonald view that the chiefs of Clan Donald, with all its multitude branches, were the undisputed lords of the Gaelic world.

The inhabitants of the little valley of Glencoe were the smallest branch on the tree of this great family. They called themselves Clan Iain, or Clan *John,* after their ancestor *Iain Og nan Fraoch,* Young John of the Heather. The land of the glen had been given to Young John as a gift early in the fourteenth century by his father, Angus Og of Islay, who had brought MacDonalds in large numbers to fight for the mighty Robert the Bruce at Bannockburn.

Following the burial of John of the Heather on the island of Iona in 1338, Clan Iain had been ruled by a succession of eight more Johns. Most of the inhabitants of Glencoe, therefore, considered themselves *sons of John,* or Maclains. The Maclains possessed an ancestry of which any Highlander might be proud, from the present chief Alasdair back twelve generations of Maclains to John of the Heather, to Angus Og and Angus Mor and Donald and Ranald and Somerled himself, yet further back to Colla the Prince and Conn, the High King of Ireland crowned on the Stone of Fail.

The MacDonalds, therefore, at least by their claim, possessed the largest, most royal, and most sacred genealogy in all the Highlands.* And as could be said of most Highland clans, they felt they owed ultimate loyalty to none but their own chiefs. They especially resented the increasing southern attempts to subdue them and to compel their allegiance to a centralized form of national government. Theirs was a centuries-long tribal tradition in which nationhood meant nothing, clan everything.

Through the centuries, tension had increased between these two opposing ways of life—the old tribal tradition and the new, more centralized form of society developing in many parts of the world. For centuries, one English king after another had attempted to subdue the wild Scots of the mountainous north. Lowland Scotland, nearer the border, meanwhile had gradually allowed itself to be assimilated into English culture and government.

As the eighteenth century approached, the Highland chiefs could see their ancient ways dying out. Some, such as the leaders of clan Campbell, at last gave in to the march of progress. Those who went along cooperatively with the new order were rewarded. Money, grants of land, and positions of power were extremely effective inducements to the laying down of clan traditions, along with the swords and rifles that accompanied them.

Others of this proud race, however—notably the MacDonalds—remained fiercely determined to keep hold of their independence, their individuality, and the legacy of their Celtic past. They would bow the knee to no man but the chief of their clan . . . and the *rightful* king of their land.

---

*British names can be confusing in an historical account such as this. Each clan has many subclans or "septs," each with a different surname. There are dozens of distinct MacDonald septs, for example, all of which are affiliated and trace their roots back to the original Donald, grandson of Somerled. When different surnames evolve on this complex family tree, clans gradually develop more than one name. In the case of what are called the "Glencoe MacDonalds," the sept name was Clan Iain or Maclain and the chief's name in 1692 was Alasdair, nicknamed "the Red." Confusion results when, in the common practice of the day, such a man might be known by any of his names—or by his home itself. Thus the chief might be called any of the following: "Alasdair Maclain" or "Maclain" or "Maclain of Glencoe" or "MacDonald of Glencoe" or "MacDonald" or even simply "Glencoe." So when the king and John Dalrymple in London spoke together about "Glencoe," they were generally not referring to the place, but specifically to Alasdair Maclain, chief of the Glencoe branch of the MacDonald clan. And Alasdair's *son*, also named Alasdair, would possess the same list of appellatives.

Robert Campbell of Glen Lyon, Alasdair's counterpart in the Glencoe drama, at least possessed only one surname, which lessens this confusion somewhat. He was known equally as "Campbell" and "Glenlyon."

Further confusion results when men were known either by title or by the name of their estate or the title of their peerage. Thus Sir John Dalrymple, King William's secretary of state for Scotland, who was the Master of Stair, is often referred to in historical documents simply as "Stair," as if it were his actual name.

No one man more implacably represented this determination than Ginevra's great uncle, chief Alasdair Maclain of Glencoe.

Neighboring the Glencoe Maclains, both to the south in Argyll and eastward on Rannoch Moor, lived large numbers of Campbells who were loyal to the new king and disdainful of the Jacobite cause. For a hundred years Clan Campbell had profited from alliances with London and Edinburgh. As a result, it had grown and increased its holdings, while Clan Donald had its lands taken away for opposing the crown.

By the final decades of the sixteenth century, King William III and his advisors had come to view the Campbells as the most reasonable of Scotland's clans, and the earl of Argyll as one of the king's most trusted supporters in the Highlands. In MacDonald eyes, therefore, their neighbors to the south and east were the worst kind of national traitors.

But the rivalry between the two clans had local roots as well. As joint occupants of the western lands, they had thieved and raided one another's herds for centuries. It was in this spirit that Alasdair "the Red" Maclain, giant chief of the Glencoe MacDonalds, carried out one of his most successful plunders in 1689. Returning from the victory at Killiecrankie with his men, still resentful that no Campbells had joined them in battle, he marched through the Campbell stronghold of Glen Lyon west of Aberfeldy, across the Black Mount, and north across Rannoch Moor, thence descending down into their native glen along the banks of the Coe. On their way they made off with thirteen hundred Campbell horses, cattle, sheep, and goats, as well as many household goods.

It was a monstrous raid. In the Highlands, livestock represented wealth and social standing as well as means to feed one's people. The Campbells claimed losses in excess of £7500, a huge sum. Many in Glen Lyon vowed to get even.

Campbell and MacDonald—they were the mightiest of Caledonia's ancient names, with much shared blood between them. But they remained rivals and enemies, and only one would lead Gaeldom into the future.

⊞   E L E V E N   ⊞

By the autumn of 1691, Brochan and Ginevra had treasured many happy times together on the moors and mountains and each in the village of the other, where despite the rivalries between their chiefs both were well known and loved. They had also spoken—Brochan with words, Ginevra with eyes and her heart—of their future together.

But the season when Brochan stalked rabbits with bow and arrow was past. A sword and dirk now hung to the side of his plaid, for he had grown to be a man of twenty-one. The years when adulthood's mantle must rest upon his shoulders had come. He was one who must know his worth, his mettle. Could Highlander and Gael expect less from himself?

Not Brochan Cawdor. If he would be worthy of *her,* he must first prove worthy to *himself.*

Therefore, a-soldiering he must go. It was the way of his clan . . . the way of his nation.

He came to the glen one day knowing it would be his last visit for some time.

Ginevra had become a quiet maiden, beautiful now even in the eyes of her own villagers, tall, graceful, well-proportioned, and modest. She rarely danced about now with hands waving, but could be seen walking beside loch or stream, in village or on distant hillside, with serenity of carriage and grace of expression. Still the faraway look distanced her demeanor and countenance from all others. Different she would always be. But hers was now the faraway expression of an angel, not of a half-wit.

Even those who in younger days had plagued her now stood not a little in awe. Some were afraid of her. Others greeted and spoke to her. A few, it is true, avoided her when they saw her approaching, in time to cross the road or change their course, for the looks she occasionally cast could still be disconcerting and unnerving. Not everyone knew how to return them. But these were not many. Most, indeed, held her in a similar sort of veneration as they did bard Ranald of the Shield.

Ginevra could not, of course, be more silent than she had always been. Yet somehow her silence seemed to have deepened. Whenever she and Brochan were together in the sight of those in the glen, she was shy about his affections. Often a pink blush might be seen about neck and cheeks. Alone, however, she could be as animated as ever. Brochan knew every look and expression and movement and glance and twitch of lips, and knew what each signified. Sometimes he felt richer for Ginevra's silences, for they made him know *her* better. In one other thing she had changed: she had learned not merely to giggle, but to *laugh*—a rich, alto, robust laugh of joy.

On this occasion of Brochan's visit, however, there was no laughter between them. He had just told her that he was going away.

They walked hand in hand along the banks of the Coe, then higher into the glen. The waters beside them were gentle and quiet, gathering strength for their winter rushes and tumbles.

For a long time Brochan was as silent as Ginevra. These tidings could not but bring her sadness. Yet they were at peace. Both had learned that in silence did the best within them meet in the profoundest way. They did not fear silence, but sought it—she because she could not help it, he because he loved her and would know this deepest part of her nature and what it had to teach him.

When at last he broke the spell of the stillness, it was that together they might remember their times. For in this coming season of their separation, they would have only happy memories to sustain them.

"The day when I first saw ye," Brochan was saying, "I was so angry that ye made me miss my rabbit, but afraid too for what I might hae dune . . . an' spellbound by yer antics all at once. I was sich a loon, I didna ken what t' say. . . .

"An' du ye remember," he went on, speaking in a peaceful voice, "win we were oot up on Stob Dubh—during the storm, the unco rout o' thunder an' watching the water tumblin' doon all aroun' us, an' racin' doon t' the glen tryin' t' git t' yer cottage afore the rain . . ."

As he spoke, Ginevra nodded and smiled with pleasure.

" . . . but then the clouds aye let loose . . . an' there we came rinnin' into yer puir mither's hame wet an' lauchin' like twa bairns. . . ."

How could he ask if she remembered? She would never forget a single happy minute they had spent together these four years!

"Jist last week," he was saying, "I saw a stag, an' it put me in the mind o' when we tracked the one t' the old crag on Bhuiridh last year. I think 'tis the same one. Ach, but I haup one day t' lay eyes on the white stag again. Remember hoo we came upon it—"

Suddenly, in the midst of his speech, Ginevra darted away. A moment later she returned with a tiny violet. She held it toward Brochan with the searching, inquiring eyes he had learned to read.

"Ay, I remember," said Brochan, "when we found that bed o' wee floers by the burn. An' ye made me bend doon an' look, 'cause I had eyes only for the fish I was tryin' t' git. An' ye made me smell them. Ay, I mind the day."

He paused, then began digging into the leather sporran that hung in front of his kilt.

"Look," he said, "I still hae the ones ye pressed for me, atween this scrap o' paper."

Ginevra smiled to think that the great, strong man who was about to become a soldier would keep her few dried flowers.

Again they resumed their stroll. Brochan continued peacefully to reminisce. He knew he had to speak for both of them, framing their memories into words that they might enjoy them together.

"An' the night we crossed the loch in yer father's boat in moonlight t' the north shore atween the twa lochs," he went on. "Yer eyes were so full o' the moon that night, I thought gien e'er yer tongue wad loose and ye'd speak, it wad hae been that night."

There were not many occasions when Ginevra longed for the power of speech. But when Brochan spoke like this, she could not help wishing she could say something, if only to make him happy.

"All I want, sometime in my life, lassie MacDonald," he continued, "is t' hear my ain name on yer bonnie lips. Jist the ane word *Brochan*, an' I'll dee a happy man. Canna ye say it, Ginevra? Canna ye say it, jist fer me?"

But only the familiar, treasured smile met his question.

He turned toward her, then leaned down and kissed the silent, expressive lips. As he drew back, Ginevra's eyes were full of tears.

If only she could speak, what torrents would her heart pour forth! But only with her eyes could she open her woman's heart to the world. Now they flooded with the liquid of love.

They walked some distance in silence, then turned and began the return to Carnoch.

"Those were aye times when we both were free," Brochan said at length. "Time doesna move on for you, but it moves for me. I maun gae next week, Ginevra. I'm at last to be in my uncle's regiment."

Now at last did the chill seize Ginevra's heart. He saw it on her face.

"Dinna fear fer me, dear lassie MacDonald," he said. "'Tis what I've always wanted t' du. I'll be a soldier at last. An' I'll come for ye ane day, an' we'll marry an' build a wee cottage up the slopes o' Aonach Mor where first we saw ane anither. An' we'll hae bairnies an' grow old in oor cottage together, wi' heather all around an' the blue o' the Highland sky abune us. An' our bairns'll—they'll be half Campbell, half MacDonald. We'll teach all oor people that the clans maun be one, jist as we are one. But I've got t' be a soldier first, Ginevra, my ain lassie MacDonald. 'Tis my dream."

Ginevra nodded. She understood. Brochan had helped her understand many things.

But her bones remained cold. And she could not help being afraid. She would not lay eyes on him again until that snowy evening when she saw him arrive once more in the glen of her home with the other soldiers of his clan.

⊠   T W E L V E   ⊠

After the ruthless slaughter of his army by the Highlanders at Killiecrankie, the English king determined to crush the rebellious spirit of the clan chiefs who remained obdurate in their support for James VII.

The Highlanders, in William's eyes, were the most present and visible obstacle to a complete political union between England and Scotland. Their outdated tribal society, backward customs, ridiculous kilts, and uncivilized language . . . they had to be rooted out, destroyed, their independent spirit broken, their defiance humbled. Clans like the MacDonalds were thieving, savage marauders. If they would not submit, they deserved but one fate.

The word that began to be discussed behind the closed doors of London between the king and his closest advisor, Sir John Dalrymple, himself a Scot and a member of the king's Privy Council, was *extirpation.* At length King

---

*The multitude and confusion of names in this drama may be helped by a brief cast of the principal characters along with the various names by which they were known.

King William III of England—William of Orange, became king in 1689, son-in-law of deposed King James VII.

Sir John Dalrymple—Master of Stair, secretary of state for Scotland, also known as "Stair."

Sir Thomas Livingstone—King William's commander in chief in Scotland.

Chief Alasdair Maclain of the MacDonalds of Glencoe—"Alasdair the Red, the old fox, Maclain of Glencoe, Maclain, MacDonald of Glencoe, MacDonald, Glencoe."

John Maclain—eldest son of Alasdair, who succeeded him as chief.

Alasdair Og Maclain—younger son of Alasdair, "Alexander the Younger," married to Sarah Campbell, niece of Robert Campbell of Glenlyon.

Ruadh Og—son of Alasdair Og, grandson of the chief.

Archibald Campbell, tenth earl of Argyll—known simply as "the earl" or "Argyll."

Captain Robert Campbell of Glen Lyon—known as "Campbell" or "Glenlyon."

Sir Colin Campbell of Ardkinglas—sheriff of Argyll, known as "Ardkinglas."

Colin Campbell of Dressalch—sheriff-clerk of Argyll, office in Edinburgh, known as "Dressalch."

Colonel John Hill—governor of Fort William.

Lieutenant Colonel Sir James Hamilton—appointed deputy governor of Fort William.

Major Robert Duncanson—commander of the Argyll regiment sent by Hamilton from Fort William to Ballachulish.

Captain Thomas Drummond—delivered dispatch from Duncanson to Robert Camp-

William, advised by Dalrymple, decided upon an ultimatum from which there would be no retreat nor compromise.

He issued a proclamation ordering all Highland clan chiefs to sign an oath of allegiance to the English crown. If they complied by the last day of December 1691, there would be no further consequences. Upon those who did *not* sign, the punishment would be carried out by fire and sword.

Word of the ultimatum came to the deposed king James VII, exiled in France. He knew his son-in-law was a dangerous man and that this was no bluff. He sent word back to Scotland releasing the chiefs from their remaining loyalty toward him. They must, he said, swear allegiance to King William. The Jacobite cause was over.

Most of the chiefs complied. They were weary of the fight. It was clear they could not hope to win.

By year's end, only a handful had not yet signed the oath. Mostly the holdouts were of the MacDonald clan in the northern and western Highlands. The chiefs of Glengarry, Sleat, Glencoe, and Clanranald of Moidart had proved most obstinate. One of these infuriated Dalrymple by his obstinacy more than all the rest—the elderly chief of the smallest branch of MacDonalds, Alasdair the Red of Glencoe. He seemed to represent everything about the Highlands that Dalrymple hated, and thus came to embody the focus of his venom.

Whatever happened, Dalrymple was not about to let this particular chief go unpunished. In his own mind he had already begun to plot how to destroy him, even if the man *did* sign.

But secretly Dalrymple hoped he would not.

---

bell on February 12.

MacDonald of Inverrigan—Robert Campbell's host in Glencoe, known as "Inverrigan."

Sergeant Robert Barber—Brochan's commander, hosted with his men by MacDonald of Achnacone.

Others mentioned: Sir John Campbell, earl of Breadalbane (known as "Breadalbane"), Alasdair the Black MacDonald of Glengarry (known as "Glengarry"), Allan MacDonald of Clanranald (known as "Clanranald"), Sir Donald MacDonald of Sleat (known as "Sleat").

❈   T H I R T E E N   ❈

That Alasdair Maclain of Glencoe was a thief who had spilled the blood of his enemies, there was little doubt. But in the Highlands there existed codes of loyalty to justify such things.

A century before, for their help in combating disorder in Scotland, the Campbells of Argyll had been granted huge tracts of land by the Crown— land seized from the MacDonalds. Ever since had the two clans remained the bitterest of enemies—with thieving, looting, burning, massacring going both ways between them.

As the seventeenth century drew to a close, it was still the Campbells who held the Crown's favor. At their stronghold of Inveraray sat the court and jail from which the king of England meted out justice in the north, presided over by Archibald Campbell, tenth earl of Argyll. No greater satisfaction could exist for any man at Inveraray than once and for all to put an end to the raids by Glencoe's men. It was the dream of many a Campbell to see Alasdair Maclain one day swinging on the end of a rope.

It would have taken a high-built gallows. Even in his old age, Alasdair presented an imposing figure, at six foot seven, with long, wild hair and a flowing mustache. In his youth, the hair had been red, and he had displayed a temperament to match. It was scarce wonder he was one of the most well-known—both loved and hated—rascals in the Highlands.

Argyll had had his chance in 1674, when Maclain had been imprisoned in the Inveraray Tollbooth. But though he was already in his sixties at the time, the huge man had managed to slip from behind Campbell bars and make good his escape back to Glencoe.

And now, seventeen years later, his red crop and mustache grown white, old Alasdair remained the same rogue he had always been. The years, however, if they had not made him repentant, had at least added a dose of realism to his hatred of the Campbells. By the end of 1691, he had finally accepted the inevitability of compliance.

After Christmas, therefore, Alasdair Maclain reluctantly set out for Fort William in Inverlochy. His head was now topped with the color of snow on the mountains, not the red of a peat fire. But he still presented a fearsome image, for a glow of the fire of resistance could yet be detected in his eyes.

Alasdair arrived at Inverlochy on December 31, the very last day before the ultimatum expired, presenting himself to the commander in charge and governor of Fort William, Colonel John Hill.

He was ready, he said, to take the required oath and swear allegiance to the king.

FOURTEEN

This was not the first time John Hill had seen service in Scotland.

He had been here at the beginning of his military career, briefly occupying the same post he held now—first as deputy, then as governor of this northern outpost under the shadow of Ben Nevis, the highest peak in all Britain. The Highlanders knew the outpost as *Gearasdan dubh nan Inbhir-Lochaidh,* the Black Garrison of Inverlochy. He had made many friends among the Highlanders at that time and had governed well.

For the next thirty years, Hill had moved through the empire as he climbed the military ladder to the position of colonel. Now in his late sixties, he was back in what was now called Fort William, renewing acquaintances among the Highland chiefs with whom he had managed to make peace more successfully than most of his peers.

Hill was an honest and relatively simple man, not a particular favorite among those who had now come to power in London, especially John Dalrymple. He was perhaps too principled. A good soldier, willing to gain native loyalty by friendship rather than threats, Hill was also set apart by his literary acumen and knowledge of the Scriptures, both of which bolstered a strong Protestant faith. His health was gradually failing, and the loneliness of age was setting in, which both his books and Bible helped alleviate. Events were soon to overtake him, however, for which he would find no comfort in either.

Hill was a sad figure, not because he had no scruples but because he was one of the few among the figures involved who did. Yet he was powerless to employ them to alter what more and more appeared the inevitability of disaster.

On this particular December day, a sense of impending doom fell upon him as heavily as the wet, clumping snow outside his office. For a moment he sat stunned as Maclain's words echoed in his ear.

"Why do you come to *me!*" he asked.

"I have come to swear the oath," repeated Alasdair in thick, Gaelic-encrusted English.

"But the proclamation is unambiguous," insisted Hill. "*The oath must* be taken in the presence of the sheriffs, or their deputies, of the respective shires where any of the said persons shall live. Those are the orders you all received. You know as well as I do that I am no sheriff."

Alasdair stood stoic and silent.

Colonel Hill looked over the stern, wild figure towering above him, the green-and-red kilt of his tartan dirty from travel, the dirk at his waist, the snow still unmelted on his shoulders, lips unmoving beneath the thick white mustache.

"I have no power to administer the oath," Hill added, exasperated. He had done everything in his power to forestall a disaster. Now this old fool had come to the wrong place!

"I am a military officer, not a magistrate," he persisted. "You must go to Ardkinglas at Inveraray. He's the sheriff in this area."

"Inverary's a Campbell toon," returned Maclain stiffly. "I hae not been there sin' the day I escaped frae its jail. I'll nae willingly set foot in sich a place."

Hill now realized why the old chief had come to Fort William rather than Inveraray. How could the proud MacDonald chief take such an oath of submission before a *Campbell*?

"I realize it may seem unthinkable, Maclain—" nodded Hill.

"MacDonalds have swung on Campbell ropes at Inveraray," interrupted the chief to bolster his point. "I dinna fancy being the next."

"I know all about your feuds," continued Hill. "But believe me, if you take the oath before Ardkinglas, no one will put a rope around your neck. Ardkinglas is a reasonable man."

"He's a Campbell."

"Dalrymple's threats are not to be toyed with, I tell you, Maclain. This is serious business."

It was more grave than Hill dared reveal, but he could not tell all he knew. The proclamation of last August had stated the risk clearly: *"Such as shall continue obstinate and incorrigible after this gracious offer of mercy shall be punished as traitors and rebels to the utmost extremity of the Law."*

Hill, after all, was a colonel in the king's army. He could not tell that troops were already amassing in preparation to march on the strongholds of the septs who refused the oath, that some of the regiments were on their way here even as they spoke.

"For once in your life, Maclain," Hill went on, more gently now, "you *must* listen to reason. The lives of your people depend on it. This is no time to be stubborn. I tell you, the danger is real and imminent." The softness of his voice made it all the more urgent.

He paused briefly. His eyes bored solemnly into the Highlander's. Then he added, "Don't you understand the danger?"

As he stood listening, at last the proud, stoic, stubborn, thieving chief began to apprehend the true state of peril in which he stood. He knew Hill to be an honest man. The man's tone was worrisome.

The chief grew uneasy, then slowly began to nod his head.

"Good," sighed a relieved Colonel Hill. "Now you have only twenty-four hours, and with this weather, you'll never make it in time. But I will write to Ardkinglas telling him that your attempt *was* made within the time-table prescribed by the king's order. I am sure he will accept it."

Hill took paper from his desk, wrote a few brief words, then sealed and folded the letter. He rose and handed it to the chief, then led the way from his office. The two walked together to the main gate.

"You must make haste, Maclain," Hill urged as they went. "The danger is great, both to you and your people."

With that final entreaty in his ears, the chief mounted his shaggy pony and headed south again through the snow.

The direct journey south to Inveraray on the shores of Loch Fyne crossed some of the most rugged terrain in Scotland. It would have been an impossible trek overland in the middle of the terrific winter's snowstorm blanketing the Highlands this last week of the year. Taking the long way around, more than a hundred fifty miles, the chief did not arrive until January 3. There he discovered that the king's sheriff, Sir Colin Campbell of Ardkinglas, was away.

For two days Alasdair Maclain waited. Finally Ardkinglas returned. The chief presented himself. The Campbell railed at him for being late. Stoically the chief handed him Hill's letter. Ardkinglas read Governor Hill's appeal.

"Maclain," Hill had written, "has been with me, yet slipped some days out of ignorance. But it is good to bring in a lost sheep at any time, and will be an advantage to render the king's government easy."

Ardkinglas shook his head again. The deadline had been set, he said. The law was the law. He could not now administer the oath.

Suddenly the aged, towering man of rival clan broke down in tears before him.

"Administer the oath," Maclain begged. "Upo' my honor I promise I'll order all my people t' be loyal t' the king. If ony refuse, ye may imprison them or send them t' Flanders t' fight in the king's army."

How could even a Campbell resist such a humbling of pride? The sheriff weakened. The humanity of the old man pricked his own.

"Come to me tomorrow," said Ardkinglas finally, "and it will be done."

On the morning of January 6, 1692, therefore, Alasdair Maclain of Clan Donald, before sheriff and clerks and other officers, swore and signed the oath of allegiance to King William and Queen Mary, asking their pardon, their protection, and their indemnity.

Maclain returned to Glencoe under sunny skies. The storm had passed. Already the snows were melting. A fire was built atop Signal Hill by which the chief summoned the men and women of the glen. Ginevra stood with her mother and father and other members of her clan to hear the chief announce to them that he had taken the oath on their behalf. Standing weary but straight-backed before them, the old man instructed his people to live peaceably under King William's government, adding that they would have nothing to fear as long as they abided by the terms of the oath.

Ginevra listened to the announcement with a mixture of indifference and hope. Indifference because this world of oaths and kings seemed so far removed from her own world of village and mountain. Hope because she wondered if this occasion might somehow bring her Brochan sooner home to her. If all was to be well, as her great-uncle was proclaiming, surely she would see her love again before long.

All was not as well, however, as the chief might hope.

Papers arrived in Edinburgh from Ardkinglas a week later at the office of the sheriff-clerk. A list was included of all those who had taken the oath at Inveraray. Hill's letter regarding Maclain was also included. Ardkinglas instructed the clerk to send the papers on to the Privy Council in London in evidence of compliance with the king's proclamation.

The clerk, however, one Colin Campbell of Dressalch, had lost several cows to the Glencoe men in the raid of two years before. He looked over the list, noting with interest the date of Maclain's oath: January 6.

Should it be accepted as valid? Dressalch consulted with other officials in Edinburgh. The matter was discussed among several Campbell lawyers.

The end result of their discussions was that, before the papers were sent to London, Dressalch scratched two or three black strokes of his pen through "Alasdair Maclain of Glencoe," removing the name from the list.

As the year 1692 opened, no one in London knew exactly how many chiefs had taken the oath. The king's commander in chief for troops in Scotland, Sir Thomas Livingstone, was put on alert for what might be required.

Sir John Dalrymple was delighted when he learned that up to a half dozen MacDonald chiefs had not taken the oath.

Having accidentally killed his brother as a boy in Scotland, young Dalrymple had been exiled to the Netherlands by his parents. As he grew to military age, he had made the acquaintance of William of Orange, gradually becoming one of his most trusted advisors. He had returned from the Continent with the new king, now as the Master of Stair, and had been given a high position in the new government. His sense of gratitude and loyalty to the king was as powerful as his resentment toward the Scotland of his childhood. As secretary of state for Scotland, Dalrymple now held the matter of the Highlands largely in his own hands. He was determined to make an example of the troublesome chiefs that would not soon be forgotten.

A large contingent of troops was amassed at Fort William for an assault on MacDonald of Glengarry, and whomever else it might be necessary to punish.

Even as this military buildup was under way, however, assurances were coming in from throughout the Highlands, relayed by Colonel Hill, that all the chiefs would submit in time—from MacDonald of Sleat and Coll of Keppoch to Clanranald of Moidart and the other vigorous holdout, MacDonald of Glengarry. Hill was not eager to see blood shed over the matter and was relieved that the great and widespread Clan Donald seemed at last ready to accept the new order of things. A peaceful resolution appeared at hand.

Colonel Hill's sympathies, however, were not shared by his superiors.

On January 7, Dalrymple dined with the earl of Argyll and the earl of Breadalbane, both Campbells, to discuss what ought to be done to solve the Highland business once and for all.

"Maclain of Glencoe," said the earl of Argyll, "did *not* sign by the first of the year."

Dalrymple nodded, then took a sip of the fine wine the earl had provided. Gradually a cunning smile spread across his lips. It had turned out just as he had hoped.

A plan began to take shape in his mind of a secretive strike against

Maclain and his brood, at a time when they were most isolated and could not hope for help from any of their cousin clans.

Dalrymple left the fortuitous dinner. Alone that same night in his own quarters, he drafted a set of orders to Livingstone. The next day they were signed by King William. The orders began:

YOU ARE HEREBY ORDERED AND AUTHORIZED TO MARCH OUR TROOPS WHICH ARE NOW POSTED AT INVERLOCHY AND INVERNESS, AND TO ACT AGAINST THESE HIGHLAND REBELS WHO HAVE NOT TAKEN THE BENEFIT OF OUR INDEMNITY, BY FIRE AND SWORD AND ALL MANNER OF HOSTILITY; TO BURN THEIR HOUSES, SEIZE OR DESTROY THEIR GOODS OR CATTLE, PLENISHINGS OR CLOTHES, AND TO CUT OFF THE MEN. . . .

To these instructions Dalrymple added, "My lord Argyll tells me that Glencoe hath not taken the oath, at which I rejoice. It's a great work of charity to be exact in rooting out the damnable sept, the worst in all the Highlands."

At their meeting, the earl of Argyll had also expressed concern for the soldiers of his own regiment, who had been sent to Fort William under Major Robert Duncanson in case Glengarry did not sign. The earl cautioned that his men did not have rations for more than a couple weeks. The fort was too crowded to house everyone adequately for such a buildup of troops. Along with the orders, therefore, Dalrymple also told Livingstone to make some arrangement for provisions for the men of Argyll's regiment.

The orders were sent north, the Master of Stair confident that Livingstone had been given full power in the plainest possible language to mete out the king's punishment against the rebels.

A few days later, Dalrymple and the king conferred to discuss the other holdouts.

"It would not be wise at this time," William said, "to provoke a widespread war in the Highlands. If only the remaining chiefs would sign the oath, I would be inclined to overlook their tardiness."

"Even Glengarry?" asked Dalrymple.

"His men would be more useful fighting for me in Flanders than dead," replied William. "If they will but sign the oath, I will not quibble over the date."

"But you agree," added Stair, "that Maclain of Glencoe must not go unpunished? An example must be made."

"Do what you must do," answered the king. "I will sign the order."

"We may have a slight problem with Colonel Hill at Fort William," said Dalrymple. "I fear he is more sympathetic to the Highlanders than suits our purpose."

"Is anyone else in the region dependable?"

"There is Sir James Hamilton."

"His rank?"

"Lieutenant Colonel."

"Then appoint him deputy governor at the fort."

"Hill would still be his superior."

"A technicality," replied William. "I am king and superior to them both."

"What do you propose?"

"Bypass Hill. Carry out the orders through this Hamilton."

Dalrymple nodded. That same night he wrote letters of new instructions to Livingstone and also to Colonel Hill and Lieutenant Colonel James Hamilton.

To Commander Livingstone he wrote, "For a just example of vengeance, I entreat that the thieving tribe in Glencoe be rooted out in earnest."

As soon as it had been set in motion, however, Dalrymple's plan was thrown into jeopardy. Suddenly word reached London that Maclain of Glencoe *had* in fact taken the oath, and *sooner* than had Glengarry and several of the others.

Dalrymple thought the matter through briefly. The news, he concluded, need change nothing. He would not even bother the king about it. Even if Glencoe had sworn the oath, he was still late—and would still serve as an example to the others.

Once more he wrote to Livingstone.

"I am glad that Glencoe did not come in within the time prescribed," Dalrymple wrote. "I hope what's done there may be in earnest, since the rest are not in the condition to draw together to help. I believe you will be satisfied it will be of great advantage to the nation that the thieving tribe be rooted out and cut off. It must be done quietly."

Upon receiving his orders from Dalrymple, Livingstone now wrote to Hamilton, "It is wished by the king that the thieving nest at Glencoe be entirely rooted out. The orders from the court are positive not to spare any. I desire you would begin with Glencoe. Spare nothing which belongs to him. But do not trouble the government with prisoners."

Hamilton read over the communication from his commander, then shrewdly considered the best method for carrying out the order. Well had

Dalrymple chosen his man, for the two thought alike.

Slowly a plan entered into Hamilton's mind—cunning and devious. He would use the fort's overcrowded condition as pretext, aided by the relation of one of his captains to the Maclain brood. He would send a regiment to Glencoe and demand billeting for troops. Under the guise of requesting hospitality, he would sabotage Maclain's defenses and catch him off guard.

He would, of course, keep quiet about his intent until the moment was right to spring the trap.

Hamilton drew up the necessary orders. He immediately dispatched Captain Robert Campbell of Glenlyon, with two companies of men, to Glencoe.

✣   SIXTEEN   ✣

As sixty-year-old Captain Robert Campbell, fifth laird of Glen Lyon, led his men south from Fort William toward Ballachulish, where they would cross to Glencoe, he thought back gloomily on the circumstances that had landed him here.

The face that once had caused women to swoon was now lined and aging. And at the moment very cold. He was a tragic yet cowardly figure in the drama of which he did not yet even realize himself a part. Cowardly not because he had no heart—but because he yet possessed the vestiges of one. And therein lay the tragedy of Robert Campbell of Glenlyon, forever after known as the Judas of Caledonia's tearstained legacy. For surely he would live the rest of his days with the guilt of what he was about to do. Yet he did not possess even what cowardly courage it took to hang himself when it was done.

Like Hill and old Alasdair, Campbell was past his best years, if "best years" anyone would call them—years filled with drinking, gambling, and the financial strains brought on by both. In his early days he had cut a wide and dashing swath through the Valley of Glen Lyon between Rannoch Moor and Loch Tay, perhaps nearly as beautiful a place as the Glen of the Coe. Young Robert Campbell had been handsome, jovial, and polished, loved by men and women alike. But his self-indulgent lifestyle had brought him soon into debt and bankruptcy, and he remained in debt to half the men in the region. He had lost land, looks, and health. By the age of fifty he had become, if not a broken man, certainly a humiliated one. Others of Clan Campbell, to whom he was an embarrassment, had forced him to place what remained of his estate in his wife's name to prevent his gambling it away.

Only a year before, he had taken a commission in the earl of Argyll's regiment in order to raise what meager income he could. Eight shillings a day would not be enough even to keep pace with the interest on his debts. But it might keep him from starvation . . . and decently supplied with whisky.

Upon receiving his orders from Hamilton, anger from the former rivalry had stirred in Robert Campbell's blood. He had suffered his own share of losses from the recent rash of Maclain raids in Glen Lyon, and he hated the MacDonalds like the good Campbell he was.

But the ride in the freezing wind, under skies that portended snow, and thought of Maclain's whisky gradually moderated his bitterness. Young men might enjoy the rigors of military duty, but he did not. Perhaps a few days in Glencoe would not be so bad, he thought. And the fact was that he was himself related to Clan Maclain, by marriage if not by blood. He was uncle to the wife of old Alasdair's second son. So he would make the most of a bad situation by enjoying a visit with his niece Sarah.

Even now, Robert Campbell did not suspect what lay in Lieutenant Colonel Hamilton's mind, and that he had been sent to Glencoe as a pawn in a much wider scheme.

SEVENTEEN

On the evening of February 1, the files of two mounted companies of soldiers were seen by several Glencoe men crossing in small ferries over the narrows from the north shore of Loch Leven to Ballachulish. They immediately sprinted toward Carnoch. The chief must be warned.

Nor were they the only eyes to witness the approach, though she who had observed the soldiers from behind some trees was now thinking thoughts not of warning but of great joy.

The men from Fort William disembarked on the southern shore of the loch, then remounted. At the head of the earl of Argyll's regiment of approximately one hundred twenty men rode Captain Robert Campbell of Glenlyon. They approached the entry of Glencoe between Ballachulish and Laroch.

Clad in the king's red, not the Campbell green, the regiment presented a curious intermingling of English and Scots. Some wore fur caps, others

Scots bonnets. The Highlanders of lower rank spoke Gaelic, of which their English sergeants could not understand a word. A piper accompanied them for drills.

The day was February 1, 1692.

Campbell gave the signal to halt.

Ahead, a company of about twenty of Maclain's men awaited them on foot. Hearing of their crossing and approach, the chief had sent his sons John and Alasdair out to meet them. Their numbers increased every second, for by now every boy from most of the small villages was running to catch up.

Campbell rode out several paces ahead of his men. The sons of Maclain came forward.

The younger greeted his wife's uncle. He returned the greeting politely. What was his business? the elder Maclain asked.

Campbell turned and signaled. A rider came forward and handed him the order he had received from Deputy Governor Hamilton. Campbell stretched down his hand. John took the paper. The brothers read it.

The fort at Inverlochy was full, said Campbell as they perused the order. Several regiments were on hand. A march against Glengarry had been planned. Billeting was therefore requested among the inhabitants of Glencoe for these hundred and twenty troops.

"That is your *only* intent?" asked Alasdair suspiciously.

"We come as friends, I assure you," replied Campbell. "On my honor, no harm shall come to your father or to any of his people. We will be grateful for whatever lodging you can find for us. It will be a matter of days only."

The sons of Maclain pondered the situation. The suspicion between the two clans was undeniable, as well as between their father and this particular Campbell.

Behind him in the ranks sat one of Campbell's young horsemen whose thoughts were neither on his duties, nor the conversation taking place ahead of the file of horses, but upon this glen to which his heart belonged. In the distance, as they approached, he had spied a figure behind a low hill. Everything within him had yearned to cry out, to break ranks.

But Brochan Cawdor was a soldier now, riding as he had always dreamed behind a captain of his clan. He must keep his own tongue as still as hers. From Ginevra he had learned to value silence. Now he had no choice but to content himself in that quiet she had taught him to treasure.

Perhaps, Brochan thought, if they remained a few days, he might contrive to see her. Whether or not it was she he had just observed, she probably already knew he was here, he thought with a smile. She always knew.

Meanwhile, Robert Campbell sat waiting, having no inkling of the infamy these two weeks would bring to his name. He had only been told to march south, seek billeting from his relatives, and await further instructions.

"You and your men will be welcome in Glencoe," said John Maclain at length, extending his arm in a handshake of welcome.

He turned and led the way, walking back toward his father's house alongside Robert Campbell's horse. Ahead of them ran the boys and young men who had gathered, calling out the news everywhere that soldiers from Fort William were on the way to their homes.

▨   EIGHTEEN   ▨

For two weeks, the soldiers were fed and offered every hospitality, two to five in a home, in the cottages of the Maclains of Glencoe. Whatever cautions existed when they rode into the glen, they soon disappeared in the commonality of shared Highland roots and the camaraderie of the mutual roof. The weather warmed briefly. The temperature rose above freezing during the daylight hours. Some of the streams began to melt.

Campbell himself was put up in the home of MacDonald of Inverrigan. Many evenings he dined at the spacious Carnoch home of Chief Alasdair. The two managed to put aside their former disputes, drinking together often to drunkenness, while listening to the pipes or enjoying song from the lips of the bard. On other occasions Campbell played cards and backgammon with the chief and his sons and enjoyed meals and drink with his niece Sarah and her husband, Alasdair the younger.

Long before the stay showed signs of coming to an end, friendships had been formed and a genuine neighborliness appeared to be breaking out between both soldiers and hosts who were of the two clan septs of Glen Lyon and Maclain. Spirited games—both cards around the table and wrestling or caber tossing in the meadows—warm fires, congenial conversation, wine, whisky, music, and the generosity of simple provision bound together the longtime rival clans in the bonds of Highland fellowship. The mutual respect for their shared Celtic roots and traditions gradually came to outweigh the reminders of the feud between them.

It was an environment that tended to force people together. At such a time of year they had to keep mostly indoors—in stone houses exactly like those the Campbell soldiers lived in back in their own glens. The smaller cottages were of one or two rooms, of dry-packed stone covered in the direction of the wind with dried mud or slabs of turf. No chimneys existed, only a hole in the roof at the highest point to allow the escape of smoke. In the middle of the dirt floor below, throughout the months of winter, burned a hot fire of peat. With no draft to suck it skyward, smoke filled the house, meandering gradually upward and blackening everything inside until it eventually discovered the small overhead passage into the outside air.

As the Campbell soldiers sat sharing the warmth of the peat with their hosts, therefore, eyes red and cheeks stained, nostrils filled with the stench of nearby animal byres and dungheaps, lungs hacking from the smoky haze that filled every dwelling, they knew that back home their own wives and parents and children were huddled about identical fires with identical red eyes in identical cottages under the same sky from which fell the same snow.

Whatever one's clan, the Highlander's life was a simple, hard battle against the elements. All were gradually discovering—though few might have actually *said* it—that there really was not so much very different between a Campbell and a MacDonald after all.

Yet the growing rapport was far from universal among either villagers or troops. For the English soldiers, this was indeed an odd interlude in the soldier's life.

"Why are we here so long?" commented one to his comrade as they walked together after one morning's drill on the frosty ground. "It's a peculiar place. I can't understand a word out of the mouths of these people."

"They say there's no provisions at Inverlochy."

"But there's been time by now. I'm ready to get out of this place. I don't like it—mountains glaring down on you from every direction. Something's up, I tell you," he added, glancing up toward the mountains he had just mentioned, then pulling his coat more tightly around his shoulders and shivering, "—and I don't like it."

Neither did Sarah's husband, Alasdair the younger, who all the while remained suspicious. Backgammon and wine, jokes and stories and laughter had done nothing to alleviate his uneasiness.

He did not like the daily drilling of the Campbell soldiers in the glen, with prominent display of muskets and bayonets. Nor was he alone. Not everyone in the glen was comfortable with Campbells wearing the red coats of the English king's army under their roofs.

Halfway through the stay, a company of men went privately to the chief.

"Send 'em away, Maclain," said one. "Oor women are anxious. Their English sergeants shoutin' oot orders in the southern tongue, the marchin', the drills . . . I tell ye, Chief, it bodes nae gude."

Around him many others nodded and voiced similar objections. But it was clear the great man was growing angry as he listened.

"I winna sent them away," he replied at length. His voice was stern. "Hae we not broken breid t'gither? I got nae love fer Glenlyon in my hert, but he's aye given his word. He's a Highlander. We're all Highlanders t'gither. No harm'll be done, no offense given. We've oor *ain* honor t' think o'."

The men of Maclain's clan went away to make the best of it. Perhaps the chief was right. Hospitality given and hospitality accepted were indeed sacred in the Highland code.

❋   N I N E T E E N   ❋

All the while, the peat smoke swirled and whisky was consumed, and the games and conversation and laughter drew the people of the glen and the Highlanders of Glenlyon's regiment closer. But the English regulars grew more eager to get out of the place.

At Fort William, meanwhile, Colonel Hill knew nothing of the treachery his deputy had set in motion. He intended no further action against the MacDonalds. In fact, he had sent confirmation to London in the plainest possible terms that peace had come everywhere in the Highlands. All the chiefs either already had or had promised to take the oath. There was no need for further action.

Yet he could not help feeling ill at ease. Something was up. In his quieter moments, Hill realized that Dalrymple was losing trust in him. He suspected the Secretary of State might be going behind his back. But he had no idea to what an extent Hamilton was already involved.

Hamilton, meanwhile, was growing impatient. Without divulging his darker intent to his superior, he sent Major Robert Duncanson south with four hundred men. The major was now camped out on the north landing of the Ballachulish ferry, at the narrows between the two lochs.

Finally arrived yet another communication from Dalrymple to Hill: "You cannot receive further instructions . . . be as earnest in the matter as you can . . . be secret and sudden . . . be quick."

At last Colonel Hill realized further action would be carried out with or without him. To refuse would be treason, and Hamilton would report him if he hesitated now. He could do nothing to prevent what he had so long dreaded.

Sickened by the thought of what might be coming, at last Colonel Hill yielded. With a weary sigh, worn out from the fever which had been with him for almost a year, he sent for his deputy. Hamilton came and stood before him.

"This business grieves me," said Hill. "I do not like it. And it is all so unnecessary. But I shall leave it in your hands. You may carry out your orders."

Lieutenant Colonel Hamilton wasted no time. He left Hill's office eagerly and sent off a quick letter to Duncanson to coordinate the attack. Then he himself set out immediately from the fort. His own detachment of four hundred would march from Fort William through Kinlochleven and descend into the glen across the Devil's Staircase. Duncanson would cross by ferry to Ballachulish and approach from the west.

Late that same day, Major Duncanson received the following order at his secret encampment some three miles from Glencoe:

FOR THEIR MAJESTIES' SERVICE,
TO MAJOR ROBERT DUNCANSON OF THE EARL OF ARGYLL'S REGIMENT,
FORT WILLIAM, 12 FEBRUARY, 1692

SIR,
    PURSUANT TO THE COMMANDER IN CHIEF'S AND MY COLONEL'S ORDER FOR PUTTING INTO EXECUTION THE KING'S COMMAND, YOU ARE TO ORDER YOUR AFFAIR SO AS TO BE AT THE SEVERAL POSTS ALREADY ASSIGNED YOU BY SEVEN O'CLOCK TOMORROW MORNING, BEING SATURDAY, AND FALL IN ACTION WITH THAT PARTY OF THE EARL OF ARGYLL'S REGIMENT NOW UNDER YOUR COMMAND, AT WHICH TIME I WILL ENDEAVOUR TO BE WITH THE PARTY FROM THIS PLACE. IT WILL BE NECESSARY THAT THE AVENUES ON THE SOUTH SIDE BE SECURED, SO THAT NEITHER THE OLD FOX, NOR NONE OF HIS CUBS GETS AWAY. THE ORDERS ARE THAT NONE UNDER SEVENTY BE SPARED THE SWORD, NOR THE GOVERNMENT TROUBLED WITH PRISONERS, WHICH IS ALL I HAVE TO SAY TO YOU UNTIL THEN. SIR, YOUR HUMBLE SERVANT,

                        JAMES HAMILTON

Upon receiving his orders, Duncanson now wrote out another message.

He folded the paper, put it in an envelope, stamped it with his seal, and sent for his captain, Thomas Drummond.

"Take these orders to Campbell," said Duncanson when Drummond appeared. He handed him the envelope. "He is lodging at Inverrigan, as I understand it. Then stay the night with him. Make certain he obeys. I will join you in the morning."

Drummond nodded and left Duncanson's tent. The wind was up. Snow had begun to fall. Another storm was nearly upon them.

✖   T W E N T Y   ✖

It was mid-evening when the dispatch from Duncanson arrived in Inverrigan. Robert Campbell was playing cards with the two sons of the chief at Inverrigan's house when Captain Drummond entered.

Campbell arose and approached. The two men saluted. Drummond handed him the envelope. Campbell opened it.

Stoically he read the orders, his face divulging nothing. To one side, Drummond eyed the chief's grown sons warily. He had not been in the glen enjoying their hospitality for two weeks. He possessed no feelings of goodwill toward anyone in Glencoe, especially the old fox's brood.

Once Campbell read the command, there could be no more doubt of the deed he had been sent to carry out.

The orders were gruesomely explicit.

FOR HIS MAJESTY'S SERVICE,
TO ROBERT CAMPBELL OF GLENLYON

SIR,
    YOU ARE HEREBY ORDERED TO FALL UPON THE REBELS THE MACDONALDS OF GLENCOE AND PUT ALL UNDER SEVENTY TO THE SWORD. YOU ARE TO HAVE SPECIAL CARE THAT THE OLD FOX AND HIS SONS DO NOT ESCAPE YOUR HANDS. YOU ARE TO SECURE ALL AVENUES, THAT NO MAN ESCAPE. THIS YOU ARE TO PUT IN EXECUTION AT FIVE OF THE CLOCK PRECISELY, AND BY THAT TIME, OR VERY SHORTLY AFTER IT, I WILL STRIVE TO JOIN YOU WITH A STRONGER PARTY. IF I DO NOT COME TO YOU AT FIVE, YOU ARE NOT TO TARRY FOR ME BUT TO FALL ON. THIS IS BY THE KING'S SPECIAL COMMANDS, FOR THE GOOD AND SAFETY OF THE COUNTRY, THAT THESE MISCREANTS BE CUT OFF ROOT AND BRANCH. SEE THAT THIS BE PUT IN EXECUTION WITHOUT FEAR OR FAVOUR, OR YOU MAY EXPECT TO

BE DEALT WITH AS ONE NOT TRUE TO KING OR GOVERNMENT, NOR A MAN FIT TO CARRY A COMMISSION IN THE KING'S SERVICE.

EXPECTING YOU WILL NOT FAIL IN THE FULFILLING HEREOF, AS YOU LOVE YOURSELF, I SUBSCRIBE THIS AT BALLYCHYLLIS, THE 12 FEBY, 1692.

ROBERT DUNCANSON

Campbell folded the paper and stuffed it into his pocket. The evening of wine, laughter, and gambling was clearly over.

Keeping a straight face, betraying nothing, he looked toward John and Alasdair.

"My orders have come," he said.

"You will be leaving, then?" said John.

Campbell nodded. "My men and I are most grateful for the hospitality of your people," he said. "But now I have much to do."

The brothers departed Inverrigan's home for their own. Campbell and Drummond nodded somberly to each other.

Then Glenlyon went out into the night to pass the orders along to his various commanders.

❊   T W E N T Y · O N E   ❊

Throughout the ensuing hours as the fateful hour drew near, Robert Campbell found sleep more and more difficult.

Notwithstanding the camaraderie of the last two weeks, he felt no deep love for old Alasdair. His raids and thefts had added their own weight to the financial ruin that had forced him to take this miserable commission at such an age. Yet he was loath to carry out such a slaughter. If only the old fool hadn't been so stubborn in the matter of the oath!

But, Glenlyon did his best to convince himself, he had no choice. To disobey now would insure him the same fate as awaited Alasdair.

Throughout the glen, those soldiers with consciences, chancing to get wind of what had been ordered, sought in cryptic ways to warn their hosts. In the Highlands, hospitality was considered inviolable. Few greater sins existed than the betrayal of one's host. When they heard what the next morning was fated to bring, many of Argyll's men were so disgusted and revolted that their consciences waged war as never before against their sworn duty as soldiers.

One of the Campbell soldiers at supper on the Friday evening with his hosts fingered the edge of a warm woolen plaid. "'Tis a good plaid," he said, glancing toward the woman of the house. "If this were my plaid, I might put it on and gae oot tonight and luik after my cattle."

He paused, then stared at her all the more intently, then turned his eyes upon her husband. "If this plaid were mine," he added in solemn tone, "I wud put it around my shoulders, and I wud take my cattle an' my family oot to a safe place."

The man of the house understood his guest's meaning well enough and did just that. When morning came, his house was empty.

One of his comrades sat that same evening at his own supper table, especially quiet. For two weeks his hosts had treated him almost as a son, and the young private had grown to love them. His heart was heavy for the evil tidings he had just heard from his sergeant. At length he sighed deeply and spoke to the dog lying beside the fire in the middle of the cottage.

"Gray dog," he said, and then looked up to his hosts with solemn and significant expression, "if I were you, despite the snow, I would make my bed this night in the heather."

The man and the woman went to bed whispering quietly amongst themselves as to what the young man could mean. Long before morning they realized his intent, for strange comings and goings could be distantly heard outside. Quietly, in the middle of the night, the man roused his wife. They left their cottage for the hills.

Ginevra herself, feeling heavy of heart in the dusk that fell that same evening as she wandered toward the village where Brochan was staying, hoping for a chance to speak with him, came upon one of the Campbell soldiers standing alone. The man was leaning against the projection of a great boulder that jutted at an angle out of the ground. A pained expression was on his face.

She paused. The man stared at her with an odd, almost compassionate look.

She returned his gaze. Their eyes met.

The soldier glanced away toward the stone beside him.

"Grit stone of the glen . . ." he began.

He paused, then turned toward Ginevra with significant expression.

"—ye hae the right t' be here, stone . . . but if ye kenned what is coming afore dawn, ye would be up and away."

Again came a penetrating stare at the girl he did not know. "Du ye hear me, grit stone—flee like the Stone o' Scone. Up and away . . . afore dawn."

Only a moment more did Ginevra remain. Suddenly her feet were flying beneath her as she ran away from the strange man. She glanced up. Clouds were approaching over the mountains. Suddenly a great chill swept through her.

Meanwhile, suspicions had returned to Alasdair, youngest son of the chief. He could not sleep. He had not liked the look on the face of the captain who delivered Glenlyon his orders.

In the middle of the night he arose and went out, keeping from sight. A bitter wind swirled through the glen. A few flecks of snow stung his face. Too many soldiers were awake and milling about.

Alasdair crept to his brother's house and roused him. John did not share Alasdair's concern. But he agreed they should tell their father. Together they went to wake him.

The chief, however, was of a surly disposition after being aroused from sleep on a cold night when another storm was blowing in. They were worried about nothing, he told his sons. If they wanted to look into it, that was their concern. He was returning to bed.

Eventually both of them did so as well.

▨   T W E N T Y - T W O   ▨

All night those few of the Campbell regiment who had been told what was coming struggled with their consciences.

Some drank. Others tried to steel their minds against what they must do. Few slept.

At last the hour arrived.

Between four and four-thirty, Campbell's men rose. In the house of Inverrigan, the nine members of the household were roused from sleep, tied, and gagged. They could not be killed until five, as the order stated. But Campbell needed the house to make preparations and as a temporary headquarters. His men began quietly preparing their muskets and pistols for the five-o'clock hour.

Meanwhile, throughout the long, dark hours Ginevra lay agitated. Dreadful visions played themselves over and over in her brain, but she could make no sense of them. She could not rid her mind of the cryptic words of the soldier by the stone.

A stone . . . a stone . . . why should a stone flee its natural home?

Again came tears. They were not now for herself, but for some terrible calamity she felt was coming.

She knew where Brochan was staying in the village of Achnacone, just beyond Signal Hill. In the past weeks, they had managed to find many a stolen moment to be together. She must warn him. She must tell Brochan to flee like the stone!

Ginevra rose, dressed warmly, and went out into the night. The hour was four-thirty.

In the corner of the same room, her mother lay awake, eyes wide with terror. When Ginevra left, she too rose and began bundling up Ginevra's young brother.

As Ginevra left Carnoch, soldiers were about. There was much movement. Six or eight members of the Campbell regiment were marching toward the chief's house. They were carrying rifles and taking care not to be heard.

The snow now fell in earnest.

But Ginevra was experienced at not being seen. She kept out of sight as the soldiers passed, then hastened out of the village in the opposite direction.

Her mind was occupied with Brochan. She did not pause to think what the rifles might portend.

❋   T W E N T Y · T H R E E   ❋

A knock sounded on Chief Alasdair Maclain's door.

He awoke. It was still dark. Momentarily confused, he waited briefly, thinking his sons might have come again. A servant entered the room with candle in hand to wake him. Several of the Campbell men were at the door, he said. They had come to thank him for Glencoe's hospitality.

Maclain rose, told his wife to fetch wine for their departing guests, then began to pull on his trousers.

Suddenly behind him the room filled with soldiers. Two shots rang out in the morning. Screams from his wife echoed through the house.

The next instant Alasdair Maclain, proud chief of his clan, lay dead on his face on his own bed, trousers loose, one bullet in his back, the other having blown all the way through his head. Moments later two more shots were fired at the servants now attempting to run from the house. They fell dead on the frozen ground.

Emboldened by what they had done, the soldiers now turned to the chief's hysterical wife. One grabbed her from behind while his fellow yanked and tore at her rings. But they were tight and would not come off. He set his teeth to the frantic woman's fingers, pulling and tearing until he felt the rings loosen and fall into his mouth. Now they ripped the clothes from her body and threw her naked to the floor. Two others dragged Maclain outside into the snowy morning, where his blood, still warm, oozed onto the ground and there began to freeze.

All over the glen the slaughter was now on.

At Inverrigan's house, Glenlyon was in the process of cruelly repaying his hosts for their hospitality. When five o'clock came, Campbell ordered that the nine they had bound be taken outside and thrown onto the frozen cattle dunghill. His order was carried out.

Campbell raised his pistol and shot his host in the head. Screams of horror sounded from wife and children. One at a time the others were shot with muskets, some knifed through with bayonets. After eight lay dead, only one young man of twenty remained.

Suddenly Glenlyon hesitated. He raised his hand and took several paces between his soldiers and the young man, then uttered but a single word.

"Hold," he said.

Had he been seized by a sudden pang of conscience? His own men waited. A strange look of sudden revulsion filled their captain's face.

"What are you doing, man?" cried Drummond. "Don't forget our orders—kill him!"

Still no one moved. Campbell stared back and forth between his soldiers and the single man left trembling on the dungheap.

Muttering in disgust, Drummond raised his own gun. The next instant the young man slumped over two or three of the other bodies with a bullet through his head.

Behind them a boy of twelve now ran from somewhere out of the darkness. He grabbed at Campbell's legs and begged to be spared.

"I promise . . . I will serve you!" the frantic boy cried. "Please . . . please don't kill me. I will go anywhere . . . I will do whatever you—"

Drummond turned to the detail. "Shoot the boy!" he cried, "and be done with it."

Several shots rang out. The boy slumped dead at Glenlyon's feet.

Their business with that household done, the troop turned and set the thatch of Inverrigan's house and barns ablaze.

In the darkness throughout the glen with gunshots filling every village, women fled for the hills with children in their arms, other youngsters struggling to keep up at their sides.

At the first sounds, servants awoke both of the chief's sons. They had just time to escape with their families toward a stand of trees on Meall Mor before detachments came to administer the same fate that had already befallen their father. Behind them, smoke rose from several houses and byres. Musket fire, yelling, screaming, and muffled shouts of terror sounded through the early morning air.

More straggling survivors came after them. The brothers sent them higher up the slopes. There they would at least be safe from the treachery, if not from the impending blizzard. John and Alasdair quickly ran back down to the glen, working their way carefully along the frozen Coe. Locating what frightened survivors they could, they sent them toward the hills in the direction where others were gathering among the trees on Meall Mor.

Meanwhile, the terrifying betrayal continued. Men were butchered in their beds with bayonets. Others were thrown on the dungheaps of their own cattle, as if in final insult, then shot. Whatever sympathies may have existed the night before, those who now carried out the atrocities were equal to the task set before them. An old man of eighty and several children of less than five years were shot. A wounded old man crept into a hut to hide. Rather than go in after him, the soldiers who saw his retreat set fire all around, then watched as he perished in the blaze.

⌗ T W E N T Y · F O U R ⌗

When Brochan awoke, he heard whispering.

Thinking he must be dreaming, at first he could not believe his ears. His own commander, Sergeant Robert Barber, was talking in hushed tones.

" . . . wake your men . . . march in sections to all the houses of the township . . . do as we've been commanded . . . no prisoners. . . ."

It couldn't possibly be what it seemed!

He must warn them! He must warn Ginevra!

He dressed frantically, then wrapped himself with overcoat and blanket. He crept out of the house unseen. Snow was falling furiously. He could hardly see through it.

Before he had taken many steps, suddenly a voice called out behind him. "Cawdor!"

Brochan turned. There stood Barber.

"Where are you going?" said the sergeant angrily.

Both stood staring, well knowing what was in the other's thoughts.

"Get your gun, Cawdor," said Barber. "We have orders."

"I heard the orders," said Brochan.

"Come with me."

"I winna be part o' it."

Behind them, Brochan saw several of the men of his own group now surrounding the house of MacDonald of Achnacone. He knew that at least nine family members were inside and that MacDonald's brother from Achtriachtan had spent the night.

"You have no choice, Cawdor," said Barber. "Do as you've been ordered, or you'll wind up like the old fox and those about to die right now behind us." He nodded toward the house behind him.

"I winna du it, I tell ye!" Brochan yelled.

He spun around and took two more steps.

"If you're trying to warn that brat of Maclain's brood I've seen you with," yelled Barber after him, "it's no use—she'll be dead before sunrise. Stop, Cawdor—I order you."

Brochan hesitated and glanced back one last time. "No!" he shouted. "The king can jist hang me!"

"If you don't obey, the king won't have a chance to hang you—I'll shoot you first."

Brochan turned and dashed away through the snowy morning. As he ran, Brochan spied an outline through the snow.

Ginevra!

He must tell her to stay away! She mustn't come closer!

Suddenly came that which for years he had longed to hear. But its sound was to warn him of treachery behind him. The word rang with no joy, but resounded across the morning with pain and dread.

"B-r-o-c-h-a-n!" shrieked the great, otherworldly cry.

The single name through the darkness sent a chill and shudder through the bones of all who heard it. Never before had that voice been heard in twenty-one years. And with the single name of her beloved on her lips, Ginevra Maclain at last joined the world of men and women.

But in the same instant the innocence of her former existence was shattered. For the warning came too late to halt the finger of Brochan's English commander.

Her shriek in the ears of Sergeant Barber was eerie and strange. The next instant his own gun silenced it.

A great explosion rent the air. Thirty yards in front of her, Ginevra saw the light fade from her beloved's eyes. He staggered, then fell to his face in the snow.

Another tremendous scream sounded, followed by the long, forlorn wail of the precious name.

Young Brochan Cawdor had been struck down in the prime of his youthful manhood. His blood stained the snow redder than the hair of the maiden whom he had loved.

Ginevra's cry floated through the snow on the echo of gunfire, over the village, waking many to the betrayal that was upon them. Her warning had been too late for one, but it would save many more.

Inside the house to which Robert Barber now returned, the brothers Mac-Donald, who were enjoying a morning's drink while the household huddled close to the fire, heard the sound.

"What lass's voice was that?" said one.

"I dinna ken," replied another, "but 'twas a dreadful howl."

But whatever warning Ginevra's scream might have given to others, it did not come in time for the house of MacDonald of Achnacone.

Suddenly Barber and a dozen men burst open the door and shoved rifles through the windows from where they had surrounded the house. Musket shots exploded. Half of those seated about the fire fell dead instantly. The white smoke from the musket blasts, mixed with the black soot from the peat fire, quickly filled the house so densely that nothing could be seen. Two or three of the wounded ran from the house. More shots followed.

"Cut them down—every one to a man!" cried Barber.

He groped his way inside the house, then dragged the wounded body of his host out the door to be killed. The sergeant stood the householder up against the wall of his home and raised his rifle. But suddenly, and with great effort, MacDonald of Achnacone heaved his heavy plaid off his shoulders, threw it over the sergeant's head, and sprinted away into the darkness as shots sounded from every direction.

Hot tears streaming down her face, burning in the cold of the air, Ginevra sprinted back toward home.

But she had not far to go. For now she saw her mother, who had followed her out in premonition of dread, coming toward her. Her young son was wrapped in the hurrying mother's arms.

Suddenly more shots rang out, closer this time. Again Ginevra screamed in an agony of despair.

The poor woman who had loved and given birth to the mute maiden would never know that on this morning her daughter's voice had been found. Before Ginevra's very eyes, mother and brother now fell dead from the same bullet in the snow.

The sickening wail of the forlorn orphan filled the murderer with such fright that for several moments he could do nothing but stare after her. By the time he came to himself and reloaded his musket, the phantom with red hair had disappeared in the darkness.

Frantic now, Ginevra fled in a frenzy of confusion and horror, hardly knowing which direction her feet were taking her.

As what MacDonalds remained alive in Achnacone also ran from their village in terror, some saw the form of her whose eerie voice they had heard a few moments before. She was ahead of them in the snow and making for the hills higher up in the glen.

All Glencoe that morning was full of the cries of many Rachels and Ginevras weeping for their husbands and lovers, their brothers and children . . . their clan and their land.

But though they wept and mourned, they refused to be comforted, because they were no more.

✼   TWENTY-FIVE   ✼

Ginevra's escape in the hours that followed took her along the very path she had run eight years before when her destiny lay ahead of her. Now it lay behind.

Unconsciously as she fled, her steps led up the glen, then south into the hills in the same direction where she had first seen Brochan. In her grief she was drawn to the slopes where she had found such happiness with the boy who dreamed of being a soldier.

While the slaughter continued, Ginevra ran through the snow, thankfully now not bare of foot. She was seen by several as she passed, including the dead chief's grandson, grown now to a lad of sixteen, and two or three others who had tormented her in their youths. It took them not many moments to

realize that the strange maiden with the second sight represented their best
chance of survival. Without hesitation they were off to follow her. This time
they had no thought in mind but to keep her in sight, knowing their lives
might depend on it. Other fugitives observed them in turn and likewise followed in the predawn darkness. Behind them shots continued thudding dully
amid screams of torment, the sounds eerily muffled in the silent snowfall.

By the time Ginevra took refuge in the cave which was one of her summer
retreats on the slopes of Bidean Nam Bian, six or eight who had followed
her to safety straggled inside behind her. They ranged in age from sixteen to
fifty-three. Some had thought to grab blankets and what little food they
could carry. Behind them, smoke rose from the villages of the glen where the
houses they had left had been set ablaze.

They rested awhile but knew they must get further away before day
broke. Search parties would surely be sent out to follow their tracks. They
had no idea how many might have survived. If these were the only survivors,
then sixteen-year-old Ruadh Og was now chief of the clan. He was too
shocked for the moment, however, to do anyone much good.

The acknowledged leader of the little band was Ginevra, who now gave
orders and offered encouragements as if she had been capable of speech her
entire life. Her tongue loosed, she spoke with intelligence and clarity, her
voice melodic and pleasant like the waters of these hills in springtime she
had always so loved. If any had considered her the village simpleton the day
before, none did now. They sensed that they could trust her with their lives.
And that they must.

"Ye maun be away," she said. "Ye maun git higher, further frae the glen."

"We canna go anither step into the mountains, lass," objected one of the
men. "We'll surely dee in the snow."

"No one o' ye will die," said Ginevra calmly. Gradually she was coming
to herself and found her thoughts returning to practicalities . . . and to Brochan. "'Tis anither cave, higher an' east," she went on. "Ye can build a fire
there and warm yerselves. There are peats inside."

"An' how du ye ken that, lass?" asked the man.

"I put them there. Noo gae. I maun return t' the glen. I will be back. Wait
if ye like. But ye may be safer to git away noo. Ruadh Og, ye know the passes
as well as I. Ye can lead them to Dalness."

She turned and left the cave, disappearing into the snowy darkness.
None thought to question further.

Even as Ginevra led the small band safely out of the glen of their home, at the same time, miles to the west, the two sons of the chief, John, now chief of the clan, and his brother Alasdair led a party of survivors that had grown to over a hundred, south from Laroch and Carnoch and Inverrigan across the slopes of Meall Mor toward Appin. They had by this time found their mother, wrapped her against the cold, and nursed her as well as they could. They heard now for the first time how their father was killed.

The new chief was worried about his son. He had not seen him since the family had scattered with the first shots. He feared the boy had suffered the same fate as his grandfather.

But he needn't have been anxious. Young Ruadh Og had been led safely off into the snow-filled eastern hills by the once silent maiden of Glencoe.

⊠   T W E N T Y · S I X   ⊠

As Ginevra crept back toward the village of Achnacone, a thin light began to show through the snowfall. Dawn was near.

Fires burned everywhere. Shouts could be heard in the distance. But the ferocity of the attack seemed to have spent itself. Most villagers were either dead or gone, and the soldiers had now moved down the glen.

How much time had passed, Ginevra had no idea. Thirty minutes, an hour, even more? Was it possible he could still be alive?

She retraced her steps. There was the house, its roof nearly burned through by now, the flames mostly reduced to breezy plumes of smoke. The byre behind was burning.

Ginevra ran forward.

There still lay her beloved facedown in the snow!

She darted to him, heart pounding in mingled fear and hope. She knelt in the white powder and gently tried to rouse him.

"Brochan . . . Brochan, please," she pled desperately, "—please wake up." Her voice was soft, her whisper urgent.

With great effort she turned him onto his side, then smothered his face and lips and eyes with kisses.

The skin was cold . . . but with the chill of snow, not death!

"Brochan! Oh, please, Brochan . . ."

A faint groan sounded.

"Brochan!" cried Ginevra with joy. "Oh, come . . . you maun get up! I ken ye're hurt. But I maun git ye away afore they find ye."

Another faceful of happy, desperate kisses was enough to rouse the young man sufficiently to remember what had happened. Groggily and painfully his brain awoke to his peril. His wound was serious. But thankfully the snow had nearly frozen it, effectively stopping the flow of blood.

With Ginevra's help he labored to his feet. Using her lithe but wiry frame as his crutch, the two hobbled off through the gray dawn.

After more than an hour through the fresh snow, their feet nearly frozen, at length Ginevra managed to get Brochan back to the first cave. The others were gone.

The only reminder of their presence was a single tartan blanket, neatly folded and placed on a stone near the mouth of the cave.

Ginevra recognized it instantly. The last time she had seen it, it had been draped around young Maclain's neck as she had spoken to him about leading the escape party to Dalness.

Ginevra smiled. She knew Ruadh Og had left it for her return.

4

CALL OF ANCIENT ROOTS

An auspicious gathering had convened in a dimly lit but expensively appointed back room of a pub in Knightsbridge.

Surrounded by dark oak and mahogany tones of paneled wainscoting and furnishings, one Dugald MacKinnon, the man who had masterminded the strategy behind the events leading up to this evening, stood drink in hand at one end of an ornate sideboard upon which several bottles sat. A smile was on his face as he listened to a select circle of colleagues offer congratulations on the triumph of the previous day.

The results of yesterday's general election throughout the United Kingdom were now complete.

The long reign of the Conservative Party in the United Kingdom had come to an end late in the 1990s with Richard Barraclough's overwhelming victory. It was a titanic shift of the country back toward the left for the first time since 1979. Everyone expected Prime Minister Barraclough to remain at the parliamentary helm for as long as Margaret Thatcher had, if not longer. His youthful good looks and dash seemed perfect for a long ride. No one expected such a close race in this, Barraclough's first reelection bid, following as it did just one month after Charles III's Stone-less coronation.

However, a squeaker it was. Suddenly the prime minister faced having to deal with parties other than his own to keep his grip on power. Labour's meager eight-member plurality, well short of an outright majority, suddenly brought Barraclough face-to-face with the necessity of a coalition government. It was either that or call for new elections, which in the day's uncertain climate might be dangerous. Barraclough could lose power altogether.

Nor had the modest gains of the Liberal Democrats and the huge advance of the Scottish Nationalists been anticipated. Both would have to be considered for widely expanded roles if Labour hoped to rule for long. That was exactly what MacKinnon, the acknowledged leader of the Scottish Nationalist Party, or SNP, had been counting on.

Already one bottle of Glenfiddich stood empty on the sideboard. A second had been half consumed, while the ebullient toasts and cheers flowed as smoothly from the mouths of the celebrators as the twelve-year-old whisky from Dufftown passed between their lips.

This private coterie had been called together not merely to celebrate, however, but to discuss and plan. Any potential coalition would necessarily be thin. It was doubtful Labour could hold the reins for another full term. The SNP's window of opportunity would be of unpredictable duration. They thus had to devise a strategy that would enable them to move into action the instant circumstances aligned themselves favorably. At the same time, with suspicion about the Abbey break-in continuing to hang over their heads, they felt they needed to keep a relatively low profile.

"Well, Dugald," one of the number said, raising his glass, "I honestly did not think your scheme would work when you proposed it several months ago. I salute your foresight and courage!"

"My thanks, Buchanan, for your kind words," laughed the recipient of the evening's praise. His accent was distinctive for this cultured part of London and rang thickly and unmistakably with reminders of its northern origins. "Who can predict how the political winds will blow these days? The important thing is that Prime Minister Barraclough now owes us a tremendous debt. Believe me, I do *not* intend to let him forget it."

More toasts from MacKinnon's Scottish Nationalist colleagues followed.

"He gave his promise of yet more widely expanded Scottish sovereignty without understanding just how seriously we would take his words. We all know Major's gesture with the Stone in '96 was made in hopes of gaining enough of Scotland's vote to salvage his government. That gambit failed. But now the good Mr. Barraclough has stepped into the same trap of underestimating the Scot. When it comes time that we may hold the key to keeping his government together, we will not let him forget his promise."

"Here, here—you are a hero," added Lachlan Ross, reelected MP from Glasgow, who had already had a glass or two more than the rest and was beginning to wax a bit too eloquent, even for this occasion.

"Yesterday's vote warms us nearly as much as this amber brew in my hand, Dugald," enjoined still another, whose tone carried more skepticism than had yet been voiced. "But do you realistically believe it is possible for us to advance yesterday's result to the realization of our dream of independence?"

"I do indeed, William."

"To be honest," Campbell went on, "I am surprised we fared as well as we did with the Stone theft unresolved and people wondering if we had something to do with it."

"In the polls I've seen, public judgment is evenly split between Scottish and Irish radicals in the affair. In any event, I doubt it affected the vote."

"Perhaps not," added Buchanan, "but it's been unnerving having the police around. I don't like it."

Comments of agreement circulated throughout the room. Everyone in the party had been hounded and interrogated since the break-in, though no connection with anyone in the SNP had been found.

"Well then," said Campbell, returning to the previous point, "we await the next phase of your proposal, Dugald, to which you alluded when you called us here. The Stone notwithstanding, you have accomplished what none of us, and probably no man in Scotland, thought possible. You have put a greatly expanded role for Scotland's parliament on the government's manifesto.* Barraclough may have intended it as a mere token, but it upped the stakes and heightened interest. He doubtless had no idea where it would lead. But how far can we go beyond these recent advances? Devolution is a fact. We have our parliament. What now?"

The room fell silent. One or two took thoughtful sips from their crystal tumblers.

MacKinnon allowed the hush to descend to an almost reverential quality. He continued to stand unmoving at the sideboard.

"It is quite simple, gentlemen," said the leader of the small but outspoken party at length. "We will give our complete and unwavering support to our Labour brethren, exactly as I have assured the prime minister we will. Then we await events. A critical juncture is bound to come when the prime minister's coalition will find itself threatened. That is the moment I will play my IOU—and then the stakes will be far greater than a mere puppet parlia-

---

*The proposed platform of legislation upon which a party bases the nationwide campaign of its candidates for Parliament.

ment. When the time comes we will place one of our own in the position of Scotland's first minister. That done, we wait . . . and we watch.

"As long as Hamilton is at the helm of the Liberal Democrats," put in the Deputy Leader of the SNP, Baen Ferguson, "your plan does not have a chance." His statement was a trial balloon, for he alone of the group possessed information as to the potential future disposition of Hamilton's loyalties.

"I admit the odds remain long," MacKinnon was saying. "But we will take one step at a time. For now the election is past, certain advances toward home rule have been promised us, and we have placed ourselves in a position where the prime minister needs us. All these developments are significant gains for the cause of Scottish independence."

He paused, then added in a tone of concern, "We must, however, keep our eyes on developments. If it were to be discovered that some radical element within our own movement were indeed involved in the Stone's theft, everything could be ruined."

"Perhaps the destiny of the Stone's future legacy has come," suggested Ferguson.

"Acts of radicalism may, as our friend Campbell suggested earlier, prejudice the public against us," insisted MacKinnon. "It is only through the political process that we will achieve our ends. We just have to hope the Yard finds the culprit, and that no Scot is involved. In the meantime, we set our sights on the next rung of the ladder, await the right moment, watch for our opportunity."

"We have no Robert the Bruce today, around whom all of Scotland will unite," observed Campbell wryly, ". . . unless *you* are prepared to take up the banner, Dugald. Do you intend to stand for first minister?"

The words were spoken but half in seriousness. Yet the room grew suddenly still, as if mere mention of Scotland's legendary hero had permeated the air with an ancient presence.

"No," replied MacKinnon with a faraway look in his mind's eye. "I am not the one." He was a politician and a pragmatic man, well enough aware of his own limitations. He had felt the presence more keenly than the rest, and he knew what it portended.

"I am merely a forerunner. There will come another," he went on, his pragmatism and vision now fusing as one. "For now we must be patient. We cannot always see the circumstances that will thrust a hero up from the ranks of common men to change nations and redirect history. When Alexander III died suddenly in 1286, Robert Bruce was a mere lad of eight. No mantle of heroism yet clung to his boyish shoulders—it had to be earned later, and it was shaped by the events and demands of his era."

He paused briefly, then added, "Events will come in our time as well. Devolution has begun a process from which there can be no turning back. Yet what most do not realize is that devolution and the new parliament in Edinburgh are only the beginning. The Act of Union must ultimately be undone."

The room was still as they pondered their leader's words.

"Our own hero-king will arise," MacKinnon went on, "—a *new* Bruce, mounted upon the political war-steed of *our* times. He will wage the contest not with axe or spear or longbow, but with a heart that fears not the challenge.

"The election just past will, I am confident, precipitate events as did Alexander's death seven centuries ago. I believe the sort of man of which I speak *will* soon emerge upon the national scene."

The silence which followed this time was lengthy and pregnant with reflection.

Each of the small company felt drawn in one accord back centuries in time, as if they stood with that ancient king of legend on the eve of Bannockburn's battle, each considering his role in the historic events soon to follow.

"My comrades and kinsmen," concluded MacKinnon, his voice taking on the ancient timber of a Celtic bard, "the day approaches when the Sassanach will again rule his own land . . . *and we ours.*"

"Hear, hear!" slurred Lachlan Ross.

"Hear, hear!" added two or three others, now solemnly lifting their glasses.

"The moment has come for us to lay claim once more to the land of our heritage. It is time Scotland again belonged to her own people. Not in part . . . but in full."

He raised his own glass now, in response to theirs.

"To Scotland!"

"—and ancient Caledonia!" added Buchanan.

"*To Caledonia!*" consented the others enthusiastically.

✵   T W O   ✵

A week following his reelection, Andrew Trentham again journeyed north.

Several receptions and speaking engagements were planned in appreciation for the vote, and to give him a chance to mingle informally with the people of his constituency. His thoughts of late, however, had been occupied more with the Glencoe story than with the election. The fact that the Stone of Scone had not been recovered and that the theft continued to baffle Scotland Yard also served to keep Duncan's homeland at the forefront of his thoughts.

He had not seen Blair since the fateful luncheon prior to his previous trip. Nor could the Glencoe story but remind him, in his more morose moments, of the betrayal he felt at being dumped by her. It was a ridiculous parallel, he tried to tell himself. She had not *betrayed* him. Yet he could not prevent the reminder from stinging.

At the first available opportunity, Andrew dressed for the weather and headed out the front door.

"Where are you going, Andrew?" asked Lady Trentham, emerging from the drawing room behind him.

"Out for a walk, Mum," replied Andrew cheerfully. "Maybe a visit to Duncan."

"Why him, Andrew? There are more important people you need to see while you're home."

"I like Duncan, Mum. One can't always be hobnobbing with three-piece-suit types. I get plenty of that in London."

"Your father was just the same when I first met him. But you can't be forever out wandering the hills and spending your valuable time in a sheepherder's cottage. You need to pay more attention to your social obligations. You've let Blair slip away, and all you can do is go out walking. You're an MP, for heaven's sake, not a mystic."

Andrew sighed but did not reply. What could he say? Slowly he turned and continued on to the door, feeling the intensity of her puzzled and disapproving stare on his back.

Walking away from the house, Andrew struck out along the hillside pathways, doing his best to put the incident behind him. It had been so long since he had visited Duncan's cottage with any regularity and heard him speak of Scotland. Now all of a sudden, everywhere one looked Scotland was in the news. Despite his mother's comments, he found himself hungry for more of the old man's tales. As he walked, Andrew's thoughts unexpectedly returned to yesterday's briefing with the press.

A smile came to his face as he recalled the question that had been delivered with an unmistakable American accent. The discussion had centered around the upcoming second reading of a foreign aid bill. He had just commented that if division came on the bill, he anticipated no delay in its passage. Then the hand had gone up, and he had acknowledged it.

"How serious do you see such a potential division in the House?" came the blurted inquiry from a young woman to his left.

A brief snickering followed.

He had felt for the poor reporter as the eyes of London's coterie of news veterans turned round to see what manner of foreign amateur had committed such a *faux pas*. He had tried to answer her matter-of-factly, though her reddened face showed she already realized her mistake.

The briefing had continued, and there had been no more questions from that quarter.

Andrew's thoughts returned to the present.

⬚ T H R E E ⬚

Patricia Rawlings sat in her London flat replaying yesterday's events over in her mind.

How could she have been so stupid!

She had heard the term "division" many times before. It shouldn't have thrown her. Now she had made a fool of herself in front of the very colleagues whose respect she was trying to gain.

The mortification was so severe that she could still feel the eyes turning to fix themselves upon her as MP Trentham gently corrected her.

"A division, Miss, uh—"

"Rawlings, sir," she managed to reply.

"Yes, Miss Rawlings—a *division* is a vote in the House of Commons, sometimes taken after the second reading of a bill and subsequent debate. The term indicates no dispute or conflict, only that a vote is being taken."

How many times in this business had she wished she could get rid of her American accent, especially its slight southern twang. She had tried to sound more British, even taken some private lessons in learning what had previously been called the Queen's, but now would probably be referred to as the *King's* English. But her efforts had accomplished little. Every time she opened her mouth she had the feeling everyone was watching her, waiting for her to put her foot into it.

She had certainly done that yesterday! Both feet—all the way to the ankles! And her colleagues with the press had been more than ready to help her swallow.

At least *he* hadn't chuckled at her mistake. Mr. Trentham had been a gentleman, his response entirely gracious. She even sensed that the smile accompanying his words *might* have been conveying sympathy.

It was a nice smile, she thought, allowing herself a respite in the midst of her self-inflicted drubbing to reflect on the MP's face. A subtle smile, with just a hint of mystery to it. She would like to know more about him. Something about him struck her as being different from the rest. Maybe it was the faint understanding look he had cast her in the midst of her awkwardness—something that said he didn't hold being an American against her.

It was hard enough to make it in the news business, she mused. Every station and network had their few token women, but it was still mostly a man's game. And here in London, doorways to power were even more tightly guarded against intrusion by foreigners. She knew well enough how lucky she was to have this job at all.

That fact did not prevent her from being unsatisfied. She wanted to move up. It had always been her dream to conduct on-camera interviews. She wanted to be someone people recognized as a news personality, as a television reporter and journalist they could trust and rely on. She went so far as to envision having her own feature spot, even co-anchoring one of the major news programs someday.

They were lofty ambitions, to be sure. She was not a young woman anyone could ever accuse of aiming too low. After yesterday, though, her dreams seemed more unattainable than ever.

Well, she couldn't stall forever. Her boss would have heard all about the incident by now. She had called in two hours ago to say she would be late. But she could not put it off any longer.

❀ F O U R ❀

Patricia Rawlings, or *Paddy*, as she was known to her colleagues and few London friends, made her way downstairs, out of the building, and along several blocks to the Chalk Farm Underground station. Once seated on the northern line, she would have about a twenty-minute ride, with a transfer to the central at Tottenham Court Road, out to the BBC headquarters at White City in Shepherd's Bush.

She had been in London six years now. Mostly she loved it, despite the personal grief that had come her way a year ago. Yet she felt she had made little professional progress here, and she sometimes wondered whether it would be better just to go back home to Atlanta. She could probably get one of the daytime on-camera spots easily enough. But this job meant too much, and she remained hopeful of moving up within the BBC.

Not just hopeful. She was determined. She *would* make it here. She *would* prove she could do the job as well as any of them, even if she was an American, and no matter how much of her own natural reticence and timidity she had to hide in order to do it. She wanted at least to last until her American accent was no longer a liability.

Paddy walked into the news building, crossed to the elevator, and punched the appropriate button. Two minutes later she was moving down the hall toward her fate, still thinking about yesterday's events. She would rather daydream about the handsome MP than see the gruff face of her boss, whose office she was now approaching. There was no sense even going to her own desk first. She had to face him.

She knocked on the door, then walked into the office of Edward Pilkington, head of the news division of BBC 2. She sat down in front of his desk without comment, only casting toward him a knowing expression intended to convey remorse, apology, chagrin, and what-do-I-do-now? all in one.

Pilkington looked her over for a few seconds, then sighed.

"Give me one good reason I shouldn't sack you right now and send you back to the States," he said.

"I can't think of any," she replied. "But please, if you'll just give me another chance."

"A chance to do what, Paddy?" he said in a refined cockney as recognizable as was her own native tongue, "—bring the BBC's reputation down to the level of the American networks? You tell me you want in on the bigger stories, and then you pull a move like this. What kind of journalism do they teach you in the States?"

"I am sorry, sir. But please—just let me have an on-camera assignment. I promise I won't muddle it up."

"I can't have you making a fool of us—especially on camera. Kirk tells me they laughed—they actually *laughed* at you."

Paddy glanced down, both mortified at the reminder and irritated that the network's star reporter, who had broken the Queen's bombshell in front of the Palace, had carried news of her gaffe so quickly back to their boss.

Pilkington sighed.

"I like you, Paddy," he said, "and I've nothing against Yanks. I think I've given you a fair enough shake. But over here, image is everything."

"I know . . . I know."

"People don't forget these kinds of things."

"What *do* I have to do to get on camera with a microphone in my hand?" she asked, leaning forward slightly in her chair, anxious to divert the conversation away from yesterday's blunder.

Pilkington leaned back slightly in his chair, interlocked his fingers behind his head, and drew in a deep, thoughtful breath. The office was silent for several seconds.

"You find me a story no one else has," he said at length, "and then we'll talk about it again."

❈   F I V E   ❈

The hawk overhead was circling slowly, its wings barely moving, intent no doubt on spotting a mouse or rabbit for dinner. Andrew found himself staring upward as he continued his solitary stroll, envying the freedom of the winged hunter.

What would he have been, he wondered, had his name not been Andrew Trentham? Who was he really, beyond who he was expected to be—or more truthfully, what his mother expected him to be?

Perhaps, he thought, the question ought to have been: What was he beyond what he expected *himself* to be?

Was the confidence he wore innate to the real him, or merely assumed by virtue of his name and position?

He was beginning to realize that he sought an identity that came not from being someone's son, or someone's brother, or being a member of Parliament, but from who he was . . . *just himself.* Could he ever disengage that identity from the confused and tormented little boy at the funeral?

Now the memories were back again. The rain, the black umbrellas, the dour faces of important men and women from London, the sniffling silence, the dull thud of earth falling on the wooden coffin, his mother's jerking and unstable breaths as she listened to the long line of condoling well-wishers, the long walk back to the car, during which his future had been determined—all part of a moment of time that was seared into his being. Those images would be with him forever.

Was his whole life nothing more than the attempt somehow to make up for Lindsay's death? Would he never escape the oppressive obligation—self-imposed, it may have been, yet no less real—to live out both her life and his?

Again came the reminder of the helpless American reporter.

His heart went out to her in sympathy. Yet as he now recalled the momentary exchange, he realized he also felt admiration. *She* wasn't afraid to buck expectation, to stand unflinching in the face of opposition, even ridicule, let come what may.

Actually, he rather liked the sound of her accent. He didn't care what some of his stiff English colleagues thought about the upstart colonials— he *liked* Americans. Their openness and informality, even their brashness at times—they appealed to him. Maybe he wished he had a little more American bravado.

Was that an intrinsic difference between Americans and the English— the willingness to take risks, to go against expectations rather than conform to them, to find out who you really were . . . anyone you wanted to be?

As much as he enjoyed politics, sometimes he couldn't escape feeling trapped by who he was, by his name, his past, trapped within the expectation of what he was supposed to do with his life, trapped within a culture that defined everything about him without his having much say in the matter of carving out an identity of his own. It was the British way—one did what was *expected* of one.

But that American journalist—she was free of such expectation. She was trying to do something out of the ordinary, something that defined her as an individual in her own right. He wondered if *her* mother approved of a reckless journalistic career in a foreign land? Were American parents less bound by familial, societal, and cultural expectations?

What had he ever done like that? Andrew thought to himself. What had he ever done that took courage, that demanded something more from him than what he had always been?

What had he ever done that was not somehow bound up in the unspoken question of what his mother would think?

▨   S I X   ▨

Andrew continued his way across the fell toward the Scotsman's cottage. As he picked his way around rocks and scrub brush, the legendary stone again came to mind. He had read an interesting piece on it the other day in *The Highlander*, one of many complimentary magazines that came to his office.

The author had attempted to piece together the origins of the Stone, citing first a Celtic myth about an assembly of gods known as the Tuatha de Danaan. One of the assembly's most prized possessions was said to have been the Stone of Fal, which supposedly cried out whenever it was stepped upon by the rightful king. Thus it had come to be used at all of ancient Ireland's coronations, so that the veracity of each new ruler would be known.

There were other myths, widely divergent, about the Stone—the most prevalent form being that the Stone had been taken from Ireland into Scotland, as the Scots from Eire overran the Picts and gradually established their stronghold there, to be used to crown kings in the new kingdom. Another version had the Tuatha fleeing from the Philistines in Greece and journeying directly to Scotland, then later moving on to Ireland but leaving the Stone behind. Still another myth ascribed the Stone's origin to the pillow used by patriarch Jacob at Bethel when he dreamt of the heavenly ladder, later brought to Scotland by Scota, daughter of an Egyptian pharaoh, by way of Spain and Ireland.

Andrew smiled to himself, picturing the slab of sandstone as he had seen it many times in the Abbey. What *were* the Stone's origins, he wondered.

Where had it really come from? It didn't really look all that different from the stones that jutted out from the hillsides of his own father's estate.

What was the story Duncan used to tell about that primitive man, the ancient he said was the first man to explore these regions? He had come from the south, driven northward from someplace far, far away.

What had Duncan called him—something like the explorer . . . or the traveler?

Andrew could not quite recall enough specifics to piece together a coherent memory of the tale. It was from the big book the old man was so careful of, whose pages were brittle with age.

The reminder of the book and its contents sent a thrill of expectation up his spine. And with the newly enlivened memory of those former times, into his consciousness came old Duncan's voice, speaking to him after the book was closed.

"Ye'll be a great man yersel' someday, laddie," he could hear Duncan say, as the Scotsman set the story-filled volume aside and stared intently into Andrew's wide and impressionable eyes.

With the words suddenly flowed back others in a torrent of memory—mysterious prognostications that Andrew had all but forgotten.

"Ye'll be jist like the auld Celt yersel'," he had told him. "Ye mayna wander sae far, but ye'll hae a hand in the future o' yer ain kin. Eh, but whate'er second sicht I may hae is pointed at yersel'. Ye're but a wee laddie noo. But ye'll be a great man ane day. I know God's got ye in his sights, laddie. An' once he's got somethin' in mind fer a man t' du, he doesna let up till it's dune."

What had it all meant? Andrew understood the strange words no more now than he had then.

"Ye'll grow intil a braw ane. The call o' greatness'll be upon ye, laddie. I ken. 'Deed, he's yer ancestor jist as sure as his verra bluid flows through yer veins, whoever's oye ye be. Ye'll mak it yer ain one day. I'll tell ye a' in yer ain time. Ah, wee Andrew . . . 'tis a braw land, ye ken. 'Tis yer ain land, ye'll see."

❖ SEVEN ❖

This location was the last place in the world the well-dressed visitor from London would have chosen to spend an afternoon. Notwithstanding his name, he hated it up here, especially in winter. Leave the moors and the mountains to the wind and goats—he had better things to do with his time than freeze in this godforsaken wilderness.

The instructions, however, had been explicit. And given the scrawled signature at the bottom of the single sheet, he was hardly inclined to refuse. Unfortunately, the social aspect of the tryst had quickly given way to a heated disagreement.

The two figures spoke in hushed tones. Their voices had grown angry.

"It was my understanding—"

"Look, I gave no promises. I only said I would consider my options when the time came."

"Well, the time has come."

"Yes, and I have considered my options. The answer is no."

"I thought we had—"

"It's no use playing that card with me. What do you take me for, an amateur who buckles to every pressure that comes along? I've been in this game a long time. I'm not so easily seduced as you might have thought. Besides all that, this is the wrong moment, I tell you. And your promises are none too reassuring. Politically, I simply cannot risk it."

A tense silence filled the air.

When the younger of the two again spoke, it was in a greatly altered tone, quieter, almost sinister.

"Politically, I don't think you can afford *not* to do as we say. The risk, as you call it, lies entirely on the opposite side of the fence from where you would place it."

"Just what is that supposed to mean?" snapped the Londoner, who had become so polished through the years that few would have guessed his roots.

"Very simple. The fact of the matter is this. Evidence has been planted—*compelling* evidence I might add, implicating *you* along with the SNP in the theft of the Stone of Scone . . . among other things."

"*You* stole the Stone!" he exclaimed.

"I did not say that. I only say that you could very easily find yourself in a position you would be hard pressed to explain. And I do not mean as a mere accessory, but as the mastermind of the affair. It would ruin your career."

"Don't be ridiculous!"

"I wouldn't risk it if I were you."

"Are you actually trying to blackmail me?" he sneered. Around the edges of the sound, however, could be detected a hint of concern.

"It is such an ugly word. I would rather call it an understanding, an arrangement."

"No one will believe a word of it."

"Even if they don't, they might believe the other, shall we say, items of interest we have compiled. There are photographs, you know. It really was rather careless of you. Now it is my turn to repeat your own words back to you—what do you think *we* are, amateurs?"

"If for no other reason, even if you discount our relationship, I would have thought better of you."

"Tut, tut—all that's beside the point now. We know what we are doing. Believe me, Scotland Yard will be extremely interested in what we have arranged to be found, if . . ."

The voice trailed off significantly.

"Bah—the thing's absurd. Maybe I *am* willing to risk it—that's how little I think of your amateurish threats. And here I thought you . . ."

His voice halted in disgust.

"You owe me everything," he began again. "It is I who put you where you are."

"As I said, all that is beside the point now."

"It is I who shall expose *you* . . . all of you. Scotland Yard will have you behind bars within twenty-four hours."

He paused and stared across the table, shaking his head with disdain.

"I should have known," he said. "I should have seen the deceit in your eyes all along. It's clear enough now."

He rose, then turned to go. Without another word he left the pub and strode angrily down the narrow cobbled street. His annoyance was directed as much toward himself for allowing himself to get mixed up with such people. One little lapse. Now he was in this pretty fix.

Within seconds he heard the door close. Feet ran behind him to catch up.

He did not turn around. His hired car was up ahead, parked along a lonely stretch of the roadway beside the deserted docks. Even now his pride did not allow him to apprehend his danger.

The footsteps slowed and drew alongside.

"You *must* change your mind," said the familiar voice beside him.

"You're daft!" he retorted, not slowing his step. "After this eye-opening little conversation, you couldn't offer me enough. If you thought the votes of our party were for sale with such tactics, you were—"

They were the last words he ever uttered.

The razor-thin blade of an expensive Highland *sgian dubh* suddenly shot upward into his side and back, piercing two ribs and slicing through the back of the heart. He was dead instantly.

Even before he had a chance to slump, the killer shoved the still-erect body off the embankment along which they had been walking. It tumbled with more a plop than a splash into the grimy waters below.

The thin figure above continued walking as if nothing had happened. Out of sight below, the body slipped silently into the slow black current of the River Dee and floated away in the direction of the sea.

※   E I G H T   ※

Duncan did not seem surprised to see Andrew, nor did he remark on receiving a second visit this quickly after the first. He greeted Andrew warmly and led him inside. Soon the water was in the iron pot and Duncan was stoking the fire.

As the old man blew and coaxed the peat flames to warmth, Andrew made his way around the room, taking in objects, textures, and memories of the place, almost as if he had never seen them before, though they had been familiar to him since childhood. He beheld everything with a full and quiet heart, noting especially the single bookshelf with a sensation not unlike reverence.

"Congratulations t' ye, lad," said Duncan, bringing Andrew back to the present. "Ye'll be back in Parliament again. The people are fortunate t' have ye t' speak their mind. But 'tis a heavy responsibility, I'm thinkin'."

"Especially with things like ever-expanding home rule to consider," replied Andrew.

"For Scotland, ye're meanin'?"

"It's about as hot a political potato as there is. The future of the UK is at stake."

Duncan nodded thoughtfully, taking in the statement with keener interest than he revealed. He asked Andrew several more probing questions concerning his current activities. The conversation continued for several minutes, then subsided briefly.

"The best things always take time, laddie," added Duncan, more seriously now and with the reflective tone Andrew recognized from his boyhood.

"You mean things like Scottish independence?"

"Perhaps. If it happens, 'twill indeed have been a long time comin'. 'Tis like the Lord's work in our lives as well—slow and steady, and often unseen."

"The Lord's . . . *work* in our lives?" repeated Andrew.

"Ay."

"How *does* he work in our lives?" asked Andrew, surprised at his own question. It was not something he had considered before this moment.

"'Tis different fer every man an' woman on earth," answered Duncan. "The Lord's got something he wants t' du in every one, but each has t' discover it fer himself."

"How does one know what that something is?"

"Ye maun ask him, an' then give him time, as I was sayin', t' show ye."

"Does he show *everyone*?"

"Everyone that wants t' be shown, an' that patiently listens fer the Voice when it comes. The moment comes t' all when he'll speak. 'Tis the moment o' truth, the moment o' decision. Then is the time when ye've got t' decide whether ye *want* that work within ye that the Lord's been waitin' t' du."

"You say, when that time comes, it's a moment of decision?"

"Ay. Jist as the Lord's waitin' till the right time t' hear a man or woman say yes t' him, he yet gives every one the right t' say no. Though he's calling oot t' us in a thousand ways, tellin' us he loves us and that we can trust him, he yet leaves oor response t' that love in oor own hands."

✇   N I N E   ✇

A long pause followed, during which Andrew contemplated the old Scotsman's words.

"The heather an' the peat's the slowest growin' o' nearly all things in makin' the heat they give," Duncan resumed as if continuing the previous track of conversation. "Peat's one o' the ancient wonders o' life, laddie. 'Tis one o' the mysteries the Creator put in the good earth he gave us."

He paused again briefly, a faraway look crossing his face momentarily. "Du ye recollect me tellin' ye aboot what the colors o' the heather put me in the mind o'?" he asked after a moment.

"No . . . no, I don't think I do," replied Andrew.

Duncan was silent, and another pause in the conversation ensued.

Andrew glanced up and waited. But the old man did not resume the conversation in that direction, and his visitor did not feel like pressing.

"'Tis one o' the reminders o' the auld times," Duncan went on at length. "The auld men an' women wha spoke the Gaelic tongue—'twas peat that kept 'em alive, laddie . . . the heather abune, the peat below . . . an' the hue o' its blossom tells the story only a few eyes can see."

The cryptic words from the old Scotsman sent Andrew into a renewal of his pensive mood. He sat staring into the fireplace, where heat now emitted in earnest from the hot-glowing sides and corners of the black peat bricks. Their legendary warmth was not merely physical, but emotional and cultural as well, symbolizing a heritage now kept alive only by a very few, like Duncan MacRanald. He was one who had not allowed the flow of modernity to rob from his sight the capacity to look back . . . and remember.

"But what did you mean before," said Andrew, "when you said the tale about the maiden of Glencoe would tell me what makes a Scot a Scot, that at Glencoe one discovers the essence of Scotland?"

"What makes a Scot who he is, is the spirit of the Highlands, laddie. 'Tis what the maiden's story is aboot, an' the wind upon the moors sings her faint lament."

"But what makes the spirit of Scotland so unique?"

"T' answer that, laddie, I'd have t' tell ye the whole history o' our land . . . an' I doobt ye hae time fer that!" he added laughing. "The good book o' Scripture tells the Hebrew tale o' salvation, an' ye ken hoo long that story is! But the like tale o' Scotland's liberty is still one that's in the process o' being lived oot. An' 'tis one that's not widely known in the world. But 'tis a tale that will soon come t' light, I'm thinkin'."

"Well," laughed Andrew, "however long it may be, I'll make time."

"'Tis oor history that makes the land get into the bones o' oor people, an' makes it so that the Scots *canna* rest till their land's their own again. The very stones cry oot fer it, like the stones o' Glencoe's still hae the blood o' the curse upon them."

"You make it sound like the Stone of Scone, that cries out when touched by the king."

"Ay," nodded Duncan. "The stones o' the Highlands are all one. They all cry oot for freedom."

A lengthy silence intervened. This time both men were, as of one accord, brought back to the present by the awareness that a vigorous steam and gentle boil was rising from the water in the cast-iron kettle hanging above the fire. Even without a microwave, the contents were by now well capable of producing a piping hot pot of tea. Duncan rose, swung the sweep out from the fire, removed the kettle from its hook by means of a thickly padded hand-mitt, and carried it to the counter beside his sink. He poured out the steaming liquid over the tea, which had been waiting in readiness in the adjacent teapot, then refilled the kettle with cold water and replaced it at the fire to begin the process once again should more tea be wanted.

Within five minutes Duncan had again taken his seat, a tray of tea makings and a plate of oatcakes sitting on the low rough table between the two men's chairs. Each poured out a cup to their liking, and both were soon sipping and munching contentedly.

"You know," remarked Andrew, "being here twice in such a short time brings so many pleasant memories to mind from my boyhood."

"Ye were here mony a' time, laddie."

"It's funny how time gets away, how you overlook your past for such long periods. Then something will happen that will remind you. And suddenly you realize you've lost touch with something important—something valuable. Do you know what I'm saying, Duncan?"

Duncan nodded. *He* had not forgotten. As the Hebrew story was always with him, so was that of his own land. And he felt that its climax was approaching. He dared hope his people's dreams would come to fruition in his own lifetime.

Andrew pondered again for a moment. The next words out of his mouth were in a different direction.

"Tell me, Duncan," he said, "you're a Scotsman—what do you think of the theft of the Stone?"

"There's mony a legend aboot its origins," answered Duncan cryptically.

"What about Scottish independence?" persisted Andrew. "Do you think that's where all these changes will lead?"

Duncan smiled. Though the politics of Andrew's situation were new, the question was far older than either man's years.

"The answer t' that one hings by the string o' self-knowledge," he replied at length, answering Andrew's question in the veiled manner which was often his custom. "Liberty must always come in the end. The question is one o' hoo, when, an' through whom."

The young politician was oblivious to the older man's deeper meaning.

"But what about the political implications to the union, to the kingdom itself?" he asked.

"I canna say as I hae an opinion aboot it, laddie. But I think 'tis a matter o' a man kennin' his roots, o' kennin' whaur ye cam frae . . . o' kennin' what it means t' be a Scot. That's the end trowth o' the matter—kennin' who ye be . . . and what's a Scot."

A knowing expression overspread his face while a happy twinkle played in his prophetic eyes as they stared into the fire. It was clear he cherished more opinion in the matter than he was willing to divulge. In the very asking of the young man's question was being fulfilled the old man's lifelong desire that the heir of the Trentham name and the Derwenthwaite estate would discover the roots and the past that bound them together. It was a very personal desire, for Andrew was heir of the same legacy which had brought Duncan's *own* people down across the border with Lady Fayth Gordon so many generations ago.

Gradually the conversation flowed into other paths and channels.

※   T E N   ※

The fire in the cottage burned low.

The two men—the one with his life before him, the other with his behind—stared into its fading embers with wide eyes and thoughtful gazes.

"You used to tell me so many old stories," sighed Andrew at length, pulling his eyes from the red-orange embers and glancing over at Duncan. "I'm sorry to say that I've forgotten probably three-quarters of them."

"No all o' them, I haup."

"No, not all. But time blurs the memory."

"There's times' for tellin', an' times for rememberin'."

Andrew smiled.

"Then this must be the latter for me."

"Why du ye say that, laddie?"

"Being here again, memories begin to come back—tales you used to tell me, things you would show me when I'd go out with you over the moors when you were tending your sheep—all kinds of little details and bits and pictures, almost like a film from out of my younger years."

Andrew paused and smiled in fond reminiscence.

"When I was home a couple weeks ago," he went on, "I was out walking up to the top of the Crag. I looked out across the Solway and saw the Galloway hills of your homeland. Then I smelled the peat from your fire. That's when I realized I needed to come visit you, and I came straight here. Now here I am again."

Duncan pondered the younger man's words.

" 'Tis *yer* land jist as it's mine," he said after a moment.

At first Andrew did not seem to hear. After ten or fifteen seconds, all at once the words registered with a jolt in his brain.

"What was that you said?" he asked abruptly, turning toward Mac-Ranald.

"That it's *yer* land jist as much as 'tis my ain."

"*My* land!" repeated Andrew. "What do you mean? I'm no Scot."

"Ay, ye are, laddie."

"To tell you the truth—and I hope you won't take this the wrong way— I always sort of laughed the notion off," said Andrew with a thoughtful smile. "I suppose I assumed that whatever links there were in that direction had grown so diluted as to be negligible."

"Hardly that, laddie. Once the Scots blood flows, 'tis there t' stay. Whaur else du ye think the name *Gordon* came frae but the hills o' the north? Ye aye got more Scot's blood in ye than ye may realize."

Unconsciously Andrew rose and began wandering aimlessly about the cottage.

"A Scot, you say?" he murmured.

"Ay."

His steps came to rest after a few moments in front of the bookshelf he had noticed earlier.

"I . . . the thought had never . . . such a thing didn't strike me in exactly that way," said Andrew, in an even more subdued tone. "I suppose I have always been aware that there is Scottish blood in our line. The same could no doubt be said of three-quarters of the people in England. But it never occurred to me to actually *call* myself a Scot.''

Even as he spoke, he had begun browsing through the tiny library of old volumes of ballads and history that had once been such a treasure to him but that he hadn't opened in years.

Sensing that the moment had come for which he had long waited, Duncan smiled. The mystery of their mutual heritage beckoned the young heir of a legacy he was about to discover as his own. The fulfillment of his own ancestral charge was at hand.

"I'll jist throw some fresh peats on the fire," said Duncan, though his guest hardly heard him now, "an' add water t' the pot for tea gien ye like.''

"Yes . . . yes, thank you . . . that will be fine," mumbled Andrew. "Maybe I will look through some of your old books, if you don't mind, and see if I can't find one of those old tales you introduced me to when I was a boy.''

Already he had located the oversized volume he had thought of when walking earlier and was turning the leaves over with care to the first tale he had been trying to recall to mind ever since. His eyes fell upon the full-page engraving of the ancient Celtic traveler of prehistoric byways, spear in hand, giant behemoth lying dead behind him.

The very sight of the old black-and-white woodcut transported him back in time.

He was a boy of seven again, wide-eyed, eager, engrossed in the tale. Slowly he stepped backward, holding the book with both hands, eyes riveted to the page, and eased back into the chair.

He was unaware of the old Scotsman pausing behind him before leaving the room, taking one final look at the important young politician seated with the open book in front of the enlivened fire.

Duncan MacRanald smiled.

He was needed no longer. It was time for the magic of his homeland to weave its spell. He left the cottage and was soon on his way to check on his sheep.

Meanwhile, Andrew's deep green eyes were as wide as they had been as a child. The years, the decades, the centuries, finally even millennia tumbled away, as he was carried away, back to the era when man first began to come to this island he called home.

Migrations Of
Wanderer's Grandsons

JOURNEY OF
THE WANDERER

5

The Wanderer

Antiquity

ONE

The man rose from where the body lay. A solitary tear formed in his eye.

He did not know the word *wife*. His elemental language made no distinction between woman, wife, and mother. But he had spent nearly ten years with this friend, and he cared for her. She had made him warm in their crude hut overshadowed by the White Mountains. And she had borne him a son.

The year, by reckonings still millennia in the future, was some two score of centuries before the time of Christ. But the man knew neither years nor dates. He knew there were warm seasons when the soil could be dug, when his woman planted seeds that produced food. He knew there were cold seasons when the mountain became covered with white and the land was hard and unfriendly.

He and his fellows in these lands north of the Great Sea others called Mediterranean were only beginning to harness the incipient fragmentary powers of their minds. Humans of embryo civilizations in the deserts of the pharaohs and the dynasties far to the east had taken rationality a few steps further. But among the races of which this man was a part, the process of thought remained as rudimentary as their tools, their weapons, and their homes. Conjecture and analysis yet lay outside the matrix of familiar exercises for their brains. Instinct, hunger, and the elemental emotions of their humanness drove them in equal share with their dawning intellects. They did not know that in this fertile region of rivers and valleys north of the Great Mountains, they were slowly becoming a people whose influence would spread throughout the world as surely as that of the Sumerians, Egyptians, and Chinese.

As the climate gradually warmed and they spread farther north into the verdant plains between the three great rivers, these herdsmen and hunters had only begun to experiment with techniques of planting and harvesting. Those who occupied this vast region were loosely linked only by their common emergence out of a prehistoric complexity of related peoples who had made their way here from the Mesopotamian crescent where life itself had begun. It would be another two or three thousand years before they would assimilate into the warlike confederation of tribes who, with forged iron swords, would dominate the landmass north of growing Rome and west of dying Greece.

To later Greeks and Romans, these people would seem a large, wild-eyed, and hairy race of savage barbarians. But the man standing over the corpse of his dead wife knew nothing of what his people would later become. He only knew what he felt in his heart—the anger, the grief, the love.

For he was a Celt. Or such he would one day be called.

These tribes of the southern Germanic plains would gradually coalesce into a powerful race that would sweep over the continent like a raging wildfire, vanquishing all who dared stand before them. To the diverse breeds of their progeny, the Celts would give the color red—the red of fire . . . the fire of energy, creativity, passion, cruelty, conquest, and vibrant life.

This man, however, would by then long have left the central European continent behind him. As the sky brought seasons of change to the land, so the ill fortunes of man's barbarity had brought such to him. The future race whom the Greeks called the Keltoi would have to rise and conquer this land without benefit of *his* progeny.

He would take his lineage elsewhere, to sire a people far away.

He was a big man for his time, though erect he would not quite have measured six feet, muscular of limb, with wide shoulders, bare of covering and hairy. His hands and feet were disproportionately large and needed to be, for they were the primary tools of his survival. The light brown hair that spread in all directions from his head, tangled and plentiful, did not stop at his neck but spread down across his back and brawny frame. His cheeks and chin and lips, large featured and abrupt, were covered with beard, which likewise spread downward over his neck and onto an expansive, rippling chest. This was the warm season, and thus he was clad in soft animal skin only about his midsection.

⁂ T W O ⁂

The man stood, raised his fist in the air as if vowing vengeance, then let out a mournful wail over his woman's body.

He felt no shame in the tears that displayed his grief. His were a people whose energy fueled itself with powerful emotions as natural as eating and hunting. Even before the echo of his outcry faded to silence, his lips began moving again. From the depths of his throat the crooning of a strange melody could be heard, lonely and full of doleful distress. Gently his body rocked back and forth.

As the chant rose and fell, he lifted his face to the sky in unknowing supplication to powers and forces he knew not. In his own way, he committed the soul of his companion to the elemental dominions of the universe which intuitively called out to him at this moment.

He did not cogitate upon such things. The brooding song lay hidden in his deepest being. It now emerged from the vast implanted reservoir of human feeling, filling the air with melancholy strains.

After some moments the chant too, like the great wail that had proceeded it, drifted into silence.

Turning, he saw his nine-year-old son running toward him in answer to the cry.

The boy had followed at some distance as they had returned from the hunt. As he now caught up, he saw the tears on his father's face. A look of fearful inquiry filled his eyes.

Instinctively sensing he must shield the lad from his mother's broken form, the man ambled quickly to meet his son and led him away.

"What is it, Father?" asked the boy in a consonantal tongue now long dead.

"Nothing, my son," replied the man. "It is time for us to seek the river. We may no longer stay in this place."

"Where is Mother?"

"Your mother will remain here."

"Why, Father?"

"She must remain here—forever," he answered. He could not prevent bursting into another wailing howl.

There were many in the tribe over the hill who would immediately have charged forth with reckless unconcern for their own lives to avenge his wife, to seek and kill and mete out death for death. Such was the way of men. Of such was justice made.

But it was not this man's way. He would not make his son an orphan. Love filled his breast, for both wife and son, with more potency than the primitive urges of conquest, greed, and retaliation that guided the footsteps of most of his era.

Revenge, he knew, would be futile. He only regretted that he and his son had been away hunting when the Helvetii had come. He knew the marauding bands had been sweeping out of the White Mountains, plundering, killing, and stealing. It had not occurred to him that they would come this far.

Had he gone with the rest of his tribe, the Boii, to live in the valley, perhaps this day would not have come. But he had always been a loner, a nomad. When he had arrived from along the Danubi fifteen years earlier, they had branded him a wandering minstrel. His parents had also been Boii. They had migrated north along the river Danubi when he was six, after one particularly severe winter. And when twenty-five years later he trekked back, the Boii who remembered him had called him the Wanderer.

The name remained, along with the lonely call of his heart. A Wanderer would he forever be.

The Boii were his people, but this was no longer his home. Wander he must. This time far away. But not to return again down the river where his parents had gone. With his son, he would travel northward, down the other great river called Rhinii. The Boii maintained relations with the Belgae far to the north. He would visit them, perhaps travel farther to lands yet unknown.

The man did not know that land ended. He did not know that seas existed or that rivers like the Rhinii and Danubi flowed into them. He only knew that the rivers brought life, and that by staying near their banks he could hunt and kill what he and his son required to sustain life.

They would wander. And they would survive.

⬚   T H R E E   ⬚

The Wanderer left the valley known as Rhaaran, which lay one range of hills removed from what the Teutonic descendants of the region would call the Bodensee. With his son he made his way, taking but few personal belongings. These consisted chiefly of hunting implements, flints for making fire, a handful of scrapers and awls and crude knives for cutting and working hide and wood, a few bone weapons and carving tools, and as many skins for warmth as they could carry.

Survive, this father and son did. For they were of Celtic blood—proud, strong specimens of a virile people whose star in the world's history was on the rise.

Northward down the swelling river they traveled, mostly by foot, occasionally on what makeshift boat they could fashion from a dead pine or fir or what raft could be fabricated from smaller fallen birches.

Where they found food, they remained, until weather or scarcity or the wandering urge compelled them onward. Sometimes days, sometimes months would they spend in a place. But always the impulse to explore new horizons propelled them onward.

The boy grew as they went, made strong and sinewy by the constant struggle against nature and the elements. As years passed, the hair on his face gave the father pleasing evidence that they were no longer mere father and son. Now they were two men adventuring together, roaming where Boii had never been.

At last they could hunt the big elk, because there were two to outsmart the beast. Perhaps one day they might even hope to bring down a giant mammoth, whose white tusks the man coveted both for their beauty and for the sharpness of their points.

As they traveled, the Wanderer revered the memory of the woman who still lived in his heart. He taught his son likewise to honor her who had given him life and suckled him at her breast. They spoke of her often, that the memory of her face and the sound of her voice would not fade. He now called her Eubha-Beanicca, "the living woman," to remind the boy always that not only his mother's blood, but also her spirit, lived on through him.

As they went, the man met others who shared their Celtic blood. Never again, however, did the urge to settle among them rise within him.

When he reached the far north, the river became so large as to be fearsome. It was by foot, on the river's south shore, for shore it was indeed by this time rather than a mere bank, that he first beheld the awesome sight— two gigantic flowing bodies of water tumbling straight one into the other in white, frothy fury, creating a new river of monstrous proportions surging out of sight, toward the sea of the north the man had never seen.

He dared attempt no crossing of this wide torrent. Without knowing it, the Wanderer and his son now stood at the lowest point of the continent.

One day these places would be called the low countries. The Wanderer and his son had gradually descended since leaving the White Mountains years behind them, always moving with the flow of the great river. But after this day, toward whatever point of the sun they turned their faces, the water would be flowing downward against them. Their journey, though they knew it not, had reached a dividing region of no return.

Three days they remained at the conflux, the crashing, turbulent echo of great rivers in their ears, mesmerized by the sight that few if any other of their species would ever see.

On the fourth day the Wanderer arose, scanned the two rivers as they rushed headlong into each other, a sight that still struck both fear and joy into his breast, then turned his gaze away from the rising orb over the horizon in the east. The time had come again, as it had so many hundred times before. His feet had become restless.

It was time to continue on. They would now follow the new river from its violent collision with the Rhinii up its unknown current, westward to see where it might lead.

Water was water, and it carried life, no matter from which direction the water came. Against the flow of this new river he and his son could no longer hope to navigate any makeshift craft. But their time would be easier on the riverbank and its environs. For spread out before them, and to their south as far as the eye could see in all directions, lay the flat, open plain of the huge delta.

This new river to which they had come his descendants would name the Themii, the "dark river."

On they marched, unaware that they had turned their backs forever on one season of their heritage. With this crossing of the great plain they were launching new streams for their proud bloodline to follow toward diverse destinies. For within the lifetime of the son's grandchildren, a repeated series of violent seismic tremors of the earth's surface would subjugate this lowland to the encroaching waters of the sea.

The plain that father and son now traversed would sink with catastrophic suddenness as the land wrenched itself apart. The jarring shifts of the globe's unsettled plates would transfigure the joining of the two mighty rivers into two wide and separate mouths a hundred miles apart, spilling into the newly created sea channel between them. It would scar the Dover coastline with miles of jagged cliffs of unusual and notable coloration. They would be called "white," or the cliffs of Alban, by the Belgae who followed. This

Celtic tribe would thus give the land toward which these first adventurers walked, and to which future explorers would venture by boat, its first Celtic name, linked by the common thread of primitive language to the White Alpine Mountains they left behind.

As they crossed the plain later to be called a strait, behind them lay the continent which, in the thirty-six centuries to come, would see the descendants of the tribes of these two men rise to great heights. Though the Celts in Europe would never build a city, nor forge a governmental empire, nor even establish an absolute ethnic unity, their many strains and breeds—from the Parisii, Cornovii, and Belgae in the north to the Remi, Treveri, Helvetii, Boii, and Vindilici farther south—would loosely coagulate into a force that would lay the economic, social, and artistic foundations for most of the northern European civilizations to follow.

They would give to the Athenians and Italians who assimilated them a host of inventions—art, metallic technology far in advance of its time, the iron plowshare, the rotary flour mill, a wheeled harvester. They would grow into a dynamic, warlike, fierce, vigorous people. It would later take the full might of Caesar's legions to subdue them throughout Gaul, Asia Minor, Spain, and the rest of northern and eastern Europe.

All these events and empires and conquests that lay ahead, however, would come to the regions now at the backs of the man and his son as they left the joining of the two rivers. They would not be part of it.

Before them instead lay a *new* history, a new destiny.

For they, and the handful who had preceded them, and the many of like Celtic origin who would pursue their nomadic footsteps over the wide isthmus and across the water which eventually overflowed it, would people a new land, soon to be an island known as Alba or Albion. They would imbue it with their Celtic energy, their pride, their language.

Most of all they would give this new land their blood, and the fire of their passion.

FOUR

The Wanderer and his son traveled west, then gradually northward once the Themii became narrow enough to navigate upstream and cross.

The son matured in strength and stature, and in the ways of living in an untamed land, as his father taught him. It was the only life they knew, the only life most of mankind knew. They hunted, they fished. Rarely did they remain long enough in one place to fashion more than a temporary shelter.

They were not the first to cross into this lush and uncharted land. They therefore met occasional beings of the homo sapiens species—though many more creatures who were not. Human encounters, in fact, were infrequent, for the population here was but a scant fraction of what it had been where many tribes were scattered throughout the valleys of the Rhine, Danube, Rhone, and Seine, whence they had come.

Here and there they came upon tribes of strange sorcerers, passed their crude stone monuments to the sun and moon, and wondered silently what they might mean. But there was no reason to tarry, for these were a queer people . . . and yet more northern lands beckoned. Out of the Wanderer's origins near the White Mountains, the inward pull of snow drew him.

In the hilly regions north of the great river's fount, the boy took a wife from one of the native tribes—of Celtic root like himself, though neither knew it, of a branch of the Belgae who had migrated two centuries before. She was of strong stock, powerful in her own right, brawny for a woman and standing as tall as most men, with fair skin, keen bright eyes, and shining black hair, long and straight. She could hunt with the men of her extended family and had killed beasts twice her size with her own hands. And yet she possessed as well an aesthetic temperament, inherited from her father and his Belgae forebears.

Her father had begun experimenting with stone, wood, and bone to produce ornaments and jewelry. She applied her craft to simpler expressions of the artistry of their breed. From an early age she had been singularly able to create images of animals and human shapes with the point of a stick or sharpened bit of flint. Now in the years of her early adulthood, she discovered how to make rudimentary colors from various plants to enhance the figures on animal skins or dried pieces of wood or bark. They were of no particular use. But the creating of such visible representations of the world brought a quiet joy to her heart.

Both the Wanderer and his son were drawn immediately to the daughter of the Belgae warrior. She reminded each in their own way of their departed wife and mother. She was big enough to survive and live long, keep a husband warm in bed, and endure childbirth without frailty.

The Wanderer immediately consulted his son, then held counsel with the young woman's father. The arrangement was concluded before many more days.

When the pilgrims continued their northern trek, therefore, they were now three instead of two. Happy days were these indeed, for the sound of the woman's voice, laughter, and song now accompanied the Wanderer and his son.

The young man called his new wife Eubha-Mathairaichean, "source of life," for all his life his father had taught him to revere the spirit and reproductive mystery of womanhood. The son of the Wanderer and his wife came together and produced two sons, then a daughter, then another son.

The Wanderer, by now an old man and growing weary, found himself at last desiring rest. The small family settled for several years in what would later be called the Cumbrian Mountains. As their steps took them northward, the air had grown steadily colder, for they were not many centuries behind the glaciers whose retreat had made these lands habitable. With cooler temperatures came rougher terrain, different breeds of grasses and wildlife and trees, more rocks, hills higher and more jagged, longer and colder nights in winter, and more sustained periods of light in summer, though the sun did not beat down with such heat as before.

Especially there was more water—under their feet, all around them in magnificent lakes, and falling with greater regularity and intensity from the sky above them.

It was a wet land, a windy land, and a solitary land.

Nowhere at that time, upon the planet called Earth, had clusters of the subduing forces of men grown numerous. Even the beginnings of cities in Egypt and Babylonia were yet meager, rural, and agrarian. But here, in the northern climes to which the Wanderer had come, isolation reigned supreme.

The land itself, more than the scarcity of men, forbade colonization. The icy winds as they swept down from the north, laying flat the coarse grasses of open moorland with their chilling blasts, called out to all who would pursue their trek farther, "Go back! Return to the South. These regions are home only to wind and mountains, ice and snow, and those few beasts brave enough and strong enough to subsist. You dare not settle here!"

This was not a friendly land. It wanted no men.

These northern places yielded few treasures. The soil was thin and soggy and unfertile. It offered little life. Wild fruits and vegetables grew only in short supply. Only the hardiest of breeds made their homes here—reindeer, boar, elk, red deer, wolf, bear, and numerous small creatures. Those not stout enough to battle the elements for an equal share in the claim to subsist either died or migrated back to more temperate regions.

Those who came here would fight but for one thing—the right to remain, the right to live, the right to endure. This was a land destined not to spawn empire, but to fashion a peculiar and robust breed of inhabitant.

This was a land of the determined and rugged loner. Those who tramped northward and persisted in making their homes in its wild wildernesses would become a breed set apart. They would be men among men, women among women, a race of stalwart victors in the most elemental contest of life.

None but the hardiest would survive.

※   F I V E   ※

It was a general warming trend in the boreal hemisphere that allowed the Wanderer, and those who followed him, to make this land a permanent home.

As the glacial ice receded to allow mankind's northward advance, however, it also scarred the land and left unmistakable imprints on a geography that would forever influence the history and character of its inhabitants.

This ice lay heavy on the land with a weight beyond comprehension. Moving along at inches a year, the deep-packed glaciers extended far below the ground's surface, scraping, clawing, pushing, and readjusting entire landscapes as it went—tearing away topsoil and vegetation, carving deep gashes where the earth's crust was weak. It thus created lakes and rivers, valleys and marshes, coves and sea channels, and long and numerous sea inlets or firths, and left exposed the bare rock and jagged mountain peaks strong enough to withstand its force. The ice shaped the face of the land.

The movement of glacial ice also took a share in the creation of a rocky substrata that, working in combination with the cold and wet of the climate, would give rise to perfect conditions for the natural production of the miraculous burning substance known as peat.

The most important legacy bequeathed by the Ice Age, however, was the simplest of all. The ice left behind nothing more nor less than another form of itself. For the geographic and climatic conditions created here came to be dominated by that most elemental of substances upon which life depends—water. A watery landscape became the defining substance of the region. Water fell from the sky. It lay in every hole and crevice. Its seas surrounded the land.

The ice returned every winter from above, covering the land with thick blankets of snow. The sea penetrated the coasts with long, fingery firths and scattered it about with islands. Persistent rains kept rivers full with swift, amber, peat-stained flow. And moors and water-soaked marshes were unable, because of the rocky substrata, to drain effectively.

❊   S I X   ❊

Water, terrain, and climate together insured that the region was slow to settle.

By the Wanderer's time, icebergs no longer floated off the shores of the land. A livable degree of warmth had come, as if borne on the breezes of the southern winds, though the winters remained frigid. Vegetation and trees covered the land, however sparsely.

Those few humans who ventured here found in the wide, cold, windy spaces a correspondent melody from within their own souls. In the whispering of lonely winds through rocky clefts and in the eerie wail of gulls along high jagged coastlines, the sounds of desolation gave rise to a solitary joy of personhood unknown to those content to bask in the warmth of plenty and in fellowship with others of their kind. From out of the barren bleakness of wide gray moors came a silent, answering sense of home into the breast of those who felt the call of the north.

It was a call not heard by the many, but the few.

Eubha-Mathairaichean, who came to be called simply Mathair, or "source," which later took on the same meaning as *mother*, was of similar temperament. Her Celtic blood was like that of her husband and his father. Nature spoke to her of mysteries and secrets, though she could only feel, not understand them. She often rose early, with young ones still asleep, and sought the lonely places, to look up and wonder. It was sensations from such moments that drove her to express herself with hands, in images of what she had seen, to make beauty, to communicate in a medium that required no words.

As the Wanderer and his son traveled, they had seen and learned much that enabled them to continue. Now the young wife joined them, taking an equal share in taming the land, adding strength when needed as well as fresh insights into difficulties they encountered. From occasional encounters with other men, they observed tools and implements not seen before. No metals yet—they would not come to this region for two thousand more years—but varied and cunning uses of stone, shells, tusks, and wood.

To the cagey skill with which the two men had become adept at stalking and killing wild game was now added the woman's resourcefulness in making wider uses of what nature provided them. It was in her nature to improve, to create, to bring warmth and homeyness to their lives in a multitude of subtle ways. Her artistic bent enabled her to see what they could not—potential uses and possibilities for whatever they owned or encountered. The result was a multiplying source of skins and other beastly material with which to barter and trade.

Their inventory of implements slowly widened, a good many of feminine design, as well as ornaments like she had seen her father make, of symbolic and artistic rather than practical use. When necessary they traded such items from her hand in exchange for what they needed. Those they encountered were eager to display and adorn themselves with representations of objects which they felt possessed supernatural powers.

What they could not trade for, they studied, then, with the woman's help, fashioned for themselves. As skill with hands and fingers became more dexterous, so did their minds. To the facts they learned, they added that great human uniqueness—ingenuity.

The most useful of these instruments proved to be what amounted to a crude saw or long-knife. A series of razor-sharp seashells—for which they had traded many skins to a tribe of fisher-people at the western shores of the sea they finally reached—were fastened in a long row, tightly bound with dry-tempered leather thongs against a slab of hardwood. The edge created along one side of the wood, with its evenly spaced, sharp-pointed shells in a precise line, made it a cutting instrument of much wider utility than mere sharpened stone or flint.

The fragility of the shells was of little use against the trunk of a tree. But they discovered it could be employed to great effect by cutting deep into the earth itself and sawing through it to extract large chunks of the grass and heather and matted root system, which extended many feet below the surface and held the soil together in a tightly bound mass.

They could not know that the boggy turf beneath their feet, so ill suited for so much and so difficult to traverse during the rainy months, in fact contained a cache of wealth that would enable them and their descendants to survive—not against hunger, as did the soil of the south, but against the elements of the weather itself. These first inhabitants sought only the insulating thickness of the sod to use for shelter. For their progeny farther north, however, the peat would provide a greater and more palpable warmth, the discovery of which would enable them to finally subdue this hostile environment and make it permanently livable for their kind.

Father, son, and daughter-in-law constructed a crude home for themselves and the son's family from tree trunks. These they thickened against the strongest gusts of wind and rain with slabs of turf, which their shell-saw enabled them to cut from surrounding wastelands.

Inside, the wife hung skins she had cured and drew pictures and shapes on their smooth sides, adorning their dwelling with designs she hoped would keep the spirits of nature pleased. She occasionally carved designs on tree trunks as well, or scratched shapes onto rocks and boulders. As they moved about the land, the etchings came to tell the story of their travels. The Wanderer, his son, and his daughter-in-law would in turn explain the meanings of the shapes and designs to the four children of their family, thus beginning an oral tradition which they would themselves carry on to their progeny.

The youngsters were growing now too, the three sons big enough to help their father and grandfather slice down into the moist earth and drag the heavy cuttings from the moor. The daughter assisted her *mathair* with preparing the ground and planting what little could be grown there.

Meanwhile, the Wanderer, his hair white and his legs weary from the miles he had trod throughout his long life, watched his growing brood with all the pride of a primitive clan chieftain, which in reality he was.

▩   S E V E N   ▩

It was toward the end of a summer season that the youngest of the Wanderer's grandsons spotted the giant prints.

They were sunken so deep into the springy earth as to leave hardly a doubt that they belonged to some behemoth of a beast. The seasonal warmth had no doubt brought it down from the north, or up from the south. Never before had they seen the likes of such prints.

The moment the Wanderer heard of it, his heart began to pound. He followed his excited grandson, eyes wide with anticipation. The moment he had dreamed of was at hand!

The lad hurried back toward the bog where he had seen the tracks, father and two older brothers running at his side, the old white-haired forebear lumbering after them as well as he was able, with labored breath and heavy step.

A few minutes more, and all five stood in a circle, breathing quietly from the exertion, staring down at the huge imprint of a foot.

The Son of the Wanderer, a muscular man now in the full virility of his prime, looked at his father. Both men knew what the moment signified. They had spoken of it frequently as they made their trek to this land, when the son was no older than his own sons were now.

The three youngsters—the eldest, in his teens, his twelve-year-old brother, and the eight-year-old discoverer of the print—glanced with wide eyes back and forth between father and grandfather, wondering what would follow.

The decision took scarcely a moment.

After a few seconds, the aging patriarch slumped to the ground and sat, still beholding the print with wonder. He would conserve his strength for this one final primordial contest between man and beast, this hunt for which he had yearned throughout his lifetime. Already his son and grandsons were hurrying back to retrieve spears, lengths of twisted vine-cord, slings, and their three stone axe-clubs. Whether the weapons that had brought the deer, the elk, and the hare into their power would likewise prove of effect against larger game, only time would tell.

There were five of them. Mostly they brought to this battle the cunning of mankind's developing mind.

Ten minutes later the hunt was on.

The two eldest walked in front, father and son, each wielding spear and club in his two hands. The lanky and confident seventeen-year-old followed a few strides back, and several paces farther behind came the two youngest, whose wide eyes and uncertain knees evidenced that fear accompanied them toward the engagement in equal proportion to the anticipation of victory.

The tracks were fresh. The hunters had examined the holes with probing fingers and keen eyes sufficiently to determine that they had been made only a short time earlier, well after last night's freeze and this morning's thaw. The flatness and uniformity of the indentations, as well as the distance between steps, made it clear the beast was moving slowly. They should be well able to overtake it.

The five warriors hastened on.

Nothing was said. This was a moment that would bind together the ties of their family, and their bonds as men, forever. Their feet fell silently on the soft earth. Each knew the peril ahead. Such only heightened the blood-tingling anticipation racing through limbs and brains.

Suddenly the Wanderer's son held up his right hand. His father and sons froze.

With noses bent into the slight breeze, as if in one accord they sucked in deep drafts of the morning air.

There was no doubt. The odor of animal flesh carried in the wind. Faintly accompanying it drifted into their ears the sounds of heavy tramping through the brush of a small forest ahead.

Wanderer's son lowered his hand and signaled them to follow. Once more they marched forward, quieter if such were possible, fingers clutching yet more firmly the implements of death they carried. Into the wood they walked, peering ahead with eyes alert. Glancing this way and that, each silently hoped to be the first to spot their prey.

Providence fittingly chose the eldest.

The old man, his white hair fairly bristling with expectancy, stopped suddenly. Eyes aglow as from a lifetime's dream realized, he raised a hoary arm and pointed through the trees with bent finger.

There stood the magnificent beast!

Never had their eyes beheld such a creature! Yet they knew the giant mammoth in an instant, for no behemoth on earth could rival it.

The furry flanks shone reddish brown, covered sparsely with coarse long black hair. The hulking shoulders loomed higher than two men. The skin from a single such beast, erected on poles, could house an entire family for ten winters! Its flesh might feed fifty families!

Such thoughts raced through the son's brain. His father, however, had eyes only for the prized tusks of white ivory, strongly curved outward then back toward the center. He had lusted after their beauty and sharp tips for more years than his son had lived.

The two older men looked at each other, formulating even in their silence the plan with which they would make their attack. A few gestures, questioning glances, shakes of the head, pointings and nods, were sufficient.

The beast's eyes offered the only logical target. In no other part of its frame did a vulnerability exist that would enable such as they, mere ants of men, to overpower the beast. Clubs and stones and anything else they might throw would only bounce off the thick, hulking carcass with no more potency than a leaf falling from one of the surrounding trees. But a flint-tipped spear striking deep into the massive head through the doorway of the eye would bring the animal down eventually, even if they had to track it for days. Once it fell, its strength at last given out, they could follow the first attack by finding soft flesh underneath its belly in which to drive more spears. Finally they could club it to death between the tusks with the stone heads of their axes.

The plan was daring, but the objective so enormous as to be worth the risk. It would require that the father of the three youngest put his life into the very path of what by then might be a charging demon of Herculean size, hold his ground until the final moment, and then launch his spear with perfect accuracy.

There would come no second opportunity. If he missed, he would be dead.

The Wanderer's son now signaled his eldest boy to follow. Slowly they crept leftward, to begin a wide detour through the trees, out of sight, and around toward the front of the beast. The grandfather and the two younger boys waited some minutes, then began inching their way in the opposite direction. The five would stalk their quarry in a slowly tightening circle, silently, with stealthy step, surrounding it until there was but one direction open—toward the waiting, powerful arm that would send a sharpened spearpoint into one of the only openings in its skull.

The mammoth had stopped its heavy-footed tramp and was now sending its trunk about the ground and tree foliage, foraging for edibles. So silent was the approach against him that it was the sensitive tip of its snout that first signaled an enemy was at hand.

The blowing, sniffing, noisy quest for food suddenly halted.

The animal lifted his massive head, the great fleshy ears widening in search of sound. The huge trunk rose into the air, its smaller end probing to and fro with breathy inquiry, like some strange finger of an other-worldly abnormality, seeking from what direction came this odor that dared interrupt his privacy.

A snort of challenge issued from a mouth rendered nearly invisible by tusks and trunk. Fear was no component in the makeup of a monster such as this. But he did not like what he could not see, and the unknown contained a certain element of inherent angst. Slowly he lifted one of his giant forefeet and plodded again into motion.

Two steps only he took. Suddenly some moving creature stood before him, barring his path. Another snort followed.

Glancing around, trunk flailing with seeming disregard for order, his eyes took in other minuscule forms closing toward him. Throwing his tusks upward and his trunk high, he opened his mouth. A great roar of anger echoed through the forest. The steps that followed did not plod, but tramped through the brush with the recklessness of urgency and defiance.

In its very path, the mighty warrior stood his ground—a mere nothing before this giant!

The human knew that to discharge his weapon prematurely would only enrage the beast and perhaps turn it toward father and sons. His heart pounded within him. Unconsciously he let the club fall from his left hand so that his entire strength could be amassed into the single motion required of his right.

Onward the colossus came, in a full charge now, issuing another great roar of intimidation against this tiny erect two-legged creature who had the effrontery to bar his way.

Still Wanderer's son held his stance. Slowly he raised the spear above his shoulder, fingers tightly gripping the slender stalk of wood. Even should he succeed, how could he avoid being trampled to death? He drew in a deep breath.

The beast was nearly upon him now.

He pulled the spear back to the full extent of his reach, gathered himself for the supreme effort, then hurled it forward with the power and momentum of one mighty thrust.

The shaft released from his hand.

He lunged sideways to escape the animal's enormous charging feet.

His spear flew through the air without a sound, finding its target with deadly precision, striking the left eye of the beast just above center, slashing through the surface and lodging its stone tip deeply at the outer extremity of the mammoth's brain.

A great shrill explosion of pain and fury rent the forest.

Red squirted from the wound, spilling in great splotches over trunk and tusks and forest floor, while a thick black oil oozed out of the blinded eye and down toward the creature's mouth.

One of his feet stumbled momentarily. The falling man tumbled sideways, out of the way of the treacherous feet and to safety. Another screaming bellow silenced the five human voices now shouting triumphantly. The great mammal lumbered off through the forest with the spear dangling and whacking back and forth against the two ivory tusks.

In great excitement, the Wanderer ran to his son and pulled him off the ground with shouts of victorious exuberance. His three grandsons ran to join in the celebration.

A moment more and all five were off after the wounded ogre. The slashing, crashing, breaking sounds of its feet trampling through the forest were easy enough to follow, amplified by thunderous bellowing and braying roars. Energized by their apparent success, they followed on foot, barely managing to keep the wobbling monstrosity within range of their sight.

For two hours the chase ensued.

Occasionally the mammoth stumbled to one knee, but always recovered itself. That the wound was mortal there could be little doubt. The spear had penetrated deeper than any dared hope. Blood continued to spill before their steps, and however far the chase led them, their ultimate triumph was only a matter of time.

At last the creature lurched, then tripped again, this time to two knees, and did not rise.

The five pursuers approached warily from behind, then stood some yards off. They well knew an enraged beast near death was most dangerous of all. They would wait.

Silently they watched, listening to the mammoth's lingering cries of anger and anguish. At length one of the two knees upon which it supported itself gave way, and the huge form toppled awkwardly onto the side of its head. Exhausted from both the run and the loss of blood, the beast rolled over on the great bulk of its whalelike right flank.

To all appearances their prize was dead. The old man rushed forward, heedless of the cries of his son, whose watchful eye yet detected the movement of breath from powerful lungs housed deep inside the mighty form. His father ran forward to the head, grabbed one of the tusks, and ran his hands up and down the smooth trophy. The wounded eye was black and void of sight, crusted with blood and a thick oily discharge. But had the Wanderer—less observant now with the advancement of his years—examined the other eye carefully, he would have seen yet the gleam of lingering wrathful life.

His son hastened cautiously to the back side of the head, shouting warnings to stand away.

"Away . . . get away, Father!" he cried.

Mesmerized by the color and texture and feel of the great tusk, the old Wanderer hardly heard him. He remained standing in the very face of the beast. His son raised the stone axe high in the air, then brought the blunt edge of stone crashing down upon the head of the mammoth just above the eyes, from one of which still dangled his spear.

A great crack could be heard as the skull began to split.

A final roar of death sounded as the giant brute let out the spent conclusion of its fury. Suddenly alert to his danger, the Wanderer jumped back from the bellowing open mouth as his son raised his club for another blow.

But as Providence had shed its light on the aged man only moments earlier, now that light was extinguished by its dark counterpart called Fate.

It was too late for him to escape the tangle of tusks and suddenly twisting trunk. As it roared its last, the beast raised its head in one final frantic, jerking motion off the forest floor. The powerful serpentine trunk caught the old man's legs, trapping him, and threw him to the ground.

The second blow from the son's club fell with perfect aim against the huge wrenching head. The stone accomplished its work. With its neck arched upward, the beast breathed its last, and its twisted head now fell lifeless back to the ground.

But even in death it had its revenge. For one of the smooth, thrusting tusks found the Wanderer's torso where he had fallen in a tangle with the trunk and was now struggling to free himself. The sharp tip gored him through. He was pinned to the ground by the very treasure he had sought. Man and beast emptied their lungs together in a lengthy gasp of death.

The great cry that now rose heavenward from the forest floor was uttered by him whom the gods had suddenly made eldest among them. It was an honor unsought, and accompanied by huge tears of grief and wails of torment for not keeping his father away. As his father had done for him so long ago, he immediately shielded his own sons from the gruesome sight.

Quickly he led them away, that they might grieve in solitude. The tusks and skin and whatever meat they might retrieve must wait.

Their elder was dead. It was a solemn occasion. Honor was due, and they displayed it by kneeling and weeping.

At length the Wanderer's son rose. They returned to the grisly scene of death. Somehow, with the help of his sons, they must extricate the corpse of his father from the tusk of the mammoth.

It took some time to wield the shaggy head such that the limp body could be pulled free.

Bloody, repulsive work it was. None of the four would forget this awful day. At last the son who had traveled far lifted the broken form of his father in his arms and bore him home, followed silently by his three weeping but stalwart sons.

Manhood did not come easily to those who made this region their home. It must often be won at great price. Though only hours earlier two men and three boys had gone in search of the great mammoth, four men now returned, bearing the lifeless body of their patriarch before them.

▨   E I G H T   ▨

It took two days for son and grandsons to prepare the Wanderer's grave. Eubha-Mathairaichean made a new drawing on a small piece of hide depicting a colossal beast and a white-haired warrior facing each other in mortal combat. She would lay it on his breast, bordered with intricate interconnected links and shapes symbolizing the continuity of life. She would say by her art that the great man lived on and had gone to become one with the earth.

The grave was not of great depth. It did not need to be. The earth spirits would soon take the body. No man nor creature was likely to disturb it then.

They lined the trough with what thin pieces of rock they could gather, pointing the venerable white head toward the north, whose frontiers he had pursued all his long life. In the crypt, along with the drawing, they placed a chunk of the tusk that had ended his earthly sojourn, to bring him pleasure and comfort during the travels toward whatever world now lay before him. At his side they laid the long shell-saw, dulled with years of use, which he had fashioned decades before with his own hands and with which those who remained had sliced his grave out of the turf. They had since replaced the tool with new and better, but this had always remained his favorite. A handful of his most cherished flints they set in his cold, stiff hand, and alongside his body a skin filled with fresh water should his journey require it.

A brief ceremony followed, with suppliant chants to the unknown powers above and below in whose hands their revered father now rested. The four men and two women joined hands around the grave, gave the white beloved face a final, tearful, stoic farewell, then silently took hold of the three great slabs of turf set alongside the hole and gently lowered them onto him. Then followed the gathering of many stones to pile atop the grave as protection against beasts, and as a monument with which to remember the fallen Wanderer.

The chief of their tiny clan was now gone.

The next days were busy ones. The great fallen beast, won with such a sacrifice, now offered a variety of wealth to the migrant family.

They could only hope to salvage a small portion of the flesh. The afternoon of the Wanderer's death they had torn off what was possible to eat within a few days and taken it back to roast over the fire. The tasty meat, however, had contained no savor in their mouths, and they had consumed it in silence. Meat was necessary to survive. But nothing could remove the bitterness that went down with every bite. They would dry an additional quantity in the reasonable hope of storing it a few months. But it was too early in the year and there was no snow about to freeze more. The rest they would have to leave to the buzzards and the wolves.

The thick hide, if with their crude knives and scrapers they could tear it off in nearly one piece, would serve as enormously valuable protection against the elements, both above them as a roof, and around their bodies as warmth. There was easily enough to make new shoes and garments from the scraps and leg sections. Teeth, bones, and hoof-nails could be used as implements for a variety of life's needs. The second tusk as well as several of the huge rounded ribs they were able to cut out and dislodge from the hulking mass would serve as strong and sturdy plows with which to dig in the hard soil.

It was a tedious and bloody process. After four days, the putrid stench from the giant open carcass became nearly unbearable. When his own three sons could tolerate the rancid fumes no longer, the Wanderer's son excused them to stand watch and guard him against incursions from other even more dangerous wild beasts who were prowling daily closer and closer.

They built three large fires to surround the scene of their labors, the reeking shell of blood, fat, muscle, gut, and bone in their center. They hoped the smell of the smoke would confuse the nostrils of nearby carnivores. If not and they ventured too close, the flames would dissuade them of further approach.

On the fifth day, the Wanderer's son still worked on, standing knee-deep in rotting entrails between the open bones and the stomach he had cut apart with his long, sharp shell knife, beating against the base of one large rib bone with a great stone held in both hands, trying to break it off at its base.

With a loud crack, suddenly the bone split and gave way at his blow.

The weight of the stone and the force of the swing threw him headlong off his feet. He fell facedown into the fetid mire with a bloody, liquid squish. Struggling to his feet, covered with the blood and viscera of his own victim, he staggered a moment, then retched violently, then again and a third time. His own vomit spewed onto his legs and feet, mingling in sickening warmth with the cold chill of death under him from the mammoth's rotting innards.

Holding his heaving stomach and pulling himself together as best he could, he staggered away, out of the disgusting pit of death, and to the solid ground where his teenaged son watched with revulsion.

It was enough! There was nothing more they could take from this beast. The time had come to leave it to whatever other animals could yet make use of it. The rest could rot.

He gathered his sons to help him retrieve the last of the booty. They would haul it to their camp while he sought one of the small nearby lakes in which to remove from his skin the last memories of the animal who had killed the man he loved.

⬚   N I N E   ⬚

One morning a month after his father's burial, Wanderer's son, the mammoth slayer, rose early.

A chill breeze met his face, portending storms a few months distant, readying themselves even now in the arctic to sweep southward toward the lands of men. The moment of restlessness had come again, as it always eventually did. He had anticipated this day, though it saddened him that his father could not enjoy it with him.

He squinted, then breathed in deeply.

He knew that tangy smell of northernness. He and his father had pursued it since he was nine. Always it had called them farther up, farther toward its origins. Away from human habitation they had trekked, into the face of the wind and the cold itself—northward, ever northward.

Now it was an odyssey for him and his own woman and their children to continue. The blood of the solitary septentrional pilgrim pulsed in his veins more strongly now that he found himself the new head of the infant clan.

The urge to move filled his soul. And he could not remain in this place of his death.

He turned to walk back to the hut. There stood his wife waiting. She had heard him leave and knew what he felt. She felt it too.

Their eyes met as he approached. They smiled. Both knew the call of the north had spoken.

That very day, with one accord, they began making preparations. With wife, daughter, and sons, the Wanderer's son gathered their belongings, heaping all of the mammoth's wealth they could pull on their two wooden sledges, and took up once more the exodus into the unknown, in the direction toward which they had pointed his father's head and toward which, he had no doubt, the old man's spirit was still bound.

Through the hilly region of lakes the Wanderer's son led them, then down onto a plain until, encountering the body of water that would come to be known as Solway Firth, he was forced inland. Making his way slowly around it to the east, through the boggy mouths of several rivers and streams at its head, he finally turned northward again, entering at last into the land which, though given many names through the years, would always be known by those who loved it most deeply as Caledonia.

Wherever he journeyed in those northern regions, his stories and tales and recountings of past travels always grew out of his love for the father with whom he had spent a full life. And it was from that father that he chose his name.

He could have been called many things—Mammoth Slayer, or Adventurer, or He Who Sojourned from the White Mountains. But in his own estimation, and by the love that pulsed in his heart, there was but one thing that set him apart with such worthiness as to give him an individuality and identity.

He thus ever after let himself be known simply as Son of Wanderer.

His own sons would continue the example, taking *his* name by which to designate their own, thus perpetuating a genealogical appellative pattern whose roots lay in remembrance of the fathers and chiefs who had gone before.

But with this patriarchal pride, he would also pass to his wife, Eubha-Mathairaichean, she who was the *mathair*, the source of life to daughter and three sons—and in memory also of her who had given him birth, her whom his father had called Eubha-Beanicca—the prerogative to extend his own heritage to his sons. Did not life spring from woman? Should not she, therefore, pass on its legacy?

Thus, early in this land's history, out of the reverence of the Wanderer and his son for the latter's mother and wife, did matriarchy come to share honor with patriarchy in the hearts of the people of this land.

❊ TEN ❊

It was a harsh and unforgiving land the descendants of the Wanderer occupied, and over which they took gradual dominion as millennia gave way to millennia.

What had lured them in this direction, even the Son of Wanderer himself could not have told. He was driven by what flowed in his veins—the urge to explore, to move, to gaze beyond the next river, to climb and look past the farthest peak.

Season after season, as he moved steadily northward, he came to lands where cold and water made settlement difficult, where economic and political oneness would be hard to come by in future centuries. The ruggedness and wetness of the terrain discouraged homogeneity and unity. The scars left by the retreating glacial ice—mountains raised high, and valleys carved low, with lakes and swampy bogs everywhere—provided built-in barriers to movement and settlement.

The first of these encountered by the family of Son of Wanderer was a quagmire of swampland that ran east and west between the firths of Clyde and Forth. Only in one spot could this boggy morass be breached. At the location which would one day be known as Stirling, the ice had left a narrow ridge of solid ground and natural rock, over which the east-west bog could be traversed, overlooked by a towering miniature mountain of solid stone. This site would in time become the land's most strategic fortress and would hold the two halves of the country together.

But for now the Son of Wanderer did not cross this natural bridge but settled his family in the fertile lowlands between the two great Caledonian firths.

His own sons would in a few years bring this prehistoric odyssey to its end. It would be they who reached the northern extremities of this arm of the European continent. From the few forests that existed, though they were neither dense nor high, they would fashion boats with which to subjugate the isles that lay off the western shore. They would hunt the animals that roamed the land and the fish that swam its seas, both of which would give them meat to live. They would learn to make the land's very starkness their chief ally in combating enemies of their own kind who would one day rise from the south against them.

Before his own days were done, the Son of Wanderer would know what had driven his father toward the north. Many would be the sights to meet his eyes in the soaring Highlands that would one day be his final home. His heart ached that the old man might see them with him. He would behold other beasts, magnificent in their own way, though none so mighty as the mammoth, that would speak to his spirit concerning this land to which he had come.

The Wanderer's three grandsons, each in their turn as manhood overtook them, extended the Wanderer's clan into the farthest reaches of west and north.

The eldest, known as Hunter, Son of Wanderer's Son, would migrate east, across the fertile plain between the Clyde and the Forth where his father had settled, managing to cross the treacherous bog which made of northern Caledonia essentially an island, and thence up its eastern coast.

The memory of the giant mammoth-kill never left him. Though it brought grief to his heart, the elemental clash for supremacy, pitting brain and ingenuity against the terror of sheer size, remembering the image of his father's bravery facing the charging beast, kindled within his bosom a restless impulse to match his own humanity against the fierceness of the lower species. Ever after, the pangs of hunger in his stomach could be sated only by meat outmaneuvered and slain by his own hand.

The nomadic spirit drove Hunter's steps, just as it had driven his grandfather before him. He explored the lowlands along the northeastern coastline, inward to the edges of the central Highlands, and northward around to Moray. For the rest of his days he sought the footprints of those whose kind had killed his grandfather. Though he never saw their like again, his canniness was challenged to its full by the great brown bear which stood higher than he himself, by the mighty stags with racks of antlers, and by the most feared predators of all—ferocious packs of pale-eyed wolves.

He was the first of the homo sapiens genus to lay eyes on the long, narrow loch called Ness. The hunting there was not good, however. It revealed little evidence of creature life. The region surrounding the fog-enshrouded, murky body of water seemed eerily somber and empty, as if some preternatural presence lay near. Even the few birds that chanced to fly overhead glided silently on the breeze, whatever invisible spell that warned beasts away silencing their overhead songs as well. Hunter remembered the thrill of following his father and grandfather after the elephantine prints. But no such feeling filled his breast walking through *this* valley beside the strange water.

Sensing ominous forebodings which not even his fearless instinct desired to question, the Hunter shivered, then turned his back and with his own son began making his way northward toward the coast. If by chance there was some beast here, it did not belong to the earth and was not one he wanted to encounter. This was no place for man.

Boatdweller, second Grandson of Wanderer, would ply his skill toward proficiency in crafting boats and learning to sail them. He would explore the Western Isles of Mull, Uist, Skye, and Harris, and as far north as Lewis, before sailing south to the largest of all the islands which would come to be called Ireland, where his progeny would remain for centuries.

His descendants would not only learn to navigate upon the deep greenish gray waters, they would develop ingenuity in taking their sustenance from under it as well. The sea gave life. Boatdweller's descendants would discover its secrets. They would come both to fear and love it.

Out of his loins would come a hundred generations of fisher people, scattering and spreading themselves north, south, east, and west through hundreds of islands besides the Green Isle, eventually peopling the encircling coastline of the entire Caledonian mainland, and in time returning from Eire to *reconquer* this very land of their origins.

The Wanderer's only granddaughter, the third-born of his son, carried on the artistry of her mother and the Belgae grandfather she never knew. During her own lifetime she left behind hundreds of etchings, carvings, and artifacts which told the stories she had heard when her father and his father had come to this land, as well as those her mother passed on about her people. She found a husband from another group of Celts who had recently arrived in the vicinity, and passed along to her own daughters the nurturing strength and practical creativity that would infuse generations of their female descendants.

Two things remained that Wanderer's generations of sons and daughters were unable to vanquish. Never would they moderate the fierce wintry snow, hail, and sleet that swept down in icy blasts from the frigid polar cap, a yearly reminder of the ice-glaciers which had only recently departed this region. Nor would they tame the mountainous inlands and rocky deserts in the far north known as the Highlands—not nearly so high as the White Mountains from whence the Wanderer and his son had begun their quest, but rugged, austere, desolate, vacant, and grim.

In spite of its gray, dreary inhospitableness, this land yet possessed a curious capacity to infect the soul. The Wanderer's grandsons and granddaughters for a hundred generations to follow would thus remain here, would prevail in spite of the natural environment's brutal hostility, would even come to cherish it.

The Wanderer's third and youngest grandson, with his wife and young brood, ended his own trek in a tiny sheltered glen beneath two high mountains. The mysterious Highlands somehow bespoke to him the prophetic essence of what Caledonia would become. Ever after would he call these high barren hills and rocky peaks his home, giving parentage to a clan that would trace its origin to the Highland Mystic, Son of Wanderer's Son.

From these original dwellers of the Highlands, future generations would know of the one stag among ten thousand, born with white coat rather than red, and what he would come to symbolize for the people of this land. More than any other in the world of beasts, the stag would come to signify the mystique of the beloved Highlands.

When Highland Mystic first set eyes on the resplendent creature he had till then only heard about from his father, standing atop a high peak, rays of brilliant sunlight reflecting off its light-hued coat and enormous crown of antlers, he felt the stag's message, and was forever changed.

As Mystic's own sons grew, they listened to tales and haunting ballads, songs, and poems of the arrival with his father in Caledonia of this first of its bards, with striking remembrances implanted into their young memories of the old Wanderer himself. These they would carry forth into the fabric of legend, which would interweave among many branches of the clan they would one day become.

Wanderer's Son and his aging wife traveled north to spend their final years with the family of their youngest son. As they stared into the orange embers of fire at night, the mysterious words and tones from the Mystic-bard's voice entered the hearts of his sons, imbuing their deepest souls with an identification with this place, and what it meant to be one with this land, its beasts, and its multitude of wonders. They listened to the tale of the great mammoth, and of the legend of the white stag. And as their grandfather listened too, his own hair now white, his heart was filled with many memories of those years with the Wanderer, when he had been no older than they.

Saoibhir sith nan sian an nochd air Tir-an-Aigh.
Is ciuine ciuil nam fiath ag iadhadh Innse Graidh,
Is easgaidh gach sgiath air fianlach dian an Dain
Is slighe nan seann seun a siaradh siar gun tamh.
Saoibhir com nan cruach le cuimhne laithean aosd,
Sona gnuis nan cuan am bruadair uair a dh aom;

Soillseach gach uair an aigne suaimhneach ghaoth.

Rich is the peace of the elements of night over the Land of Joy,
And rich the evenness of the calm's music round the Isles of Love,
Every wing flies urgently in obedience to nature
While the path of the old spells winds inexorably westward.
Rich the breast of the hills with memories of bygone days,
Serene the face of the seas
With dreams of the times that are gone.

When the Son of Wanderer finally breathed his last, his youngest son wept, sang a doleful lament, then went in search of a suitable and fitting place to lay his father in final peace. He found a great slab of stone, nearly flat on its top, under which some animal had once carved out a now unused den. After enlarging this cavity, they buried the old man beneath the enormous rock of a shrine, filling it in with stones.

For days after, it was the old man's wife—she known as *Mother* and *source*, now the eldest of the family—who, alone with her memories, chiseled upon the giant gravestone with sharp flint and stone a series of figures. On this stone she would tell for all time of this man she had loved and what they had seen and done together. It was she who passed into the future the legacy of her man who now dwelt beneath the stone and gave his blessing to their mystic son. With hand upon his thoughtful head, in her strong yet aged voice, in a tongue long forgotten, she intoned the words Highland Mystic would never forget.

The land, its creatures, all nature is one, and we with it.
Revere nature, honor life, forget not that existence is a circle without
   end.

Her voice broke into the song of a strange melody of mingled lament and rejoicing.

Look up, look around, look beyond, my children, at those who make the
   earth their home.
Look up and wonder.
Behold the sky, the stars, the clouds, the winged creatures, the empti-
   ness.
Look about you and wonder. Wonder at the storm. Wonder at the brightness of the sun.

Behold the creatures and trees, the stones and brooks, the fields and the
   sea.
Behold those with whom you share life, for they have much to teach you.
The fertility of the earth brings life, but nature takes life in its time,
For is not life a circle without end?

Mystic's own wife heard the words and melodies with the rest. They
entered her soul, and in her turn after years she likewise passed Mystic's
blessing and her own carvings and symbols and their meanings on to their
sons and daughters. Mythologies of nature worship grew out of such beginnings and gave rise to yet more symbolic art. Statues of stone and wood,
later metal, came to replace drawings on leather, as idols representing a host
of creature-deities. And out of the honor these patriarchs of antiquity bestowed upon their women were laid down the roots of what in later years
would be a succession of kingship through the women of this prehistoric
Caledonian clan.

Ever after, as long as Mystic's family dwelt near that place, they would
return periodically to the great stone, stand for a few minutes atop it, gazing
upon the crude-carved story of a life, in silent contemplation of him who lay
beneath it, remembering the men from whence they had come who had
brought them to this land.

❊   E L E V E N   ❊

The grandsons and daughters and families which sprung from Mystic's
seed and that of his two adventuresome brothers and artistic sister were
followed by many others.

Hunter, Son of Wanderer's Son, taught his descendants to kill and eat
the boar, the deer, wild cattle, proliferative grouse and small game, as well
as many land birds.

The progeny of Boatdweller, Grandson of Wanderer, gathered fish from
the sea and shellfish from its beaches, as well as an occasional stranded
whale. This would lead to the making of the first bone whaling harpoons by
his fearless great-grandsons, as more and more methods were tried and discovered to extract life from the tempestuous ocean waters.

Those who succeeded Highland Mystic, Son of Wanderer's Son, in making the wild and lonely spaces their homes also hunted for their meat. They

also gradually learned to till what soil they found in the protected valleys and glens of the mountains, and as they migrated back southward into the low-lying and more fertile regions. In the absence of mammoth bone or tusk, antlers from highland deer provided the earliest form of plough with which they dug and worked the earth and put into it things to bring forth food on vine, root, shrub, stalk, and tree.

One of the Mystic's sons migrated west, across a wide moor, and down into the protected valley which future generations would call Glencoe. There he settled, and there his family and descendants remained. Neither he nor his brothers nor sisters forgot the great slab of stone and what it signified. As generations passed, many forgot its exact location. But there always remained a few throughout the generations who knew. For bard followed bard, and mystic followed mystic. It was their duty to remember.

Not only did the Highlands give Caledonia the snow of the arctic—its very terrain provided the means to *endure* that cold. One of the Mystic's sons unearthed a remarkable fact, for the Celts of ancient Caledonia a discovery as vital to survival as fire itself. The mystery was simply this: The same turf upon which they built their crude homes, and which they had learned as far back as the Wanderer's time to cut into slabs to stack in piles to fend off the blizzards which came every year, or to partially seal the mouth of a cave against icy chill, was not dirt at all. It was a remarkably dense organic material which, when dry, burned hot and slow. It was the single discovery which, more than any other, would make life in the Highlands for the Mystic's successors possible.

And so did the descendants of the Wanderer explore and settle the land of the north. Future historians and archaeologists, sifting through the sparse implements his people left behind, and through the cloudy, mythical stories perpetuated by the Mystic's descendants, would wonder who came with the Wanderer to this land. Scraping through fragments and traditions and dusty legends of the past, they would speculate whether his Celtic bloodline was the first to settle. Or were the Wanderer's people but one of several such ancient roaming peoples to migrate toward the extremities of the world's landmass?

As the climate continued to improve for the fifteen centuries after the Wanderer's arrival, more stalwart nomads of his Celtic race followed, in small though increasing numbers. Celtic tribes on the continent rose and expanded. Their dynamic energy pushed at the boundaries of colonization. By now the earthquakes and crust shifts and tremors had cut this land off from the rest of the continent. But across the created channel of water they steadfastly came, following if not in the Wanderer's footsteps, at least in the direction of his path.

The small transplanted race of Celts flourished, if not in numbers, certainly in hardiness and courage. A mixing and blending of Celtic blood took place. Family and tribe remained the unit of strength. Out of the mingled origins of tribe and filial loyalty was born the clan. And though most of the derivative shoots which eventually occupied Caledonia shared common racial beginnings, their Celtic origins also infused within them a fierceness capable of erupting against rival families and clans as readily as against a common enemy.

As this was no tame land, likewise its inhabitants were no tame breed. They were, however, an emotional and intuitive people, who venerated their chiefs and bards. Spinners of tales—poets and storytellers and singers all in one—rose from within their ranks to carry on the tradition of the Mystic. They spoke and sang of past adventures, aided by crude musical instruments. Harps were made from willow, ideal for lightness, density, and resilience. Strings were fashioned from long, sturdy strings of intestines, cut and dried after a hunt, attached top and bottom with carved bits of bone. The willow was considered a sacred tree, which gave the music a magical significance. Poets and storytellers and singers of ballads placed the foundational folk epics and allegorical narratives into melody and rhyme. These bards came to be venerated alongside the chiefs of emerging clans.

They also revered their gods, for they were a polytheistic people. As Mathair, the Source, had taught them, they believed the supernatural lay all about, in the spirits which pervaded men and rivers and animals and mountains and sun and moon and all of nature.

The storyteller in time also became a religious leader. He spoke not only of what had come before, but of the invisible world all around, gradually infused with druidic influences from the south as learning and awareness expanded and overlapped. The bard entertained and instructed. He taught his people to think and seek meaning, though he yet himself knew little of the greater God to which his pantheistic deities dimly pointed.

Thus was added to the fire of Celtic emotion the kindling of religious fervor. This spiritual passion would flow through time as a constituent characteristic of these people and a dynamic force to influence the later history of their land.

Out of the Wanderer's and *Eubha-Beanicca's* mutual seed eventually emerged the animal tamer and soil tiller whom paleontologists would call Neolithic, or "new stone" man, whose dominion on the land lasted until approximately the first millennium B.C. The era was characterized by the development of increasingly sophisticated uses of stone, later pottery, then metals, all of which led to wider and more stable sources of food supply.

Slowly these men and women *settled* the land rather than merely drifting back and forth across it.

The foraging existence of the ranging hunter and fisher gave place to a more systematic life. As more people arrived, a cross-fertilization of discoveries resulted, leading to improved implements and methods, and greater understanding of plants, seeds, techniques, and new foods.

Celts were curious after their own kind. As the Wanderer had adopted the shell-saw from a chance encounter eons before, so men continued to observe one another. Faraway civilizations brought advances to the outskirts of human settlement, carried on the feet and tongues of new generations of nomads and wanderers.

As the diversity of tools and instruments widened, forests were cut so land could be tilled. Gradually man felled larger trees, crafted longer and wider boats, fashioned both stone and wood to build larger structures.

Primitive settlements formed. Implements improved. Metalwork was refined in the early years of the first millennium B.C. as the use of bronze was developed, changing weaponry and toolmaking forever. Men cleared and worked the land and soil to make the earth yield more of its fruits. Planting, cultivation, and harvesting became more effective. Not only was land cleared for growing, it was cleared for pasture. Man took dominion over domesticated animals and began altering earth's environment to suit the purposes of his expanding rule.

Steady colonization by the expanding tribes of the Celtic race followed in increasing numbers the Wanderer's dim historical footprint. To Ireland they came, and to all parts of Britain and Caledonia, the Western Isles, the outer Isles, the Orkneys and Shetland. They came from the continent, from the Mediterranean, from the north, round the Iberian peninsula, along the coast of France, along Brittany, up the Irish Sea and to the Hebrides.

The Celtic race approached the zenith of its power and creative energy on the continent. As they arrived to these western regions they were ab-

sorbed into the ancient brotherhood of those who had come before. These
new Celt arrivals carried with them a knowledge of society and technology
far in advance of their predecessors. They brought major developments in
metal technology. Swords, knives, chisels, cauldrons, sickles, axe heads,
spear tips were fashioned and put into use, and an immense variety of additional tools and devices. Gold and silver were melted down and crafted
into jewelry.

Stout explorers continued to brave the North Sea and turbulent channel.
The ancient Celtic tribe of Belgae—whose very legends told of one who had
wandered through their primitive camps long before, whom one of their chieftains' daughters had married and whom some of their people had followed
westward—settled in great numbers in the south.

Though in time he was all but forgotten to memory, nonetheless did the
Wanderer's blood flow throughout all the branches large and small that went
to make up this surging tide of human occupation.

He was the father of this land, the Adam of a people into whom were
grafted a hundred generations of newcomers. Had the old wandering nomad
been able to rise up out of his grave and gaze out of the past toward the
continent whence his steps had brought him, he would have seen a thriving
race. They were, after all, a people of his own origin—still vigorous, still
strong, still proud.

And they continued to spread the life and energy of his bloodline, as he
himself had done, outward into a world still young.

6

SHAKE-UP IN WESTMINSTER

ONE

Andrew Trentham closed the great book of childhood memory, set it aside, stood up and stretched. Would he himself ever have a family, he wondered, a heritage to pass down to others? What a privileged thing—to father a dynasty as the Wanderer had done.

He had been so caught up in reading the story that he hadn't noticed the descending dusk. The afternoon was obviously well advanced. Nor had he paid attention to the whereabouts of Duncan MacRanald. Now for the first time he saw that the fire in the hearth had grown cold.

He called out to Duncan. But there was no reply.

Andrew rose and walked to the door. He stepped outside. No sign of the Scotsman met his gaze, nor did a sound from the small barn adjacent to the house indicate his presence.

He set out to walk around the cottage to see if Duncan was up on the hillside behind it.

He had just rounded the corner of the stone building when the sound of horse's hooves interrupted his thoughts.

Andrew turned toward the downhill path. A rider was galloping toward him holding the reins of a second mount, riderless but saddled. Andrew recognized the Derwenthwaite groom.

"Mr. Trentham!" called the man even before he had his horse well stopped, "I came to find you, sir."

"Yes, what is it, Horace—" replied Andrew, "is something wrong?"

"You've had an important phone call, sir—from London. It was your office, sir."

"What did they want?"

"That you ring them up—immediately, they said, Mr. Trentham."

"What is it about?"

"They didn't say, sir. Only that it was most urgent, and that I must get word to you without delay. I brought your horse."

"Yes . . . I see that . . . thank you," replied Andrew. "How did you find me?"

"Your father saw you strike out across the hill earlier in the afternoon, sir," the groom replied. "And your mother remembered that you might be coming here."

Andrew took the reins, glancing once more about for some sign of Duncan. He would have to pay a return visit at the earliest opportunity.

Reaching into his pocket, he pulled out a pen and hastily scribbled a note, which he handed to the groom, with instructions to leave it in a safe place for the old man. Then, his thoughts still preoccupied with the ancient Celt and with his neighbor, the Scotsman of more recent pedigree, Andrew grasped the leather firmly and swung himself into the saddle. The next instant he wheeled his mount around and hastened off downhill, around the Bewaldeth Ridge, and across the heath toward Derwenthwaite Hall.

⊠   T W O   ⊠

Member of Parliament Andrew Trentham looked to the right and left along Bridge Street, then dashed into the open space between two oncoming cars.

The traffic, noise, and hubbub of the city contrasted with the quiet of Cumbria even more sharply than usual, he thought.

A glance toward Winston Churchill's bronze presence across the street in Parliament Square silently reminded him of the solemnity of his duty as he made his way toward the imposing Palace of Westminster, where the Houses of Parliament were located. He would check there briefly first, then get back to his office in the Norman Shaw building.

Andrew loved London no less than Cumbria. He enjoyed his life here.

He functioned in the very hub of Britain's affairs, even the world's. Something about his truncated visit to his northern home, however, had pricked more deeply than usual. The walk up Bewaldeth and the pleasurable hours spent reliving the trek of the Wanderer had made him less than eager to resume the city's pace.

So much, it seemed, had come all at once—the breaking of his relationship with Blair, the theft of the Coronation Stone from the Abbey, old Duncan's curious statement about what made a Scot a Scot. And the stories . . . the maiden of Glencoe, the tale of the Wanderer.

His brain was full of many new things. And now had come this shocking news which had shortened his visit to Duncan's cottage.

For the dozenth time Andrew replayed in his brain the fateful telephone conversation following his ride back from MacRanald's cottage.

"Mr. Hamilton is dead," had come the numbing words.

"What . . . Eagon?" said Andrew in disbelief.

"Eagon Hamilton is dead, sir," his secretary had repeated. "Most of the other party members are here . . . everyone is returning immediately."

"But . . . what happened?"

"No one knows, sir. A heart attack, they say."

"Heart attack? Eagon was fit and feisty as a Highland bull!"

"Yes, sir . . . Scotland Yard has released no further details."

"Scotland Yard!" Andrew had exclaimed. "What do they have to do with it?"

"I don't know, sir. I think you had better come back to London as soon as possible."

"Yes . . . yes, of course," he had stammered. "I'll drive to Carlisle this afternoon and catch the overnight train."

Andrew had set down the receiver, stunned at the news, and slumped into the nearest chair, where his father found him motionless a few minutes later. Soberly he recounted the news to the two elder Trenthams. After an early light tea with his parents, he had been on the road by five.

Yet even as he hurried back to the city for the investigation—if Scotland Yard was sniffing around, what else could it legitimately be called?—and to help, if he could, with plans for Hamilton's funeral, Andrew felt that he was leaving something important behind.

His reflections as he walked toward the Houses of Parliament were interrupted by a voice he recognized only too well.

"Mr. Trentham! Mr. Trentham. If I could just have a moment of your—"

"I just arrived back in the city, Luddington," Andrew interrupted the reporter running toward him, microphone in hand, followed by a cameraman doing his best to keep up.

"I won't take more than—"

"I'm sorry—I know nothing," Andrew replied firmly. He stepped up his pace several notches. He was in no frame of mind for an interview. "The leader of my party is dead. Beyond that, I don't know a thing."

"But if I could only—"

"I'll have a statement for you tomorrow."

With those words, Andrew brushed past the persistent correspondent, showed his identification to the guard at the gate, and walked briskly on toward the Palace and inside.

⬚   T H R E E   ⬚

The late afternoon's memory of the setting sun still glowed pink and red at the horizon, though most of the low-lying valleys and dales of the mountainous Cumbrian countryside were already enshrouded in the shadows of approaching night.

It had been a remarkably lovely day for late winter, thought Duncan MacRanald as he set down the final load of wood next to the large open fireplace. He sighed and looked over his stores. Plenty of logs and peat for another two weeks.

He straightened his aging but sturdy frame, and walked outside again for a final look at the remnants of the gloaming before it gave way entirely to nightfall.

His was a constitution that could scarcely have been more suitably reflective of the land of his ancestors. There was nothing the man could be but a Scot.

His features seemed hewn out of the rocky granite of the Highlands, as if its mountains had *grown* him of themselves, just as many of the ancient castles and fortresses of the region appeared to have naturally emerged out of rather than been built on top of the stones that comprised their foundations.

MacRanald's eyes had seen a great deal and had grown wise from the season of waiting. In the economy of man's earthly sojourn, they were not quite yet ancient eyes, for MacRanald was still three years short of fourscore. But they were old enough to have learned to look forward as well as back, safeguarding their aspirations in silence—hoping not for vindication of past wrong, as did Glencoe's peaks . . . but for fulfillment of future dreams.

Notwithstanding the pleasant hours just past, Duncan thought, it would be chilly tonight. Unless his nose betrayed him, the wind would shift before morning. A storm was likely hurrying this way even now.

MacRanald's mood, as if drawn by recent physical proximity, had remained gathered all day around his famous young friend. If he did possess any scant quantity of the Glencoe maiden's ability to sense things beyond the ken of normal men and women, such a second sight had no doubt been activated by Andrew's presence both yesterday and the month before.

Seeing Andrew again had kindled many memories in the heart of the aging shepherd.

Duncan had himself romped these hillsides and woodlands and explored its streams and pathways and lakes and hidden caves many years ago with Andrew's father, Harland. Duncan had grown up in this very cottage, the only son of an elderly Scots man and woman who had done what they could to keep love of all things Scottish alive in their son. They had married late and were gray by the time Duncan's earliest visions began to gather vaporously about them into definable memories.

Duncan's mother had served Lady Kimbra Trentham as had her mother served Lady Ravyn a generation earlier. Such service, however, was carried out in a steadily reduced capacity as the years progressed, for the former Victorian English lady had brought her own maids to Derwenthwaite after marrying Andrew's great-grandfather Bradburn, only four years before the end of the great queen's long reign. In former times, even further back in the previous century, Duncan's people had resided at the estate after coming from Scotland with Lady Gordon for her marriage in 1866 to John Trentham. But as English blood came to predominate in the modern Trentham pedigree, the onetime bond between the aristocratic family and their loyal Scots servants had steadily been lost to the sight of the former, although Duncan's father had continued to be provided the cottage rent free, out of respect for the past and in exchange for what limited services might still be required of a gamekeeper for the estate.

Duncan had grown up not exactly alongside, but in proximity to Harland Trentham. Their playful childhood friendship, however, had gone the way of many such, fading with the passage of time.

Andrew's father had gone south to boarding school during the war, then embarked early on the career that followed—not a particularly distinguished one, but one that certainly proceeded along normal and expected pathways. Later in his life he would become known more as the husband of the feisty MP Waleis Trentham than for his own name and accomplishments. He and Duncan scarcely saw each other now, though he like his father before him allowed the cottage to remain in the MacRanald family rent-free.

By the present era, no one at the Hall exactly remembered the reason for the connection between the family Trentham and the final remaining unmarried scion of the MacRanalds. Andrew's father was the only one alive whose roots extended far enough back to make him privy to whatever information existed. But he scarcely remembered his own father and mother speaking a word about it.

❋   F O U R   ❋

The same pinks and reds glowed down over the snow-covered mountains that overlooked the valley of Glencoe. In the north, however, they had mostly by now given way to purples and deep blues that would soon be black.

The man driving through the lonely darkness had planned to meet his seductive colleague here, when the dust settled from both the election and Scotland Yard's investigation, to celebrate privately as well as to plan what should come next. The sudden death of their unwitting Irish Liverpudlian associate had thrown a new wrinkle into the scenario, although it might not change much in the long run. Still, they needed to talk.

He had notified her when he would arrive, but had received no confirming reply. Nor had he been able to reach her since. A gnawing suspicion or two had crossed his mind, but he had quickly dismissed them.

It was cold by the time Baen Ferguson arrived at the cottage. He was looking forward to the fire and tea Fiona would doubtless have prepared for him.

As he drove up the lonely mountain road, however, no sign of life was evident. No lights shone from the windows. No smoke rose from the chimney.

He parked the car and approached the cottage. It was nearly dark now. The door was locked.

He opened it and went inside. Cold lifelessness met his face. He felt the chilly stale odor of nonuse on his skin and in his nostrils. He turned on the light.

A quick glance told him the place had remained unvisited since their visit the previous November.

Now for the first time a premonition of deception seized him. She should have been here a week or two ago with their prize. Even if she had been delayed, she should certainly be here now.

Suddenly memory upon memory of Fiona's face returned to him. He had tried to convince himself that she loved him. Had he been a fool all along? Suddenly he could see cunning and duplicity in those eyes.

He spun around. His hand crashed down violently on the table as an angry oath exploded from his lips in the night air. A great rage filled him—both at himself and at Fiona and whomever she might be involved with.

What was her game? he wondered. Whatever it was, he would get to the bottom of it! If she had set him up, this would not be the end of it. And if she had—

Ferguson's brain was reeling now.

—what if she planned all along to implicate *him* in the theft?

He turned on his heel. There was no use his hanging around. There was nothing here for him now. Besides, if she had double-crossed him, she might at the same time have put Scotland Yard on his tail.

He had to find out where she had disappeared to. And what had become of the others. And the Stone . . . there was no sign of it here. Had she never intended to bring it at all?

He flipped off the light and stormed from the house—and was soon driving recklessly down the mountain through the night.

▨   F I V E   ▨

After the death of his own parents, Duncan MacRanald had been left to tend his sheep, help neighboring farmers with their animals, and enjoy his solitary peace . . . and hope for opportunity to carry out the familial charge as best he could in the life of the next younger in the Trentham line.

Duncan could still hear his mother's words.

"Ye maun serve the bairns hooe'er ye can, my son, as I hae aye done these mony a year t' their father an' his brither, though they didna pay muckle heed t' the auld stories nor the auld ways."

The imperative of her words was never far from the mind of the aging Scotsman. Through the years of Andrew Trentham's childhood, MacRanald had tried to honor her charge by planting curiosity, wonder, and a hunger for ancient times.

"Ne'er forget the auld tales . . . ne'er forget the auld homeland," persisted his mother's voice in Duncan's memory. *"They maunna forget. 'Tis oor heritage, an' that o' the wee bairns too. They maunna forget."*

He knew young Andrew had been far away, about his country's business. But the moment he had laid eyes on him several weeks ago, he had felt the lad was at last ready to know more of his roots. He hoped the moment was now at hand that the old tales would begin to work their magic upon Andrew's full-grown consciousness.

The water was hot, thought Duncan, glancing toward the kettle that hung above the fire. A second pot, hanging from another hook, contained boiling potatoes. Andrew's grandfather had had electricity installed for them in the cottage forty years ago. But Duncan still boiled water for tea, potatoes, and oatmeal as his people had for centuries. He would keep the past alive by whatever means were possible.

A few minutes later everything was ready. He bent his head in a few moments of quiet thankfulness to his Lord as the source of all provision and pleasure. He then opened his eyes and proceeded to enjoy what he considered the second-best of the great "high teas" known to man. In his mind, it was surpassed only by that simpler and therefore *highest* high tea of all, comprised of but two chief components: *oatcakes* with butter, and *tea* with sugar and milk.

The austerity of his lifestyle was entirely a matter of Duncan Mac-Ranald's own choosing. In truth, he was well able to afford whatever he might want, given that his tastes were humble and that he preferred simplicity over luxury. The Trenthams had been generous to his family, and the latter had taken care to wisely use what came to it over the years. As a result, Duncan wanted for nothing in the way of pleasure or comfort.

He was known throughout Cumbria as a man honest as he was shrewd in any and all things having to do with sheep and the wool they produced. Thus, what appeared little more than an old crofter's cottage and a few dozen acres of land to go with it had in fact, through the years, been a relatively thriving little shearing, dyeing, and veterinary enterprise. Because his needs were so simple, however, Duncan MacRanald had probably given away more than he had spent on himself.

When supper was past, Duncan cleared the few things from the table, then poured out the final cup of tea from the cooling pot and sat down in his favorite chair in front of the same hearth whose aromatic smoke had drawn Andrew to his very doorstep a month or so earlier.

His reflections still circulated about Andrew Trentham . . . Andrew *Gordon* Trentham, Duncan added to himself. How often had the boy sat right here, in front of this very fireplace, just as they had yesterday, staring into it just as he was now, listening fascinated to stories of the old land?

It took time to know and appreciate roots. Now Duncan found himself silently praying murmurs of thanks that such a time had apparently come.

"Thank ye, Lord, fer the friendship ye've given me with the lad, an' that he's come t' sich esteem in th' world, without harm bein' dune his character. Du yer work in him, Lord. Draw his hert t' yer own. An' when he comes t' ken his roots, help him t' see that ye're the Father o' us all."

Slowly, after a minute or two, Duncan rose and threw two more logs and another peat brick into the fire. He stood, slowly gazing around at the four walls of this, the largest room of the cottage.

He approached his bookshelf. There were not many volumes here. But what treasures!

He reached up and reverently drew down the same worn and ancient history that had kept Andrew entranced for much of yesterday afternoon. He thumbed casually through its pages, every leaf filling him with nostalgia for bygone days.

Moving through the book as if centuries were passing under his hands, he paused over a large woodcut drawing of a towering figure of a man, clutching a sword most mortals would scarcely be capable of lifting.

Slowly a smile spread across his face.

"Eh, Bruce," he whispered. "Ye're still, for a' that an' a' that, the greatest Caledonia's e'er seen."

He paused, then added, "When will we see yer likes again?"

A moment more he gazed at the drawing, in a silence that hovered in the shadowlands between awe and reverence. He set the book back in its resting place on the shelf.

Lifting down two or three others, he returned to the hearth and eased again into his chair to enjoy the renewed crackling cheerfulness of the fire and the fellowship of the authors whose companionship he had selected for the evening.

An hour passed. Duncan's eyelids began to grow heavy. He dozed, fought the sleep away, read again, dozed again, and finally slept in earnest.

The fire in the hearth burned low. Duncan awoke from his snooze. All around the cottage the wind whistled and whipped about.

"Ay," he muttered, rousing himself to groggy wakefulness. "I kenned it was comin'."

With an effort he set aside the books and struggled to his feet, then ambled slowly toward his small bedroom.

He would sleep well tonight. His brain was already half full of the dreams that would pass through his inner sight before morning.

SIX

". . . the Cumbrian MP was not available for comment upon his arrival in London yesterday. He assured this reporter, however, that a statement would be released today. Kirkham Luddington, BBC 2, reporting live from Westminster."

The brief film clip showed Andrew Trentham's back as he hastened by. The camera then cut again to the reporter, standing in the early morning's drizzle, on the scene with a full film crew to capture the revelations he was certain would develop as the day unfolded.

"More tea, sir?"

Andrew glanced up from the morning news on the television. His housekeeper stood before him with a freshly brewed pot.

"Oh . . . yes, thank you, Mrs. Threlkeld."

She set it down in front of him, then began to clear the breakfast things from the table. The telecast continued its report on the death of the prominent MP Eagon Hamilton, leader of the Liberal Democrats.

Andrew had been out till after eleven the previous night, involved in meetings and discussions with Larne Reardon, the heir apparent to the party leadership, and with other colleagues and members of the party, trying to piece together a strategy for meeting the immediate circumstances. The press would be on them today no less than if word was leaked about a new Jonathan Dimbleby exposé. It was important they present a united response.

He and his colleagues had also discussed at length what could possibly have been the cause of Hamilton's death. Scotland Yard had questioned all his intimates thoroughly. Officially it was still being called a heart attack—though whether the press would believe the lie for another twenty-four hours was doubtful.

The Yard obviously suspected foul play. Just the fact that they were withholding the body said there was more to the story than they were letting on. A rumor was circulating that Eagon's corpse had been fished out of the Dee, floating near an abandoned Aberdeen dock, but the Yard would neither confirm nor deny the report.

Given the mysterious circumstances, it had been an especially difficult call that he and Reardon had made upon Hamilton's family yesterday. Reardon had been closer to Hamilton than any of them. He was leaving today to accompany Eagon's widow to Liverpool for a few days.

The ringing of the telephone interrupted his thoughts. He rose even before Mrs. Threlkeld summoned him.

"Andrew," a voice on the other end of the line greeted him. "I wanted to extend my condolences personally."

"Thank you, sir," replied Trentham respectfully.

"Britain has lost a great leader. I am extremely sorry."

"It is very thoughtful of you to say so, Miles."

"Commons won't be the same without him."

"I should think not . . . though on the practical side," Andrew added pointedly, "it will make *your* job easier."

"I meant no such thing, Andrew. Eagon and I may have had our differences—"

"Strong differences," interposed Trentham.

"True enough," consented the other. "But I had the utmost respect for him. He was true to his convictions. No one can fault a man for that," Miles Ramsey went on. "As was your mother—tell her we Conservatives need her here to get our government back."

"I'll convey the message," laughed Andrew.

"As to what impact Eagon's death will have upon my position," Ramsey added, "the answer to that may rest with *you*, my young friend, and your colleagues. If we could somehow persuade your party to join *us* in coalition rather than your Labour brethren . . ."

His voice trailed off significantly.

Andrew knew the powerful leader of the opposition Conservative Party was probably right. Suddenly the Liberal Democratic Party was going to be thrust into the limelight as it had never been under Hamilton's tenure as party leader. The whole balance of national politics could be affected.

Miles Ramsey knew it. Prime Minister Richard Barraclough of Labour knew it. His own Liberal Democratic colleagues knew it. They had spoken of little else last evening, though Larne Reardon, the deputy leader of the party, had been understandably subdued. Notwithstanding his somber mood, all had deferred to him as though he were already the duly elected head of the party. That vote, however inevitable the outcome, had yet to be taken.

"We need to talk, Andrew—and soon," the opposition leader said.

"It is Reardon you need to speak with, Miles," replied Andrew. "He will be head of our party soon."

"That may be so. But Reardon and I have never exactly been political friends, if you know what I mean, any more than Eagon and I were. But you and I understand one another, even if we represent different parties. I am hoping you will be able to use your influence with the party. . . ."

"Many are more senior than I am, Miles."

"Ah, but your star is on the rise, young Trentham. In any event, I hope you will consider me an ally and friend. With you I always know I'll get a fair hearing."

"I appreciate your confidence, Miles," said Andrew, smiling wanly to himself. "But surely it can wait a few days."

"I will not object to that—just not too long."

"I'll be in touch to arrange something after the funeral."

Andrew hung up the receiver, reflecting on Ramsey's words.

Well, he thought, *it's already begun*. The subtle attempt to woo him, this time with flattery and praise—it was sure to come from both sides. And the pressures would get stronger and less subtle as time went on. He may have been young, but he had been around Parliament long enough to realize that politics was a man's sport, not a boy's game.

Andrew returned to his chair, sat down, and took a swallow of tea from the half-empty cup in front of him. Again his attention was drawn to the television set. The BBC reporter Kirkham Luddington was just presenting his biographical portrait of Eagon Hamilton.

". . . outspoken critic of the Conservative government's policies during the Thatcher and Major eras, and leader of the increasingly influential Liberal Democratic Party—found twenty-four hours ago, reportedly in Aberdeen, dead at age fifty-six.

"The controversial Northern Irishman, who traveled to Liverpool in 1964 in hopes of seeing the Beatles firsthand, soon made the great western seaport his permanent home. He worked on the docks as a young man and eventually worked his way up to become one of the city's six MPs. Yet he never lost his Ulster brogue, nor forgot his humble roots, and he became known throughout the United Kingdom as the champion for lost causes. During recent years, a peaceful settlement to the Irish question filled his agenda, an issue which largely frustrated the attempts of Scottish Nationalists to win over Hamilton's support to their cause. Fighting with dedication against any break between Northern Ireland and the rest of the United Kingdom, Hamilton was on record as saying that, however sympathetic in principle he may have been to the notion of Scottish home rule, he could not allow that sympathy to jeopardize what he was trying to do for his own homeland. Having succeeded in bringing Scottish independence to national attention, the SNP has been carefully monitoring the climate in the Commons—a climate which now seems to have changed dramatically.

"To repeat—the Honorable Mr. Hamilton, Liberal Democrat Minister in the Labour government, is dead. It remains to be seen what course Hamilton's successor, likely his deputy and close friend Larne Reardon, will follow, and in which direction he will take the Liberal Democrats."

Andrew stood and turned off the set.

It was time to face the day.

⌗   S E V E N   ⌗

Andrew knew from this morning's newscast exactly where Kirkham Lud-dington and his film crew would be positioned. If he took a taxi or limousine straight to the front entrance, there would be no escape. Therefore he opted to try blending in with the busy sidewalk pedestrian traffic along the Victoria Embankment until he was close enough to slip through one of the side gates into the Norman Shaw building.

His party colleagues had given him the assignment of releasing a state-ment on their behalf today. But he had other things to do first. There were people he needed to talk to, and Inspector Shepley from Scotland Yard had promised to announce something more definite about Hamilton's death be-fore noon.

Andrew had decided to call a press conference for half-past one that af-ternoon—sixty minutes prior to the convening of the House of Commons. He would make the notification as soon as he arrived at the office, hoping it would at least secure him the morning free from the press.

The streets were busy, crowded, full of blaring horns and the smell of diesel, the rumble of buses, taxis, and trucks. He hurried along quickly, ducked through the gate, and soon was entering his office. There was hardly time to greet his secretary before the telephone on her desk rang.

"It's the prime minister, sir," she said a moment later.

Andrew smiled. He had known it would be a frenetic day.

"I'll take it inside, Mrs. Blanchard," he replied, then walked into his inner office, removed his coat, sat down behind his desk, and drew in a deep sigh before picking up the receiver.

"Prime Minister," he said, "how good to hear from you."

"Good morning, Andrew. Terrible business, this, about Eagon. I wanted to let you know how sorry I am."

"Thank you, sir. I appreciate your sentiments."

"Reardon's office said I should talk to you. Any more news from the Yard? The press is on me for some kind of statement."

"Me too. But I've heard nothing this morning."

"You still on for this afternoon?"

"Right."

"Would you like me to share the heat with you, field some of the ques-tions? I'd be happy to, Andrew. Eagon was a good friend."

"Thank you, Richard," replied Andrew. "That is a very kind offer, but

I think it best if I handle it as planned."

The prime minister would like nothing better, thought Andrew to himself, than to share the limelight with him at the press conference, mourning the loss of Eagon Hamilton together, and conveying the unmistakable message that the Labour-Liberal Democrat coalition was as strong as ever.

It was too soon for all that. Andrew didn't want to begin accumulating political debts before Eagon was even buried. Neither he nor Reardon nor any of his colleagues had any intention of breaking the coalition, but they had to have time to adjust to the new circumstances.

"The Scottish Nationalists have already contacted me," Barraclough went on, "wondering where the LibDems will line up on Scottish issues."

"You'd think that after the fiasco with the Stone's theft," said Andrew, "they would lay low for a while. Their favorability polls aren't all that high at the minute."

"MacKinnon insists that the Abbey break-in had no connection to their movement. He would like us to think it was the Irish, but I don't believe that for a second. Any thoughts on it yourself, Andrew?"

"Nothing more than what I've heard in the news."

"In any event, Dugald MacKinnon and his Scottish Nationalist friends knew Eagon was the roadblock to much they would like to accomplish. To tell you the truth, I shudder to think where MacKinnon wants to take all this. Devolution seems hardly to have appeased him. I'm sure they'll be talking to you and Larne Reardon soon enough."

"No doubt. I'm surprised we haven't heard from them already."

"There are other matters we have to discuss, Andrew," added the prime minister.

"I'll tell you the same thing I told Miles Ramsey—no discussions until Eagon is buried and our party decides if it wants Larne Reardon to lead it," replied Andrew firmly. "When the vote is taken, then you can talk to Larne. I am only acting as party spokesman on a temporary basis during his absence."

"You've already spoken with Ramsey?" The prime minister's voice was wary.

"He called to extend his condolences."

"He will do his best to lure Reardon into his camp, and he'll use you to do so if he can. These are tense times, Andrew. We mustn't let either the Tories or the Scots bring down our coalition."

"I shall keep my wits about me."

"I suggest you do just that, Andrew. Ramsey may promise you the moon, but let's face reality—a Conservative-Liberal coalition is impossible to imagine, even if all you Liberal Democrats were reelected. And you would lose the Social Democrats again."

"Conservatism isn't dead yet, Prime Minister," laughed Andrew. "You might just lose your Labour-led coalition altogether. I'm betting you won't call for elections quite yet, even though I admit we are sitting a tight wire."

"Have it your way, Andrew. But I tell you that you and your colleagues belong with Labour—something Eagon Hamilton understood."

"I'm sure we will have many opportunities to discuss these matters in the future, Prime Minister," replied Trentham. "But I really must try to get my statement prepared."

Barraclough laughed heartily.

"I know when I am being brushed off, Andrew. But yes—I'm sure we shall. In the meantime, I hope that either you or Mrs. Hamilton will let me know if there is anything I can do, or if she would like me to say a few words at the services."

Andrew hung up the phone, then began flipping through the stack of calls and messages on his desk.

Half were marked urgent.

He stood, walked to the window, and stared outside for several long moments. How suddenly things could change.

❈   E I G H T   ❈

By ten minutes till one, Andrew had a double-Excedrin migraine and was glad he still had a supply of pills left from his last trip to the States.

The day's developments had made him regret a dozen times over that he had ever called a press conference. To back out now, however, would only add more fuel to the fires of speculation.

He leaned forward at his desk, resting his head in his hands.

If this was any indication of what leadership of his party was like, he was glad Eagon's friend was going to inherit the position. Many days like this and he would go mad. Faithful Sarah Blanchard had done her best all afternoon to handle the calls and keep the pressure off him. But there were many he had no choice but to take.

The call he had just received had topped the day off with the worst possible news he could imagine.

Scotland Yard was about to issue a statement revealing more details of Eagon's death. In view of his upcoming press conference, they wanted to give the news to him first. And then, Inspector Shepley had added, they would appreciate his coming over to the Yard for a private and more in-depth interview.

He picked up his pen, leaned forward, scribbled across the page of notes, then pulled out a fresh sheet of paper. He would have to redraft an entirely new statement in light of the Yard's disclosure.

A knock sounded at his office door.

Andrew glanced up. His secretary held a delivery in her hand.

"This just came for you from Mr. Reardon's office," she said. "They didn't know whether it could wait for his return, or if you should see it." She handed him the parcel.

Larne Reardon's name was neatly typed on a sealed envelope. He recognized the seal on the corner immediately. It was from Dugald Mac-Kinnon, Scottish Nationalist MP and party leader.

He had expected this, but not so soon. Richard Barraclough had been right—the Scots wasted no time. He thought they would at least have had the decency to wait until after the funeral.

Slowly Andrew slit the seal, removed the single sheet inside, and read the brief and relatively straightforward communiqué, then sat staring for some minutes straight ahead.

If MacKinnon's words accomplished anything, it was to derail Andrew's mind even more thoroughly from the press statement he was trying to write.

※   N I N E   ※

The press briefing opened to the fading strains of Big Ben's somber strike of the half hour.

The crowded sidewalk was buzzing as Member of Parliament Andrew Gordon Trentham strode to the front of the crowd, where a bank of microphones was positioned in readiness.

"Ladies and gentlemen," he began, "I have a statement to give you regarding the death of my colleague and friend, Eagon Hamilton. First of all, I would like to express what I know are the sentiments of all of us in this city and throughout the country—our sympathies and heartfelt condolences to Mrs. Hamilton and her family. Eagon Hamilton was a dedicated public servant whose voice in this nation's affairs will be sorely missed. I have spoken with both Mr. Barraclough and Mr. Ramsey. I speak for them and their parties as well as the rest of Parliament when I say that we are all shocked at this sudden news, and we grieve the passing of one whom we all considered a friend, as well as a staunch and loyal colleague . . . and loyal Briton."

Andrew paused and cleared his throat. Several hands shot into the air immediately. He ignored them and went on.

"As to the pragmatic matters which such an unfortunate event forces upon us, the fifty-one remaining members of the Liberal Democratic Party will meet as soon as possible to elect a successor. No major changes in the party's policies are anticipated at this time. Deputy Leader Larne Reardon, who left the city with Mr. Hamilton's family this morning, is expected to take the reins.

"A by-election for Mr. Hamilton's seat in Mossley Hill will be conducted as soon as can be arranged."

There was another pause, this one briefer than the first.

"The funeral will be held on Thursday of this week in Liverpool. Most of Mr. Hamilton's party colleagues will be in attendance, as well as, I have been informed, both Mr. Ramsey and Mr. Barraclough. Mr. Larne Reardon will be asked to represent the family to the press at that time.

"That concludes my prepared remarks. Thank you very much."

Trentham made no attempt to leave. He knew questions would follow in a frenzy. Therefore he stood and allowed the blitz to come.

He acknowledged one of the twenty hands that were in the air the next moment.

"Where is Mr. Reardon now?" said its owner.

"With the family. That is all I care to say."

"You say Deputy Leader Reardon is considered the front-runner to become the next leader of the Liberal Democratic Party?" shot out someone from the rear.

"Mr. Reardon is well capable of the leadership necessary to articulate the views we hold."

"Will he continue your party's loyalty to Labour's coalition?" asked another.

"That will of course depend, as in the past, on the issues involved."

"Do you anticipate a change?"

"No, but it is not my place at this time to speak for the entire party."

"You say you have spoken with the prime minister?"

"That is correct."

"Was policy discussed?"

"No."

"Did you agree to keep his coalition intact?"

"I repeat—substantive matters were not part of our very brief conversation."

"You say Miles Ramsey has also contacted you?" came another voice.

"I have spoken with the opposition leader as well, yes."

"With what result?"

"He was merely conveying his sympathy over Mr. Hamilton's death, as was the prime minister."

A brief pause came. Andrew took a breath, but the lull was short. Suddenly the gathering erupted again with questions. The most importune of them took him by surprise.

"What do you know of the report just released by Scotland Yard?" the questioner asked.

"To what report would you be referring?"

"The report stating evidence of a knife wound through Mr. Hamilton's heart?"

"I did not know you were aware of that report," rejoined Andrew, doing his best to keep from showing his surprise. He had assumed that Inspector Shepley's call forty minutes ago would give him at least an hour's lead time over the bloodhounds. He was not prepared with an answer.

"We are all aware of it, sir," the questioner added. "The statement was given out thirty minutes ago. What is your opinion, Mr. Trentham? It was obviously murder!"

At the word, a heightened buzz spread around the crowd.

"It is far from conclusive that such is the case at this point," replied Andrew. "I believe the Yard is also investigating the possibility of suicide."

"No one stabs himself in the heart!" laughed one of the outspoken reporters in jest. "Not at that angle. And floating in the river—come on, Mr. Trentham, what are you trying to hide?"

"I'm hiding nothing," Andrew shot back testily. "I am merely waiting for all the facts."

"Who would want him dead?" shouted a voice.

"You knew Eagon Hamilton," put in another voice over the mounting din. "Can you describe his recent mental state?"

"His recent mental state was perfectly fine," rejoined Andrew a bit too quickly. He could feel his even temper wearing thin.

"Then you *do* subscribe to the murder theory. Whom do you think was responsible?"

"I subscribe to no such thing."

"But the wound obviously rules out natural causes—"

"The Yard's report is not so decisive," rejoined Andrew.

"What about the rumor that the knife was Scottish, a sgian-dubh?" called out another.

"I have not heard that," answered Andrew.

"Do you think there is some connection between the murder and the unsolved theft of the Stone?"

"I have no idea. But I really must insist we move on to other matters. Scotland Yard will release the details of Eagon Hamilton's death in due course as they carry out their investigation. Until then it is pointless to speculate further. Now . . . I will be able to take another question or two."

Again hands shot into the air. The sound of a dozen voices erupted around him.

One, however, stood out from the rest. How could he not give her an opportunity to redeem herself?

"Yes, Miss Rawlings," said Andrew, acknowledging the attractive young American.

An uncommon hush came over the gathering in spite of the traffic behind it. No one wanted to miss a word, however her accent might grate upon their ears.

"It seems clear," Paddy said, perhaps trying a bit too hard to sound forceful and confident, "that Eagon Hamilton's death will place Mr. Reardon in a more controversial limelight than merely as concerns the coalition in Parliament. And the same might be said of you," she added.

She paused briefly, seemingly for effect, but in reality to take a steadying breath. She knew she was on display. She was trying her best not to reveal her jittery nerves.

"—Tell me, Mr. Trentham," she went on, "what do you think the odds are that the issue of greater sovereignty for Scotland will come up soon for *division* in the House of Commons?"

Her emphasis of the word, showing that she was not afraid to poke fun at her previous mistake, struck a positive chord. Most of those present, though half expecting another blunder, were willing to recognize her improved presence of mind.

Only a second or two did the quiet last. Then could be heard, first from one, then three or four, a sporadic applause, accompanied by a few nods and looks of good-natured surprise—in recognition that she had handled herself well.

"A very perceptive question, Miss Rawlings," smiled Andrew, "—as your colleagues are well aware," he added, glancing around. "You've put me on the spot, and they know it!"

Now laughter broke out in earnest. The American reporter was obviously relieved.

"But, to answer the question you raise," Andrew went on, his face again turning grave, "I honestly don't know."

From where she stood, Paddy's eyes met those of the young Englishman. His penetrating gaze held hers for the briefest instant. The edges of his lip hinted at a smile, as if to add his own private and unspoken *Well done* for the pluck she had shown.

"It would seem," Paddy persisted, "that your rising influence in the party may increase the likelihood of such."

"That I would not want to say at this time. And my rising influence, as you call it, is nothing more nor less than simply the fact that none of my colleagues want to face any of you today! When the services are over and all this is behind us, Mr. Reardon will speak for the direction of our party."

"Eagon Hamilton was no friend of the SNP."

"Eagon always acted on what he felt was best for the United Kingdom and its people. Such will continue to be the policy of the Liberal Democratic Party, and that of Mr. Reardon as well."

He turned his face away. Paddy knew her brief moment in the spotlight was over. But she was satisfied. That one instant of eye contact, and the smile he had given her, made the whole day worthwhile!

Again voices clamored for the MP's attention.

"Yes . . . Mr. Luddington," said Andrew, acknowledging the BBC reporter.

"You mentioned both Mr. Barraclough and Mr. Ramsey," Luddington said, seizing upon the opening his American colleague had given him. "Have you spoken to Dugald MacKinnon as well?"

"I have not spoken recently with the Scottish leader," replied Trentham.

"There are rumors that the SNP is about to become more aggressive in pursuit of its causes. You must admit, would you not, as Miss Rawlings indicated, that your leader's unfortunate death changes, if not the SNP's agenda itself, then certainly its potential timetable, especially given their apparent implication in the theft of the Stone of Scone?"

Andrew wanted to deny any knowledge of anything to do with the SNP's plans. He didn't want questions surrounding Eagon Hamilton's death further stirred up by this contentious issue. Unfortunately, he could not deny it. He had just read MacKinnon's letter back in his office, outlining the precise steps by which the SNP intended to bring the matter of Scottish independence to the forefront of national attention now that one of their chief adversaries, Eagon Hamilton, was out of the way.

"I can see where you're going with this, Mr. Luddington," he replied. "However, this seems a highly inappropriate time for any of us to speculate upon the future activities of the SNP. I would suggest you direct your questions to Mr. MacKinnon himself."

"What is your position, Mr. Trentham," persisted Luddington, "on the matter of Scottish independence?"

"As I tried to indicate to Miss Rawlings, it is too soon to speculate on such things. My position is irrelevant at this point."

"I am not asking you to speculate whether the matter will come up for debate. I am asking what is *your* position on the matter. If the SNP manages to pressure the prime minister to bring it front stage onto the agenda, would *you* go along with Labour on it?"

"I can only repeat that it is pointless for me to speculate about things that may or may not come up in the future. That is all the questions for today, ladies and gentlemen. Thank you very much. Good afternoon."

The Liberal Democratic spokesman turned quickly and strode toward the Palace.

▓ T E N ▓

It was different returning to Derwenthwaite this time. Andrew Trentham had not been to Cumbria so often within such a short time since last summer's recess.

The two stressful meetings early that morning, another interview with Scotland Yard, the ride to Liverpool, the funeral, and now this long ride north had exacted their toll. Andrew was spent. By the time Horace pulled the automobile into the tree-lined approach to Derwenthwaite it was well past dark, and rain was coming down steadily.

The sound of the tires crunching along the gravel drive, and the illumination of the headlights against the large beech and sycamores along either side, warmed Andrew's spirits as he approached the ancient stone dwelling. Gradually the faint lights of the house appeared, adding yet further to the homey feeling.

He hurried inside and greeted both his parents. As they entered the drawing room—where a crackling fire waited—there was the tray of tea things approaching in Franny's two faithful hands. Within moments, the ill effects of the difficult day and the afternoon's journey had already begun to fade into memory.

After tea and a scone and forty minutes' light conversation, Andrew retired to his room. In weariness he undressed, only managing half a page in his Father Brown novel before putting it aside in favor of what his sagging eyelids were telling him.

He awoke eight and a half hours later to shafts of sunlight blazing through the windows.

In place of the roar of London streets, he gazed out now upon cold, sunny silence. Above was pure blue, unbroken by a single cloud.

Andrew dressed and made his way quickly downstairs. Sounds came from the kitchen, but he kept straight for the door and outside. He made his way around the imposing east wall to the expansive gardens and wooded pathways north of the house. The morning air was chilly, yet not so cold as to have frozen the multitudes of droplets left over everywhere from the night's rain. Given the season, the temperature actually felt pleasant.

He paused for a moment, breathing deeply of the clean, bright air. He glanced toward the lake, then again left, allowing his eyes to drift across to the pastureland where, in summer, his father grazed a small prized herd of thoroughbred horses. Thence he gazed beyond, toward the hills.

An involuntary glance back toward the house revealed the form of his mother in an upstairs window. He pretended not to notice. It was what he continually expected to feel somewhere over his shoulder—her watching eyes. He never knew exactly what she was thinking. But he always knew he sat under the unrelenting microscope of her inspection.

He set out slowly across the wet lawn for a short walk. But he knew his parents would be down before long, and he hadn't visited with them long the previous evening. And he was ready for a cup of Choicest Blend.

The thought of morning tea made him unconsciously increase his pace. A minute or two later he walked through the dining room door. His mother and father had only moments before taken their seats.

"Are you feeling better this morning, Andrew?"

"Much, thank you, Mother—as long as tea is brewing!"

"The water was poured two minutes ago."

"Good! In that case, yes—I feel well rested . . . and glad not to have the sounds of London echoing in my ears for a change."

"You've always liked the fast-paced life," commented his mother. "I can't think how many times I've heard you say you couldn't wait to get back. Your sister, on the other hand, always said—"

She stopped and said no more.

Andrew pretended not to notice. "Maybe I'm changing, Mother," he said.

"This wouldn't have anything to do with Blair?" she asked, her voice probing for more information.

Andrew shrugged. "Maybe it does, maybe it doesn't," he replied. "All I know is that I find myself thinking about new things these days—more country things than city things."

He took a seat. Within a short time the three were enjoying toast, tea, and hearty conversation. Mr. and Lady Trentham were always interested to hear every detail about the public life of their son, and they were especially eager to hear the latest developments in the Eagon Hamilton situation.

There wasn't a man who knew him who did not love and admire Harland Trentham. His soft-spoken demeanor and dry wit insured that he was a favorite in any and all company. But in public it was Lady Trentham who had always been out front and in the news, vocal and controversial. Many whispered privately, especially in the early days of their marriage, that she was the one who wore the trousers of the family. But her husband seemed not to mind her forthrightness and drive. He was along for the ride and enjoyed life as he went. He hadn't realized he was marrying the conservative political version of a feminist. But as that's how things had turned out, he had made the best of it.

That Lady Trentham loved him in turn was clear enough, though her husband's phlegmatic personality did nothing to dissuade her from the opinion that women were more suited to lead anyway, and that the world was lucky it had managed this far with men at the helm. But new days were coming. She had been part of it and had cherished the hope, now gone, that her daughter would take such leadership even higher. Even so, she maintained a lively interest in the London activities of her only son.

"I see you mentioned in the *Times* every day, Andrew, my boy," laughed Mr. Trentham. "Seems like the old days—just as when I saw your mother on the news almost every evening. You won't need to call us ever again—we can find out all we need to know about our son from the papers!"

As he spoke, he held up that morning's edition, pointing to a caption halfway down the page: "Reardon, Trentham both silent on LibDem future."

"You don't have to remind me," groaned Andrew. "I'm well enough aware of it!"

"Has the Yard made progress in the Hamilton affair?" asked Andrew's father, marmalading a slice of toast.

"Not much."

"Dreadful business, that," he said, "—imagine, a knife between the ribs. I didn't know Hamilton kept such company."

"Nor did I," replied Andrew.

"Any sign of the weapon?" asked Lady Trentham.

"Not a trace, Mum. The Yard's got nothing much to go on. They're trying to track down two roughs in the East End, but without much success. I'm not sure what the connection is."

"Any idea as to motive?"

Andrew shook his head.

"What do you think, son?" asked his father.

Andrew was quiet a minute or two before replying.

"I am puzzled, Dad," he answered at length. "I thought I knew Eagon Hamilton nearly as well as anyone. Obviously not as well as Larne. But I haven't the slightest notion who would want him dead. His involvement in Irish affairs always makes one wonder in that direction. But to my knowledge he was highly thought of in both Northern Ireland and Eire. I just don't know."

❋   E L E V E N   ❋

By midday, Andrew's early morning good spirits had begun to give way to reminders of the reflective mood which had driven him out of the city twenty-four hours earlier.

He walked outside and toward the stables. Within ten minutes he had saddled his favorite gray mare, Hertha, and was cantering away from the house, up the gently rising slope in the opposite direction from the lake.

It was quarter past two, and he could not have imagined a finer afternoon. The sun shone brilliantly overhead, and the waters of ocean and lakes reflected of the deepest blue.

In no apparent direction he rode, pausing halfway up the northern slope of Bewaldeth to behold the sea in the distance. It was one of those twice-in-a-year days when you could see almost forever. The haze had been cleared off by last night's rain, and the horizon seemed magnified in its brilliance.

Sight of the blue expanse reminded him of a favorite childhood overlook. To him as a boy, the incomprehensibly wonderful fact of being higher than the gulls as they circled in the windy inland eddies in front of the cliff below had never failed to seize him with a special mystery and delight. To fly himself would have been best of all. But to be capable of looking *down* upon a flying creature had given wings to his own sense of fantasy and wonder. It had filled him with quiet sensations of boyish power and sent his imagination off in a thousand directions at once.

He smiled as the images refocused themselves on the lenses of his memory. He would visit the overlook again!

He hoped the gulls were playful today. Watching their aerial games would suit his nostalgic mood.

Unconsciously he quickened the pace of his mount along the thinly discernible trail winding slightly upward and to the east.

It was not far. In less than ten minutes he dismounted and tied the mare's reins to the branch of a tree. The final ascent he would make on foot.

Andrew walked for only a moment or two, then set off in a run up a slight incline. After some fifty yards he turned all at once onto a track leading to his right and found himself, after another half dozen paces, halting quickly at a clifflike ledge overlooking a small lake. This had been his most cherished vantage point when he was a boy.

Looking at the spot now with the realism of years, he found it a wonder his mother had ever let him come here alone.

The lake below was not deep, nor was it large. Most natives of this region would scoff at calling the little thing below known as the Tarn Water a lake at all. Scarcely two hundred yards from end to end, and only perhaps fifty wide, the tiny expanse rated not even a mention in the tourist guides alongside the likes of Bassenthwaite, Ullswater, and the Derwent Water. All the more reason for him to love it, Andrew thought. He had always considered the tiny lake his very own.

But the Tarn Water was unusual in this—that when approached from the direction he had come, by the trail leading to the peak of Bewaldeth Crag another quarter mile up the hill, it lay glittering beneath a steep drop-off. The path seemed to end with astonishing abruptness. One found oneself suddenly looking down at the surface of the Tarn from a height of a hundred or more feet. The water could be reached easily from below by other paths. But from this one spot, the first glimpse over the sudden precipice was enough to bring a momentary quiver to anyone's knees. It was no place for carelessness.

Andrew crept out onto the stone promontory overlooking the peaceful and protected lake, then sat down on the rough foot-high stone next to the path and drew in a deep breath of the unseasonably warm air. The few gulls visiting the inland lake from the seashore swirled about along the steep cliff face with an occasional shrill cry, just as he remembered them.

Of course, there were other memories too.

How could he not think of his sister here? They had both loved coming here . . . until that fateful day. For a while he had revisited the spot every so often, as if hoping to exorcise the haunting ghosts of the incident. But it had been no use. He had not been back in years.

And now he found his mind drifting toward yet another of MacRanald's tales . . . not of the Wanderer this time, but rather the story of the two brothers who loved each other.

Now he remembered . . . they had had a lake with a high-cliff overlook too, just like this.

Their adventures had always been among his favorites.

What were their names . . . odd and ancient tribal names. . . ?

Try as he might, however, Andrew could not now recall them.

He turned, walked slowly back to his horse, remounted and rode on.

Memory of his two recent visits rushed back upon him. The smoke . . . the smell of peat . . . thoughts of old Duncan . . . the tales of the Maiden and the Wanderer . . . then Horace's appearance and the call from London that seemed destined to change his life.

Time to visit old Duncan again, thought Andrew. This time he would not leave until he knew more about his own past!

Andrew wheeled his mount around, and the next instant was cantering over the uneven terrain as rapidly as was safe, upward and yet deeper into the hilly region of the Scawthwaite Fells.

▒   T W E L V E   ▒

In the dimly lit nave of the ancient church named for St. Bartholomew the Great in northeast central London, two men walked slowly toward a deserted corner where they would not be disturbed.

They did not sit down. The interview would not be a lengthy one.

The robed member of the duo felt a pleasing sense of dark affinity with the atmosphere here in one of London's oldest churches. He had chosen the place for its mystical symbolism and imagery—though his own religious inclinations were in the opposite direction altogether, and with roots far more ancient than the good St. Bartholomew.

His suit-and-tie-clad colleague had agreed to come here, not because of the church's mystical vibes, but because he could not afford to be noticed. Should the two be seen together, each could have much to lose. Both were well known in their respective fields—disciplines as far removed from each other as it would have been possible to imagine. Circumstances, however, had brought them together for a common purpose, of which it was in the best interest of both that the public remain unaware.

"The people I brought into this thing are not the sort who are known for their patience," now said the suit. "They will expect payment upon delivery."

"All will be completed in due course," replied the robe. "They needn't worry."

"Soothing words will do little to placate their anxiety. They are eager to get out of the country."

"They must be patient."

"Look, Dwyer, I don't—"

"Keep your voice down," interrupted the mystic. "You of all people should know that the powers can be trusted. Where is the . . . object now?"

"It is safe—here in London."

"London!"

"Of course—the last place they will look for it."

"Has transport been arranged?"

"When the time is right. But I shall require assistance with customs."

"It will be done. You will carefully supervise the movement? It must be intact or power will be lost."

"It will be well crated, I assure you."

"Then when the time comes, I will meet you at the Green."

⌘ T H I R T E E N ⌘

As Andrew rode up the wet moorland toward the farthest boundaries of the Derwenthwaite estate, a gust of chill wind met his face. His eyes squinted against it, but just as quickly it died back down.

Andrew glanced northward.

Black clouds seemed to be massing at the horizon. How quickly the sky could change in this region! When he left the house, it had been clear as far as the eye could see.

Andrew knew what the clouds contained. The temperature had already dropped several degrees since he had set out an hour ago.

He drew in a deep breath. He recognized the fragrance. There was snow in the air.

Andrew's first impulse was to turn back for home.

No, he thought. Let the weather come and do its worst. He would not leave this errand uncompleted a second time.

Within ten minutes he was reining in his mare in front of the familiar old stone cottage set in its protected dell. Duncan MacRanald had just walked outside to gather a supply of fuel for his fire. He too had detected the change in the weather.

Andrew hailed him, then leapt from his horse.

Their greeting was filled with that rich affection true men extend toward one another. Truly did this old Scots shepherd and this young English politician love each other.

"See to that fine cratur o' yers. Git her brushed and under cover wi' some oats, then help me with these peats an' wood," said Duncan. "I was jist aboot t' light a fire. There's a cauld wind blawin' in."

Within half an hour both men were settling themselves inside. Again Andrew made his way slowly about the cottage, once more eying the books.

Meanwhile, Duncan crouched on the floor, first laying, then lighting the fire in the hearth. With breath from between his two wrinkled lips, he gently encouraged the newly lit flame underneath paper and wood scraps into greater robustness of life.

Such was the only use he ever made of newspaper. Old editions were brought to him by the same woman in the village who supplied him with bread, for the sole purpose of furnishing flame beneath his chunks of peat. He scarcely looked at a word printed upon them, and though he knew that the son of the man who had been his childhood friend was a member of Parliament, he possessed not the slightest notion of the new prominence into which Andrew had risen. Nor did he realize that for the previous week he had been using to ignite his fire the very photographs and articles about the young man who now stood watching him that the rest of the country had been reading over its morning tea and toast.

Once the fire was well lit, he rose to his feet with a sigh of satisfaction.

"An' hoo has it been since the last time I saw ye?" the Scotsman asked, now setting about to the boiling of water and the making of tea—a necessity of equal importance to the fire for the drawing out of happy conversation between companions of the heart.

"Hectic and sometimes busier than I would like," replied Andrew. "Which is why I rode out to see you again," he added after a brief pause, "—to try to get in touch with some things that I'm wondering if I haven't paid enough attention to."

He paused thoughtfully. "I've found myself remembering another time, years ago," he went on after a moment. "I couldn't have been more than

eight or ten. You took me up to the top of Bewaldeth—I'm sure you remember."

Duncan nodded.

"You pointed out over the moor, to the sea, and beyond to the hills.
You said to me—and suddenly I remember it so clearly!—you said, 'There's
the land o' yer ancestors, laddie. Someday ye'll ken . . . someday.' "

Duncan smiled at Andrew's use of the old Scots tongue, as poor as was
the attempt. His heart warmed to hear that Andrew remembered the day.

"I guess the time has come," Andrew resumed "that I *want* to know all
I can about the land north of those hills. The real land, the real story. You
know, it's strange. I never paid much heed to the place except as a setting
of storybook adventure, in those tales you told. Or as something we learned
in history lectures. Or as a place I go for meetings. But suddenly it has become important to me to know *everything* I can."

"Why, laddie?" said Duncan. "Why has it become so important?"

"I suppose it's become more personal now?"

"*More personal*," repeated Duncan. "How . . . why?"

"Because of what you said. Don't you see? If Scots blood is in my own
veins, then Scotland's past is not *mere* stories. It's not *mere* history. I've been
drawn up into it now *myself*, drawn in a new way, drawn into the story as if
I am *part* of it . . . because it is my story too."

"Ye're aye knockin' away at trowth in the matter, laddie, when ye speik
aboot bein' drawn up intil the story like it's yer ain. I kenned such a day
would come when ye was a wee bairn an' I held ye in my ain two hands."

"What—you held me as a baby?" laughed Andrew. "I've never been told
that."

"Yer father was prood t' have a new son. He invited me doon t' the
hoose fer a wee peep."

The words pierced Andrew with a strange fondness for his father.

"The moment I held ye, somethin' inside me kenned that the Lord had
great things fer ye, lad," Duncan went on. "An' I believe it still."

Andrew took in the words deeply, and as the conversation went on asked
many questions, and told the old Scotsman much of what he had been thinking. Duncan listened more than he spoke. Everything would be known . . .
but he would rather his young friend make the important discoveries for
himself.

The fire burned. Logs and peat were added. The cottage warmed. Neither was aware of the continued drop in the temperature outside.

Slowly afternoon gave way to evening. Tea was consumed, oatcakes eaten, followed later by boiled potatoes with butter and cream. Steadily night drew down over the fells.

Still the tea flowed and the peat burned . . . while they spoke of many old and pleasant things.

⬚   F O U R T E E N   ⬚

As the dusk turned black, the young man and old man, as of a single mind, found themselves reflecting together on eras that once had been . . . and of the men and women who made of them times to remember.

After some time Duncan rose and ambled to the door and slowly opened it. Large silent white flakes were falling thickly in the blackness, illuminated by the faint glow from the fire inside.

"We'll be buried in a blanket o' white afore mornin', laddie," he said, staring out. "Gien ye're goin' t' mak it t' Derwenthwaite, ye'd best be on yer way afore it's too thick underfoot. It'll be a hard enough ride fer the mare noo, even wi' a bright torch shinin' in front o' her hooves."

Behind him he heard no reply. Andrew's thoughts were far away. Parliament, parties and majorities and coalitions, the Stone of Scone, and Eagon Hamilton's murder, all of which had recently been at the center of his thoughts—they had now grown hazy and distant.

"I think I would just like to sit here awhile longer, Duncan," said Andrew.

But even as he spoke, he unconsciously stood. Without forethought his steps found themselves moving slowly toward Duncan's bookshelf. A moment later his favorite old volume was in his hands. He clutched it almost reverently, then eased back into his chair. Already he was flipping through it for the story he had remembered while looking down upon the Tarn Water.

"Suit yersel', laddie," Duncan said in response to Andrew's previous words. "When ye canna stay awake, jist make yersel' a bed there on the couch like ye did when ye was a bairn. There's two o' three tartan blankets t' heap o'er ye gien ye're cauld."

But already Andrew was lost between the pages of the well-worn book of legends. He did not see his host fill the fire with peats, give them a few stoking jabs with the poker—all peats, no wood this time. He would make circumstances as favorable as possible for the mystique of Scotland's past to envelop his young friend. Within another three or four minutes, Duncan left for his own bed.

Meanwhile, Andrew had located the story.

The book opened just as he remembered it as a boy. As he began to read, he could recall Duncan's voice intoning the ancient ballad of the people who lived in the remote northern region of Caldohnuill.

A chill of adventure swept through him.

If he let the vision of his imagination stretch further toward the north, in his mind's eye he could just barely make out the two spear-carrying descendants of Hunter, Son of Wanderer's Son in the distance. . . .

Region of Caldohnuill

Black Water

Tuarie Brora

Tri piuthar

KILDONANOID

An Stoc-bheinn

Loch Tigh na Creighe

Valley of the Cave

Loch Bruid

Loch Craggie

Muigh-bhlaraidh Ecgfrith Forest

Aethbran Ion a Sgeulachd

Journey of the brothers & the Bard's son

Falls of Bruid

Loch Cracail Mor

Lochan na Gaoithe

Aethbran nan Bronait

Aethbran Srith

Cnoc a' Choire Bhuidhe

Loch an Lagain

Beinn Donuill Hill fort & broch of Laoigh

Loch Laoigh

Place of the wild boar

Dungal na Mhaghafrith

Muirenthryth Wood

Rossbidallch

Loch Durcellach

Strath Dungal

The cave of meeting

Durcellach Bay

The Dark Waters

10 Miles

Matrilinear Line of Descent Among the Pritenae of Caldohnuill From Approximately the 5th to the 2nd Centuries B.C.

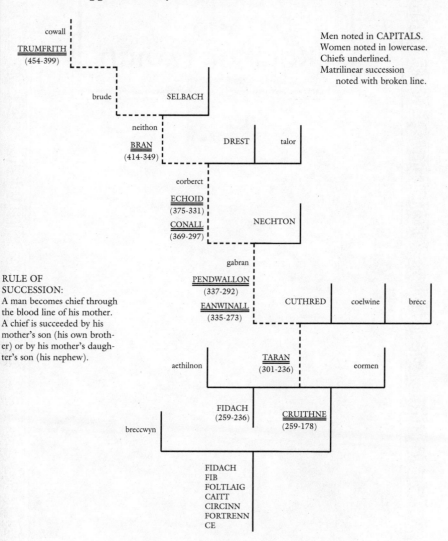

Men noted in CAPITALS.
Women noted in lowercase.
Chiefs underlined.
Matrilinear succession
    noted with broken line.

RULE OF
SUCCESSION:
A man becomes chief through
the blood line of his mother.
A chief is succeeded by his
mother's son (his own brother) or by his mother's daughter's son (his nephew).

cowall
TRUMFRITH
(454-399)

brude   SELBACH

neithon
BRAN   DREST   talor
(414-349)

corberct
ECHOID
(375-331)
CONALL   NECHTON
(369-297)

gabran
PENDWALLON
(337-292)
EANWINALL   CUTHRED   coelwine   brecc
(335-273)

aethilnon   TARAN   eormen
(301-236)

FIDACH   CRUITHNE
(259-236)   (259-178)
breccwyn

FIDACH
FIB
FOLTLAIG
CAITT
CIRCINN
FORTRENN
CE

Years and Successions of the Chiefs

Trumfrith (415-399) succeeded by his sister's daughter's son Bran.
Bran (399-349) succeeded by his mother's daughter's (his sister's) son Echoid.
Echoid (349-331) succeeded by his mother's son (his brother) Conall.
Conall (331-297) succeeded by his eldest nephew (his mother's daughter's son) Pendwallon.
Pendwallon (297-292) succeeded by his brother Eanwinall.
Eanwinall (292-273) succeeded by his nephew (his sister's son) Taran.

The line of Taran's mother Gabran ends with no matrilinear heir.
Taran chief 273-236

· HILL FORT ·
AND
BROCH OF LAOIGH

LOCH AN LAGAIN

THA
AONACHD
AN BRATHAIREAN

AETHBRAN
NAN
BRONAIT

BEINN DONUILL

BROCH

HILL FORT OF LAOIGH

DUN

7

FATHER OF THE CALEDONII

237 B.C.

❈ ONE ❈

The hunting was not good that year.

A young man, bare chested, wearing skins below his waist, crouched in readiness behind a large boulder. He held an eight-foot iron-tipped spear firmly in both hands.

He had come that morning to the edge of Muirenthryth Wood hoping to locate a wild boar. He had found one, but for an hour it had eluded him. Now, angry and nearing exhaustion, the vicious beast was all the more dangerous and his tusks the more lethal. Surely the buzzards above knew death was close at hand. But would it be the enraged swine's . . . or the man's?

A few minutes more the young man waited. The forest was silent.

Suddenly a wild screaming rent the air from amongst the trees some fifty yards distant. A seeming madman, also clad in skins, sprinted with frenzied motion on bare feet across the scraggly grass that bordered the wood. His arms flailed wildly, and ear-splitting skirls poured out of his mouth. Before him, at full speed on his stocky legs, scudded the boar, directly toward the giant rock.

Judging the proximity of the brute from the approaching squeals, the first young warrior crouched and continued to wait. He must not spring until the precise moment or they would lose their quarry.

He would have one chance. If he failed, the deadly tusks would gore him to a hideous death. More than one in his tribe had thus met his end.

A moment more . . .

At last he leapt from his hiding place and spun to face the beast as it pounded toward him. Sensing its peril, and knowing it was too late to alter its course, the animal shrieked in a delirium of fury, lowered its tusks, and charged straight toward him.

The huntsman planted his feet firmly. Stretching upward and back, he held his huge spear aloft with both hands. Just as the hulk was upon him, he jumped deftly aside and thrust the spear forward and downward with all his might.

A bloodcurdling screech told him he had found his mark. The sharp iron tip plunged deeply into the boar's left shoulder just behind the stout neck, spewing out dark red blood. Clutching the shaft of his weapon, the young man drove it in yet further before the beast could turn on him.

But the wounded creature was suddenly empowered by desperate strength. Writhing in the agony of death, it wrenched the spear from its assailant and ran berserk, still howling and shrieking, off across the heath. The tiny legs tore along with surprising speed, but the animal could only sustain the effort for a short distance. At last one of its front hooves caught on the turf. The other foreleg gave way, and the beast stumbled and fell. Its long snout crashed into a fallen log, and one of the tusks glanced into it sideways, wrenching its head backward. At last the boar was still.

"You did it, my friend!" cried the approaching comrade who had flushed the boar from the wood. "What a masterful stroke!"

"You chased him straight toward me, Fidach," replied the victorious killer, beaming. "I must either kill or be maimed."

"Our father will be pleased."

"Yes, fresh boar meat will not only satisfy his tongue, but will do his body much good," added the young man known as Cruithne.

"You are right. For too long he has had only fish and barley cakes."

He threw his arm around his companion as they walked toward their dead prey. Thirty minutes later the two young men had begun the four-mile trudge back to their home, the heavy boar, its hooves tied with leather thongs to the spear that had ended its life, hoisted between their shoulders.

It was a long way to come for a kill. But no boar had been located all season west of Loch Laoigh or south of the river known as Aethbran nan Bronait. Fish had been plentiful in the small freshwater lochs that dotted the region, as well as in the inlets from the sea—the Aethbran Frith to the north and Durcellach Bay to the south. And they had their cattle and sheep, of course—the tribe had possessed small domesticated herds of tame beasts for many generations. But flesh of the kind the chief preferred had been scarce.

Taran, chieftain of the Pritenae tribe occupying the region of Caldohnuill, had always walked with one of his two large feet out of step with the march of advancing times. He was of the old times, and desired his meat wild.

TWO

Taran remembered well the construction of the broch. The undertaking had been envisioned and carried out when he was a boy, during the chieftainships of his two uncles Pendwallon and Eanwinall.

But when his own elders had urged the expansion of the dry stone wall to encompass living and livestock quarters, bake ovens, and the smaller tower, creating a hill-fort to protect them from all threats, he had resisted.

"Let them come!" he had shouted, standing to the full six-and-a-half feet of his measure and raising a fist in the air. Truly he was a giant of a man, an imposing chief and worthy successor to the tradition of the Wanderer and his grandson the Hunter, whose blood flowed in Taran's veins. His elders allowed him to speak, while they sat in silence.

"Let the Taezali or Maeatae from Sutherois or Inbhir Nis come! Let the Smertae from beyond Kildonanoid in Gallaibh come down to meet us! Let even the Scothui from the mountains beyond Bruid or even from Eirinn itself come to us! We will defeat them! We have no need to hide ourselves behind stone walls and towers and barricades!"

The elders listened with patient respect. They knew their chief was a fighter after his own kind, filled with the blood of many generations of hunters and warriors, who had killed their food with their own hands, and who had had to kill to hold the ground they chose to call their own.

The wild blood of Taran's Celtic stock ran hot with thrill for the hunt. He was like, and yet also different from, his dear friend Pendalpin, in whose veins and heart mingled the pedigree of both Hunter and Highland Mystic, Sons of Wanderer's Son. Pendalpin vented his own Celtic fervor in verse and tale, and with lyre and lute, harp and syrinx.

So they had listened. But in the end the hill-fort had been built. And Taran had consoled himself by listening to the melancholy strains of Pendalpin's voice as he sang of seasons now gone, times past remembering, and legends whose roots were obscured by the primeval haze of historical beginnings.

Caldohnuill was changing. All the land was changing. The elders knew it, but saw no way to stop the flood of new arrivals.

Though the old men knew nothing of the fact that they occupied a portion of an island, they had heard tales of a huge land across the Dark Waters, a land of tribes and peoples who were growing and moving and bringing boats to their land. Neither did they know that the Borestii and Maeatae and Selgovae, and most of all the Belgae—that half-Germanic tribe who had brought their warlike spirit and druidic religion to the southern portion of the island a thousand years earlier, and even before that had given a wife to a certain aging nomad—were in fact sharers of their own primal Celtic blood. All they knew was that these other tribes were pushing ever closer.

The blood of the Wanderer and his Celtic cousins had been so intermingled as to seal the brotherhood of these peoples for all time, even as it obliterated their common roots. Now Celtic tribe battled Celtic tribe for supremacy. As the Belgae settled in the south, the tribes of the Vacomagi and Maeatae and Taezali and Venicones had moved further north, while the more ancient tribes that had long occupied the regions of Rois and Caitt, including the Pritenae of Kildonanoid and Caldohnuill and Rossbidalich, struggled to maintain their hold on territories that had once been so wide and free that few other humans were to be seen.

Even the Scothui from across the water in Eirinn to the west were making more and more forays this way. They carried the seed of Boatdweller, Grandson of Wanderer. But common blood notwithstanding, they were intruders. Taran and his people felt the squeeze in the unfolding slow stretch of territorial muscle.

Strife over the land was not the only change coming to Caldohnuill, though it was the chief reason that stronger fortifications were necessary. The coming of the age of bronze and iron centuries earlier had greatly advanced the ability to make weapons, but it had also tremendously improved the agricultural possibilities for Taran's people. Like many of the tribes indigenous to the area, the Pritenae were now clustering more and more into small settlements where they might tend crops and raise cattle and sheep. The life of the nomadic hunter was coming to an end.

Now, with the hill-fort completed and his people at peace and much of Caldohnuill as his domain, Taran was an old man, whose white beard and stooped shoulders gave ample evidence that the giant warrior represented a passing era. Fortunately for the future of this land, the archaic Celtic ritual from the continent by which aging chiefs were disposed of by the knife had long before given way to revering them, and Taran was held in great esteem by his clansmen.

His consolation as the years progressed was that he might be blessed as no chief before him with the joy of knowing his own son would succeed him as ruler of the tribe. In the matriarchal system of lineage which determined chieftainship of the Pritenae, never had a son succeeded a father. But the line of Taran's mother Gabran had ended with him. Both of her brothers had been chief before him. She had no sister, and thus no nephew to whom the line might pass.

Taran's two wives had each given him a son. It would be one of them, Taran hoped, probably Fidach, the eldest, who would succeed him. Of course, the elders must ultimately decide, and it might be that they would choose some other as ancient Cowall's more legitimate heir.

▓ T H R E E ▓

The two young men, each carrying an end of the long, thick spear with the dead boar jostling from side to side between them, mounted a small incline, then stopped to rest.

Beyond them, about five hundred yards distant, lay Loch Laoigh. Behind them, only barely visible now in the gathering dusk, sat the fringes of Muirenthryth Wood, which they had left an hour earlier. They had another's hour or two journey ahead of them. It would be late when they arrived home. But not too late to bring rejoicing at the gift they bore the chief.

"What do you think, Fidach?" said the one as he set down his end of the load. "Are the boars returning to Muirenthryth?"

"We can only hope," replied his companion. "For myself, I would rather hunt the great stag of the north."

"Not so dangerous, eh?" chided the other good-naturedly.

"You laugh, my brother," rejoined Fidach. "But it was I, you recall, who nearly fought you for the privilege of holding the spear today. Even though, for our father's sake, I deferred to your strength, I did not fear the danger. But it is the glory of the stag I admire. He runs so mighty and free. He represents a challenge, the challenge of this land to conquer and subdue. Knowing that only by cunning will the quest be successful, that he can easily outrun our swiftest spears, that he can hear us coming while we are yet many yards distant—that is what summons me to the hunt!"

"A magnificent creature, you are right in that," the other mused, beginning to be caught up in his brother's enthusiasm.

"Let us go to Muigh-bhlaraidh Ecgfrith, Cruithne! Let us see whether the great white stag has not returned to the forest."

"He has not been seen in many years, Fidach."

"My heart beats within my breast, telling me a change is coming to Caldohnuill. Perhaps the stag's return will signal it."

"You always know such things before they come to pass. I have learned to trust what you feel. Has some voice spoken to you about the stag?"

"No," laughed Fidach. "Only a wonderful dream that you and I were stalking him. We had been following his track for days, and at last we cornered him at the end of a small hollow. The trail led straight up rocky cliffs all around. The two of us guarded the only entrance to the place. Slowly we crept toward him. At last, when we stood but some twenty paces from him, the stag turned to face us. His giant eyes looked into mine. And those eyes— Cruithne, they pierced through me. They held no fear, but more a look of . . . recognition. It was as if no mere animal stood before us, but a creature almost human. And suddenly I sensed he had known all along that we followed, that he had led us into the ravine after him."

Cruithne opened his mouth to comment on the improbability of such a thing, but then he held his tongue.

"Then, for what seemed an eternity," Fidach continued, "the stag's eyes held mine. You and I both held our spears poised, yet neither of us could move. The animal's eyes seemed to say, 'Why must you kill? Know you not that we are brothers of the land?'

"Then suddenly the stag sprang toward us, reaching the point where we stood in two bounds that seemed less than the blink of an eye! Still we could not move. As he reached us, the magnificent creature leapt into the air and flew over our heads, and in the same instant we were released from our trance.

"Quickly we spun around, but the white stag had already receded from sight. He had grown wings and soared into the sky. We watched him circle around and upward until we could see nothing but the blue. And as we watched, a wave of . . . of tenderness came over me . . . for the beasts . . . even . . . for our enemies. I began to weep, and the same moment I awoke."

They were silent several moments.

"And you think you will find this winged stag in the forest to the north?" posed Cruithne at length.

"Perhaps not. But I hope to discover what I was meant to understand."

"Meant to understand?" queried his brother. "Who would mean you to understand something in a dream? What are dreams but nonsense?"

"Not always, Cruithne. Pendalpin says I have the second sight."

"Bah! Pendalpin is so full of tales, one must be careful what to believe."

"Our father listens to him."

"As do I, Fidach. But not about everything."

"A dangerous word to speak about the tribe's bard."

"I respect Pendalpin. But I do not know if I believe in the second sight. Even Domnall does not claim to possess it, and Domnall is his son."

"Nor do I make such a claim. I only say I have dreams, and I try to know what they mean."

Fidach paused, then added, "Will you come to Muigh-bhlaraidh Ecgfrith with me?"

"Certainly!" answered Cruithne jubilantly. "You follow your dream, and I will follow the great stag. Perhaps together we will find what we seek."

They rose, again lifted their burden to their shoulders, and started off on the remainder of their trek. It would lead them beside the shores of Loch Laoigh and westward to the hill-fort where dwelt their people.

❈   F O U R   ❈

Both young men—the practical huntsman and the lover of the stag—were of twenty-two years. They were not twins, however, but half brothers, sons of their father's two wives. Born late in Taran's long life, the boys had since birth been nearly inseparable, bound closer to each other than any half-shared link of blood to the chief could explain—a fact rendered all the more remarkable by the antipathy that existed between their mothers.

Fidach, witness to the unseen and dreamer of dreams, was the older by almost four months. His features were soft, his skin pale, and his hair black as the pools of water on the moors in the dead of winter. He had inherited his father's keen mind, as well as the poetic nature of the ancestors about which the bard Pendalpin sang with his harp.

Perhaps his mother's nature was more in evidence as Fidach grew older. A quiet, even-tempered woman, Aethilnon did not, like many wives of the tribe, strive to make her matriarchal influence felt. As the chief's first wife—many said she was still the favored one—she could easily have lorded it over the other women. Instead, she took upon herself as wife of the chief an incumbency to serve her kind. She regarded the chieftainship, and thus her position, as a sacred duty, not as an authority to be flaunted. Whence came this view of her calling it would be difficult to say. It embodied raising the very essence of clan motherhood to the high stature of a loving servant. As old Taran carried the blood of the Wanderer and his son, so she carried that of *Eubha-Mathairaichean,* the mother, the wife, the source of life.

Aethilnon could not have been more unlike her rival for the chief's attentions, Cruithne's mother Eormen. The question of what had possessed a man of otherwise sensible judgment like Taran to bring under his one roof two such opposites as the scheming and fractious Eormen and the gentle, unselfish Aethilnon was one that had been asked many times by the wisest minds in Caldohnuill. Now that his years were advanced, his two sons now men, and the line of his mother Gabran without a clear successor, it had been widely anticipated that a rivalry would break out between the two sons.

But such had never occurred. The rivalry dwelt only in the heart of Eormen. The vision of one day rising above other women as mother to the chief had become her consuming passion.

As for Cruithne, he was clearly of his father's mold—tall, a muscular man who relied on his hands and feet and prowess of strength and limb. The angularly precise features of his face and the thick, dusty gold thatch of hair atop his head made him always the most instantly visible in any crowd, his natural charisma enhanced by a wide mouth full of white teeth and always ready for a smile or roar of laughter. In a sprint of less than two hundred yards, no man of any age in the tribe was his match, though at longer distances his leaner brother, who might run ten miles or more out of the sheer joy of testing his physical and mental limits, overtook him and left him out of sight. No man in all Caldohnuill was more chieftainlike in his bearing and imposing carriage than young Cruithne, son of Taran.

Cruithne had also been blessed with a large heart. He loved his brother and would sooner die than seek preeminence over him.

Indeed, the two youths, for all their vigor and strength of body and mind, rejoiced more in the successes of the other than in their own. Some of the older men had considered the boys feeble of brain in their earlier years because of the sensitive bonds they displayed toward one another. As they grew into adulthood, however, most of these old hunters and warriors and fishermen came to respect Fidach and Cruithne all the more for the ties of their brotherhood.

Neither boy cared a squirrel's tail for the chieftainship. It seldom occurred to them that one of them might actually be chief someday, since no son within memory had ever directly succeeded his own father. But then, this was an unusual time, for Gabran had no daughters, no nieces, no nephews. Taran was the only living member of a long line that had preceded him.

If only, Taran had mused many times, Cruithne might become the warrior chief to lead the people with his strength, and Fidach become the dream-inspired bard to uphold the hearts of the people in song. Together they might rule in harmony.

There could, however, be but one bard, and Pendalpin was already preparing his own sixteen-year-old son Domnall to follow after him.

And there could be but one chief.

▩ F I V E ▩

Two hours after their rest, the sons of Taran began the final ascent up the hill to their home, passing the dun, used now for storage of grain, metal tools, or fishing implements, and continued up to the hill-fort. Fires burned in many of the huts as they approached, and from inside the fort, smoke still rose from two of the bake ovens.

It was young Domnall who first spied their approach.

"Fidach and Cruithne have returned!" he shouted. "They carry a wild boar!"

The two set down their porcine burden as a number of the men wandered out of their stone huts to investigate the commotion.

From around the western wall, Fidach's mother Aethilnon walked into view.

"You have returned home I see, my son," she said. "Good evening to you as well, Cruithne. Your hunt has been successful!"

"As we had hoped, mother of my friend," returned Cruithne. "How is our father?"

"Not well, I fear. He sleeps now. Your mother is with him."

"The meat will revive him," said Fidach.

"He has longed for fresh boar," added the woman with a sad smile. "Though I fear it may be the granting of a dying wish rather than an omen of returning vitality."

"Do not speak so, Mother. Surely he—"

"We can talk of it later, my son," said Aethilnon softly. "The time comes to all. It is not unexpected. But now I must go down the hill. Coelthryth expects me. She too is suffering."

"Ah, Mother," sighed Fidach, "is there not one in all the camp who is not your charge?"

She laughed. It was a musical laugh, full of pleasure in the unknowing compliment her son had given her.

"It is my duty to serve our people, Fidach," she replied. "And my happiness. It is what sustains my health and gives me joy."

"You are a good woman, Aethilnon," said Cruithne. "If only all sons might be blessed with such mothers," he added wistfully.

"What does Coelthryth need, Mother?" asked Fidach. "May I be of help?"

"Only some meal. I bring her barley from our stores. But you might see to her fire. She could surely make use of more wood or peat. The night looks to bring cold with its darkness."

"With pleasure, Cruithne," he said, turning to his brother, "will you see to the boar while I go with Mother?"

"Domnall will help me," replied Cruithne as the bard's son now ran up to meet them. "We will carry it to Uurcell to begin preparations for the chief's feast tomorrow."

"I will see you in the morning, then," said Fidach. He turned with a wave of his hand and then accompanied his mother down the hill toward a small group of rude huts about a hundred yards away.

For a few moments Cruithne watched them in silence. Then he turned back to young Domnall, who stood awaiting orders.

⊞   S I X   ⊞

Forty minutes later Cruithne ducked low and entered the dry-stone house where he dwelt with father, mother, and his father's other family.

The chief's was the largest dwelling of the clachan, or community, supported across the top of its twenty-foot width with large timbers. Under its thick roof of turf and peat were positioned two nearly separate rooms wherein dwelt the chief's two wives, Eormen and Aethilnon, and their two sons. Each had its own separate hearth, above which a one-foot round hole in the roof emitted the fragrant smoke from peat and occasional oak fires beneath. The floor was of hard-packed dirt, with here and there an animal skin lying upon it. All the walls were two feet thick, constructed of skillfully set stones without mortar. On the windward side of the perimeter, the outside wall of stones had been packed with turf to the height of the roof to protect it from the freezing winds out of the north. Over all the roof was spread a network of dried grasses and thatch that, along with peat, managed to keep out a good deal of the rain and snow which came to that region.

The accommodations of the chief and his two small families, by the standards of the day, were reasonably comfortable. But though the thick peat kept the weather outside at bay, the living arrangement inside was a stormy one. Not because Taran had two wives. Many men had more than one, and his own father Cuthred had had three. But in the case of his parents, the line of succession had always been distinct. There had been no dispute, therefore no rivalry, for Gabran's line was clear. Neither of his two stepmothers, Brecc or Coelwine, mistook their position in the family. From his earliest memory, Taran had known that his uncle Eanwinall would succeed the chief Pendwallon and that he would himself succeed Eanwinall.

But under his own roof, life had been anything but harmonious, despite the conciliatory efforts of Aethilnon and the close friendship between the two boys. Eormen scarcely spoke to either Aethilnon or Fidach and was increasingly possessed by the chiefly ambitions she cherished for her son.

As Cruithne squinted in the low light from the fading fire, he heard her light voice from the other end of the room. "Is that you, my son?"

"Yes, Mother," answered Cruithne.

"Are you alone?" queried Eormen.

"Yes. Fidach and Aethilnon went down the hill to see Coelthryth."

"Ah, that is good! Come . . . come, my son, we must talk."

Cruithne approached and sat down on a reindeer hide next to his mother. "Your father sleeps."

"Is he. . . ?" Cruithne paused.

"He is no worse. He sleeps fitfully, calling out first for you, then Fidach, then sleeping again. He will not get better. You know that, Cruithne. That scheming mother of him you call your brother knows it too! She—"

"Aethilnon is no schemer, Mother. She is a kind woman. As for Fidach, he *is* my brother . . . and my friend."

"You and your dull-witted notions of friendship! Have you no desire to be chief?"

"Not at the expense of Fidach. He is not only my brother, he is my *elder* brother."

"Elder, ha! By a few days . . . a week or two!"

"Three and a half months, Mother. You of all people should not be able to forget fifteen weeks of carrying your own son in your womb while the infant cries of another filled the very walls wherein you lay."

"Stop, I will not hear such insults from you! It matters not!"

"It may matter a great deal. He is indeed the firstborn, and I will do nothing to dispute his claim."

"He has no claim, I tell you! His mother is no better than the old women she so tirelessly serves. It is I who bear the blood of old Cowall in my veins."

"Which you have been trying to prove your whole life without success."

"I shall prove it! It may be but a distant relation, but the line passes through me! It shall be known . . . and you shall be the chief one day."

"Is it really so important, Mother?" said Cruithne softly. "I would be happy just to—"

"Important! How dare you question the only thing that has ever mattered to me? Do you not know that I live for you, that I would die for your sake?"

"Then for my sake, why will you not leave this relentless chase in which I have no interest?"

Silence fell for a moment. The low flames of the dying fire now and then sent out a stream of light which reflected the avaricious gleam in the woman's eyes. Cruithne did not like what he observed. Sometimes he wondered if this were really his mother. She seemed inhabited by a sinister spirit he did not know.

"Do you see him, Cruithne, my son?" she said at length. Her voice was soft, barely above a whisper as she pointed across the room to where Taran still slept. "Look closely, Cruithne. See how he labors for breath. Death lingers close. It comes. I can feel its presence stalking round about the hill, approaching the walls, coming nigh this place."

Cruithne did not reply.

He glanced over at his father, then back to Eormen. Though her voice remained calm, on her face glowed the insidious passion of lust—greed to hold power in her grasp. He could not look upon it without a wrenching ache seizing him. The look was one of consuming hate. He could not witness it without a sickening revulsion filling his stomach. How could he have come from this woman?

"The time is not far off, Cruithne," she went on, smiling now, but with a grin of diabolic intent. "The moment approaches when we must seize the mantle of the chieftainship."

"Such does not lie with me," said Cruithne, looking away and sighing deeply.

"Who else, then?"

"It is not mine to determine."

"Are you a coward?" she challenged, the blood in her voice rising again. "Are you not willing to fight your rival, to put an end to his claim?"

"He is not my rival, Mother," replied Cruithne. "How can you speak so? I will *not* fight Fidach. I will never fight him! And Fidach will be the next chief, Mother. Do you not understand? It is *his* destiny, not mine."

"He will never be chief!" she growled in a low passion of rage.

"He will be, Mother," replied Cruithne. "And I tell you, I will serve him with humble and joyful heart."

"Such are the words of a swine! My own son a coward!"

She rose and stalked to where lay the weak form of her husband. She eyed him for a long moment, then turned back and thrust her fist in her son's face.

"He will not be the chief," she said, in a tone of yet deeper determination. "That woman he calls his mother will *never* look with pride at the leader of our clan and know him to be her son. That is—that has always been my right! It is I who will look upon the face of the chief and know him to have come from my womb. Do you hear me—it is my right! I ask you again, if you would be my son—will you take upon you the cloak that is yours?"

"If you mean will I attempt to steal from my brother what rightfully belongs to him—no, Mother, I will not!"

"Then you leave me no choice! What I do, I do for you, my son!"

She stormed over to her personal cache of belongings, gathered up some bits and pieces of food and clothing, and stalked toward the door.

Cruithne rose and attempted to stop her. She shoved him back with a strength he had rarely encountered.

"Mother," he implored. "Come back!"

"He will never be chief!" she hissed back over her shoulder. She continued her enraged course out of the walled compound and down the hill to the southwest into the night.

She did not return for three days.

❈   S E V E N   ❈

Meanwhile, with the fire attended, two or three nights' fuel stored nearby, and his mother softly comforting the old woman Coelthryth, Fidach walked back up the hill. He did not hear the argument between his brother and step-mother, nor did he observe her shadowy figure descending the opposite side of the hill.

On his return he stopped at the bard's house, the largest in the clachan other than his own father's. He entered to find Pendalpin sitting with his son before a warm fire.

"Come in!" cried the old bard pleasantly. "A hearty welcome, son of my friend!"

"Thank you," replied Fidach, giving the man the grip of his hand. He turned to Domnall and attempted to tousle his hair. The boy shot out an arm to fend off the playful attack.

"Domnall, you grow too rapidly for me!" laughed Fidach. "You are nearly a man yourself!"

"Soon I will go with you and Cruithne to hunt the wild boar!"

"Perhaps sooner than you think."

"Why?" said the boy, eyes widening.

"Surely you know of the stag?"

"My father tells me many stories, Fidach."

"You must know all the tales, Domnall, for you must pass them on to our children, and teach them to tell their children."

"So Father has instructed me since before I can remember."

"The bard's is a sacred calling. And your father is the best teacher of the past we have known."

Fidach turned toward Domnall's father.

"The stag has returned to Caldohnuill, Pendalpin," he said. "I dreamed of him."

"I have learned to heed your dreams, son of Taran. If he becomes chief—" he added, speaking to his son, "—you must learn to trust them too, Domnall. We may call ourselves the bard and the bard's son, but Fidach possesses the second sight. You must listen to what he tells you."

"I do not know," laughed Fidach. "I only know that you tell me my heart sees what no man's eyes are able to."

"A bard can learn stories and songs. But no one can predict within whom the prophetic eye will be implanted. It is a gift to be guarded."

"Why does it not fall to the bard of the clan?"

"I have indeed heard of bards with the gift, but only a few in any generation of men possess it. Who can tell why certain men are chosen? But tell me of the stag, Fidach."

"I do believe he has returned," replied the chief's son. "The dream was no ordinary one. Cruithne and I will soon go search for him. Perhaps Domnall can join us."

"May I, Father?" asked the bard's son excitedly.

"We will decide when the time is at hand," replied the bard. "Your first duty is to learn what I teach you while I yet live. The bard's is no lesser trust among our people than the chief's."

"Your father speaks wisdom, son of Pendalpin," said Fidach.

Domnall nodded.

"Yet there is much Cruithne and Fidach can show you as well," the old minstrel went on. "One of them will be your own chief. The other will be your friend. They will teach you what even I cannot, for new times will come to our people. Sometimes old men like Taran and myself do not observe the coming changes in time to do what is needed. The eyes of the old become fixed and unable to see the new. Therefore, it is good for you to learn from those who will lead our people of a new generation."

Pendalpin reached behind him for his small harp, which he brought to his lap. He himself had helped his father choose the willow from which they had fashioned the frame, waiting until the angle of the sturdy branch was of the perfect shape and strength. They had then cut it and hollowed out the heavier bottom portion, stretched it over with skins, and attached it top and bottom to a column of heavy oak. He now began softly to pluck at its strings.

"Neglect nothing your father has for you, Domnall, Son of Pendalpin," said Fidach. "Within the heart that beats in his breast has been placed a huge storehouse, containing more fragments of wisdom than all the pieces of grain we keep in our granaries. It is more than merely the tales and legends. It is the man he has become, the knowledge that resides within him. All that wisdom from the reservoir of his years and his experience and his thoughts—you must seek to discover it all, so that you can implant it from his storehouse into your own. You must not merely memorize what he teaches. You must watch him, observing the wise judgment that displays itself not only in words but in the stature of his manhood. Do you understand how important this is, Domnall?"

Domnall nodded seriously.

"There are tales of peoples across the waters," Fidach continued, "where the past is preserved on great sheets with marks and pictures, perhaps like the drawings we make on our stones and pots and ornaments. I do not know—I cannot understand how stories can be told without sound of human tongue. But I do know that what the bard preserves for us through his memory and his voice is a treasure greater than any our people possess. The bard tells not only of feats and happenings, but of meaning, for all is housed within the storehouse of his mind and heart. It falls to every bard's son to preserve the same treasure and add to it. The bard's duty is greater than the chief's."

Fidach paused.

Pendalpin strummed his harp tenderly, his thoughts now far away. Both Fidach and Domnall remained silent. They sensed what was coming. Both had sat thus around this very fire late into the night many times, listening to the honored poet and musician sing and recount tales from the ancient past, tales he had learned from his own father and grandfather, as they had learned them from theirs, back further into time than any man was capable of remembering.

"We revere the bull and raven and boar, the wolf and bear and ram," said the bard softly. "We dance to the gods of the sky and sea and oak. But none is greater to our own people than the white stag, for it is said he actually comes to visit our kind."

"Does he speak to man, Father?"

"All the creatures speak, my son. One must learn to listen how to hear their voices. It is said the stag speaks with his eyes, with a look that is full of knowing."

"Yes!" said Fidach. "Yes, that is how it was in my dream. He spoke with his eyes!"

The old bard nodded thoughtfully. "It is said the white stag first came to this land before man's foot trod these regions," added Pendalpin softly. "That was when the snow and ice covered the land. When the great winter went away from the land, the white stag was left behind with its whiteness upon him. He remained in Kildonanoid and Caldohnuill, wandering the hills to remind the men who came that they were not the first inhabitants of this place."

The bard paused. All was silent.

Tongues of flame from the fire licked out into the air as if trying to snare invisible specters from the night. A faint popping and crackling from its hot coals was the only sound.

"The white stag has returned," Pendalpin went on. "He has come no doubt as a sign."

"What does it mean, Father?"

"It is not for me to know, my son," answered the bard. "My vision of such things comes and goes. Perhaps you should ask your friend, the chief's son."

But Fidach remained silent, staring deeply into the fire, lost in his own thoughts.

"Our chief is not well," Pendalpin went on. "I too am old. I know not what the stag portends. But perhaps it is a sign that death approaches. Perhaps it is a reminder that our heritage rests not in the lives of individual men, but in the generations of our people, an enduring heritage like the land."

He began again to strum the instrument in his lap. On its stretched-skin soundboard was drawn, surrounded by ornate and colorful designs, an image of the very stag about which he sang. After a few moments, in melancholy tones, the voice of the bard began to sing:

An old man stirs the fire to a blaze
In the house of a child, of a friend, of a brother.
He has overspent his welcome.
Night draws down over Caldohnuill.
He is beckoned to rise, to journey
To a new place he has never seen.
It is a land of light, he is told,
But in his heart resides fear;
It is a land he knows not.
The days, grown desolate, whisper and sigh;
Hearing the storm through the roof above,
He bends to the warmth and shakes with cold,
While his heart still dreams of battles and loves
And friendships, and the vigor of youth,
Mingled with cries of the hunt from the hills as of old.
The fire burns low.
The old man kindles it once more, but there rises no flame.
Life ebbs from the coals, and from the man.
A land of light and warmth and youth awaits him.
The white stag beckons him come
To a land where all is at rest and where all are One.

Yet his soul fears, for he sees only with his eyes,
And they cannot behold what lies beyond the darkness.

"Have you seen the stag, Father?" asked Domnall after several minutes of silence.

"Only once, when I was a young man of twenty."

"What was he like?"

"A majestic creature! He stood on a distant peak. I caught but a momentary glimpse of his giant form. My father had taken me northward over Aethbran Ion a Sgeulachd. We journeyed for some days toward Kildonanoid. My father had much to tell me."

"What did he tell you?" asked Fidach.

"You have heard the stories of old many times, son of my friend."

"I choose to hear them again, Pendalpin," replied Fidach. "Tell me of the first men who came here after the stag."

"It is said the first man to lay eyes on the stag," began Pendalpin, "was himself old and covered with hair nearly as white as the stag's. I do not know if tales of this man are myth or fact, but I trust the legend as my father learned it from my grandfather. He said the man was already advanced in years when he journeyed far into the region of the stag. He met the animal one afternoon when he was hunting to feed his family. When the grizzled face of the man met that of the stag, the thought of harming it never occurred to him. They stared at each other for long moments, in an awe of respect, for neither had seen the likes of the other before. At length they turned, and each walked quietly away through the forest from the direction he had come.

"The hunter returned to his family without food. He told his three sons of the beautiful creature, adjuring them, if they ever laid eyes on the beast, not to harm it. The old man, says the legend, lay as one dead for three days, and thereafter for many weeks could not speak at all.

"Each of the three sons is said to have journeyed to different regions. The youngest was the first bard, so the tales say. He taught his own son of the things past—taught him to pass along to his sons and daughters and all those who would follow the story of what his father had seen. Thus it comes to me, after generations too numerous to number, to pass along to my son as well.

"The sons of the old white-haired man were but the first of many to come. As the men moved north from the lands below and came from across the Dark Waters, the stag moved ever deeper into the mountains and forests.

For it was not every man's destiny to lay eyes upon the white stag, but only those chosen to receive his message."

"What is his message, Father?" asked Domnall.

"Ah, my son, only those who are chosen to look into his eyes can know such things. But the tales that are spoken tell of love for this land. They speak of peace between man and man, brother and brother, man and beast, and between man and the land that feeds him. The tales speak of brotherhood. They speak of respect for man and creature, respect for the earth and forest and moor and lake and stream and sea, which feed all living things. But sadly, most often the legends are but tales sung by old bards, while men of youth continue to fight and grasp and seek to dominate one another.

"In times not nearly so ancient, times of my own great-grandfather, new peoples began coming to the north. Brown-faced tribes came from the distant south. The Scothui from Eirinn journeyed eastward. And though the land remains bountiful, they seek to wrest control from one another. We of the tattoos, whom they call the blue-painted ones—we have always been here, since the days when the white stag roamed these highland places alone. Now other warrior tribes would drive us out."

"Do you foresee war, Pendalpin?" asked Fidach.

"I do not know," answered the bard. "Perhaps there will yet live many generations in harmony after us. But I fear the future bodes not well for this land and its discordant inhabitants. We are too different, and the blood of too many runs hot for battle. Though the stag summons us to harmony, and though the common blood of the ancients flows through us, I fear the plants of this land will be fed more by the blood of feuding brothers than by the gentle rains of peace."

"Perhaps it is you who has the second sight after all," reflected Fidach.

"Only the passage of many years will tell if what I have spoken be true," replied the bard. "The words come not from my father, but from my own heart. The illness of your own father has weighed heavily upon me, Fidach. Many thoughts have come while I sat at his side and my chief lay sleeping. I have felt evil forebodings. And your dream of the stag sends chills through my spine. I fear he is not happy with us, with the way we quarrel among ourselves. He summons us to brotherhood, but we have not the eyes to see him, nor ears to heed his call. Only few see him, Fidach—like you and Cruithne. Do not neglect this gift which has been given you, this gift of seeing with your heart. Teach it to your people when you are chief. Teach it through your life, through your deeds."

"Is that the true second sight?"

"Such I have always considered it. Others may speak of being able to foretell the future or may speak of visions. For myself, the 'sight,' given to so few, is to see that life's meaning comes from harmony with this earth and its beasts and with our fellows. You of the next generation must not forget. You must teach these things to those who come after you."

"We will not forget, faithful Pendalpin."

"And you, my son? You will before many years be bard of Caldohnuill."

"I will not forget what you have taught me, Father," answered Domnall.

"It is good," said the old man. "I can rest in peace."

He sank against the wall, still staring into the fire. He had spent a great energy. He had discharged a portion of his duty, and now retreated into thoughts of deeper things. Truly Pendalpin carried in his soul the blood of the Mystic, and was no less one himself.

Slowly Fidach rose, bade both the young man and his father a restful night, and left. When he reached his own quarters, the only sounds to greet him were the night sounds of sleep.

▨   E I G H T   ▨

The next evening, shortly before dusk, the two sons of the chief had climbed to the top of the broch together. They now stood leaning against the topmost parapet, gazing westward toward the setting sun.

"It is a beautiful land, is it not, Fidach," sighed Cruithne.

The elder nodded. His spirit was still.

"I never tire of coming here and looking into the distance," his brother continued. "On a clear day, I often imagine I can see the Dark Waters. But I fear it is only my eyes playing tricks upon my mind."

"The water can be seen, Cruithne," replied Fidach, speaking at last. "Down through the valley of Dungal, Durcellach Bay is plainly visible. But even the eastern sea lies not too far distant for mortal eyes."

"Perhaps not for yours," laughed Cruithne.

"But on this evening my eyes gaze not to the east, my brother, but rather to the north."

Now it was Cruithne's turn to be silent. He did not reply, and after a moment his brother went on.

"He is out there, Cruithne," Fidach said softly. "I feel him. He calls . . . he beckons me to come."

"Who?"

"The stag, Cruithne. He calls us to seek him."

"Stags do not call men to hunt them, Fidach."

"Perhaps they call for different reasons."

"You have been talking again to Pendalpin!"

"This is no mortal beast."

"The mysticism of the bard has seized your brain, my brother!"

"Perhaps. But what the bard sees is true."

"And you follow where his eyes see?" Cruithne laughed. "Our people may wind up with two bards if you do not keep at least one of your feet upon the solid rocks of the earth. One man with his head in the sky is enough for any clan!"

Fidach laughed too. "It is good of you not to mock me for my fantasies."

"I would never mock you," said Cruithne seriously. "I may not see what you see, but I trust you to be true. I would follow your sight over that of any man in the clachan, however practical he might be."

Cruithne grinned, then added, "Though I might chuckle now and then at some of your notions and visions."

"So will you come with me?"

"You are still convinced you will find the stag in the forest of Muigh-bhlaraidh Ecgfrith?"

"Perhaps. But even if we do not find him, it would be good to visit An Stoc-bheinn Mountain to celebrate the coming of spring. We can take young Domnall with us! He will delight in the cave."

Cruithne studied his brother's face a second more, then grinned and nodded. "It is good! I too am eager for such an adventure."

"So you do not mind following my fancies?"

"You pursue what your second sight shows you. I will take my spear to hunt the one you dream of . . . and we will show the son of our bard our place of solitude on the distant mountain."

While the two young men thus made their plans, below them in the fort, Taran and Aethilnon spoke quietly around their fire.

"I am pleased you feel better today, my husband," said Aethilnon as she gently wiped the old chief's brow.

"The meat of the boar brings strength," he replied in a weak voice. "And it rests my tired soul for Eormen to be away. Has no one in Laoigh seen her today?"

"No one, my chief. I have been to everyone in the fort and all the huts."

"She grows anxious for her son, I fear."

"Surely she worries for your health," protested Aethilnon softly.

"You know better. She would see me dead if it suited her purposes, which no doubt it would. But you must not worry. It is your Fidach who will be the next chief."

"You cannot be certain of that," said Aethilnon. "I have no claim by blood. Eormen does."

"A claim as false as the prophecy that the moon will turn black! A claim hatched in her own scheming brain to wrest power from my hand!"

"There may be truth in it."

"She is no more of the line of Cowall, Brude, and Neithon than are the Scothui from beyond Loch Bruid! I tell you, Fidach is the one I have chosen to follow—my eldest son . . . son of my first wife Aethilnon."

He reached out a feeble hand and stroked her face.

Aethilnon smiled. "Gladly will I serve my people," she said, "as the chief's wife, or as the chief's mother. But the elders must decide how to rule on the succession."

"They will rule as I tell them to rule," insisted Taran. "There is no precedent. They will do what I say. Fidach shall be chief."

"You must not exert yourself with such talk," said Aethilnon, pulling a blanket of skins up around him. "Rest, my husband. I will bring you more of the meat."

"Yes, yes . . . that will be good," sighed the chief with feeble voice. "They are good sons . . . sons to make a man proud. And you are a good wife, Aethilnon. You make an old man's bones warmer with your care than any flame of fire."

She knelt down with a smile and kissed his wrinkled cheek.

▨   N I N E   ▨

Two days later Taran, son of Cuthred and chief of the Pritenae of Caldohnuill, watched his two sons make their way down the hill, away from the encampment, and across the wide valley toward the peak known as Beinn Donuill. In truth it was no mountain. But in these regions none of the peaks were of great height, a fact which in no way lessened their severity when fierce snows came.

They made him proud, but he was also sad, for the trek would keep them away from home for many days, perhaps a week or two.

Beyond Beinn Donuill, which they would skirt to the east and north, they would ford the Aethbran nan Bronait, still brown and frothy and swollen with the winter's runoff from the high places, in the safest spot for two miles in either direction, just below Lochan na Gaoithe. In that loch, or perhaps its sister, they would fish and hope to catch their supper before striking out into the rugged region between those lakes and Loch Cracail Mor, where they would make camp their first night.

The chief watched as they receded from sight, the two sons of his late years, one of whom would soon replace him, the sons whose mothers he had loved, one of whom had brought so much bitterness into the camp. Away they walked, as they did two or three times a year, to be together. Their friendship made him content inside, as did their kindness toward the son of his friend Pendalpin, who now trailed them eagerly. It was the first time he had been invited to accompany the two young men on their odyssey for meat and companionship.

Slowly Taran turned back inside the stone hill-fort and again sought the warmth of his fire and the comfort of the one wife he had truly loved all along.

The course that Cruithne and Fidach, with Domnall between them, pursued lay across a well-worn path through a rugged valley of heather and bracken that separated the hill-fort and broch from Beinn Donuill. The wide expanse was actually little more than a river valley, which widened as the flowing current of Aethbran nan Bronait swept round the base of Donuill toward the inlet from the sea that bore its name and opened up in the direction of the hill-fort.

It was a solitary region through which they walked. Indeed, this whole part of the earth was desolate in its very essence. Taran's nearest neighbors, the Caleborstii of Kildonanoid and the Roismaeatae of Rossbidalich were yet twenty miles distant. The three young men would likely trek the entire forty or fifty miles of their journey to An Stoc-bheinn and back without encountering another human soul.

A random amalgamation of bare hills, partially hidden glens, and wide-open heaths and moors made up the area through which they walked. Each little valley or strath possessed its own stream, nearly all flowing with the rich-hued amber waters of peat runoff. Mostly the aspect was of gray and brown, but the coming season had colored the region with pleasant periodic interruptions of green, not numerous but lush where they chanced to burst out of the earth. On the stream banks grew here and there a rowan tree or a silver birch or alder, watered by the foaming waterways as they ran around big stones and under occasional cliffy banks, and long green spring grasses grew to their very edges.

Had the pilgrims been blessed with the visage and vantage point of the lone falcon which wheeled lazily several hundred feet above them, to the east behind them they would have beheld, several miles distant, the great, expansive northern sea, clear and cold. Over the pale gray-green ocean hung an even paler thin blue sky, dotted here and there with a few cold white clouds sitting offshore miles higher than the falcon himself would have dared venture. A chill wind blew—keen but not angry, as the winds of that land often seemed; keen enough, however, to crisp up into white foam the tips of the waves in patches here and there as they made their way to shore.

Toward the distance in the opposite direction, low hills and valleys of heather, bracken, scrubby shrubs and brush, and coarse grasses rolled away westward, interspersed with numerous bogs, giving way at no great distance to mountains with snow on their crests. Far away on the horizon, where the mountains and clouds conducted business together, the more distant highland peaks rose to grandeur—still ablaze, this early in the year, with a pure, deep white that reflected the fiery rays from above but felt no compulsion to absorb them. The snowy peaks seemed to laugh at the sun's feeble attempts to spread warmth across a land that would stubbornly resist his efforts for several more months.

Few trees were visible to the west, though occasional clumps of Scots pine could be seen, and several of the hills and mountains guarded small forests on their slopes as homes for the thousands of tiny creatures and hundreds of roe, elk, and deer, which were as plenteous as men were scarce. Wolves there were as well, friendly to no man or beast, but they kept mostly inland, in the remotest of the high regions. Of boar there were few, though there had once been many, and their numbers would increase again. Cattle and sheep were now mostly domesticated. The sheep's cousin, the scrappy highland goat, was multitudinous and prolific.

How this variety of beasts sustained its existence, only their creator knew. For that matter, how the hundred generations of men and women who had not only survived but, in a manner of speaking, had thrived since the days of the Wanderer was also a fact of existence that only a power greater than the men of those generations could have known. The answer was no doubt born out of the reality that both the people and the beasts of this region were not unlike the land they inhabited. A sinewy and hardy lot they were, content to carve out whatever life they could from a land that was the only home they had ever known.

The stark border region between the low-lying coastal areas and the more mountainous terrain farther west yielded its bounty grudgingly, and every winter seemed determined to wipe every trace of life from its face. Somehow, nevertheless, the consciousness of nature always managed to sleep under the thick blankets of snow, held in a suspended frozen warmth against the frigid blasts sweeping across the surface of the planet, until spring sent forth its miracle from unknown depths, as it had thousands of times before, and visible life had once more come to the land.

Chilly though the air was, spring was abroad in the north, and for the day at least, the whole land lay bathed in sunlight. Quietness reigned on the earth, and above the earth, while underneath the feet of the three walkers, in the very earth herself, life—quiet, waiting, eager—readied itself for the blossoming of the new year.

In the very bowels of the boggy areas they crossed, between the roots of the surface vegetation and the rocky plate that made up the subsurface stratum ten to twenty feet below, lay the remarkable substance known as peat— that partially decomposed, tightly compacted organic material which the ancient grandson of the Wanderer had discovered could be taken from the earth, dried, and then burned with remarkable effect and great heat. These very bogs over which the three made their occasional way, appearing to the eye as uninviting and useless as ever landscape could be, were the storage closets and wine cellars and reservoirs of the sun, collecting and stockpiling its miracle of warmth, the very cordial of life.

The countryside could not have by any description been termed pretty unless you knew, not so much where to look, but rather how to perceive its beauty. Neither was it friendly unless one lived upon it for sufficient generations to make of it a friend. It was a rugged place, beautiful not with vivid splashes of color, but with infinite subtle hues and variety of lonely terrain, sparse but full of the wide majesty of pure northernness. The solemnity and stillness and solitude of the region itself was alive.

Little was said as the three young men made their way across the mile or so that separated the hill-fort from the rounded bare summit of Beinn Donuill. Though they had walked this way many times, today they would not climb the path that led to the lookout there. Instead they swung wide around Donuill's base, walking almost to the bank of Aethbran nan Bronait, where the river took a wide southerly loop, before turning and heading westward to the point a mile and a half upriver where they would cross the waters.

They walked around the shoulder of the hill that closed off from their view the wide lowland behind them. Now they entered a narrower section of the valley, through the bottom of which the river ran, and up from whose banks on either side the hillsides sloped more steeply.

As the sheer cliff of Beinn Donuill's more precipitous face loomed ominously skyward at their side, the sun disappeared behind it, leaving them for a time walking in an enormous dark shadow from the mountain. A good many patches of snow still lay about here, and halfway up the granite crag, in a protected little hollow that only saw the sun's brightness for a few days toward the end of every July, the white drifts rose to depths of ten or fifteen feet. Where the valleys opened northward and where hills shielded the sun from reaching the ground, the earth often remained frozen for as many as six months of the year.

Through such a place they now walked. The ground crunched beneath their leather-clad feet. The sun shone high in the sky. Here and there tender green shoots gave evidence that he was doing his yearly work of attempting to awaken the land. The shadow of Beinn Donuill reminded Fidach especially that the ball of fire overhead was but a wayfarer in these northern wastes of hillside and mountain and valley and moor. Even during the summer he was not able to enter into every nook and cranny with complete freedom. And now, with summer still far off, his heat was more visual than actual, and the crannies were cold and the nooks black with ice.

Fidach noticed all this and pondered it in his heart. Meditations on the meaning of these things mingled with thoughts of the stag inside his mind, and he was silent as he walked along. He was a Celt, full of mystical idylls and undefined emotions.

Cruithne exulted in the zestful adventure inherent in the physical substance of life. He led the way with a merry step and a smile on his face, sucking in deeply every so often of the nippy air, clutching his stout spear, whose blunt end now served as a staff to assist his steps over the uneven ground, and relishing in anticipation of the rigors ahead. In his heart were no poems, but rather the hope that he might be the man finally to achieve the conquest over the great stag that none of his tribe had ever attained.

Cruithne too was a Celt. His blood ran hot with love of a challenge, and his fine iron-tipped javelin was ever at his side.

Domnall followed the warrior-chief and the poet-chief. At sixteen, he was still a boy in many ways, but already the ways of the bard were deepening within him. His sensitivities to the land and its creatures and people grew every passing year. From his father, at whose knee he had heard the ancient tales, he had also been given eyes and heart to learn what it all meant. His hands had strummed the bardic *clarsach* from the moment he could sit. Now the countless ballads that comprised Caldohnuill's history had deeply woven themselves into his being and made up the very matrix of his consciousness.

As Domnall walked along behind, therefore, unconsciously he hummed a haunting melody of unknown origin. The adventure had already begun to mark itself into his heart, to be added in later years to the tales he would pass to his own son. For he too was a Celt, and a bard's son besides. His soul was full of an ever-recurring impulse to break out now in melancholy chant, now in happy song, to tell what has been and what might yet be.

The three young men, so distinctive of temperament, yet bound by bonds of clan and friendship, blood and lifelong camaraderie, made together a threefold cord of Celtic character—the multisighted mystic, the hot-blooded adventurer, and the historian-bard. As they followed their course across the frozen ground, the very expressions on the three faces offered fit symbols to epitomize the varied character of their clan and their race.

Several hours later, as the afternoon shadows lengthened toward night, they yet trudged on. They had covered some six or seven miles, and had rejoiced along the way in a successful catch of eight or ten fine freshwater trout. With the dried salty venison and baked hard cakes of ground oatmeal mixed with water and melted fat from the slaughtered boar, their catch would make them a feast around tonight's fire.

The wind still hounded them, softer now, but colder with the approach of darkness. They were nearing the vicinity of Cracail Mor, rounding the short end of a small lake in the midst of rugged and rocky hills. Walking here was difficult even when the light was good, and it would shortly grow treacherous.

The hills hereabouts offered a very picture of desolation. What little vegetation dared peek its greenery from between the rocks was still mostly white from a remaining dusting of snow, or with the frost that already anticipated the night. None of the shapes of rocks or bushes or even trees contained much beauty. All was gray and brown and seemed worn, hopeless, and tired—and so very cold!

The walkers would not make it out of this wasteland tonight as they had planned. They now sought a tolerably flat piece of ground, protected by a ledge or large rock from the southwesterly direction of the breeze, where they might make their camp and build the fire that would see them through the frigid black hours. How thankful they were for the warm pelts and skins they wore, and for the extras they carried.

An hour later, they were sitting around a brightly roaring blaze, sheltered from the wind, and laughing as only the young can laugh, heartily enjoying the end of their first day and the rewards of their labors at the loch.

❈   T E N   ❈

Far away, some thirteen to fifteen miles almost due south, in a forlorn cave across the waters of Loch Durcellach, another fire burned. It was smaller, though the heat required from it was not so great, for the blood of the three who sat talking around it ran hot enough to make up for the cold.

A woman—old, the wrinkles under her eyes accentuated by the bright flickers of flame, but still feisty and vigorous—sat in animated speech with two men. The gestures of her hands and face suggested it was with difficulty that she made herself understood. Her eyes within their network of wrinkles shone with a fire of dubious origin. The clenched fist accompanying her words disclosed the intensity with which she spoke.

They came from different tribes, she and the men with whom she shared the fire, though all three possessed similar origins, and thus much commonality of tongue. The men were of the tribe Roismaeatae, meaning they were people of Celtic Maeatae extraction who had migrated north and settled in Rois. She had sojourned south to meet them from Laoigh in Caldohnuill. Though the two tribes would not exactly have considered themselves enemies, in these times, even with shared strains of blood, few indeed were the affiliations that would have led them to consider another tribe a friend. The woman and two men were no exception. Self-interest alone guided the motives on each side of the fire.

At present the woman was speaking.

"Time is short, I say. You must act without delay!"

"We cannot march against the hill. We would be slaughtered as we made approach from the plain."

"Have you not been listening, you fool?" rasped the woman. "You must infiltrate the camp, and when the time is right and the boy is alone—"

"It will have to be at night."

"Without question."

"How will we know him?"

"Leave that to me! When the time is right, I will give him a greeting you will not mistake."

"A mistake will cost you your head, old woman!"

"We must pick a moment when my own son is out of the camp. Then you must move swiftly."

"What has your son to do in this matter, cousin of the Maeatae?" asked the other man.

"Hold your wicked tongue!" retorted the woman. "Even in this foul place, do not speak that word! I have all but convinced the old hags of the place that I am one of them. If they knew my son's veins flowed with your blood, he would never be chief."

One of the men laughed deeply. It was far from a merry sound, and it echoed only a twisted pride in the woman's guileful deception.

"What makes you think he will be chief anyway?" he asked, laughing again, this time in something more like derision.

"If you do as I tell you, they will have no choice. You will kill that old fool who is my husband and his bastard offspring. Then I will make certain my son returns to drive off the savage raiders. He will be acclaimed a hero."

"So, that is what you would call us—savage raiders?" asked the first man, with menace in his tone.

"Keep your blood calm, you fool! I was but thinking what they will call you after."

"Insolent wretch. No one calls me a fool!" He rose from the fire, and his hand sought the huge blade at his side.

The woman sat unmoved, the flicker of a smile playing at her mouth. If there was the slightest trace of fear in her heart, not a hair on the back of her crinkly neck moved to show it.

"You are a dangerous accomplice," she said at length. "But I do not think you will harm me."

"You push me far."

"Yes, and you will fall in with my plan if you know what is good for your people. But the dark powers roast you if you lay any trap for me."

"I do not plan to get close enough to you again to allow your hot breath or the fires from your pit to singe so much as the hair of my arm!"

"Say what you will," growled the woman. "It is I who can put wealth in your hands."

"What can you give that we cannot take for ourselves? That is the one flaw in this daring scheme of yours, my evil-minded cousin—yes! I will call you by the word, if only to show you I fear the words of no woman! You summoned my brother and me here to hatch your sinister plot. But I have heard nothing yet that would benefit us. What do we gain?"

"I can put wealth in your hands," she replied, eyes aglow. "Precious silver bowls and trinkets, finely smithed jewelry and exquisite stones from far across the Dark Waters. Neck pieces and hair adornments for your women. There is abundance of silverwork in the hill-fort, but only I can lay my hands on it for you. I will bring it all to you after my son has driven you off."

"You expect us to run in fear from a mere boy?"

"A boy, you call him!" she shrieked. "My Cruithne is a mighty warrior, worth any three of your kind!"

"And it is from fear for our safety that we must come when he is away from camp?" rejoined one of the men with a throaty chuckle.

"He would slay you with one deadly aim of his spear if you dared approach uninvited!"

"Let him try it, and you will see your son's blood soak into the ground along with the other's."

"If you attempted to harm his brother, he would lift your severed head in his hand before you could raise your knife an inch against the soft-brained interloper!"

She stopped momentarily and gazed into the fire as her voice grew pensive.

"That is my son's only weakness," she went on, "—his distorted affection for the whoreson scoundrel of that baseborn woman."

Then just as quickly, she shot her glance back up toward the two men and again addressed them in vehement tone.

"I will see to it that he returns in time to drive you off. The black death take you if you harm a hair of his head. I will do the work for him and plunge a dagger into both your breasts! But do what I say and run like the cowards you are, and seven days later, when the moon is high, I will bring to this same spot enough wealth to satisfy even your greedy fingers!"

"How do you propose that we enter the fort unseen and unheeded, without the rest of the men raising the call against us? They will surely know you as a traitor and us as the enemy when they witness our taking counsel together."

"You must come as friends."

"Impossible."

"There is a way."

"You cannot reveal us to your relatives. We would be walking into certain death."

The woman fell silent for several moments. She stared into the dying embers, even as the two cousins she had not seen for almost ten years stared into the fiery orbs of her eyes. They mistrusted her, yet were bound in an ancient bond of blood unknown to anyone in Laoigh, including Eormen's own husband.

"It can be done, I tell you," she said at length, dark cunning in her voice. "You must paint your chests with the reindeer or the wolf. They will take you for one of the tribes from Kildonanoid. I will greet you as distant members of my family, for old Cowall is said to have migrated down from the north with her sucklings and husband."

"Tattoo our bodies with the emblems of our enemies?" rose the voice of one of the men. "You speak words of betrayal!"

She laughed, amused at the thinness of skin and stiffness of brain in the one she had played with as a child.

"I said *paint* your chests, not tattoo them. The designs need not be permanent. Mix the blood of a rat and black water squeezed from wet peat with the dye of Kermes. The design will serve our purpose. You can swim Loch Durcellach when your mission is complete, and by the time you reach your borders, all trace of your temporary treason will have washed its way toward Durcellach Bay."

"And if the heavens turn against us and the sky empties itself of rain?"

"Then cover your chests, you fool! And make sure you keep the images of those ugly entangled snakes on your backs covered as well, or the people of the hill will know in an instant the Maeatae whom they hate."

"You would have us walk into the wolf's lair, as they call Laoigh, with a painted tattoo as our only protection?"

"The wolf is old, and his eyes weak. Come bearing him a gift, and mind that you do not approach from the south. The old fool has a passion for the flesh of wild boar. Come carrying a dead pig on your shoulders with words of greeting, and he will welcome you. Bury the weapons you will need in the bowels of the beast. I will take care of the rest. You may trust me."

Now it was the men's turn to laugh, and they did so. But the sound was far from a pleasant one.

"You are an old witch," said one. "If danger should lurk behind Taran's walls of stone, it will be your flesh my knife shall slit."

"There will be no danger if you do as I say."

"And if the silver is not as you promised, and not so bountiful," added the other, "a second raid may come to Laoigh one night when you least expect it. But yours will be the only neck the sharp blades of Roismaeatae seek!"

"You troublesome fools," said Eormen, rising. "You will get your pieces of silver when my son is chief."

She turned and made her way toward the mouth of the cave. The voice of one of her cousins stopped her.

"Be vigilant, old woman. Our druids will offer the sacrifice of a virgin in the sacred grove that we may be successful. Then we will come when the sun rises high in the southern sky, not more than fifteen days from this time. If we discover that you have betrayed us, it will be your gore we will next sprinkle on the oaks."

She merely nodded, then disappeared into the night.

Neither of the two men said anything for many long minutes. Together they sat watching the final flames of the fire flicker to their death and give way at last to glowing embers. When finally they arose to leave, the inside of the cave was black, and only a thin trail of smoke remained behind them.

❈   E L E V E N   ❈

The morning was well advanced when the three stalwart young walkers reached the Falls of Bruid. Sounds of whitewater tumbling over the rocks and crashing downward reached their ears many minutes before the spectacular sight came into view. The fact only heightened the wonderful terror of the perilous place.

Loch Bruid, the greatest inland loch for many days in all directions, had been carved out of the highland granite thousands of years before by retreating glacial ice. In one of nature's creatively humorous moments, it had been left perched nearly atop a range of encircling peaks, a basin some two thousand feet high into which the waters from many streams poured melting snows from the mountains, but out of which there was but one natural means of egress. A narrow aperture at the southeast end of the loch, between two jagged cliffs, sent a narrow but swift, and at certain seasons deep, torrent of water on an exciting journey that would, some eight miles distant, empty into the headwaters of Loch Durcellach and thence flow eastward to the sea.

The remarkable feature of the course of Loch Bruid's overflow, however, was not the two-thousand-foot descent in elevation, but the fact that more than half of it occurred within some five hundred lineal feet along its path, at approximately the halfway point between Bruid and Durcellach. Following a steadily downward yet not unleisurely course, the stream wound southward, gaining both speed and volume from small tributaries along the way, until suddenly the very earth beneath it seemed to give way. Without warning, the current cascaded downward in a rush, over boulders and stones, frothing itself into a positive frenzy of turbulent whitewater.

Then suddenly, in a geological moment of genius seemingly too marvelous to be wasted upon a wilderness where scarce eye could see it, the downward surge hesitated and, in a narrow, smooth, and nearly level trough of some thirty or forty feet, gathered itself in a final rush, shot straight out over a single slab of overhanging rock, and plunged gloriously through the air some three hundred feet straight down. There it thundered into a great pool of unknown depth, which had apparently been hewn out of the rocky terrain for no other purpose than to receive the magnificent cataract.

It was at a point about a third of the way down the waterfall that Cruithne, Fidach, and Domnall now stood, beholding in silent awe the sight before them. Domnall had been to the falls only once before, as a mere lad with his father. But all morning, as they walked, the two sons of the chief had heightened his expectation of what he was about to behold with their own tales of its splendor.

As he stood gazing upward toward the point where the watercourse shot out as if propelled by some great invisible force from the very mountain itself, then turning his eye downward to behold the constantly churning tarn below, the bardic imagination of the boy was not disappointed. Through his brain pulsed not only the sight and sound of water tumbling over stones, but also enshrouded images of seasons and eras, of heat and cold, of ice and sun and clouds and rain that all combined somehow to have made the water and now caused it to run so.

"Eh, Domnall!" said Cruithne, with inquiring tone. "As we promised?"

"Magnificent . . . yes!" replied the son of Pendalpin in a soft voice.

Neither Fidach nor Domnall could gaze upon such a sight without sinking into reverie, wondering, each in his own way, what so wondrous a gift to their senses might mean.

Had Fidach been told what even the wisest bards in the land could not dream of—that the waters of the lochs and rivers and the great sea itself returned invisibly to the sky, then fell in their season back again to earth, such a truth would have deepened the mystery tenfold, binding together the earth and heavens in a closed circle of incomprehensible beginnings and endings. That the visible, finite stream before him should both come from the rain and snow of the heavens and be fated to return one day to the sky— such an idea would have sent the thoughtful brain of Fidach, son of Taran, into an agony of joyful wonder. As it was, his heart only felt what his brain did not know, and his sense of almost holy marvel was enlarged. He watched, he listened, and inside was glad.

As the two young philosophers contemplated the wonder of the place, however, the energetic Cruithne was eager to be about his favorite business at the falls.

"Come . . . come!" he shouted, leading the way downward along a barely visible, precipitous path that wound to the foot of the falls. "The sun is warm today. We must cool ourselves before we continue on!"

This was the one aspect of their plans for the day the two older youths had intentionally left for Domnall to discover in the panic of the moment.

With a broad smile spreading over his face, Fidach followed his brother. "Yes, the water beckons us," he said. "Come, Domnall . . . we will swim in the pool below!"

Domnall looked down again toward the thunderous base of the waterfall. Any attempt by man or beast to even set a foot in the turbulent pond was sure to meet with certain death! But before he could even get a word of objection out of his mouth, his two companions were out of sight down the steep incline.

Hastily Domnall scrambled down the ridge that banked the terrifying falls, the overwhelming sound of the water silencing every other sensation. Climbing down the side of a mossy slope and skirting a huge boulder, he found a space of a few yards where he could run for a few paces.

But catching Fidach and Cruithne was hopeless. Straining his ears, he could just barely hear their shouting voices ahead.

When next his eyes caught sight of them, they had nearly reached the ledge over the invisible pool. As he emerged from a thicket of close-growing pine he beheld the two, with the deafening fall seemingly now right beside them, and having already cast off every vestige of clothing from their well-formed bodies, sprinting side by side toward the turbulent, churning, lethal lake.

"Stop!" Domnall shouted, but in vain. The sound of his voice was swallowed in the fulminating pounding of water.

He raced after them.

Suddenly Cruithne halted, then Fidach, and both turned back.

"You must not do it!" cried Domnall. He ran to them and stopped. "The water is too dangerous! It will pound you underneath, and you will never see the surface again!"

"Nonsense!" returned Cruithne. "Do you not think I am able to swim strongly enough to meet the challenge?"

"No man can survive in such water!" insisted the youth, gesturing toward the falls.

"Off with your skins, Domnall," now added Fidach with a smile. "We all will swim, and conquer the mighty Falls of Bruid!"

As he spoke he turned away and sprinted off. The next instant Cruithne followed.

"No, you mustn't!" implored Domnall, chasing after them.

But he was too late.

Before he could reach them again, suddenly Fidach leapt from the path as if to make a running dive into the lake. Instead he disappeared from sight. Cruithne followed, flying into midair.

Domnall reached the spot of their departure just in time to see the ends of Cruithne's feet disappear into the water of a deep pool positioned some twenty feet below that which received the falls, hidden from view until the last instant, and separated from the main course of the river by a sheer cliff of rock.

The two sons of Taran had been here many times since discovering the spot. Few things offered them as much pure animal pleasure as bounding off the ledge and shooting through the air headfirst into the frothy mass, out well beyond the tame fall of water that fed this tiny pond from the larger one above. Each time it was the same: they would attempt to swim up and under the small falls, yielding for a time to the sport of the bubbling water, allowing themselves to be tossed and tumbled about, before jumping out, panting and blowing, then scrambling up the cliff to begin all over again.

Out of the water two heads now rose, laughing in joyful abandon.

"Come, Domnall!" shouted Fidach. "The water here is deep. There are no stones or hidden ledges."

"But I thought—" he began in consternation.

Cruithne climbed onto the bank and headed up the cliff to join him. "You do not think we are such fools as that!" he laughed, nodding to the other lake above. "Even the fish do not survive in Bruid's Falls!"

"It looked like you were about to dive straight into it."

"Ah, Domnall, we deceived you," panted Cruithne as he reached the top. "An innocent joke played on our friend. It was for the hidden pond that we brought you here . . . for this!"

He dove again, arching his back perfectly as he floated out past the small falls, plunging in with a great splash. When his head again appeared, it was accompanied by a mighty whoop of pleasure and triumph.

"But is it not cold?" called out Domnall loudly.

"Like the very ice from which it comes!" replied Fidach, who had by now himself regained the summit and was readying himself for another leap. "Too cold for any but a wild man to enjoy!"

He darted back several paces, turned, and, shouting wildly, tore again toward the edge of the cliff. With a scream of delight, Fidach followed his brother and sailed off the ledge toward the frigid glacial pond. The next moment, Domnall's skins lay in a heap on the ground and he was soaring through the morning air after them.

At one time the main course of the river had no doubt continued its downward plunge through this very spot, the pounding water hollowing out the deep basin in which the three now frolicked like children. But time had altered its path, and now, after its several-hundred-foot fall, the river bent sharply to the right, plunging and cascading on down the steep valley toward its destiny at Durcellach, while to the left but a trickle remained to spurt out over the ledge from which the youths leapt, feeding the chilly hole that now gave them such sport.

To one unaccustomed to the waters of this region, the clear brownness of the pool, with the white, frothing foam, natural enough in these mountain streams but made all the more bubbly and turbulent by the falls and the crashing of the river over and around the stones and boulders of its rocky course, might have appeared strange. Here surely was no ordinary water of blue or green, but water from some altogether strange and unknown source.

Indeed, the waters of these districts had not originated from mere snow and rain and ice. Because once they began their downward flow, either above the surface or beneath it, they flowed over and around, and most often through, great fields and bogs and mountains of peat, which stained their waters and lent them a radiant bronze luminescence. Loch Bruid itself for most of the year shone a pale blue from the melting snow that continually fed it. As its water emptied into the stream below, however, and as the stream was augmented by the burns draining the surrounding moors and hilly slopes, it gradually took on color. By the time it reached Bruid's Falls, the water's blue had been transformed into a rich, earthy, amber brown. Even the stones over which it rushed were no longer colored their natural gray, but brown from the stain.

As the earth loosed its ice-bound hold on the moisture that had fallen upon it throughout the winter, the channel filled every spring, and its contents poured kaleidoscopically down, through the deep-worn brown of the gorge—fierce, dark, wild, unable to rest until it reached the end of its journey in the glens far below.

In and out of these cold brown waters the three youths plunged and dove, shouted, laughed, and cavorted, relishing the perfect pleasure and safety of their merrymaking all the more because it was set within close proximity to such a terrifying display of nature's power. But the cold was an aspect of nature's character too, and one they could not easily ignore for long. After ten minutes of revelry, they were forced to assume once again the posture of their kind.

Up and down the path they ran several times to warm up and partially dry off before donning their skins and beginning the ascent back up the side of the falls the way they had come. They would stop in another clearing known to Cruithne and Fidach, one that opened up beside the very top of the falls themselves, so close that they could almost reach out and touch the mighty current as it shot over the cliff and into uninhibited space. There they would pause and rest and eat of their cakes of oat and their leftover bits of fish from the previous night.

Perhaps after they had warmed themselves, eaten, and rested, they would swim again. Then they would resume their journey, moving now in a north-easterly direction, hoping to reach the shore of Loch Craggie by nightfall.

Of course, everything depended on what they found that afternoon.

They would search Muigh-bhlaraidh Ecgfrith for signs. If the stag had indeed returned to the forest, they would know it.

⊠   T W E L V E   ⊠

No two hunters in all Caldohnuill could locate the whereabouts of game with the skill and craft of the two sons of Taran.

Either alone would not have stood immeasurably above his peers of the tribe. Each was skilled in his own way, but not unusually so. Together, however, they were so capable of divining the other's thoughts and actions ahead of time that scarcely a beast had a chance against them.

One of their hopes in bringing young Domnall with them on this occasion was to teach him what they could of their peculiar mode of stalking the creatures of the land—a method that relied not on the might of one's arm nor the speed with which one hurled the spear, but rather on one's ability to think as the creatures thought. For the rest of the day after leaving the falls, first Cruithne, then Fidach, spoke to the future bard, relating this technique or that, recounting stories of things they had seen and done on various hunts.

The eyes of Fidach were far-seeing and calm, those of Cruithne keen and eager. The connection between the two had always more resembled that of twins than half brothers. It took but a glance, a lift of the eyebrow, an imperceptible nod of the head, a wink, a slight curve of the lip to communicate worlds from one to the other. Their souls were one and thus required few words to hold communion.

With this love came trust. When Cruithne detected a certain look on the face of Fidach, he knew his brother had felt the presence of some animal. He would instantly drop into a crouch of utter stillness, watching Fidach's face for further sign of what approached and what he should do.

Fidach, likewise, trusted absolutely in Cruithne's marksmanship with the spear. It caused the pulse of his heart to quicken not a beat to find himself charged by boar or elk if his brother was near, for he knew he was in no danger.

The only dispute between them might have been in this—that Cruithne felt his brother cared more than was reasonable for what the beasts might feel, while Fidach worried that Cruithne too greatly enjoyed the conquest of killing. They resolved this difference by never killing for *mere* sport. What the sustenance of their people required, Fidach would gladly kill, and he allowed Cruithne the pleasure of the hunt when wolves or other predators threatened the hill-fort or the tamer beasts.

They had not yet spoken about whether they would actually *kill* the white stag if they came to such a moment. Cruithne spoke of hunting the great stag for the food it would bring Laoigh. Fidach knew, however, that his brother's zeal lay in deeper regions. This was one of the few unspoken barriers that had arisen between them, and Fidach was not at peace concerning it. The time would come when a decision must be made. He wanted merely to set eyes on the great white stag. Cruithne desired to conquer it. Beyond that difference, however, Fidach's so-called second sight could not see.

For the present, as they walked, they explained their methods to Domnall.

"The secret is in working together," said Cruithne. "Beyond the necessity for food, most men hunt to satisfy their own thirst for power and supremacy. To their minds it is a competition. Thus they often work against themselves. To be against one's fellow is to be against oneself."

"This does not sound like Cruithne, the hunter."

Cruithne laughed. "I have learned much from my brother the philosopher!" he replied. "He has taught me to hunt with more than my arm and my spear. He has taught me many things of the heart, of the mind. From him I have learned the advantage of cunning."

"Is this true?" asked Domnall, turning with interest to the oldest son of Taran.

Fidach merely smiled. "It is not cunning that I have taught my brother," he answerd. "I have merely helped him to see that we reach our greatest skill *with* others, not apart from them. The hearts of most brothers such as we, sons of a chief, of nearly equal age, would burn with rivalry, each attempting to better the other for his father's attention."

"Why does not such jealousy consume you?"

"Because we know that together we can become greater than either of us is on our own."

"What has that to do with hunting?"

"It has to do with all of life. It may be Cruithne's spear that finds the heart of the boar, but it may have been my stalking of the beast that drove him into Cruithne's path. Attempting to outdo each other, perhaps neither of us would be successful. Together, we can outwit almost any animal."

"And the stag?"

"Should we succeed in stalking the great beast, it will be because the two of us, working in harmony not separately, outsmart and outmaneuver him as no single hunter could."

They continued to talk as they walked. By degrees the landscape changed from the wide treeless plateau they had been crossing into a vast forest of green, lush with undergrowth, shrubbery, grasses, and species of flora not found anywhere else in these northern latitudes. In some quirk of nature, having to do with the winds and the lay of the mountains surrounding Loch Bruid, as well as those to the north and the east, the region of Muigh-bhlaraidh Ecgfrith received perhaps twice the rainfall of any other place in all the east of this land, and the soil conditions were such—with more soil and less peat—that vegetation flourished in abundance.

The three young men followed no path as the forest of Muigh-bhlaraidh Ecgfrith closed round them. The brothers had been here many times, but always they sought a different route through the dense wood. Today they would go wherever the signs led them. Perhaps they would stay the night in the depths of the forest. If they saw no sign of the stag, they would reach the other end, continue on, and encamp near Loch Craggie.

▧   T H I R T E E N   ▧

As the trees grew taller and more close, the solemnity of the place deepened. Talk gave way to silence as the spell of the wood came over them.

The forest was alive with a presence of its own. To speak was to intrude upon the live conversation that was the very essence of the place.

"He is here," whispered Fidach at length. "Do you not sense his presence, Cruithne?"

"Your second sight plays mischief with your brain, Fidach," replied his brother. "You feel only the silence of the forest."

"It is more than that," Fidach answered back, still speaking softly. "I told you before that he was calling us."

"So, Domnall," laughed Cruithne, "do you see what I must put up with in this starry-eyed brother of mine? He gives all things a meaning that no one else can see. He feels and hears with senses not reserved for mere mortals. And now he hears the great stag calling us, as if the beast would hasten its own death."

Fidach laughed too at his brother's good-natured jests. They were accustomed to making sport of their differences rather than quarreling over them.

"My father says the stag's presence in Caldohnuill portends a change," said Domnall.

"The bard of our people seldom errs in his forecasts," said Fidach seriously.

A brief silence followed.

"You will not *kill* the stag, Cruithne?" Fidach asked at length.

Cruithne hesitated.

"I am a hunter, my brother," he finally replied. His voice too had grown reflective. "The Pritenae must hunt and kill to live."

"Our quarry today is no ordinary beast."

Cruithne was silent again as he thought about Fidach's words. "I must hunt," he said slowly. "I hope you will help me. What I will do if we find him, I cannot say. But I will allow nothing to drive division between my heart and yours. I care more for you than I do the stag."

Fidach did not reply. For the moment the answer was sufficient, and they continued deeper into Muigh-bhlaraidh Ecgfrith.

Over their heads, the blue vault had receded behind a tangle of branches and trunks and newly greening foliage in the treetops above them. Underneath their feet, the softly carpeted forest floor was springy with moist mosses and brown fallen leaves. The trees of birch, aspen, alder, and rowan were not huge, though they passed an occasional old Caledonian pine of several feet in thickness. Neither were their trunks so dense as to make finding a course through them difficult, though thickly growing everywhere else was a great variety of highland heather and other woody shrubbery.

Whether there had been rain here recently it would have been difficult to tell. Even in high summer the place was unusually damp. Now, in early spring, every inch dripped with moisture. Wherever the sun could penetrate, millions of droplets hanging from every branch and leaf and slender shoot of green danced with the many colors of reflected miniature rainbows. In late afternoon, the fading sun made the place bewitchingly enchanting with infinite hues of light and shadow.

The whole was pervaded by the mingled odors of wetness, earth, wood, growth, and decay. Leaves and needles from millennia of past autumns lay under their feet with the moss. Here and there a rotting log, with new growth springing up from either around or within it, gave evidence of the continually dying, ever-renewing cycle of life and death and new life—the essence of creation itself. Flowers, too, could be found in their season—though scantily, and it took a watchful eye to know where to look for them. High wild rhododendron maintained a lofty perch but seemed stingy about bestowing too frequent a glimpse of their purple blossoms to would-be visitors. A few delicate ground flowers, where they could push their fragile way through the tangled mass, came and went. At this season some hardy breeds of primroses—yellow, purple, white, and blue—could occasionally be seen peeking up from the forest floor from amid their rough-textured protective leaves.

Truly it was a paradise, a quiet, somber, hidden, private world all its own. When the brothers had first walked inside its depths years before, an irresistible spell had come over them. Even the joy and laughter of the falls and the warm comfort of the fires back at the hill-fort could not match the quiet pleasure they felt here. Whether any man had set foot in the seductively wondrous wood before, they had no way of knowing, though they never encountered a human soul there. But both immediately felt it calling to them from its depths, *I am yours to enjoy, and you are welcome to all my treasures!*

Through the wood they now walked slowly, reverently. Domnall's awe was evident. Both brothers took quiet pleasure in knowing what he felt, for neither had forgotten his first day here. They made their way gradually eastward and occasionally northward without specific intent of direction.

Neither Fidach nor Cruithne led. They walked forward purposefully, yet in no hurry. An eerie silence accompanied them. Neither sparrow nor robin nor wren nor finch, usually plentiful in the trees above, could be heard. Only their footsteps and their occasionally whispering voices broke the tranquil stillness. Some presence other than their own seemed to have settled over Muigh-bhlaraidh Ecgfrith, commanding everything in it to repose.

The sun was now well past its zenith. The shadows from their own forms, broken by those from the surrounding trees and forest images, were lengthening in front of them when suddenly Fidach stopped. For several moments he stood motionless. Cruithne and Domnall waited at his side.

"I hear him, Cruithne," uttered Fidach solemnly.

Unconsciously Cruithne's fingers tightened around his spear. "In which direction?" he whispered.

Behind them, Domnall's feet stood unmoving, as if they belonged to the earth. He struggled intently to divine whatever snap of forest twig or step of cloven hoof had reached Fidach's preternaturally keen ear. But he heard nothing. All remained deathly calm.

Fidach turned his head slowly this way and that.

Cruithne and Domnall searched his face for some sign of his thoughts. But though his countenance was alive with meaning, for once Cruithne could not apprehend its purport.

Slowly Fidach crept forward, on his toes lest he cause any forewarning sound. The others followed.

Through a deep thicket of pines they went, treading softly on the blanket of fallen needles, carefully avoiding the multitude of small dead branches that lay strewn over the brown carpet. Emerging from the grove, Fidach sent his gaze out across a grassy clearing, surrounded by trees. At its far end stood a gnarled ancient hawthorn alive with a wild, queer, beautiful grotesqueness.

His eyes scanned the small open field, then came to rest upon the hawthorn. Steadily he stood as one transfixed, then slowly turned his head in Cruithne's direction. As their eyes met, he motioned with one hand.

Cruithne knew his meaning instantly. He retreated several paces back into the pine wood, then slowly began to work his way around the perimeter of the green meadow while remaining under cloak of cover within the trees. Not a sound could be heard from his steps.

Fidach turned to Domnall and signaled likewise in the opposite direction. The son of the bard, following Cruithne's example, understood his task and immediately crept away. He had learned well the lessons of his two elders from earlier in the day.

Fidach waited until the two were perhaps a third of the distance in their respective directions toward the hawthorn, then gingerly stepped forward into the grassy meadow. With steps of tiniest degree, he inched his way forward in absolute silence.

When he had traveled some ten yards—traversing the distance had taken some three or four minutes of stealthy deliberation—suddenly a great commotion reached his ears from the wood beyond the meadow. The next thing Fidach heard was a shout from his brother. But he had time to apprehend no words.

The same instant, from behind the trunk of the great hawthorn, there suddenly emerged a great stag, with antlers of points too numerous to count and a huge majestic head of white that faded down his neck and along his back into a light gray.

Whatever silence had previously descended upon the place was utterly shattered. The stag crashed out of the forest in a dead run, in a tumult of legs and hoofs, bending brush and breaking branches, with echoing shouts behind him. The tempest of flurry and sound and movement, however, lasted but a moment. The instant the stag broke free of the wood, he saw Fidach directly in his path. As suddenly as he had sprung into flight, he now stopped.

The giant animal seemed to sense he had no retreat to the right or the left, where Domnall and Cruithne were poised in readiness. And he could not go back, for they would cut off his path before he reached the hawthorn again. His only course lay forward, across the clearing.

From thirty paces, the eyes of the beast met the wondering gaze of the youth who would become chief. They held each other for several long seconds. It seemed an hour.

Fidach would fain have approached him. Yet he could see that the eyes of the one he had so long sought glistened with fear. The huge round black orbs shone from the center of the white head with an uncanny and mysterious cognizance that the one standing before him was no enemy. The powerful silver flanks gave not so much as a shiver to betray their muscular readiness to bolt again. Neither did the tiny thin tail divulge the slightest twitch. The great white stag stood motionless as a statue of stone.

Fidach timidly held forth his hand, then took another step closer.

To his right Fidach heard his brother's step plunging out of the wood. The head of the stag turned quickly, perceived his danger, and sprang forward. Cruithne's spear rose above his shoulder and the brawny strength of his arm flexed backward to heave it toward its mark.

"Cruithne—no!" shouted Fidach.

But already the beast was gone.

In two giant bounds he came straight toward Fidach, then leapt mightily into the air.

Cruithne arrested his javelin. To send it forward now would endanger the brother he loved.

To the left of Fidach, and nearly over his shoulder, the great stag flew, landing in full stride well past him. In another instant he was receding from sight into the pine wood from which they had just come, vanishing in a light blur against the dark forest.

Fidach spun around to follow the movement, and then stood gazing after the stag in wonder, a great smile of awe and joy on his face. Feelings indefinable filled his breast. Slowly Cruithne approached and placed his arm around his shoulder.

"We have seen him, my brother," he said.

Fidach sighed and nodded. "It was worth everything, for just that moment," he said softly. "I do not understand all he had to tell me, but in time it will come clear."

"You were right," said Cruithne. "It would have been wrong to kill so magnificent a creature. I do not know why I was unable to understand that before."

"If only that fear in his eyes could be banished—from both beasts and men."

"I regret raising my spear against him, Fidach. I did not think to kill him. I found myself taking aim almost in spite of myself."

"Think no more of it," replied Fidach, pulling his gaze away from the forest, and now looking intently into his brother's eyes. As he did, Domnall approached from the other side of the meadow. "We all have much to learn," Fidach added, "not only about the beast and the land and about our fellow creatures . . . but also about ourselves."

It was enough. No more needed be said.

They turned again toward the hawthorn. Arm in arm, with young Domnall at their side, they continued their journey.

Each of the three knew they would not see the great white stag again.

▒ F O U R T E E N ▒

It was beyond midafternoon the following day when the two brothers and the bard's son ascended the final slopes of the mountain known as An Stocbheinn.

It was the highest mountain in the region, and though its peak stood less than four thousand feet above the surface of the Dark Waters, the northern latitude ensured that snow remained on it for nine months of the year. It was a rugged place, extremely rocky, with little vegetation above three thousand feet, and it took no small amount of skill and stamina to conquer its height.

After an early start from the edge of Muigh-bhlaraidh Ecgfrith, the three youths had reached the mountain's base before noon. There they had rested and refreshed themselves before beginning the strenuous and circuitous assault on the summit. Now, breathing hard and perspiring freely, they climbed at last to the peak and paused to gaze around them.

To the north, beyond Tuarie Brora, which ran far below them toward the sea, they could easily descry the three sister lochs, Tri piuthar, which signaled, along with the river, the borders of Kildonanoid. To the west, from their bird's-eye vantage point, they saw spread out below them the low-lying expanse of moorland which steadily ascended toward the range of snow-capped peaks that cradled Loch Bruid. Toward the southwest they gazed down upon the dark green tops of the trees of the forest where dwelt, for the present, the white stag. And toward the southeast they saw, spread out between the two great inland rivers, the gradually descending plain that connected, in a series of hilly intervals and broken by valleys and burns and hollows and glens innumerable, the Dark Waters eastward and the rocky peaks of the snowy highlands to the west.

It was not for the exercise of the climb, however, nor for this magnificent panorama upon which their eyes now feasted, that the brothers had come here. After a pause of several minutes, therefore, they pressed on, passing the summit and moving down around the mountain's northeasterly slope, where under shadowy overhanging ledges the snow piled in high white drifts of twenty and thirty feet in thickness. Their destination was a tiny hidden valley situated perhaps some thousand paces from the lookout point at the peak but only some one or two hundred feet less in elevation.

The glen extended but two hundred feet in length, was perhaps fifty feet wide, and appeared to have been scooped out of the mountainside like a gigantic dish—no doubt the geological work of some icy glacial hand in millennia long past. Its western and northern edges were walls of vertical granite that shot straight up to the peak of An Stoc-bheinn. Thus the flat little hollow on the side of the great mountain was almost completely protected from the blasts of wind that swept down from the highlands to the north and west. Opening toward the south and east, in certain seasons it even boasted here and there some grass and patches of heather. It was the only such place on all the mountain, which otherwise resembled a single gargantuan hunk of granite that had been thrust skyward from the center of the earth during some prehistoric upheaval.

Even now, however, they still had not reached their chosen destination. This scenic and protected glen was not the reason the sons of Caldohnuill's chief had adopted this unknown locale as their second home. What they were seeking was the cave they had discovered when, at sixteen, they had wandered from the peak of An Stoc-bheinn down to the hidden valley for the first time. Since then they had sojourned here at least twice yearly, and had gradually turned the cave into a shelter in which a man might survive comfortably the year round if he so desired.

The cave sat square against the northern cliff of the glen, partially obscured by a ledge that jutted out from the mountain, and thus directly beneath the peak they had just left. Its mouth was not large, and might even at a second glance be easily mistaken for a shadow thrown from the ledge above. Fidach barely cleared the entrance with his head, Cruithne had to stoop slightly to enter, and only one at a time could walk through the opening. Once inside, however, the unpromising entry gave way to a magnificent open, flat-floored hall measuring twelve feet at its narrowest and twenty at its most expansive, with seven to eight feet of clearance above at all points.

When Fidach had years before first wandered inside, he knew even by the dim natural light that he had chanced upon what to a sixteen-year-old lad could be described as nothing other than a veritable paradise. Quickly he had called to his brother, and the two had ignited a hastily assembled fire as quickly as their trembling fingers and beating hearts would allow. As the firelight brightened the cave's interior, they had glanced this way and that, beside themselves with ecstasy, talking and pointing and looking and laughing and shrieking all at once.

They had discovered their own private retreat—from all discernible evidence, known to no human in all the world but themselves!

Animals had apparently been to the place. There was evidence of dried dung. But no creature seemed to have claimed the cave as a permanent dwelling. No odor of recent occupation could be detected.

Immediately on that first visit of discovery, as if by common consent, they had begun preparations to turn the cave into a hospitable dwelling. Before many days were out, the brothers had excitedly hauled as much wood as they could gather from the lower slopes of the mountain and as many chunks of peat as they could cut from the plain beneath, back up to the valley and into the cave, to dry in preparation for their next visit. They kept their fire alive and slept cozily there that first night, envisioning all they could do to make the place more habitable.

Indeed, the cave was rendered even more suitable to their purpose by the presence of two or three fissures in the rock of the roof overhead. These, they concluded, extended all the way to the surface above, for smoke found egress through them. Yet the cracks apparently twisted and turned through the solid granite of the mountain in such a manner as to reach the surface a good distance below the summit, projecting in a downward direction, for never a drop of moisture reached the cave. In the wildest of rainy storms, no matter how furiously the wind swirled, or during the most rapid of snowy thaws, the hole in the mountain remained utterly dry. And whatever the temperature outside, the youths discovered they could quickly heat the place with a peat fire carefully placed so as to induce just the right flowing draft between the door of the cave and the fissures in the ceiling above. After many trials, they had learned the precise spot where a fire would burn hottest, expend the least fuel, and smoke the least.

This was the first visit they had made to the valley of the cave with anyone but themselves. As they entered, young Domnall's exclamations of delight could hardly have been greater than the brothers' inward pleasure, undiminished after more than a dozen visits.

Against one wall stood a great stack of dried, cut peat and pieces of wood, large and small. Fidach gathered a stack of these to assemble a fire. While he worked with the stones and iron and bits of twig and straw to ignite what he hoped would soon be a warm blaze, Cruithne led their awestruck young visitor around in the semidarkness, explaining what he could see in his mind but Domnall could only guess at from the dark shapes.

Within moments, Fidach's nimble and experienced fingers, working in perfect harmony with gentle puffs of his breath, had created from a random momentary spark that most marvelous of man's discovered creations—a barely smoldering single piece of dry grass. It only remained to convert that single stalk into two, then four, until at last suddenly a tiny flame burst forth, igniting a handful of the tinder.

Twigs came next. When they were caught, he added small scrapings of peat dust. The peat gave the infant fire heat and helped larger fragments of broken branches ignite. These in turn provided a slightly elevated cradle upon which to set one- and two-inch chunks of crumbled peat, which, with flames now burning around them and a draft of air flowing from underneath, soon glowed bright orange around their edges. Within ten minutes the fire was secure and had begun to produce both warmth and light within the surrounding enclosure of the earth.

Fidach rose from his knees and joined his companions.

Domnall was still gazing around him with mingled amazement and sheer childish delight.

"But . . . how could you have done all this?" he exclaimed. "There are provisions here for an entire tribe . . . wood . . . peat . . . skins . . . and—is this . . . yes—even food!"

Cruithne and Fidach laughed in unison.

"We come here often," said Fidach. "We must be prepared."

"Prepared . . . for what?"

"One night," Fidach went on, "when we slept in the cave, we awoke in the morning to twelve feet of snow. It had piled up in huge drifts and completely blocked the doorway. Had it not been for our provisions, we would surely have frozen to death. As it was, we stayed for five days, comfortable, warm, and well fed."

"We had not only dried venison," said Cruithne, "but barley and wheat grain, and oat groats."

"All the water we needed we took from the snow," added Fidach. "We had already brought in pots . . . and stone slabs to cook upon."

"We ground grain, mixed it with the snow water," went on Cruithne enthusiastically, "and even put together oatcakes which we baked on hot stones over the fire. That was truly a wonderful visit. We got much work done in the next room."

"The next room!"

Again the brothers laughed.

"Certainly, Domnall, son of Pendalpin," said Fidach with a smile. "You do not think two young men such as we could be satisfied unless we enlarged our mountain home."

He grabbed a pole from where it stood in readiness against one of the cave's walls and thrust one end of it into the blaze.

Clearly intended for that very purpose, the formed mass of peat soaked in boar-fat, clumped and securely attached to the tip of the pole, slowly took the flame onto itself. A moment later Fidach raised his burning torch aloft. "Come, Domnall," he said.

Shadows and light danced intertwining from the two sources of radiant light as Fidach crossed to the far end of the cave. He stooped low, followed by the bard's son, then Cruithne, and led the way into an adjoining chamber about a fourth the size of the larger room. All about were evidences of human labor.

"You see, Domnall," said Cruithne once they were inside, "this room is of our doing."

In truth, almost from the moment they discovered the place, the brothers had conceived the idea of developing it into a more congenial dwelling than a mere highland cave. To it they had carried not only supplies and provisions and necessities for fire making, but also what tools they could spare from the hill-fort. Other tools they had fashioned for themselves out of stone and iron and wood, and for the last six years had lost few opportunities to use them in this remote place on the slopes of An Stoc-bheinn.

Gleann nan uaimh, they called it, valley of the cave. It was their private world under the mountain, and much had they managed to accomplish with the might of their arms and the skill of their hands.

Searching the perimeter of the cave's granite walls, by and by they had discovered that the density of stone was not all uniform. Softer spots they had hollowed into shelves and ledges in the great interior sphere, and even chipped out a low-placed bench that would accommodate two persons. But the greatest discovery of all was the deposit of limestone at the distant end, farthest from the mouth. Once they realized what their tools would accomplish against this softer stone, they were well begun on a second cave inside the first.

This, over the years, had grown into a complete second room, in which they now slept, and which they continued to enlarge at every opportunity. Slowly they excavated the limestone from its depths, carrying the chunks outside and tossing them down, shaping the private chamber as much to their liking as was possible.

"As you can see," said Fidach, "the smoke does not so easily find its way out of the inner cave and must meander back into the big room. But otherwise we find it most comfortable."

"It is wonderful!" sighed Domnall.

"And yours are the first eyes to see it besides ours," added Fidach. "We hope you will come to understand its meaning with us."

"What does it mean, then?" asked the bard's son. "Is it in preparation to hide away during an attack? Are you preparing a raid into Kildonanoid?"

"We will explain everything later, Pendalpin's son," said Cruithne. "First, let us make ourselves comfortable, and prepare the fish and rabbits we were fortunate to kill. We will feast. Then we will hold counsel together."

⬚   F I F T E E N   ⬚

As dusk descended, the three young men gathered what sticks and brush they could find and heaped them up in the middle of the glen.

When all was ready, Cruithne climbed back up to the mouth of the cave, while Fidach and Domnall took positions safely removed from the pile of combustibles.

"This is something my brother always tries," explained Fidach. "He has some notion of the technique's value in times of battle, and he takes the opportunity whenever we come here to perfect it."

"What is he going to do?" asked the bard's son.

"Watch and see," replied Fidach.

Cruithne disappeared inside the cave momentarily, then returned holding a long spear, on whose tip he positioned a burning chunk of peat he had stabbed from the fire. Drawing back his arm, he let it sail. The ball of fire arched through the night from the cliff onto the pile below.

A few flames slowly spread out as Fidach and Domnall cheered. Cruithne scampered back down the hillside and ran to meet them.

"A direct hit!" exclaimed Fidach, "—your most perfect shot yet."

"An unusual way to start a fire," remarked Domnall.

The two brothers laughed.

An hour later the night was dark. A thin moon had risen high in the black sky.

The air was cold, both from the season and the elevation, but was not intolerable. While the small fire of peat continued to warm their sleeping quarters above, the three now sat talking around the blaze that had been ignited below from Cruithne's incendiary lance.

Though the bonfire would be neither a long nor a hot one—for it had been necessary to add to it fuel that was not dry—it served the youths' purpose. Its crackling, hissing flames and dancing patterns of orange light mesmerized the spirit, calling forth many undefined thoughts and feelings as they sat gazing into its depths.

A chance traveler, observing the scene from the top of the cliff above, might have thought to ask himself, "What does it mean? Why do they make such a great fire for none but themselves to see?"

But where the two sons of Taran were concerned, being together was reason enough for such a celebration. There was no greater pleasure. They were two uncommon young men. To say that their mutual affection was ahead of its time would imply that humankind would one day come to understand, perhaps in some future eons distant from this, the joy of putting another above oneself—a prediction perhaps too far-reaching to prophesy concerning any era.

Suffice it, therefore, to affirm that in the midst of and in spite of their differences of personality and temperament, each man cared for the other— if not more than for himself, at least in equal measure. During their younger years they had been playmates of more than orthodox harmony. In their youth they had been comrades in the hunt, companions in discovery, makers of the cave, climbers of the mountains, explorers of the forests. Now, in their young manhood, they had become staunch allies with a mutual concern for what their role would be amongst their people.

It was no secret that Taran's remaining days were few. Neither were they unaware of the bitterness of the dispute over the succession and of how the tongues of the old women of the hill-fort wagged in support of one or the other of their mothers' sons.

Both would readily have relinquished his own right of potential chieftainship in willing service to the other. Both, in fact, had expressed an eagerness to do so. Yet they jointly recognized that more was at stake than the title of chieftain. With Taran's passing would dawn a new era in Caldohnuill. Competition for hunting grounds with neighboring tribes could not but increase. Encroachment by those tribes to the north and the south seemed inevitable.

In this new time, with its new challenges, both Cruithne and Fidach longed to serve their people *together*. They had by degrees arrived at the reciprocal hope that they might lead side by side, with neither as chief preeminent over the other, and thus demonstrate leadership by cooperation and service rather than sovereignty of authority. It was a lofty goal, ambitious with the idealism of youth. It was to open this vision to their young friend, who would one day serve alongside them as bard to their people, that they had brought with them sixteen-year-old Domnall, son of Pendalpin.

The three of them sat silent a long while, and then the melodic voice of Domnall began softly to croon an ancient melody. To the brothers, the sounds seemed almost to come from the fire itself, and the words from out of the very hill surrounding them in darkness.

> Se Coire cheathaich nan aighean siubhlach,
>   An Coire rùnach is ùrar fonn
> Gulurach miad-fheurach, mìngheal, sùghar,
>   Gach lusan fiùar bu chùbh-raidh leam
> Gu molach, dùbhghorm, torrach, luisreagach,
>   Corrach plùranach, dlùghlan grinn.
> Caoin ballach dìtheanach, canach, mìsleanach;
>   Gleann a, mhilltich 's an lìon-mhor mang.
> 'Na ghlugan plumbach air ghoil gun aon-teas,
>   Ach coileach bùirn tigh 'nn a grunnd eas lòm,
> Gach sruthan ùiseal 'na chuailean cùl-ghorm,
>   A ruith 'na spùta 's 'na lùba steall.

> My misty Corrie, haunted by deer,
>   My lovely valley, my verdant glen,
> Soft, rich, and grass, sweetly scented
>   With every flower I love;
> All thickly growing, and brightly blowing.

Upon the sides of its dark green lawn,
Moss, cannach, gowens adorn its mazes,
   Through which lightly skips the graceful fawn.
Thence bubbles boiling, yet coldly coiling
   The newborn stream from the darksome deep;
Clear, blue, and curling, and swiftly swirling,
   It bends and bounds in its headlong leap.

"That was beautiful," commented Fidach when he was through. "As you sang, I imagined the beginnings of the waters of Loch Bruid."

"You are indeed nearly a bard," consented Cruithne. "Your father could not have sung the old ballad with more feeling."

Again silence fell. Each of the three stared into the dancing blaze, their eyes enraptured by its bright movement.

"Nothing so wondrous exists anywhere," murmured Fidach after a long pause in their conversation. "To sit upon a great mountain, breathing the blessed air of the lofty places, with sea and valley and river and gleaming loch spread out below . . ."

"But it is dark," said Domnall. "We can see none of all that."

"Ah, my young friend, after your song I took you for more bard than that. Can you not see everything with the eyes of your imagination? We have beheld all that, and more. We will see it again. With the dawn will visions of everything be renewed! But tonight, just to know it is there fills my soul!"

As if in answer to his words, the orange and red flames flickered and cracked, shooting a shaft of fire up toward the night sky.

"My brother speaks of the marvels of the night," said Cruithne. "But it is of a yet deeper marvel that we want to tell you, Domnall—one of life's hidden mysteries."

His manly voice held an earnestness Domnall had never before heard in it. He waited. The two were his elders and might one day be his chiefs. He would listen for what they would tell him.

"You are young," Cruithne went on. "But it is time you should know of the things that burn in our hearts."

"The mystery," put in Fidach with quiet passion, "lies in a single word—bràithreachas. Brotherhood rather than strife and competition."

"Bràithreachas," repeated Domnall slowly.

"You must not think it is because we happen to be brothers that we speak of brotherhood," Fidach went on. "Our common blood is but a chance of nature. It has allowed us to learn of bonds deeper than blood can ever produce—

the binding of hearts . . . hearts joined by the laying down of preeminence one over another."

"You see," added Cruithne, "Fidach and I were born of different wombs. Our looks are different. I am more muscular and can lift heavier loads. He is slender and can run farther. We are of different personalities. Fidach is a thinker. I am a hunter. Do you see my meaning, Domnall?"

The bard's son laughed. "All in Laoigh know these differences."

"But whereas most men and women strive to gain ascendancy, as even my own mother would do, Fidach and I have come to care more for *each other* than we do for ourselves. Gladly I choose to lay down what is *I* in order that what is *we* may become greater."

"We desire to lead our people as one," said Fidach, "whichever one of us happens to become chief. We will rule together . . . and show our people the power of unity and brotherhood—*aonachd . . . bràithreachas.*"

"There will be no strife between us that cannot be resolved," added Cruithne.

"Only so will tribes and peoples be kept from the feuds which destroy," said Fidach. "Though most do not consider such fighting wrong, they must one day see that it is in harmony that greatness is achieved."

"Ah, the folly of my own mother," sighed Cruithne. "She is consumed by the evils of jealousy and ambition, thinking I must rise above other men so that she can rise above other women. It is a vain aspiration, doomed to end in despair and loneliness. The happiness she seeks cannot live in the blackness of her heart. As for me, to find myself over Fidach would mean my ruin, not my triumph."

"I have heard my father speak of such things," said Domnall, "but why are you telling me all this?"

"For the future, Domnall," answered Cruithne. "For the future of our people, for the future of our land. You must understand the mystery of unity. As bard, you must speak and sing of these things. In story and proverb, you will hold power to sway men's thoughts.

"It is not enough that Fidach and I live as brotherhood, for we too will grow old. We will die and go the way of our father. But the people who come after us must also know what we have learned. They must know for all time. Otherwise they will continue to strive against one another. The land will constantly be divided, brother at war with brother, tribe against tribe, family against family, clan against clan, while all the time there is no joy, no harmony, and our enemies will be easily able to subdue us."

"You speak as a prophet, my brother," said Fidach somberly. "Perhaps more of the second sight is yours than you think."

"I will leave prophecies to you."

"Everything my brother says is true, Domnall," continued Fidach. "Strife within the heart of man is the most lethal of enemies. No enemy from without can vanquish a people who are strong within. With one of us as chief, and the other at his side, and with you as bard, our people can be taught to live this wonderful mystery. It is for the future of the land and our people that we share this with you, and that we now bring you into our *bràithreachas.*"

"You speak of noble things," said Domnall, his voice now solemn. "I am honored that you have taken me into your confidence. I will seek to be worthy of your trust."

The three fell into a thoughtful silence, their eyes fixed on the glowing embers of the dying fire.

It was Cruithne who suddenly broke the solitude after several long minutes.

"I have a thought," he said. "Let us erect a monument . . . *an carragh!* Let us enshrine what we would see among our people with stones pointed toward the sky."

"Yes . . . yes!" replied Fidach excitedly. "Two great pillars, standing strong like two men . . ."

"With a single slab of stone on top stretching across from one to the other," suggested Domnall, catching the vision, "the two pillars becoming united as one."

"Spoken with vision and wisdom!" said Cruithne. "You are indeed a true bard's son."

On they talked, late into the night, after the fire had dwindled to mere dying coals.

When at last the three young men rose and walked slowly up to the cave for the night, their thoughts were full of the undertaking to which they had committed themselves. Their hearts swelled with love for one another. This love that had not been taught them. It had been breathed into their souls by a Power, of whose presence they possessed only faint and broken hints, as of an echo of a far-off song whispering mysterious messages, whose meanings were yet too dim for men to comprehend.

They slept contentedly in their warm shelter, full of dreams for the future of the people they loved.

Five days later, a boy who had climbed to the top of the broch of Laoigh spotted Fidach, Cruithne, and Domnall crossing the valley to the east, approaching their home. Quickly he called to his fellows. The small group of shouting youngsters ran out of the hill-fort moments later to greet the returning travelers.

The three young men had remained two more nights at *gleann nan uaimh* and then had marched down the valley of Sgeulachd toward Laoigh. The entire way they had discussed plans for their monument and the story they would carve in pictures upon the stones.

Fidach argued for a drawing of the stag, to represent the mystical link between man and beast. Cruithne favored the likenesses of men—two, perhaps three, linked arm in arm. In the end they had decided to make use of all the figures, though in what arrangement and configuration they yet had to determine. The stones they would erect on the peak of Beinn Donuill, in view of the hill-fort. They would call the monument *ann an aonachd tha bràithreachas*—"In Unity Is Brotherhood."

The sun was setting behind Loch an Lagain as they strode across the valley and ascended to the hill-fort of Laoigh. Word had quickly spread through the stone houses of the settlement that the sons of the chief had returned, carrying a catch of fish for their father. Before they had walked halfway up the incline, they saw Aethilnon hastening out of the gate and down the path to meet them.

"Hello, Mother!" cried Fidach cheerfully as she approached.

She embraced her son warmly, then Cruithne as well. "So, Domnall," she said, "did you have an adventure?"

"I am certain you would not ask if you did not already know the answer," laughed the youth. "These two are indeed worthy sons of a mighty chieftain!"

Aethilnon's face turned grave.

"Your father is very ill," she said to the two older boys. "I fear his time may be short."

Without awaiting another word, Cruithne and Fidach set out running up the remainder of the hill. "Your father is with him now," added Fidach's mother to Domnall. Then the two of them hurried along after the two sons of the dying chief.

Reaching their stone house, they found Pendalpin seated at Taran's bedside, softly humming an ancient melody. The place was but dimly lit, and the fire had burned low. There was no sign of Eormen.

Aethilnon entered a few moments later. "He collapsed this morning," she said softly. "He has been lying still ever since, breathing thinly. He will take no food or drink. Whenever he wakes, he asks for both of you."

Fidach stooped to one knee and reached out his hand. At the touch upon his shoulder, the old man seemed to know its source. His eyelids lifted slightly. Inside their sockets his eyes searched for sign of some figure before him. He was unable to move his head.

"Is that you, my son?" came the feeble question from his lips.

Realizing that Taran could not see him, Aethilnon motioned to her son. Fidach crept down near his father's feet, where he now came into the old man's line of vision. Taran weakly motioned the others away. Cruithne and Aethilnon immediately turned and walked out of the hut. Pendalpin rose and likewise left, with his son beside him.

When the two were alone, Taran lifted a weary hand toward his eldest son. Fidach came toward him and clasped it firmly in his own.

"My son," came the chief's voice, so weak that Fidach had to lean forward to make out the words, "you will soon be chief."

He paused. His eyes closed once more.

The few words had taxed him. But after a moment he labored on, with many breaks and hesitations. Fidach listened, tears gathering in his eyes.

". . . I have told Pendalpin . . . and . . . elders . . . my wish . . . that you . . ."

Again he stopped, breathing heavily. Fidach waited, his heart aching. He would have tried to persuade him to conserve his ebbing strength, but he knew such imploring would prove useless. His father was discharging a duty with these final words. Nothing would deter him from saying them. Therefore Fidach remained silent, gazing into the old man's pale, wrinkled face with eyes of love that only a faithful son could possess. Patiently he waited for Taran to continue.

"My mother . . . no heir . . . the elders must—"

His voice broke in a fit of coughing. But he struggled to finish.

"—they will decide . . . I have spoken my will to them . . . when you are chief . . . our people . . . serve . . . you must—"

He struggled to continue.

"But . . . but you must . . . you must beware of—"

He could not go on.

"I understand, Father," said Fidach, speaking at last. "If they choose that

I succeed you, I will be faithful to your wishes. I will serve our people as you have done."

Taran nodded, then motioned toward the door with his free hand.

"Cru—" he began.

"I will bring him to you," said Fidach, beginning to rise.

He hesitated, then glanced back toward his father and chief. Suddenly a paroxysm gripped the old man. Fidach felt his own hand squeezed as if pressed between two stones. Quickly he knelt back down and placed his ear close to his father's lips.

The old man was clearly struggling to speak, but only indistinguishable sounds came from deep in his throat.

Fidach felt the grip of Taran's hand go limp.

The next instant he pulled back and sought his father's eyes. The pupils had retreated inside his head. All that met Fidach's gaze was white.

He knew his father was dead.

A moment more he knelt, pressed his lips against the wrinkled forehead, then rose.

Fidach hastened outside. With his eyes and a quick nod of his head toward his brother he made the truth known. Cruithne ran inside to stoop down beside the body of his father and chief.

Fidach embraced his mother, weeping silently.

SEVENTEEN

The sun rose high in a clear sky.

Two days of driving rain had impeded the brothers' progress. Today, however, promised not only brightness again but also warmth. In the smell of the warming earth could be detected hints of the coming summer, whose promise already flowed throughout the land, through roots and stems, stalks and trunks, branches and buds of the shrubs, trees, flowers, and grasses.

It was a fine day to resume work on the stone monument planned first as a symbol of brotherhood—now also to be dedicated as a memorial to the dead chief.

Long had ancient legends surrounded an enormous flat slab near the summit of Beinn Donuill. The hazy stories had been passed down to them when their people settled the area by a few scattered relations now too distant to recognize who still populated the nearby forests. The huge stone, it was even said, overspread the remains of some long forgotten settler to the region. Hints of fragmentary shapes upon it might faintly be detected, mostly worn away by centuries of harsh wind and rain. Fidach had noticed them in his youth and had done his best to find meaning in them. It was obviously the largest stone for miles. But as it could not be moved, and was considered too sacred to mar with inscriptions, the brothers would find smaller stones to commemorate their own father's life.

The day after their return, therefore, Fidach and Cruithne, driven by their common vision but also as a balm for the grief they now shared, had set out to locate stones large enough for their purpose but small enough to be managed with enough men. They had found them high on the far rocky sides of Beinn Donuill. Foundation holes near the summit had been dug to receive them. One of the stones had even been dragged around the crest of the hill to within thirty feet of the site.

Then the rains had come.

But today, with the sun shining down once more, and with every man and boy and half the women of the community ready to help, the two youths—now joint heads of their shared home and the acknowledged leaders of Laoigh, though the final decision of the elders had yet to be made—hoped to have the first stone in place by nightfall.

It would not be an easy task to erect the two upright pillars or to hoist the flat slab atop them. The completion of *ann an aonachd tha bràithreachas* would require every muscle as well as all the technological insight to be found in Laoigh, for the brothers had indeed selected gigantic stones that no ten men could budge. It had taken twenty men, pulling with ropes and with slender logs underneath, to roll, push, pull, haul, and drag the first stone around the uneven mountainside, then up the remaining portion of slope.

The death of the chief, along with the suggestion that *ann an aonachd tha bràithreachas* would be erected partially to memorialize the site of his tomb, had energized the settlement. Fidach and Cruithne knew they would have all the help they needed to complete their task.

Even as the rain had poured down, Fidach had ventured across the plain to Beinn Donuill with his metal chisel, his pounding stone, and other tools, to begin the process of inscribing upon the stones the message of the monument. There were many carvings to make—figures that told not only the story of the stag and the brothers who walked in unity, but also of their father's reign as chief—and they could be more easily begun while the stone lay flat on the ground.

Cruithne joined his brother an hour later with some of the larger implements. The first stone was reasonably flat on one end. But a protruding jut at the top of the other had to be removed to render it useful for their purposes. It was to this task that Cruithne now bent himself. So as Fidach carved and chiseled the beginning outlines of the figure of a stag on the stone lying near the hole, on the other side of the hill, he could hear the dull clanking sounds of his brother's blows against the other.

By midafternoon, wet and cold and with shoulders and arms aching from pounding and hammering against the stubborn granite, Fidach and Cruithne had huddled in their shared home around a fire to which they had just added several large peats. They were shivering, yet their eyes glowed with accomplishment. The beginning outline of a stag had formed under delicate and well-placed blows from Fidach's skillful hand. And the second large stone, where it lay, now possessed a top flat enough to balance the lintel stone securely, with all former bumps and uneven extrusions heaped on the ground beside it. With these beginnings accomplished, they had settled in to await a change in the weather.

It had come. And now, by midday, Fidach and his crew of sixteen men and nearly as many boys had lugged the stone upon which he had already expended so much effort the remaining distance to the site and had positioned its heavier end at an angle next to the foundation hole. That completed, Fidach ordered the boys to stand away. With a heavy line of vine-braided rope encircled around the top of the stone and stretching some distance down the hill in front of it, he and ten of the men grasped it firmly to pull, while the other men bent their shoulders under the stone to push.

At Fidach's signal, the rope stretched taut, and the top of the great stone slowly rose from the ground. Its heavy base pivoted toward the three-foot-deep hole into which it would be sunk.

Slowly it rose.

No sounds could be heard other than the grunts of exertion from the warriors and hunters, now become laborers and builders and movers of stone . . . until at last they began to feel an easing of the load.

As the stone approached the perpendicular, the shifting weight sank with a quiet, sliding thud into the hole. Gradually the uphill pushers and the downhill pullers relaxed.

The stone, though sunk three feet into the earth, yet rose some eight or nine feet above the surface and was perhaps three feet in diameter at its base.

"Easy now!" shouted Fidach. "We mustn't topple it over the other side!"

The pushers stood back, then shifted quickly around to the downhill side. As the wielders of the rope pulled the top its final inches, the others now stretched out hands ready to balance it into place lest it come too far.

At the exact moment that he perceived the stone to be standing at level, Fidach shouted, "Now, boys!"

All the youngsters who had been poised in readiness immediately began hurling rocks and pebbles into the hole around the stone's base to secure it into position. Fidach let go his hold on the rope and joined them, while the other men continued to hold the stone firmly. In a few minutes the void was half filled. The men now relaxed their hold and joined in, refilling the remainder of the foundation hole with stones of all sizes and chunks of the peat and earth that had been dug out to make it. In another ten minutes, with the giant rock pointing toward the sky, secure and immovable, and with a figure about halfway up it that hinted of a stag looking downward from the slopes of Beinn Donuill toward the hill-fort, they stood back and gazed upon their work with a weary but elated satisfaction.

"Well done, men and boys of Laoigh!" said Fidach. "My father would be proud!"

Meanwhile, some fifty yards away, Cruithne and his crew of men labored steadily, inching up the hill from its opposite side with the second giant stone to stand alongside the recently erected obelisk.

"Come, let us help our comrades!" shouted Fidach. He ran across the slope toward his brother.

"You have done well," said Cruithne, pausing to greet Fidach and admire the stone resting silently in its place. "Perhaps now we will be able to move this beast with greater speed. I fear it is too much for these few of us."

"You have already brought it far," said Fidach.

"We have moved it," rejoined Cruithne. "But far . . . I do not think so, my brother!"

Fidach laughed. "In any case, now that the first stone is in place, we will join our efforts on this brute."

"And hopefully drag it the rest of the way before every man in Caldohnuill collapses in exhaustion!"

"The day you collapse in exhaustion, Cruithne, son of Taran," said Fidach, "will be the day all the water dries from the lochs of Caldohnuill! You have more strength than any four men I have ever seen!"

"I am too tired to argue the point," laughed Cruithne. "But I fear we will not be capable of erecting the great slab atop the two pillars, even with every man we have underneath it. Perhaps we will be able to tow it to the site. But to hoist it eight feet in the air will require a hundred men, many stout ropes and timbers, and—"

"All in good time," broke in Fidach. "Perhaps we can journey to Kildonanoid for help. Our neighbors are said to possess knowledge of such things."

He stopped. Neither spoke for a moment.

When Cruithne broke the silence, his tone had grown somber. "I do wish our father could be here to see the united efforts of the people on his behalf."

Fidach sighed. "We must believe that perhaps he does see, and is pleased, though his spirit is gone from us."

As if reminded by the memory of their father of the urgency of the duty at hand, the young men stooped down and stretched their fingers tightly around one of the stout ropes wrapped around the giant stone, and threw it over their shoulders. In silence, each remembering in his own way their dead chief, the men of the settlement all took up their positions, half above the stone, pulling on the dozen ropes wrapped around it, and half below it, shoving with hands and shoulders against the stone itself. With silent consent all renewed their energies, pushing and pulling upward, inch by tedious inch, over the four wooden poles that rolled beneath it on the ground.

By nightfall the job was done.

With aching limbs, hands swelled and in many places raw, and legs scarcely able to support their spent frames, the men and boys stumbled back to the hill-fort. Most crawled home to their suppers and beds. But Fidach and Cruithne headed together for the broch and slowly climbed the steps to its top. When they reached its height, they leaned against its parapet wall.

"This climb has never been such a long one to these legs of mine," sighed Fidach.

"Nor to mine," agreed Cruithne. "I think we will not accomplish more labor for several days."

"The lintel slab may have to wait, as you say, perhaps for help from one of the tribes of the Kildonanoid."

"We can rejoice, at least, that it is not so far away as the others. Yet even the hauling of it must wait. We must have rest, and there are yet things to do concerning our father."

"But look . . . our labors have not been in vain," sighed Fidach, pointing toward Beinn Donuill.

There they could see, in the descending dusk, the two giant columns of stone pointing upward into the night sky.

"I hope our father is pleased," he added.

"I am sure of it," said Cruithne. "Through our efforts, he will be remembered. Whatever the meaning of the great slab nearby, it has already been forgotten. But our monument will stand forever. The people of the future must remember the legacy of Taran, son of Cuthred. And they will remember as well what we, the sons of Taran have learned. Through us, our father's legacy will be one of brotherhood."

"They will remember! We will inscribe the stones to depict the vital message. Your beginning of the stag is well done. We will not allow them to forget."

"If the elders do make me chief," said Fidach, "as Pendalpin says they will, you will rule with me . . . alongside me. It will be my first command."

"It will be my joy to serve you, my brother," said Cruithne.

As silence again fell between them, the two brothers continued to gaze out into the dusk toward the mountain known as Beinn Donuill. Then their eyes looked out slowly around in all directions over the land, now their domain as sons of Taran, known as Caldohnuill.

After a few minutes more, Fidach turned and threw his arm about his brother's shoulder. The two ambled slowly, to the extent that their sore and weary legs would tolerate, back down the circular stairway of the broch toward their mutual home, where they would pass a much-needed night of sound and dreamless sleep.

EIGHTEEN

The aches in the arms and legs of the men of Laoigh had not entirely disappeared, though Fidach had used the intervening days to make further progress on his stone etchings, when three men from the north appeared.

They came from the plains across Aethbran nan Bronait. If further identification than the direction of their march were necessary, the deep-blue tattooed reindeer on the open chest of the one and the wolves on the other two easily marked the visitors as coming from one of the friendly tribes in Kildonanoid. On their shoulders, two of the men carried the ends of a stout pole, from which dangled a dead boar.

The children playing outside the encampment saw them first. With shrill shouts, they carried the news swiftly up to the hill-fort.

Cruithne's mother was first to leave the gate. She descended a third of the way down the hill, stopped as if to peer more closely toward the approaching men, then turned back to shout at several women who had gathered about the entrance to the fort.

"They are of my old people!" Eormen shouted with apparent joy, then hastened down to meet the strangers.

When she returned with them several minutes later, a crowd had gathered in welcome, including Cruithne, Pendalpin, and several men of the community.

"These are cousins of my grandmother's folk!" said Eormen in high spirits.

"The news of the loss of your chief traveled quickly to us," said one of the men with grave countenance. "We have come in peace, bearing a gift in memory of the old warrior, and to pay our respects to his wife and clan."

"Wives," corrected Cruithne.

His mother shot a glance in his direction, but did not allow her face to lose its composure.

"You are most welcome in Laoigh," he added. "We mourn yet for my father. But we do not despair in our grief, but remember him as he was. We mourn by erecting a monument to his memory, with which perhaps you may help."

"Gladly," replied one of the visitors.

"We will show you the monument tomorrow. Today, however, you must rest from your journey. Come."

Cruithne led them inside the encampment. "Surrender your burden to our women," he said. "They will take it to Uurcell to begin preparations to roast it."

"No, please," replied the man hastily. "We come to honor Taran and his people. We will roast the pig ourselves. If you will simply show us where we might be comfortable, we will rest for a brief while and then begin our work for the feast."

"You are most generous."

"It is only unfortunate your father could not be among us."

"He enjoyed nothing like fresh boar," replied Eormen kindly. "All of Caldohnuill feels his loss sorely."

"We grieve with you, my cousin."

"I must tell my brother of your arrival," said Cruithne. He turned to go.

"Your brother?" inquired one of the strangers with raised eyebrow.

"Yes," replied Cruithne. "My older brother and Taran's eldest son, who will soon be chief in Laoigh."

"We must meet him."

"You will. I shall bring him."

"I will see to their comfort, my son," said Eormen. "The small dun at the foot of the trail should suit them. They can roast the boar in the pit beside the broch."

Cruithne nodded, then strode away, in high spirits to see his mother with a smile on her face. Eormen took their guests back outside the wall and partway down the hill on the side opposite of that from which they had come. They carried the heavy boar as they went, the four speaking quietly amongst themselves.

They were still speaking in hushed tones ten minutes later when Cruithne again approached, this time with Fidach at his side. Eormen saw them coming.

"Son of my husband," she said, glancing up at Fidach with a smile such as she had never before bestowed on him. "Come, offer a hand of welcome to our guests, my people from the north!"

She walked toward him and greeted him with a kiss on the cheek, then turned back to her cousins. "This is he of whom I spoke," she said with enthusiasm, "the dear friend of my own son."

Fidach came forward smiling. He welcomed the three once more and again offered help with the boar, which again they declined.

Cruithne said nothing. By now he had come to observe the proceedings and his mother's ebullient spirit with a cautious and unsettled eye.

The following afternoon Cruithne and Fidach—with the boys and girls of the hill-fort running after them with spirited shouts—took the three Kildonanoid visitors out to *ann an aonachd tha bràithreachas* on the slopes of Beinn Donuill. With the help of the other men, they had been struggling to haul the great flat slab of stone down from Donuill's summit to the site of the monument. Only a few hours before, that very morning, they had succeeded in lugging and pulling it the final twenty feet, and now the slab lay at an angle, partially leaning against one of the two upright stones.

"We understand that you of the north have constructed such monuments," said Cruithne. "We hoped perhaps you would be able to enlighten us concerning your methods of hoisting giant stones into the air. As you see, we have progressed as far as the mere strength of man will allow."

The strangers glanced at one another for a moment.

"Uh . . . yes," replied one, "there have indeed been such standing pillars and slabs raised in Kildonanoid."

"You will help us then?" said Fidach expectantly.

"Let us consider the task tomorrow. Shortly we feast on roast boar. Tonight we will listen to the songs that tell of your people. Tomorrow we will bend our minds to the task you have set for us."

The five began the return walk down Beinn Donuill toward the hill-fort. Fidach turned and glanced back at the two pillars raised high, with the nearly completed tomb of his father beside it.

How fitting, thought Fidach to himself, *that the very symbol of brotherhood should be completed with the aid of men from a neighboring tribe— related by blood, and working with us in harmony.*

With a smile of satisfaction, he turned and continued on with the others. Smoke already rose from the burning pit beside the giant broch. The aroma of roasting boar hung pleasingly in the air.

The night was late after the feast when Fidach and Cruithne approached their stone home together. Had their father been alive, they would have been laughing. As it was, the sound of Pendalpin's melancholy voice echoed through their brains, along with thoughts of their father. Their spirits thus remained, though quietly joyful, yet subdued in the loss of one they both had loved since earliest memory.

In the darkness they heard the gentle breathing from where Aethilnon lay sleeping peacefully.

The brothers clasped hands silently in brief farewell for the night, then each went to his own room. Fidach lay down near his mother and was soon lost in deep slumber. Cruithne lay down upon his skins, wondering where his own mother might be. He had not seen her around the fire earlier.

Sleep for Taran's younger son did not come so quickly.

When it did arrive, it was fitful and troubled.

❈   N I N E T E E N   ❈

Cruithne half woke to dreamy, confused impressions in his sleep-dulled consciousness—images of stone and reindeer, of boars and wolves, of a great stag, and of a danger he could feel but not see. His spear was raised in readiness, but he could not find the enemy. His brother was in danger! The tip of his javelin was poised to protect Fidach from the attack. But from what direction would it come?

Wolves! How could he, with a single spear, keep the whole pack from Fidach!

Shivers of fear tingled through his chest. The wolves were silent. No sound betrayed their whereabouts. They crept ever closer. But try as he might, he could not detect their movements, nor their position!

His body trembled. He turned over on the hard floor, becoming gradually more alert.

The vague light of predawn had begun faintly to gray the sky. Dreams still swirled through his head. It was cold. The fire had burned low.

Whispers of haste sounded somewhere close.

Cruithne tried to open his eyes. His mother was speaking near his face, but he could scarcely make out her words, nor the features of her agitated countenance.

"My son . . . come," she was saying. "There is danger." Her voice was soft but urgent.

He shook himself into semiwakefulness.

"You must rise and come," she insisted.

"Why, Mother?" he tried to respond. His voice remained full of sleep.

"Shh . . . quiet, my son," she replied, placing an imperative hand upon his mouth. "You must rise, I tell you, and come. I fear they will desecrate your father's crypt!"

In an instant Cruithne sat up, coming alert. "Who, Mother—what is this desecration you speak of?"

"I do not know," Eormen whispered. "Strangers . . . enemies. I see men across the plain approaching Donuill."

"How many?"

"Two . . . perhaps three. It is yet dark."

"We will drive them off," he said, rising to his feet. "I will awaken Fidach."

"No, no, my son! Let him sleep. There is no need. You are easily able for the task."

Still suffering from what remnants of sleep clung to his brain, Cruithne did not pause to question her words. He grabbed his iron-tipped spear as he sprang from bed and hastened outside. He ran to the wall, peered through the haze of the gray dawn across the plain to the northwest. But he could distinguish no movement in the valley or beyond it.

Still without questioning, only fearing for his father's remains, he ran for the gate and sprinted down the hill toward Beinn Donuill.

Meanwhile, Eormen, too, had left the stone enclosure to follow her son. She moved with stealthy step, watching his movements, remaining behind the walls of stone that were as hard, cold, and impenetrable as her heart.

She wanted only to see, not be seen.

The moment Cruithne was safely out of the enclosure of the hill-fort, she hastened to the opposite end of the perimeter wall, out a narrow opening, and down the hill toward the dun where her guests of treason were waiting.

"Come quickly!" she called as she approached. "The moment is ripe! My son is away. Strike while you can. He will return in less than ten minutes."

The woman's cousin, prepared for the summons, emerged from the stone dun.

"Come . . . come, you fool!" she urged. "Make haste! I will go, even now, to fetch your silver. You have only to—"

She was interrupted by a scornful laugh.

"Ha! ha! ha! What have you to give us? We will *take* all your silver, and everything else we want from Laoigh!"

The other two visitors from Rossbidalich emerged into the morning air. They were followed by three more, then six. Their open chests were bare of skins and still revealed the temporary markings of friendship. But twining up upon their shoulders from behind could now be seen the hideous snakelike tattoos of the enemies of Laoigh. Suddenly the look of urgency on Eormen's face turned ashen with the horror of betrayal.

"What. . .?" she stammered angrily, but with an uncertain premonition in her tone. "Who are all these?" As she spoke she backed slowly away. She did not like the leering looks on the faces all now turned upon her.

"The plans have changed, my vile cousin," said their leader. "Your feeble husband did not have the courtesy to wait for us to slit his throat. What did you do, decide to retain the pleasure for yourself and slip poison into his brew?"

"What has my husband to do with today?" Eormen spat. "I brought you here on another mission."

"You brought us!" he rejoined with derision. "You thin-brained old crone! Do you not think us capable of coming and going where we choose?"

"I sought counsel with you."

"And now, as I said, the plans have changed. You can see we have brought with us many warriors of the Roismaeatae."

"What need have you for warriors? There is but one I have told you to kill."

"You shall give us no orders! Now, begone, old hag! It may be that I will allow you to live—but only if you stay out of my sight."

With the fire of hatred in her eyes, Eormen spun around and ran back up the hill. As she entered the compound, she cast a hasty look behind her. Already her cousin had left the dun and was walking after her, followed by no fewer than eight of his companions. In their eyes gleamed a lust for conquest. In their hands they bore cold iron knives and murderous swords.

Now observing the shadowy forms of a dozen or more warriors rising from their hiding places on the plain south of the broch, Eormen raced back to her dwelling, which had given such life to the settlement but would from this day forward breathe life no more. The whole tribe of the Roismaeatae was upon them!

There was still time, she thought frantically, to succeed in her plan! She would slay the interloping fools by her own hand, then rouse the wrath of her son against the foul invaders. He would kill them all with the might of his sword, thinking it was they who killed his brother! Then everything would be as she had dreamed!

Blindly she stumbled into the darkened hut and squinted until her eyes caught the glint of the chief's long sharp hunting dagger. With trembling hand she clutched it tightly, then groped her way into Aethilnon's enclosure.

It required but a moment to end for all time the rivalry for her husband's affections and her own position of power. She shivered involuntarily as the blood from the neck of Taran's first wife spurted warm onto her murderous hand, then drenched the dead woman's sleeping robe before soaking into the dirt below. Aethilnon made scarcely a sound, only a momentary choking, then it was over.

In feverish haste, Eormen moved toward her son's brother and friend, her hands quivering now in demonic abandon. Fidach stirred at her approach and opened his eyes.

As he saw the mother of his brother bending over him, Fidach's face filled with a smile of kindness.

"Eormen," he said, reaching out his hand to greet her. "What is—" he began to ask.

They were the last words to leave his lips.

A look of such hatred as Fidach had never seen suddenly consumed the old woman's eyes.

"You baseborn usurper!" she spat.

With one swift thrust of her old but still-powerful arm, she plunged the long blade deep into his chest and directly through his heart.

Fidach's body slumped back, the knife of his father still protruding from the gushing wound. Within seconds he was dead.

Eormen rose, barely conscious of the blood upon her hands and arms. Shuddering with evil madness, she staggered into the cold morning air. All around her were the sounds of looting and slaughter. She made for the gate which led toward Donuill.

Cruithne was barely halfway across the plain toward the mountain when he heard the sounds of massacre behind him. He looked behind him. In the distance he saw a figure dash out of one of the duns outside the stone wall, followed by a large man who cut the screaming woman down with his sword, then ran back up the hill in search of further victims.

In an agony of dreadful foreboding, Cruithne now turned and raced back the way he had come, already fearing he would be too late. Screams and moans and shrieks of terror filled the air.

Halfway up the hill, Cruithne saw his mother emerge from the gate toward him.

"My son . . . my son!" she called. A horrible look of triumph lit her eyes. "Drive them away and you will be chief, the greatest man in all Caldohnuill!"

"Mother, what has happened?"

"All is well, my son!" she answered. "Swing your sword about, and they will all flee before you!"

"But . . . but, Mother," stuttered Cruithne, at last beginning to divine the grisly truth, ". . . what is this . . . blood on your hands?"

"It is the blood of conquest, my son!" she cried. "The blood of victory! We have won, do you not see the truth? You are now the chief!"

"I seek not to be chief!"

"But it is our destiny!"

"I must go to Fidach," he said, pushing his way past her. "I must fight with my people against this enemy that has come into our camp!"

"Fidach is dead—don't you understand!" she yelled behind him. "Now there is only you!"

Cruithne spun around. A stricken look of chilling horror spread across his face.

He stared for a moment at the woman who stood before him, with the sickening sound of her hideous laughter ringing in his ears. Now, in truth, she did feel the passion of the chief in his eyes as he bore down upon her. Some stab of inner cognition told her that he would never again, from this moment forth, be her son.

"What is this evil you speak?" he said slowly. "What have you done, you cursed viper?"

"What I have done, I did for you, my son," she whimpered.

"For me!" he thundered.

But even as the words roared from his throat, with them came a mournful wail of despair. "You have destroyed the most important thing in all the world to me! You have taken my heart's desire—to serve my brother as chief. And you would do such *for me?*"

Again a pitiful shriek burst from his lips. Hot tears of bitterness gushed from his eyes.

In vain Eormen tried to cling to him. But he shoved her away. She fell to the ground. Cruithne hastened weeping toward the encampment.

As he attempted to enter the gate, suddenly young Domnall burst through and ran headlong into him.

"Come, Cruithne!" he yelled. He grabbed at the older man's arm to prevent his going farther.

"I must find Fidach . . . Aethilnon . . . we must save our people," mumbled Cruithne in a daze. He scarcely recognized the son of the bard.

"No, Cruithne," insisted Domnall. "It is too late. They are dead. The stench of treachery is among us. Death is all about! It is you and me they now seek. Come . . . we must flee!"

"Pendalpin . . . we must go to—"

"My father is dead! Many are dead! Our only hope is to escape ourselves, then find what others of our people have been able to flee to safety."

Still Cruithne stood in shock, gazing impotently about him. He listened to the sounds of his people screaming as they ran down the hill away from the plundering swords.

"Come . . . come, I tell you!" begged Domnall, tugging at his arm. "We will go to *gleann nan uaimh!* There we can hide in safety—then come back another day!"

Bewildered and stunned, Cruithne followed his young friend, whom the wicked betrayal had suddenly elevated to bard of his clan.

As they ran down the hillside, Eormen attempted to stop them.

"My son . . . my son!" she pleaded. "You are chief now. They will not harm you. I will give them silver! Come back . . . come back, my son!"

Not heeding her cries, they ran down the hill and across the plain toward the river of Aethbran nan Bronait.

They did not see, and neither did Eormen, the approach behind her of the man she had disdained to call her cousin. Slowly down the hill he came, huge knife drawn in readiness, to where she stood calling pathetically after her son.

While the ruthless leader of the Roismaeatae completed that portion of his task he had most eagerly anticipated, the new young chief and younger bard of the Pritenae of Caldohnuill ran from immediate harm.

They would gather what remained of their people. They would repopulate the region. And they would make of Caldohnuill both a land and a people to be remembered for all time.

Today as they fled, however, there were no thoughts of the future.

Cruithne only glanced back once, pausing before the eastern face of Beinn Donuill. With aching longing for the brother with whom he had dreamed of completing it, he gazed at the unfinished monument of *ann an aonachd tha bràithreachas.*

An urgent tug from Domnall's hand came to his arm. Unwillingly, and with wet stinging eyes, he who would become the father of the Caledonii turned and staggered away behind the fleeing feet of the young bard.

8

LEADER OF THE LIBERAL DEMOCRATS

Andrew Trentham set down the great book on his lap and glanced at his watch. The hands showed a little after two-thirty. He had been sitting absorbed in the old tale for more than three hours! Duncan had gone to bed hours ago.

It was too late now to make an attempt for home. He would do as Duncan had suggested and curl up on the couch under several of the old plaids.

The names of the ancient tribes and clans themselves contained such unexplorable mysteries . . . *Borestii, Maeatae, Pritenae, Scothui* . . .

The mere whispered sound of the old Celtic words on his lips sent a shivering tremble of filial affinity through his body.

He opened the book again and flipped through the oversized pages to the story he had read a week ago. He remembered something . . . there it was—

. . . nonetheless did the Wanderer's blood flow throughout all the branches large and small that went to make up this surging tide of human occupation.

Now he scanned again through the story he had just read, locating another passage.

The wild blood of Taran's Celtic stock ran hot . . . other tribes were pushing ever closer . . . sharers of their own primal Celtic blood . . . that blood had been so intermingled as to seal the brotherhood of these peoples for all time. . . .

Was the idea too far-reaching that these might be narratives not only of the beginnings of this northern region of Britain, but the beginnings of his *own* family tree as well?

Andrew's eyes began to grow heavy. He reached across to the couch and pulled a tartan blanket toward him. He draped it unceremoniously across shoulders and knees. As consciousness slowly faded, his visions of the old adventurer and the two brothers began to mingle with his own dreams.

As sleep overtook him, unsettling sensations began to gather about the scene of the two ancient brothers on the overlook to their private loch and falls. But the scene was no longer a happy one.

The faces slowly changed.

It was he and Lindsay now, not the brothers of the story . . . they were playing, running toward their own clifflike vista . . . laughter, a summer romp over the fields. Suddenly Lindsay slipped . . . now his sister was falling, her head hitting against a stone . . . his own mouth opened wide to scream after her, but no sound came out . . . the silent splash into the lake below . . . now he was running, running, his clothes wet, tears streaming down his face, panic and fear and guilt seizing his heart . . .

Suddenly with a jerk Andrew awoke.

He drew in a deep sigh of relief, then another, glancing about Duncan's silent cottage trying to collect himself, remembering where he was. He pulled the blanket more tightly around him and after some minutes began to doze again. The nightmare did not revisit him.

Before Andrew was even well asleep again, the new image of an intrepid pilgrim came into view in the scene of his mind's eye. While dressed in skins and carrying a long, crudely made spear as he ran across a vast moor of obviously Highland locale, this new adventurer bore a striking resemblance to one who would one day represent the north of England in the Parliament of Westminster. He sped over the ground bare of foot, eyes aflame with purpose, and suddenly was standing not on open heath, but on a concrete corner before the Houses of Parliament. All around passersby and reporters clamored toward him, taking pictures and thrusting microphones in front of him. But the only sound to emerge from his lips was in an ancient and long-forgotten tongue that none could understand.

Now boldly he walked past the guards and toward the doors of the great modern Palace of Westminster, and a great hush descended upon the city in anticipation of what would happen. But gradually the images faded, and dreamless sleep followed. . . .

It was thus that Duncan MacRanald found his young friend five hours later, head slumped back, open book still in his lap under the colorful wrap, sound asleep and dreaming of the ancient beginnings of a people he was already beginning to call his own.

❈   T W O   ❈

Andrew awoke a little before eight to a blazing fire. To one side hung the small black cast-iron kettle with steam pouring out its top in anticipation of its coming duty in the matter of the tea.

"Weel, laddie!" exclaimed the old Scotsman, approaching him from behind the moment he saw his young guest rousing, "'Tis plain t' see ye slept sound enouch!"

"Very well indeed, I am happy to say," laughed Andrew. "After I finally fell asleep sometime in the middle of the night!"

"Ye'll be thirsty fer a drap o' tea, nae doobt," said Duncan, swinging the kettle toward him out of the fire. "I've already seen t' yer mare in my wee barn. She was a mite hungry, but none the worse fer her night away frae hame. She's breakfasting on oats."

"Thank you," said Andrew.

He threw the blanket from his chest and discovered there the book still open where he had left it. Setting it aside, he stood and stretched to shake off the remnants of drowsiness and make himself ready for the day.

Snow had indeed fallen that night, to a thickness of about six inches. When Andrew opened the door and took a few steps out, the sight greeting him was of a winter fairyland. The clouds had journeyed south with the storm, and a brilliant cold sun was just beginning its climb up the sky in the east. The first arrows of its light shot across the glimmering surface as if igniting a million frozen water-jewels into tiny crystals of light that shot in every direction.

The dazzling white blanket spread out silently in all directions, broken only by wintry trees whose thin branches did their best to retain their thin white treasures as long as possible, and by the stone dikes, white-topped but gray-edged, that meandered throughout the countryside. All nature save the sun seemed dead under the white sheet. Yet how could it be dead, for the life contained deep inside the earth cannot be killed, any more than can the inner life of the men and women who inhabit it. In truth, even now, frozen though it was, *life* was in that earth—awaiting fresh opportunity for resurrection.

Andrew took in the sight with relish.

As he stood at Duncan's door, the keen air sent the warm blood to his cheeks. Immediately his heart began to beat more rapidly. But he would have to get back home before long, he told himself. There were things to attend to.

Alas, his duties in London beckoned. He must be back on Monday morning.

▒▒▒   T H R E E   ▒▒▒

The darkened atmosphere of the Knightsbridge pub was noticeably more subdued than it had been upon the evening when the same six men had gathered some weeks earlier.

The intent of this gathering was ostensibly to mourn a fellow parliamentarian. Beneath the somber tones and lugubrious comments, however, a discerning eye might have detected here and there a twinkle of repressed gaiety. Their sympathy was genuine. Yet it could hardly be denied that the honorable gentleman's death, shocking though it was, could have the effect of advancing their cause.

The Glenfiddich tonight flowed somewhat freely from its slender green neck into the crystal tumblers throughout the room, and from the latter into the mouths of the assembled Scots politicians, gradually igniting the orbal fires and loosening the tongues of those thus gathered.

"To Hamilton!" toasted Glaswegian Lachan Ross for probably the fourth time. It was the simplest and quickest method to justify sending repeated swallows of his favorite evening fare down his throat, and thirst was not lacking for the barley brew.

"Hear, hear!" came two or three sober rejoinders, followed by the sound of chinking glass.

It was silent a moment. At length the stillness was broken by the beginnings of a muted chuckle. Then, as if that had been a spark set to dormant flame, several more deep-throated murmurs of humorous response began to sound softly. When they gathered just after the election, their elation over its outcome had been tempered by the knowledge that their true goal was far from realized. Now suddenly the opportunity they had long dreamed of seemed at hand—the chance to push forward their agenda with a reasonable promise of success.

"I told you all before," said their leader, "that if we awaited events, a critical moment would come. Not that I would have wished for it to arrive in such a manner. But as it has happened, we would be foolish not to make the best of it."

"Your gambit has obviously succeeded, Dugald," Gregor Buchanan said to MacKinnon. "I didn't believe it would, but the campaigning of *our* people for *their* candidates in the election five years ago certainly played a role in Labour's strong victory and got devolution on their manifesto. And they know well that, had it not been for our support, they may have lost this recent contest."

"I didn't think it would help," said one Archibald Macphersen. "I was certain the prime minister included it merely to get Scotland's vote and our support."

"Oh, I have not the slightest doubt, Macphersen, that you precisely represent the good Mr. Barraclough's intent," laughed MacKinnon. "Both parties have been playing that game since Mr. Major's passionate speech about returning the Stone in July of '96. But we will not let the prime minister forget our role in his coalition. And now perhaps the time has arrived to remind him that we are a constituency whose needs he must continue to address."

"Twenty-one seats in six hundred fifty-nine hardly gives ground for us to remove our offices to Edinburgh along with our Scots' parliamentary colleagues just yet," commented William Campbell, bringing a note of dubious realism to the discussion.

"True enough," rejoined MacKinnon. "But I would not have gone to Barraclough before the elections with, shall we say, my proposed *bargain*, if I did not think it a gamble unquestionably worth taking. I would assume that you, Campbell, with the dark history surrounding your name, would not be one to flinch in the face of great odds."

"It is not the odds that worry me," responded Campbell, ignoring the sly dig at his heritage, "but the practicality of our efforts. So I ask you, MacKinnon, what do you actually propose to do now?"

"As I promised him, we have been faithful on every issue. We have been, for all intents and purposes, Socialists ourselves. We have given Richard Bar-raclough our complete support."

"Well and good, Dugald," pressed Campbell again. "But what *now?*"

"I believe Hamilton's death gives us the opportunity to press him further."

"Press him?" repeated Campbell.

"By threatening to withdraw our support."

"He could carry the coalition without us by keeping the alliance."

"LibDem support may change—don't forget that. The prime minister may not be able to count on it so automatically now, with Reardon at the helm of the Liberal Democrats. I have the feeling the threat of a *No* vote from us may make Barraclough consider bringing full home rule onto the agenda. He will not be at all eager to lose us right now."

"As much as he has tried to curry Scotland's favor, he still views Scottish issues as fringe matters," remarked Buchanan.

"And he is mistaken," rejoined the Scottish Nationalist leader. "He will underestimate the power of yet greater sovereignty to capture the imagination of our people. As I have said, devolution is but the tip of an iceberg that neither Labour nor the Tories fully see. Wales may be satisfied with a regional parliament. But I for one am not satisfied with such for Scotland's future. And neither, I suspect, are most of us."

"Sounds to me as if you like to attempt the impossible," remarked Archibald Macpherson.

"Our cause has been viewed as impossible since the National Party was formed in 1928," replied MacKinnon. "Yet look how far the movement has come in that time. We had one MP in Parliament in 1970, and by 1983 only two. The referenda of 1979 and 1997 had their effect, each in its own way. Now there are twenty-one of us, devolution has come about, Scotland has her parliament. Many of us would have termed *that* impossible even ten years ago.

"I tell you," he went on, "what we have seen is only the beginning. These are but the first steps in the complete eventual reversal of 1707."

A long pause followed as his colleagues reflected on MacKinnon's stirring words.

"By the by," said Macphersen, "do we know any more on the cause of Eagon's death? I worry about a backlash in our direction, especially if we move too soon."

"I wouldn't concern yourself," replied MacKinnon. "Nothing about the affair can point toward us."

"I'm not so certain. The way the Yard still suspects us in the Abbey theft . . . I don't know, I think they'll see a connection. Especially in that if we move too quickly we may be seen to benefit from his death."

"We haven't had the slightest connection with Hamilton," remarked Buchanan. "Our hands are clean."

A brief discussion ran round the room.

"I said an opportunity would come," said MacKinnon at length. "It would appear that moment is now at hand, though it has arrived much differently than anticipated. It now appears that our best chance for influence may lie not so much with the prime minister, but with whomever the Liberal Democrats choose as the new leader of their party."

The only man who had not spoken, and who indeed had remained uncharacteristically silent throughout the exchange, was the Deputy Leader of the Scottish Nationalist Party, Baen Ferguson.

⊠ F O U R ⊠

It was midmorning by the time Andrew finished breakfast, saddled Hertha, and swung into the saddle for the ride back from Duncan's cottage.

The sun had risen high by then and actually felt warm beating down on his bundled shoulders. It had not even begun to thaw the snow from last night's fall—that would take a week or two, if more did not descend in the meantime. But it was a spectacularly gorgeous day, notwithstanding cold hands and feet, to ride across the virgin blanket of white and to let his thoughts wander where they would.

It didn't take long for the story he had read the night before to float to the top of his mind—and with it, the recent death of his party's leader. He could not avoid seeing a parallel between the two. As he considered it, he found his own opinion gradually tilting toward some unknown political motivation in the unsolved case. What else could it be? he thought as he rode. It wasn't just the ancients who could go to such lengths to further a cause.

Neither had he forgotten the dream that had haunted him in the middle of the night. And now, as the mare picked her way across the rocky fell, he realized he needed to stop at the overlook again—to attempt once more to come to some kind of terms with what had happened there.

It was strange how snow could change the look of a place, he thought when he finally stood again at the spot where the path dropped off over the lake. The covering of white seemed to soften the edges of the landscape, transforming it into something both familiar and strange. He brushed the cold powder from the rock he had used as a seat countless times, then sat down and stared out over the expanse of cold water below. He could almost hear Cruithne, Fidach, and the bard's son Domnall laughing and crying out in glee as they dove into the pool from high above the Falls of Bruid.

But then other cries intruded into the ears of his memory, replacing the cries of happy adventure with sounds of terror. He knew well enough that the silent sounds in his mind came from his own mouth, for he had relived the incident over and over since that fateful morning.

It had been warm, a magnificent day of high summer. The sun had shone as brightly as today, but the hillsides had been green with the fragrance of moist and vibrant growth.

He and Lindsay had tethered their horses some way down the slope and had run and laughed their way up to the overlook. His sixteen-year-old sister had been in a gay mood, full of frolic and fun and spirited teasing.

She was always good to him in ways that many an older sister would not have been to one so young in her eyes. When they rode and romped together, though she was six years his senior, she treated him as an equal and a friend. She taught him to ride, to swim, to recognize plants and flowers, and let him accompany her on many youthful adventures in the hills around their home.

They had visited the overlook many times before. Though steep, it was actually not as dangerous as it appeared, for after the first drop-off the ground gave way in a succession of naturally terraced ridges rather than a single sheer plunge. But two days of rain had drenched the district, and on that particular day the earth was soft and soggy, the footing not the best.

They reached the favorite spot and plopped down to enjoy the view of gulls and water. But the sun and warmth and ride made Lindsay giddy and carefree. Too carefree. The next instant she was scrambling over the edge, stretching her legs down to the ledge about four feet below the top.

"Lindsay, don't go down there!" cried Andrew in his high ten-year-old voice as he ran up a few seconds after her and saw what she was doing.

"But look—there's a wild lily. They smell just lovely, and I haven't seen one all year."

"But it's too close to the edge."

"Look, I'm down already," she said gaily, turning to stoop toward her prize.

"Be careful!"

But now Andrew's sister was down on her knee, reaching past the ledge amongst a loose collection of stones for the little yellow-and-white bloom as her brother watched in terror.

She tried to draw close to it. But her toe shoved through a soggy bit of sod near the edge of the supporting ledge.

It gave way. She gave a little scream and slipped. One of her legs dangled over the side.

"Lindsay!" cried Andrew.

All thought of the blossom was immediately gone. His sister finally realized her danger. Frantically she clutched at the thick grass and tried to pull herself back onto solid ground. But it was wet and loose. If she pulled too hard, it too would give way.

"Help me, Andrew," she said. Her voice was quiet and full of controlled fear. "See if you can reach down and get hold of my hand."

On his knees now Andrew stretched down over the top edge as far as he dared. She reached up. Just as their hands met, Lindsay shifted her weight for one more upward thrust. The clump of grass in her left hand pulled loose.

She tumbled from the ledge with a scream.

"*A-n-d-r-e-w!*" sounded the wail of her voice in his boyish ears.

He watched in horror as she bumped and fell, crashing and twisting helplessly against the rocky face of the steepening slope. At last came a splash in the black water below.

Andrew looked down where she had fallen. But the shoreline was obscured from his sight. No more sounds came from below.

Already he was running back for the horses as fast as he could. He leapt onto his mount and in seconds was galloping at full speed along the trail that led the long way around down to the lake. Miraculously the horse didn't stumble as he urged it down the slope. Three minutes later he dismounted. The water of the surface was slowly calming from the disturbance. He found himself praying it had been caused by some rock her fall had set to tumbling.

"Lindsay!" he screamed. "Lindsay . . . where are you?"

Nothing but silence met his ears.

Frantically he ran about the water's edge. He came to the spot of impact. From the disturbed bank and traces of mud in the water, he knew that more than a mere stone had fallen into the lake.

He didn't think to tear off his clothes but dived in. He struggled below the surface and felt about. His hands reached the bottom. But he felt only mud. Kicking and thrashing violently, he struggled to search and probe about.

He surfaced, took a gulp of air, and went down again, widening his frantic swim. But the lake was deep and its water, even at the best of times, murky. He could not see more than six inches in front of his face.

Again Andrew surfaced . . . and dived again—again and again, until exhaustion threatened his own safety. Panting desperately, lungs aching, he saw nothing, he felt nothing.

Up he came for a final time, gasping desperately for breath, then scrambled onto the shore, glancing about desperately in the hope she might have appeared in the meantime. But there was no sign of Lindsay anywhere.

Genuine panic now set in. His eyes reddened and filled with tears.

He flew to his horse and galloped back to the Hall faster and more recklessly than he had ever ridden in his life, crying shamelessly and freely.

"Mother . . . Mother!" he cried while a long way off. "Mother!" he screamed, ". . . it's Lindsay—she's fallen!"

By the time he reached the door his mother was already outside.

"She fell . . . she fell in the Tarn Water!" he blurted out hysterically. "I couldn't find her . . . I tried . . . she wouldn't come up . . . I looked and looked . . ."

Already Lady Trentham was calling for Horace and some of the other men. Within minutes they were on their way with horses, a wagon, ropes, and blankets.

But all the afternoon's rescue efforts proved of no avail.

Lindsay's body did not surface until late that afternoon, with a tremendous gash on the side of her head where she had been knocked unconscious during the fall.

It was in the hours between, after he had explained to her what had happened, and before Andrew's father returned, that Lady Trentham and her son had the brief private talk that had so deepened the impact of the incident in his impressionable young mind.

"I think it best, Andrew," said the woman in the shock of realizing her daughter had drowned, "that we tell no one that you and Lindsay were together today."

Red-eyed and whimpering, yet struggling to be brave, Andrew looked up into her face with a questioning look and nodded.

"It would cause too many questions, you see," she went on. "Of course you didn't do anything wrong, Andrew. I know that. But there might be talk, you understand. I simply want to protect you, and the family, from any more unpleasantness. We will just say that Lindsay was riding and had an accident, which is the truth. It will be our secret, yours and mine. And we won't need to talk about this, will we? We'll just put it behind us and keep it to ourselves."

Again Andrew nodded, his eyes wide, the words penetrating deep into his soul. His mother was always in control. He would do as he was told.

Whatever her reasons were for such cautions, even she could not have said. The poor woman's brain had nearly ceased to function. She spent the next few days in a stupor of pale shock, which continued through the church service and burial. True to what she had said, they had never spoken of it again.

Ever after would he and his mother be linked by a secret that could do nothing but increase his guilt over the affair. No doubt she quickly disregarded, or even forgot, the vow of silence she had enjoined on him. And she never knew its effect.

So many questions had plagued him since. Why had he not gone to Duncan's cottage, closer than home by half? It might not have done any good, but the thought haunted him. Why hadn't he tried to dive just once more? Why hadn't he gone deeper . . . done something different? He had been so frantic, so powerless!

And ever after that day, like Cruithne, he had been destined to assume a mantle of family elderhood—he could hardly call it chieftainship in this modern day—that should have belonged to another, and that, however long he wore it, he would gladly have relinquished could the personal history of his family be rewritten.

Did that explain why the old tale had struck such deep root within him as a teenager? Without realizing it, had he shared Cruithne's pain at the loss of his dear Fidach? These were questions he had never before considered, questions that now deepened all the more this soul-searching season of personal reflection.

Andrew rose from the spot, drew in a deep breath, and continued his ride back to the Hall.

If only, he thought, like Cruithne, he might rise above the pain and loss of the past, and, though the younger, yet prove to be a worthy heir to the legacy that fate had cast upon him unsought.

▩   F I V E   ▩

The fifty-one members of the Liberal Democratic party gathered a week after Eagon Hamilton's funeral to elect his successor to party leadership.

The mood of the gathering was quiet, as befitted the sobriety of the occasion. Discussion between them kept returning, as it had for the last week, to the unbelievable circumstances of their former leader's death. Yet they all recognized, despite their grief and shock, that they needed to move forward with the business confronting the party.

Deputy Leader Larne Reardon, looking uncommonly wan, with his suit uncharacteristically rumpled and sparse hair in disarray, presided over the vote.

The first ballot was taken. Surprisingly Reardon did not come away with a majority. Party secretary Charles Wilcox, from Kent, read the tally:

"Larne Reardon, twenty-two votes," he said—

A few puzzled glances went about the room.

"Maurice Fraser-Smythe, fourteen," Wilcox continued. "Edwin St. John, six, Andrew Trentham, five, Sally Lutyens, two, and Charles Wilcox two."

The surprised looks and glances, with a few mumbled comments of astonishment, evidenced the fact that each of the twenty-nine who had not voted for Reardon had expected his own vote to be one of very few such cast. But apparently more of their number than anyone could have predicted had chosen to express their admiration for others in their ranks, assuming their vote would make no difference in the outcome. What it had done, in fact, was to prevent the Deputy Leader from achieving a first-ballot majority.

"To speak truthfully, my friends and colleagues," said Reardon with a peculiar smile, "I am not surprised at this result."

He paused with serious expression. They could tell something momentous was on his mind.

"I have been somewhat ambivalent about my future since the night I heard about Eagon," he went on. "You can imagine what a dreadful blow it was. I do not think it is that I am afraid for myself—though perhaps I am. In any event, I have found myself questioning whether leadership of the party is what I really want, at least now. I have my family to consider. I think I am going to require more time to reflect upon my future. And this vote we have taken . . . well, it only confirms the direction I feel I should take."

He paused briefly.

"What I am trying to say," he resumed, "is that I feel it best for the moment that I withdraw my name from further ballots. I think the Liberal Democratic Party will best be served with one of you at its helm."

More vocal expressions of astonishment went round the room, accompanied by no fewer than a half dozen objections and counterarguments that loudly extolled Reardon's accomplishments and qualifications.

"I am afraid my mind is quite made up, gentlemen and ladies," insisted Reardon. "I should have made my announcement before. Perhaps I felt a lingering sense of duty should the vote have been strongly indicative that you felt I was the only one possible. But such is not the case. These of my esteemed colleagues for whom you have cast ballots—any of them will be well capable of filling Eagon's shoes. At this point, I'm afraid my decision is final. Because I remain acting deputy leader, however, I will continue to preside over this election. Now, with my name no longer under consideration, we will vote again."

The room continued in a hubbub of mumbling and astonished comment. But Reardon stood calmly in front of them, waiting, unmoved by their attempts to persuade him to reconsider. Then one by one, as they finally realized he was in earnest, the party members again took their seats and quieted before setting about the suddenly unanticipated and newly unpredictable business before them.

This time the vote took nearly twice as long.

Again the MP from Kent read out the results, which came as an equal surprise from the first ballot.

"Maurice Fraser-Smythe, thirteen," Wilcox said. "Edwin St. John, seven. Andrew Trentham, *nineteen*—"

That most in the room, including the fourteen who had switched their votes in his favor, were taken aback the moment Wilcox, with slight emphasis in his inflection, uttered the word, was more than obvious. Again a low buzz of astonishment spread among them.

"—Mrs. Lutyens, six," continued the secretary, "Thomas Parsons, four, and Charles Wilcox, two."

"Well," laughed Reardon, displaying the first sign of humor they had seen from him in more than a week, "this is proving more and more interesting as we go. It looks as if we shall have to do it again."

"I must speak up," now added Secretary Wilcox, still standing beside the deputy leader, "to ask that my name be withdrawn. If you would like me to continue in the capacity of the party's secretary, I am happy to serve. But more than that I do not feel appropriate."

A few nods of acknowledgment followed.

Thomas Parsons, MP from Wales, now rose from his seat. "While I appreciate the confidence of those who entered my own name," he said, "I must follow Mr. Wilcox's lead. My family simply could not take the added strain at this time. I respectfully request that no more votes be cast on my behalf."

"Any of those who remain would certainly be capable leaders," said Reardon, glancing about the room. "Let us vote again."

A third time the room quieted as the members considered their party's future. Four minutes later, Wilcox announced the results of his latest computations.

"Maurice Fraser-Smythe, eleven," Wilcox began, "Edwin St. John, five—"

The dropping numbers of the others already more than hinted at what was coming.

"—Mrs. Lutyens, *four*. . ."

Wilcox paused for obvious effect, drawing out the word.

"—*and Andrew Trentham, thirty-one!*"

A few cheers and sporadic applause briefly broke out.

"It looks like that is it—congratulations, Trentham," said Reardon, beckoning Andrew forward. "It looks as if the new head of our party is a Cumbrian."

His mouth open in a half smile of disbelief, Andrew rose to his feet.

"Get up there, Trentham," said Edwin St. John beside him. "You're our man now."

Still amazed that his name had even been considered, yet not feeling at liberty to withdraw it without compelling reason, Andrew stumbled forward, the bewildered look on his face gradually giving way to nods of gratitude to those around him.

"Come on up," persisted Reardon, extending his hand in congratulations, "the gavel is yours."

Andrew took it. Reardon sat down. Shaking his head slowly back and forth as he gazed upon his colleagues, Andrew found himself at a loss for words.

"I hardly know what to say," he began. "The only thing that comes to my mind is to ask if you are all sure you want *me* as your leader and spokesman."

Laughter broke out. Slowly it gave way to applause. Gradually the sound grew louder and louder. Andrew stood, still shaking his head, but unable to keep himself from smiling as his colleagues clapped and cheered their rousing endorsement of the results.

"Yes," said St. John, standing and walking forward to shake Andrew's hand. "We *do*. You are the right man for the job."

"Here, here!" added Maurice Fraser-Smythe, rising and coming forward also to extend his personal and enthusiastic congratulation.

One by one, the rest followed suit. With the vote less than five minutes behind them, already the sentiment seemed strongly confirmed in the minds of all that they had made the right decision.

"In fact," said Maurice Fraser-Smythe above the congratulations, "I move that we make the vote unanimous."

"Here, here!" came voices from around the room. Another and even louder round of applause followed.

SIX

The first Patricia Rawlings knew of the unexpected turnabout at the top of the Liberal Democratic Party was from the afternoon's edition of the *Post*, which startled all of London.

"Cumbrian Trentham Named New Leader of Liberal Democrats!" read the headline.

Her eyes probed the photograph of Andrew Trentham, as if the black-

and-white image would tell her something if she stared at it long enough. Slowly a smile spread across her face.

"You have something to tell me, don't you, Andrew Trentham?" she said softly to herself. "There's a story here. I don't know what it is yet, but I'll find it. And somehow you, Mr. Trentham, are at the bottom of it."

She grabbed a pen and tablet from her desk, and then began to read the article, taking notes as she went, and jotting down the names of the principal players in the unseen drama she was certain lay somewhere between the lines of this news report.

Twenty minutes later she had been through the article twice, with numerous pauses for thought.

Her tablet, between doodles and cross-outs, contained several queries to herself, which she now underlined and circled for emphasis:

> *What connection Stone and Hamilton?*
> *Links between SNP and LibDems?*
> *Why Reardon's withdrawal?*
> *Motive for murder—political . . . religious . . . nationalistic . . . other?*
> *Motive for theft—same?*
> *What connection Trentham with above?*

At the bottom of the sheet she listed several names. Around them she now drew a little box, as if to highlight that at last her search for a story had some specific leads to follow. She would talk to them all, she said to herself—obviously all except the first . . .

> *Eagon Hamilton*, former leader LibDem
> *Andrew Trentham*, new leader LibDem
> *Larne Reardon*, deputy LibDem
> *Dugald MacKinnon*, leader SNP
> *Baen Ferguson*, deputy SNP

—and she would begin immediately.

Tucking the tablet into her bag next to her portable tape recorder, Paddy rose and left the office.

⚜   S E V E N   ⚜

Andrew's telephone was ringing even as he walked into his flat the evening of the balloting.

"I called to reiterate my congratulations and wish you well," said a familiar voice as Andrew answered it.

"That is very gracious of you, Larne," replied Andrew. He set down his briefcase and threw his coat over the couch. "I must admit I am still stunned by the sudden turn of events."

"Within days it will seem quite natural. You'll see. And I want you to know that you can count on me for anything you need."

"I appreciate that, Larne. It means a great deal, coming from you."

"I hope I may be able to do some good behind the scenes, as it were. I will help guide you through the political land mines however I am able. I hope you will feel free to turn to me often."

"I am happy that the party decided you should continue on as my deputy leader."

"I am honored to do so. By the by, did you hear any more from Scotland Yard while I was out of the city?"

"Only that they are trying to trace the movements of some East Ender."

"Who?"

"I don't know. They managed a partial print from some papers they think were Eagon's—they found them on an embankment upriver from where the body was located."

"Hmm, well—that's . . . uh, good news—that there appears to be progress. What kind of papers?"

"Inspector Shepley didn't say."

"Have they found the fellow?"

"Not yet. I think there's a connection to a pub—O'Faolain's Green . . . ever heard of it?"

"Uh . . . no, I haven't," replied Reardon.

"What it has to do with the fellow they're looking for, I'm not sure."

A few more pleasantries followed. Andrew hung up, still shaking his head at the turn of events, and went to change clothes.

Just one day ago he had been but one of 659 members of the British House of Commons. Now the Liberal Democrats had chosen him as their new leader. At age thirty-seven he would, in the tradition of Paddy Ashdown, become leader of Parliament's third-largest party. Given the technical aspects of what was required to keep the government's coalition intact, that position would make him one of the most influential men in the United Kingdom.

❈   E I G H T   ❈

Andrew telephoned Derwenthwaite Hall later that same evening.

"Well, son, it would appear congratulations are in order," said his father. "I heard of your election on the news."

Andrew laughed. "Quite a shocker, eh, Dad?"

"My money was on you all the way! Was the vote close?"

"Three ballots," replied Andrew "Then they made it unanimous."

"Well, you have my heartiest congratulations. Imagine . . . *my son* the leader of his party at the ripe young age of thirty-seven. And Barraclough knows that he needs you to hold on to his government."

"He's already called," laughed Andrew. "Very gracious and congratulatory as you would expect. As did Miles Ramsey of the opposition. They're both already trying to win my loyalty."

"As I would expect. If Ramsey could turn you, it would put the Tories back in power."

"I'll need time to sort it all out."

Father and son continued to chat lightly for several minutes.

"Ah, here's your mother," said Mr. Trentham. "She's been storming and ranting ever since the news broke, waiting to talk to you!"

Andrew could picture his mother doing exactly that. He wondered if this latest twist of his fortunes would heighten her confidence in him.

"What are you going to do about the Scottish question, Andrew?" his mother asked the moment she had taken the receiver from her husband.

He could feel her uncertainty across the 340 miles that separated them.

"You must have been watching the news," commented Andrew wryly.

"And reading the papers. You're everywhere these days. But I want to know how the thing looks to you."

"I don't know, Mum," sighed Andrew. "The pressures have been mounting from all sides since Eagon's death. Now it's bound to get worse."

"The Scottish Nationalists?" queried Lady Trentham.

"This is the chance they have been waiting for to up the stakes toward independence, and they're throwing everything they have into it."

"What I want to know is, do Labour and the SNP stand a chance of passing anything without your support?"

"If they got *every* Labour MP, *every* Scottish Nationalist, and *all* twenty-four MPs from the minor parties, that would give them exactly the 330 majority needed. No," Andrew went on, "I would rate the chance of that happening at about one in ten thousand. A coalition like that would provide the perfect opportunity for one man to control government single-handedly. *One* of those twenty-four would be bound to vote against the coalition, if for no other reason than to be known as the man who toppled the Labour government."

"That places you in a powerful position."

"Or a vulnerable one," remarked Andrew. "How would you like to take my place, Mum?"

The light comment had just slipped out. The moment he said the words, Andrew wished he could retrieve them. He knew well enough who his mother would have put in his place if she could.

A brief, and for Andrew awkward, silence followed.

"I don't think the Liberal Democrats would have me," replied Lady Trentham after a moment. Thankfully she did not add an allusion to Andrew's sister.

Another brief silence followed.

Suddenly everything had changed for the young MP now engaged in conversation with his mother. There were decisions that would soon fall to him as the new leader of the all-important Liberal Democrat contingent of the House of Commons. It could quite literally be said—and every editorialist in every paper from the *Times* to the *Sun* was getting ready to say precisely that in the next day's papers—that young Andrew Trentham, as a result of today's vote by his party's colleagues, would be one of the key men holding Labour's slender coalition together. At just about any moment he chose, Trentham would be capable of bringing Richard Barraclough's government into dissolution and force Parliament to go to the country for new elections a second time within a very short period.

Many questions about him, therefore, were certain to arise in days to come.

Who was this young MP who had suddenly risen so high? What did he want? What was his game? What was his personal political agenda?

By now everyone knew that the SNP was planning to waste no time forcing more and more issues concerning Scotland to the front burner of national attention. They had steadfastly disavowed involvement in the removal of the Coronation Stone and did not intend to allow either the theft or the murder of Eagon Hamilton to change their plans.

Andrew would have until September, therefore, or perhaps early October, to figure out where he stood on these Scottish questions. By then the prime minister would be calling his cabinet back for meetings at Number Ten Downing Street to put together the elements of the speech he would hand to the King.

Thus Andrew had six or seven months to sort through the issues and his thoughts on them.

Where *did* he stand? If Scotland's future did get put onto next year's agenda, and if it later came up for a second debate reading, how *would* he vote?

"Well, I wouldn't worry about the Scottish Nationalists at this juncture," his mother finally said. "They are certainly in the public doghouse over the business with the Stone."

"I'm not so sure they're behind it," said Andrew.

"I thought there was evidence," said Lady Trentham.

"*Supposed* evidence," rejoined Andrew. "But why would they do something so foolhardy after devolution has given Scotland a regional parliament, and so soon after the Stone had been returned to Edinburgh? No, I think there's more to the theft of the Stone than meets the eye."

As Andrew put down the telephone a few minutes later, a strange feeling of aloneness invaded him. This was a day that should represent the summit of his career thus far as a politician. His name and picture would now regularly appear on the front page of the *Times* and all the other papers. He should be basking in the glow of his triumph. What man in the country wouldn't envy him?

Yet strange and unknown sensations were rising up from somewhere within him. Questions about himself, about who he was and who he wanted to be—questions about his past, questions about the cultural expectations that might be said to have guided his destiny thus far.

Pinnacle of his career or not, Andrew Trentham felt he was at a crossroads. He needed perspective. Despite the press of so much demanding his attention in London, he needed to get away from the city again. Even if it meant only another brief weekend at home, the mental and emotional rest would be worth it.

⁂   N I N E   ⁂

Before Andrew could think any further about the weekend, his phone rang.

Halfway expecting to find his mother on the line again, he picked up the receiver. "Andrew Trentham," he said.

"Hello, Mr. Trentham," said a pleasant voice on the other end. He knew it instantly and did not require the identification that followed. "It's Patricia Rawlings calling, BBC 2. Perhaps you remember me?"

"Of course, Miss Rawlings," replied Andrew. "I remember you perfectly. And I must say you handled yourself very well last week," he added. "That was rather brave of you, jumping right back into the fray . . . *and* with a question about a division, no less!"

Rawlings laughed.

"Well, you were very kind in the way you fielded my blooper the first time I brought up the subject," she said. "I appreciate the fact that you said nothing to make me seem a bigger fool than I already felt!"

"Everybody makes mistakes," said Andrew. "I've made more than my share."

"In any case, you were most gracious." Paddy paused.

"The reason I telephoned, Mr. Trentham," she went on after a moment of silence, "was to ask if you would perhaps grant me an interview."

"Hmm . . . something on camera?"

"No, nothing like that. They don't trust me yet on film," Paddy added, laughing. "And I'm sure you can see why."

"Do you mean because you're American, or because of your lack of experience?" rejoined Andrew good-humoredly.

"Both!"

"Tell me what you have in mind."

"Nothing formal. I just thought you might be willing to talk casually. I really am very interested in the questions I raised that day. Is there some way we could get together briefly sometime?"

"I'm planning to leave for Cumbria tomorrow afternoon."

"On holiday?"

"Just the weekend."

"Next week?"

"My schedule's rather full—" hesitated Andrew.

"Only for a few minutes, then. I would just like to meet you in a more relaxed setting than the middle of the street. I could come to your office anytime you like. I promise I won't put you on the spot."

Andrew debated with himself. All his training told him to be cautious in such circumstances. There wasn't a single thing he could gain by an interview of this nature, and much he could lose. Hadn't he already turned down half a dozen or more requests, including a call just this morning for an on-camera question-and-answer session presided over by none other than this woman's cohort Kirkham Luddington?

Yet for some unknown reason, suddenly he found himself answering in an altogether uncharacteristic manner.

"Come to think of it," he said, "why wait until next week?—How about lunch tomorrow?"

"Oh—" exclaimed Paddy, trying to hide her astonished delight. "That would be wonderful."

❈   T E N   ❈

Because of its location just off Whitehall, Granby's at the Royal Horse-guards Hotel was a favorite dining spot for politicians. If any of Andrew's curious colleagues were here for lunch today, however, and wondered what he was doing with the lady from the BBC, neither the young woman nor the new leader of the Liberal Democratic Party took notice. They had been talking together now for forty minutes.

Paddy's salad and Andrew's plate of veal both stood only half completed. The conversation had long since diverged from what would be termed a political "interview." The young American had been quizzing the MP on some of the finer points of the parliamentary system.

"As long as I've been here, and as hard as I've studied trying to understand everything," Paddy was saying, "I still find myself in situations where my background doesn't prepare me for the way you do things here. When

I first got on with the BBC, they had me doing other things. What's most embarrassing—I really *do* know what *division* means! I guess when I heard the word that day, my brain called up the American usage before I even had a chance to think—then suddenly I'd blurted out that idiotic question!"

Andrew threw his head back and laughed.

"But it still is beyond me," Paddy went on, "how you run a government as you do, when every bill that comes before the House of Commons *has* to pass. It's so foreign to our way of thinking in the States. What purpose does the opposition even serve?"

"To articulate opposing viewpoints and to represent their constituencies," replied Andrew.

"But they have no power. Why do they bother coming at all, if every vote is a foregone conclusion?"

"It is important to give voice to all sides, even if the government dictates the agenda."

"It's absolutely antithetical to our system, where the president and the two parties in Congress have to battle it out over every issue, and where some bills go one way and others the opposite—and that's another thing," Paddy went on. "The government's agenda. Is all legislation really established a year in advance?"

"Pretty much. The Queen's speech—pardon me, I mean the King's speech—sets the agenda for the year."

"And the prime minister and his cabinet decide the agenda, I know that—but what happens when things unexpectedly come up?"

"The prime minister can introduce something not on the agenda if need be."

"And is the government obligated to bring up every item from the majority party's manifesto for a reading in the Commons?"

"Not obligated. But if they don't take some action on most of them, they will likely not be returned in the next election."

"What are your thoughts about being a leader in Labour's coalition?"

"That sounds strikingly like an interview question. So I will give you the stock political response—it is too early to comment."

Paddy laughed. "You are pretty good for having been a party leader such a short time."

"When you're in politics you learn—"

Andrew stopped abruptly. Where she sat across from him, Paddy followed his eyes to the other side of the room. They had magneted on a tall man and blond woman just entering the restaurant.

"Pardon me for a moment, please, Miss Rawlings," Andrew murmured. He rose and slowly approached the newcomers.

"Hello, Blair," he said, then nodded slightly to the man at her side.

"Andrew!" she replied with a start, then quickly recovered. "—How are you?"

"Well. And you?"

"I'm fine—oh, Andrew, it is good to see you! And you've become so famous all of a sudden."

"Hardly that."

"I hear about you everywhere." She glanced in the direction of the table from which Andrew had come. "And I'm so happy you've found someone else," she added.

A puzzled look came over Andrew's face, then he smiled thinly. Suddenly he realized how very different he and Blair were. The insight pained him afresh. It would be pointless to explain. It had only been a few short months, yet suddenly he felt they were worlds apart.

"But I am forgetting my manners," she went on. "Andrew, do you know—"

"Yes," interrupted Andrew, now shaking hands with her escort, "—hello, Hensley. It's been a while."

"Trentham," nodded the man called Hensley.

"Still writing those press briefings for the Yard?"

"Keeps meat on the table."

"What do you hear about the Stone these days?"

"Nothing much. Got our boys more than a little mystified."

"Well, nice seeing you, Hensley . . . Blair," said Andrew.

He returned to his seat while the two were shown to a table on the other side of the restaurant.

"Friends?" asked Paddy as he sat down.

"A former acquaintance," said Andrew in a sober tone.

"From that look on your face, I would say a *close* acquaintance."

"You are very perceptive, Miss Rawlings," he said with a pensive smile. "But you're a reporter, and that is personal."

"Oh . . . I'm sorry," replied Paddy, embarrassed. "I meant nothing—"

"No problem," smiled Andrew.

"I suppose I'm also an American—blunt, forward, tactless . . . all those qualities we are famous for. . . ."

"Miss Rawlings, please . . . I meant nothing of the kind—only that I'd rather not go down that road. But you are right in what you said—she is someone I cared for very much. Yet seeing her again . . ."

His voice trailed off.

"Maybe I'm changing more than I realized," he added after a moment. This time Paddy said nothing in reply. A lengthy silence followed, during which she busied herself with her salad, he with his veal.

"But wasn't that Fred Hensley with her?" said Paddy at length. "I read something he released to the press about the Stone. It seemed to raise more questions than it answered."

"It certainly has been a mystery. Frankly, I'm surprised the Stone hasn't shown up by now."

As the conversation continued, they chatted further about the British system of politics. Scotland was mentioned. Then the subject of Paddy's name was raised. She had just mentioned that her friends called her Paddy, with d's not t's.

"Why *Paddy*?" Andrew asked. "Isn't it a man's nickname, and an Irish one at that?"

The American paused. A reminiscent expression of mingled nostalgia and pain crossed her face as she recalled the first time the name *Paddy* had sounded in her ears. What a happy day that had been—a memory that had now turned bittersweet. No, she wasn't quite ready to open *that* box of memories for her new acquaintance Andrew Trentham.

"Let's just say it is a nickname a friend gave me when I first came to England," she sighed at length. She forced a smile to pull herself back to the present.

"Why are you interested in Scotland?" he asked, diverting the conversation in another direction.

"That's supposed to be my question!" Paddy rejoined. "I'm the one who asked you about Scotland, remember?"

Andrew laughed. "Just curious," he said. "I'm rather fond of the north, you see. I was raised just a stone's throw from the border, though to tell the truth, we rarely ventured across it—my family's interests have always focused toward London. But now that recent responsibilities have been thrust upon me, I feel an urgency to understand as much as I can about the issues coming up. I always did my best to stay informed. But now I feel I need to know more—not just the facts but what is behind them. Understanding Scotland and its history suddenly seems vital to me."

"All right—I can see that. But you must realize that you may now very well become the center of the entire debate."

"Right now I would prefer not to think about it. What do you say we change the subject?"

"All right, then. Let me ask you about your recent election. Why did Mr. Reardon step down?"

"I honestly don't know—family, personal reasons. Actually he didn't share many details with us about it. But I'm not sure that was enough of a subject change to suit me, Miss Rawlings," laughed Andrew. "So *I'll* have a go at it. What's it like being a reporter—do you enjoy it?"

"That *is* a one-hundred-eighty-degree turn!" she rejoined. "But to answer you, yes. Of course—I love doing what I do. Though if I was to be absolutely truthful—"

She paused and glanced into Andrew's face.

"—off the record?" she added.

He nodded.

"To tell you the truth, aspects of the job are hard for me."

"How so?"

"I'm afraid I'm really not as forceful as you have to be to make it in this game."

"You could have fooled me!"

"You have to put on a journalist's persona. I love news—the process of investigation, being in touch with what is going on. But it's often difficult to be the kind of person you have to be to succeed. Sometimes I wonder how long I will be able to keep it up," she said. "And you?"

"What about me?"

"Do you like being a politician?"

"I would give you the same answer you gave me—of course, though it too has its difficult side."

"Such as?"

"Off the record?"

Paddy nodded.

"That's not good enough," smiled Andrew. "You have to promise me that what I say will remain just between the two of us."

"You are a shrewd one. All right then," she replied. "I *promise*." She extended her arm across the table.

They shook hands to formally seal the pact of confidentiality.

"All right then," Andrew said, "I too find that the persona I must wear weighs a bit heavy at times, simply because of who I am."

"How do you mean?"

"I mean my mother and her reputation, not to mention her expectations . . . and everybody in the city knows my father . . . and here I come, the young scion carrying on the Trentham name. I don't know—lately I've found myself wondering who I am all by myself, if there is a *me* that represents something deeper than all the external things people see when they look at me."

"You're going through a time of personal reflection—is that what you'd say?"

"I suppose. I'm wondering as well about my roots, about where I came from."

"But don't you know?" she persisted. "I mean . . . your family is an old one, right? I thought you would have, like a coat of arms or a family archives or something."

"I suppose perhaps we do, somewhere. But you have to understand I come from a long line of modernists . . . yes, even my Conservative mother in her way. We've never been much for tales of the old days."

"But that's changing now, you say . . ."

"Something's changing." He shook his head. "I don't really know where I'm going with all this. Suddenly it just dawned on me that, here I am—well-known, my name in the papers, journalists—like you!" he added with a grin, "—wanting to talk to me . . . and I find myself wondering if I've ever stopped to try to figure out who I was."

"Did Eagon Hamilton's death trigger all this introspection?"

Andrew thought for a moment.

"No, it began before that. Actually, I think the theft of the Coronation Stone may have had more to do with it than what happened to Eagon. But whenever someone you know dies, you can't help but grow pensive." Andrew smiled. "A fateful lunch with the young lady over there," he added with a smile, "contributed its share. And come to think of it, actually your question about division helped stimulate my thoughts too."

"I'm glad something good came of it! But how could *that* have had anything to do with it?"

"I don't know . . . that you were willing to launch out into uncharted waters."

"American accent and all!"

"Exactly. I found myself envying your being in a position different than would be expected of you."

"Certainly none of London's journalists expect it of me."

"I look at what you're doing and I see a freedom I'm not sure I've ever known."

A brief silence fell.

"And then a visit to an old Scotsman who lives on our estate up north added to my reevaluation," Andrew said, as if picking up the previous thread of conversation. "That did it most of all."

"So all this *does* have to do with Scotland?"

"Suddenly this has a sound very much like an interview."

"No, I promise. I'm just interested."

"To answer your question—no, I don't think it is the home-rule issue so much as my own personal role in it. *Roots,* as I said before."

"That statement has very much the ring of an eldest son trying to forge an identity as his generation rises to prominence in a well-known family."

"Did you study psychoanalysis as well as journalism?" laughed Andrew. "That statement has very much the ring of someone trying to get inside my psyche!"

"As I said, I'm just interested. *Are* you the eldest in your family?"

Now it was Andrew's turn, as she had done a few moments before, to draw down over his thoughts the protective cloak of silence. It was obvious from the expression that briefly crossed his face that there was more pain to the answer than he wanted to divulge. Neither was he ready to open *his* box of private memories just now.

"No," he answered softly after a moment. "I had an older sister—"

He paused, then added, "—she died when I was ten."

"I'm sorry," said Paddy, nodding thoughtfully.

It was clear there was more to MP Andrew Trentham than even she had realized.

When she arrived back to her office after lunch, Paddy took out the list of individuals and questions she had drawn up earlier. To the bottom of the paper she added the words:

Also keep track of for related interest: . . . Fred Hensley, Scotland Yard . . . as well as Andrew's former friend—blond . . .

Paddy's hand paused momentarily as she briefly replayed the incident in her mind. Then she added—

. . . shifty eyes . . . a user.

She put the paper away, smiling to herself. Were her instincts accurate? she wondered. Or had a hint of female rivalry risen up to cloud her perspective?

※   E L E V E N   ※

The early spring's snow still lay thick on the hills when Andrew arrived again in Cumbria.

After Saturday's breakfast, as Andrew passed through the entryway, his eyes fell upon the four family portraits that hung symmetrically on the wall to his left—his mother and father, Lindsay at fifteen, a year before her death, and he upon his graduation from Eton.

He gazed into his sister's eyes and upon her smile longer than was his custom, then wandered into the expansive drawing room, where a cheery fire burned in the large hearth. He stood a minute or two glancing around the room, so familiar since his boyhood. Antique furnishings, thick red carpet, two massive sideboards, three couches, and six or eight overstuffed leather chairs were spread about the room. On the wall over the enormous fireplace hung a huge and ancient fading tapestry. On each side were mounted heads of a red mountain stag and a great horned ram. On the opposite wall hung a large mirror framed in ornate carved oak.

Andrew took in each item in its turn. Suddenly, as if beholding them all for the first time, he found himself wondering where the antiques and mirrors and stuffed heads and tapestries had come from. Till this moment, it seemed, he had taken everything in this house for granted.

Who had brought them all here, he now pondered. And when?

He ambled toward the wide and expansive staircase that rose majestically from one corner of the drawing room toward the upper floors of the house.

Methodically he took the great stairs one slow step after another, gazing now to the right, then to the left at the gallery of paintings hanging on the walls—men and women, scenes, houses, castles, landscapes as familiar to him as his own hand. The sight of every one sent stabs of nostalgic longing through him—but for what he did not know.

He recognized each face distinctly. Yet now he realized he knew them not at all.

Who were these people, whose silent expressions had gazed down from these walls upon him during all the years of his life, never offering comment, never passing judgment, never changing expression through the years? Whose were these eyes that now seemed to stare so intently into his consciousness with their concealed messages of antiquity, as if waiting for him to discover the secret that *they* knew . . . but that he had yet to uncover? What were they trying to tell him? What were their secrets?

On he climbed, turning round one landing, then another—up to the first floor now, where a length of gallery leading to his right opened as a loft above the room he had just left, while in the other direction the staircase bent round again and continued its upward ascent. He was at the level of the goat and stag heads now, opposite him, flanking the fireplace below.

Up he continued. More faces adorned the walls. Relics from the past sat on shelves and upon benches that were formed into the stone walls under the windows at each outside turn of the staircase. A giant bell . . . a bronze statue of a horse and rider he remembered loving to touch as a child . . . a handsomely painted miniature ship . . . more portraits of what he could only take as representations of his own ancestors. . . .

His eyes fell on the portrait of an ancient warrior in green-and-black kilt and full accompanying Highland dress. It hung in a heavy gilded frame among the others. Funny, Andrew thought to himself, he didn't remember noticing that painting before.

Andrew stared up, gazing deeply into the ancient Celtic eyes, trying to apprehend what the man would tell him if he could but speak.

Who are you? thought Andrew. *Why are you here, old Highlander, watching silently over this English estate?*

Was this old portrait of a Gordon . . . could the fellow be a Trentham ancestor?

Slowly Andrew continued upward, still turning the matter over in his mind, and arrived at the second floor. He left the staircase and approached the Derwenthwaite library two doors down the wide corridor. He opened the large double doors and stepped inside.

As with everything he had seen this day, a wave of melancholic nostalgia swept through him at the sight and smell of this familiar yet all at once unknown place. Everywhere sat more silent reminders of the past. Though there was a large contingent of newer volumes, the bindings and the dusty aromas of the older books drew him with sudden sensations of long-past mystery.

Here were stories and tales and legends innumerable! They had been right in front of him all his life.

Standing before the bookshelves of the Derwenthwaite library, pale light coming in from the tall window behind him, he recalled the tales of the Maiden, the Wanderer, and Cruithne. With the remembrance came a realization that had escaped him before—that the Wanderer had no doubt settled very near here, just south of Scotland's border.

He turned and left the room, returning down the stairs in a tenth the time it had taken to ascend them.

He found his father seated in the private sitting room on the ground floor.

"What is it, Andrew?" Mr. Trentham asked in some alarm, seeing the expression of urgency on his son's face.

"I've got to know a few things, Dad," Andrew replied.

"About what?"

"About the family. For instance, who is that old Highlander upstairs?"

"Old Highlander?" repeated Trentham.

"The portrait up on the second floor."

"Oh . . . right. Now that you mention it, I do seem to recall some strangely attired fellow up there. Rather imposing-looking, if I recall."

"But why is his portrait hanging in Derwenthwaite? Is he in the family?"

"He's been there since before I can remember, to tell you the truth. No doubt he is an ancestor of some kind, now that I think of it. There were some Scots in the family, you know, back in the last century."

"What about the other portraits?"

"I'm sorry, Andrew," said Trentham, "I just can't help you. I don't think one of those paintings has gone up or come down since I was a boy. I'm afraid I don't know a thing about most of them."

"What about my name? How did you and Mum choose it?"

"*Andrew*—that was your grandfather's name."

"And my middle name?"

"*Gordon*—that is a family name too."

"Where did it originate?"

"I can't actually remember—let's see . . . somewhere way back, one of my . . . hmm, it would have been my great-grandfather—maybe my great-great-grandfather—married a woman named Gordon."

"Who was she?" asked Andrew with continued importunity.

"I can't recall—we'll have to get out the old family records. But why the sudden interest? What's the matter with you, son? Till now you've never paid any more attention to them than I have."

"Just curious, I suppose, Dad."

"Why now?"

"Somehow it just suddenly seems to matter a great deal."

"Without going into the records," sighed Mr. Trentham, "I'm afraid there's not much I can tell you. It's all there in some book in the library. But tell me," he went on, attempting to turn the conversation toward politics, "how are you and the PM getting on? Is everything I read in the paper about Barraclough true?"

"More or less," answered Andrew distractedly. "I'm sorry, Dad—I'm not in a political frame of mind right now."

He turned and left the room, leaving his father puzzling over the strange swing of his son's mood since the morning.

Much of the remainder of the day Andrew spent upstairs in the library, digging out several books from its shelves that he hoped would be able to shed more light on the next period of Scottish history which had begun to fascinate him.

✖   T W E L V E   ✖

The scene in Edward Pilkington's London office late that same day was much different from the last time Patricia Rawlings sat here nervously wondering if she would still have a job at day's end. Her American newshound's personality had surfaced and she paced about the small room with obvious agitation.

"I tell you, Mr. Pilkington," she said, "there is more going on in the mind of the Honorable Andrew Trentham than anyone realizes."

"Meaning what?"

"Nothing I can put my finger on exactly," replied Paddy. "But this Scottish thing goes deep with him—deeper, I'm convinced, than anyone in this city realizes."

"Nearly every MP backs devolution and the recent changes. It's the wave of the future. It's not *news* that Andrew Trentham's for it too."

"It's more than that. It's personal with him."

"Personal—how do you mean? Are you on to some skeleton in the closet of the, quote, Honorable gentleman?"

Paddy shrugged. "I doubt that—I'm not even sure what I mean. It's just a sense. Isn't that what reporters do—rely on instinct and intuition?"

"In books and movies," replied Pilkington sarcastically. "In real life, it's facts that count. What about the *real* news—say, for instance, the murder of Hamilton and the theft of the Stone? You get me some hard news on those items, Rawlings, and you can write your own ticket."

"I'm working on it," rejoined Paddy.

"Yeah—how?" asked Pilkington, obviously intrigued.

"I'm going to talk to some people. I've got some theories."

"Anything you care to share with a seasoned veteran?"

"When I'm ready," smiled Paddy. "But did you mean what you said? If I get you facts, as you say, on either—"

The door opened behind her. In walked an impeccably tailored Kirkham Luddington.

"I understood there was some discussion concerning possible new information on Andrew Trentham," he said. He sat down and eyed the two.

"How did you hear that?" snapped Paddy. She turned toward the newcomer with a look of anything but welcome on her face.

"I know what goes on around here," replied Luddington with an unmistakable superior air. "Tell me, what's up?"

"You keep out of this, Kirk—this is my story!"

"Everything around here is my business, *Miss* Rawlings—tell her, Edward. Doesn't she know how seniority works?"

"Not if I get something you don't have," Paddy retorted. "Then where is your seniority?"

"If you'll pardon my saying so, a respected member of Parliament is not about to divulge any tidbits of news or inside scoops to a novice American whose knowledge of British politics is almost as inept as her use of the English tongue."

The smile that followed the words of the veteran television personality aroused the fury of her sex and the independent blood of her nationality.

"We shall see, *Mister* Luddington!" said Paddy, making no attempt to hide her ire.

Face red, she now turned to Pilkington, who sat behind his desk, rather enjoying the heated exchange to liven up an otherwise dull news day.

"You told me not long ago," she said, "that if I found you a story no one else had, we'd talk again about my getting a shot to go on camera. Well, I'm ready to talk."

"Do you have such a story?"

"I may . . . before long."

"Bring it to me and we'll see."

"No deal, Mr. Pilkington. If I'm going to stake my career on something, I want to know you won't just hand it over to Kirk."

She glanced toward Luddington, who sat listening with that infuriating smile on his face, amused at the notion that this upstart American could ever land a story he wouldn't know about first.

"Do you have an angle?" asked Pilkington.

"I'll get one."

"Not so easy with parliamentary leaders. They guard their flanks."

"Trentham's different."

"None of them are *different*," put in Luddington with derision in his tone. "They're all the same."

Paddy kept her eyes focused toward her boss.

Again Pilkington leaned back in his chair, thinking.

"You bring me something really good," he said at length, "something no one else has and something with some news value and punch—all right, I'll give an American a chance on the BBC. You bring me such a story, and I'll put a camera in front of you and see what you can do."

"And Kirk's seniority?" she added, eyeing her boss, and this time not even glancing in the direction of her competitor.

"I'll let you go with whatever you uncover," replied Pilkington. "Seniority will not apply."

"Thank you, Mr. Pilkington." She turned to go.

"But if you slip up again, Rawlings," Pilkington's voice sounded behind her, "it will be the end of what little seniority even you have."

Paddy nodded.

She turned and exited the office. As the door closed behind her, she heard the sound of Kirkham Luddington's voice in mumbled comment, followed by the sounds of both men chuckling.

Let them laugh, she thought. For once it didn't annoy her. She would show them what kind of reporter she was.

When the camera zoomed in on her face to report her findings to the country . . . they could see who was laughing then!

▨ T H I R T E E N ▨

He was next on her list anyway, Paddy thought as she left the building. She had been trying to set up an interview through official channels without success. She would try the direct approach. It had worked with Trentham.

She caught a cab and headed straight for the Norman Shaw building, where the office of MP Larne Reardon was located. It was forty minutes before Commons convened. If she was lucky, she might be able to nab him as he left his office.

Conning her way past the guard and into the building with a fake ID, Paddy took the stairs to the third floor, then slowed her pace. She kept her eyes on the busy corridor, trying to monitor the traffic without being too conspicuous.

She drew nearer to Reardon's office. The double doors were closed. She sauntered past, continued on for some distance, then casually turned. Someone was bound to notice her if she hung around too long.

But wait—the door to Reardon's office was opening!

A figure emerged and strode down the corridor in the opposite direction. Paddy glanced at the newspaper photograph in her hand and took note of the narrow face, the thinning hair.

It was Larne Reardon. She was sure of it! She hastened after him.

"Mr. Reardon," she said as she drew alongside, "I hoped I might have a moment of your time."

"If you don't mind walking—I'm on a tight schedule."

"No, not at all," replied Paddy, doing her best to keep up. "I wondered if you might be able to tell me why you withdrew from the election for your party's leadership."

"Personal reasons," replied Reardon. "Why?"

He paused slightly and glanced toward Paddy. "Who are you, anyway?"

"Patricia Rawlings, BBC2."

"Ah, a reporter . . . I should have known. I think I've already given the only statement I care to make to the press. How did you get into the building?"

"Would you sit down with me sometime and discuss the matter in more detail?" persisted Paddy, thinking it best not to answer him.

"I really doubt I would be interested in—"

Reardon hesitated. Paddy glanced toward him in time to detect a slight flush of apparent anger in his neck. Her eyes followed his down the hall to a tall man near the elevator. Though they appeared not to know each other, the eyes of the two men had clearly met.

The next instant Reardon recovered himself. He glanced with a smile toward Paddy.

"—I really don't think that would work at all," he said. "I am interested in no more public dialogue on the matter. Good day, Miss Rawlings."

He hurried off and left her standing in the hall, watching his back recede as he moved away from her. Instead of taking the elevator to the ground floor, however, Reardon turned toward the stairs. As he opened the door, Paddy detected a slight nod of his head toward the other man, who followed him a moment or two later.

Without pausing to think what she was doing, Paddy hurried after them.

Cautiously she opened the door. The corridor was deserted. The sound of the two men's footsteps came up from the stairwell below. As softly as they were attempting to speak, portions of their heatedly whispered argument echoed up into Paddy's ears.

". . . no idea what you're talking about . . . never heard of someone called Fiona. . . ."

The speaker was Reardon. Now came the other man's voice, in a thick Scottish brogue.

". . . did with Hamilton . . . won't work with me . . ."

". . . voice down, you fool . . ."

Other words followed that Paddy couldn't make out.

". . . madder than a March hare . . ."

". . . druids took . . ."

". . . imagine you think I had anything to do with . . ."

". . . can't double-cross me . . . where is she . . ."

". . . do you think . . . didn't come down with yesterday's rain . . ."

". . . Celtic compound . . ."

"Never heard of it."

". . . don't believe you . . . if I find you . . ."

". . . call the police if you try to threaten me . . ."

The door below opened. Suddenly the voices were gone.

Paddy hurried down the stairs after them. She emerged from the building but saw no sign of either man.

So, she said to herself, *the plot thickens!*

But what plot? What was it all about? And druids, for goodness' sake—why were they talking about ancient pagan priests? And what compound?

With many new mysteries suddenly to unravel, Patricia Rawlings slowly returned to her office.

She didn't yet know a lot of people in London. Nor had she accumulated enough favors—that elusive commodity that lubricated the engines of both politics and journalism—to shake a stick at. But she had made a few friends in several of the right places.

Her thoughts immediately turned to Bert Fenton, a would-be novelist whose day job at a travel bureau had turned him into something of a computer whiz, if not a hack.

She would call him.

❊   F O U R T E E N   ❊

The following morning, on Sunday, Andrew was up and away from home early. He had planned to go to church in the village with his parents as he did most Sundays when he was home. But at the last minute he decided on this drive instead.

Yesterday's image of the old Highlander staring down from the wall of the house still haunted his memory, blurring with the woodcut of the Wanderer. How near to this very place might have been the Wanderer's home?

Is your presence still haunting these regions, old wandering ancient, he thought . . . *filling your descendants with the same northward beckoning that lured you?*

Might even some of the mammoth's bones be lying under the ground nearby, Andrew wondered, lost to the centuries in a burial crypt of dirt and stone and peat?

Who were all those people hanging upon the walls of his home? Was it from Cruithne's stock they had come?

Perhaps someday he would find out. Today, however, he was after another piece of the puzzle, one suggested by yesterday's research. He had decided to drive eastward to Carlisle, then northeast through Brampton to the remains of Hadrian's Wall north of Haltwhistle. He had visited there once before, as a schoolboy, but little remained in his memory other than vague impressions of rocky ruins. Now, with his adult interest newly piqued, he wondered what he might learn.

A driving rain set in as Andrew followed the road along the ancient Roman boundary, watching for bits of the wall that remained across the countryside. His first stop was at the ruins of the Roman fort at Housesteads.

After ten or fifteen minutes in the gift shop and museum waiting for the downpour to let up, Andrew bundled up as best he could and set out for the half-mile walk up the hill to the ruins. A biting wind whipped past his ears and stung his nose and face. Gradually the rain eased.

Though all that remained of the fort were stone walls and the outlines of rooms a few feet high, as he walked slowly among them he felt a great sense of ancient reality. Thousands of men had actually lived in forts just like this—solitary outposts that represented the final reach of the Roman Empire. What a difficult life it must have been! The weather alone would have been daunting if today's fierce blasts, speckled with hail, were any indication. Yet the remains showed solid construction. And the still-visible floor pillars of the bathhouse gave evidence of Roman technology intended to keep the cold at bay and provide some degree of luxury even on a faraway frontier like this.

From the edge of the fort itself, Hadrian's Wall stretched down across the fields to the northeast. The only sign of life visible as the stones faded in the chilly distance were a few sheep. They cared as little about today's wind and rain as they did about the history of the ground upon which they grazed.

How had the Romans been driven away, Andrew wondered. How had the northern people done it? How had primitive people managed to reduce these once-massive and seemingly impenetrable forts to ruins?

He turned and made his way back across the soggy ground to the parking lot, then continued on his way to Hexham. After a brief walk through the center of the historic market town, he drove on to Corbridge and the ruins of another first-century Roman fort. The rain had let up by now. Though the wind continued to whistle among the stones, occasionally a ray or two of sunlight did its best to shine through.

The fort in this season did not attract many visitors. Andrew took the opportunity to question the woman in charge of the visitor's center.

"What was it that destroyed this fort?" he asked.

"There were actually two forts built at this site," she answered. "The first dated from the governorship of Julius Agricola in the early 80s A.D., when he conquered this region. It was originally destroyed by fire."

"Fire?" repeated Andrew. "How could these forts have been burned?"

"The circumstances have been lost to history. Some six or seven Roman forts were all burned around the same time."

"But everything is made of stone," said Andrew.

"The ruins we see at present, as I said, dating from the second, third, and even fourth centuries, are mostly reconstructions. The original first-century forts were largely made of wood. Some had stone foundations, but most of the roof supports and interior walls were of timber. Trees were much more plentiful in those days, you see. After the burning of many of their forts, however, the Romans resorted to more stone, higher walls, even slate for the roofs."

"But *how* were the forts burned?"

"It is one of the mysteries of early British history. Along the north of this border, from coast to coast, the natives of early Scotland apparently repulsed the legions of Rome from further advances."

"When did it happen?"

"The year was 105 A.D."

Andrew thanked her for the information, browsed a bit more, purchased two books, then walked out to the site. After a brief walk through the remains of the fort, he made his way to a solitary portion of the outer wall. There he located a large, partially dried stone protected by a remnant of wall face, sat down, shifted the pack from his back, and took out the luncheon he had packed for himself.

He wondered if the descendants of Cruithne and Fidach might have been among those Caledonian tribes who withstood the Roman advances.

Andrew opened one of the books he had just bought. As he quietly ate his lunch, he began to read about that epoch between vague prehistory and known history. It had been then, in the first and second centuries A.D. that the Roman Caesars had attempted to subdue the most distant reaches of their empire . . . that northern portion of the isle they had named Britannia.

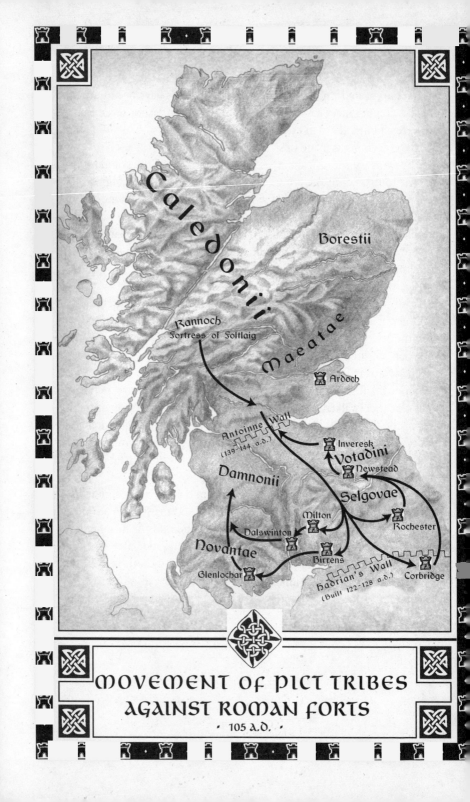

Caledonii

Borestii

Maeatae

Rannoch
Fortress of Foltlaig

Ardoch

Antoinne Wall
(139–144 a.d.)

Inveresk
Votadini
Newstead

Damnonii

Selgovae

Milton

Rochester

Dalswinton

Novantae

Birrens

Glenlochar

Hadrian's Wall
(Built 122–128 a.d.)

Corbridge

MOVEMENT OF PICT TRIBES
AGAINST ROMAN FORTS
· 105 A.Ð. ·

9

TO WITHSTAND AN EMPIRE

A.D. 105

✖ ONE ✖

The young man called Foltlaig, son of Gatheon, was twenty-two when he went out with his father and thousands of their tribesmen to fight the Romans. The day was etched in his brain like the hot coals of fire into which he stared at this moment.

How proud he had been, how strong and virile, marching side by side with his father and following the great general Gaelbhan to battle!

None of the inner turmoil of his later years had plagued his soul that morning. He had felt only the thrill of approaching battle, the challenge of facing the foe and emerging the victor.

The anguish had come several hours later when suddenly, at his side, his father had stumbled and fallen. . . .

Foltlaig turned. At first he could not comprehend the unthinkable. He glanced around . . . why was blood splattering about him?

Then came the horrifying realization. It was spurting from his father's chest!

He fell to his knees, then burst into boyish sobs, babbling words he would never remember afterward. Gently he attempted to lift his father's head, then cradled it in his arms only long enough to see a feeble smile and hear the weak words of farewell.

"Do not let them . . . take it . . . they mustn't take it from us," the warrior struggled to say. "Keep . . . protect the land . . . do not let—"

The words broke off. The dying soldier attempted to draw in a breath.

"I won't, Father," sobbed Foltlaig. "I will fight the strangers until they are gone."

"They mustn't . . . can't have our land . . ." The voice was faint.

"I won't let them, Father—I promise."

" . . . have to protect—"

Then a choking sound, and the whispered words that Foltlaig alone could hear in the midst of the battlefield tumult. It mattered not—they were meant for him and no other.

" . . . my son . . ."

Then the light faded from his eyes, and he was gone.

The reminder of his youthful tears brought Foltlaig back to the present and the importance of the mission they were discussing. A little more than twenty years had passed since the day his father fell. Foltlaig was now a man of forty-two, a leader among his people. He had taken his father's place and now had a son of his own. And still his people faced the encroaching presence of the swarthy-skinned invaders from the south.

Now he sat with his own and the chieftain of a neighboring tribe in a wide stone dwelling laced with great timbers, dark and primitive, yet containing many of the implements, tools, weapons, and other accouterments of a steadily advancing culture.

He was an eighth great-grandson of Cruithne, ancient ruler of the great Pritenae tribe now called the Caledonii.

Across the dirt floor, though this salient fact was known to neither, sat listening an equally distant descendant of the ruthless kinsman who had murdered the old chief's mother.

On the present occasion, however, Foltlaig—so named after the third son of Cruithne—was joined in conclave with his own chief and their distant Maeatae cousin for purposes of common intent.

Though the matrilineal line of descent among the Caledonii excluded him from the line of chiefs, Foltlaig was widely respected as a battle strategist—perhaps the greatest among the Caledonii since old Gaelbhan had roused the north against the Romans a generation earlier. It was perhaps a strange honor for one who was also one of the gentlest men in the tribe, one who would kill neither man nor beast without necessity. In truth, Foltlaig had inherited not only Cruithne's prowess and battle sense, but also the sensitivity and tenderness of his brother Fidach. Thus did the bonds of their ancient brotherhood—as well as the tension between their two natures—live on within his breast.

It was Foltlaig's inheritance from Cruithne, however, that was now required—for this meeting was nothing less than a council of war.

His own chief, Coel, leader of the district of mountainous Athfotla between Loch Lochy and the Firth of Tay—the southernmost of the Caledonii chieftains—had requested that his Maeatae counterpart join them in serious counsel.

They sat in the Caledonii chief's stone, wood, and turf dwelling. Construction of such homes had made great advances in the course of the previous three hundred years, as their people drifted southward into the Highlands north of Loch Rannoch. The peat fire between them was unchanged, however, in the years since the ancients had learned of its heat-giving properties. The same remarkable fuel now glowed as brightly as when it had warmed the hands and feet of the northland's inhabitants in years back beyond memory. It still burned hot, still smoked with singular odor, and still contained the essence of life in this frigid and inhospitable land.

Perhaps in the very flames now burning between them lay also the solution to the common difficulty which had brought these two rival chieftains together in an uneasy peace.

The visiting Maeatae chieftain, a somber-faced warrior named Ainbach, had just spoken.

Coel of the Caledonii waited, then cast his eyes over at Foltlaig. He had learned to depend upon his warrior-commander in such matters. The reach of his own influence had grown wide precisely because of his willingness to trust in Foltlaig's judgment.

Foltlaig extended his hands toward the fire that had prompted his brief interlude of reflection, then rubbed them briskly together. At length he spoke in answer to the question just posed by their visitor.

"You are wise to be cautious," he replied thoughtfully. "In truth, I do not know whether our brothers to the north and west will join us."

"If not, I see no possibility that your plan can succeed," said Ainbach.

Foltlaig glanced at his own chief, who still offered no comment on the matter.

"My plan requires no great numbers," Foltlaig said. "Only courage . . . and the united support of all the tribes in the region."

"You think to defeat the Romans without a great army? You think you will accomplish what your own Gaelbhan was unable to do?"

Ainbach's apparent doubt at last roused Coel to speech.

"What choice do we have? What choice do any of us have?" spoke the Caledonii leader. "If they are not turned back now," Coel went on, "they will overrun your people in Ochils and eventually proceed to Strathmore.

And then beyond! Conquest is their only purpose. They will swallow your people, then mine. They must be stopped, I tell you. Do not discount Foltlaig's plan, my Maeatae cousin."

Coel spoke from no hollow, groundless fear. During the previous century, scattered Pritenae had drifted southward below the Clyde, even as far south as the Cheviot Hills and Tweed. Some returned with tales of a conquering people from a distant land who were marching northward in great legions, vanquishing all who attempted to withstand them.

Nor had the northern tribes long to wait before witnessing the truth of these reports with their own eyes.

Neither Coel nor Foltlaig nor Ainbach nor any of their people knew anything of the place from which these trespassers came. They knew nothing of Rome except that it was far away across the waters. The name of the Roman governor Agricola, who had pushed the Roman presence far to the north, had carried no meaning to the ears of their fathers, and these men presently gathered scarcely knew that Agricola himself was no longer in Britain. Certainly they would not have recognized the name of the current Roman emperor, Trajan. They only knew that the Roman forces had advanced northward two generations before, building their stone-and-timber forts all the way from Carlisle to the Forth-Clyde line and carrying out deadly forays into their own regions. A few expeditions had extended as far north as Moray, where the great battle of Foltlaig's youth had been fought, and where his father had died.

Now Roman forts and outposts dotted the landscape in the regions of the Selgovae and the Votadini. The northern tribes all feared for the day when the urge for conquest would again fill the minds of the foreigners.

Thus Coel had sent a messenger to Ainbach, requesting this council. At the same time he had summoned his own commander, Foltlaig son of Gatheon, to begin preparations for a plan to protect their region from the encroaching southern menace.

"Perhaps the Selgovae and Damnonii will assist us," said Ainbach at length, "and the Votadini."

It was the very suggestion Foltlaig had hoped to hear. He knew the tribal rivalries were more severe in the south, where borders were closer. If he misstepped in trying to bring the tribes together, a great intertribal war could result. Such would be worse than sharing their land with the Romans. Thus he had waited, hoping the idea of the tribes joining together would come from one of the chieftains.

"I am certain of it," now replied Foltlaig enthusiastically. "And the Novantae. Every tribe lost men during the time of my father. The Selgovae have sought vengeance against the intruders ever since they began erecting their fortresses. They require but a spark to ignite their thirst for revenge."

"Do you speak for yourself as well, son of Gatheon?"

Foltlaig hesitated a moment before he spoke. "My father went to his death behind Gaelbhan. I vowed no revenge on that day. Such is not my way. But I do seek freedom for our land. I must do my duty to his memory by keeping my people, and yours, free from these who would conquer us."

"You cannot succeed alone."

"That I realize only too well. We must lay aside the strife that has divided the many tribes of our land. We must join hands as one."

As Foltlaig spoke, he glanced toward each of the two powerful Celtic tribal chieftains, the one of his own Caledonii, the other of the powerful Maeatae. He knew what pride and independence drove such men. He knew that the mere suggestion that they relinquish a portion of their authority to join with those who had in times past been their enemies was a bold and precarious proposal. If his plan was not well received, he could pay for his imprudence with his life. Yet Cruithne and Fidach's vision lived on in him. Deep in his being, he knew that in the uniting of the tribes lay their best chance for success.

"The usurpers think we are savages," he went on. "But we will use cunning to prevail against their numbers and their swords and the metal in which they dress themselves. *If we unite,* they can be turned back."

"You speak with boldness, son of Gatheon," remarked Ainbach.

"And in boldness we shall defeat them!" rejoined Coel. "If the others will heed my Foltlaig's plan."

"You have taken the first steps?" asked Ainbach, now turning toward Coel's trusted general.

"We have already sent messengers to the Borestii in the north," replied Foltlaig. "They too await vengeance for hostages taken twenty years ago. Messengers have also gone out to the tribes of the Damnonii, your neighbors. All that remains is for you to gather the chiefs of the Maeatae and for us to convince our Caledonii brothers. That accomplished, we will entreat the Selgovae, the Novantae, and the Votadini also to join our cause."

The Maeatae chieftain cast a long, appraising look at Foltlaig. "I will do what I am able," he said at length.

"The snows of winter will soon be upon us. We will await word from the other tribes and then reconvene with the first spring thaw. If we rouse our people as one and swoop down upon them before the winter's sleep is gone from their eyes, victory will be ours!"

"I shall return in the spring, then."

"A summons will be sent," added Foltlaig. "Bring others of your people who can help us."

Coel and Ainbach rose and clasped hands, an occurrence that had not been seen between chieftains of the Caledonii and Maeatae within generations of memory. Foltlaig sat where he was, his heart full as he quietly observed the handclasp. Not until this moment had he dared dream they would go along with his plan. Now suddenly success seemed possible.

If these two peoples, he thought, enemies from beyond memory, could henceforth begin to behave as the brothers they indeed were, their mutual Celtic blood would unify them against the common enemy to their shared inheritance, the land of their ancient ancestry.

▘▘   T W O   ▘▘

On the mainland continent of Europe, which the Wanderer and those like him had left behind longer ago than men remembered, those of their shared Celtic blood had by this time risen into a great civilization and waned.

These people who had originated in the valleys of the Rhone, the Rhine, and the Danube under the northern shadow of the Alps were by any standards an amazing race—a stalwart breed of warriors and wanderers whose collective personality could perhaps most accurately be described by the archaic word "puissant." The Celts were a *puissant* people—strong, mighty, virile, zealous, fervent, forceful—full of intensity, energy, drive, emotion, inventiveness, and creativity.

They worshiped nature, and honored as many gods as there were mysteries about the world they did not understand. The creation of idols to their deities—as well as accouterments of battle and everyday life—was aided by an artistic sensitivity and advanced skill in metal and enamel work. Their priests, called druids, were given to barbaric ritual, gathering yearly for solemn assembly at holy sites where they left altars stained with human blood. Yet these druids were also learned in advance of their time, adept at plant and animal lore, astrology, and music, and would be largely responsible for Celtism's enduring influence.

As recently as the time of Cruithne's father, Taran—around 300 B.C.—the Celts had held sway from the North Sea to the Mediterranean, from the European Atlantic coast to the Black Sea, which looked eastward toward Asia, from the north of what would soon become known as Britannia to the south of the peninsula where the city-state of Rome was slowly growing in might. They had occupied the very center stage of Europe's development. The cities of London, Geneva, Lyon, Strasbourg, Bonn, Budapest, Vienna, and Belgrade were all Celtic settlements. Celtic tribal names left their mark across the entire European map: the Parisii in Paris, the Remi in Rheims, the Helvetii in Helvetia, later called Switzerland, the Belgae in Belgium, the Boii in Bologna and Bohemia. From their Latin name *Galli* came the name for the Galatians in Asia Minor, as well as the Gaelic tongue.

In one aspect of advancing modernity, however, the Celts did not excel. They lacked centralized organization. No cohesive form of government held their empire together. No single head nor king nor capital rose preeminent. Theirs was a fierce *individualism* that prevented organizational *unity*. Their culture, therefore, remained tribal and heterogeneous.

Though the Celts at their height sacked Rome and pillaged Greece, the civilizations of Athens and Rome possessed features that would enable them ultimately to outshine Celtic influence—centralized government, a preserved and documented language which contributed to the development of literature and libraries, a sophisticated tradition of engineering and architecture, and a uniform economy upon which to base business and trade.

But in the fragmentation of the Celtic civilization . . . in its proclivity toward individuality and separateness . . . in its preference of loyalty to family and clan rather than to region and nation . . . in the divisiveness of its rival factions . . . can be descried the factors that centuries later would draw history's curtain down upon Celtic culture.

Romans were loyal to *Rome*. Where lay their pride? In being *Roman* citizens. The independent Celts, however, were loyal only to tribe and family. This *individualism* was both the pride and the doom of the Celt. The very strength of Celtic heritage was the Achilles' heel of potential nationhood.

The might of Rome eventually reached its zenith in the first century called anno Domini and continued its spread outward across the globe. Fragmented and disunited, the waning Celtic confederation was by then unable to stop Caesar's mighty legions. As their civilization gave way to the Romans, the Celts migrated in droves throughout the western world—to the west in the direction of England, France, Ireland, Wales, Scotland, Belgium,

Holland, and also east to the steppes of Hungary, Bulgaria, and Russia. The trickle of previous millennia became a migratory flood.

Year by year, the Celts found themselves pressed farther and farther from the central regions of the European continent they once dominated, pushed ever more toward its outward extremities—toward the north, toward the west, toward the waters and across them . . . to escape the Latin advance.

In the far north of the land the Romans called Britannia, however, unmolested by the turbulent changes sweeping through Europe, and unseen by those continental races of Celts to whom they owed their heritage, another scion of tribes had through the centuries been growing on the worldwide Celtic ancestral tree.

They were a people rising into prominence even while their continental Celtic cousins were being overrun—a people still strong, still energetic, still puissant with the hot blood of Celtic passion.

▓   T H R E E   ▓

Foltlaig, son of Gatheon, left the stone enclosure of his chief and walked slowly outside the camp.

His steps took him to the shoreline of Loch Rannoch, from whose waters his people drew much of their sustenance, and on, upward along a steep path sloping ruggedly away from the lake. He arrived, after a lengthy climb of more than thirty minutes, at a high overlook from which he could see the long outline of Loch Rannoch spreading out in front of him, with the Caledonii settlement led by Coel on its banks.

The day was cold. Foltlaig pulled the animal pelt more tightly about his shoulders and chest, then sat down on a great stone and gazed upon the buildings below. Smoke rose from most of the stone and turf dwellings of the fortress and wafted toward him on the light wind. He found the aroma a pleasant one. It spoke to him of comfort and protection against the elements, of his people's capacity to subdue nature and even to put it to use against itself—making fire from the earth's treasure house to keep out one of its most lethal perils, the cold of winter's snows.

This was a good land, he thought, and it gave his people a good life. It provided fish and many four-legged and winged creatures to eat—as well as food for the sheep they raised in their fields. From the soil, rocky and boggy though it was in many places, they were able to coax grains and vegetables.

The skins of the beasts who roamed the earth and the peat from under the earth kept them warm.

He drew in a deep sigh and stretched his gaze around in all directions—beyond the loch and the settlement below and toward the great mountains in the distance, some already capped with snow.

Yes, it was good land, and he loved it with every fiber of his being.

If only . . .

The sigh of pleasure turned melancholy.

If only the men who inhabited it were as compatible with one another as the land and its creatures were with themselves, as its elements were with those who found ways to use them.

For it was *man*—not the beasts, not the elements, not the snows nor the hail nor the freezing colds nor the poor soil—who was enemy to survival in this place. And it was the enmity of his own people against themselves—one tribe against another—that threatened them more than the encroachment of the soldiers from the south.

It had warmed his heart more than any peat fire to see the clasp of hands between Coel and Ainbach. The rare show of unity and brotherhood had touched him so deeply that he had hurried to be alone on this beloved outlook overspreading the valley of his home.

He knew it probably couldn't last. Conflict between the rival tribes was bound to be renewed, breaking out again as through the generations. It saddened him to think of it.

Complex stirrings swirled within the breast of the Celtic paladin, vibrations of race and ancestry pulling at him from opposite directions, setting the diverse natures of the two ancient brothers against each other in the bowels of his soul. He was by nature a man of both pragmatism and poetry, of peace and war, of thought and action.

It was an inner warfare with which he had struggled most of his days. For he was a paradoxical man, this reflective Caledonian warrior. Those of his kind who were driven by more primal instincts said he thought too much. Perhaps they were right. Yet he would become a progenitor of his race as surely as the two brothers of old. The turmoil of his broodings would lay foundations for much of the future history of the realms upon which his eyes now gazed.

The meeting with the two chiefs and the thought of the approaching conflict could not help drive his memory back twenty years, for the tension within his soul stemmed from his personal experience as well as the intrinsic paradox of his nature. How much of his contradictory emotions grew from what he had heard and seen on that fateful afternoon when his whole personal history had been altered forever?

Moisture filled his eyes. He did not try to prevent it.

⁂   F O U R   ⁂

Foltlaig recalled little of what happened on that day after the moment he realized his father was dead. He only remembered lifting his face to the sky and shrieking in mournful agony.

He was left fatherless in the heat of battle. Yet he could neither pause to mourn, nor even move the warm corpse of the man from whose loins he had come. Charging Roman horses and infantrymen ran about in a frenzy of arrows, lances, and flailing swords.

How the day passed, Foltlaig could not remember. When it was over, blood covered every inch of his body, though he was not himself wounded. Whether it was Roman in origin or came from his own people, he did not know. He may have killed, he may have struck down a dozen soldiers in the fury of his grief—he remembered nothing. He had seen only the blood.

He returned at the end of the day, searching through the carnage for the only body that mattered to him. He found it mostly unchanged, though the flesh had grown cold, stiff, and unfriendly. He picked up what remained of his father and carried it to a nearby wood. There, weeping without shame, he buried the man he had always considered the bravest and most invincible of all the Caledonii.

His people had been slaughtered that day, his father and countless others. Throughout the sleepless night that followed—and many sleepless nights and days as he returned to Rannoch—the words he had uttered to his father came back to him again. They were all he could recall of what he said that day, but he remembered them with a vividness that would never leave him.

I will fight the strangers until they are gone, the words from his own mouth rang in his brain.

I promise, Father. I will not let them take the land.

In the lonely despair of those nights, however, Foltlaig also made another vow—this one to himself. If he ever had a son, he would keep the boy from facing the horrible loss he had just experienced. He would live a long and full life with his son, and they would grow old together.

That same year, Foltlaig's wife gave birth to his son, Maelchon.

Foltlaig never forgot his vow. As the boy grew, no father and son among all the Caledonii were as inseparable as Foltlaig and Maelchon. They loved each other not only as father and son, but as bosom friends.

Neither did Foltlaig forget his promise to his own dying father. His vow was not to avenge that death by spilling Roman blood, but to prevent such from coming upon them again—by driving the encroachers from the land.

The two promises seemed set at odds against each other. But he could ignore neither. He was both a son and a father, a warrior and a man of peace. Thus within his bosom grew the conflict between his promise to his father and the vow he had made within himself to live a long and peaceable life with his son.

As the years passed, Foltlaig could not escape destiny's call. He knew he would ultimately be forced to make a choice he was loath to contemplate. It was the dread feeling that it would one day rest with *him* to take up the sword of Gaelbhan . . . and face the same foe in battle.

Again had risen up two distinct persons within his breast, battling for supremacy. It was the inner battle between the warrior and the father.

Which Foltlaig was highest—the son of Gatheon, or the father of Maelchon? To whom did he owe greatest allegiance—his clan and its land . . . or his family?

Such destiny was unsought. Foltlaig desired to be no hero of his people. He was an unwilling warrior, one who would gladly live out his life without lifting his sword again. He remained determined that no war would take from *his* son what had been so cruelly snatched from him at the height of his youth—a father.

But he was Coel's greatest strategist, after all. He could not show himself coward before eyes of chief or son or clan. Thus he occupied his position as tribal leader, and kept his fears and personal dreams hidden away in the secret places of his own heart.

F I V E

Foltlaig smiled. His melancholy faded as memories of his conflicting promises gave way to thoughts of the daring scheme those very promises had caused to unfold.

By and by a plan had taken shape in Foltlaig's mind—a way to defeat the intruders *without* the shedding of Caledonian blood.

Perhaps they could make this land so inhospitable to the Romans that they would leave—if not of their own accord, at least with some unpleasant encouragement.

He would outwit the Romans rather than amassing an army against them!

Such an objective lay at the core of the plan he had eventually shared with his chief—a plan not of cowardice, but of cunning. Coel hated the Romans, but he was not eager to go to his death in another battle such as that of Mons Graupius. The chief, therefore, heartily agreed.

Foltlaig gave himself to working out every conceivable detail, bringing Maelchon into the planning with him. As he became more and more convinced of success, his inner anxiety diminished. He would accomplish both purposes to which he was dedicated—he would fulfill his promise to his father by driving the Romans away, *and* he would enjoy long life with his son.

His thoughts were interrupted by the sound of a footstep approaching along the rocky path he himself had followed a short while earlier.

He glanced up. As if in response to his thoughts, there stood his son.

"Maelchon! How did you know where to find me?"

"I saw you leave the camp, Father," replied the youth, a lean but muscular twenty-year-old.

"You knew I would be here?"

"Where else? I know where you go to think, and from your slow step I knew your mind was full. Is all well, Father? Did the two chiefs agree to your plan?"

"Yes, Maelchon, they did."

"Then we will be victorious!" said his son with the enthusiasm of youth.

Foltlaig nodded.

"I only regret that it is always through battle that such matters as these must be solved."

"The intruders are our enemies," said Maelchon. "They must be stopped. I have heard you say it yourself many times."

Again Foltlaig nodded.

"Perhaps you should take my place as Coel's commander."

"Not so long as *you* live, Father."

The young man sat down and gazed over the blue-green water below. Even Maelchon, as well as he knew his father, did not fully comprehend the sympathetic, thoughtful, and tender side of Foltlaig's being . . . nor the price his father paid in attempting to reconcile the diverse natures within him.

The two remained silent for some time, then gradually resumed their conversation, discussing the new developments in the plan they had devised together.

Fidach's haunting sensitivities had been temporarily subdued in the heart of Foltlaig. They had spent themselves remembering the past. Now within the bearing of the man who was Coel's trusted commander, the warrior Cruithne had emerged dominant again over the present.

When the two descended the hill together an hour later, arm of father over shoulder of son, they spoke excitedly about what lay ahead, eager to implement their designs on behalf of the Caledonians and their Celtic brethren.

✦ S I X ✦

Three centuries had passed since the two Pritenae brothers had first practiced the ideal of unity that would one day be the hope for their land. The conquering Romans who discovered their descendants did not know they were the distant offspring of the same Celts their Roman forebears had battled on the European continent. Taking them for a new, previously unknown race of people, they had therefore given these fiercely independent northern tribes a new name.

These people would be identified by the conquering legions, and forever known to later generations by the tattoos on their skin. The Romans called the tribes *Picti*—"the painted people"—and *Pritenii*—"people of the designs."

These northern Celts left behind no written accounts of their civilization. Yet they possessed considerable skill in working with the most prevalent commodity their land produced: *stone* . . . the essential building block of a nation—granite, in all sizes and shapes—from pebbles to giant boulders no fifty Goliaths could budge. By these stones they documented their legacy.

The Picts took stone and with it raised dwellings, wheelhouses, forts, ovens, furnaces, circular duns, and monuments. The most remarkable such construction was the *broch*—ancestor to the stone castle—a circular tower up to fifty feet in diameter and rising to heights of forty or fifty, with walls up to fifteen feet thick at the base and stairways rising to the parapet walks atop them. In the enclosed center, an open central area provided living quarters as well as protection from enemies. This Pictish fabrication was carried out without the use of mortar—a drystone construction.

The Picts also left behind monuments of giant standing stones, upon which they carved their own unique style of decoration. In the absence of written records, their living quarters and these stone landmarks, in addition to the murky tales and myths passed down through the centuries, provided the most substantial links to their culture for those who followed them.

When records eventually began to be kept by the Picts, the most prominent was a list of the kings that had evolved out of their ancient tribal chieftainships. The most distant records revealed the name of an ancient Celt by the name of Cruithne, who came in later years to be considered their first king. When the Irish later migrated to the land and encountered these Picts, they gave to their whole race the name *Cruithne* after this first king. Cruithne, it was said, had married and fathered seven sons who ruled after him, dividing the kingdom of the Picts into its seven provinces.

It was not until the year 55 B.C. that the Roman general Julius Caesar, with all of continental Europe and parts of Africa and Asia Minor under his feet, turned his eyes across the English Channel and himself sailed from Gaul across to Dover.

Rome was in a headlong rush to conquer the known world. Never had a people—from Palestine to England—successfully fended off its might. Over the course of the next century the island the Romans called Britannia, like most of Europe and the Middle East, was also overtaken by the ruthless efficiency of Caesar's legions.

Fortresses were built and soldiers sent to man them. Communications stretched between these outposts. Roads were laid down for Rome's armies. Fleets moved up the eastern coastline while the legions tramped northward by horse and foot. Latinized names were attached to every place on the great island. Indigenous tribes everywhere were brought under Roman control.

All but the northernmost segments of the island were eventually secure. These were the regions dominated by two major Celtic tribes—the Caledonii and the Maeatae—and four smaller.

Thus it was that when the Roman governor of Britannja, Petilius Cerealis, reached Carlisle between A.D. 71 and 74, he sent reconnaissance forces farther north to establish outpost fortresses, in order that the Romanization of the island might at last be completed. Gnaeus Julius Agricola, who replaced Cerealis in A.D. 78, pressed the advance with even more vigor. By the year 80 he had penetrated to the Firth of Tay on the east coast and begun to construct still more outposts. Four years later, far to the north, he had laid waste a huge indigenous army of the painted barbarians led by him they called Galgacus at the place the Romans called Mons Graupius, defeating them handily, taking hostages, and putting many more to the sword.

Indeed, by the time Agricola was withdrawn from the region and recalled back to Rome, most of the north appeared to be under the empire's power. The governor had constructed some thirty forts in all, each skillfully situated and modern of innovation and design.

What Agricola did not know, however, was that among the natives dwelt a survivor of Mons Graupius who might well prove his equal. When the time was ripe this warrior, now grown, would match his cunning against Rome's might, to avenge a father who had fallen on the battlefield, slain by Roman sword.

Though nowhere else in all the empire had its legions been forced to retreat before a native people, Rome had not yet entirely subdued the Cruithneach, known as the Caledonii.

SEVEN

As the gentle but determined Caledonian warrior predicted, the snows came early. And thick. It was the coldest winter in Foltlaig's memory. The white powder still lay in drifts the following May.

The snow and its cold had not brought idleness, however. Foltlaig had spent the snowy winter months perfecting a very different strategy to defeat these latter-day Romans than his continental kin had used five centuries earlier to sack the city whence originated these interlopers. On his mind was no raid on Rome itself, but rather a conquest that would prevent its soldiers making further penetration, and perhaps drive them from the north altogether.

Throughout the winter, Foltlaig had been unable to quiet the disturbing voices within him. He remembered the old Caledonian leader Gaelbhan well, remembered his courage and the stirring words of his call to arms. Would that crusty old warrior consider him a coward for going out to meet the enemy in the dead of night rather than mounting a great pitched battle as he had done?

And yet, Foltlaig argued with himself, Mons Graupius had shown that the Pritenae warriors could never defeat the more organized and efficient Roman soldiers in direct battle. Something more than sheer numbers was needed.

The nature of that something more would be the subject of the upcoming meeting that Coel had now called again with the Maeatae, as well as with leaders of the Borestii from the east and the Damnonii, Votadini, Selgovae, and Novantae from the south.

The hour would soon be at hand for them to reclaim their land, hold it, secure it, and drive the Romans from it, as Foltlaig had promised his father. Such could be accomplished only if the various tribes could lay aside their feuds and disputes and rally together as one.

To this purpose, Foltlaig and Maelchon had traveled tirelessly throughout the winter months garnering support among the tribes north of the Solway. For the past three weeks, Maelchon had sojourned to the northern brethren of their own Caledonii, as well as the neighboring Borestii. He was due back at the fortress any day, and Foltlaig eagerly awaited his return.

Word had arrived yesterday that the Maeatae chieftain, Ainbach, true to his word, had convinced the Votadini to link with their cause. He himself would arrive with the Votadini chief early next week. Foltlaig had personally extracted promises from the three southwestern tribes to join them as well.

A messenger interrupted his thoughts.

"Your son has entered the settlement, Son of Gatheon."

Foltlaig glanced up. Quickly he rose and followed the bearer of the happy tidings outside.

❋   E I G H T   ❋

Several hours had passed.

Foltlaig and his son Maelchon walked out of the settlement and across the wide expanse of heath. Most of the snow in this open space had melted. There had been no fresh fall for ten days, though clumps and mounds of white still clung to the shadowy recesses.

They continued for some time in silence. The elder man's strong muscular arm stretched around the equally muscular shoulders of the youth, who was actually a finger's width taller than his father. Little could they know how similar they were in display of shared love—for which there was no shame among those who drew ancestral strength and vision from their emotion-rich

Celtic blood—to some of their own notable patriarchs.

"The news you bring gladdens my heart, my son," said Foltlaig at length. "I confess, I harbored an anxiety that our brother tribes to the north might not agree to join us. Neither their land nor that of the Borestii is yet threatened, so I feared they might not come."

"You and Coel remain their leaders, Father."

"Perhaps. But it seems they grow more independent each year."

"Perhaps I shall have to marry one of their chieftains' daughters and become chief myself."

"A worthy plan to keep the Caledonii united," laughed Foltlaig. "But what of the girl's mother and brother? You know as well as I that one does not become chief among the Caledonii so easily!"

"There are the ancient seven sons of Cruithne."

"An unusual case among our kings."

Foltlaig took his arm from around his son. They continued to chat casually.

"Will they really come, Father, do you think?" asked the younger man after a brief silence.

"It begins to seem so, Maelchon," replied Foltlaig, "if all the reports are true. You yourself have brought the good news from the north."

"Even if they do not, we could still carry out our plan with men from our own tribe."

"You are right, of course. But it is not merely great numbers we need, but rather the precedent of working together. If we do not do this now, how will those who follow be able to do it in the future?"

"Why is it so difficult for our people to join in common cause?"

"Because men find it easier to dispute than to unite. Easier to fight than to live and work together."

"I have heard you say it often, Father," said Maelchon. "Yet you yourself are a fighter."

"I do not fight unless it is the only way. I would always rather seek resolution by other means. Nor do I fight with my own, but only against a clear enemy."

"You are commander of all the Caledonii."

"Because our chief has made me so. He values my ability to outwit both man and beast. And he thinks I possess a certain courage."

"You are the bravest warrior in the land, Father! Everyone knows it."

Foltlaig smiled.

"Perhaps that is why so many even of our own people find it difficult to understand me," he replied. "You remember our saying, *Na sir 's na seachain an cath.*"

"I remember."

"Neither seek nor shun the fight. When the enemy shows himself, only a coward turns away. When fighting is required, none worthy of being called a man will shrink from the confrontation. Yet many are the battles a wise man does not have to fight, but into which fools rush headlong. A man displays no lack of courage by using intelligence and strategy to prevent hostilities. It is a matter of wisdom, not cowardice, to discover where a man may agree with his fellows."

"But in this matter of the southerners," asked Maelchon "—is this not a time when we must fight?"

Foltlaig was silent a long while. How could his son comprehend the depths in the question he had posed? It had taken Foltlaig himself twenty years to know how to face it. That the question now came from his very son's lips made the answer all the more difficult.

"I believe it is just such a time," he said at length. "But we will fight not to kill, but to demoralize. I would take no life unless it is required. Killing *may* be required but is not the chief duty before us. What is important is that we drive the Romans from our land. If they persist, then we may have to kill, but not before."

Again a silence fell. As in one accord, both men turned and began walking slowly back toward the fortress. Maelchon reflected on his father's words.

"Why do you say," he asked after some time, "that the tribal leaders must join together now so that those who come after them will also be able to?"

Foltlaig smiled.

"It is another one of my habits that some of the men tire of," he replied, "—always looking ahead, trying to see into the future. But to answer you— I am concerned for those of our people who will follow us, for your grandsons and their grandsons, and theirs after them."

He paused and gazed all about them where they stood.

"Look around you, Maelchon—what do you see? A beautiful land, but a cold, hard one as well. You and I love this land precisely because it is such. Only the strongest and fittest choose to dwell here. This will never be a land of ease. Those who make their home here will forever do so because they love the loneliness of its vast reaches. Those who come after us will never be able to hold this land without recognizing their brotherhood upon it."

Foltlaig paused briefly. He thought again of his father. "The Maeatae and the Selgovae are truly our brothers," he went on, "united to us from long ago by ties of blood. Yes, there have been times I have had to fight against them. I have occasionally even fought against those among our own Caledonii who have risen against our chief. But such must not be our way.

"There will always be enemies. There are tales of treachery from times past, among our own people, which swirl in vague mists, mingling the legends of our first and mighty king. That was many generations ago. We must no longer be our *own* enemies. Only in unity will we hold this land.

"In common blood and heritage and purpose we *must* join, we *must* unite. We must make mutual cause against these interlopers, or you may be assured, my son, that the day will come when those who follow us will lose this land."

❋   N I N E   ❋

The representatives of the other tribes came, just as Foltlaig had hoped.

By late spring all had convened at the Caledonii fortress of Rannoch. The gathering of Pict leaders was unprecedented. The seven tribes represented had battled amongst themselves for two centuries to maintain and expand their respective territories. Occasional alliances had formed between two of the tribes, but only for the purpose of making war against some third.

That the chiefs of all seven had now come together against a common enemy would not have been believed by any of them had a seer foretold it a year earlier. But each now realized the enemy from without was too strong for any of them to resist alone.

Even united, most wondered what chance they had. The Roman fortresses throughout their region had been standing and manned for twenty years. The great leader Gaelbhan had been thoroughly routed at Mons Graupius. Twenty years before that, farther to the south, the revolt of the now-famous warrioress Boudicca had likewise ended in defeat, with the mighty Celtic queen taking her own life by poison. No one who had tried to stand against the Romans had succeeded for long. How could they possibly hope to succeed now?

And yet they came to Rannoch, some twenty or thirty of them, all seven chiefs and many of Foltlaig's counterparts from their tribes. Four women were among them—one chief and three warrior generals. Boudicca's reputation had spread, with the result that more and more Celtic women were rising up to rival the males of their clans in military might. The chieftainess from the Damnonii had risen to her present position by parading through her village with the head of her predecessor, a man, on the end of her sharpened, metal-tipped spear. She had only been challenged once since, with the same result.

Most of those present were large, the women as well as the men, and powerful. A few displayed reddish and purple markings on their faces. On the arms and shoulders and chests of the men and of one woman who wore no covering above the waist could be seen great variety of artful tattoos, in pattern and design much like those that adorned their symbolic standing stones, pottery, and other carvings. The men as well as the four women wore about their necks and wrists jewelry made of silver, bone, and shell.

When food and drink had been sufficiently consumed and the assembly seated around a blazing peat fire—for the cold of winter had not altogether retreated before springtime's advance—Coel nodded to Foltlaig. He now rose to address the gathering.

"My fellow warriors," Foltlaig began, "on the eve of the battle when my own Caledonii brothers took arms against the southerners, I myself sat listening as the great Gaelbhan addressed his army. Never have I forgotten his stirring words. They were filled with challenge and hope. Yet before day's end they became a bitter memory, for I watched my own father die that day."

Foltlaig gazed intently at his hearers. His voice grew soft and reflective.

"Let me tell you again the words the great man spoke to us before the dreadful defeat of that day, to remind us that the same challenge is now before us."

Again he paused briefly, then raised his voice and began to recite from memory the words that, in equal proportion with love for his only son, had burned within him during the twenty years of his manhood.

" 'I believe,' Gaelbhan said, 'that what we do here today will mean the beginning of liberty for all of us. So many have fought against these foreigners, and now the final hope rests in us. We are here gathered, my Caledonian brothers—the last free men on this isle. The plunderers of the world, after exhausting the land with their devastation, have now advanced on us.

" 'We, the most distant dwellers upon the earth, have been protected from their advance until now. Our remoteness has kept us safe. But now they have come. And we will either become their slaves or send them back where they came from. As for me, I will never submit to them. I will stand with my back to the sea and my sword in my hand and await my destiny.' "

Foltlaig paused, eyes closed, bringing the next words to mind.

" 'Look back, my brothers,' he said. 'Beyond us lie no more tribes, nothing but waves and rocks and cliffs. Before us . . . the enemy.' "

Foltlaig stopped again and drew in a breath before completing the climax of the battle speech that once had so inspired him.

" 'But they have yet to subdue us,' Gaelbhan concluded. 'And they never will. We will show them how sharp are our spears, how valiant our hearts! So to battle! Think of your ancestors . . . and of your posterity!' "

Foltlaig's voice trailed into silence. The gathering fell somber.

In a culture where there were no written reminders of the past, such an oral tradition carried great weight. The flames of the burning peat danced silently into the air in the middle of the wide circle in which they sat. Every man and woman stared into its red-orange depths, pondering this message given, as from the grave, to those who now carried the future of this entire land on their shoulders. It was as if, through his remembered words, mighty Gaelbhan had come to life in their midst.

Foltlaig waited for his words to penetrate. He then resumed in a moderate voice.

"But despite the challenge of Gaelbhan," he said, "our people were slaughtered by the thousands that day—slaughtered by the swords of this same enemy we now face. Were the words of Gaelbhan then in vain?"

Again he waited.

"I think not," Foltlaig answered his own question. "It is still true that only by united effort will we succeed in preserving the freedom of the land that our ancestors possessed before the tramp of foreign armies was heard in the north.

"But it is all our tribes that must join together, not just the Caledonii. Never has there been such a gathering of tribal leaders, laying aside past hostilities and disputes over land and regions. I say that we will indeed join as the brothers of ancient blood that we are. We are, as Gaelbhan prophesied, the last dwellers on this remote corner of earth's shores. We must now show what manner of warrior we bring to the defense of our land!"

"Is that why you have summoned us here, to rouse the men and women from our tribes to united attack?" asked Deargicca of the Damnonii, the single female chief among them. She was a woman of enormous frame, with long reddish brown hair and deep voice. A knife was strapped to her colored tunic, and her muscular wrist and forearm indicated that she knew well how to use it. She wore a twisted torque of gold about her neck and bracelets on both wrists, and a large brooch upon her chest fastened the cloak about her shoulders. One look in her eyes confirmed that an adversary would be foolish to underestimate her. "I am no coward," she said, "but I do not relish Boudicca's fate."

"What if they come out with thrice our muster?" added a Borestii warrior. "I too fought as a young man at Mons Graupius. I have no wish to see our people cut down again."

"We will fight to the death when we must," added another. "But to do so is foolish if the cause is lost before it is begun."

Foltlaig raised his voice above the clamor of dissent that began to rise. "We must not only unite," he said. "We must employ cunning. What I propose is to a different purpose than the mere raising of weapons."

"Warriors such as the Romans understand only the sword!" called out another.

"Superior armies will never be ours," rejoined Foltlaig. "The defeat of Gaelbhan proved that merely to raise swords against them is not enough. It will never be enough. Should *all* the tribes of Pictland join together, and *every* man and woman go out into battle . . . it will not be enough. This is a thinly peopled land. The enemies from the south will always possess greater numbers. So we must be shrewd. We must bring our wits to the aid of our swords."

"This is fool's talk!" exclaimed one of the generals.

"To go out with mere weapons," Foltlaig answered levelly, "would be to face defeat again. I ask you—are you content to share your land with these Romans?"

A general murmur throughout the gathering—resembling more the growling of angry dogs than a council of war—indicated the answer clearly enough.

"Then we must achieve such an end with smaller numbers. I am certain the chieftainess of the Damnonii understands my meaning," he added, glancing toward Deargicca, then the other three women present. Deargicca returned his gaze coldly, without expression. "The women of our kind do not rise to such positions of leadership among many men without superior wits and cunning."

One or two of the women answered by inclining their heads slightly in assent. Still the Damnonii chieftainess stared.

"What is your plan, Foltlaig?" asked Ainbach of the Maeatae, who had the advantage of already having heard its general outline. "We will listen."

"To attack quickly, and by night—with a force so small as to be invisible."

"They fear us," objected another, "with our war cries and our painted bodies. We are no cowards to steal about in the darkness!"

"When the time is right for battle, we will face them with cries and our swords. But our numbers are far too small to confront their entire force. Far better to strike at the heart of their army, yet without losing our own. The blow that will carry throughout the land must be struck with stealth."

"How, Son of Gatheon?" asked Deargicca. At last she was intrigued.

Foltlaig did not respond immediately. Now that he had their attention, he would choose his words with care.

"With the coming of the first frost, send me forty of your strongest, swiftest, and most agile warriors from each of your seven tribes. There must be at least two skilled spearsmen among them. With these two hundred eighty, we will defeat this empire."

"You would defeat Rome with less than three hundred!" said the astonished Selgovae chief.

"Perhaps not the entire empire," replied Foltlaig, "but the corner of it that would bring *our* land under its domination."

"Bah! I ask again . . . how?"

"The men you send—or women of equal skill—must be fleet of foot, able to survive in the wilds, and willing to obey my every command. Give me such individuals, and the legions will draw back across the southern hills from which they came."

This was not what any had expected. Except for Ainbach, each of the other leaders had come anticipating an invitation to amass their troops and descend upon the enemy in all-out war.

The gathering fell silent. They pondered now the unexpected claim of Coel's commander. They respected the reputation of the son of Gatheon. He was surely no fool. They would have to hear more.

When the convocation broke up forty minutes later, each of the chiefs was satisfied. The way Foltlaig had laid out the details of his plan, the risk seemed small for so great an objective. Once he had gained the confidence of the wild-haired Deargicca and Ainbach, the others quickly joined in support.

"Will druids accompany the forces so that the gods are with them?" asked the Borestii chief.

"Your druids must offer their prayers and sacrifices in your villages and holy places, but may not accompany us. Speed and invisibility will be our allies. There can be no extra men or women among us."

A few murmurs went about. They knew their priests and magicians might object. If they agreed to Foltlaig's plan, this was a chance they would have to take.

"Why should our warriors travel all the way north to you, only to return southward again when you make your attacks?" asked the Selgovan leader. "Why do you not amass your troops nearer the fortresses of the enemy?"

"The training will be the most vital phase in our success," replied Foltlaig. "It can only be carried out far from risk of discovery. Your lands are too crossed with Roman byways."

Nods went around the group. At last all the questions had been satisfactorily answered.

That same evening, the Caledonii of Rannoch treated their guests to a great celebration, a lavish feast of wild boar and highland venison. How long the leaders of the seven Pict tribes would remain on such friendly terms as to eat and drink, sing, and make merry together might have been a question to ponder. For now, however, none seemed inclined to raise past disputes. By the time the fires of the camp burned low and they retired to their beds, it was very late, and most of the guests were more than half drunk. The Caledonii had spared nothing in their hospitality, even to the liberal provision of the best wine and ale from Coel's personal stores.

When the visitors left for their home regions two and three days hence, all had agreed to the plan of Coel's trusted general. When the warmth of summer was past, the assembling would commence of the two hundred eighty Picts who would withstand an empire.

Until then, Foltlaig and his son continued to work out the tactics whereby they would coordinate the companies of tens and seventies that would provide the foundation of their force.

Father and son spent the months of summer scouting through the land like Moses' twelve, yet with the faith of Caleb and Joshua, traveling to and spying upon their intended targets. Under the very noses of their enemy, joining with local natives selling livestock and produce, they managed to

penetrate most of the forts. There they silently observed and mentally practiced what must be done.

Thus were the details of their scheme perfected.

※   T E N   ※

In late August, Foltlaig and Maelchon returned north to Rannoch through
the lands of the Maeatae. At least temporarily there was no fear of harm
from the southern descendants of their ancient Roismaeatae cousins who
had slain King Cruithne's beloved brother.

As they were crossing the central plain between the forests of Ard and
the Great River, which centuries hence would be called the Forth, Foltlaig's
thoughts bent themselves toward the distant northlands from which the ancestors of the present Caledonii and Maeatae had migrated.

He had been waiting years for the right moment to take his son to the
ancient stones and there, within sight of the deserted hill-fort and broch of
Caldohnuill, to explain their meaning. His own father had made that same
northern sojourn with him shortly before they left with the rest to fight for
Mons Graupius.

Such had been the Caledonii tradition, his father had told him, since the
days of Cruithne himself. One by one the old king had taken his own sons,
when they were well advanced into manhood, to the place where he had spent
his early years. There had the king told to each the meaning of the stones
and enjoined upon them the duty of carrying on the tradition. And there, for
generations to come, the descendants of Cruithne had likewise taken their
own sons.

"Your own sons must be told," Gatheon had told Foltlaig, "though that
is not enough. You must not only tell them of Cruithne and Fidach. You must
also teach them to tell their sons and their sons after them. Otherwise the
message will die out in a few generations. Though bards pass along stories
of the past, every father must be a bard to his own sons and daughters. You
must take them to the stones, as I have taken you, that they might feel the
ancient vision with their hands and also observe the cost of failing to heed
it. Our grandsons must be told to pass it on to their grandsons and to teach
their grandsons to do likewise—into future generations . . . for all time."

As Foltlaig grew older he had come to see the wisdom of old Cruithne's
patriarchal charge, dedicated to a principle that would extend in perpetuity

to future generations. For the truth to be permanent, the generational links must not be broken.

As great as was his confidence in the plan he had devised, thought Foltlaig, when man went to battle one could never be certain of the outcome. Within two moons of his own visit to the monument as a young man, his father had fallen dead on the field of battle. Now was the time. He could wait no longer. Maelchon would father his own sons and daughters before many more years. The charge must be given.

When father and son arrived back at Rannoch after their final scouting mission, Foltlaig announced to Coel that all was in readiness. They now awaited only the proper season to strike. He then begged leave to journey to the north with his son. They would be gone perhaps three weeks.

Coel nodded his assent. He understood the importance of the standing stones and the slab of Laoigh. He too was descended from Cruithne, through the line of Circinn, and he too had sons. And they were all descended from him who was said to rest under the great sacred stone.

Three days later, Foltlaig and Maelchon set out on their northward journey, pursuing a course through the rugged Highlands. Many settlements and encampments of their own Caledonii brethren lay along their route. But they kept to themselves. This was a time for father and son to talk and laugh, to hunt and eat, to stalk game and share dreams, to sit and talk by the fire long into the night as two men—as comrades in the spartan challenge that life presented to those of these regions. Though their steps were hundreds of miles removed from those of their most ancient patriarchs—the Wanderer and his son—the feet of these two yet fell along the same pathways by which the old Celt's three grandsons had first carried the ancient Boii bloodline into these northern climes.

As they went, Foltlaig recounted to his son, as he often had before, many tales and legends of antiquity. Though the night rarely blackened their land during these warm months, it yet brought a subdued and quiet atmosphere. During its hours of solitude, Foltlaig broke occasionally into wailing chant or mournful melody as they sat by the fire, harmonizing in curious combination the characteristics of both his venerable ancient forebears—the Hunter, from whom he derived his wiles and prowess, and Highland Mystic, from whom emerged the poet and bard.

The legacy of these early Celts of the north had been passed down in this way from father to son and mother to daughter, by word of mouth, over the ages. Eubha-Mathairaichean had given the charge to the Wanderer's three grandsons. Taran had passed his life—and Pendalpin, his bard, had instilled a veneration for the past—into the two brothers who, centuries in advance of their time, understood how man had been appointed on this earth to relate to his fellows. The son of Gatheon now passed the same tradition of both bard and father on to his son.

Arriving finally at Beinn Donuill, father and son took seats on the great jutting slab down the slope from the peak, as was the custom, gazing toward the two raised stones a short distance from them, and beyond across the valley floor to the disused ruins of the hill-fort of Laoigh. A long silence fell between them—the healthy silence of contemplation.

"*In unity is brotherhood*—such is the meaning of the stones, my son," said Foltlaig at length.

"You have told me of them many times, Father," replied Maelchon softly. "Now that I have seen the stones, and felt them with my own hands, I know they could not have been brought here, and raised upon this mountain, without many men laboring in brotherhood and unity."

"As we must now do against the intruders."

"Is that why you brought me here now?"

Foltlaig nodded. "The stones are indeed fit symbol of the truth they reveal," he said. "For our time and, as Chief Cruithne knew, for the times of all men."

"I will remember everything you have told me this day. So too shall my own sons remember."

"They must tell their own sons after them and teach them likewise to pass on the truth of brotherhood to their descendants."

"I will not forget, Father. What about this giant stone we are seated upon?"

"Legends abound, my son," replied Foltlaig. "It is said that the earth below it contains the bones of the most ancient pilgrim to this region. But the tales grow faint with the passing of years. Most of what I know concerns the nearby monument of the brothers."

Maelchon nodded. He set his hand upon the great stone below them and slowly rubbed his fingers back and forth across its rough surface, wondering if the legend could be true. Gone now, after centuries of weathering, were the images Fidach had noticed more than three centuries earlier, carved originally by her who had truly become a Source of life to the stalwart race who now occupied the land.

After a few moments more, the two men climbed down off the prehistoric tomb and walked back down the mountain slope. They now stood pondering the standing pillars of the monument.

"Why do we not raise the flat stone upon the two standing stones?" asked Maelchon.

"What is your proposal?" laughed Foltlaig. "That we two do what the great Cruithne was unable to accomplish?"

"I do not mean alone, Father. We could bring others, *many* of our men! When we are successful in driving out the soldiers from the south, why should we not signify the event by *completing* the monument?"

Foltlaig smiled in fond reminiscence.

"I asked the same thing of my father," he answered. "Youth are always full of the dream to surpass what their fathers have done."

"What did my grandfather tell you when you asked?"

"He gave me the same wisdom that I shall now pass on to you," replied Foltlaig. "My father told me that the stones must be preserved as they are—as you now see them begun but unfinished, with the images upon them incomplete."

"But why, Father?"

"Such was Cruithne's wish, which his seven sons passed on to those who came after. They must remain such as a reminder of what fleeting thing is the goodwill these stones represent—how fragile is unity, how easily broken."

Maelchon nodded. At last he apprehended the deeper significance of the monument.

"Unity is a high thing for men to seek," his father continued. "But when they forget brotherhood, it is undone. These stones of an unfinished monument not only help us remember the dream, they also remind us of the consequence when brotherhood is cast aside."

Maelchon observed the partially carved outline on the stone. "Tell me again of the white stag, Father," he said.

"It was the stag who caused the brothers to raise the monument—who summoned the men of this land to harmony. The brothers said that such was the message in his eyes."

"Is it true that King Cruithne could have killed him?"

"It is another of the stories from the old times. My father said that the stag appeared to the brothers. Whether either had it in his earthly power to do the beast harm, who can say?"

"When will the white stag be seen again in Caledonia, Father?"

Maelchon knew the answer he would hear. He had asked the same question a dozen times throughout his life. It was part of the tradition that bound these people together, to ask and to listen. It was his duty as a son to ask the question, and to hear over and over the same answer he would give his own sons when he had taught them to inquire of the stag. It was a tradition that had come through the bardic line of their people from Pendalpin to Domnal down to the present time.

"The stag will return," answered Foltlaig solemnly, carrying out his portion of the sacred prophetic charge, "when brotherhood has come to our land. He will then allow men to gaze upon him. At last he will be pleased with them, for they will then have lain down the disputes that divide them. His return will signal that freedom will have come to Caledonia. When the land is one day united under a single king, legend says he will stand upon the great slab of antiquity. Upon it then will he take his crown, as symbol and reminder of those who came before, from whose loins we all have sprung."

An hour more father and son remained among the stones of *ann an aonachd tha bràithreachas.*

At length they made their way back down Donuill's southern slope to the hill-fort of their ancestors. Dusk was descending. They would sleep within the crumbling walls tonight, hoping to absorb the spirit of their former chieftains, leaders, and bards.

They would begin the trek homeward on the morrow.

ELEVEN

The frosts came, and with them the first of the two hundred eighty warriors Foltlaig had requested.

Over the next week they continued to arrive from all corners of the tribal region of the north—forty from each of the seven tribes, including twenty-seven bold young women. Each, according to Foltlaig's instructions, came with stores and supplies to sustain himself or herself for two months. They would spend the next fortnight by the shores of Loch Rannoch while Foltlaig and Maelchon personally trained them in the assignments that lay ahead.

The first step was to divide them into smaller groups. At the heart of Foltlaig's scheme lay a twofold division of the warriors—first into four companies of seventy, with each of these in turn divided into seven units of ten. From the whole, Foltlaig selected nine men and one woman to serve, along with himself and Maelchon, as leaders—twelve in all, three over each of the four companies. All of the smaller ten-person units included individuals from each of the seven tribes.

Foltlaig's objective in this organizational scheme was to allow bonds of trust to grow between men and women of different tribes as they carried out this important mission. He hoped this would have the ultimate effect of creating new permanent levels of brotherhood among them. His objective concerned the Romans only in the immediate. He was equally dedicated to future unity. Pictland could survive unchallenged from without only if it remained strong within.

Day by day over the next two weeks, Foltlaig was gratified to see his hopes rewarded. For as the gathered warriors studied the details of the plan, as they honed their skills and practiced their tactics . . . all the while eating and drinking and talking together . . . the warriors of the seven tribes gradually began to merge into a single entity . . . a united force dedicated to fighting for the freedom of all Picts. The twelve leaders, too, as Foltlaig's inner council, grew closer in purpose and learned to work out their differences.

The day of their departure drew closer. As Foltlaig reviewed the progress of his specialized army, a new desire came into his mind. The tradition held that the stones must not be moved. But why should they not complete the depiction of the legend upon them? What better way to insure that his united army would carry his teaching back to their people than by allowing representatives of all the Pict tribes to take a united hand in carving the stones dedicated to brotherhood?

As soon as the campaign against the Romans was done, Foltlaig told himself, he would take his eleven leaders north to the hill country of Laoigh. There they would complete the drawings on the monument, though no stone would be moved. Thus might men know for all time the full meaning of *ann an aonachd tha bràithreachas.*

That night he explained to Maelchon what had come into his heart to do. Then he climbed into his sleeping skins with a heart full of peace and a mind full of plans.

On the eve of their departure, Foltlaig gathered his fighting men and women, instructing them to sit together in their twenty-eight bands of ten. Foltlaig now rose to address them.

"You have been chosen by the chieftains of your tribes," he began, "to embark upon a mission the likes of which has not been seen in this land before. Your descendants will tell of the fame you win for yourselves. They will call you heroes, for in your hands their future freedom rests.

"Get ready, then, to cross the Great River into the south. Have courage, that we may retain possession of the land our forefathers have given us. But remember, it is only through brotherhood that we will be capable of keeping it. Do not forget these words of mine, nor let them later slip from your hearts. Teach them to your children and to their children after them. Keep the exhortation by which I bind you this day: Only in the unity of our peoples will our freedom survive. Take these words to heart, that you and your tribes and families may live long in the land your fathers have given for your heritage.

"But be careful. Do not forget the command I am placing upon you this day. For if you or your descendants do not follow it, you will certainly be uprooted from this land we now possess."

Foltlaig paused, gazing slowly to the right and left upon the company under his charge. Then he opened his mouth in a final great voice of challenge.

"Now, faithful men and women of the Caledonii, the Borestii, the Maeatae, the Damnonii, the Selgovae, the Votadini, and the Novantae, let us rise up as one and take full possession once more of the land of our fathers, so that the days of our children might be many and prosperous in it!"

❊   T W E L V E   ❊

The force of two hundred eighty set out from Rannoch in the first week of October.

The year was A.D. 105, though none of their number would have called it such. Their method for distinguishing the passage of the moons and seasons and years vanished with the passing of time. To the unsuspecting Romans, safely ensconced in their forts throughout the region in anticipation of the coming winter, the date would have been reckoned at 858 years after the founding of Rome. Neither Pict nor Roman yet knew of nor apprehended the significance of Him whose birth a century before, in that far opposite end of the empire called Palestine, would someday mark a watershed for the centuries. Both peoples would one day know of Him well enough, for His story would eventually change both this land as well as the far-flung Roman Empire . . . indeed, all of human history.

As the united Picts of Caledonia set out on a bright, chilly dawn, they hardly resembled the invisible force Foltlaig had described to the assembled chieftains the previous spring. But once they split into their smaller constituent units and set about their work, they would be invisible enough.

It would be a cold and unpleasant winter for those legions under the Roman emperor Trajan who had the misfortune to be stationed in the far reaches of the Wanderer's domain.

The burdens of Foltlaig's warriors were light. Each carried a modest amount of food and drink, their clothing, skins for shelter against the cold, and weapons—long dirk knives, short *dubh* knives, swords, and spears. Food and water beyond what they carried would be available in abundance as they went. They were all skilled hunters. They could survive in these wilds.

To the twelve who had been chosen to lead was entrusted the fire.

Burning coals they must have in ready supply if their daring plan was to succeed. Five carts followed, four heavy laden with dried bricks of peat, the fifth carrying other needful supplies. One each of the peat-wagons, along with the hot-pots of burning coals, kept alive twenty-four hours day and night, would follow each of the four seventy-man companies.

Maelchon led a small but swift band of runner-scouts. They went before, beside, and behind them at distances of twenty to forty minutes. The large force *must* not be seen by the enemy. It was the job of the runners to make certain they passed through the central lowlands and then into the southern hills of the Roman territory without detection.

The danger would increase after they passed the Great River and the plains south of it. In these regions the Roman presence was more pervasive. There would be greater likelihood of encountering traffic between the southern forts and the two Roman outposts of Ardock and Inveresk, on the shores of the Great River.

The force moved into the region of the Maeatae, whose two leaders among the twelve led them dexterously through the bog and moss. They then crossed the great east-flowing river while yet avoiding by many miles the Roman bridge.

On the southern shores of the Great River they encamped for the night. Here they tripled the night watch and braved open fires in order to dry themselves thoroughly. It would be the last night they would enjoy such heat. Henceforth would their rations of peat be reserved for other purposes.

It had now been four days since they left the waters of Rannoch. As on the night prior to their departure, Foltlaig stood once again to address his band. As he did, he was filled with the spirit of the ancients and with the wisdom and vision of Cruithne, whose son and heir, now more than ever, he truly was.

"We have now crossed the Great River," said Foltlaig to them. "Tomorrow we venture southward, deep into the heart of the enemy's territory. Many of you are familiar with these regions—for some, this is your home. Yet we must be doubly vigilant now. Our discovery by Roman scouts will place all we have worked for in jeopardy. We are many, easily seen. Therefore, we must be wary and watchful.

"We will journey to the heart of the Selgovae, there to divide our company three or four days hence. The enemy will know nothing of our presence until we strike at our most distant targets. Then, while retreating northward, we will destroy the rest of their outposts. After that, we will not meet again. When your work is completed, you will return to your own people. But do not forget the lesson of our victory. Every place where you set your foot shall be known as the land of Caledonia. Be strong and courageous."

The next day they reached the Roman road connecting Milton with Newstead. They crossed the road safely and without exposure, and made camp that night in the western Cheviot Hills.

That evening, Foltlaig called together the eleven he had chosen as leaders. Late into the night, they held counsel together. He was about to send them out at the head of the four companies. He must make certain every detail was clear. Coordinated timing between the companies and the individual units was vital. Once they parted, there would be no further communication between the eastern and western flanks of their force.

He had originally planned for Maelchon to lead the two companies striking west, and he the two to the east. He now determined, however, that they should go together. He wanted his son at his side as they consummated this venture for which they had so long prepared. Turenna of the Damnonii, daughter of the chieftainess Deargicca, had shown herself gifted and capable and would skillfully lead the two westward columns.

The following morning long before daybreak, as the autumn chill hung in the air, the Pict force split in half. Two of its companies, led by Turenna, would pursue a westward course toward the region of the Novantae. The remaining two, led by Foltlaig, would march eastward through the hill country south of the lands of the Selgovae. Six of the twelve leaders accompanied each group. They would remain together another thirty-six hours before cleaving again. Turenna's two companies would encamp that night and pause for the following day, allowing the two eastern companies to make closer approach to their targets.

The plan was as daring as it was shrewd, and Foltlaig had established as precise a timetable as was possible to coordinate between two groups of seventy individuals each, traveling independently and over different terrain.

Yet two days further would be given for his two companies, now divided and traveling separately, to reach the Roman forts at Rochester and Corbridge. By that time, Turenna's companies would be in position at Milton and Birrens. Ten days after setting out, therefore, each of the four companies of seventy should be in readiness for the first strike of their campaign.

The most important work must be done under cover of night. They would have to invoke the skies against rain, or the plan would be doomed.

❊   T H I R T E E N   ❊

Foltlaig and Maelchon stood together under cover of the edge of a small wood in the forest called Wark. Through deepening dusk, they gazed across the two hundred yards of moorland that separated them from the wooden structure that had been their objective—the rectangular Roman fort of Corbridge. It was now six days since they had crossed the Great River.

"The hour has finally come," said Maelchon quietly.

"I only pray our brothers and sisters are all in place."

"They will be, Father. You have trained them well."

"If one of the companies should be even a few hours late, the Romans with their swift horses would be able to give warning."

"We will strike together, Father. Turenna and the others understood your orders."

"Are the fire pots ready?"

"I checked before coming out to join you—we will have five full pots of coals ready by nightfall."

"And the smoke?"

"There is a slight breeze from out of the northeast. We have positioned the pots so that the smoke drifts away from the fort. Their long Roman noses will detect nothing."

"Is it visible?"

"If they looked for it, they might see a hint of white. But it will be dark soon. I made certain only the driest of the peats were used."

"Good. Now we await darkness, and the night's quietest hours. Then we strike."

Maelchon returned to their men.

Foltlaig remained where he was several minutes more in quiet contemplation. If all went well tonight, he would discharge his debt to his father and his people. He would accomplish revenge after his own fashion, then he would grow old with his son.

❈   F O U R T E E N   ❈

Four hours later, every warrior of Foltlaig's seventy had taken his appointed place. Each knew precisely where he belonged.

At four separate locations, positioned so as to take most effective advantage of the gentle northeasterly breeze, ten men stole across the moor toward the high walls of the fortress.

The preparatory hours had been spent in two activities undertaken so silently that they had been carried out successfully within but a few yards of the Romans themselves. First, they had dug a series of holes under the foundation timbers on the windward outer wall. As some were thus engaged, their comrades were gathering armloads of brush and dry wood from the surrounding forest and piling them in readiness near where trees gave way to moorland. Even if they could only get a foot or two beneath the foundation, it would be enough to set the wall ablaze. As soon as night fell they silently stuffed their fodder into the holes and leaned the excess against the foundation at other strategic points along the windward and two adjacent walls.

Foltlaig would give the signal, but not until he had personally crept around the entire walled fortress to make certain each of the four units was in readiness. The first he told to count for sixteen minutes, then begin. He began the cadence they had carefully practiced. When their rhythm was synchronized, he left for the next company, continuing to count four minutes as he went. The next unit he told to count for twelve minutes. Continuing on his way around the fortress, he instructed the third unit to wait for eight minutes, and at length he arrived at the fourth and final company of ten. He himself counted the final four minutes, then nodded.

Within mere seconds, each of the groups began to empty their pots of peat coals at the base of the wooden structure and into the holes they had dug, quickly heaping the glowing embers high with quantities of the dried peats they had carried from the supply cart in the wood. Huge flames did not result immediately, though it would not take long for much heat to be generated. Though some of the brush and wood that followed the peats onto the pile was not completely dry, the summer just past had done its part to aid the speed with which the four fires took hold. As the fires spread up from below, especially where placed beneath foundation timbers, the favorable wind blew them toward the fort, gradually setting great sections of the wall first to smoldering, then into flame.

By the time the sentries inside the fort realized they were surrounded by fumes not generated from within the camp, it would be too late to prevent the blaze from engulfing them.

Now finally did the genius of Foltlaig's plan reveal itself. Notwithstanding summer's rains, early autumn provided the best opportunity for sizable quantities of dry fuel. Yet with winter only a month away, there would be no possibility of rebuilding the forts before the snows set in. This timing guaranteed the most devastating impact. It was indeed a shrewdly designed scheme, for winter here without shelter was fatal. If the fires completed their incendiary assignments, those who dwelt behind these walls would have no choice but to move southward.

Meanwhile, after assisting their brothers in hauling burnables to the fire sites, two more units of ten positioned themselves at strategic locations within clear sight of both the front and rear entrances of the fort. The critical responsibility of these twenty was twofold: to guard their comrades while the blazes got underway, and to prevent the escape of a rider from the fort to warn other fortresses of the attack. It would be too late for Rochester, of course, for the northern seventy should simultaneously be dealing that fort a like fate. But it would be days before they reached Newstead, and that great stronghold must not be warned, for it was the most strategic of all their targets.

The two guard units thus stood now with spears poised in readiness, watching the gates and the walls through the thickening smoke.

Once Corbridge was completely in flames, the entire company—all seventy together—would prevent escape by retreating northward to meet their brothers from Rochester. They would then move toward their next two targets by such a route as to cut off any rider trying to make for them. Thus would they prevent communication between the various Roman posts until all eight lay in smoldering heaps.

It was not Foltlaig's chief design that many would die from the fire. The buildings within the fortress were spread out enough that even with its walls and dwellings in flames, there would probably not be great loss of life. They would merely contain the Romans within the burning walls sufficiently so that they could not spread warnings. Massacre was not the objective, but forced withdrawal.

As the four groups set the fires and two others stood guard, the seventh and final unit of ten targeted the two granaries and the workshop. In most cases, these stood inside the ramparts. Here at Corbridge, however, they had been built outside the walls. At this hour they were unmanned, full of much dry fuel, and blazing high within minutes. Destroying provisions for both sustenance and the capacity to rebuild, with winter fast approaching, was sure to add impetus to a southern retreat.

With granaries and workshop in flames, they would likewise attempt to burn the bathhouse outside the walls. This would be more difficult, in that it was constructed of both turf and timber. It was an optional target, in that the destruction of its hygienic function would not greatly alter the disposition of the emperor's troops. The elimination of the recreational service it offered in such a forsaken outpost as this, however, would further demoralize the Romans and render their withdrawal more likely.

As four or five perimeter fires began to heat up and grow, Maelchon flung a coiled rope to the top of the outer wall at a point where it appeared unlikely he would encounter a guard. Yanking hard to make sure it was secured tightly against one of the upper beams, he pulled himself up the outside of the rough wooden planks.

Reaching the top of the wall, he carefully peeped over. No sentries were nearby on the elevated interior walk. Maelchon scrambled hastily over the parapet and onto the walkway.

On the ground below, guarding him as he thus penetrated the Roman stronghold, stood both his father and the third member of their leadership team. Both held spears in hand, prepared to send to his death any Roman sentry who made an appearance.

The outer rampart-wall upon which Maelchon stood ran rectangularly around the entire camp. Enough structures abutted against it that, with the wall in flames, the fire would eventually spread throughout the interior. His present assignment, however, was to make sure the Romans were not able to contain the blaze merely to the circumference. He would now strike into the very heart of the fortress.

Maelchon glanced quickly to his right, then his left.

The *principia*, or headquarters building, in the middle of the compound, was probably unreachable, though the barracks might be within range. The latrines and various storehouses were not vital. Near them sat another free-standing structure which Maelchon recognized as the hospital. Foltlaig had given specific instructions to leave it untouched.

Glancing about further, he spotted what he had been looking for—the stables.

It would have been better had he been able to scale the wall fifty yards closer, but this would have to do. Their summer's scouting had paid off. He hoped his counterparts this night at Milton, Birrens, and Rochester were finding themselves equally well positioned to inflict the most important and damaging blow of all—that which would send the interior of the fortress up in flames.

He signaled down to his father and Rhodri to follow on the ground. Maelchon loosened the rope's coil. Carrying it as he went, he crept quickly southward beside the parapet toward a point that would give him the best chance for a perfect shot. Though all was still calm in the fortress, he could already smell the burning peat. One or two sentries roamed about below, unconscious as yet of their danger.

When he judged himself near enough, Maelchon stopped.

He attached the coil of rope to another wall-post and signaled down to his father. Moments later he was hoisting up, by means of the very rope that had enabled his ascent, a long spear. On its tip was rigidly impaled a brick of peat that had been prepared in one of the fires and now burned brightly.

Suddenly a shout sounded from below.

The flaming lance had been seen against the night sky!

More shouts followed. He had not a second to lose.

Maelchon loosened the rope from the end of his blazing weapon, then took firm hold with his right hand at its balance point. He drew back his arm and sent the fiery instrument of freedom toward its mark.

In seconds the straw beside the horse stalls had ignited into a rising ball of flame. A minute later it was out of control and spreading about the building. In the meantime, Maelchon had sent the end of the rope back to the ground for a second spear, which he now likewise unfastened.

Again he cocked his arm in readiness and, with a mighty thrust, heaved a second flaming missile with all his might. He feared it would fall short. But it landed on the barracks building. Its roof of thatch was ablaze in seconds.

All about the fortress, pandemonium now broke loose. Soldiers poured out of their quarters, yelling, pulling on tunics and boots and paenula as they ran, trying to ascertain the cause and direction of the attack.

Their running steps converged upon the burning stable buildings, where whinnying, terrified horses were bolting for freedom. Quickly the realization spread that the native attack against them involved far more than a single fire.

By the time arrows were being fired in Maelchon's direction, he had leapt back over the wall and was scrambling down the rope to the ground, flushed with the exertion of success.

"Well done, my son!" cried Foltlaig. He could see the smoke rising from inside. Encircling the entire fort, the ring of wall-fire now began to take control.

"And to you, Father!" rejoined Maelchon. "Your plan has worked to perfection. They are in confusion inside, while their fort rises in flames."

"Would that it were daylight, that we might see evidence rising in the sky that Milton, Birrens, and Rochester have likewise been set to destruction."

"Our brothers will succeed—have no fear. Now we must be away!"

Noises and angry shouts of the fortress coming awake as the soldiers roused themselves was all the indication any of the fire-builders needed that their job was done. Foltlaig's instructions had been clear. Once the fires were well set and the walls burning on their own—the time for retreat had come!

Foltlaig, Maelchon, and Rhodri sprinted round to the front of the fortress. They were met by two of the fire units and one of the guard units. All hastened to the prearranged spot well clear of the fortress. They must secure the northern road leading away from Corbridge against the escape of messengers.

Quickly they all ran, carrying ropes, spears, and other provisions as they went, retreating not as cowards but as victors. They were joined presently by the guard and fire units from the opposite side of the fort. Both fire units were doing their utmost to make haste, hauling the fire carts behind them.

Within five minutes, breathing heavily, seventy members of the united tribal force stood at a distance of some two to three hundred yards, watching as the blaze spread and joined into a great circle of fire. Radiant orange in the night, it gradually engulfed the entire fortress.

Not a single man or woman of their company had been lost.

Now they would begin a gradual retreat northward on the Roman road, spreading out in a planned pattern to guard the road and other potential routes. Their comrades would be doing likewise as they retreated from Rochester—a much more vital task, given its proximity to the largest of the forts—until they met, two days hence, to join forces in a similar attack first on the great strategic fortress at Newstead. After that, continuing still farther northward, they would complete their campaign at Inveresk.

As they went, Turenna's forces farther west would remain in their separate companies of seventy, the one moving from Milton to Dalswinton for attack the following night, and the other inland from Birrens to Glenlochar.

Thence would the two western companies, their work more quickly done, retreat northward through the western wilds of Carrick, disbursing quietly to their own tribes.

※   F I F T E E N   ※

Seven days had now passed since the first flames had been set to the Roman fortresses at Corbridge, Rochester, Birrens, and Milton. The only failure had occurred at Milton, where a brief rain had foiled the attack. The threescore-and-ten company of Picts, however, had more than avenged themselves the next night at Dalswinton. Their companions had been equally successful at Glenlochar and had already disbanded.

Meanwhile, Newstead had been burned to the ground by the united efforts of the two companies under Foltlaig and Maelchon. Now smoke had begun to rise as well from around the walls at Inveresk.

The Romans here, however, had not been altogether surprised. When this truth began to dawn, Foltlaig assumed that a horseman from Newstead, or perhaps Milton or Dalswinton, must have gotten through with the message that danger was approaching.

In actual fact, the treason lay much closer.

A cowardly Pict youth, anxious to ingratiate himself with their conquerors, had slipped away in the early morning hours from the Selgovae fortress at Eildon Hill, where Foltlaig and his men had refreshed themselves with their southern cousins en route to the attack. The traitor had traveled north to Inveresk, even as Newstead rose in flames, to warn the Roman commander on duty at the northern fortress on the mouth of the Great River.

As a result of this subversion of kinship, Foltlaig's men found themselves at Inveresk engaged in battle of both fire and sword. It was not the first time the land of the Picts had seen kinsman betray kinsman. Nor would it be the last.

Even as the combined groups numbering one hundred forty began to set fires around the circumference of the enclosed rectangle, they heard shouts from inside.

Within minutes fully outfitted soldiers appeared round the parapet walls. Moments later, archers, spearsmen, and slingers were raining down arrows, lances, and stones upon them, their counterattack aided by a near full moon that bathed the fort and its surroundings in a pale glow.

"Back . . . fall back!" Foltlaig commanded his men with great shouts.

The guard units surrounding the fortress returned the Roman fire as best they could. They had not prepared for full confrontation, however, and their battle provisions were scanty.

Foltlaig ran toward them, waving his arms and shouting to arrest their attention.

"Break it off—follow the others!" he cried. "You must retreat!"

Within minutes, all were making for the high ground, with its protection of boulders and a few trees, that lay across the open heath from the fortress.

Maelchon, meanwhile, delayed a few moments more to carry out his assignment.

From a position which he hoped was in the approximate vicinity of the stables, Maelchon prepared his burning spears. There was no time to scale the wall if he hoped to get away with his life. They would have to be launched from here.

He grasped the first flaming lance, drew back his arm, and with a great heave aimed it up and over the wall. He hastily prepared another, sent it after the first, then turned and sprinted after his father. Foltlaig was already halfway across the heath to safety. The fire and guard units were there making for the small wood as fast as they could.

Both front and rear gate of the fortress now swung upon.

A column of Roman cavalrymen rode out the front. A company of light infantrymen poured through the opposite gate behind.

Escaping on foot, the painted natives were no match for the horsemen. A slaughter seemed about to begin. The treachery of their own had surely placed every man of them into the Romans' hands!

They continued sprinting toward the wood.

Maelchon, behind his fellows from his business with the spears, saw perhaps better than all the rest their grave peril. He ran alone, at an angle to intercept his comrades. But suddenly, to his horror, he saw that a single figure lagged behind.

It was his father!

As he watched the drama unfold, all at once the words from his father's lips echoed in his brain: *Na sir 's na seachain an cath*—"Neither seek nor shun the fight. When another shows himself an enemy, it is only a coward who turns away...."

Almost as if Foltlaig had likewise heard the same words he had spoken, suddenly the Pict leader ceased his flight. He stopped. In an almost unconscious moment of sacrificial decision, he turned alone to face the approaching column of soldiers, placing himself between the cavalry and his escaping men.

"No, Father!" yelled Maelchon. "Run ... run!" The same instant he broke off his retreat toward the wood and sprinted shouting toward his father.

But Foltlaig heard nothing. And Maelchon was too far away to help.

Rising to the full stature of his height, he now deliberately began to walk forward, reaching across his body as he did, and slowly withdrawing the sword that hung at his side.

The lead Roman officer hesitated at this strange sight of painted native warrior approaching fearlessly with a look of death in his eye. He reined back his horse, suddenly oblivious to the fact that across the ground in the distance the rest of the natives were escaping to safety. The Roman's chest was covered in an armored vest of leather and metal strips over his tunic, and a red cloak hung from his shoulders. Because of his haste from the fort, his head was unprotected by helmet. In his hand he held a two-edged, sharply pointed sword.

Behind him halted the cavalrymen and foot soldiers, awaiting the result of this confrontation.

Maelchon saw it all and divined his father's intent—to delay the Roman charge long enough for his own men to reach the protection of the wood on the other side of the hill.

"Father—no!" came a final bloodcurdling cry of protest from his throat as he ran frantically toward the scene.

But it was too late.

Already the Caledonian warrior had risen tall and was engaging in mortal blows of the sword with the centurion who had so warily eyed his approach. Foltlaig could hardly hope to unseat his adversary from the ground. His only thought at the moment was the protection of his son and his men.

Even as the two swords struck against each other, clanging repeated blows, the son's loud cry was heard over the field of battle.

Knowing whose voice shouted across the plain behind him, Foltlaig glanced toward the sound.

A thousand emotions tore his breast to see his son running and imploring him to give up the fight and make good his escape. Yet perhaps for the first time in his forty-three years did Foltlaig understand why his own father—and fathers before and after him throughout all time—had marched to battle. Men fought, and men would always fight . . . the foe *must* be faced.

To call oneself a man required bravery. This was no land to make heroes of cowards. With fortitude and strength had it first been explored. With valor had it been won. And only with courage would it be held—whenever and however the summons to courage was demanded. . . . If he did not face this rival, his son and all the others might die. What would bonds of love mean then?

On the field of battle, a man must be one with himself, or he is lost. The thinker would have to remain silent. The warrior had risen up. The Fidach of his nature could not meet this Roman enemy. Today Cruithne had won the inner struggle.

For a brief instant the eyes of father and son met. The next, Foltlaig waved him away.

Maelchon hesitated, torn between obedience to his instinct or to his father's gesture of command.

In the split second that the exchange required, a punishing blow fell from the centurion onto the shoulder of the Caledonian warrior. Blood spurted from a great gaping wound that sliced through the muscle of his upper arm. The sharpened blade did not stop until it struck bone.

A great deep cry of agony rent the air.

Seriously weakened, and with the help of his other hand, Foltlaig attempted to lift the sword in defense. But the fingers clutching its handle, as well as the entire limb, were already lifeless.

Another blow came crashing down, this time to the side of his head, though fortunately with the blunt edge of the Roman's weapon.

Foltlaig slumped to the ground.

Meanwhile, hearing their leader's cry, looking back, and seeing Foltlaig fall, every remaining Pict arrested his flight away from the fortress. All turned now and rushed forward to engage the Romans. If the freedom of this land required their blood being spilled on its soil along with his, they would give it.

Hearing the piercing war cries of his comrades approaching from the hill of retreat brought Maelchon to his senses.

In a mad frenzy of passion and rage, he resumed his forward flight. Before he knew what had happened, his own sword was dripping red halfway to the hilt with the blood of the Roman centurion, who lay dead on the ground, his horse sprinting away riderless.

The screaming of a hundred forty maniacal, painted Picts, throwing spears and brandishing swords as they ran, and the sight of their own leader so suddenly cut down, brought to the minds of every Roman cavalryman and infantryman the tales they had heard since Agricola's time about these murderous barbarians. Thinking it perhaps better to engage this enemy from behind the safety of the fort's high walls, they fell back toward the gates. The frenzied mass of attackers swept past father and son after them.

Unaware what a poignant scene he was playing out from among his father's worst fears, Maelchon stooped down to the bloody and broken form of his father. Foltlaig was unconscious but yet breathing.

Tears gathered in Maelchon's eyes as he tenderly stretched his hand under the older man's limp neck.

"Father . . . *my father*," he whispered.

But there was no time for deliberation. Grief would have to wait. With the sounds of battle echoing behind him, Maelchon gathered the fallen warrior in his arms, lurched with difficulty to his feet, then staggered back up the hill and to the safety of cover.

Behind the shelter of a large rock, he carefully lowered Foltlaig to the ground. His own arms and chest were covered with the terrible sight of the very blood which now ran in his veins. Maelchon attempted to make the suddenly frail general as comfortable as possible. As he did he spoke in gentle tones of comfort, then set about to wrap the ugly gash tight with leather strips and thongs to stop the flow of blood. He was attending the wound, tears flowing down his cheeks, when the sounds of the companies rushing back to join him met his ear.

"They are beaten back inside the fort."

Maelchon glanced up at the bearer of the message.

"For good?" he asked, rising.

"Only for the present, I fear. But much of the fort is in flames."

"Then we must make haste from this place," replied the son, who was now in command. "A full cohort will soon be sent after us."

The mission for which Foltlaig had gathered them was done.

They were now in the region of the Votadini, and not far from that of the Selgovae.

Once they were gathered together again and had taken stock of their casualties—few indeed apart from their commander—Maelchon told the leaders of the companies, "We will split up immediately. You may each return to your own tribes. But move stealthily as you go. Stay in hollows and among trees. Make the darkness of night your ally. Thus we will hope to confuse their attempt to pursue us."

With their Damnonii and Maeatae comrades, therefore, Maelchon and his Caledonii brethren, bearing their commander in one of the carts that had remained in the woods during the attack, took a westward heading along the shores of the Great River. They must make what speed they could, not only because of potential danger behind them, but to get Foltlaig as hastily as possible to more assistance than they were here able to provide him.

Little could any of them know that this treachery of brother against brother by the collaborating Selgovae, in centuries to come—in a tiny glen only a short distance to the west of the Caledonii home across Rannoch Moor—would even more brutally doom the brotherhood that had brought victory against the Roman invaders.

▩   S I X T E E N   ▩

The journey was arduous and slow, but at last, Maelchon neared the fortress of Rannoch. Beside him in the cart that had originally carried bricks of peat rode the broken form of his father and general, lying unconscious but clinging stubbornly to life. Behind him stretched a final remnant of the column the fallen commander had himself led southward three weeks earlier.

They had been seen long before the shores of Loch Rannoch met their eyes. Their kinsmen poured out of the settlement to meet them, led by Chief Coel himself and followed minutes later by the Caledonians who had returned from Turenna's command, and by Maelchon's mother, who was that same night made a widow.

Home and safely among his own, the spirit of the great man relaxed its fight to live. Whatever his thoughts as he lay, attended to by his wife and the faithful son he loved, no one ever knew. No more words passed his lips. An occasional tear rose in his eyes when Maelchon's face came before his, the only evidence of the hope that was dying with him. Even his son, however, would never know the dream he had so long cherished and had sacrificed on the field of battle—of a long, shared life with his son.

That night Foltlaig's soul slipped away to that higher region the people of Caledonia yet knew little of. The smile on his face, however, as he lay surrounded by chief, weeping wife, and stoically tearful son, gave evidence that already the dying warrior was being privileged with glimpses of those greater Highlands to which he was bound.

The month of October was nearly done.

Snow would shortly cover the mountains.

It would be a cold winter, coldest of all in the heart of Maelchon, son of Foltlaig—frozen from no bitterness at his fate, but by the loneliness of losing the best friend it was possible for a son to possess: a virile, smiling, energetic father who loved him and with whom he shared the best of life's joys.

The moment had arrived for the son of Foltlaig to step into his heritage, to take his place among the ranks of those sworn to pass along the story of his fathers. Upon him, at a youthful single score of years, now came to rest the ancient imperative that future generations should never forget the men who had won this land and preserved its freedom.

That very night, Maelchon determined that neither would he let *his* father be forgotten. The next day, he sent out messengers calling together once more the ten leaders from the other Pict tribes.

"We will journey northward," he said when they had gathered together once more and he had explained his father's wishes. "We will leave immediately, before the onslaught of winter. We will do as my father had planned."

His comrades listened intently, sensing by his voice the change that had come over their new leader.

"We are only eleven now," Maelchon went on. "My father gave his life in the battle to which he led us. It is our duty, as those who remain, to carry on what we were taught when we were twelve.

"Let us journey northward to the stones."

▧   S E V E N T E E N   ▧

A frigid blast of wind met the face of the lone youth. Laced with specks of icy moisture, it was the kind of wind that boded ill for travelers without shelter, fire, or food.

The young man leaned into the breeze, seemingly unmoved by its warnings.

He was only days short of his twenty-first birthday, but his eyes revealed depths far in excess of his years. He had witnessed death, and its distress had matured him.

He stood on the same hill where he and his father had stood when the air was warm, looking down upon the monument of stones to which his father had brought him and to the abandoned hill-fort across the valley in the distance. The storm in the air would wait a few more days, he hoped, before unleashing its fury. If it arrived sooner than he estimated, he would take shelter in the home of the ancient chief just as he and his companions had done for several previous nights. If a white blanket fell so thick as to prevent travel, he would no doubt die here before winter was out.

His aim, however, was to finish his task here and then return southward, following the steps of the ten he had sent back to their homes yesterday.

Turenna had been the last to go, for they had grown close on the journey north. "Let me stay and return with you," she had urged.

"This I must do alone," Maelchon had replied. "I will come to you again in the spring."

Thus they parted. He had spent the night alone in the ancient stone dwellings from which his people had come. This morning he had walked back across the moor, a barren wasteland now, and climbed the slope of Beinn Donuill, there to make his final peace with the ancients, with his father . . . and with his duty as a son of both.

His eyes rested upon the oblong pile of stones set off to one side from the monument of Cruithne, which would now become a shrine to two great men of Caldohnuill.

He and his comrades had laid his father to rest beneath them three days ago. They had dug out a narrow tomb and set inside it the body which his mother had prepared for the journey as best she could, but which, according to the smell, was well past the time for burying. They then had carried out the ancient ritual themselves, in place of chief, or bard, or druid, covered the grave with turf, and finally marked the site with stones. The fallen warrior had thus been laid to rest within an easy stone's throw of the place where the bones of Taran still lay and not many paces farther from him who, in more distant times, had brought their Celtic blood to this land with his father.

Once the Caledonii general was laid to rest, his son and remaining ten had set about the task for which they had made such a long—and, in view of the season, dangerous journey—putting to use the implements and tools, mostly a variety of iron chisels and wooden mallets, they had carried with them to inscribe the three stones of Cruithne according to Foltlaig's dream.

Working together, they had taken three days to complete their task. The labor was not so backbreaking as that of their Caledonii ancestors to drag the stones to the site and raise the two pillars into their present positions, but it was nonetheless exacting and painstaking.

On the three stones, they had completed the design of the stag.

"To the carving we will add a representation of the ancient legend of Cruithne," Foltlaig's son explained to the others. "When that is completed, we will add the story of our recent assault upon the forts of the south."

"Is not the old tale of more importance?" asked one.

"My father's intent was indeed to preserve the ancient legend for posterity," replied Maelchon. "But I would make certain that those who come after us and who chance to read these standing stones of Laoigh will know not only of ancient Cruithne of the Caledonii, and the story of the white stag and its meaning, but also of the bravery of Foltlaig, son of Gatheon, who united the seven tribes of Pictland against the Roman intruders."

The final carving upon the stones, however, Maelchon reserved for himself.

This day he would spend in solitude with his father on the mount, alone with his memories. With his own two hands he would add to the original name of the monument as envisioned by the two ancient brothers. As a posthumous reminder of his father's words and the example of his father's deeds, Maelchon would inscribe the symbols to convey the additional message: *ann an aonachd tha neart Caldohnuill*—"In Unity Is the Strength of Caledonia."

The work was finally completed late in the day. Maelchon rose stiffly, straightened his back, and took one last glance about. He sighed, and rubbed at the tears seeking to rise in his eyes. His was that same grief that had been felt by all sons since Wanderer's Son wept over him who had been slain by the mammoth's tusk, as each young man for himself entered that manhood only the passing of a father brings.

A moment more he stood, then began the slow walk down the hill called Donuill.

He was ready to return to his home at Rannoch. There he would take his own place in the history of the people known thereafter by the retreating

Romans—whose expanding empire had been halted in its tracks—as *Caledonians.*

❈   E I G H T E E N   ❈

The Romans did indeed retreat from the northland.

After more than twenty years of attempting to subdue its native peoples, the invaders from the south finally gave up the effort. The united efforts of the Pict tribes against the Roman army, along with declining interest in the region on the part of the Caesars themselves, eventually led to a gradual and steady withdrawal of the Roman forces southward into lands they had been more successful at taming.

After the burning of their forts at Newstead, Dalswinton, Glenlochar, and the other locations, the Romans kept their forces withdrawn below the Forth-Clyde line. Even at Milton, where Turenna's company of seventy had been unsuccessful, before winter was out the troops had begun a systematic dismantling of the entire fortress in preparation for permanent departure. So complete was the evacuation that nails were clawed out of timbers and buried to keep them from use by the natives, pottery and glass were broken into tiny fragments, structural posts were dug out of the ground, flagstones were removed, and what remained was burned.

Hadrian acceded as emperor of Rome in 117. Not long afterward, following a renewed outbreak of united Pict effort against his troops, led by Maelchon, son of Foltlaig, the new emperor ordered a fixed stone border to be erected from Carlisle across to Newcastle to mark the permanent northern frontier of Roman Britannia. Hadrian's Wall, erected between the years 122 and 128, served a more defensive purpose than similar Roman walls erected elsewhere. Its purpose was to keep the mischievous Picts out, rather than providing Rome with a frontier outpost to keep its inhabitants in.

Hadrian's successor, Antoninus Pius, repented of Rome's decision to abandon Caledonia and commissioned a new more northerly wall to be built between 139 and 144, signifying a fresh effort on his part to hold the Forth-Clyde isthmus. But in 154, in his late sixties, Maelchon—still a determined warrior and following in the footsteps of his father—mounted yet another Pict revolt against this northern encroachment. Again the Romans were forced south behind the wall of Hadrian.

The great Caledonian commander was struck down in the effort, however, and died from the wounds. Representatives from every tribe of Pictland came to Rannoch to mourn with the Caledonii the loss of a mighty leader, whose reputation by this time exceeded even that of his father. The sons and daughters of Maelchon and Turenna, grandchildren of Foltlaig and the warrior-chieftainess Deargicca, were all mighty among their people, having inherited the best that these two Celtic strains of manhood and womanhood could give them.

Fighting persisted on and off. But never could Roman forces subdue the Pict tribes. Maelchon had fitly inscribed the ancient stones, for indeed in their unity was found their strength against the empire. The Romans were driven out of the north for the final time in the early third century by the Maeatae, the Caledonii, and other tribes.

By then, however, the various Pict clans no longer possessed Caledonia to themselves.

From over the sea-channel to the west began to venture descendants of the Wanderer's seafaring grandson, a people from northern Ireland, a land then known as *Scotia*, or Eirinn.

Named for their homeland, these newcoming *Scots* voyaged freely across the north channel in the third and fourth centuries, into the nearly unpopulated west coast and islands of Britain's northern mainland, and eventually built homes in the new region. By the late 400s, the various Scots settlements were well established. The Scots colony in Caledonia was called Dalriada.

Nor were the Scottish descendants of Boatdweller the only people encroaching upon what had once been exclusively the domain of the Picts.

When Rome's worldwide empire crumbled at the end of the fourth century, its evacuating retreat suddenly made vast lands accessible for the occupation of yet more new peoples. Northern Britain was thus opened to the northward migration of another Celtic network of tribes from the southern west coast known as Britons.

By this time, midway into the first millennium, the Pict tribes had gradually fused into one and become known by the name of their most powerful tribe—simply as *Caledonians*.

All three tribal groups—the Caledonian *Picts*, the *Scots* from Eirinn, and the *Britons* from the south—were of Celtic blood, and spoke languages with common Celtic roots. All three now became the mutual inhabitants of the land north of Hadrian's Roman wall, the land of *Alba*.

By now the new religion of Christianity, which had become the dominant religion of Rome itself, was spreading into the islands of Roman Britannia. Unbelieving tribesmen provided a natural object for the sights of Christian missionaries. In the closing years of Roman rule, a Strathclyde native Briton called Ninian traveled to Rome, where he was consecrated a bishop in the Catholic church. Returning in the final years of the fourth century, he established a monastery at Whithorn, and from it he sent missionaries northward.

It would remain, however, for the Scots from Ireland to bring a widespread evangelization to Caledonia. In the fifth century, St. Patrick brought the gospel to tribal Eirinn with remarkable success, and by the opening of the sixth century, Ireland had been predominantly converted to Catholicism. In the 540s, the first Christian missionaries journeyed from Ireland to the islands of Scottish Dalriada. Churches were established on Iona, Mull, and Tiree. Many of their monks and missionaries, however, died of a plague that swept the area in 548, before the missionary effort could be taken farther onshore.

By the middle of the sixth century, memory of ancient Cruithne had nearly dropped away save for the most obscure of legends recalled by a few scattered bards. His name, however, survived in the Gaelic word for the Pict people, who were known as *Cruithneach*.

The king of the northern Caledonians at that time, a certain Brude macMaelchon, rather than being called by the name of his blood father, chose to be known as "mac" or *son of* his second-century ancestor Maelchon, who was the son of Foltlaig, son of Gatheon, son by the generations of Cruithne, son of Taran, son by the generations of both Hunter and Mystic, sons of Wanderer's Son . . . who was the only son of the Wanderer.

10

SPRINGTIME OF
DISCOVERY

Andrew Trentham had been back in London a week or two.

Spring had arrived. At least so the calendar indicated. Here and there could be seen hints confirming the fact. The ground in St. James's and Regent's Parks had thawed sufficiently to allow any number of early floral varieties to bloom. Many species of trees were budding out nicely. Kensington Gardens, though not yet approaching the glory it would display in May and June, was attracting more and more birds and tourists daily.

Andrew's thoughts, however, were constantly of the north, and of the icy grip that, according to reports on the BBC and his telephone conversations with his parents, still held the land captive. At sight of the face of merry daffodil or delicate colorful crocus in Hyde Park, he immediately found himself wondering if any of the happy yellow heralds of spring or the tiny purple-and-white wonders on their slender juicy stalks had broken through the ground anywhere yet in the Scottish Highlands.

Ever since his afternoon at Hadrian's Wall, and with the tale of Foltlaig and Maelchon fresh in his consciousness, Andrew found himself thinking about leadership in new ways. How might their example, he wondered, enable him to step up more firmly to articulate a vision for leadership of his party?

He located a small green-and-gold-embossed 1885 Routledge edition of Robert Burns in an antiquarian bookshop and had taken up the habit of going out for a long walk every morning with book in hand. Burns' poetry gave him such a heightened appreciation for nature and the events of Scotland's history.

Many, varied, and rich were the discoveries made during those long, pleasurable hours before the day began—discoveries that took him at first to many of the small parks nearby in South Kensington and Chelsea, but eventually also to parks and lawns and wooded areas of London he never knew existed, and that carried him soaring on the words and songs and rhymes of the world's poet-Bard.

The day he returned from the north, refreshed and invigorated and feeling enthusiastic and equipped for the political battles at hand, he had begun arising earlier than had been his custom, usually between five o'clock and half past the hour, preparing a pot of tea—Mrs. Threlkeld did not arrive until seven o'clock—and then diving into his Burns or one of Sir Walter Scott's Waverley novels until the awakening of the day allowed him to bundle up and go outside.

As the season advanced and the sun rose sooner and sooner, earlier became his walks, until they replaced the pot of tea as the morning's first activity. He found himself easing into bed each night with anticipation already welling up for the morning's excursion with Burns or Sir Walter—approaching each new place he might explore as an adventure.

Gradually he became more comfortable with the look and meaning of the strange Scots dialect—aided by a dictionary of the old tongue. He even undertook to learn a few of his favorite poems and passages in the mother tongue in which they had been penned, practicing aloud as he walked. More than once he found himself startled into embarrassed silence by the curious looks cast his way by other morning pedestrians whose approach he had not seen in time to temper his attempted northern soliloquies.

Fortunately, he thought, BBC's Kirkham Luddington had not made the discovery that one of London's hottest news personalities was walking alone along the streets every morning exhibiting a most peculiar form of behavior!

It was a season for Andrew Trentham of discovery and newness, when life seemed a good and exciting thing.

❧ T W O ❧

The detectives prowling around with flashlights in the dark and muddy passages and drains beneath the Palace of Westminster had been here before. But with the case still unsolved, pressure was mounting for some kind of break. The underground network was cramped, dank, and smelly. A salamander, maybe rats, might be able to move comfortably in here. But not grown men.

But they had not just been sent back into the maze through which the thieves had penetrated the Abbey for the fun of it. They had been *ordered* to find new evidence.

"I say, what's this?" said one of the men. He scraped about on his hands and knees. "Bit of a scrap of paper, what?"

He reached gloved hands toward it, where it lay in the corner, wet and half buried. Two of his colleagues approached for a closer look.

"Piece of a business card torn in half, I'd say," remarked one.

Shining his light upon it, the finder now turned it over from the side on which a few all-but-illegible scribblings had been made. Whistles from all three followed.

"I'd say we'd best get this to Shepley immediately," he said.

❧ T H R E E ❧

Inspector Shepley of Scotland Yard turned the torn card over in his hand several times. It would be some time before they knew whether any of the three partial prints they had lifted from it matched anything in the computer file. In the meantime, he had to try to extricate some clue from what little was here.

The personal card of the late Eagon Hamilton! What on earth was *it* doing near the hatch where the thieves had escaped to the Thames?

All he had to go on were a few numbers scrawled on the reverse—possibly a partial telephone number—and the cryptic letters . . . L-E-N-C. . . . What came before and after was either torn or too muddied to read.

It was a long shot, but he would try to trace the number—if it was a telephone number at all. It could be part of an address. It could be anything.

Whatever it was, there was no guarantee there was any connection to the UK. It might just as well have been written by someone on the continent.

Shepley again turned the card over in his palm.

It wasn't much. Unfortunately, at this point it was all he had.

⋇   F O U R   ⋇

The late April morning's sun streamed through a large rectangular window facing northeast from the small top-floor corner flat.

Patricia Rawlings stood, coffee cup in hand, looking out across the small street separating the long row of genteel Georgian houses from the sloped greenery of Primrose Hill off Regent's Park. The three-room apartment high in one of the white stone buildings had been a lucky discovery three years ago, and the price reasonable considering the location. She had grown to love this quiet little corner on the western edge of Camden Town, some three and a half miles from the center of London.

She had arisen rather earlier than usual today, had brewed her two-cup pot of coffee, and now stood enjoying its aroma until it cooled sufficiently to sip.

She stared out the window with little more on her mind than the vague contentedness that accompanies a brilliant sunny morning. Suddenly her gaze was arrested by a lone figure strolling along the sidewalk across the street. She was jolted instantly more awake by the sight than any anticipation of her coffee had achieved.

What could he *be doing here!* she thought, . . . *and at this time of the morning?*

Before she could narrow her focus to make sure the walker was in fact who she thought he was, the familiar form had turned into the park and was gone.

She turned back into the room and sat down. Slowly she began sipping at the cup in her hand.

The following morning Paddy again arose early—this time, however, by design. She filled and turned on her coffee maker, dressed hurriedly, then pulled a chair up close to the window. A few minutes later she took a seat with mug in hand to observe Primrose Hill and see what she might see.

An hour later, disappointed, she rose. She had seen no one familiar. Not to be deterred, however, she followed a similar routine the following morning, and the next after that.

On the fifth day, she was at last rewarded. Prepared this time, Paddy tracked the morning walker carefully with her gaze.

It *was* him! The gait was leisurely but unmistakable as he made his way up the hill. He carried no briefcase and was dressed casually. He was obviously not on his way to a breakfast meeting or anything of an official nature.

She leapt from her chair and was halfway to the door when a pang of hesitation seized her. What would he think to turn around and see her running along the sidewalk after him? It would hardly be a dignified opening to conversation.

Slowly she returned to the window. She would have to rethink her strategy. Besides, he had already disappeared into the park again.

Paddy glanced down at her watch. It was six-thirty-five.

She would be up even *earlier* tomorrow . . . and ready for the appearance of the honorable gentleman.

Paddy's alarm rang the following morning at five-fifteen. By quarter till six she was strolling leisurely along Regent's Park Road bordering Primrose Hill. Occasionally she wandered onto its side paths, hoping to intersect whatever might be his morning route.

By six-fifty, growing tired and with a whole day of work still ahead, Paddy gave up the attempt and returned to her flat.

For four successive mornings she adhered to the same routine. But all met with identical lack of success. She wondered if he walked in the park on weekends too.

She would do her best to find out.

⸙   F I V E   ⸙

The morning was a brilliant one, and unseasonably warm for the first weekend of May. Andrew Trentham had been walking through Regent's Park—his favorite haunt for the last couple of weeks—for twenty or thirty minutes, and was by this time beginning to perspire. He crossed Prince Albert Road, as he had done two or three times lately, and continued across the lawn of

Primrose Hill. A bench at its summit was his goal. With his open Burns in front of his face, he had paid only enough attention to the few other early-rising souls present at this hour to keep from bumping into them.

"Why . . . why, Mr. Trentham—what a surprise seeing you here!"

The merry voice sounding ten yards in front of him as he rounded a bend in the path momentarily startled him. Andrew glanced up and paused in midstride.

"Oh . . . hello, Miss Rawlings!" he said with a smile as he recovered from his surprise. He closed the book into one hand and dropped it to his side. "I didn't know you to be one of the city's early birds."

"Not every day, I confess," replied Paddy. "But I like to come out when I can. It is such a wonderful time of the day."

"I couldn't agree more!" rejoined Andrew. "It is a recent obsession with me. Getting out early has made this the best spring I've had since moving to London.—Which way are you going?"

"Oh, nowhere in particular. I live just over there."

Andrew glanced in the direction of her nod.

"Well, then, if you don't mind, I'll walk along to nowhere with you for a while!" he said, turning and resuming his walk in the opposite direction. Paddy fell into step beside him.

"Do you enjoy living here along the park?" he asked.

"I love it," replied Paddy. "I don't suppose it's all that fashionable. But there's such a neighborhood feel to it—little shops, Sesame Whole Foods, the bookstore, Odette's, sidewalk cafes . . . it's nice."

"I live on Hereford Square off Gloucester Road."

"South Kensington—now *that* is fashionable."

Andrew laughed. "It's a pleasant street," he said, "but a rather busy part of London. You can always hear the traffic from Old Brompton Road. Not that I'm complaining. It's a good central spot. Convenient and all that."

"Out here, it seems that people aren't quite so much in a hurry. You can get a cappuccino and a roll and read a book on a nice day and almost imagine you're in some quaint little village."

"I'll have to come up again with my book and do just that."

"I'll treat you to coffee at Cachao."

"What's that?"

"My favorite little bakery, down at the end of the street a couple of blocks from my place. So what *is* that you're reading?" Paddy asked.

"Robbie Burns, the Scots poet."

"I'm afraid I don't know much about his work."

"Nothing in the world like it."

"How so?"

"The way he captures the land, the culture, the mystique, the history of his homeland."

"Scotland again!" laughed Paddy. "It seems we get around to it whenever we cross paths."

"Scotland's what I'm interested in these days."

"Why is that?"

"I don't see your interviewer's note pad," laughed Andrew. "But I'll answer you with another question—have you ever studied genealogy?"

"Not much."

"Neither had I. But recently I'm finding it fascinating to go back into the history of a kingdom, a continent, a nation, a family, and try to find where one's own roots intertwine with the people and events that have influenced the direction of that land's past."

"What does that have to do with Burns and Scotland?"

"Burns is *the* Scottish bard," replied Andrew. "*Scotland* is the country whose roots I'm trying to untangle."

"What does that have to do with *you?*" asked Paddy. Almost as the words were out of her mouth a light of revelation dawned on her face, and she added, "Why—*you're* not Scots?"

"I just may be, Miss Rawlings," answered Andrew seriously. "Somewhere back in my lineage there seems to be some Scottish blood. I'd never given it much thought until recently. Now that I *am* thinking about it . . . let's just say I am intrigued."

Paddy nodded, taking the information in with a knowing expression.

"—But that's off the record," added Andrew with a laugh. "For now, at least."

"You know the rules, Mr. Trentham," said Paddy with a sly smile. "You have to claim confidentiality beforehand. Otherwise your comments are fair game."

"So this *is* an interview!"

"No. But the reporter in me always lurks near the surface."

"Well," rejoined Andrew with a crafty expression of his own, "if you want more from me later, I think you'll honor my request."

"Are you saying you will give me a story?"

Andrew walked a few more steps in silence.

"*If* there's a story, Miss Rawlings," he said after a moment, "I'll call you first."

"Then I'll honor your request," said Paddy. "But you don't have to be so formal with me—I'm an American, remember? Can't you just call me Paddy?"

"I'll call you Miss Rawlings," replied Andrew with a smile. "Some American ways are a little too loose even for a new-generation liberal like me. I like to preserve respect, without giving in too soon to informality. But I haven't forgotten the cappuccino invitation."

They walked on for several minutes in silence. When the conversation resumed, the subject of ancestry—either Scots or American—did not come up again between them.

✖   S I X   ✖

As Andrew Trentham walked back through Regent's Park, his thoughts were full of the serendipitous conversation with the delightful American journalist Patricia Rawlings.

Why had he allowed so much time to elapse since their lunch together? His thoughts suddenly flitted to the garden party he was scheduled to attend during the Chelsea Flower Show later this month. He would invite her to accompany him.

It would be fun. Why not set people to buzzing about something other than his politics for a change? And what a scandal it would be—a respectable English gentleman with a scrappy American journalist.

Whatever percentage his blood contained from his northern heritage, Andrew thought with a smile, maybe it had been derived from a Scottish rogue!

When he walked into his flat the telephone was ringing. He quickly strode across the room to answer it.

"Hello, Andrew," said a musically accented voice on the line.

"Blair!" he exclaimed.

"You sound surprised."

"Well, yes . . . I am. I would have to say you are rather the last person I expected to hear from," replied Andrew. He tried to recover from his shock and keep his voice sounding halfway normal.

She laughed good-naturedly. "I deserve that," she said. "Why *would* you expect to hear from me?"

The sound of Blair's voice in his ear, especially her laugh, sent Andrew into a brief whirlwind of enchantment, mingled with a renewal of confusion over what had happened. Her question had been rhetorical, and before Andrew could collect his wits to reply, Blair spoke again.

"Seeing you last month at Granby's," she said, "reminded me of a lot of good times we had together. I've been thinking about you ever since. Perhaps I was wrong."

Andrew's brain reeled at the words.

"I'd really like to get together," she added. "I want to talk to you."

Andrew's first impulse was to drop everything and rush to her immediately. But something within him spoke a word of caution. If the long walks and hours of reflection and newfound self-awareness had done anything, perhaps they had made him a little more self-protective. If he was suspicious, it was because he was not eager to be hurt again. If, as he had come to realize, he hadn't really known Blair that well, a brief telephone call wouldn't change that fact. He would have to give this situation some thought.

The silence on the phone lasted but two or three seconds. "I'll ring you," said Andrew after a moment. "Are you still at your flat?"

"Actually, no," Blair replied. "I'll give you another number."

Andrew took it down. They exchanged a few more pleasantries, then hung up.

He sat down and exhaled deeply. The call had shaken him. Slowly his mind drifted back to Patricia Rawlings and their walk in the park.

Call from Blair or not, he would still ask the American to the flower show!

§§§   S E V E N   §§§

The knock on Inspector Shepley's door sounded urgent. The owner of the hand that made it did not bother to wait for a summons to enter.

"I think we've got a break, Inspector," he said, walking in.

"What do you have, Burford?"

"That card the boys found in the sewer tunnel paid off."

"You've isolated a phone number?" exclaimed Shepley, rising to his feet.

"Not only the phone—we've traced down the location . . . an exact match on the four letters below the numbers."

He handed Shepley the report. The inspector scanned it quickly, then glanced up with wrinkled brow. A look of disbelief spread over his face.

"I thought you might find the owner of the property interesting," said Burford.

"I find it more than interesting . . . and more than coincidental. What's the connection with Hamilton?"

"I don't know, Inspector. I just analyze the clues—you figure out what they mean."

"Well, I don't know all of what it means yet," rejoined Shepley, reaching for his coat and heading for the door. "But I know this much—you'd better pack your bags, Burford. You and I've got to catch the next flight to Glasgow."

✳ E I G H T ✳

Waiters bustled about with drink-laden trays, while people clustered for small talk, spreading in all directions among the hedged pathways and abundantly flowering walkways. Water from two fountains sprayed into the air, then fell back with a pleasant tinkling sound onto ornate ponds where large koi and Japanese carp moved about lazily.

The sound of tennis balls could be heard from the courts in the distance, rhythmically punctuating the delicate strains of a small four-piece chamber ensemble playing Borodin's String Quartet No. 2 in D Major. A grand piano and concert harp stood silent to one side, giving hopeful promise of more music later.

"I'm not very comfortable in situations like this," said Paddy as they walked onto the expansive lawn. "I never know anyone, and I'm self-conscious about my American tongue. I feel like everyone's waiting for me to stumble over myself."

"You have nothing to worry about," laughed Andrew. "Your accent is wonderful. Believe it or not, some English actually *like* Americans. And you'll probably know more people than you think—the press loves to hang around functions like this."

The crowd spreading through the grounds of the eighteenth-century Chelsea estate was well sprinkled with lords and ladies from all segments of the peerage. There was talk, some said, of the King making an appearance.

"King Charles has quite a green thumb, you know," Andrew said.

"Will you introduce me?" asked Paddy excitedly.

"If he comes, and if we can get close enough, I'll try," replied Andrew.

"I say, Trentham," said a voice, approaching from one side, "any more news about the Hamilton affair?"

Andrew turned.

"Hello, McGrath," he said, shaking the other's hand. "No, nothing that I know of."

"The Nationalists are making it difficult for you, though."

"No more than they did when Eagon was alive," replied Andrew. "Everyone has his agenda. I don't suppose anyone can fault them for pursuing theirs aggressively.—But here, Miss Rawlings, I'd like you to meet Duvall McGrath. Mr. McGrath. . . . Patricia Rawlings."

The two shook hands and exchanged the normal pleasantries.

"Well . . . welcome to England, Miss Rawlings. I hope you enjoy your stay," said McGrath, turning to go. "—Trentham," he added with a nod of departure.

"You see what I mean?" said Paddy when he was gone. "The instant I open my mouth, people make assumptions about me, like his thinking I had just arrived from the States."

"But he meant no disrespect," replied Andrew. "And besides, you have to be your own person and not worry about what anyone thinks."

Even as the words fell from his lips, Andrew paused to reflect how ineptly he had been able to heed his own advice. But he would not brood upon that just now. "How long *have* you been here, by the way?" he asked.

"A few years."

"What brought you to England?"

"Uh . . . a series of events, actually," she answered with a sigh. "It's a long story."

Andrew detected a change in her disposition. "I hope not *too* sad a one," he said.

"I don't know the ending yet, so I can't really say."

A pause intervened.

"How did you get such a good position in such a short time?" asked Andrew.

"Now it's *you* who is interviewing *me*!"

"The British press is hardly known for letting in newcomers," laughed Andrew. "Especially a woman. And a foreign one at that."

A sardonic look passed over Paddy's face. "Just lucky, I guess," she said. Andrew saw the expression but did not press further.

"Let's go over and listen to the music," he said. He took her elbow and steered her across the lawn, greeting several men and women as they went.

The next words they heard, however, were directed toward her.

"Say, Rawlings," came an approaching voice, "how's that investigation—"

Quickly gathering her wits, Paddy interrupted.

"Why, Bert—I haven't seen you in ages!" she said. She tried to sound confident but was noticeably flustered. "Here, let me introduce you."

"Mr. Trentham," she said, turning toward Andrew. "I'd like you to meet my friend Bert Fenton. Mr. Fenton, this is Andrew Trentham, MP from Cumbria."

The two men shook hands. Paddy did not give them time to speak.

"Mr. Fenton," she said to Andrew, "works for the Midland Travel Service. Bert, er, Mr. Fenton, I'm sure you know that Mr. Trentham is the new leader of the Liberal Democratic Party."

"Of course," replied Fenton. "Everyone in England knows the name Trentham by now."

"Mr. Trentham," said Paddy, turning to Andrew again, "would you mind excusing me for a few minutes? There is something I've been needing to discuss with Mr. Fenton."

"Not at all," said Andrew.

Paddy made her departure with Fenton in tow. They moved quickly away from the musicians and their listeners. She rejoined Andrew ten minutes later.

The remainder of the afternoon passed without incident.

❈   N I N E   ❈

Since Andrew Trentham's election as their new leader, his Liberal Democratic colleagues had given him complete loyalty and support in his new role. Given the unpleasant circumstances, the transition in leadership had been remarkably smooth.

Prime Minister Barraclough kept his majority coalition intact with less difficulty than had been anticipated by the editorialists primed for a dogfight over control of the House of Commons. Andrew and the prime minister spent a good deal of time together, discussing the latter's program.

Trentham's support in and of itself was sufficient, as Hamilton's had been, to insure a comfortable majority for the Barraclough's Labour government. In spite of the noises it was making regarding greater moves toward independence, the Scottish contingent continued to back Barraclough as well.

In the month since his return from Cumbria, following up on the communiqué sent by Dugald MacKinnon to Larne Reardon, Andrew had had two lengthy meetings with the Scottish Nationalist leader. MacKinnon continued to dismiss allegations of Scottish involvement in the Stone's theft.

Meanwhile, Scotland Yard reported that it had apprehended two suspects in the death of Eagon Hamilton, though neither had yet been charged. The Yard had been unable thus far to link the crime with any higher motives. The mystery of the affair deepened.

Patricia Rawlings' nose twitched when she heard of the arrests. She was certain they had been made merely to quiet public speculation—that Scotland Yard's *real* interest, and their ongoing investigation, lay elsewhere.

If she could just get some angle on one of the people on her list.

Deputy Leader Larne Reardon continued to interest her most of all. After their brief encounter, he remained at the top of her list of suspects.

Two stories had run in the tabloids, one in the *Star*, the other in the *Sun*, claiming that the murder was political in nature and quoting an interview or two—insignificant and unsubstantiated—alleging that the SNP had ordered the assassination in order to remove the chief roadblock to their cause. No one paid much more attention to the charges than to what was normally printed in the two papers along with monthly reports of the capture of the Loch Ness monster.

It could not be denied, however, that people were talking about the articles.

▨   T E N   ▨

Though on many evenings he did not arrive home until eight or nine o'clock, throughout the spring Andrew tried to end his day as he had begun it. This involved an hour or so immersed in the depths of one of the volumes he had borrowed from Duncan MacRanald or in one of the books he gradually accumulated of his own.

Through the afternoon he would find himself anticipating the moment he could put the day's politics behind him, sit down with a cup of tea and a plate of milk-chocolate Hob Nobs, and lose himself in the history of the land whose future was being thrust onto the front pages of the nation's interest.

Summer came to England, and for Andrew Trentham, something he had anticipated far more than long, warm days of sunshine—the recess of Parliament!

He had been planning a trip north for some time—farther north than Cumbria and his home at Derwenthwaite. He wanted to understand more deeply this land whose magic and mystique was infiltrating him. More and more he was realizing he could not do this merely from reading books about legendary heroes of the past, nor from long walks memorizing the verses of Burns, nor by visiting the Tartan Shoppe or the Scotch House in Knightsbridge to admire woolens and purchase oatcakes and shortbread.

All these had deepened his affection for things Scottish. But to truly understand these things, he realized, he needed to know the land itself. There was only one place that could happen—*in Scotland*.

One piece of unfinished business he had to deal with before he left, however. That was Blair.

Her call had been gnawing at him. After the devastation from a few months ago, he found himself wondering if he really wanted to resume their relationship. So much had changed since that fateful luncheon.

Yet it could not be denied that the sound of her voice on the phone had struck chords within him. Whether he loved her or not, he had to see her again. He had to work it through one way or another.

He would try to see her before he left for the north.

⚏ E L E V E N ⚏

The week of Parliament's recess, Paddy sat down at her desk after lunch. She checked her voice mail. She had one message waiting.

It was brief: *Call Bert.*

Without putting down the receiver, she immediately returned the call.

"Bert . . . it's Paddy."

"As I told you at the flower show, I've been doing some more computer sleuthing on those names you gave me," said Fenton, "and I finally have something that might interest you. That fellow Reardon, the MP—he's booked on a flight out of Gatwick. I don't suppose there's anything so strange about it, but I noticed the destination and . . . well, let's just say I thought you might be interested."

"I'm listening—where's he flying off to?"

"Dublin."

Paddy whistled under her breath.

Without thinking what might be the implications, she asked, "Can you get me on the same flight?"

"For the day after tomorrow? Kind of late notice."

"I've got to get on that flight," persisted Paddy.

"Let me see . . . hmm—" muttered Fenton, punching in a few words on his computer. "Looks like it's full. How about the next flight to Dublin . . . there's another one ninety minutes later, from Heathrow."

"That won't do me any good. I'd have lost track of him before I even get there. Bert, it's *got* to be the same flight he's on."

"I'll see what I can do—call you back in five minutes."

Paddy waited anxiously. Four minutes later her extension rang. She grabbed the phone.

"You're first standby," said Bert's voice. "Best I could do. Be at the gate and ready. I got you the advance ticket price."

"How'd you do that?"

"Don't ask. But you owe me one."

"Right," replied Paddy. Her meager supply of favors was shrinking fast! "Thanks, Bert. Can you arrange for a car for me?"

"No problem. What's going on anyway, Paddy?"

"Can't say. I'll tell you when it's over . . . *if* anything comes of it."

"I hope you know what you're doing. I've heard strange things about Reardon."

"What kind of things?"

"Oh, just spiritualistic mumbo-jumbo—more wacky than dangerous. Still, I avoid those types." He paused.

"You know," added Fenton after a moment, "there is one thing a little strange about the whole deal. Reardon's also making arrangements to transport a large box."

Paddy's ears perked up. "What kind of box?" she asked.

"I don't know—just a box, a wooden crate . . . like a tiny coffin. But the information on it—at least what's in the airport's computer—says *Nonscannable, security cleared.*"

"What does that mean?"

"That it's not to be scanned."

"What's in it?"

"Doesn't say. It's already been cleared through Irish customs on this end. I have the feeling it got through security with high-level help of some kind."

"Why do you say it's strange? People ship things all the time."

"Because its weight is listed at three hundred seventy-five pounds."

Paddy's mind sprang alive with possibilities.

"One more thing," she said. "How good are you with computers, Bert?"

"Pretty good."

"Can you get me a couple of phone numbers?"

"Piece of cake."

"Unlisted?"

"Takes a little longer, but no problem."

Paddy gave him the name.

Now Bert whistled. "High circles, Paddy! I can get them. But I'll say what I did before . . . I hope you know what you're doing."

As Paddy hung up the phone, Bert's sobering tone made her think perhaps she ought to take one more precaution against Reardon recognizing her.

TWELVE

The day following his decision, Andrew picked up his telephone and rang the number Blair had given him.

A man's voice answered.

Momentarily taken aback, he hesitated.

"I . . . uh, was calling for Blair," said Andrew.

"Blair?" the man repeated, as if he didn't know the name.

"I must have rung the wrong—"

Suddenly Blair's voice interrupted on the line.

"Hello."

"Blair? . . . Blair, hello! It's Andrew."

"Andrew—I wondered if it might be you."

"I thought I had the wrong number. I didn't expect anyone else—"

"Just a friend who dropped by."

"In any event . . . I've been thinking about your call," said Andrew. "I said I'd return it, and . . . here I am. Parliament's out of session, and . . . I guess I'm ready to get together."

"Oh, Andrew," she replied. "You couldn't have caught me at a worse time. I'm afraid I'm leaving in a few hours. I'm nearly just walking out the door."

"Where are you going?" asked Andrew.

"Away . . . uh, on business."

"Out of the country?"

"Not exactly. But I *would* like to see you, Andrew. We have so much to catch up on. May I call you when I get back?"

"Yes . . . yes, of course," replied Andrew. "I'm taking some time off this summer. You can reach me in Cumbria—you have the number."

"I'm so glad you called. I'll get back to you—I promise."

The following day Andrew returned to Derwenthwaite.

His plan was to set out for Scotland in a day or two.

THIRTEEN

At last Paddy settled into her seat on the Aer Lingus plane bound for Dublin. She had arrived early and kept out of sight. Not that the man she was following would remember her face, but she wanted to take no chances. From a vantage point across the gate area, she had watched her quarry arrive, then board. Fortunately he was on the plane before they began calling the standby names. She had cut her hair, and in its new style she could not help feeling that she stood out like a sore thumb. But no one else seemed to notice.

As Bert had promised, she was first to be called from the standby list. She checked her one bag, then boarded, taking her seat near the rear of the cabin. She did not see Reardon. She was in a middle seat, so would not be overly visible if he chanced to look around or walk along the aisle.

Paddy fastened her seat belt and took out a magazine.

Well, she thought, *here goes nothing!*

❋　F O U R T E E N　❋

The afternoon prior to his scheduled departure for Scotland, Andrew rode out to Duncan MacRanald's cottage. As the two men talked, gradually Andrew found himself opening his heart and mind to the old shepherd about personal dilemmas he had been wrestling with recently.

"I don't know, Duncan," he said, "sometimes I wonder what my mother thinks. She can be so silent. Here I am at the center of what I thought she always wanted for me. Yet from her expressions sometimes, I can't help but think I still don't measure up in her eyes to what Lindsay would have been."

"Yer mither's a good woman," replied Duncan, "but a wee bit confused. She has always been a mite hard on ye—an' yer dear sister."

"Hard on Lindsay!" exclaimed Andrew.

"Ay—worse'n wi' yersel'. The lass couldna please the puir woman whate'er she did. Nae doobt ye were too young at the time t' see it."

Andrew sat stunned—not only by what Duncan had said about Lindsay and his mother, but also by the fact that the old man was aware of such things.

"If only I could free myself from the weight of her expectation," he said after a moment, "and the constant undercurrent of her disapproval."

" 'Tis a burden I've seen ye were carryin'—an' ye bear it well, lad, though the day'll come when the Lord'll free ye frae it. We can only pray that yer mither'll let loose o' her ain weight in time fer it t' du her some good in this life. It'll be lifted from her in the next. But t' find peace here an' noo, she's got t' let loose o' it hersel'.

"In truth," he added, "'tis a severer burden on her shoulders than yer own. Ye're comin' t' feel a peace wi' who ye be—though ye're also tryin' t' be more a man than ye are noo, which is what matters more. But she's a woman not at peace wi' hersel', so hoo can she be at peace wi' those around her? I ache fer her—'tis a sad plight fer a body."

Andrew had been silent, pondering his words. "But you say God will free me from the weight," asked Andrew. "And my mother too. What do you mean? How will he do that?"

"I already see it happenin' in ye," replied Duncan. "'Tis plain that the good Lord's at work already. As fer yer mother . . . who's t' say but it won't happen as weel. For her, 'twill simply be a matter o' laying doon the false expectations she's been carryin', which she's put on ye and yer dear sister.

"In yer case, though, I dinna think 'tis so much a matter o' lettin' go as it is trusting God t' git inside ye in a deeper way and make himself t' be yer strength. Don't git me wrong, lad—I got no doubt ye believe. But belief isna the same as givin' yer whole heart t' the Lord t' make o' ye what he will. When that day comes, an' it comes t' all, ye'll no more need t' worry aboot what anyone thinks o' ye. Ye'll jist be happy an' content t' du God's will. Ye'll be a man in the eyes o' him that made ye then, an' that'll be all that matters."

Andrew took in Duncan's words thoughtfully. It was silent a minute or two.

"I don't know, Duncan," he said at length, "you would think that a man of thirty-seven, especially one in my position, relatively successful in the eyes of the world—wouldn't you think that by now I should be out from under the shadow of my mother and be secure in who I am. But even now my mum's at home stewing about this trip to Scotland I'm planning, thinking I ought to be doing social and political functions rather than taking, as she views it, a personal holiday. Why can't I just laugh it off? But it's just not so easy."

"Ah, laddie," replied Duncan, "none o' us in this life is ever altogether free o' the expectations oor mamas and papas put on us—not kings nor queens nor prime ministers, or shepherds like me. Look at puir King Charlie and all the princes afore him—and Victoria's son the King, God bless him, who ne'er was much his own man. Nay, all of us live wi' oor parents' silent expressions inside us. 'Tis what makes us who we be, but sometimes it makes us *doobt* who we be at the same time."

Duncan paused, nodding to himself thoughtfully. Andrew waited.

"O' course there are parents," the old Scotsman continued, "who ken hoo t' lead their sons an' daughters in the right way wi' their maker, an' who gi' them confidence in themsel's. Yet even then, 'tis perplexin' hoo different youngsters can grow in the same home an' reap different harvests from the same upbringing. 'Tis why ye canna lay it all at the feet o' the parents. Young men an' women need t' find fer themsel's who they be, take the good wi' the bad an' make the best o' it. But I du allow that yer mum has given ye, an' Lindsay afore ye, a tough row t' hoe."

"Am I destined to be filled with self-doubts all my life?" asked Andrew.

"Self-doobt isna really so bad a thing, laddie," said Duncan with a chuckle. "'Tis what the Creator gives t' keep us humble. So long as it doesna cripple ye an' make ye so ye canna do a thing, a little self-doobt can du ye guid. 'Tis the seasoning o' a gracious soul to keep it from thinkin' too highly o' itself."

"Self-doubts are rough to cope with in my position!"

"Ye may be right. The Lord's tellin' a different tale w' each o' us. But the curse o' the human lot is either thinkin' too *much* or too *little* o' oorsel's. There's self-doobt and there's pride—an' everyone's got one or the other. Likely enough, everyone's got a heap o' both! But 'tis usually one or the other that's the inner cross o' character we each must bear till the guid Lord's work in us is dune. Speakin' fer myself, I'd rather walk through life wi' the heavier dose o' the doobt than the pride. 'Tis perhaps a wee harder t' bear up under. But the one grows the fruit of Galatians Five in us if we let him have his way, but the other's a sure ruin o' character if we don't."

Again Andrew contemplated Duncan's words.

"Dinna ye fret, laddie," said Duncan at length. "Ye're a man. An' ye're a man that's walkin' down the right road wi' yer face held t' the light. Ye're just a mite more openhearted than most aboot the struggles ye got inside. But all men'se got 'em. All the men in yer Parliament, an' yer prime minister—they're all fightin' the same battles. 'Tis jist that most never let anither see 'em. An' there's some that winna look them square in the eye themsel's. Ye're *more* a man, Andrew my lad, fer facin' yer doobts an' trying t' win through them, not less."

⊠   F I F T E E N   ⊠

By the time Paddy's plane touched down at Dublin's airport, the flaw in her plan had revealed itself. In the time it would take her to pick up her hired car, the good Mr. Larne Reardon would be long gone!

Well, she thought, she would just have to play it by ear.

She waited in her seat until the 737 was mostly empty, busying herself rearranging the contents of her small bag so she wouldn't be noticed by those exiting. The moment the coast was clear she got up and hurried out.

There was Reardon up ahead, walking briskly toward the ground transportation exit. He apparently had no checked bags to worry about, nor was doing anything right now concerning the mysterious heavy box. By the time Paddy emerged outside the terminal, he was already ducking his balding head into the back of a taxi.

She'd have to come back for her suitcase and the rental car. At the moment all she wanted to do was keep Reardon in sight.

Paddy hurried forward, hailed the next taxi in line, and got in.

"I can't believe I'm going to say this," she muttered to herself, "but . . . *Follow that cab ahead of us,*" she added, now more loudly, to the driver.

It was not a long ride.

Both cabs pulled to the front of the Doyle Skylon Hotel between the airport and the city. Paddy waited until Reardon was inside, then got out, paid the driver, and followed the MP into the hotel.

Dusk was descending. Whatever he was up to, it looked like Reardon planned to spend the night here. At least it wasn't a five-star hotel, thought Paddy, though still it would probably be more expensive than Pilkington would allow on her expense sheet. But she had no choice, she told herself. She had come this far—she had to see it through. Though for all she really knew, Reardon was on holiday and this flight to Ireland nothing more than an innocent excursion. If this turned out to be a wild-goose chase, her producer wouldn't pay so much as a pound of her expenses!

Paddy took a chair in the lobby and pretended to busy herself with a newspaper lying beside her until Reardon was on his way up the elevator. She rose and walked to the desk, hoping they had an available room.

After she had checked in, and once she was satisfied Reardon would be inside for a while, she would return to the airport for her suitcase and the car Bert had reserved for her.

▨   S I X T E E N   ▨

The morning following his eventful talk with Duncan, Andrew said good-bye to his parents. His father was jovial and talkative, perhaps trying to make up for his wife's silent disapproval of the proceedings.

He shook Andrew's hand. "Good luck, son—enjoy yourself. But please—don't come back wearing a kilt!"

Andrew laughed. "I doubt my fascination with Scotland will extend quite that far, Dad!"

He turned to his mother.

"Good-bye, Mum," he said. He approached and gave her a hug. She was stiff.

"Andrew," she said as he backed away, "you and I are going to have to have a little talk when you get back. If you intend to get anywhere in London, you're simply going to have to take your responsibilities more seriously."

Andrew sighed inside, but did his best not to show his frustration.

"Right, Mum," he said cheerfully. He turned to his waiting car before the conversation could go any further down that road.

"Well, cheers," he said. "I guess I'm off."

Already his mother was walking back toward the house. Andrew waved one last time to his father, then started the engine and backed away.

He glanced toward the house. His mother stood watching at the doorway. He gave a little wave, then accelerated down the drive.

"Mother, Mother," he sighed, shaking his head, "you carry the weight of the world on your shoulders."

Andrew drove away from Derwenthwaite and toward Carlisle by his normal route. Turning left in the middle of the city, however, instead of south, sent a feeling of exhilaration and adventure through him that rose even higher twenty minutes later as he passed the blue "Welcome to Scotland" sign on the M74.

The route was familiar enough. He had attended countless meetings in Glasgow and Edinburgh over the years. But as he drove north through the hills of Dumfries, every mile now appeared different to his excited eyes. Now it was *his* turn, following in the Wanderer's footsteps, to explore this land . . . northward, ever northward, toward mountainous unpeopled regions not seen by many, appreciated only by those few capable of detecting their magic.

The Burns verses came into his head:

The winter it is past, and the simmer comes at last,
And the small birds sing on ev'ry tree.

It summed up just how he felt—happy and alive. For now all the pressure of Parliament, and even his mother's watching eyes, lay behind him.

The land of Caledonia beckoned!

He would drive and hike the moors, the forests, the mountains, the open spaces. He would ferret out little-trod pathways. He would gaze in all directions from Scotland's rocky peaks. He would walk its islands and stand upon its cliffy shores.

Glasgow held little appeal to his present adventuresome outlook, nor did any city. More lonely places called out to him.

Andrew therefore drove straight through the great northern seaport and metropolis, making his way westward along the banks of the Clyde toward the watery rugged coastline of the western isles and the Highlands. At Dumbarton he bore north around the shores of one of Scotland's two most fabled lakes.

❈   S E V E N T E E N   ❈

Back at Derwenthwaite, Harland Trentham sought his wife inside the house.

"Weren't you being a little hard on Andrew?" he said in an uncharacteristic moment of criticism. "It wasn't a very pleasant way to wish him a good trip."

Lady Trentham stared at her husband, not sure she had heard him correctly. "I know how things in London work, Harland. He would do well to ask my advice about these things."

"Perhaps he wants to stand on his own two feet."

"He simply has to learn how the political game is played," she replied a little testily.

"I for one happen to think he's done pretty well for himself."

"Then why is he off gallivanting about like this?"

"He's had a strenuous year—he deserves a little break. And it wouldn't hurt you to say you were proud of him once in a while. Don't you know how much your approval means to him?"

"Pshaw. He knows we're proud of him."

"Maybe *we're* proud of him, but are *you* proud of him? I've never heard you say so . . . and I'll wager neither has he."

Lady Trentham stared at her husband blankly, as if the concept was utterly foreign to her way of thinking.

After a moment her face went pale.

"I . . . I think I'll go lie down," she said. "Suddenly I'm not feeling very well."

✵   E I G H T E E N   ✵

Andrew's mood quieted while driving along the famous loch, with thoughts of the bittersweet love anthem in his brain.

> *By yon bonnie banks and by yon bonnie braes,*
> *Where the sun shines bright on Loch Lomond . . .*

The words and haunting melody stole over him, and he quietly murmured and hummed the solemn Scottish ballad.

> *. . . And ye'll tak' the high road,*
> *An' I'll tak' the low road,*
> *An' I'll be in Scotland afore ye . . .*

A short time later, with the sad, nostalgic strains still weaving in and out of his brain, he passed the sign reading: "Crianlarich, Gateway to the Highlands." An inexplicable thrill surged through him. He was about to touch the *essence* of what had for months occupied his heart and soul. The bare starkness of the hills called out to him. So empty they seemed in comparison to his own Lake District, which teemed with visitors and tourists at this time of year. The terrain around him spoke to his soul of wide expansiveness, of adventure . . . of myth and legend.

Still unconsciously wrapped in the subtle folds of Lomond's musical spell, which added its own distinctive melancholy to the compelling recipe of mystery, Andrew drove northward up onto Rannoch Moor—home to

Foltlaig's ancient tribe and to Brochan Cawdor of Clan Campbell—then down through the narrow, twisting gorge into Glencoe.

As the surrounding mountain peaks rose towering over him on each side of the roadway, he relived once more the captivating story of the maiden and the young soldier. On which of these slopes had Ginevra and Brochan met? Where had they escaped during that fateful February night?

He had made advance accommodation for his first night at the Balla-chulish Lodge, nestled at the foot of Beinn a' Bheithir on the shores of Loch Linnhe, where the Campbell troops had crossed by boat from Fort William.

The following morning he rose early and drove back into the glen. He parked at the visitors' center and walked along the banks of the Coe for an hour before breakfast, reliving again the compelling tale from long ago.

His second day's drive took him south along the shores of Loch Linnhe to Oban, where a ferry took him across the Firth of Lorn and Loch Linnhe to Craignure on the Isle of Mull. After a leisurely afternoon's drive across Mull's lonely southern hills, Andrew found himself standing at the water's edge in the small village of Fionnphort, looking across the glittering, choppy sea to that Genesis point of spiritual beginnings of Scotland—the tiny historic Isle of Iona.

The ferry ride across the Sound of Iona filled Andrew with many sensations—the sun, the sea air, the sense of mystery. This was the very place Columba's mission had begun. The same rocks were here today that those early missionaries and pioneers had trod over so long ago.

He and the few other passengers disembarked. As they set foot on the island, it was almost with a sense of reverence that all grew quiet. With his heart peaceful and full of feelings he could not identify, Andrew made his way to the hotel to check in. Here he would spend the night, then take the ferry back to Mull in the morning to continue his journey north.

A brief walk about the village followed, then a visit to the abbey and the nearby grave of former Labour leader John Smith, the Scotsman whose sudden heart attack had stunned the nation a few years earlier.

After dinner that evening, with book in hand, Andrew went out into the early twilight to walk about the sacred isle and make his way over the rocky rise to the opposite shoreline of open sea.

Twenty or thirty minutes later he stopped at the water's edge, pondering the wide expanse of Atlantic stretching out in front of him.

⌗   N I N E T E E N   ⌗

For Paddy Rawlings, journalist and amateur sleuth of late, suddenly MP Larne Reardon—whom she had been doing her best to keep track of for the last forty-eight hours—was far less intriguing than the green-and-white van ahead of her.

More particularly, she was interested in what was inside the crate that sat in the back of the van!

She had spent an uneventful day and a half at the hotel where, as far as she could tell, Reardon had not done much of anything interesting. Of course, he might have been making any number of telephone calls. But she couldn't bug his phone, so she had had to satisfy herself with eyeball surveillance. Then suddenly an afternoon delivery truck from the airport had shown up . . . then fifteen minutes later the van.

Reardon met both in front of the hotel, then supervised the unloading and loading of a large box. It looked exactly as Bert had described. When they brought out a portable hoist she knew it must be of great weight.

Once the loading was complete, Reardon climbed into a car and drove off in the opposite direction. At that moment Paddy had a decision to make: Which vehicle was she going to follow? She still wouldn't allow herself to believe what she was thinking. But she wasn't about to lose sight of that cargo now!

She hurried for her car, then pulled away from the hotel after the van.

That was ninety minutes ago. All that time she had been driving through the spectacularly beautiful Irish countryside. They had come forty miles out of Dublin to the southwest, passing a few minutes ago through the town of Carlow. They had just gone by a country pub whose sign displayed faded green shamrocks, a tipsy leprechaun, and the name *O'Faolain's Green*.

Now at last the van began to slow.

Paddy braked and pulled to the side of the road. That was the hardest part of trailing another car—the constant tendency to creep too close. She didn't *think* she'd been seen, though she couldn't be sure.

Several hundred yards beyond the pub the van signaled, then pulled off the road to the left. Slowly it continued up a paved but obviously private road toward what must be an estate not visible from the highway. A minute or two later it crested a small rise and was lost to sight among the trees.

She obviously couldn't follow it. Her presence would be too obvious.

Slowly Paddy turned her car around and returned to the pub. She would park and wait.

Twenty minutes went by . . . then thirty . . . and forty.

Suddenly she spotted the van heading back down the paved drive from the small cluster of hills where it had disappeared earlier. It turned back onto the main road, gradually picked up speed, and returned the way it had come. Was her brain playing tricks on her, or did the rear suspension seem to be riding a little higher as it went by?

The moment the van was out of sight back toward Carlow and Dublin, Paddy started her car and proceeded from the pub along the road, turning left onto the mysterious entryway. Cautiously up the hill she drove, then down through a slightly wooded region. The road took several bends, then rose again into a clearing.

Paddy gasped in astonishment. Spread out before her at a distance of about half a mile was an imposing stone castle. Behind it, in the midst of a luxuriant carpet of green grass comprising at least two or three acres, stood twelve or fifteen upright stones set into the earth in a semicircular pattern. They were of varying sizes—two or three huge ones, and the others no larger than two or three feet in height.

She remembered this place now! She had read about it a year or two ago—the castle and Standing Stones of Carlow.

This was the Irish equivalent of Stonehenge! Druids gathered here once a year from all over the world to tap the great supernatural powers of the ancient stones. She remembered something about an uproar among the locals a while back. The BBC had interviewed some disgruntled ale-drinking farmers at a local pub—perhaps that same pub she had passed.

She crept forward down the drive until she came to two great iron gates closed against further approach. To the right, carved into a stone sign with heavy Celtic script, were the words, *Celtic Druidic Center.* On the other side, anchored into the ground at automobile height, stood a remote-coded keypad and intercom.

She wasn't about to press the button to seek entrance. The sooner she got out of this place the better!

Suddenly she saw three or four men in the distance. Two wore what she took to be druids' robes. The other two burly fellows were attired as workmen, one carrying a shovel over his shoulder. Between them, from what she could tell, was the crate from the van.

If only she had a pair of binoculars! The second workman was pushing the box along on a hand truck toward the open grassy area of standing stones. He appeared to be straining to keep the load moving.

It couldn't be possible. . . .

With all of Scotland Yard involved in a massive three-month search throughout the whole country . . . had *she* actually managed to stumble on to it?

Things like this just didn't happen. Not to her.

But there it was.

If her suspicions were on the mark, how had Reardon been able to get it out of London right in the middle of Scotland Yard's investigation? And then past customs and airport security into Ireland? Even MPs didn't have that kind of clout. Reardon must have some kind of high-placed connection. Maybe, thought Paddy to herself, the answer was in that castle down there behind these imposing iron gates.

She would have to find out later. Right now, this place gave her the shivers. She had no intention of getting involved with druids!

She backed up to a wider spot, turned around, and then drove back down the entryway. It was time to return to Dublin and see what Larne Reardon was up to.

▨   T W E N T Y   ▨

It had been a long and awkward day for Harland Trentham.

His wife was not accustomed to words of reproof from him. She could take any amount of criticism from her political adversaries, and fling it back in kind. But her husband was a different matter. He did not usually speak his mind quite so bluntly. As a result, she had been silent and grumpy most of the day and had kept to herself.

Andrew's father had thought it best to be away at dinnertime. He had gone out about eleven and had not returned until a little after two. By teatime that evening, however, he thought the chill had gone on long enough. When Franny began to set out the tea things, he went upstairs to his wife's sitting room. She sat motionless, staring out the window toward the lawn behind the house.

"Coming down for tea?" he said, giving his voice as cheery a sound as he could.

She turned, then rose, exhaling a little sigh intended to convey that she was still hurt, invitation to tea notwithstanding, and that they both knew who was responsible.

Mr. Trentham stepped aside. She passed him and led the way downstairs to the dining room. They entered. Franny was just pouring boiling water into the pot on the table. Andrew's father turned toward his chair.

The next instant he heard the sound of a crash behind him.

He spun around. His wife had collapsed over a corner of the table.

Franny gave out a scream. The boiling water spilled onto the middle of the table even as Lady Trentham's body pulled cloth and dishes from one edge of it tumbling down upon her as she collapsed to the floor.

Andrew's father was on his knees at her side in a second. She was unconscious, her face ashen, her eyes closed.

"Franny, call an ambulance!" he cried, still on the floor. He leapt up, sought a napkin and glass of water, and attempted to revive his wife. He spoke tenderly and frantically as he dabbed at her face and forehead with the damp cloth. It was obviously more serious than a mere fall.

He now jumped up and rushed to the phone himself, which he took from Franny's hysterically shaking hand.

⌗ TWENTY-ONE ⌗

As Andrew continued his stroll about the legendary island of the Hebrides, a great sense of reverent history stole over him at the mere sound of the water lapping against the jagged stones of tiny Iona's coast.

The evening was warm and calm—unusual, he had been told, for this far north. Evocative smells from the sea water and rocks and coastline lifted gently into his nostrils, mingling with scents from the close-cropped flowering turf just inland and filling his head with haunting pleasure. The deep blues and greens of the ocean, arrayed with the varied and multihued colors of shoreline, rock, sea grasses, and sand, combined to remind his senses more of the Mediterranean than the North Atlantic.

Ahead, a fisherman was lugging in his nets and tying up his small boat for the night. Andrew approached.

"A good day's catch?" he asked.

"Ay, middlin'," the man replied.

"Do you fish here all year 'round?"

"Canna git oot much in the winter."

Andrew nodded.

"Seas be too fierce," added the man, more to himself than to Andrew, for rarely would a Highlander give out excess information to a lowlander. "'Tisna a friendly place when the water's angry. I ten' my beasts an' hire mysel' oot on Mull an' wait fer the weather t' turn again."

"Why do you stay if the living's so hard?"

The man paused and stared, as if wondering whether to continue the conversation with a stranger. Then he answered, "The sea's my life, laddie. I love the sea. Couldna be happy wi'oot its waves in my ears an' its salt spray in my nostrils. If I canna be upon it wi' my wee bit boatie, I still must be near it."

Andrew nodded. "I can see that a place as beautiful and peaceful as this would get into your blood," he said.

"Iona's like no place on earth, lad," said the fisherman, waxing strangely philosophic. "'Tis my home, an' my parents' before me, an' theirs before them. 'Tis why I stay."

Andrew continued on. It would be easy to find oneself beguiled on a day like this, he thought, into believing this a more temperate climate than it actually was. But as the man had said, the Atlantic was no tame sea. It took a singular breed to make a life here—like the fisherman he had just left. The lives of those who braved crossing it for their faith so long ago were far from easy ones.

Encountering a few sheep and an occasional cow, Andrew worked his way gradually up the small mountain called Dun-I. When he reached the top, he had arrived at the high point of the island, from which most of it was visible. Slowly he turned his gaze all about him.

Behind him stood the sacred abbey on the site first established by the venerable saint called Columba. Andrew had not expected to be so moved at first sight of it a few hours earlier. But a silence had swept through him as he gazed on St. Martin's cross and the edifice rising out of the stones of the isle—a silence that had deepened into awe when he had some moments later gone inside.

Until recently, he had not been a man much given to praying. But now, as he stood on the mountain overlooking the place where Columba was conjectured to have landed, Andrew Trentham found no other response that seemed appropriate *except* to pray.

As Andrew gazed contemplatively out upon the calm waters, he wondered what must have been in Columba's thoughts when he set sail from his native Ireland.

It had been an expedition that had sent the spiritual roots of a new religion down into the rocky soil of this region of the world. What the Romans had failed to do in three hundred years, Columba accomplished in a lifetime.

Andrew sat down on a stone and breathed deeply of the fragrant evening air. He opened the book he was carrying and began to read the ancient account of the first landing here . . . a landing that changed Scotland forever.

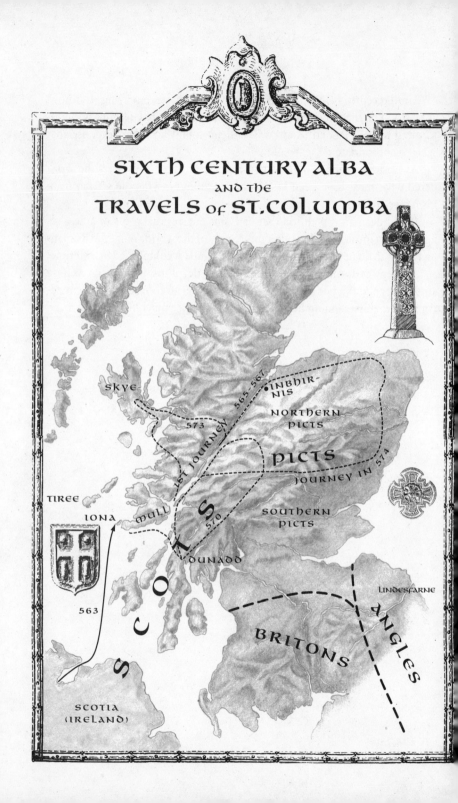

SIXTH CENTURY ALBA
AND THE
TRAVELS OF ST. COLUMBA

SKYE

565-567

•INBHIR-
NIS

573

NORTHERN
PICTS

1ST JOURNEY

PICTS

JOURNEY IN 574

TIREE

MULL

570

SOUTHERN
PICTS

IONA

S C O T S

DUNADD

LINDESFARNE

563

ANGLES

BRITONS

SCOTIA
(IRELAND)

11

COMING OF THE DOVE

A.D. 563

☒ O N E ☒

Tears of impending dread filled the eyes of the twelve-year-old girl.

She was marching in a solemn procession of Celtic ritual up a gentle slope. On its crest ahead grew a towering oak. A moment of high and sacred import had come for the people of her village. But her heart did not rejoice to be part of it . . . for she herself was to be the sacrifice.

The girl was terrified for her life. But in her youthful and ignorant way, she also possessed some vague sense that this rite was horribly and shamefully wrong.

She had always been an unusual child for the culture into which she entered the world. These remnants of a now-vanished Celtic empire were what might have been called an innately spiritual people, but theirs was a crude spirituality and its forms of expression were base and pagan. She felt, on the other hand, the higher callings of that spirituality. She was seen as strange—possessed, some said, by devils of the dark powers.

The girl's odd behavior as she grew confirmed the suspicion in which she was held. She did not fear the power of the world, as did most, but relished in it. From an early age she was more at peace away from the village under the open blue sky, beneath the stars that sprinkled the vast blackness of night, even amid the fiercest of black clouds when they roared and unleashed bolts of fire and sent icy pellets of hail or rain whipping across the land. She might be found in the midst of such fury, face gazing up into the tumult, laughing with pleasure.

Nature delighted her. The world made her happy. Yet she did not worship it, as did so many of her kind. Though but a child, she sensed that the earth and sky and sea—all its creatures and growing things—had been created by something above them all. The wonders of the earth had been given and she had been placed in their midst . . . to enjoy not deify.

Though she would not have been capable of forming the rational conclusion that she could *think* in more significant and abstract ways than the eagle or the bear or the mighty stag of the forest, somehow she knew herself to be greater than all these manifestations of that Higher she sensed but knew not of.

The girl's name was Diorbhall-ita.* She was the daughter of the king.

As this day approached, she was told that to be offered to the Great Oak at the High Place was the highest honor that could come to one such as she. The druidic priestesses said she should rejoice to have been chosen from among all the young virgins of the village. The great god Bilé, who dwelt in the oak, and Danu, the mother goddess who watered the oak from heaven, would be greatly pleased. They would drink her blood and bestow the blessing and prosperity of harvest to her people.

In her heart, however, Diorbhall-ita knew that her father, King Brudei of the northern Picts, had selected her because he hated the sight of her. She reminded him of her dead mother.

He had done away with that one when he was through with her. Now he would be rid of the daughter too.

"You will be highly exalted by the gods," High Druid Broichan told the king, "for offering your own seed."

Thus had it been arranged.

Diorbhall-ita already suffered a girl's worst agony, that of knowing she was despised by the man who had given her life. She hated him, and she hated the evil man Broichan. She would kill them both if she could. She would kill them with her own hand!

But she was just a child. Her father was the king, and Broichan was the High Druid. What could she do against them?

As the procession now approached the sacred High Place above Inbhir-Nis, twelve-year-old Diorbhall-ita, already extremely tall for her age, trembled in terror. Behind her the column of druids and druidesses chanted in solemn cadence.

In front of the bloodstained altar ahead stood the horrid towering form of Broichan. She could not prevent her wide, petrified eyes from seeing the great knife beside him. That sharp blade was meant for her neck!

---

*Pronounced *Dee*-ah-leeta, as might in English be spelled Dialeta. Diorbhall is the Gaelic form of Dorothy, which means "God's gift."

The procession stopped. Hands forced her to her knees and now bent her head toward the stones of the altar. A cry escaped her lips. Above her the evil shadow of Broichan rose into the air. His deep voice began to chant in dark tones.

She did not want to die!

Out of the corner of her eye she saw his hand move toward the huge knife. He clutched it, then drew it toward her. Now rose the chants of the druidess procession to a loud frenzy of—

Suddenly Diorbhall-ita squirmed loose.

A gasp of astonishment went up from the druidic assembly. A few hands grabbed at her.

"No!" she screamed. "I won't let you kill me!"

She darted away across the top of the hill.

An angry curse exploded behind her. It was the voice of her father. Another shout followed from Broichan. Running footsteps came after her.

But she was young and swift of foot. And she was running for her life. None of those present could catch her now.

She ran and ran, knowing not where, heedless of direction. She sprinted over the hill, into a wood, down into a ravine, up the other side, then followed a stream bed until she came out onto open heathland.

Still she ran . . . on and on and on.

Several hours later, she found herself at the edge of the River Nis some two or three miles upriver.

She lay for some time exhausted and tearful. She could not move another step.

In the agony of terrified desolation, as her weary lungs at last slowed, young Diorbhall-ita began to whimper, then broke into sobs of loneliness. For many long minutes she wept uncontrollably, until at last the storm began to pass.

"Help me," came a murmured cry from her lips, "please . . . help me!"

Within moments she was sound asleep.

She had no idea to Whom she had prayed. She had always harbored a vague sense that more existed beyond her sight than the oak and Bilé and Danu. But that the whispered, despairing cry of her heart was actually *heard* by a personal Being greater than Broichan's inanimate deities—was a truth that lay outside the scope of her imaginings.

But her prayer had indeed been heard. And even now a savior was being prepared who would be sent to this land to deliver her from this season of her sorrows and afflictions.

❈   T W O   ❈

Diorbhall-ita awoke to rude shakings and angry voices.

The brusque hands of her father's men grabbed and yanked her to her feet. Binding her wrists, they shoved her cruelly ahead of them back toward the village.

A merciless beating at her father's hand followed her return to her home at the palace. She lay motionless in bed for a week, bruises scarring her face, welts up and down her back, one eye blackened to the top of her cheek. She was kept alive only by the ministrations of a compassionate servant woman.

Broichan came to the king.

"I adjure you solemnly, King Brudei," he said. "As humiliated as you are before the people and the gods, you must not kill the girl. To murder one intended for sacrifice would bring her wickedness down upon you, and with it the curse of the gods."

"Let us bind her hands and feet and take her back to the altar," said the king, still incensed. "She will not escape us a second time!"

"She can no longer be used," replied the druid. "She is now defiled. The gods must have a willing sacrifice. They would repudiate such a gift and rain down fire from the heavens. No, she is no longer worthy."

"What am I to do with the miserable cur!" shouted the king in a white wrath.

"There are ways to be rid of such, my lord king," replied the druid.

"She has been a curse to me since her birth."

"Leave all to me, my lord king. I shall find her a suitable marriage that will ease you of the burden, and bring upon the head of the wicked child a fate such as she deserves."

Two months later, Diorbhall-ita was given in marriage to a man from a neighboring village whose reputation was well known to Broichan.

This Gairbhith had his way with the twelve-year-old daughter of the king of Inbhir-Nis. When he had gained what pleasure it suited him to take from her young body, he rented her to others of his low class. As Broichan had known only too well, such was Gairbhith's means of having amassed a not insignificant level of wealth. When his youthful brides failed to satisfy his customers, he sold them as slaves to a seafaring people from the north with whom he maintained dealings of commerce.

And thus did Diorbhall-ita become an outcast and castaway from a society into whose royalty she had been born. Delight died within her. She no longer sought the open spaces. Life became a torment of pain, misery, and abuse at the hands of evil and pleasure-seeking men.

When her so-called husband died six years later, she was left as an exile and wanderer, without means, with no friend to whom she could turn, and with no home of her childhood to which she might return. Even now, had her father been able without incurring the wrath of the gods, he would have arranged for her murder.

As the next years passed, she did all she knew to survive and gave herself to the low men who continued to seek her.

Seven years went by. She sank into mere existence. Her tears dried, for they had been spent. Her soul numbed. No more did she feel its aches, its yearnings, its whispered callings to life's higher dreams and purposes. The death from which she had once run, should it come to her now, would be a blessing and relief.

But the cry of her child-heart beside the river long before had risen on the invisible messenger-wings of angels. It had been heard by Him who made little girls and angels, hailstorms and mountains and rivers altogether. And even in this bleakest hour of her misery and destitution, he had not turned away his face of love.

He only awaited the appointed moment when the answer to her plea would come back down from heaven . . . this time sent to her on the wings of a dove.

▨   T H R E E   ▨

The bird of her deliverance was nineteen when Diorbhall-ita was born, thirty-one when she was marched up the hill as intended sacrifice to the deities of the oak.

Like her, he was born of royal lineage. He was born not as a dove but as Crimthann, a *fox*, prince of the Irish O'Neills of Donegal. At his christening his name was changed to *Colum* O'Neill. Like Diorbhall-ita he would be forced from his home and would never rise to rule his land.

The destinies of these two would intertwine as they rose into their mutual inheritance in a new Kingdom . . . and as son and daughter of its new royal family they would together help change their world.

As the Irish lad grew, he was placed into the care of Cruithnechan, the priest who had baptized him Colum, *the dove.** Upon returning from church one day, Cruithnechan witnessed a vision of fire hovering over the face of the sleeping child. Surely, he told the parents, it was a sign that the Spirit of God dwelt within the boy. As a result, they destined him early for the priesthood.

Among the superstitious peoples of the post-Roman world, spiritual leaders were viewed as more powerful even than kings. In order to further his ecclesiastical training, therefore, in his teen years young O'Neill was given over to the tutelage of an aging Christian bard by the name of Gemnan. His tutor curiously intermingled ancient Celtic craft with the new Catholic faith which had been introduced to Erin in the previous century by Saint Patrick. Columcille learned well from Gemnan's instruction. He himself would ultimately elevate the bardic priesthood—Christian rather than druidic—to new heights of influence in the Celtic world.

Of powerful intellect and physique by the time he was twenty, Columba soon made his impact felt in Ireland—in both the political and spiritual spheres. He entered a monastic seminary, was ordained a priest, and within a short time demonstrated that he was at the forefront of a rising new religious generation of Irish leadership.

Gifted with magnetic personality and filled with youthful zeal to expand throughout his country what was still a relatively new faith, at only twenty-five, Columba founded a monastery school at Derry. In 553 another followed at Durrow, and the following year still another at Kells. By the age of thirty-three the apostolic mission of Colum O'Neill's life was set—to establish monasteries and churches, like the three already in existence, throughout a pagan land.

Such a vision carried political implications. The fact that an atmosphere of miracle had surrounded the young priest since his birth insured that he would be drawn into the affairs of his nation. So did his family name, which was linked to Irish royal descent. By the age of thirty-five, Columba was a national figure. And a controversial one. Some said his noble birth gave him a right to the throne.

But King Diarmaid of Eire was not about to relinquish power to a young

---

*Also known as Columcille and Columba.

upstart priest, kinsman or not. The rivalry between supporters of the two grew heated and bitter. Columba's public criticism of Diarmaid over the killing of another Irish prince expanded the quarrel and drew in all of Ireland's leading families. Hostilities eventually erupted in the bloody battle of Cuildremne. Ireland's future leadership was at stake.

It was a rivalry, however, that Colum O'Neill was destined to lose. From influential, even miraculous beginnings, fate seemed now to turn against him. Suddenly the cousin of the king was also his enemy. Church leaders had to make a choice of allegiance. Most sided with king against priest. Columba was censured publicly, excommunicated for a brief period, and suddenly found himself in disgrace.

Time had come for a change. Whatever claim his noble birth might have entitled him to make, he now decided to leave his homeland. He would seek a new mission field . . . across the waters to the east.

If he was bound for exile, it was a convenient one, for escape from Eire might be the only way he could stay alive. His future lay in the land of northern Britannia. Whatever motivations stirred within his heart—whether he was a spiritual outcast, an outlaw, or merely one whose ambitions had been curbed and whose pride was humbled—at forty-two, Colum O'Neill now sailed from the land of his birth.

Ahead lay the land of the wild pagans known as the Picts, on the western shores of whose territory his own native Celtic Scots had begun to establish a foothold in what they called the kingdom of Dalriada. In the land to which he was bound, his destiny would bring him sainthood . . . and the stature of legend.

He and the twelve companions who sailed with him were hopeful of both evangelizing the Picts who controlled most of Caledonia, and strengthening their fellow Irishmen—the Scots of Dalriada, who had several years before suffered a crushing defeat at the hands of the natives.

The motives of his sojourn were thus threefold: personal, political, and spiritual.

F O U R

A long, narrow boat of pine and oak sliced through the waters of the North Channel. On the prow and gazing into the distance for sight of land stood the Irish priest responsible for the voyage.

By the standards of any age he would have been considered a giant among men. Tall, commanding, confident, bold. A visionary, perhaps. Passionate, certainly—to the point of being hotheaded, said some. A dove is the last image these latter would have affixed to their memory of him.

Whatever the mix of traits, and whatever his temperament, this Celt from the Irish race known as Scots was destined to change not merely the history of the Picts, but of all Caledonia.

Columba stood at the front of the vessel observing the white water thrown aside as the wind carried them forward. In the distance off starboard could barely be seen the island of Islay. The wind had blown uncharacteristically from behind them, and the crossing thus far had been without incident. The next landfall would be the tiny chunk of rock just off the tip of Mull.

What would they find at Iona, he wondered. There could not be much left following the plague of fifteen years ago. Three churches had been established in these outer islands two decades earlier, but most of the priests had died of the dread disease. Thereafter the beginning efforts to bring the faith to northern Pictland had been frustrated. Hopefully Columba and his companions would be able to reverse that setback.

"What are you thinking, my cousin?"

Shaken from his reverie, Columba turned.

"Ah, Baithen, my friend," he replied with a smile. "I was just reflecting on how delicious this southerly breeze felt in my hair, and how wonderful is God's sweet-smelling provision of the sea!"

"Is that all? The look on your face spoke of weightier concerns."

"You know me well!"

"It must be difficult for you, now that Erin is out of sight behind us, not to know when you will see your homeland again."

"Perhaps there is a certain melancholy in my heart, I cannot deny it. Yet Alban-Dalriada is also in Erin's domain—we are merely bound for a different corner of our own kingdom."

"And one in which you will be recognized as a religious leader, rather than an outcast."

Columba smiled pensively but did not reply.

"What else are you thinking?" asked his cousin, younger by a dozen years.

"I was wondering what we are likely to find on Hy*, and what the Almighty has in store for us in this adventure."

"Do you think he will open the mainland to us?"

"It is my hope," replied Columba. "Much will depend on what we learn from my kinsman King Conaill."

"You will visit Dunadd?"

"As soon as is possible. Conaill, after all, rules over Hy."

"And then?"

"There is a great deal we can do among our own people to be sure. And the pagan Picts in the north are greatly in need of the church and its gospel."

"It is they who stand most in the way of the expansion of the Dalriadic kingdom as well."

"You have spoken shrewdly," rejoined Columba. "Their conversion will certainly serve the political purpose of our nation's expansion."

Master and protégé fell again to their contemplations of the early summer's sea.

It was midday and they should see their landfall soon. They had set out from Derry at dawn, Columba and his faithful companions: Echoid, Baithen, Grillaan, Brenden, Rus, Rodain, Scandal, Luguid, Cobthach, Diormait, Tochannu, and Cairnaan.

The sound of the waves slapping against the sides of the small ship turned Columba's thoughts poetic. By the time the rocky shoreline above Port-na-Curaich was in view an hour or two later, the verses were in his brain that he would write down that same night during his time of contemplation and prayer:

> That I might listen to the thunder of the crowding waves
>   upon the shore;
> That I might stand in the sanctuary of the surrounding sea,
>   and hear its roar;
> That I might observe its noble flocks in winged flight
>   over the watery ocean;
> That I might witness the greatest of its wonders, leviathan
>   in powerful motion;
> That I might watch its waters ebb and flood,
>   outstretched for me therein;

---

* A form of the old Irish Gaelic name of the island (*Hi,* or *Ia,* or sometimes merely *I*), whose adjectival form in Latin, *Ioua,* was misread *Iona,* which is Hebrew for "dove."

That my mystical name might be,
   I say, Cul ri Erin.*

❊   F I V E   ❊

The land the Irish nobleman and cleric would evangelize was part of a Celtic world steeped in heathen tradition.

It was a paganism hideous to modern sensitivities whose practices involved occult rituals. Like its continental cousins, these Celts took pleasure in placing the heads of slain enemies on stakes in dedication to their gods. It was a paganism not so different from that of the Hittites, Canaanites, Perizzites, Amorites, and Amalikites of the ancient Middle East.

The druids who presided over Celtic paganism were of an ancient priesthood of magicians and sorcerers, sprung from the great Amairgen of Ireland. In the eyes of the masses, they possessed enormous spiritual power. Through dark and mysterious rites they maintained their grip upon tribal society, incorporating into one the roles of bard, poet, priest, fortune-teller, seer, prophet, and witch doctor. It was everywhere a primitive world, and in its Celtic corners the druids conducted Satan's business.

But even in the midst of this darkness, mankind yet found ways to progress intellectually. Druids also served as the lawgivers, teachers, and judges for their communities. Their educational and magisterial function was equal to the spiritual. Learned in mathematics, geometry, art, physics, Latin, and Greek, druids were the primary educators of an illiterate people. Important families sent their princes and sons to be privately tutored in druidic learning.

Yet it was a primitive culture gradually being displaced by the dawning religion and civilization of Europe and the Mediterranean. And in one small corner of the Celtic world—the Ireland from which Columba sailed—the Judeo-Christian heritage had already begun to infiltrate druidic tradition.

When Christianity came to the Celts, however, it did not instantly change all tribal customs. Christianity changed the *foundation* of religious belief. But many old forms and methods remained. Even when the Christian God replaced traditional idols as the object of worship, many superstitions, demonic symbols and chants, and much art and folklore remained.

Cul ri Erin—"turned toward Ireland."

The result was that many subtle forms of druidism's pantheistic tradition continued. Thus did the entire material world continue to be seen as endowed with deified elements of the supernatural. Animal and other nature cults, worship of sacred oak trees, water and celestial gods and goddesses, and hundreds of aboriginal superstitions, therefore, intermingled their way into the complex structure of primitive Celtic Christianity.

Nor was this a purely Celtic phenomenon. In many parts of the world, an incoming Judeo-Christian belief system often *adapted* more to the conventions of pagan cultures than *eliminated* them.

The Hebrews of the Old Testament—with Moses and Joshua and David and Solomon and the prophets to guide them—continually lapsed into the practices of their heathen neighbors. How much more, in the early years of its influence in other regions of the earth, did residual paganism interfuse with the modes in which Christianity was expressed. Especially was this true in the Celtic world.

A sort of dualism, therefore, emerged between Christian belief and pagan tradition. As the new religion gradually took hold, it retained many customs from the old ways. Celtic missionaries did not demand that every element of paganism be cast aside. They were themselves Celts. A primitive and idolatrous sort of *religious* perspective was inbred in the Celtic temperament. The culture of their race spawned a harmony of outlook which allowed the old and new to coexist together naturally.

Many Christian priests, moreover, had themselves been taught by druids. Most of the early Christian monastic schools in Ireland had once been druidical schools. The *new* thus flowed out of the *old*.

The result was enormously practical: Christian Celtic monks allowed the transition out of paganism to occur slowly.

This was a far different kind of evangelization than had occurred in other parts of the world and in other cultures. The apostle Paul and his colleagues were outspoken in their judgments against imperial Rome. For the average Roman to accept the Christian faith meant going against everything he had been taught throughout a lifetime. Christianity was *antagonistic* to what the Roman Empire stood for everywhere.

In Britannia, on the other hand, Christianity was easily accepted because it *tolerated* what had come before. The pagan heritage of Columba's race formed an intrinsic foundation for the particular form of Celtic Christianity that now rose up.

Thus, when Christianity slowly swept across from Erin to Alba, then south to England, and ultimately across the continent back in the direction of Rome itself, many of the old Celtic ways lived on within it.

▓   S I X   ▓

The first Scot to venture across from Ireland had been Cairpre Riata, late in the third century. This ancestor of the great Conn of Eire and son of Cormac macArt, founded the first Irish, or *Scotian*, settlement on Alba, a settlement which his son Colla Uais and grandson Eochaidh expanded.

And now the mainland fortress of Dunadd, between the Sound of Jura and Loch Fyne at the narrowest point on the Argyll peninsula, was strategically located to give Irish Dalriadic king Conaill a well-placed base for his Alban kingdom.

These Irish emigrants, or *Scots*, had been hounded by the Picts since their first migrations to the western shores of Caledonia. But Dalriada maintained its bridgehead. Now it was Conaill's hope that Columba's arrival might give him opportunity to expand the kingdom. He was anxious to offer the abbot whatever help lay in his power. Any spiritual influence Columba might exert could only strengthen Dalriada.

Within a month of his arrival at Iona, Columba sailed across to the fortress of Dunadd on the mainland at Argyll. He and the king discussed many matters, not the least of which was the most mutually advantageous strategy for establishing contact with the Pict king, and how to convert him to the Christian faith.

"Brudei is a strong leader," said Conaill. "If you win him over, his people will follow."

"Is he a man of reason?" Columba asked.

"I have never spoken with him. But I understand he surrounds himself with powerful druids capable of great sorcery."

"Sorcery is no match for the power of the gospel," rejoined Columba.

"There is a particular wizard by the name of Broichan. It is said he is more powerful with his magic than all the rest."

"Is anything known about him?"

"He was Brudei's tutor as a boy. The king places great store in him."

"Then that is how I shall win them over to us," said Columba, "—by defeating his magic."

They spoke further, and did not part until certain arrangements had been made in view of Columba's proposed mission.

"Without protection, you would be dead before reaching the Great Loch," said Conaill. "I will send word of your coming to the Picts. I will tell them you are a holy man in the line of Scotia's kings. They will allow you safe passage."

Conaill paused.

"There is one more thing," the king added solemnly. "I intend to grant you full possession of Iona from which to carry out your mission."

"I am honored with the confidence you place in me," replied Columba respectfully. "You will not regret this decision."

Though religious affairs in Erin and Dalriada at the time were as political as spiritual, in his own way, Columba was a deeply devout man. He was proud and ambitious, it was true—some still called him by his given name of Crimthann, *the fox*, not Colum, *the dove*. But his was an ambition not primarily on his own behalf or for worldly gain, but rather for nation and tribe . . . and for the gospel.

Though his influence in Irish politics was enormous, Columba remained in a certain way a simple monk. Private contemplation and prayer came in for a heavy share in his daily schedule. He had no desire to build monuments to himself, nor gather wealth or possessions. He lived an austere personal life, was never too proud to sleep on bare ground or remove the shoes of the monks under his charge to wash their feet. He ate no meat, drank no ale.

From the beginning to the end of his days—in the midst of controversial involvement in the secular affairs of the world—Columba remained dedicated to that most fundamental of priestly duties, a painstaking copying of the Word of God. Books were of the world's greatest treasures. They could be made available only through reproduction by hand. Columba's favorites were the Gospel accounts and the Psalms. Wherever his travels took him throughout the years, he toiled in his priestly cell laboriously duplicating whatever manuscripts he could lay his hand on.

He found himself especially drawn to the miracle passages. The stories of healings, and the conflicts between demons and angels, the power of God over beasts and events and men . . . these became as real in his mind as they had been to he whom he called Master. Columba perceived in the Gospels a story he could step into *himself*, and whose truths he too, like Jesus, could embrace and live.

From an early age he had seen people healed at his hand. As he grew, so did Columba's faith to believe that whatever he prayed would come about.

❈   S E V E N   ❈

Eight months passed after Columba's visit to Dunadd.

He and his comrades put the winter to use making their quarters on Iona permanently livable. They began to cultivate the protected portions of what land contained sufficient soil. Though several buildings survived in tolerable repair from the first missions here, much new construction was necessary. Living quarters, animal barns and pens, a kiln, and a church all had to be built. Several voyages were made back to Erin for supplies.

On stone foundations, they made initial huts and structures from wattle-and-daub—interwoven twig mesh, over and through which they spread mud and cob, a mixture of clay and straw. To this they added what wood was available, as well as stone, and finally thatch for roofs. As long as such dried mud walls were thick and kept dry, the structure proved strong and serviceable.

As time went on, gradually monastery buildings grew in size and in the sophistication of their construction. Sheep and cattle were brought across from Dalriada.

The following spring and summer more strides were made toward permanency and self-sufficiency. Personal cells and the chapel were completed. More animals were ferried from the mainland. The garden area was expanded. Many crops were planted. Great quantities of peats were cut, and other winter stores laid aside. A new barn was constructed.

By the onset of his second winter on Iona, Columba's thoughts and prayers began to turn toward the mission for which he and his comrades had left their homeland. Now that his base was well established and secure, he was free to set his sights on his next objective—the Picts in the north.

One morning Columba walked about the grounds in prayer. *The time approaches,* he thought to himself. *I will journey north as soon as weather next year permits. There I will seek audience with the powerful Pict ruler Brudei.*

Throughout the winter, the small island drew the priest to its remotest places. By the emergence of spring he knew every corner and rock on the tiny isle from *Carraig ard annraidh* in the north to *Port a churraich* in the south and had explored each of its two dozen bays.

"It is only three miles long and one and a half wide and surrounded by water," Columba was often heard to remark in later years. "Yet as cut off from the rest of mankind as our small troop is, when I walk this lovely island in the midst of such vibrant blue-and-green waters, I sometimes feel that the whole world is my own possession and that I am afloat on the seas of time."

He was not so far wrong. He had written the words many times as he had copied out the Scripture *Blessed are the meek, for they shall inherit the earth.* Whether or not he was yet one of the meek was only for God to determine. But Columba knew that on this island he *felt* the inheritance of the whole world. To walk its lonely pathways in prayer was blessing indeed.

"Could more suitable spot exist than this wonderful little island from which to launch the Christian enterprise?" Columba said to his fellows the week before they embarked for the mainland. "Here both dawn and sunset tinge the sea with their glories. Here waves lap against warm silver sands, and, when the storms rage down upon us, crash violently against sharp jutting cliffs. Could any other place serve as such fit sanctuary in which for men to offer up their worship unto God?"

EIGHT

In late May of the year 565, Columba set out on a combined political and spiritual mission that would change the course of Britain's future. In the next few years foundations were laid upon which the nationhood of Caledonia would be built.

From Conaill they gained familiarity both with the route they would use and the Picts to whom they were going. The Dalriadic king supplied them guides and two Irish Picts, Comgall and Canice. They could interpret the strange Pict tongue and hopefully alleviate whatever potential difficulties might arise with the natives.

Columba and his companions traveled by boat around Mull and into the Sound of Lorne, then northward through the four lochs, Linnhe, Lochy, Oich, and Ness—carrying their craft overland between them. The journey through the great series of glens bisecting the mainland lasted three weeks. At last, rowing down the Abhainn Nis, they drew within the environs of the mouth of that same river, the place known as Inbhir-Nis.

In 565 this region was the seat of power of the northern Pict kingdom. It was ruled over by the twelfth great-grandson of the old Pict warrior who had, with his father, burned the Roman forts at Corbridge and Newstead. Through the twisting lines of peculiar Pictish lineage, Brudei macMaelchon now occupied the same chieftain's role as had his great ancestor Cruithne, by whose name his very people were now called.

Columba's adversary would be the powerful druid Broichan.

Though a Christian monk, Columba was sufficient believer in supernatural manifestations of both druidic and Christian origin to be affected by the shadowy sorcery of the times. Superstition lay in the very fiber of his race. His character, therefore, was woven from the same cloth as Broichan's. As Christian priest his method was not apologetic like Paul's in Galatia or Athens. He would rely heavily upon the miraculous to persuade the Pict king of the gospel's truth.

Columba brought a *new* supernatural myth to lay over an *old* mythology. He was the most prominent among many who now redefined the metaphysics of an old world by bringing Christian "miracle" to a Celtic culture. The Celts were a people who made cult-idols of their kings and warriors. Now came priests and monks telling of new *Hebrew* heroes. Later they would make hero-saints of the humble monks themselves. Still later would they deify the clan chieftains of their beloved Highlands. Christianity neither drove out the hero-cults nor the old myths. It recast and infused them with Christian identities.

While the conversion of heathens to the Christian faith was of high concern, so was the future of Columba's people and nation. While the Picts may have been Celts, the relations with them were of prehistoric distance, stretching back in time so far no mortal remembered them. If the Scots and Picts sprang from that same ancient wandering seed, little did they now consider the fact of import.

Columba's ambition was for his *own* people, the Scots of Dalriada. He desired to help Conaill expand his kingdom. If he could establish friendly relations with Brudei—presenting himself as much a prince of Erin as abbot of Iona—it would go far in securing the future of the Dalriadic kingdom. If the Picts could be converted in the process, so much the better.

Messengers had been sent to Inbhir-Nis from Dunadd. They informed the Pict ruler that a man of high esteem and vaunted reputation was coming to seek audience at his palace. That he was reportedly a bard and holy man, whose blood ran with the kingly succession of Erin, induced the Pict leader to allow the party friendly passage through his land and to his court.

When Columba drew near to Inbhir-Nis, therefore, Brudei was expecting him.

❊   N I N E   ❊

In a stone dwelling in the fortress of Brudei, not far from the king's own residence, a boy of five ran excitedly inside the darkened enclosure.

"Father," he cried, "they have been seen!"

"Who, Fintenn?"

"The holy man—they are rowing him down the loch! May I go down to see him, Father?"

The man turned toward the door and led the youngster outside. "You may go with me, Fintenn," Aedh said, "but not alone. There may be danger. We know not this man's magic."

Satisfied, the boy took his father's hand.

"May I come too, Papa?" called out a younger girl's voice behind them.

Aedh turned and nodded to the boy's sister. The three walked toward the gate of the fortress, then down the incline toward the wide river mouth. News had quickly spread. Aedh and his son and daughter were not the only curious Caledonii of the settlement making their way down toward the water's edge. In the distance, Aedh saw two boats, without sail, approaching from upriver.

His brother would not be among those on the shore to welcome the guests, thought Aedh to himself. Even though the holy man from Dalriada was coming at his brother's own invitation, Brudei was a proud man and would not emerge from his quarters too readily. He would give no premature homage to this newcomer, nor appear too eager before his people, and thus, in his own eyes, be the weaker man. Vanity augmented his pride, which perhaps contributed to the brawn with which he wielded his kingship.

It was a vast empire over which the descendant of Foltlaig ruled, extending throughout all of northern Caledonia. Men and women throughout Pictland feared the son of distant Maelchon. But few could be said to love him.

Aedh and Brudei were both sons of Baldri, it was true, but the great king of northern Caledonia and his humble brother could not have been more disconnected of personality and character. They were as different as had been Cruithne and Fidach, but with this distinction, that the uniqueness between the former drew tighter their filial attachment, while in the case of the latter, the bonds between them since the days of their youth had been nearly nonexistent.

What could Brudei hope to gain by admitting the Dalriadic priest, Aedh thought to himself.

Was it his brother's fascination with wizardry? Perhaps Brudei was curious to see what manner of magician Dalriada was capable of producing. If the man truly was of Erin's succession of kings, and capable of miracles besides, he would be a powerful force.

Then again, Aedh thought darkly, his brother could be worried about a potential rival to his own power. It might be that Brudei had encouraged the visit in order to kill the man. Under ordinary circumstances his brother would not think twice about doing so. To take the life of one with occult powers, however, was dangerous to contemplate. Even Broichan the Magus might not possess power to save him from the tempest of the heavens brought on by such an act.

Before he could reflect upon the matter further, however, a tug of his arm let him know they had nearly reached the river.

"Come, Papa!" urged young Fintenn with the enthusiasm of childhood. "They are nearly to shore!"

A small crowd had already assembled, though none of the king's counselors or druids were among them. The two boats, seeing the fortress on the hill, had been moving generally toward them for some time, and now bore straight at the gathering welcome.

Before they reached the shoreline, a man spoke from the lead boat. "Greetings, fair people!" said the newcomer in their own tongue. "We bring you good tidings from the kingdom of Dalriada. We come as friends. We come under the authority of the abbot of Hy, Columba, son of Fedhlimidh of Donegal, who seeks counsel and friendship with your worthy and exalted king, Brudei, son of Maelchon."

The two crafts glided gently onto the sandy shore. Several of the men jumped out and hauled them thoroughly onto the beach. Since no officially appointed representative was present to receive the visitors, Aedh stepped forward from amongst his clansmen.

"I am Aedh," he said to the man who had spoken, "son of Baldri, brother to the king. My brother has taken to himself the name of our ancient and honored ancestor. He calls himself macMaelchon. In the name of our people, I welcome you to Fortress Brudei."

Now stepped out of the boat the commanding figure of another who took several steps forward, looked Aedh firmly in the eye, then extended his hand. There could be no doubt this was the one of whom they had heard. One gaze into his pale gray eyes and Aedh knew him to be a different breed of man than he had ever met.

"I am Colum of Iona," the man said, in a quiet but powerful voice and unfamiliar tongue.

Behind him, another translated the words. Aedh nodded that he had understood, then stretched out his own hand to clasp that of their visitor.

"Thank you for your greeting," continued Columba. "Will you take us to your brother the king?"

"I will take you to the fortress. You are expected. I am not, however, in my brother's council nor of his court. I do not know when he will see you."

Columba nodded. Now first he noticed the young boy and girl, hand in hand at the side of the king's brother.

"Are these your children?" he asked with a smile.

Aedh nodded.

Columba turned his face to them, then knelt down.

"What is your name?" he asked of the lad.

The translator made his meaning clear.

"Fineach-tinnean," replied the boy, clutching more tightly to his father's hand on one side of him, and his sister's on the other.

"A name fit for a grown man," remarked Columba with a smile of good-natured humor. "What does it mean?"

"A link in the chain of his kin," answered the boy's father. "He is called Fintenn."

"Fintenn," repeated Columba thoughtfully, "a good name, I would say. And what is yours?" he now said, addressing the girl.

"Anghrad," she replied.

"Also a good name."

He paused, looked back to the boy, then placed his hand on his head and gazed deeply into his eyes.

"May the Lord Jesus bless you, son of Aedh, nephew of the king. May he make you a son of his Father in heaven . . . and thus the most worthy link in the chain of your clan's heritage it is possible for a man to be."

Lifting his hand, he turned and now placed it upon the girl's head.

"And may the Lord bless you too, Anghrad, and make you and your children also faithful links, as your brother, in the Father's family."

Columba smiled affectionately, leaving boy and girl gaping in astonished bewilderment at what the strange words and accompanying smile might mean. He turned and followed the brother of the king up the hill toward the fortress, while the rest of the men of his party and the Caledonians who had come down to water's edge to meet them trailed close behind.

❈ T E N ❈

Aedh led the party straight between the stone walls of the settlement, the crowd steadily increasing in size as they went.

Following at some distance, the furtive form of a woman darted in and out between walls and shadows, tagging behind but keeping the newcomers in sight. She seemed reluctant to draw close or join the throng moving from water's edge up the hill to the king's house. The expression on her face displayed more than simple curiosity. She appeared as one mesmerized.

By appearance she could have been thirty, but was in fact only twenty-five. Hers was an ancient profession that aged women before their time, in both body and soul. She was not beautiful, though in her eyes could be seen that expression which drew low men and made them lust for such as she. But the hypnotic attraction which now pulled her along behind the crowd was from an altogether different world than the only one she had ever known.

Why she had followed the sounds of the crowd to the river, Diorbhall-ita could not have said. She had no interest in holy men or kings. How could they help her plight? Fathers, kings, and men, she had all learned to despise together. But once she had laid the eyes of her starving heart upon the tall form of he who stepped from the boat to speak with Aedh and now walked at his side, she could not take her eyes off him. His face shone with something she had never seen. It was a glow that compelled her to follow. No thought entered her mind to possess such a man, as she could be said to possess the men of the settlement who came to her in the darkness.

She could only follow and watch, drawn to the face with fascination. Her dove had arrived from up the same river beside which she had offered her childhood prayer of desperation.

The party of newcomers led by the king's brother walked through the gate of the village, which stood open, and into the central courtyard in front of the king's residence, the largest building of the place. It was barred by two large wooden doors, tightly shut.

Still Aedh saw no delegation from his brother on hand to welcome the visitors. By now their arrival could hardly be unknown to anyone for miles. The entire settlement had poured into the courtyard and now gathered about.

Though up to two hundred must have been present, the only sounds were of shuffling feet and the general bustle of movement. Not a word came from the watchers. Silently the throng observed the approach to the king's house. Many fears and superstitions mingled with its collective curiosity.

Aedh indicated the well in the middle of the courtyard where the new-comers might sit and refresh themselves, then, prefaced by a word of apology, said he would attempt to learn the king's whereabouts.

"Be not anxious about myself or my men, friend Aedh," replied Columba through the Pict Comgall. "The afternoon is well advanced. We will begin our day's vespers and thank our God for safe conduct."

The smile on the tall priest's face temporarily removed Aedh's annoyance over his brother's absence.

Before they could begin, however, a sudden commotion broke out at the back of the crowd. Suddenly it was aroused to speech.

"What is she doing here!" came a cry.

"It's the prostitute!" shouted a woman's voice.

A great pushing and shoving began against the woman in their midst who had suddenly been seen.

"Get her away!"

Some of the women struck at her.

"Out of the gate with her!"

Hearing the noise, Columba came forward. The crowd parted and slowly quieted. He reached the center of the clamor just as one of the men who had joined in the fray was poised to throw a fist-sized rock toward the woman's body.

With a strong grip Columba seized the man's wrist and held it fast. The look of rebuke with which he pierced the man's eyes was enough.

The priest let go of the man's arm.

"Are you, my friend, without sin that you would cast the first stone?" said Columba. His tone was strong and compelling.

A brief silence followed. Columba nodded toward one of his translators. The Irish Pict now repeated the words in the native tongue. A low murmur of astonishment swept through the crowd at such a bold and unusual saying. As if struck by an invisible blow from the words, the man stepped back two or three steps. As he did, he was unable to remove his eyes from Columba's face.

The stone fell to the ground with a dusty thud. The accuser backed away and was swallowed by the crowd.

Columba now turned and knelt to face the object of the crowd's derision and hatred where she had fallen. As he did, he signaled to the Pict Comgall to approach and join him.

Columba gazed into the woman's face. He saw neither Scot nor Pict, neither man nor woman, neither prostitute nor king's daughter. He beheld only two eyes of common humanity staring up at him, filled with tears.

"What is your name, my child?" he said tenderly.

Comgall translated the words.

"Diorbhall-ita," she replied timidly. Her white face was dusty and tear-stained. Her light brown hair fell straight and tangled down on all sides, partially obscuring eyes and cheeks. Unconsciously she brushed back a few loose strands and wiped at her eyes.

"Diorbhall—God's gift," smiled Columba. "What a treasure is such a name. It also means thirsty. Tell me, are you thirsty, my child—thirsty for the water of life?"

The great liquid eyes continued to stare at Columba, in disbelief that such a man as he would speak to the likes of her.

"I believe that you are God's gift, Diorbhall-ita," said Columba. "And I believe that he will satisfy your thirst."

He rose and stretched his hand down toward her. "Rise, my daughter," he said. "Come to the well and sit. Listen to our songs and prayers and see if they do not refresh your soul."

As one in a trance, she took his hand. He helped her to her feet and led her to the well. The crowd watched with incredulity, wondering what manner of man this was who had come into their midst and now made himself the friend of outcasts.

⌗ E L E V E N ⌗

Aedh now turned toward the doors of the king's hall.

Behind him Columba and his men seated themselves on the ground. They were soon praying and chanting softly. Beside the well sat the thirsty prostitute, listening but not understanding, weeping though she knew not why. Encircling them, but from a wary distance, two hundred or more Caledonians watched the strange proceedings in renewed silence.

No response met Aedh's attempt to gain entry to his brother's palace.

Surely, Aedh thought, Brudei's council of seven, and his five druid priests—none of whom had been heard from since the two boats had first been seen approaching almost an hour ago—surely they were not . . . afraid to show themselves.

He knew his brother too well to imagine such a thing. Superstitious perhaps, but *afraid*—not Brudei macMaelchon, king of the Picts!

The singing of the newcomers by now rose to a level which could be heard throughout the entire village. Their presence could not be unknown behind the doors of the king's residence and hall. And now at last the musical tones awakened action behind its walls.

Suddenly the doors before Aedh opened sharply. Five long-robed bearded druid priests strode out. In the lead came Broichan, stern faced and ominous. The doors closed behind them with a thud. A clanging of iron bolts followed from within where *someone* had obviously remained hidden behind the walls.

Ignoring the king's brother, Broichan walked briskly toward the convocation near the well.

Seeing his approach, and sensing by his long robes and bearing that he must be an important personage—perhaps King Brudei himself—Columba rose to face him. The rest of his party continued to sing in soft tones. The expression on the druid's face indicated that his mood was anything but friendly.

"You are commanded by the power of the dark sea, in the name of Brudei, king of Caledonia, to silence."

Columba met the man's forceful gaze. He displayed no surprise at hearing the words in his own tongue. Behind him, the singing of his men at their vespers now increased slightly in volume.

"Silence!" repeated the druid angrily, finding himself ignored in full view of the entire population. Columba continued to stare into the man's eyes. Each felt in the other a repository of power, though from vastly different sources.

Only a moment more did the silent confrontation last.

The druid sensed this was no man to be easily cowed. Broichan turned slightly and nodded to his four priestly companions. They now moved to positions surrounding the small circled assembly of visitors.

When they were in place, the five began intoning a chant invoking the powers of the air, the sea, and the earth to their aid in cursing the wicked tongues of these who had come among them. They would *compel* them to silence.

Now did Columba's spirit rise up against the pagan deities which held these people captive. He had come to proclaim the gospel. He would therefore demonstrate its power for all to see.

He raised a hand to still his men. For a brief moment no sound could be heard but the low chants of the druids.

In a loud tone that reverberated throughout the enclosed courtyard, Columba now raised his voice and began loudly to sing out the words of the Forty-sixth Psalm.

Is e Dia ar tearmunn agus ar neart, ar cabhair ro dheas ann an teanntachdaibh. Air an aobhar sin cha bhi eagal oirnn, ged ghluaisear an talamh, agus ged atharruichear na beanntan gu meadhon na fairge. Ged bheuc a h-uisgeachan, agus ged chuirear that a chéile iad, ged chriothnuich na beanntan le a h-ataireachd.

The thunderous chant of his first words was still echoing from the surrounding walls of stone when the maledictory dirges invoked against him ceased.

Ghabh na cinnich boile, ghluaiseadh na rìoghachdan—chuir e mach a ghuth, leagh an talamh.

Columba paused again and gazed around him. Throughout the courtyard, the eyes of his listeners were wide, their tongues dumbstruck. Curiosity now passed into fear. The five druid priests stood still as statues. They had now been commanded into silence.

Columba continued to the end of the psalm.

Tha Dia nan slògh leinn, is e Dia Iacoib a's dìdean duinn.
Thigibh, faicibh oibre an Tighearna.
Bithibh sàmhach, agus tuigibh gur mise Dia.
Ardaichear mi am measg nan cinneach.
Ardaichear mi air thalamh.
Tha Dia nan slògh leinn. *

---

*God is our refuge and strength, a very present help in trouble. Therefore we will not fear, though the earth be removed, and though the mountains be carried into the midst of the sea, though the waters roar and be troubled, though the mountains swell and shake.

The heathen raged, the kingdoms were moved—but he uttered his voice and the earth melted.

The Lord of hosts is with us, the God of Jacob is our refuge. Come, behold the works of the Lord. Be still and know that I am God. I will be exalted among the heathen. I will be exalted in the earth. The Lord of hosts is with us. (Psalm 46, selections)

His words ceased.

The native Picts stood awestruck. The tongue they heard was related to their own. Some of the older men of the village grasped a few words and phrases. But even after Columba's assistant had translated the verses of Scripture into their own Gaelic dialect, the words conveyed little meaning. These were new sayings, and strange.

Still the villagers stared, mesmerized even more than by the content of the man's words, by the tone and volume, cadence and timbre of his voice.

This newcomer possessed a force they had never seen. He spoke as one having authority, and not as the druids. Never had Broichan been silenced by any man. Surely there was some terrible and mighty power here.

Young Fintenn, who in his very innocence had perhaps been listening more attentively than many of the older tribesmen, whispered a question to the man at his side.

"Father, what does the Lord of hosts mean?"

"I do not know, son," whispered Aedh in reply.

Meanwhile, Columba began walking slowly toward the doors through which the five priests had emerged. Broichan moved to stop him but remained powerless to speak. Columba paused before the large wooden doors.

He lifted his right hand and slowly indicated the sign of the cross in large exaggeration before the entryway.

"In the name of the Father, and of the Son, and of the Holy Ghost," he said in calm but loud voice, "I command thee, kingdom of Caledonia, to be opened to the Gospel of Jesus Christ, the Son of God!"

With his hand still raised, he took two steps more forward, placed his hand against the large rough wooden slabs, and again made the symbol of the crucifixion over them. He clenched his hand into a fist, then knocked forcefully and deliberately against it three times.

Columba now lowered his hand, stepped back, and waited.

The entire courtyard was deathly still. The people of the village stood transfixed. Their five priests fain would have moved, but their feet were anchored to the ground. Columba's men stood calm and expectant.

A moment more the silence lasted.

Suddenly—and though the sound was small, it seemed to echo throughout the courtyard as if thunder had shattered the silence of the sky signaling victory to the man of God—the metallic bolts clanked back.

The two doors swung wide. Columba stepped back.

The next instant, to the magnified astonishment of his druids and the disbelief of his citizens, King Brudei himself strode out, followed by the seven members of his council.

Without hesitation, he approached Columba, extended his hand reverentially, and spoke words of respectful welcome.

The spell was broken. The entire village broke into spontaneous movement and animated voice.

Once friendly relations had been established with their king, all clamored now for a closer look at the new arrivals. Somehow in the movement and excitement, Broichan managed to slip from the courtyard unnoticed and was not seen for many hours. So too did Diorbhall-ita shrink back to her lonely hovel at the edge of the village, which was the only home she knew. All the people of Pictland struggled to survive, for in this land merely to eat and keep from freezing meant victory. But the poverty of this poor lonely soul was more grievous than all the rest.

A great feast was held that night in the palace. All the important men of the settlement were invited that they might hear from their honored guest.

In a surprising show of respect for his brother, Brudei asked Aedh also to attend.

As he was leaving his own enclosure, young Fintenn approached. "Father," he asked, "what does the Lord Jesus mean?"

Aedh gave the same answer as earlier. "I do not know, Fintenn," he said. "The holy man from the south speaks of many new things."

⁂   T W E L V E   ⁂

Two weeks passed.

Columba and his men had been treated with honor and respect since their arrival in Inbhir-Nis, and had been shown every courtesy and luxury possible. After their questionable reception, a more satisfying turn of events could hardly be imagined. Columba and his companions visited in many homes, of both rulers and peasants, explaining to them the Christian faith. Not a few from throughout the region believed, for these were a people anxious after the supernatural.

Broichan the Magus and his fellow druids were angry with the obvious affection of the people toward the Dalriadic abbot and did their best to thwart Columba's every move. The king himself took delight in the contests between the two, desirous to see which man possessed the greater power.

Broichan had maintained an uncomfortable control over Brudei all his life, and the king now enjoyed seeing the druid squirm. In King Brudei's eyes, whoever's magic proved superior was the one whose religion must be the more formidable.

Even as a tense interview between priest and druid was taking place in Brudei's palace, in her hovel the prostitute Diorbhall-ita scrubbed at her body, hair, face, hands—doing what she could to make herself presentable. Strange feelings had risen up within her. She had given herself to no man since the priest's arrival. She desired to be clean in every way.

Whether she was a pretty woman, she had not stopped to ask since Gairbhith had made her what she was. It had never mattered before. She stood a head taller than most women, which made her recognizable to everyone, even had she not been an outcast. She had always wanted to hide from the stares of all who saw her. But her very size prevented obscurity. Never could she escape the looks of revulsion and disgust which had followed her.

But now something new had suddenly come into her heart, something that did not feel like hiding, but singing. Never had anyone shown her such kindness as the priest from Dalriada. With heart beating and unknown melodies seeking to rise within her from places in her heart long sealed, she tied her hair back from out of her face. She would go down to the river and wash more thoroughly.

As Columba and his men departed from the palace, they made their way down to the shores of the River Ness. As they walked along, a white pebble caught Columba's eye. He stooped to pick it up where it lay at the water's edge. As he rose, in the distance he beheld the figure of the sad young woman he had not seen since the day of his arrival. She stood alone some distance away.

Motioning his companions to remain where they were, he walked toward her. How different she now appeared.

As Columba approached, she could not prevent a smile breaking out on her face.

"My child," he said, "you have changed since I saw you. How lovely you look." Already he had learned enough of the Pict sister tongue to converse freely with the people.

His words plunged straight into her soul, and her heart leapt for joy.

How much is the kingdom of God advanced in unseen ways by simple kindness between his creatures. It is the invisible power that opens doors for the reception of the gospel. Jesus commanded his followers to be *good* people and to do *kind* things to their fellows . . . in order that the world might believe.

And now did the ministry of kindness send its transforming power into the soul of this Caledonian prostitute, who was, after the fashion of the time, about to become a child of God.

"Thank you," said Diorbhall-ita shyly. She glanced toward the ground. "I have been following . . . listening to what you say."

"I can see the change in your eyes and your smile."

"I want to believe," she said simply.

"Then come," said Columba.

He took her hand and led her to the water's edge, then a few steps into it to the depth of his ankles.

"Kneel in the water, my child."

She did so.

Columba stooped, placed his hand in the river, scooped out a handful of water, and brought it up and let it fall over her forehead. It dripped down over her eyes and onto her face. With thumb and forefinger he made the sign of the cross on the wet skin of her forehead.

"Diorbhall-ita," he said, "I baptize you in the name of the Father, the Son, and the Holy Ghost."

He now took her head and clasped it gently between his two large hands, lifted his eyes to the sky, and uttered a silent prayer for the woman he had just baptized. Then he took her hand again and pulled her up.

She rose, radiant and weeping.

"You are now whole, my child," said Columba. "You are a child of the God who created you in his image. Go, sin no more, and live as his daughter, pure and spotless from this day forward."

He turned. Diorbhall-ita watched him go, then herself turned and walked along the river's bank away from the village, pondering many things in a heart slowly being made new.

⬛   T H I R T E E N   ⬛

As Columba rejoined his companions, he took back out the white stone he had picked up earlier. He opened his palm and contemplated it a moment. A vision awoke in his mind's eye of his adversary the druid gasping for breath.

"Broichan is being severely chastised," he said. "An angel has been sent from heaven and has broken the glass from which he was drinking into many pieces. One of them has lodged in his throat. The king will send messengers to us, asking us to return to help."

He had not yet finished this speech when two horsemen galloped down from the fortress to meet them.

In haste they related events exactly as Columba had predicted them. "The king has sent us," the messenger concluded, "to request that you would return to his hall and cure his tutor Broichan. A jar broke as he was drinking. He choked on a piece of its glass. His breathing has now stopped. He appears at the point of death. The king is greatly afraid."

For reasons known only to himself, Columba sent two of his men back to the king. "Take the white pebble," he said, handing it to them, "and tell this to the king: If Broichan shall immerse this stone in water and drink from it, he shall be cured."

They did according to Columba's instructions.

By the time Columba's two men arrived, the king and his druidic tutor were so beside themselves that they immediately did all exactly as he had said. As the pebble was immersed, the king saw that it floated on the water.

"What kind of trickery do you bring into my palace?" cried Brudei.

"No trickery, Honorable King," replied the other. "Our priest and abbot blessed the stone. It now contains holy powers. Tell your priest to drink of the water while the stone floats."

With trembling hand, Brudei took the cup. He handed it to Broichan. He could barely sip at its edge. After two or three sips, he managed a full swallow.

Suddenly a violent cough erupted. Several pieces of glass flew out of Broichan's mouth. He choked again, struggled for a breath, then another and deeper. Gradually he began to breathe more easily. He now took a large drink from the cup. Within minutes he was restored and breathing freely.

The king took the cup from his hand and peered inside it.

The white stone still floated on what water remained.

Thereafter, and for many years, Brudei preserved the astonishing pebble among his treasures, and used it on water to the same effect many times among his people. Thus was the king himself able to administer a cure for various diseases.

F O U R T E E N

After that day, Diorbhall-ita followed Columba's party wherever it went, until all the settlement came to regard her as one of those who were always with the great man. She walked about everywhere unafraid to be seen, taller than most of the men of the company except for Columba himself and two or three others. Wherever he taught, she sat at Columba's feet, and would have washed them with perfume if she had possessed any and dried them with her hair as Mary of old. In her eyes glowed adoration and unembarrassed devotion. No longer did the villagers torment her, for none could deny that a great change had taken place. Most still moved away if she came close. But now they more feared than despised her.

A certain highly respected man among the Picts listened eagerly to Columba's preaching and believed in the word of life. Along with many in Inbhir-Nis, he and his family were baptized—wife, children, and slaves. Only a few days afterward, one of the man's sons was attacked with a serious illness. The attack was so sudden that even as word of it spread, already the boy was nearly gone.

When the druids heard of it, they marched in solemn procession to the home. They began bitterly to upbraid the distraught father and mother.

"You have brought this on yourselves," they said. "You have forsaken our gods. This is the result. The spirits are angry. The boy will die, the rest of you will die. There is nothing we can do."

Word of Broichan's visit to the house of their most recent convert came to Columba. Immediately he proceeded to the house with some of his companions. He found the parents mourning and the mother weeping disconsolately.

"It is too late," the father said. "He is dead."

"Be contented, dear parents, " said Columba. He took the mother's hand and gazed tenderly into her face. "Do not doubt the power of God," he said. "What room is your son lying in?"

The father conducted him to it. Columba entered alone. He fell on his knees and began to pray.

"Oh, Lord," he whispered, "has such occurred by your command? Surely this cannot be your intent. What would you have me to do, Lord Christ?"

A few moments more Columba remained on his knees. Slowly he opened his eyes, then rose and approached the body of the boy. He placed his hand on the forehead. In appearance he might indeed be dead . . . yet warmth still seemed present.

Suddenly Columba recalled to mind the words of the Lord himself. Had he not copied them over by his own hand countless times? *The girl is not dead, but sleeping.*

A great swelling rose up in his breast as he remembered the *next* words to fall from the Lord's lips. Did not the Lord say that *greater* works would his disciples do than he had done? Who was he, a mere servant of the Lord, to doubt what Jesus had said?

Columba placed his hand again upon the boy's forehead, then spoke in a bold voice: "In the name of the Lord Jesus Christ, arise, and stand upon your feet."

The boy's eyes opened. He glanced around and saw Columba, then smiled feebly.

Columba took his hand and lifted him to a sitting position. He waited a few minutes for the boy to regain his breath, for he was still very weak, then pulled him to his feet. He now led him out of the room and took him to his mother. Gasps of astonishment erupted throughout the house. Tears of weeping became those of disbelief and joy.

Columba's kinsman Baithen, watching the proceedings from one side, and observing the tender expression in his cousin's eyes, smiled and sighed softly.

"God, how you must *love* that dear man," he murmured to himself, "to have endowed him with so many gifts."

Great was the rejoicing, both in that house and in the entire village. Even more came to believe that day. Dozens were thereafter baptized in the waters of the Ness.

※   F I F T E E N   ※

With reports circulating of healings and miracles at Columba's hand, at length King Brudei sent word to his guest to come to his hall that he might make more thorough inquiry. He had heard the abbot preach and give oratory. Now he would question him.

His druidic tutor and counselor in all matters metaphysical and transcendental objected. The king denied his counsel.

"I beg you, then," urged Broichan, "allow me to be present."

"For what purpose?" asked Brudei.

"That I might prevent the Scotian cleric from seducing you or gaining mastery over you with some bedeviling sorcerer's spell."

"How would you prevent it, my learned druid?" asked the king. A hint of sarcasm laced his tone.

"By placing an incantation upon him."

"Your magic is not as strong as this man's, and I would learn why. I will be on my guard," he assured the druid. "But no less am I determined to get to the bottom of the man's strange power. Away with you, Broichan."

Columba was shown in. The king saw something in his eyes which momentarily unnerved him. He had never been looked at with such an expression. He was used to seeing men look upon him with *fear*. But he had never seen another mortal man look upon him with . . . *compassion*.

No, it could not be that. There must be some other explanation—perhaps it was one of the man's spells!

Brudei recovered himself and began the interrogation. Comgall, the Irish Pict, sat beside them.

"Whenever I have heard your words, you speak of four deities," the king began, addressing Columba while Comgall translated. "You speak of God, you speak of Lord, you speak of a Ghost, and you speak of a man you call Christ. I want to know which of these is the deity who gives you such power, and what is his name."

"They are all one," replied Columba directly, in the king's own tongue.

"They are the *same?*" asked Brudei, puzzled.

Columba nodded.

"We have many gods," the king went on, "who rule over different regions of the sky and the earth and the sea."

"The so-called gods of your druids are no gods at all, Honorable King. They are not capable of giving you eternal life. In truth there is only one God."

"Why then do you speak as if he too were many separate beings?"

"He has shown himself to mortal men in different ways. But he is one and the same God."

"As in the sun, the moon, the crane, and the oak?"

"Perhaps something like that indeed. He knows that the aspect of his nature which shows itself in a mighty ocean storm or in the thunder which rages and the lightning which flashes down from the sky must seem a dreadful and powerful thing to the small creatures upon his earth. So he sent part of himself as a man to live among us, a man who was God himself, a man who was like us, not fearsome like the thunder and lightning. He was a man who could tell us what God was like, because we could not see him for ourselves."

"Are you that man?"

"No, that man was God's Son, the Christ."

"What is your God's name?"

"He is called Jehovah, or *the Lord*."

"Who is this man he sent?"

"He is the man named Jesus."

"Where did he live?"

"Jesus was a Jew, born in a place called Palestine. Do you know of it, King Brudei?"

The king shook his head.

"It is to the east and south, in a warm and temperate land inhabited by a people called Hebrews."

"Then what is *Criosd* you speak of?"

"The *Christ*," repeated Columba. "Jesus, who was born almost six hundred years ago, is called the Christ. It means *the anointed one*, the one sent from God. His birth was foretold among the Hebrew tribes for centuries, as one who would come to live on earth, sent from God, to save his people from the death of their sins, and bring them into eternal life."

"You speak of *eternal life*. What is this life?"

"To live forever, Honorable King."

"I know of the Happy Isles, and the fruit and swords and robes and animals and maidens which Niam of the Golden Hair promised to Ossian. I find nothing new in what you say."

"But have you spoken with any man who has been there and returned?"

The king did not answer.

"The Prophet whom we honor died and then came back to tell where he had been," said Columba to Comgall in his own tongue. He must be certain he did not misspeak this central truth.

"Bah!" exclaimed the king the moment the words had fallen from Comgall's lips. He had finally heard enough to make him laugh this new religion to scorn. *Coming back from the dead!* He would sooner listen to Broichan's incantations and chants!

"Judge my words by what your own eyes have seen, Honorable Brudei," said Columba. "If the God Jehovah whom I serve, and Jesus Christ whom he sent—if they are not more powerful than deities of your druid priests, then how did the white stone float on the water? I ask you, Honorable King, has your Broichan performed the like before your eyes?"

The king remained silent.

"And when your tutor called upon his gods—which were nothing but evil spirits—to raise a hurricane against me, and I called upon my Lord Christ and his angels, and embarked in my small boat and set off into the wind, and sailed straight against it, and then the force of the gale immediately changed its direction . . . I ask you again, Honorable King, have your druids performed the like before your eyes in all your days?"

Still the king did not reply. In truth, he had been sorely moved by Columba's deeds.

"And further, I ask you to recall the incident of the boy who was sick, whom they say had died, and who, but moments after I called upon the power of my Lord God and his Christ, rose and left his bed."

Brudei recalled it well enough.

"These are only small signs and wonders, Honorable King," Columba continued. "This and more will my God do for *all* who believe in his Christ, who is the man Jesus, his anointed one."

Brudei glanced into Columba's face with an expression of new question at what he could possibly mean.

"Eternal life, Honorable King," said Columba, "—that which you asked about earlier—Jesus promised to *all* who believed in the God who is Jehovah, and who became his own followers."

"Where is this place where you say man lives forever?" the king asked.

"It is not on this earth," replied Columba. "Jesus spoke of a different kind of life. Though their bodies grow old and die, the spirits of his followers will live forever with him and with God Jehovah."

Brudei did not reply immediately. The room became silent. He had heard of such things. But none of his own druids could say where the Happy Isles were. He was a practical man. He had never seriously imagined when he ran a sword through the heart of one of his enemies, that the spirit of such was still alive, floating up over the scene.

"How can I believe what you say?" asked Brudei at length. "Have you been there? Have *you* seen the spirits of the dead?"

"They cannot be seen while we yet live on the earth."

"How then do you know it is true?"

"Because Jesus told us of it. He came from there and returned, to demonstrate that death had no power over him."

"This man you call Jesus yet lives?"

Columba nodded.

"Show him to me and I will believe!"

"He no longer inhabits the earth, Honorable King. But he lives as surely as you and I sit here together."

"You talk in circles!" exclaimed the king.

"The eternal life brought to man by God's Christ is not an earthly living forever, but an eternal life in heaven with Jehovah. He calls on us to believe without seeing. To believe by faith."

"Where is this *heaven?*"

"No man can see it, Honorable King. It is the place Jesus told us God dwells, and where his followers will live forever."

"How can a man believe what he cannot see?"

"You believe in many things you cannot see, Honorable King. Do you believe in the power of the wind?"

Brudei thought a moment, then nodded.

"But no man can *see* the wind," Columba went on. "It blows where it pleases. You hear it, but you cannot tell where it comes from. We only see its power. In the same way, though we cannot *see* Jesus or eternal life, we see their power."

The king pondered his words. This holy man was not only powerful, he was shrewd of tongue.

"You say the man called Jesus returned from death, and also came back to earth from this place you call heaven. How do you know?"

"He was seen by his friends and followers . . . by many."

"Perhaps it was a ghost."

"They felt him, touched him, spoke with him. He ate and walked with them. They put their hands in the hole in his side where his body was pierced dead with a spear and gushed blood and water. And they recorded the events for all to read of ever after. I have myself read these accounts many times."

"And this man, you say, came back from death . . . fully alive?"

Columba nodded. The king was very thoughtful. He had never heard the likes before.

"If only I could touch the hole in his side *myself.*"

"One of his own followers, before he made his appearance, uttered your very words. Jesus later told him that they were greatly blessed who did *not* see, and yet still believed. Such is your opportunity, Honorable King, and mine—to *believe* in Christ, though we have *not* seen him. Such is called *faith.*"

"How, then, if you have not seen this man, and if he is nowhere on this earth to be found . . . how do you know of him?"

"Because his followers—men and women who knew him, who were taught by him and who saw him die with their own eyes and witnessed him arise from the tomb three days after—they have written down the events of his life and have recorded his teachings. Many who have come after—men such as myself—have likewise recorded these events and sayings and teachings. Thus it is from these witnesses that we know of Jesus' life. We know the words he spoke. In them we find the eternal life he came to offer all those who would follow him."

"I would rejoice to hear of these words and events, that I might know more of this man Jesus and his God."

"So you shall, Honorable King," said Columba, "and all your people with you. With your permission, each morning as long as my companions and I are among you, I shall read the words of the gospel story which tell about the man Jesus, and tell of his deeds and his teachings, of the exploits and signs which flowed from his hands—how he ruled over the wind and waves, how he turned water to wine, how he walked on the very waters of the sea, and how he rose up out of the grave after he had been in the tomb three days."

"I give my permission, and will make it known among the people."

"You will be among the listeners?"

"I shall," replied the king.

The king hesitated a moment, then reached behind him to unclasp the great double-linked chain which he wore around his neck. He took it in one hand, then stretched it forward to Columba.

"This is my royal chain," he said. "You see the emblem of the kingship on the clasp."

Columba nodded.

"You are a holy man," the king went on solemnly. "It is my desire that you have it."

Columba took it from his hand. "I am deeply honored," he said. "It shall be a symbol, not only of your kingship, but of understanding and brotherhood between our peoples."

The readings of the Gospels commenced on the following morning. The king was indeed present. He scarcely took notice as he arrived of the tall young woman already seated near Columba's feet, gazing upon him with radiant eyes. She was so greatly altered of countenance and demeanor that had he stared straight into her face, his eyes might not have known her.

The instant she rose at the end of the reading, however, he saw her form and unusual stature. Immediately he recognized her, and cast upon her an expression of such hatred as would make a warrior tremble. But Diorbhall-ita had grown beyond his power to hurt her.

"What is the tall one doing here?" he demanded of Columba. His voice was angry.

"She is one of my followers," Columba replied.

"Now I know you speak absurdities!"

"The gospel comes to all freely and equally—kings and outcasts alike. *All* are sinners."

"Bah . . . she is—"

"She is what, King?" interrupted Columba. "Do you know her? Her heart is now pure before God."

"*Pure*," the king spat back, "—ridiculous! Do you know what she is?"

"She is a sinner cleansed. I am a sinner cleansed. You too are a sinner, King."

"Bah! Of course I know her, and I know she is anything but pure. She is my daughter, and I despise the very sight of her!"

Columba was silenced. Diorbhall-ita—the daughter of the king! He collected himself quickly, then smiled. Indeed, he thought to himself, she was now the daughter of two kings!

The king strode angrily away from him.

As a result of the readings, and also from Columba's continued good deeds and miracles among them, many in the province believed and were baptized. Columba's fame spread for miles as if carried throughout the region on the very winds he had spoken of to the king.

Among the most enthusiastic of the converts was the family of the king's brother Aedh macBaldridh, with his wife, their five-year-old son, Fineach-tinnean, and four-year-old daughter, Anghrad. Now did Columba realize their ties of kinship with Diorbhall-ita, all of whom would grow to be important links in the history of their clan, to which many new spiritual chains were now added.

⊠   S I X T E E N   ⊠

When it came time for Columba and his party to depart Inbhir-Nis, Dior-bhall-ita became quiet and subdued. Little did Columba suspect what was in her heart.

How could she live without the man who had given her life? She could not go back to what she was. What was she to do? What life could she possibly have apart from him?

On the day before their departure, Diorbhall-ita came to him. She found him alone.

"I am afraid," she said softly. Her eyes began to fill with tears. "Please do not leave me."

"I must take the gospel to others, my child," replied Columba. "The Lord will take care of you."

"I cannot remain here. Take me with you, Colum."

"*Take* you?" he repeated in surprise. "Ours is not a mission for a woman."

"I can serve you. I will help you with your mission."

"It is not possible."

"I only know I must be with you."

"There are hardships, dangers. You do not know what you ask."

"They mean nothing to me. Let me go as—"

She hesitated and glanced away, her courage momentarily failing her.

"What is it, my child?"

"Please, Colum . . . *let* me serve you," she said in a pleading voice. She cast such a look on the man of God as nearly melted his heart. "Let me serve you all my days. If I cannot go as one of your followers, then . . . then take me . . . as your wife."

The word fell upon Columba's ears with such quiet force that a silence hung in the air between them, as if waiting for its unsounding echos to die away.

After a moment, finally Columba spoke.

"Oh, dear one," he replied tenderly. "I cannot marry you."

"I thought you loved me," said Diorbhall-ita, gazing into his face with innocent, hopeful expectancy.

"I do, dear one . . . but with the love of Christ, not the love of a man."

The momentary hopefulness fell. Her face shuddered slightly, as if she had been struck a physical blow. Stunned, she turned away. His painful words brought a fresh rush of tears. A knife of cold stone had been plunged into her heart.

She could not stay here with him. She must get away. She had made a fool of herself.

Quickly she began walking away.

Columba took several strides after her. He placed his hand on her shoulder.

Diorbhall-ita stopped. It was the first time he had touched her since her baptism. His fingers sent new tingles of hope through her. Slowly she turned. The eyes that had suffered much at the hands of men now swam in rivers of confusion that her new faith could bring such a new kind of pain. With the ache in her heart was the mortification of a woman's embarrassment for what she had just done. How could she look into his face after what she had said! Yet his eyes sought hers.

"Oh, my dear, dear Diorbhall-ita," said Columba softly, "I do love you. But I am a priest. I may not marry."

"Why?" she said.

"I am consecrated to Christ."

"What makes a priest different from other men?"

"We make ourselves different, by taking a vow."

"What kind of vow?"

"To live unmarried, to touch no ale or wine, to live in simplicity."

"Must you keep it?"

"I choose to keep it, dear one."

"But you have given me life," she pleaded. "I cannot endure without you. Let me come with you as your servant."

"A woman, traveling with me in these regions? It is not possible, dear one. Our life is arduous. We will be going among people where there may be danger. I tremble to think what might happen to you."

"Worse will happen to me here," she said, turning away. She began to sob.

The difficult conversation did not last much longer. Columba's heart was sore. But as he watched the poor young woman at length break into tears, then turn and flee from him, he was powerless to allay her suffering. He could not comfort her with the comfort of a man. At this moment the comfort of God, however, was no balm for her distress.

That night Diorbhall-ita cried herself to sleep. Columba, meanwhile, found that slumber did not easily visit him.

⚌   S · E · V · E · N · T · E · E · N   ⚌

As Columba lay on his hard bed, he could not get the face of Diorbhall-ita from his memory. The interview had shaken him. He found himself thinking about the mission upon which they were about to embark farther into the land of the Picts.

His thoughts gathered themselves about Mary of Magdala. She was of the company who followed the Lord as surely and faithfully as any of the men. Why should he not also have such a one? Diorbhall-ita was right. What was there for her here after he left? Whatever danger she might face with him, she could face worse here.

Despite the ache in her heart, Diorbhall-ita had eventually managed to fall asleep. When she awoke the night was still black.

Had she been dreaming, or had she actually heard her name? Some sound had awakened her. She did not think of God's voice, for she had never heard of Samuel.

"Diorbhall-ita," came the sound again, softly in a loud whisper.

She would know that voice anywhere!

"Colum!" she said excitedly. "Where are you?" She glanced about.

"Outside. Come quickly."

She was at the door the next instant, peering out into the night. She felt his presence, though she could barely see his eyes in the darkness.

"Take these," he said.

She felt him hand her a bundle.

"What . . . what is it?"

"Clothes . . . men's clothes. Dress yourself and gather what you need for a journey."

"You . . . you are taking me with you!" she exclaimed.

"If you are willing to go as a man," he replied, "and not give yourself away. Only my closest companions will know."

"Oh, yes! Of course I will—thank you, Colum!"

Unable to contain her joy, she threw her arms about him and kissed his cheek. Then suddenly realizing what she had done, she pulled away.

"Dress now," he said. "Make yourself ready in haste. You must be gone from the village before dawn. Go upriver two miles and wait. There we will meet you."

✺ E I G H T E E N ✺

It was not many weeks that they had been traveling together before Columba knew it was not mere compassion for a soul he felt when he looked into the face of Diorbhall-ita. He realized he had known the moment she kissed him on the morning of their departure that he indeed loved her with more than merely the love of Christ. The love of a man had also sprouted within him.

Yet he buried his feelings in his priestly heart and did his work the more earnestly, in that he now must daily rededicate himself to his vow. If anything, he became yet stronger in his love for the Lord as his heart was thus opened to a woman.

Diorbhall-ita served the men of Columba's mission with devotion and faithfulness. Upon occasion she received odd looks from natives in the villages and settlements to which they traveled, and on more than one occasion questions were raised about the tall, silent member of their company.

But the disguise kept any man from approaching her. And in many invisible ways did she make her contribution to the expanding of the gospel.

When at last they returned to Iona, Columba had a small building constructed for her to dwell in privacy and peace, with an adjoining prayer cell. To both this building and her fellowship through the years were added the presence of several other women.

✺ N I N E T E E N ✺

In one thing, however, was Diorbhall-ita's life unchanged. Her past continued to haunt her.

She now began to be plagued with terrible and vivid nightmares from her former life. Images tormented her from her father's hatred and of the tormenting experiences at the hand of Gairbhith and many other men in the years after.

No prayer of her own or any of the community, not even those of Columba himself, could rid her of the memories of those evil days when her very life was a hell. The intensity increased such that her sleep was seriously affected. Fatigue set in. Gradually her health began to fail.

"Why won't your miracles work for me?" she moaned to Columba.

"I do not know, dear one," he replied.

"I am *not* a new creature. I am a wicked woman who can never escape what I was. I will never be like the rest of you."

"I pray for you daily, my child. The Lord's work takes time."

"Help me, Colum—I do not know what to do."

"I cannot help you of myself, dear one. Only he has power to heal."

She turned and left him, more forlorn than he had ever seen her.

That same night a terrifying dream sent Diorbhall-ita into a paroxysm of screaming torment. Her shrieks echoed with chilling horror over the whole island. It sounded as if a legion of demons was attacking her.

Columba awoke in his cell.

"Oh, God," he prayed, "why do these devils haunt your daughter? Give her peace, Lord, I beseech you!"

For several minutes the screaming persisted, with vague phrases, indistinct cries, and otherworldly howls.

"Go away . . . the hands . . . get away, you beast . . . leave me alone . . . get off me . . . Jesus, Jesus, help me!"

At last Columba rose thinking he must go to her.

Suddenly the sounds ceased. In great distress, he paused and fell to his knees and prayed again.

Diorbhall-ita's screams had at last awakened her to full consciousness. As sleep departed, the dreams gradually receded, yet horrible visions remained. Sweating and panting, she went out into the night. A full moon was high in the sky. She walked up the hill to her favorite outlook of the island. It was warm and still, the sea calm.

"I know I have no right to expect peace," she prayed as she went. "After what I have been, why should I not expect torment? But, dear Lord, Colum says you give peace. *Why* do I not have peace in my soul! Why do guilt and voices of accusation remain? If I am clean in your sight, why do nightmares come? Why do hands grab and grope? Must I forever relive the terror?"

Gradually as she walked, the calm of the night came into her spirit. A sense of presence filled the silence about her. Slowly a giant invisible blanket seemed to descend out of the sky, a blanket of white. She felt as though God himself were bringing it down and slowly wrapping it around her shoulders. The blanket was rich and pure. How good it felt, how clean and warm. For a few moments she felt safe, protected, enveloped in its thick white folds.

Then she felt the blanket rising up again. But even those few moments had been bliss indeed.

In her mind's eye, as she looked up she saw the blanket rising back toward heaven. But now it had changed. Suddenly it had become soiled and stained, covered with dirt and blood, its edges tattered and frayed and torn.

In confusion she stared until it disappeared from sight. She brought her eyes back toward the earth. Now in her vision she beheld a figure walking toward her. He too was dressed from head to foot in a robe of pure white. When he looked into her eyes she knew that he knew everything she had ever done. She was ashamed and tried to look away.

But she could not remove her eyes from his.

"Do not fear, my child," said the most lovely voice imaginable. "I know what is in your heart, all that you were, all you have done. And I love you still."

She could only hear the words with the ears of her heart and wonder.

"Do you not know that the blanket is gone," he said with a tender smile, "and has carried with it all the stain of your sin, and taken it to the bosom of my Father?"

Suddenly Diorbhall-ita realized that the torment of guilt was gone.

"What do you feel, my child? Do you not sense it?"

She felt as if she had bathed in a warm pool, not only her body, but every part of her inner self. For the first time in her life she felt whole and clean and pure.

"I took away your sin, my child," said the Savior. "It is gone just as you saw that blanket rise away out of your sight, carrying with it the stain of your sin. By my grace you have been washed clean. You need never again think of the past. You are mine now. You need no longer fear. No more will your past torment you."

Now in her vision, though she could not tell where it came from, he placed about her shoulders a heavy, thick robe of purest white—whiter and warmer and softer even than had been the heavenly blanket.

"This robe of purity will forever clothe you, my child," he said. "It will never leave you, nor become soiled or stained. It is the robe of my forgiving grace. It is yours to wear for all time."

Diorbhall-ita fell on the moonlit ground and wept, unable to prevent a great rush of long, tearful sobs of released emotion and thanksgiving. For ten, then twenty minutes, she wept.

At last the tears subsided. She began to breathe more easily. When she looked up again, she saw only the moonglow over the sea.

The vision was gone. She knew the Savior had taken her sin with him, where it could plague her no more, and left her a robe of white. She rose and, with gratitude and praise in her heart, slowly returned to her cell.

The nightmares did not visit her again that night, nor ever again thereafter.

Two days later a great rain fell. Diorbhall-ita rushed out to greet it like she had as a child. Her delight with the wild wonders of the natural world had returned! As her name meant "God's gift," now God gave back this gift which circumstances had taken from her.

Tears of exuberant laughter filled her eyes, washed and replenished by the pouring rain. God had made her happy!

Slowly she sank to her knees. From somewhere deep in her soul a small voice spoke. Instantly she knew that for the healing to be complete, the next step was hers alone to take. The soft words which now sounded amid the storm were ones no other mortal ever heard. But he to whom all tears are precious took them into his eternal bosom and made them—along with the tears she had shed at the hands of those whose names she now uttered— into jewels for the crown he was fashioning for her in the heavenly place which would one day be her home.

"God," she whispered quietly as the rain beat down upon her head, "I forgive Gairbhith . . . I forgive Broichan . . . and I forgive my father."

❈   T W E N T Y   ❈

Nine years passed.

The Columban church in the region of the Picts thrived.

Followers of the Irish priest, whose name would forever be associated with bringing Christianity to northern Britain, continued to travel throughout the mainland in the regions of the Scots and Picts, and even southward in time to the tribes of the Britons and Angles. Monasteries were built, that men of God, monks and priests, might study and learn together, and continue making copies of the Word of God.

It was now 574. Columba and his companions embarked at the onset of spring on their most ambitious journey yet through northern Pictland. It represented their fifth such expedition. The previous summer had been spent on the isle of Skye. Having now traveled through most of Alba, Columba realized this might be his last such extended journey. Thousands of Picts had been converted. The Dalriadic kingdom was secure and slowly expanding. The monastery at Iona was thriving. It was time for others to carry on the missionary work, while he devoted himself to writing and training new priests who would establish monasteries throughout the regions where they had sojourned.

The lad Fintenn, fourteen now, was one whom Columba knew would influence many for the faith. He had sensed it from the beginning, and had thus now invited the young man to join them. Fintenn had grown to love Columba as an uncle and was utterly devoted to him. His father Aedh, a hearty believer among the people dwelling at the mouth of the Ness and in truth more influential among the Caledonians than his brother the king, eagerly consented. The only drawback to the plan was that Aedh's daughter, thirteen-year-old Anghrad, begged also to join them, a request which circumstances forced him to deny.

"I want to know why I cannot go too," the girl had insisted feistily.

Taken by surprise, Columba looked upon her with a compassionately apologetic smile.

"Dear one, you are yet young," he replied. "There will be many opportunities for you—"

"I am only a year younger than Fintenn," she interrupted.

"I am sorry, but I simply cannot take along a young girl."

Anghrad turned and stormed away. With a look of sincere sorrow mingled with kindhearted humor, Columba glanced at the girl's father and mother.

"She can be troublesome when she does not get what she wants," said Aedh. "It is good for us all she has been converted at a young age, or she would be likely to take up the sword and join my brother's army."

Columba was glad Diorbhall-ita had remained at Iona. None in the settlement of her birth ever knew what became of her. For this present conversation it was best no one know of the one occasion when a woman *had* accompanied them.

The expedition began—with Fintenn, but without Anghrad. Yesterday, however, the boy had lagged and grown exceedingly pale. In consequence young Fintenn had occupied a larger than usual portion of his prayers this night.

"I beg your pardon, Columba," said a voice.

"Yes, Diormait," said Columba, glancing up as his faithful servant approached.

"The boy has a dreadful fever," said Diormait. "Baithen asked me to find you. He fears the worst."

Alarmed, Columba rose and followed his attendant.

He found Baithen kneeling at the form of young Fintenn. Columba instantly detected his anxiety. He knew his cousin thought Aedh's son was dying.

Columba placed his hand gently on the lad's cheek. A slight shudder coursed through the body. The skin was on fire.

"How do you feel this night, my son?" asked Columba tenderly.

"Hot . . . very hot," murmured Fintenn.

Columba turned and walked a short distance away. None of his companions heard the conversation which followed, but in the silence of his heart, he whom an emerging nation would call a holy man was pleading for the life of the king's nephew.

Fintenn's fever began to subside that night. They carried him the next day, but he was back on his feet the day after that, and strong as ever in two more. Surely God had chosen this one to be among them.

Despite his youth, the boy contributed a great deal, in both help and encouragement, throughout the remainder of the journey, reminding Columba of the young John Mark, whose travels with the great apostle prepared him to later write the Gospel account of the Lord's life. He wondered what the future held in store for *this* young man in the Savior's service.

It was Fintenn, during their journey to the northern regions of Pictland, who discovered the curious collection of stones, some small but some so large that no ten men could budge them, in the vicinity of what appeared an ancient human settlement.

In their missionary efforts among the natives of the area, a wizened Pict bard of ancient years told them the legend of the stones, that ancient kings and rulers—whether one or several, no one knew—were buried beneath them. That the stones signified something was clear enough from the unmistakable carvings and inscriptions upon the two that rose vertically into the air.

If they were stones of sacred intent, thought Columba, he and his companions must not disturb the standing inscribed stones. But why should they not remove a sizable chunk from the great slab jutting into the hillside, and carry it back with them to Iona, as a symbol of this place and its kings, to link the new center of rule and spiritual authority with the legends of those who had come before? He set his men about it immediately.

It was not until he was older that Fintenn joined them at Iona, at which time he saw his cousin Diorbhall-ita for the first time in years. He did not know her, yet something in the tall, graceful form struck a chord of recognition in the brain of the eighteen-year-old Pict youth. She was by now a radiant woman of God of thirty-eight years, held in high esteem by all the Ionan community. He had never known that the outcast who lived at the edge of the settlement of his birth was his cousin. But when Columba now told him, he was proud of the filial bond.

Thereafter the two were as brother and sister, as in truth they surely were.

❋   T W E N T Y - O N E   ❋

Another journey was planned.

Now that she had a home, no more did Diorbhall-ita accompany them. She had remained on the island for six years without setting foot from it, and was free to be herself—the woman and daughter of God's design. She had not dressed in the clothes of a man since leaving the mainland.

The evening before Columba's departure, he went to her quarters to say good-bye.

The moment he saw her, he knew from the strange light in her eyes that she was feeling a great depth of love for him.

A moment of special quiet tenderness followed as they stood before each other, both their hearts full.

"I am more grateful for your presence at Iona than you can know, my child," said Columba at length. "You are loved by all the community."

The love of God had not diminished but rather had increased and made pure the created passion of Diorbhall-ita's woman's heart. Slowly she began to disrobe before him.

"I have not been with a man since the day you arrived in Inbhir-Nis," she said softly. "Let me give myself to you, that I might know the joy of true love between a woman and a man."

It was the only gift she knew to give. She wanted to give it to the only man she had ever, or could ever love.

"I do not want to be loved by the whole community," she said. "I want to be loved by *you*."

"Dear Diorbhall-ita," replied Columba, and his voice contained great emotion. "My heart would hold you close if it were possible. But I must not, dear one."

"My Colum," replied Diorbhall-ita, "all these years I have served you. You have been more kind and loving to me than I ever thought a man could be. Do not break my heart like this."

"We must remain consecrated to our Lord," he said. "Though we possess the flesh of a man and woman, he has given us a higher calling. By this will he perfect our love, as we give it to him, and offer even that love on the altar of our service to him. Likewise is this a sacred place, this beloved island, and we must honor it with purity."

He drew the robe gently back up around her shoulders, then took her in his arms.

She was weeping, both for loss and gain. What a great man had been given her to love, a man who loved God more than he would let himself love a woman. Her heart was sore, yet it could only love him more because he was the man he had proved himself to be.

He held her close for several moments of silence, then gently released her and stepped away. It was the only time in all her life that she would feel his arms around her.

But the eternal moment would remain with her in memory for the rest of her days.

TWENTY-TWO

The arrival of Christianity to the mainland did not eliminate its tribal and territorial factions. This was an era when religious beliefs precipitated more conflict than they prevented. Dalriada was growing, and the Picts, in both northern and southern Alba, presented the greatest and most practical obstacle to that expansion. Dalriada was not a kingdom whose permanent place would be won with icons or prayers, but rather with swords.

By now Columba's authority was recognized throughout all Caledonia. When Conaill died at Dunadd, Columba claimed to have been visited by an angel and declared that Aedan, Conaill's cousin, was to be the new king.

Aedan was brought to Iona to be enthroned as king of Dalriada. It was the first occasion for the slab of sacred stone from Pictland to be used for a ceremonial purpose.

Columba instructed his distant kinsman to step up onto the stone that his men had cut in the Highlands and transported to Iona, which was about a foot thick, and measured some two and a half by three and a half feet.

Aedan did so. Columba told him of the stone's history, that he and his men had brought it from a legendary site of the burial of ancient Pict kings, and that by taking his oath upon it, he was entering into a line, not only of Dalriadic succession, but also of the lineage of the kingship of all Caledonia.

Then the abbot instructed Aedan to kneel upon the stone.

"Believe me, O Aedan," said Columba in words of consecration to the new king, "none of thy enemies shall be able to resist thee. Wherefore direct thou thy children to commend to their children, their grandchildren, and their posterity, not to let the sceptre pass out of their hands through evil counsels. For at whatever time they turn against the Lord their God, the hearts of men shall likewise be turned away from them, and their foes shall be greatly strengthened."

This injunction laid upon him, Columba rested his hands upon Aedan's head and blessed him.

Aedan stepped off the stone, now king of Dalriada.

⌘   T W E N T Y - T H R E E   ⌘

King Aedan of the Scots was even more ambitious for power and land than his predecessors. He waited six years after his ordination as king, then in 580 took up the sword against the Picts, both in the north and the south. He himself lost two of his own sons at the hands of the Picts. King Brudei of the Picts was killed in 584.

Aedan ruled for thirty-four years. As the seventh century after Christ opened, he had successfully brought much of Pictland under the domination of Scottish Dalriada. The Scots, it appeared, would be a dominant force on the northern mainland.

Columba spent most of his latter years at the monastery on Iona. The tiny isle had now become the religious center of the Celtic world. Every one who knew Columba loved him, and his influence had spread throughout Erin, Dalriada, and Pictland. He was not only a spiritual giant, but also a king maker, diplomat, and statesman who wielded perhaps more authority than any single man throughout the various Celtic kingdoms.

But Columba was aging. The year was 593. He was seventy-two and tired—tired of the strain between political and spiritual forces, drained of his worldly ambitions, and ready for the coming eternal phase of his life. He had, in fact, been praying that God would call him toward his heavenly journey.

A day of particularly great joy came in the first week of June.

"Oh, God," he whispered, alone in his cell, "I have been thirty years in Alba. I am ready for you to take me. I rejoice that perhaps the day will be soon."

A vision of angels arose before his mind's eye. His heart leapt—they had been sent to lead his soul out of its fleshly imprisonment! He saw them standing on a rock beyond the narrow sound between Iona and the Ross of Mull.

But why could they approach no nearer? Why did they stand motionless and not come for him?

Suddenly a great sadness came over the man of God as divine revelation came to explain the vision.

They were unable to cross the sound and carry him away because of the many and fervent prayers on his behalf from churches throughout the land. In answer to the entreaties of his people, God would grant him another four years of life. At the end of that time he would be taken.

The end came, as foretold, in 597, exactly four years later.

Knowing that his time was drawing nigh, in the second week of April, Columba called for the man and woman who were his two dearest companions yet remaining on Iona, Diormait, his servant and Diorbhall-ita, his friend.

He requested them to summon two others to Iona to be with him in his final days—his cousin, Baithen, whom Columba had already designated as his successor, himself now sixty-four and the presiding abbot at the daughter monastery of Maigh Lunga on Tiree, and their Caledonian convert Fintenn macAedh, Diorbhall-ita's cousin and now a mighty Christian man of thirty-seven, who had himself established a Columban monastery at Kailli-an-Inde in the Caledonian midlands among the southern Picts.

Diormait carried out Columba's instruction, while Diorbhall-ita sought the solitude of the island's rocky shores to be alone with her thoughts and prayers. She had loved her mentor and spiritual father, her friend and brother, for thirty-three years. Now she feared he was about to leave her. Her heart was ready to break over it.

By the next afternoon messengers were on their way to both Maigh Lunga and Kailli-an-Inde.

Fintenn arrived on the tenth of May. He went immediately to Columba's quarters where the venerable man was resting.

The Caledonian had not seen his spiritual father for more than five years and was immediately shocked at the change so visible upon his features. Columba had been such a vital individual, powerful of voice and frame, and even more formidable of spiritual and mental constitution, perhaps the greatest man of his generation. Now he lay tired, pale, even his wonderful gray eyes losing their luster and sparkle. The earthly spirit was indeed ebbing out of the great man's weary body.

Fintenn could not prevent tears from welling up in his eyes. He walked to the bed, knelt down, embraced the thin form, then laid his head on Columba's chest and broke into manly weeping.

"Ah, dear one, weep not for me," said Columba quietly. "Do not grieve that my time has come. Rather rejoice with me."

As he spoke, Columba placed a thin white hand on the younger man's head and patted it, affectionately remembering the first day he had seen him as a lad at his father's side only moments after stepping ashore at Inbhir-Nis.

Fintenn glanced up, his cheeks glistening and wet from the Celtic outpouring of his emotion. The glowing smile that met his gaze was sufficient momentarily to melt away his grief.

He stood and returned Columba's smile.

"It is good to see you again, my friend," he said.

"And you," replied Columba. "How goes the work at Kailli-an-Inde?"

"Well . . . very well."

"And your sister?"

"Also well," replied Fintenn.

"The fire of her Celtic blood is cooling at last?"

"I doubt it will ever cool," chuckled Fintenn. "But the fire is now directed toward the warfare of the spirit. Anghrad and Domhnall have three children now, and are spreading the faith among the people of the islands. The spiritual seeds you planted in our family continue to bear much fruit."

They continued to speak of many things. No one ever heard what Columba said to him, and though he was a man of prolific writing, neither did the Caledonian priest later record a single one of the words which passed between them. The truths of that day, Fintenn said, could be stored only one place—in the quiet depths of his own heart.

⁜   T W E N T Y - F O U R   ⁜

The following morning, after a great downpour of rain, the sun came out over the island in glorious fashion. Columba asked Diormait and Fintenn to place him in a cart that he might go out. The sun had drawn him, and it was unseasonably warm.

"And find Diorbhall-ita," he added, "that she might accompany us."

They did so. With the stately woman of grace walking beside them, the two men carried him to the distant side of Iona, where some of the priests were at work. The workers laid down their implements and gathered round the cart. Columba took each of their hands and blessed them one by one, thanking each for his hard work on behalf of the monastery.

He turned his face toward the east. Still seated as he was in the cart, he spoke a prayer of blessing over the island and its inhabitants. He was then carried back to the monastery by his two attendants. Diorbhall-ita hung several steps behind. She was softly weeping.

Not many days later, on the Sabbath Saturday, having regained his strength, Columba and his servant Diormait were walking with Diorbhall-ita. Columba turned to his servant. "Leave us a moment, will you, my friend," he said. Diormait did so.

When Columba and Diorbhall-ita were alone, Columba spoke. "I have a secret to tell you, dear one," he said, "but only if you promise not to reveal it to anyone before my death."

"I promise," agreed Diorbhall-ita, though with some inner reluctance.

"This day in the Scriptures is called a Sabbath, which means rest," Columba went on. "And this day is indeed a Sabbath to me. For the Lord has revealed that this shall be the last day of the labors of my present life, and that tonight, at midnight, as the Sabbath passes, I shall depart."

"Oh, dear Colum, please do not say it!"

"I am sorry to make you sad, dear one. But you mustn't grieve. You cannot imagine how happy it makes me. My only sorrow is that Baithen has still not arrived. I would so like to see my old friend one final time."

They returned toward the monastery.

Coming toward them, they observed Fintenn and Baithen, who had just moments before stepped off his boat from across the sound.

In spite of Columba's rejoicing, Diorbhall-ita's heart sank still lower, knowing what secret she held in her heart. She turned and walked away while Columba hurried forward to meet his old friend. The two monks who had been pilgrims together in crossing to Iona thirty-four years earlier embraced with tears of joy. Baithen, though aging, still carried the strength and vigor of manhood, while Columba seemed shrunken and bowed with old age. Diormait joined them again.

The four sat down together and fell to talking. They spent some minutes in quiet conversation. Presently they observed Diorbhall-ita walking alone on the hill overlooking the monastery. Columba rose and nodded to his friends.

They departed, and Columba slowly ascended the hill toward her.

Diorbhall-ita saw his approach and waited. They stood for some time together, gazing about. It was a gorgeous warm day of early June.

"Such a day makes it almost possible to forget the bitter cold of winter," said Diorbhall-ita at length.

Columba nodded, knowing he was enjoying this view of his beloved isle for the last time.

"Has what I said brought you grief, dear one?" asked Columba at length.

"Of course. How can it not?" she replied. "You know how I love you."

Columba nodded. He continued to gaze about, then sighed deeply.

"I shall miss you, Iona," he said at length. "And I shall miss you, my dear Diorbhall-ita. The Lord has used you in many ways to make my life rich. I thank God for you."

"And I you, dear Colum."

"He has blessed us indeed to have allowed us to share life together as we have."

It was silent a few moments, then Columba stooped down to the ground and picked up a rock. It was no larger than a walnut. For a moment he held it in his hand. Then he raised both arms into the air, his right hand clutching the pebble, and, as if in final benediction, blessed the monastery and its work:

"Small and plain though this place be," he said, "yet it shall be held in great honor for the work that has proceeded from it, not only among the Scots kings and their people, but also by the rulers and people of foreign lands. Even the saints of other churches shall regard this isle with uncommon reverence."

He lowered his hands, looked at the rock in his palm, then to the woman who had been his faithful friend. He smiled, then let the stone drop to the ground.

A gust of wind kicked up. In the distance across the sea, approaching storm clouds could be seen.

They began to walk from the place. Diorbhall-ita paused, bent down, and retrieved the stone. She carried it with her as they returned to the abbey, and there put it among her few possessions.

They descended the hill and parted, Columba to his own room in the monastery. Already the sky was darkening and the gusts increasing.

Columba lay down and rested until Sabbath evening's vespers. Thereafter he returned again to his cell. Once more he lay down on his bed of bare flagstone. There he remained the rest of the evening, his head, as was his custom, resting on a pillow of stone.

Knowing what approached, Diorbhall-ita refused to leave him. She longed to tell the saint's dearest friends what he had confided. But her tongue was constrained to silence.

Thus she alone spent the last hours in his presence.

※   T W E N T Y - F I V E   ※

The hour of the same evening grew late.

Columba dozed off once or twice. The Sabbath was nearly done.

As he slept, Diorbhall-ita sat beside his bed, gently stroking arm and head in loving ministration. Her thoughts were on that Mary of like calling as had once been her own, who had also been cleansed and forgiven the stain of that deepest of human defilements.

What, she wondered, had been in Mary of Magdala's heart toward Jesus of Nazareth? Did she dare believe that Mary of Galilee might have loved her Lord in a womanly way as well as a worshipful way? Had she doubly ministered to him both as a disciple and a woman, keeping it within her own heart?

How blessed she was, thought Diorbhall-ita to herself, to be allowed a similar privilege.

She looked down at the sleeping face, now wrinkled with age, feeling no less love for him now than when it had first blossomed within her so long ago. What might the Lord have felt toward Mary, she wondered.

If only he would open his heart to her before he went, Diorbhall-ita thought. If only he would tell her whether, in all these years, he had loved her in the way she had quietly treasured her love for him.

Slowly she bent forward to the bedside and kissed the wrinkled cheek.

The kiss roused Columba to wakefulness, though he did not know what it was that had awakened him. He looked up. There sat Diorbhall-ita, such a smile on her face as he thought he had never seen.

The candle flickering on the table could not light the whole room. But it was sufficient to send light into each of their eyes. Now Columba sought her eyes with his own. What he said with them was enough to make her happy the rest of her days.

He reached out his hand, still gazing into her face, and took hers. For several long seconds he held it tight. In that moment she knew that he had loved her, and had always loved her.

"My dear, dear Colum," she whispered, her eyes filling with tears. "Thank you!"

Several more moments of silence followed.

"I want to give you my final instructions," said Columba at length. "Write them down, my faithful Diorbhall-ita, that you may convey my words to the brethren."

He paused. She sought paper and materials to do as requested.

"These, O my children," Columba began, "are the last words I address to you—that you be at peace, and show sincere charity among yourselves. If you thus follow the example of the holy fathers, God, the Comforter of the good, will be your Helper, and I, abiding with him, will intercede for you. And he will not only give you sufficient to supply the wants of this present life, but will also bestow on you the good and eternal rewards which are laid up in heaven for those who keep his commandments."

Columba fell silent.

By and by the monastery bell tolled midnight, sounding across the sea-surrounded isle, that the Sabbath was past and that the Sunday of June 9 had begun. The tempest that had blown in from across the sea now raged over Iona.

Columba rose from his bed, anxious to get to the church for the midnight mass. He left his quarters. In spite of his weakness, he broke into a run. Diorbhall-ita hastened after him in alarm.

Columba entered the church alone, hurried quickly forward, and fell at the altar on his knees in prayer.

Moments later Diorbhall-ita entered. A sudden flash of lightning was followed by a great crash in the sky overhead. To her eyes the whole interior of the chapel was filled with bright light. It seemed to radiate from her kneeling master. The monks began to enter almost immediately and witnessed the same great radiance. With them came Columba's servant.

As quickly as it had come, the light vanished.

Diormait rushed forward into the darkness, heedless of the great storm outside that suddenly seemed to consume the island. Columba had disappeared from his vision.

"Father," cried Diormait, "Father . . . where are you!"

Feeling his way in the darkness, as the others approached from behind with candles in their hands, the faithful servant found the aged saint lying beside the altar. Diormait stooped down, gently slipped his hands under him, and raised him a little, supporting his head on his chest.

The rest of the company approached.

Diorbhall-ita reached the altar first, then Baithen and Fintenn, followed by the others. All knew their beloved father and friend was dying. Diorbhall-ita knelt down beside him and burst into tears.

Columba's eyes were wide. An expression of wonderful joy and gladness was spread over his countenance. The angels had at last been permitted to cross the waters and had now come to take him home!

Diormait took his right hand and raised it that he might bless his assembled monks. Columba could not speak, but his hand moved slightly in gesture of blessing.

A lengthy sigh sounded. What air remained in his lungs slowly exhaled. The earthly body of the man who would forever after be known as the Saint of Iona breathed its last. His eyes gently closed, as one drifting peacefully to sleep. While he lay in Diormait's arms, the brightness and smile remained upon his face for several long seconds, then slowly faded.

The whole church soon resounded with a Celtic outpouring of weeping and grief.

The assembly sang their morning hymns and said their prayers, then carried the lifeless body back to its cell, where it lay for three days and nights. During those same days the rainless storm continued to blow over Iona. At the end of three days the body was wrapped in a clean shroud of fine linen, placed in the coffin which had been prepared for it, and was buried near the monastery.

The storm ceased the moment the coffin was committed to the earth.

Columcille, the dove of the church, had flown to his new home.

Many saints of God whose names would never be known but in the Book of Life continued Columba's work of spreading the Christian gospel throughout Dalriada and Pictland.

The land was largely converted to Christianity within two or three generations, a remarkable achievement, and quickly began to influence other parts of the isle called Britain, and eventually mainland Europe.

It was a distinctive form of Christianity, to which still clung reminders of its nature-loving Celtic past.

Though they no longer worshiped objects of the universe, Celtic Christians would always revere the awe-inspiring corner of the world which God had given them. The very vistas of loveliness and grandeur to which their eyes were accustomed pointed to the glories of the life to come. The Christian faith, whose sanctuaries of worship were to be found on windswept crags and desolate moors and promontories overlooking loch and sea or quiet bay, resonated with the inborn spiritual sensitivities within the heart of the Celt. The holy places revered by the people of Columba's race were those fashioned by the finger of God, not constructed by the hands of men.

No tradition rose up here of building temples in which to enclose their worship. They valued natural order and beauty above nearly anything but loyalty to clan and race. The Christianity Columba left behind would always find a deeper soul-harmony with the wind on the face than standing before altars of wood inlaid with silver and gold, upon which linens were spread. Columban priests were drawn to earth and sky more than to tabernacles and robes, incense or ceremony. They sought no finery with which to embellish and enshrine the holy presence.

The Celtic church thus built for itself no temples of white marble, but rather plain churches of gray stone. Its worshipers found cathedrals elsewhere.

They took for the dome of their worship the open vault of blue which God himself had stretched over their heads. In the place of unyielding marble floors, Celtic priests walked the lonely heath and rejoiced in the springy turf under their feet and the fresh breezes—sometimes cold—which met them on their way. For stained-glass windows—from a thousand breathtaking vantage points they possessed an outlook of the sea with which no place on earth could compare, with infinite gradations of blues and greens and whites, and the sunset to add its transcendent purples and oranges and reds to the majestic display. For tower and steeple and arch and pinnacle and spire, what could equal the rugged peaks of the Highlands, brown or green, purple or white in their due season?

As Columba foretold, Fineach-tinnean, son of Aedh, lived to the age of ninety-two. His sister Anghrad and her husband Domhnall spent the whole of their lives in the Hebrides, mingling the Pict heritage of the former and the Scot's of the latter with the Christian belief that replaced the paganism in both Celtic lands—and foreshadowing the political union that was gradually coming to the mainland. Their daughter Frangag married a southern Pict Christian, Rhaonuill. They named their son after his uncle, one of the first Pict Christian priests, Fineach.

During the later years at the monastery he himself founded, with his sister and Domhnall already gone to follow the dove, and with Columba's words of many decades earlier weighing heavily upon his spirit—*May the Lord Jesus make you a son of his Father's, and a worthy link in the chain of your clan's heritage*—Fintenn macAedh, Pict holy man and priest, ordered that a metal box be made for him. In it he would place the treasures of that heritage, to give into the hands of his niece Frangag and her husband Rhaonuill, himself now a grown man, to be passed down to their son and his own namesake, Fineach, in his time.

Thus was the reliquary of Kailli fashioned for the aging priest—who represented one of the last men or women alive in Caledonia from the pre-Columban era—by his craftsmen monks, overlaid and engraved with silver designs of both Christian and Pictish symbols. It measured three hands long, by two wide, and approximately a hand and a half deep, with rounded silver top, hinged to open, with round brass rings on each end with which it could, with some effort, be lifted with two hands. A great deal of gold also went into the design.

When it was completed, Fintenn placed inside it a small copy of each of the Gospels and a Psalter, all of which he had copied from ornate manuscripts by his own hand . . . the silver neck chain which had belonged to his uncle, King Brudei, and which Columba had given into his hands at his ordination as a priest at Iona . . . a small silver cross, some trinkets and neck ornaments of his mother's . . . a few pieces of silver and smithed jewelry . . . a silver cup he had used many times in performing the communion ritual . . . several precious stones . . . his personal handwritten remembrances of the events of Columba's encounter with his uncle, as well as his memories of his travels with the saint as a youth . . . and the stone from Iona that his cousin, the daughter of Pict King Brudei, kept for many years, then passed on to him, as a treasured and tangible reminder of the man who had shown his family and his people the way to salvation. It was held in great reverence by all who later possessed it.

As for Diorbhall-ita, following Columba's death, with the help of her nephew Fintenn, she returned to the mainland of Caledonia at age fifty-eight, where she established the first Christian nunnery in Caledonia. There both Pict and Scot women came to live lives dedicated to God, and to be taught by one who was a closer companion to the Saint of Iona than any of them knew. When walking alone in the Highlands several years thereafter, in the distance she spied a great light-hued stag. A tremble of thrill surged through her. She sensed the magnificent animal looking straight toward her, almost waiting for her to catch sight of it. In that moment she knew that Colum had sent it to her as a sign, that his spirit remained watching over the land to which he had given so much of himself.

She lived to the age of eighty-six, and her passing was mourned almost as greatly as that of the one she still called her *Dear Colum*. For like him, she was greatly beloved. Thereafter, as Columba was considered its father, Diorbhall-ita, daughter of King Brudei of the Picts, was considered mother of the Caledonian church.

TWENTY-SEVEN

In his eighty-seventh year, knowing the season of his bodily strength was slowly coming to an end, yet still feeling fit and capable, Fineach-tinnean macAedh planned one final pilgrimage to Iona.

It was an appropriate year for remembering. The monks under his charge argued against the arduous journey, which could not help but be strenuous to his frame. It was something he must do, he insisted, in the spiritual tradition to which he had dedicated his life.

The land was changing. His own people, the former Caledonii, had, just in his own lifetime, been pushed farther and farther north and west. The Scots of Dalriada, and new tribes from the south, were exerting forceful influence, not always peaceful.

Nor was the religious climate without change of its own, likewise not always peaceful. The church had greatly expanded under Bishop Aiden, who had created an abbacy in the south at Lindisfarne on almost the very order of Iona.

There had been missions south into heathen England, to Glastonbury and Cornwall, and even across the Channel to the continent into Gaul and to the regions of the Rhine. Converts to Christianity flocked to hear the Irish and Caledonian priests. Truly had the Wanderer's ancient and now forgotten pilgrimage progressed in a great round back toward the land of his origins.

Along with such expansion, however, conflicts with the Roman Church grew as well. The pope sent representatives to Britain for the purpose of bringing the monasteries and churches into line, and to cure them of their independent ways.

Disputes in Caledonia were no longer merely tribal or territorial, but also doctrinal. Mostly they were destined to be over matters of authority. For whatever their spiritual inclinations, the Celts had by no means laid down their fiery independence. As the Picts of old had resisted the Romans, so too did their descendants resist the religious domination of Rome.

What the future held for this land of his birth and heritage, Fintenn did not know. He had never claimed the prophetic sight like the holy father from Iona. Even if he had, more and more as his years increased, he found himself looking back rather than forward.

While Fintenn crossed the sound from Mull, as the rocky island became larger and larger in his view, he could feel the years tumbling away. He had planned his arrival for this day, to coincide with the anniversary, both sad and joyful at once. By the time he set foot on the familiar shores, he was a young man again!

So many memories flooded the aging Pict priest, from the first moment he had set eyes upon the saint as a youngster of five, to the night of Columba's death thirty-two years later. An atmosphere of holiness pervaded the entire isle as he walked slowly up from the sea toward the monastery with those who accompanied him.

Everyone on Iona felt it too.

Though the humble man was completely unaware of it—his thoughts were only upon Columba. For the others, Fintenn *himself* was the center of the aura. All the current resident monks had been in keen anticipation of his coming, for he, it was said, was the only man yet alive who had been on intimate terms with the saint himself.

He was nephew to the Pict king, cousin to Diorbhall-ita, mother of the Caledonian convent. The saint had prophesied over him when he was but a child. He had been present at the palace of Brudei. He had traveled with Columba through Pictland in those early years. And he had been present the night of his passing.

Truly this man *himself* was also a saint. In his presence they could not help but feel the same awe Fintenn felt toward the saint who had been his mentor.

Unconscious of the honor in which he was held, Fintenn made his way inside the monastery. He walked reverently to Columba's cell. A yet deeper sense of the saint's presence came over him. In the small room where he had written and prayed, and where his body had lain, there Fintenn offered his greetings to Columba's memory.

His companions waited reverentially outside. This was a time, they sensed, for such a man as their guest to be allowed solitude with his prayers.

Fintenn emerged ten minutes later, eyes wet with tears. He had been fondly reliving his last private conversation with Columba in the very room he had just left.

He now walked to the church.

There he prayed, then slowly sought the temple of open spaces. He passed the venerated slab of stone cut from that great slab which he himself had first seen, as a young boy, on that first memorable journey into the Highlands with Columba's missionary party, and upon which Aedan had been made king. He paused before it, stooped down, and ran his hand back and forth across its rough surface, wondering again, as he had so many times, whether the legends of it told by the old Pict bard were true. After a few moments he rose and continued on his way.

Slowly Fintenn now made his way along the pathway, which had become a pilgrimage-walk already to many others, to Columba's grave.

There he stood in solemn silence for many minutes.

When at length he turned away, those monks of the abbey who had been standing behind him saw a strange unearthly glow in the old man's eyes. The time had come for him to begin being made ready for his *own* passage to that new kingdom where he and Columba and Diorbhall-ita, and all who believed, would reign as saints together.

The date was June 9, 647—fifty years to the day following Columba's death.

Fintenn remained with the brethren of Iona four weeks, during which time he taught them many things of the bygone days, when the Christian faith of Caledonia was in the first days of its infancy.

Then Fintenn departed the isle never to return.

He himself died five years later. The monks of Iona and Kailli-an-Inde mourned. Few others in Caledonia knew the name Fineach-tinnean, son of Aedh, nor were aware of his passing.

12

ROOTS, PAST AND PRESENT

Andrew set down the book and sighed. What a story! Might God truly be that personal and real and mighty?

It was a *compelling* tale. It could not help but get into you . . . maybe even *change* you.

Were the accounts actually true?

Could they be true?

Did such miracles . . . really happen?

Columba's story reminded him of his friend Duncan MacRanald. What was it about the Scots, Andrew wondered, that gave rise to such faith?

Andrew stood, full of the story, and slowly descended the hill. It was nearly dark, or as least as dark as it was going to get on this summer night so far north. But sleep was far from him. The whole island was still. The only sounds that met his ears were those of the faintly splashing sea surrounding him in the distance.

With thoughts of Columba still swirling in his brain, Andrew recalled Duncan's words of several days earlier.

. . . belief isna the same as givin' yer whole heart t' the Lord t' make o' ye what he will. When that day comes . . . ye'll jist be happy an' content t' du God's will. Ye'll be a man in the eyes o' him that made ye . . .

Andrew had heard the term *God's will* many times in his life—especially from Duncan himself. But he had never paused to consider what it might mean in an individual way. Did God really have a *personal* will for each man and woman? That's what Duncan seemed to mean about finding God's will.

He spoke of God as a personal friend who was always trying to do his very *best* for each of his creatures.

How much of what Duncan had told him of God through the years had gone in one ear and out the other? Had he been too young, too immature, too spiritually insensitive to heed his words . . . or had the time simply never been right?

What did it mean—God's will . . . for *him*? Was there really such a thing as God's will for *Andrew Trentham*?

If God had a certain will for Duncan MacRanald . . . or for Colum O'Neill who later was called a saint . . . or for a prostitute who became a woman of purity and established a convent . . . why not for him too?

He could feel strange stirrings within him. Was it simply from being in this remarkable place? Toward what was it leading?

Were there more kinds of roots than merely racial and ancestral? What role did *spiritual* roots also play in one's life and sense of identity—roots that extended all the way back . . . to one's origin?

Even if by some unbelievable string of circumstances it turned out one day that he discovered himself linked by blood, sprung after countless centuries from the Celtic seed of the Wanderer himself . . . was that enough? Even such a remarkable fact would still not address the primal, causative, foundational question of roots—of who he was at the *source*, at the utter core of being.

For where had they *all* come from in the beginning?

The phrase repeated itself in his brain.

. . . in the beginning.

Where else had they all originated but out of the life-producing heart, the very breath of God himself—the Creator of the heavens and the earth . . . the Creator of man and woman?

That was the beginning.

And *that* too, Andrew could see, was the import of this tiny island. That was the essence of Columba's story, maybe the Wanderer's story too . . . the significance of *all* the stories . . . the meaning of history itself.

Stories had to have a beginning, a source, as the name of the Wanderer's daughter-in-law implied.

In that awesome, terrifying, wonderful phrase in Genesis, *In the beginning God created*—in those five words was contained the energy and power that had set all humanity in motion, out of which had sprung the Wanderer and all that came after him, right down to Columba . . . and now to him, too, *to Andrew Trentham as well!*

Andrew walked on in thoughtful silence, his mind and heart exploring many inner paths he had never traveled before. He made his way slowly and quietly around the silent stone walls of the great abbey, pondering anew its meaning, then gradually back toward the hotel.

As he walked into the lobby, the face of the clerk on duty instantly lit up with concern.

"Mr. Trentham," he said, "we've been looking high and low for you."

"Well, here I am," said Andrew with a smile, "what can I do for you?"

"You had an urgent call, sir. Here is the message."

He handed Andrew a slip of paper. On it he read the words, *Call immediately*, with a telephone number he did not recognize.

Andrew quickly hurried up to his room to place the call.

⊠ T W O ⊠

When the voice at the receiving end of the line answered, "City General Hospital," Andrew immediately knew something was wrong.

"This is Andrew Trentham calling," he said. "I had a message to ring."

"Yes, Mr. Trentham, we've been expecting you. Hold a moment, please."

About fifteen seconds later, Andrew's father came on the line.

"Hello, Dad," said Andrew.

"I'm sorry to have to break it to you like this, son," said Harland Trentham. "Your mother's had a severe stroke. She's in hospital here at Carlisle."

"How bad is it?"

"Massive, my boy. She's not expected to live."

An audible gasp sounded from Andrew's mouth.

"If she does make it," his father continued, "it's doubtful she will speak again."

"What's her status now?" asked Andrew.

"She's in a coma. Her body appears completely paralyzed."

"I'll leave immediately," said Andrew. "I should be there by two or three in the morning."

Andrew paused.

"Wait a minute, what am I thinking?" he went on. "I'm on Iona without a car. The ferry's shut down for the night. The whole island's asleep. Without a helicopter, there's no way I can go anywhere."

"Right . . . I understand," said his father.

"I'll have to leave first thing in the morning."

"I don't suppose there's anything you can do in any event—except pray."

"I will . . . yes, I will do that, Dad. Call me if there's a change."

"Right, son."

Andrew put down the phone and stood a moment numbly. This was a sudden turn of events he had certainly not expected.

He descended the stairs.

"Is there any way off this island at this time of the night?" he asked the clerk.

"I'm afraid not, Mr. Trentham. Even if there were, you couldn't get from Mull to the mainland."

"I didn't think so." Andrew wandered once more out into the Ionan twilight. The air was warm and fragrant, with gentle sea breezes drifting over the tiny island. How everything had changed from an hour earlier, when he had been reading Columba's story and reflecting on its significance.

Gradually, as he walked, his thoughts took a far different turn. In his mind emerged the beginnings of an inner conversation with his mother as he reflected on what he would say to her if she were listening at this moment. But this inner dialogue, too, soon began to shift. Before long he was directing his thoughts toward Another.

Without realizing it, Andrew Trentham had begun to pray.

"Don't let her die now," he said audibly. *"Not before I've had the chance to talk to her again, not before I've made peace with her . . . made peace with the memory of Lindsay."*

He quickened his steps, not yet giving conscious thought to Whom he had begun to address the deep feelings of his heart.

"I have to talk to her again," he said. *"We must break this silence about Lindsay. Even if she cannot speak . . . maybe she won't even be able to understand . . . still I have to try to make sure she knows there was nothing I could have done . . . that I loved Lindsay too. Please . . . give me one more chance to talk to her."*

Andrew walked on, moving down toward the shore, yet keeping the hotel in sight. If another call came, he didn't want to be too far away.

▓   T H R E E   ▓

Life . . . we take it so for granted, Andrew mused, now thinking to himself. *Yet death is always close—right beside us . . . waiting . . . though we rarely see it. Birth, life, death . . . an ever-moving stream. . . .*

Suddenly all the stories he had lived with in past months returned to his mind. All seemed to culminate in the story of Columba, which now leapt into a brilliant clarity of focus and spiritual purpose. With it came words and phrases he had heard Duncan utter over the years.

He's no ancient God, lad, Andrew heard in his memory, *he's as real an' alive this very day as when his Son walked the earth. He's as alive fer ye an' fer me as he was fer old Saint Columba, or for Saint Peter himsel'. . . .*

Could it really be that simple? Andrew wondered. Was it just a matter of trusting that God was real and alive?

Was the very simplicity of Columba's faith the thing that gave him such power . . . power literally to bring forth miracles?

His mother's face was before him now. In the midst of his quandaries, he saw her smiling and full of life and health.

And there, strangely, was Columba's smiling face alongside his mother's. Andrew had no idea what the ancient saint might look like, but the *sense* of the man was there.

Suddenly Andrew realized that his personal search for identity and roots was bound up in his relationship with his mother . . . and maybe in old Columba's faith at the same time. How, exactly, he didn't know. Yet somehow they were linked.

All at once, in the silence of the night, the words were out of his mouth: *"God, help me discover who I am . . . and to know who you are."*

For a few moments his spirit was calm. All at once Andrew's brain reeled with an incredible idea.

The thought was so huge!

If Columba could exercise such practical faith . . . if Columba had courage to do nothing more than simply *believe* . . . and, if as a result of that elemental principle, rocks could float and people were healed . . .

Andrew's mind was spinning!

. . . If Columba could exercise such simple faith . . . *why couldn't he?*

If a former prostitute could forgive the pain a father had caused a daughter, could not a son forgive a mother the pain she had caused him? What was to prevent his following both these examples from the moving story?

The example of forgiveness . . . the example of faith.

And there, in the semidarkness and utter quiet of Iona, Andrew Trentham slipped to his knees at the water's edge.

"God," he prayed, *"I come to you as Columba of old did on these very shores. I ask you in the same way he did to work a miracle. I can't say that I have much faith. I don't even know if I have ANY faith. But if you are the God of power that Columba called on, and the God dear old Duncan speaks of as his friend, the God of this land and its people, then whether I have any faith or not, and whether I deserve to be heard or not, I ask you, please, to help my mother come through this, and put forgiveness and new love in my heart toward her."*

Around him the night was silent.

Andrew lifted his face and gazed into the starry expanse above him. It was not an empty expanse. Everything above, around, even inside him, was full of a great Presence.

Slowly, a deep peace descended over him, such as he had never felt before. He wasn't sure he even understood what it meant.

Slowly Andrew rose and made his way back to the hotel. He was reluctant for the moment to end, yet knew he had to get some sleep before the morrow.

He walked upstairs to his room and, notwithstanding concern for his mother, slept soundly and peacefully.

At dawn he was awake, and left the island on the morning's first ferry.

❖   F O U R   ❖

Patricia Rawlings sat in the lobby of the Doyle Skylon Hotel, a magazine in her lap, nearly out of her mind with boredom. She had to have more, she thought to herself.

Much more.

If she tried to go to anyone now with what she was thinking, they would only laugh. Reardon would deny everything. She could just see Pilkington and Luddington smiling as they listened, then breaking out in laughter the minute the door was closed behind her. She would become a greater laughingstock than before!

Everything was still nothing more than a gigantic hunch. Even if it was the Stone they were hiding in the druidic compound, by the time the police got there they could easily hide it or move it again.

The fact was—she had no *proof* of what was inside the box. Nor that Reardon was involved in something underhanded.

If she intended to write a story or go to the police, she had to get something concrete. Otherwise she might just as well go home.

An hour later, Reardon came through the elevator doors again. He didn't so much as glance her way as he crossed the lobby.

Paddy hurried through the front doors as close behind him as she dared.

❈ F I V E ❈

Andrew walked into the Carlisle hospital in midmorning. He found his father in the corridor outside his mother's room. He walked up and nodded gravely, momentarily taken aback by the expression on the older Trentham's face. It was anything but downcast.

"Good news, son!" said Mr. Trentham jubilantly, coming toward him eagerly and shaking his hand. "Your mother's out of the coma."

"What—that's wonderful!" exclaimed Andrew. "When . . . what happened?"

"Sometime late last night—I don't know, it must have been between midnight and two—all of a sudden her vital signs began jumping about. I was afraid we were going to lose her. The heart monitor signal was bouncing up and down. But the doctor said it was a good sign. Something was happening inside her, he said. It was almost as if she were being touched by some outside force, probing at her heart and brain, trying to make her respond."

As his father spoke Andrew felt goose bumps tingling through his body.

"And then a couple of hours ago," his father continued, "her eyes began to twitch, then suddenly opened. The doctors are dumbfounded. They have no idea what caused the change. Some of them are calling it miraculous, though of course, they don't mean literally. It just happened so suddenly, that's all."

Andrew stood listening, incredulous. He couldn't believe what he had just heard.

"Is . . . is she awake?" he asked.

"Only barely. She hasn't said anything. They still don't know whether she'll be able to or not. But I think she knows who I am."

He turned and led Andrew into the room.

❈ S I X ❈

The moment Andrew saw his mother so pale and weak and vulnerable, his heart stung him. Immediately it opened to her with a kind of love he had never felt before.

Andrew and his father sat down. For several minutes they remained at the bedside in silence. Both detected the moment Lady Trentham's eyelids flinched, then opened slightly. They could not tell at first whether or not she saw them. They each took one of her hands.

"Andrew is here, Waleis," said Andrew's father.

There seemed a slight movement of the woman's neck. Her eyes remained expressionless.

"Hello, Mum," said Andrew. His voice choked with emotion.

Her head turned perceptibly toward the sound. Her eyes seemed to fill with liquid and glistened in the dull yellow hospital light.

"Would you mind, Dad," said Andrew, "if Mum and I had a minute or two alone?"

"No . . . of course not, son," said Mr. Trentham. He rose and left the room.

Andrew sat for three or four minutes in continued silence, his mother's hand resting limply in his, her moist eyes gazing at him without expression. He had no idea how much she might understand, but he had to make the attempt. If God had answered his prayer, he now must do his part. Perhaps

God was extending her life so he could deal with the memory of Lindsay for both of them. This opportunity might not come again.

"Mum . . ." he said at length, then paused. The first word had been the most difficult. But now he had to keep going. He drew in a deep breath.

"I have so much to say," he continued. "I know you and I haven't really been as close as either of us might have liked. I always felt that Lindsay came between us. . . ."

Another pause . . . another deep breath. This was infinitely more difficult than addressing the House of Commons! And took far more courage.

"Perhaps I am wrong," Andrew went on, "but I felt that her memory was more important to you than I was, even though I was living and she was gone. I know you loved her, and that when she died it caused you more anguish than I will ever understand. I mean no disrespect either to you or her by what I just said. I loved you both too."

Yet again Andrew paused, struggling to keep going.

"But I was *me*, not her," he said. "I never could be her. But I felt you wanted me to be. It was an expectation I could never measure up to. Whatever I did, whoever I was, her memory would always be larger, holding up a standard I could never meet. I feel funny talking about all this right now, when you're not well. But for some reason I feel it is important for you as well as me . . . and that this is the time we must face it.

"I've been reflecting on many things recently—who I am and what that means. If I've seen one thing, it is that I can't live any longer under a shadow of expectation, where I always feel disapproval simply because I am not Lindsay. Whether it's something you put on me, or whether I put it on myself, I don't know. Perhaps it doesn't matter at this point. I have to get free of it.

"And, Mum," Andrew continued hesitantly, "I think you have to get free of it too. It is time we break this vow of silence about what happened that day. I think it was wrong to keep silent, and for you to put that on me. I know you were in shock at the time. But I was too young and afraid to know any better. And it wasn't right. You made us put our trauma into a box and seal it over with a tight lid. That prevented resolution for either of us. It built a wall between us. It's been like a secret cancer at the core of our relationship all these years. And I think it is time we rooted out that secret and brought it into the light. Your grief over what happened can never be resolved unless we get it out in the open and *talk* about Lindsay. I've struggled all these years with what happened, but at last I have come to feel a new sense of peace about it. I hope you can be at peace as well, about Lindsay . . . and about me."

Andrew stopped and again exhaled slowly. He hadn't planned to say quite so much.

He looked down at his mother's face. Tears flowed freely from her eyes. Wet tracks glistened down both cheeks. She seemed to be trying to speak, but she could not.

"I'm sorry to cause you this extra pain right now, Mum," said Andrew.

He stretched out his free hand and gently wiped away the tears with the back of his finger. A lump rose in his throat. They were the first tears he had seen her shed since Lindsay's death.

The silent eyes poignantly followed the motion of his hand. Her lips began to quiver. Still they uttered no sound.

Andrew felt a squeeze on his other hand. He returned it.

Lady Trentham turned her head away, then closed her eyes. Overcome with tenderness, Andrew leaned toward her, stooped down, and kissed his mother on the cheek. Then he rose, walked some way down the corridor to collect himself, and sought his father.

"What is the plan, Dad?" he asked in a husky voice. "What do we do now?"

"I'll see what the doctors have to say," replied Mr. Trentham. "In any event, I'm sure I'll stay the night here."

"I think I'll drive on home," said Andrew. "I've just put Mum through a bit of an ordeal. I think it will be best for the two of you to be alone together now."

His father cast him a questioning glance. "Uh . . . whatever you think, son."

"I'll call you this evening, then come back over tomorrow morning."

13

FROM EIRE TO CALEDONIA

⸙ O N E ⸙

The road leading southwest from Dublin was familiar this time.

Paddy had a good idea where Reardon was going by now, and she could follow at a safe distance.

They had left Carlow a mile or two before. There was the pub coming up on her right, with its faded sign and a red-and-white phone booth in front. The turn-off for the druidic center would be just a little farther down the road.

Unexpectedly, however, the car in front of her braked and pulled into the lot.

Paddy slowed and drove on, glancing over as she passed the pub. It was Reardon all right. What was he up to? She would turn around after a bit, then come back and try to find out.

A few minutes later Paddy pulled into the pub's parking lot. Reardon's car sat empty. She parked and put on her oversized hat—the best disguise she could manage under the circumstances—then got out, pulled her light jacket tightly around her, and walked inside.

The place was dimly lit and filled with the haze of tobacco smoke. The odor of strong Irish lager and stout met her nostrils. This was obviously no tourist spot, but strictly a watering hole for locals. Eight or ten men were scattered in twos and threes at tables throughout the room. A couple of others stood at the counter, chatting loudly with the fat, balding proprietor of the place, whose grimy white apron bulged over his stomach and upon which he wiped his hands after pouring each new draft.

Paddy slipped into the closest chair to the door. She was conscious of nearly every head in the place turning in her direction. Momentarily the buzz subsided as they eyed her. Gradually the noise of conversation, movement, and laughter, chairs scraping and glasses chinking, resumed. She could easily imagine half of those here as IRA members with guns beneath their jackets. Only one other woman was present in the whole place. It would be just her luck to have walked into a terrorist stronghold!

Paddy stared down at the worn oak table. An awkward minute passed. Slowly she became aware of a form approaching and taking up a position in front of her. She looked up. There stood the filthy apron.

"What'll ye have, miss?" said the man, looking and sounding none too pleased at the prospect of another customer.

"I'll, uh . . . I'll have a Guinness," replied Paddy. It was the only name she could think of. She doubted they served Fetzer Barrel Select Chardonnay in this place.

Without acknowledgment, he turned and walked back to the counter. He returned a minute later with a gigantic glass filled with some kind of dark brown liquid, nearly black in this light, topped with an inch and a half of creamy tan foam. He set it in front of Paddy and departed.

Trying to look nonchalant, as if she came down to the pub for a beer or two every day, Paddy reached for the glass, lifted it to her lips, and downed a healthy glug. She choked and broke into a fit of coughing.

Ugh! she exclaimed to herself. What kind of foul stuff was that! If this was Guinness, why was it so famous? Who could drink it?

A few glances and snickers crept around the room. But they were brief. Soon everyone was about their business again. As her eyes grew accustomed to the dim light, Paddy again raised the glass to her mouth, this time sipping at the foam and glancing about as she pretended to drink. She spotted Reardon seated at the far end, apparently waiting for someone. If he had noticed her, he was paying no attention now.

Behind her the door opened again. A shaft of light pierced the smoky haze, then disappeared as the door banged shut.

A man walked across the floor and sat down beside Reardon.

※ T W O ※

Andrew Trentham drove slowly from Carlisle back toward Derwenthwaite. His mind was full . . . not only of his experience on Iona, but also of what had just taken place in the hospital with his mother.

Talking to her like that had been awkward and difficult. And yet . . . what had happened in those few moments between them was nearly as miraculous as her sudden recovery.

Suddenly he realized—if not for the first time in his life, then with an awareness that went deep into new places within him—that he *loved* his mother . . . really loved her with all the affection a son should feel. He had always loved her. But her weakened condition and his honest confession had unlocked new reservoirs of feeling in his heart that had been shut away for years under the twin burdens of expectation and disapproval.

He felt such great relief.

A gigantic burden had been lifted from his shoulders that he had been carrying all his life. He knew he was at last free from having to be anyone but the person God had made him to be . . . and to become.

A silent tear slowly crept down his cheek.

I don't know what to say, God, he whispered, *except thank you. Thank you for hearing my prayers. And thank you for my mum, and what I now realize she means to me.*

※ T H R E E ※

Several long minutes passed in O'Faolain's, during which Paddy made very little progress toward emptying her tall pint of stout. She continued sipping at its edges, trying not to grimace. The foam was nearly gone. There was nothing to do now but actually drink some of the dark brown mud. The fat, aproned man again approached, looking down at her with a bemused expression.

Did she want anything else?

Paddy shook her head and attempted a smile. He nodded without further word, then ambled off toward his other patrons.

From somewhere at the far end of the pub, the form of another woman now emerged from the shadows and sat down to join Reardon and the other man. The woman's blond hair seemed out of place here, thought Paddy. She continued staring absently.

Wait—it couldn't be. . . .

Suddenly recognition dawned. She knew that face!

What was *she* doing here?

Andrew Trentham shot into her mind. Maybe *he* would know!

She rose and left the pub. Now she was sure something was up! Outside she hurried to the phone booth that stood near the front door. She fumbled through her handbag for her address book, then quickly rang the number she had managed to obtain for Andrew Trentham's flat.

She heard the phone ring twice. "Hello, this is Andrew Trentham," she heard his voice answer. "I'm away right now but would appreciate your leaving—"

No! she wailed in exasperation. *Not a machine! I hate answering machines! Now is one time I don't want a recording!*

She hung up and thought for a minute. There was only one thing to do—go back and see if she could hear anything from Reardon's table. If she couldn't get hold of Trentham, she would have to figure this out alone.

She walked back inside and took her seat. Unfortunately the pint of stout was waiting for her. She wondered if the man with the apron had any 7-Up. Her stomach was feeling funny.

Paddy strained to listen. From the back somewhere a fourth man now joined them.

Several minutes went by. She could make out very little, only the subdued sound of their voices through the drone of pub noises.

All of a sudden Paddy's brain cleared with revelation. What was she thinking? He had said he was going on recess! Andrew Trentham wasn't in London at all. He was at his estate in Cumbria!

Hastily she fumbled in her purse for the tiny book. Yes . . . there it was! She rose and again hurried out to the phone booth.

She was more glad than ever that she'd asked Bert to track down these numbers. She hadn't anticipated needing them quite so soon!

She picked up the receiver and began hurriedly punching in the numbers from her book.

⬚ F O U R ⬚

Andrew drove slowly up the familiar drive to Derwenthwaite Hall, his home since childhood.

A nostalgic feeling swept through him, almost as if he had not been here in years. He had actually been gone less than three days. But so much had changed in that brief time.

In no hurry, Andrew walked toward the great stone house, pausing briefly to gaze upon it, then continued to the front door. He walked inside. In the front entrance hung the pictures of the family, just as they had for years. How different was his response to the four faces on this day.

His heart filled with love for his father and mother as their images stared down at him from the wall. Tenderness welled up within him to see his mother next to Lindsay. A new compassion came with it. What his mother must have gone through . . . the pain, the agony of loss.

God, he silently said, hardly pausing to think how easy and natural praying had suddenly become, *I am sorry for not understanding before now how hard it was for her. Give us back the years we lost, each perhaps being afraid to open up to the other. Don't take her yet. Give me time to be a true son to her, and give her time to learn to be a true mother. Free her, God, from whatever shackles of guilt and disappointment and regret have bound her all these years and prevented her being what perhaps deep down she always wanted to be toward me.*

Gradually into Andrew's ear intruded the sound of the telephone ringing from the other room. . . .

⬚ F I V E ⬚

Larne Reardon, Member of Parliament, of ancient Irish descent though apparently a loyal Britisher throughout his professional life, had been speaking in low tones to his three associates-errant for some time. He had scarcely glanced about the pub since his arrival or taken notice of its other patrons.

Though most of Reardon's parliamentary colleagues were aware of his Irish roots, none of them possessed an inkling how deep his true loyalties, kept secret all these years, actually went. They would have been shocked to learn that he had connections high in the IRA as well as in certain Irish druidic circles and that he had been more than peripherally involved in a number of incidents that he had decried from the floor of the Commons along with his fellow parliamentarians.

This present mission was nearly done. Whether it would result in his public exposure and thus a sudden needful modification of career path—that much was uncertain at this point. But it was not *his* future that was presently on the minds of the two men and one woman at the table with him at this moment, but their own.

"It's payoff time, Reardon," one of the men was saying. "You said it would be today."

"The delivery has been made, Malloy," replied the MP. "We have to be patient with these people."

"We've been patient for a long time! Now, where is the bloke?"

"He'll be here. Believe me, the money will—"

Reardon stopped abruptly.

Suddenly his attention came instantly into focus across the room at the just-vacated table where a half-empty pint still sat.

"Did any of you notice that woman who was sitting over there a minute ago?"

The two men followed Reardon's eyes, then shook their heads.

"Now that you mention it," said the young woman with them, "there was something familiar about her. I do think I've seen her before."

"I was afraid of that. Go get her, Malloy," said Reardon, now in an urgent tone. "You too, Fogarty. Find out what she's up to. Don't let her get away from here. If she recognizes any of us, we could be in big trouble."

The two jumped up and strode quickly toward the front door.

⌗   S I X   ⌗

Mr. Trentham . . . Mr. Trentham . . . it's Patricia Rawlings . . ." came the unexpected and imperative voice on the line when Andrew answered the phone.

"Miss Rawlings!" said Andrew in an incredulous but pleasant voice, "how in the world did you find me here?"

"Never mind," replied Paddy. "I'll apologize for that later."

"I am right in the middle of a bit of a family situation. If you're working on a story, I'm afraid—"

"Please, Mr. Trentham," interrupted Paddy, "just listen."

At last Andrew realized that her insistent voice carried a worried tone.

"Go ahead," he said. "You've got my attention."

"I'm in a phone booth outside a pub in Ireland," Paddy began.

"Ireland—you mean Northern Ireland?"

"No, I mean *Ireland*—southwest of Dublin. I followed your friend Larne Reardon here."

"You . . . *followed* Reardon? But—"

"He's mixed up in something, Mr. Trentham. I'm sure of it. How well do you know him?"

"We're not close friends, if that's what you mean. But *why* on earth would you be following Larne?"

"That's why I'm calling, Mr. Trentham. I think he's involved with the theft of the Stone of Scone."

"What—Larne!" exclaimed Andrew. "Surely, Miss Rawlings—"

"And he's not alone. Remember that woman we saw in the Horse Guards restaurant—the one you went up and spoke to?"

"I remember.—What's this all about, Miss Rawlings?"

"She's here, Mr. Trentham . . . she's with Reardon."

"Blair? I'm sure you're mistaken. I spoke with her only a few days ago."

"It's the same woman, Mr. Trentham—I tell you, she's here with Reardon."

"I had no idea they were acquainted. I admit I am surprised, though I'm not sure I see anything so nefarious in it. And I still do not see why any of this is your concern, Miss Rawlings. Or mine, for that matter."

Even as he spoke, however, Andrew recalled Blair's words—*I'm leaving in a few hours*—and her reluctance to tell him anything about her destination.

"There are two others here with them," Paddy was saying. "They look like IRA types if ever I saw them. To answer your question—it is your concern because you know them both. You're an important man. You're the only one who can help. I don't know who else to turn to. If they are mixed up in the—"

Suddenly Andrew heard a cry of pain.

"Ouch . . . hey!" exclaimed Paddy's voice, "—what are you doing . . . stop!"

A scuffling followed.

"Andr—!" came a cry, instantly muffled. The line went silent.

Now Andrew was genuinely worried.

After several seconds another voice came on the phone—a masculine and angry voice.

"I don't know who you are," it said. "But if you know what's good for you, you'll keep out of it. Otherwise, this bird's dead."

The next instant the phone clicked into silence.

⊠   S E V E N   ⊠

The June sun was already climbing high in the sky, though it was not yet even eight in the morning.

Andrew stood as far forward on the upper deck of the ferry as he could get. He had left the seaside town of Stranraer on the first ferry of the day and would soon arrive in Larne, just north of Belfast. When buying his ticket, the name of the small city suddenly brought to mind Larne Reardon's Irish roots. All night since Paddy's call, he had tried to tell himself there was some innocent explanation for what she had seen. Now he began to wonder if her suspicions might contain more merit than he first thought.

After checking her incoming number through his telephone's Caller ID, Andrew spent a good part of the previous evening on the phone to London, trying to get the precise origin of her call. It hadn't been easy, but at last he had nailed it down to a public phone booth outside a pub called O'Faolain's Green near Carlow in southeast Ireland—as Paddy had said, southwest of Dublin.

The instant he heard the name of the pub he remembered it from Scotland Yard's investigation. He also recalled that he had mentioned it to Larne Reardon, who said he had never heard of the place. If what Paddy had said was true and Reardon was there, then Larne either had just discovered that particular pub . . . or had lied to him.

Whatever this was all about, thought Andrew, it was beginning to have a serious feel.

He knew he had no choice but to get to Ireland as quickly as possible. Patricia Rawlings was in trouble—that much was obvious. He could call the authorities . . . but Scotland Yard had no legal jurisdiction in Ireland. And Andrew wasn't sure he wanted to involve the Irish police just yet.

In the end, Andrew decided to go alone, at least initially, and take his own car. Driving would be quicker than trying to find a flight and would give him greater mobility. He hoped the UK plates would be no problem. He would keep his mobile phone with him every second, with Shepley's private number entered in memory. The instant he got in over his head, he'd have Scotland Yard, or *somebody*, on the phone! He was no James Bond!

He had hardly slept all night. Unfortunately, he had to wait till morning. There were no ferries at two A.M.

He'd driven away from Derwenthwaite at first light, stopping by the hospital in Carlisle to explain the sudden developments to his father. His mother had had a good night and was still asleep.

"I hope to be back in England by evening, Dad," he said as he left.

From Carlisle he drove north into Scotland, then through southern Dumfries and Galloway to Stranraer.

Now here he was with the Irish coastline approaching. He would head from Belfast down to Dublin, and then to the last place he knew for certain that Paddy had been.

Once he arrived . . . well, he didn't know what he'd do then. He'd have to improvise.

❈   E I G H T   ❈

Several hours later Andrew pulled into the parking lot of O'Faolain's Green.

A red-and-white phone booth sat in front. It must be where Paddy had called him. Nothing looked sinister in the light of day. No armed IRA guards hung about. The place appeared mostly deserted, though three or four cars were parked in front.

Andrew got out and went inside. He had dressed for the occasion in a faded plaid work shirt and old jeans. If he didn't raise his voice, hopefully he would blend in.

He glanced around, then sauntered to the counter and ordered a pint. The fat man gave him a thorough once-over as he set down the glass on the counter. Andrew nodded and took a sip. He perked up his ears to listen. He wanted to get the feel of the place before asking questions. Locals in places like this never liked inquisitive strangers. He stared into his glass, pretending to be absorbed in his own thoughts.

Scattered voices echoed about in thick Irish accents. The sound of one old fellow came through as more eccentric than the rest. He seemed a likely candidate for further scrutiny. The voice did not exactly rise above the din, but its scratchy timbre and high pitch, punctuated by an occasional laugh, made it a voice one couldn't help noticing. He seemed to be up on all the local gossip, though how much of it was true might have been open to question. Few of the others in the place were paying him much attention. His laughter and chatter indicated that he liked his beer robust and his stories exaggerated . . . and that he had already been enjoying the consumption of the one and the dispensing of the other for some time. After several minutes Andrew deduced him to be a semiretired farmer from Carlow.

Casually Andrew glanced around. The fellow was not difficult to find by following the sound. His appearance matched the voice to perfection. A worn wool cap slanted down onto the top of one ear, while out of the other side of his head shot a wild mass of curling gray hair that looked as if it hadn't split the teeth of a comb for years. His face was lined and angular and clearly spent much time in the open air. Wind and rain and sun had aged it to the rugged complexion for which his breed was noted. His companion, who had been the recipient of this day's tales, was just rising to leave.

Andrew turned back to the man behind the counter. "Give me a couple of Murphy's," he said.

The man did so, though with a quizzical look as he drew down two more tall drafts and set them on the counter.

Andrew picked them up, then turned and walked to the table just vacated by half the conversation he had been listening to. He set the glasses down and shoved one forward across the table.

"Have a Murphy's, my friend," he said.

"Thank ye, laddie—what's the occasion?" replied the man. He did not wait for benefit of an answer before sending a healthy quantity of the unexpected boon down his throat.

"No occasion," answered Andrew. "I'm new to the area, and I like making the acquaintance of a man who knows who's who and what's what. The moment I walked in, I said to myself that you were just such a man."

"*Hee, hee, hee,*" laughed the Irishman in a high-pitched cackle. "It's right ye are about that, stranger. I'm yer bloke. *Hee, hee.*"

Another swallow. "But what's a ruddy Englishman like yerself doin' in an out-o'-the-way place the likes o' this?" he said, wiping the foam from his lips with the back of a thick-vesseled hand.

"Just researching the county," replied Andrew.

"Well, it's nobody knows it better'n me, I'm thinkin'. Been here all my life, I have."

Suddenly the man stopped. His eyes narrowed as his face clouded with suspicion.

"Say, ye wouldn't be no friend o' that Amairgen Dwyer bloke, now would ye?" As he spoke, he articulated the name with scorn.

"No . . . no, I'm not," replied Andrew. "I'm afraid I don't know the name."

"Then ye'll aye be a lucky man. Stay away from 'im is all I got t' say. Most peculiar name I ever heard. Whoever called a wee tyke *Amairgen*, can ye tell me that! If ye ask me, it ain't his real name. He's a rum customer, that."

Again he paused suddenly and looked Andrew over again.

"Ye're not one o' them television blokes," he said, "what comes around t' film the comings and goings when they got their equinox thing?"

"No," laughed Andrew. "I'm not a newsman either. What equinox thing?"

"Every spring. That's when the Dwyer bloke brings in his hundreds o' queer ones, plugging up the towns an' the roads with their robes an' their nonsense. 'Fore ye know it, our cattle's drying up an' our dogs is barkin' all night at the moon. They bring nothing but ill, I tell ye."

As he listened, gradually the name came into Andrew's memory with the ringing of a faint bell. He continued to probe.

"You say this . . . this Dwyer lives around here?"

"Ay. He's the druid bloke, out t' the compound where the old stones be stickin' out o' the ground. He and his barmy-robed blighters chantin' their prayers t' the stones and the sky and the stars. The whole lot o' em's dotty if ye ask me. Just what we told them telly folks. Get the druids out o' here. The likes o' us has no use for 'em."

The farmer took another satisfying swallow from his glass. Now that a fresh supply of Murphy's stood in front of him, his tongue loosened all the more.

"Have you ever been out there?" asked Andrew.

"Ay, mate. I been there."

The man glanced about the pub, then leaned toward Andrew over the table in confidentiality. His voice lowered to a whisper. "Walked up through the woods," he said. "Wanted t' lay eyes on the place for myself, though I wouldn't go back. Set me t' tremblin' all over just t' look at it—big fence an' gates about the place. 'Twas the stones off in the field that gave me the shakes. Tremblin' from head t' foot, I was, till I got back an' got three pints o' O'Faolain's stiffest stout in me."

He stopped, eased back as if he had just recounted the heroic adventure of a knight in King Arthur's court, then took a long, slow, thoughtful drink and emptied his glass.

Andrew rose, obtained another, and returned to the table. The man, shaken by the memory, took a while to come to himself. The sight of a new full glass, however, brought a sparkle returning into his eyes.

Now it was Andrew's turn to keep his voice low. He pushed the glass toward his new friend.

"But if a fellow did want to get in," he asked softly, "past the gates—how might he do it?"

"I know that—*hee, hee* . . .'tisn't a problem," laughed the Irishman. "Though ye'd never catch *me* back there again, I'm tellin' ye."

"How then?"

The Irishman drew close across the table.

"I'll tell ye a secret, laddie," said the farmer, eyes shining in fun. "I heard him whisper the code t' one o' his druid cohorts. *Hee, hee.* I'm not so batty as they take me for."

"You heard him? Where . . . *here?*"

"He comes down t' O'Faolain's now an' then. Druids get thirsty too, ye know. Pays the likes o' us no mind, but I listens t' more than he thinks. *Hee, hee.* He's always carrying on in somber tones about getting the Stone they're missing, and when they get it, Ireland'll rise again, and talkin' about the druidical priesthood o' the ancient kings. Blarney and tommyrot, nothing more, *hee, hee.* Priesthood . . . missing stones! *Hee, hee.* He looks over t' me and I knows what he's thinking. He's thinkin' that all the lights are on but nobody's home, that I'm just an old fool. But I listen t' every word that comes out o' the queer blighter's mouth."

Another swallow of Murphy's followed.

"Where is their compound?" asked Andrew.

"Just up the hill, over the road a bit. Go up there, an' ye'll see the stones fer yerself, and likely a few blokes wandering around in robes muttering in some queer old tongue, talking t' the trees and the rocks, looking up in the sky one minute, down t' the ground the next . . . we are one with the grass . . . we *are* the grass. *Hee, hee!* Ever heard ye such foolery?"

"Were you here yesterday?" asked Andrew.

"Yesterday—why that . . . what, here?"

Andrew nodded. "I'm looking for a friend of mine."

"Well, O'Faolain didn't get so much as a pint's worth out of me yesterday, on account o' havin' t' see t' my cows. My hired bloke was sick."

"But you still haven't told me the code to get in," said Andrew, returning to the druid theme.

"That's the easy part, laddie," replied the man with a wink. He drew close again, reached across the table and clutched Andrew's shirt, and pulled him forward. "Nothing more," he whispered, "than spellin' out the word *C-E-L-T* with the numbers on the gate. That's what he said, though I never tried it myself. Just spell out the word—like on a phone, he said."

Andrew nodded, taking in the information with interest. As soon as was conveniently possible, he rose and made his departure.

▓   N I N E   ▓

As the tipsy Irish farmer had assured him, the number sequence *2—3—5— 8*, punched onto the coded keypad at the entrance to the Celtic Druidic Center, caused the black iron gate to roll instantly back on its track.

Andrew had parked about fifty yards in front of the gate, where the entryway widened, and approached the gate on foot. As the gate opened, he slipped inside. Thirty seconds later, the gate automatically closed behind him.

What he saw spread out in the distance below was the same sight that had met Paddy's astonished gaze three days earlier—a castle and compound with an enormous grassy expanse behind and to one side, in the middle of which stood the fabled and ancient Standing Stones of Carlow.

Five or six people stood out near the stones. He couldn't tell if Paddy was among them. All he could tell for certain was that one of them wore what Andrew took for a traditional white druid's robe.

Keeping to the edge of the drive near the trees and out of sight as much as possible, Andrew crept down the hill toward the compound.

The drive led straight to the front of the castle across a large paved car park. Only three or four automobiles were visible, though several outbuildings and garages surrounded the castle. Andrew saw no one nearby. He recalled to mind Columba's approach to King Brudei's palace. But he would not march to the front door of this place to demand entrance, thought Andrew. The modern day Broichan he had to face was out in the field with the stones of supposed power.

He crept to one side of the castle, shielded from the view of those at the stone site about three hundred yards away. Gradually he circled the main buildings. If he was going to get to the stones unseen, he would have to do so from an angle on the other side of the castle.

Five minutes later, still moving slowly and trying to keep one or another of the largest of the standing stones between himself and the druid, Andrew gradually drew near the small gathering in the field. Fortunately all but the man in the white robe were turned the other way. He could only see their backs.

Two of the group were women. He thought the one wearing a hat might be Paddy, although he couldn't be sure.

The robed druid stood facing him, but with eyes lifted skyward, chanting incantations in a weird and mystical voice.

Andrew inched forward. He reached one of the large upright stones and used it to shield himself from view. He peeped around its edge. When the coast was clear, he crept into the open, hurried to the next stone, and slipped behind it.

He was near enough to hear them now, and to see the druid's features. He recognized the face from news photographs as Amairgen Cooney Dwyer, the well-known druidic priest and head of the Irish Celtic Center. He was a tall and powerfully built man, imposing by stature and whatever other power he possessed. As he listened, Andrew found himself mesmerized by the cadence of Dwyer's chant.

I invoke the ancient land of Eire, much coursed by the fertile sea.
Fertile is the fruit-laden mountain with waterfalls by the lake of deep pools.

Deep is the hilltop well, a well of tribes is the assembly, an assembly of the
*   kings is Tara.*
Tara of the hill of the tribes, the tribes of the sons of Mil.
Like a lofty ship is the land of Eire, darkly sung with incantation of great
*   cunning, the cunning of the wives of Bres of Buaigne.*
But the great goddess Eire—Eremon has conquered her.
I, Amairgen, invoke the power of the sacred stone of her kings.
The stone awaits her kings who will rule the new Eire,
*   the new Eire which will rule the kingdom,*
*   the kingdom which will rule all the kingdoms.*
Her sacred stone has come.
I invoke the power of the ancient land of Eire.

With effort Andrew forced his attention back to his situation. He couldn't let himself be lulled to sleep by all that!

Again he ducked his head and crossed to another stone. From here he could see the features of some of the other figures. There was Larne Reardon all right, a few paces beyond the woman with the hat. Yes, it *was* Paddy, her face pale, her hands bound together with cord. And now suddenly it dawned on him that the other woman standing beside Reardon—that flowing blond hair—who else could it be but Blair!

Andrew could go no farther without betraying his presence. It was time to see what kind of courage he possessed.

Slowly he stepped from behind the stone and approached. Dwyer sensed the movement and glanced down. Instantly his chanting ceased. The heads of the others turned.

"Whatever you're up to, Dwyer," said Andrew, "the game is over. You can continue with this ritual as soon as we're gone, but I am taking Miss Rawlings with me."

At first sound of his voice, Paddy spun around.

"Come over to me, Paddy," said Andrew.

A cry of terrified relief escaped her lips. She started to run.

"Stop!" boomed Dwyer's voice. "Stay where you are!"

Paddy froze. All eyes locked on Andrew.

"Trentham, stay out of this," now said Reardon. "You have no idea what this is all about."

"We'll sort it out later, Reardon," said Andrew. "I don't know how you got involved in all this or even what your role is. But right now I'm taking Miss Rawlings away from here."

He glanced toward Blair with an expression of saddened bewilderment. "How did *you* get mixed up in this, Blair?"

She returned his stare without speaking. The look she cast him was not one of fondness, nor even of recognition, but the look of a stranger. Andrew sought her eyes, but they would not return his penetrating gaze. He now knew that his belated realization had been right on the mark—he had never known her at all.

"Do you know this man, Fiona?" said the man beside her whom Andrew did not recognize.

"It's Andrew Trentham," she replied, still looking in Andrew's direction. Her voice was strange and hard, as foreign as her expression, a different voice than Andrew had ever heard from her mouth.

"The bloke you were trying to sweeten up to get a line on—"

Andrew felt a knife plunging into his gut. He heard nothing more of what the man said. The whole thing had been a setup from the beginning! She had just been using him.

With great effort he forced back his composure.

"Trentham, this doesn't concern you," repeated Reardon. "There are powers here greater than you and me, greater than any of us."

"You won't get away with it, Reardon. I've encountered a power recently too, the power of God. It's greater than the power of these druids, I can tell you that."

He turned to Paddy. Her face was pale and frantic.

"Paddy . . . come with me," said Andrew.

Now the druid approached with great mumblings and incantations and threats. Paddy's feet remained nailed to the grass.

But a new source of power was indeed coming to Andrew Trentham, though even he had little idea how great was this present conflict and how truly the power of Columba's God was in the process of wakening within him.

"Stay where you are," said Andrew in a voice of newfound strength, its power surprising even him. "In the name of God I command you to stop and be silent."

The druid halted. No one spoke. The two men faced each other for a tense second or two.

Andrew again remembered Columba's encounter with Broichan. The next instant the words of the Forty-sixth Psalm were flowing from his mouth as if he had committed them to memory:

"The Lord of hosts is with us," he said in a strong voice. "Be still and know that I am God. I will be exalted among the heathen. I will be exalted in the earth. The Lord of hosts is with us."

As if he had been hit with some invisible force, Dwyer's frozen mouth twitched in stunned silence.

"You have no power over her, Amairgen," Andrew continued, "nor over me."

Hearing his assumed druidic name used in command against him, and with such authority, jolted Amairgen Cooney Dwyer into dumbfounded submission. His eyes flashed with hatred, but he did not move or answer.

"Now I tell you again," Andrew continued slowly and deliberately, "I am taking her, and nothing any of you can do will stop me. Come on now, Paddy."

At last Paddy ran forward. The others watched, still as statues. Blair's eyes contained innumerable daggers. Paddy, trembling, fell into Andrew's waiting arms.

Andrew began backing away in the direction of the castle, keeping his left arm around Paddy to steady her shaking legs. He continued to face the others, staring intently to keep them from following.

They had only retreated some fifty or sixty feet when suddenly Andrew's eyes shot open in astonishment.

With sudden disbelief he realized what he had been looking at out of the corner of his eye the whole time—a small chunk of upright sandstone stuck vertically into the ground next to the spot where Dwyer had been chanting his poetic ritual!

One of its iron rings and links hung from the top of the block. The other had been freshly buried some six inches into the ground. Standing only some twenty-one inches in height, it was by far the smallest stone of the circular collection surrounding them. But obviously Dwyer considered it the most crucial missing link.

It was the Stone of Scone!

"Paddy," he said, "do you see what—"

"Yes, yes," she interrupted in a quivering voice. "It's the Stone. They stole the Stone. They only brought it here two days ago. I saw them delivering it."

"I don't know how you did it, but—wait, what am I thinking! We've got to notify Scotland Yard."

Still moving backward, he let go of Paddy, pulled out his mobile phone and quickly punched in the necessary code to reach the UK.

"Shepley," he said when the inspector answered, "you're not going to believe where I am and what I'm looking at this instant!"

Shepley listened in disbelief.

"So Glencoe must have been a red herring," he said.

"Glencoe?" repeated Andrew.

"Never mind," said the inspector. "Tell me exactly where you are."

Andrew described the Celtic Center. "I know Ireland's not in your jurisdiction," he went on. "But I'm telling you the Stone is here, and I'm looking at the people responsible for stealing it. So get *somebody* here. Fast."

Hearing Andrew on the phone, Malloy suddenly came to himself. From somewhere he produced a gun.

"Let's go, Paddy," cried Andrew. "Run. We've got to get to my car." He turned and sprinted in the direction of the entryway, with Paddy panting beside him. Andrew shouted into his phone as they ran.

"We're not going to stick around, Shepley!" he cried. "They've got a gun, and we're outnumbered five to two. We're getting out of here!"

He glanced behind them to see Malloy taking aim across the field while Reardon, Blair, Fogarty, and Dwyer all bolted for the castle.

TEN

The sharp report of gunfire exploded behind the two runners.

Paddy screamed.

"Come on . . . we'll make it!" shouted Andrew. He led her running across the front of the compound toward the drive. She ran awkwardly, her hands still bound together.

"I don't think I can do this," puffed Paddy.

"We're nearly there," returned Andrew, reaching out both to steady her and pull her along up the driveway toward the gate.

Another shot sounded. A bullet slammed into a tree to Andrew's right, sending splintering pieces of bark flying.

They must have passed the invisible beam of an electric eye, for ahead the black iron gate rolled back. Andrew's car was only seconds away. But there was no time to feel relief as they ran through the gate. Behind them now came a new sound.

Andrew glanced back. The door to one of the garages stood open. Two well-equipped motorcycles roared out, the robes of their riders flapping in the wind behind them.

Andrew and Paddy sprinted the final yards to the car.

Only now did Andrew realize the mistake he'd made when he arrived. His car was still pointed down toward the castle! Turning around would take precious seconds. They would never be able to outrun motorcycles on these winding Irish roads!

He stuffed Paddy into the passenger side. The automatic gate was now sliding closed. The two bikers roared up the drive after them.

Andrew hurried around, got in, and flipped on the key. But instead of turning around, and without pausing to think, he yanked into gear and accelerated straight toward the gate.

He had no time for the *C-E-L-T*-code now!

"What are you—?" began Paddy. The next instant she gave a cry and ducked down.

Andrew blasted through the gate, sending the wrought-iron frame flying off its hinges. It bounced and clanked loudly to the side of the road as Andrew sped past.

The two young apprentice druids had been ordered to prevent an escape. The last thing they expected as they rounded the bend and approached the gate was a maniac speeding down upon them in the middle of the road! The car accelerated and swerved first toward one then the other.

Paddy just had time to look up. She ducked down again in terror. Before they could gather their wits, both cyclists careened off the road in front of the onrushing car. One cycle, now absent its owner, crashed into a tree. The other tumbled down the embankment on the other side into a deep ditch paralleling the entryway, depositing its druid-cyclist head over heels into brush and undergrowth.

Andrew sped on down toward the castle.

"Where did you learn to drive like that?" shrieked Paddy.

"I *don't* know how to drive like this! I'm making it up as I go along."

"You're doing pretty well if you ask me! I'm about to be sick."

Out of one eye Andrew saw Malloy running toward them. A second later a gunshot fired. A window shattered. Dwyer was running across the pavement toward the castle shouting orders to at least a half dozen more of his robed protégés as they poured out the front door of the compound.

"No time to get sick now, Paddy," cried Andrew. "Hang on to your hat!"

He crunched the steering wheel hard to the right. With a tremendous screech the car skidded around in a semicircular arc on the paved lot. Malloy had not anticipated the move. Suddenly he found himself sideswiped and thrown to the ground.

As they skidded back around in a direction generally facing the driveway they had just descended, Andrew jammed his foot to the floor.

Recovering himself, Malloy scrambled to find his weapon and get back to his feet. His aim was now wild and erratic. Several more shots sounded but missed the retreating automobile.

With the rear tires squealing and leaving a black patch of rubber stretching behind them, Andrew accelerated back up the hill, whizzed past the cyclists climbing out from among the trees, and zoomed out of the gate still picking up speed.

Dwyer and Reardon stood staring after them, then ran for one of the parked cars. They would take up the chase themselves.

ELEVEN

Ninety seconds later, Andrew's car roared onto the highway two miles west of Carlow. Paddy was struggling to free her hands from the cords that bound them.

"My car—it's still at the pub!" she exclaimed. "I just remembered."

A sudden idea came into Andrew's head.

"You have your keys?" he said.

"They're in my pocket."

Andrew braked hard and skidded into O'Faolain's Green.

"What are you doing?" exclaimed Paddy.

"Once those cyclists are back on their bikes we won't stand a chance," said Andrew. "We're going to Plan B. Come on, get out . . . hurry!"

Andrew ran inside the pub with Paddy on his heels. He hurried straight to his new Irish acquaintance.

"Hey, laddie!" called out the familiar voice. "How about another pint?"

"No time now, my friend," said Andrew, bending low and confidentially and talking fast. "Do you remember what we were talking about before . . . about getting into the druids' compound? It worked. I got in. But now the druids are after me!"

"After you! That's no good, laddie. I told ye an ill wind was blawin' about the place."

"Will you help me?"

Immediately the Irishman began climbing to his feet. He had to make an effort to keep his wobbly knees from trembling at thought of fighting off the druids, yet he summoned his courage like a loyal soldier whose captain had given the order.

"Ay, that I will, laddie. Ye can count on Coogan Mulroney."

"Then come with me!" said Andrew.

He led the farmer called Mulroney outside, then handed him his keys. Paddy followed.

"I need you to drive my car to the police station in Carlow," he said. "I want them to think they're chasing me. Can you do that?"

Mulroney nodded, ennobled if not sobered by the task set before him.

"I know you've had a pint or two of the black stuff," said Andrew, "but try to keep on the road and go as fast as you can. There'll be a commendation in it for you if we can fool the druids."

"I've never driven over twenty-five in my life, laddie."

"That will do just fine," said Andrew, feeling a sudden twinge of conscience at what he had asked the man to do. "I don't want you getting hurt—and fasten your seat belt!"

Andrew looked behind them toward the compound. "Hurry—look," he said pointing, "—here's their car cresting the hill. They're headed this way!"

"You can count on me, laddie! Fool the druids . . . I'm good at that."

Andrew helped him in. The car roared recklessly into life, then sprayed a trail of gravel behind it. Mulroney sped off, weaving back and forth across the pavement, quickly accelerating to the twenty-five miles per hour comfort level, then gradualy up to thirty.

"The poor fellow!" exclaimed Andrew. "I hope he *makes* it to Carlow. But quick, before they see us . . . get in."

They jumped into Paddy's rental car and scrunched out of sight. A minute later they heard a vehicle roar past. Andrew raised himself enough to sneak a peek.

"They've taken the bait. They're after him!" she said. "Let's go! It's your car—do you want to drive?"

"Are you kidding? I'm trembling from head to foot and haven't eaten in twenty-four hours."

A few seconds later, with Andrew at the wheel, they half skidded onto the road and now sped off in the opposite direction.

"As soon as we're good and clear of this place," said Andrew, "we'll stop and get you some food."

"What I could really use is a hot bath and a bed."

"Unfortunately, that will have to wait. By the way . . . you cut your hair—it looks nice."

"Thank you," said Paddy with a worn-out smile.

The relief both suddenly felt resulted in several minutes of silence. Paddy was the first to break it.

"Thank you for coming," she said in a quiet voice. "I was so afraid."

"What else could I do?" replied Andrew. He glanced over at her weary face, which was finally beginning to relax. "We English squires, you know," he added with a smile, "are obligated to rescue damsels in distress."

"Well if ever there was a damsel in distress," rejoined Paddy, "it was me! I was a complete idiot to try to solve this on my own."

"If you hadn't, the mystery of the Stone might never have been solved."

Behind them in the distance they heard the whine of police sirens.

"Sounds as if Inspector Shepley got somebody on the case in a hurry."

"We really still don't know all that was involved, do we?" said Paddy.

"Recovering the Stone will be a big part of unraveling it."

"It was bigger and more dangerous than I realized."

"Next time we won't make that mistake."

"We?" repeated Paddy.

"Of course. I'm in it with you now," said Andrew. "We'll get to the bottom of it. But first we've got to get out of Ireland."

.

※   T W E L V E   ※

The sun had set, but the sky promised a wondrous pink-and-orange twilight.

Andrew Trentham and Patricia Rawlings stood on the upper deck of the same ferry on which Andrew had crossed the North Channel of the Irish Sea some fourteen hours earlier. Both were exhausted but relieved to at last be bound for the Scottish coast.

"Beautiful, isn't it?" sighed Paddy with weary contentment. "Especially after a day like this."

"It's what the Scots call the gloamin'," replied Andrew. "It is a special time of day."

"You know," said Paddy, "I've never actually set foot in Scotland. This is going to be a first for me."

She paused and glanced at Andrew with a twinkle of fun in her eye. She had dozed a number of times as they drove north, and with the added benefit of a warm meal inside her was now feeling much better.

"And come to think of it," she added, "that reminds me—it was Scotland that first brought us together . . . in a manner of speaking."

"How do you mean?" asked Andrew.

"I tried to get you to tell me why you were so interested in Scotland, and you were evasive."

Andrew laughed.

"So how about it now, Mr. Trentham? Haven't we been through enough together that you could confide in me?"

"You are probably right. Whatever reasons I had for keeping it to myself no longer seem important. I suppose I was afraid of your going public with something I would see on the papers or hear on the telly the next day. Somehow I find it hard to worry about that anymore."

"I wouldn't publicize anything without your approval, not after what you did."

"I appreciate that," replied Andrew. "And you're right. We have been through quite a lot together. So in addition . . . I think it's time you called me Andrew."

"I'm honored."

"And by the way, how *did* you get my phone numbers?"

"I said I'd apologize later—so . . . *I'm sorry.* Actually, I don't suppose I can be *too* sorry. Getting in touch with you may have saved my life. As for how I got them, I'll tell you when you let me in on your mysterious Scottish secrets."

"Touché!" rejoined Andrew.

They had nearly arrived at Stranraer. It was time to return to Paddy's car on the lower deck. Minutes later the ferry docked, and Andrew continued to drive as they disembarked onto the Scottish shore.

The gloaming deepened. They began their way across the southernmost region of Scotland, directly across the Solway Firth from Andrew's home in Cumbria. Sight of this very Stewartry coast from the hills above Derwenthwaite had prompted much introspection several months earlier. As dusk descended it grew quiet and peaceful between them. Andrew drove at a leisurely pace as he reflected again on the changes that had taken place within him since then.

Their conversation slowly drifted into more thoughtful channels. Andrew began sharing with Paddy about his family, about Duncan, and then about his gradually deepening interest in his Scottish roots.

"I'd never thought much about it before," he said. "Then all of a sudden, a few months ago, I couldn't get enough of it. It was as if I had to know who I was, where I'd come from, and what role this land of Scotland might have played in both those things. That's when I started reading some of the old tales from Scotland's history, stories Duncan had told me when I was a boy."

"What kind of tales?" asked Paddy.

"About the ancients who first came here, the men and women who conquered and tamed the land, and those who brought the Christian faith to Scotland."

"This Duncan sounds like a man I would like to meet."

"Perhaps you shall one day," replied Andrew. "Curiosity about my own roots began it for me. Then Caledonia itself took over. The history is absolutely fascinating! There's none like it. I feel as if I've been living in a completely different world since I was bitten by the Caledonian bug."

"Your enthusiasm is infectious. So who *were* the first people to come here?"

Before Andrew knew it, he was recounting to Paddy an abbreviated version of the Wanderer's story. She listened, mesmerized.

"You are a marvelous storyteller!" she exclaimed when he was through. "My heart was pounding when that mammoth attacked. I've never heard history told so . . . so much like an adventure. You make it come alive. I felt like I was really there."

"I suppose that's because to me it *is* an adventure—and a majestic one."

He paused reflectively. "But it's more than that," he added. "Somehow Scotland's past has a vitality that makes me feel connected to it. I can't help but feel that these old characters of former times have much to teach me, that there are universal lessons here for our time. Cruithne and Fidach, and the importance of unity and brotherhood. And Foltlaig and Maelchon and having the courage to fight for your land."

"*Cruith* . . . what?" said Paddy, trying to repeat the strange-sounding name. "Who are these people?"

Andrew laughed. All it took was a few more questions from Paddy and again the storyteller rose up. Only now it was Andrew rather than Duncan, recounting the tales he had heard from the old Scotsman's mouth. The hours flew like minutes.

"Do you see what I mean?" he said after they had relived another era or two together. "All this that is going on with us who live today, even this crazy adventure we've undertaken today—it pales into insignificance alongside the heroism and grandeur of those ancient times."

"I *am* starting to see what you mean," replied Paddy. "Is this what you call the Caledonian bug?"

"That's it! It comes over you rather like a virus."

"I guess I've got it then. Can we just head north for Scotland right now? I want to see it all!"

Andrew laughed.

"What is it that makes Scotland's history so compelling?" asked Paddy. "I can *feel* it as you're telling me these stories. I sense it just driving through these hills, although now we can hardly see them. But what is the magic?"

"It's Caledonia itself—Scotland . . . the land, the history. It's heather and peat and battles and clans and tartans and bagpipes. It's the people, the Celtic past, the language I think to a degree, the music, the color, the culture . . . the wonder of all of it."

"You mentioned earlier about the bringing of Christianity to Scotland."

"Have you heard of Saint Columba?"

Paddy nodded.

"He came to Iona in the sixth century. I was just there a few days ago—incredible now that I think of it. It seems like a month! That's quite a story too."

"I'm listening!"

Andrew briefly told her the story of Columba and Diorbhall-ita. When he was through, again it was silent as they reflected on the story and its spiritual implications.

"But you've only told me the history of Scotland—Caledonia as you call it—up to the year 600," said Paddy at length. "I feel as if we've only begun."

"Exactly. There's *much* more to come. It gets better and better! But remember, I've only begun this quest recently myself. I still plan to do much more reading."

"Will you tell me what you learn?"

"Of course! And wait until you hear about Glencoe," added Andrew. "It is one of the later stories—from the seventeenth century. Duncan told it to me recently. It will make you weep."

"What's it about?"

"Clans and loyalty and betrayal, about changing times in the Highlands . . . and about a maiden named Ginevra and a young Highlander named Brochan."

"Sounds like a love story."

"You're right."

"Does it have a happy ending?"

"Yes and no," replied Andrew. "Its happiness is bittersweet. But even the sad endings in Caledonia are tinged with magic."

"Why do you say that?"

"You said it a minute ago . . . because Caledonia is a magical place."

They arrived at Derwenthwaite after midnight. Andrew had called ahead to Franny, who had one of the guest rooms waiting for Paddy with clean sheets, fresh flowers, and a soft pillow. After what she had been through, and especially after the hot bath Franny was in the process of drawing for her, she could have slept anywhere.

"Do you want to call your producer?" asked Andrew.

"I don't think Edward Pilkington would appreciate being awakened at this hour. Besides, I'm too sleepy."

"Then sleep well."

An odd expression came over Paddy's face. "I don't know what more to say," she said, "other than simply again to thank you . . . for everything."

"Don't mention it—damsels in distress and all that, remember."

"And thank you for all the stories. What a perfect end to the day."

"I enjoyed telling them—helped put all it into perspective."

"Well . . . good night, Andrew."

"Good night, Paddy."

❈ T H I R T E E N ❈

A bright, sunny Cumbrian summer's day dawned over Derwenthwaite. Both adventurers awoke refreshed and invigorated.

As Paddy came down from her guest room and was greeted by Franny, she heard Andrew's voice on the phone.

"Are you ready for a nice English breakfast, my dear?" asked the housekeeper.

"Yes . . . thank you," said Paddy.

"Mr. Andrew is in the dining room waiting for you."

She led the way and Paddy followed. Andrew was just hanging up the phone as they entered.

"Good morning!" he said. "Sleep well?"

"Like a baby," replied Paddy.

"I've been trying to get through to Inspector Shepley, but he's out. He's supposed to call me. And you need to call your producer."

"You're right. I probably should check in before Luddington finds out about the Stone!"

"Why don't you do it right now? I'll pour us tea."

A minute later Paddy had her producer on the line.

"Mr. Pilkington," she said. "This is Patricia Rawlings . . ."

A brief pause.

" . . . never mind where I'm calling from. I just wanted to tell you that I'll be back sometime late this afternoon, tomorrow morning at the latest. What I have for you is *big*, Mr. Pilkington—the story I was telling you about. Part of it at least . . ."

Again her producer spoke.

"Right . . . but I can't give it to you over the phone. I'll tell you this much—the Stone of Scone has been found."

Even Andrew from where he stood some distance away heard Pilkington's exclamation.

"What!" came the echo of his voice.

"I'm sure it will be all over London before the day's out," Paddy went on. "But, Mr. Pilkington—I was there. I saw the whole thing. So unless you want me taking my story elsewhere, you'll wait for me and not give it to Kirk."

Paddy glanced toward Andrew with a smile.

He winked and nodded as if to say, "Good for you!"

"Right . . . yes, thank you, Mr. Pilkington. I also want to talk to you about my expenses. I'll see you later today."

Paddy hung up and laughed. "The poor man—he didn't know what to say."

"What could he say? You had him over a barrel!"

They sat down to their breakfast of eggs, sausage, tomatoes, mushrooms, toast, and tea, but they had only begun when the telephone rang once more. Andrew jumped to answer it.

"Yes, Inspector, hello," he said. "Are you back in England?"

Andrew nodded.

"Yes . . . I see—so, what's the news on the Stone?"

As Andrew listened, Paddy watched his face. He nodded, taking in the information, then after a minute or two broke into a great laugh.

"Just an Irishman I met at O'Faolain's," he said.

Again the inspector spoke.

" . . . who I am—no, not an inkling. I didn't give him my name . . ."

More laughter.

"All right, then . . . you're right, he probably is in for a surprise . . . thank you, Inspector. Cheers."

He hung up and walked back to the table with a smile on his face.

"The Stone is recovered," he said to Paddy as he sat down. "But the compound was deserted. The Stone is under guard and the whole place sealed off. Inspector Shepley said the Irish police are cooperating nicely. The Stone will be on its way back to Edinburgh in a day or two."

"What was so funny?" asked Paddy.

Andrew began to chuckle.

"Shepley said, 'By the way, what was your car doing out there?' He said they found a car with UK plates in a ditch alongside the road about four miles out of Carlow. 'When I checked the registration,' he said, 'who should I find out is the owner but Andrew Trentham himself!' "

Paddy laughed.

"And inside the car, literally asleep at the wheel, and without a scratch on him, was a drunken Irish farmer."

Andrew broke into laughter again.

"When they finally managed to wake him up, all he could say was, 'Got t' keep the druids from gettin' the laddie . . . fool the druids . . . ye can count on me.'—I guess he didn't find the police station!"

"Now I really have an angle for my story that Kirk Luddington won't know anything about!" laughed Paddy.

"There is only one trouble with that," said Andrew. "Our friend Mulroney doesn't like television people any more than he does druids!" said Andrew.

"Then you'll have to tell him I'm with you."

"I'll see what I can do," laughed Andrew.

Later that morning they drove into Carlisle. Andrew had Paddy drop him off at the hospital. They said good-bye. Paddy then continued south to London, and Andrew went inside to check on his father and mother.

▨ F O U R T E E N ▨

A week later Harland Trentham brought his wife home to Derwenthwaite. She was able to walk, though somewhat unsteadily. Her left arm hung limp at her shoulder, and she had still not spoken since the stroke. The doctors could offer no clear prognosis as to further recovery, although they discussed treatment with a number of therapists.

Andrew remained at her side nearly every minute of the next week, attending to her every need, reading aloud, bringing her tea, helping her gradually accustom herself to a life that was dramatically altered. She seemed most relaxed when he was at her side and seemed always glancing about waiting for him when he was not.

Andrew could not have been more grateful for the opportunity to link hands of ministration with the prayers he had breathed that life-changing night on Iona. What the strong woman who had always been so in control thought of being waited on, it would have been difficult to say. She seemed to adapt to the change with more grace than might have been expected.

During the third day of the second week, Andrew came upon his mother about eleven o'clock in the morning, standing with her new cane before the second-floor window and gazing out upon the lawn and the lake in the distance. He had seen her watching him from this particular window many times. On this occasion, however, she was not gazing outside at him, but inside at herself. The window had become a mirror.

"Here, I've brought you some tea, Mum," said Andrew as he walked into the room.

At first she did not respond. He wondered if she had heard him. Slowly she turned. A most unusual expression was on her face. With her good hand, she motioned toward the coffee table. Andrew set the tea tray down. Now she motioned to the chair beside it, indicating that she wanted him to sit down. He did so. Moving carefully, she took a seat opposite him on the settee.

Andrew waited, not sure what his mother wanted.

At last she began to speak, slowly and softly, almost unintelligibly to begin with. He was so elated at the first sounds from her lips that he nearly jumped up to run for his father.

But his mother waved her hand importunately for him to remain where he was.

" . . . must finish . . . want to say," she whispered.

Andrew calmed and sat back. The expression on his mother's face was clearly one of struggle to get out every word.

"I know," she began, "wasn't easy . . . all of us . . . Lindsay . . ."

As she continued to speak the words seemed to come easier, though her voice remained slurred and soft.

" . . . Stroke hit . . . second or two as I fell . . . saw my life passing—like they say . . . saw how I had compared . . . so many years . . . unfair . . . you're right—burden of expectations . . . so clear . . . saw vividly. Yet I knew something dreadful had happened . . . losing consciousness . . . as I fell, I prayed . . . a split second . . . would have the chance to tell you myself . . ."

She turned her pale though still elegant face toward him, and her eyes filled with tears. "Then . . . woke up . . . you were looking into my face . . . so happy, but couldn't say anything . . . lips wouldn't obey my brain. . . . Then you said what you did . . . probably wondered if I heard . . . I did, every word . . . all I could do was cry."

As he listened, Andrew felt the tears rise in his own eyes as well. Though neither of them saw him, Harland Trentham in the corridor had heard his wife's voice and now stood listening at the doorway, his eyes in the same state as his son's.

"I am proud of you, Andrew," continued his mother, her voice continuing to strengthen. "You are a son any mother could be proud of . . . *should* be proud of, not just for what you have accomplished . . . for the man you are . . . man of character. Your father always knew it . . . thinks so much of you. I was afraid to think about it . . . for fear I would forget Lindsay. Maybe I was afraid to let myself be proud of you, thinking it would not be right of me toward her . . . don't know why . . . suppose I've been a mixed-up woman for many years. You have been a good son to your father and me . . . as good and honoring a son as you could be. I am so sorry for not realizing it and for not telling you . . . suppose I did realize it . . . didn't know that I did . . . never said anything to you. Forgive me."

Andrew was already on his feet. He sat down beside her on the settee and took his mother in his arms.

"I do forgive you, Mum," he said. "I've already forgiven you. We'll be all right now."

"Thank you," she whispered. "I love you, Andrew."

"I love you, Mum."

Outside the door, the one who loved them both stood choking back his tears.

⬚   F I F T E E N   ⬚

The following afternoon, after a joyous twenty-four hours in which husband, wife, and son had been able to converse together again with newfound freedom and mutual respect and love each toward the other, Andrew sat down in his favorite reading chair in the library. His father was somewhere upstairs. His mother was sleeping comfortably in her room. For the first time in years, the house felt completely at peace in every way.

On Andrew's lap sat one of Duncan's books in which he had been reading. He had been saving this particular story for just the right time. He had, of course, heard the captivating tale from Duncan's own lips, but he had never actually read it through from beginning to end in the worn and treasured old volume.

He heard a sound. He glanced up. His father entered the library.

"You know, son," said Harland Trentham, "ever since you brought up our ancestral line and asked me about those old portraits, I haven't been able to get that old Highlander up in the gallery out of my mind. I was up there just now. Now I know why his eyes got into you that day. I must confess, he's had the same effect on me. Every time I go through the gallery now, I sense him gazing down at me. Whenever I let his eye catch mine, something sweeps over me—a sense of mystery. I don't know. . . . I can't explain it. Do you know what I mean, son?"

"Yes, Dad," Andrew smiled, "I think I do."

"And now that I think about it, I do remember being told as a child about there being a Scots branch on the old family tree. There must be something to it if it has such a strange power."

"I've got an old book here you might like to read—one I borrowed from Duncan."

"You don't say? I would like to see it."

"Here, let me show—" began Andrew, starting to hand it to him.

"No," replied his father. "I'm not in the mood to read just now. I'll look at it tonight. What's it all about?"

"Tales of old men and women," replied Andrew, resuming his seat. "Duncan used to let me look at it and tell me stories from it when I was a boy."

"What do they have to do with the chap up in the gallery?"

"I'm not sure. I haven't gotten that far along in the story."

"Hmm . . . I wonder who the old Highlander is anyway."

"I don't know, Dad. But I am going to find out. I have the feeling we've only begun to unravel the mystery of our family tree."

"Well, let me know what you find out, Andrew, my boy."

"I will, Dad. I am determined to find what legacy that old kilted Highlander has left us."

"Well, you've got my curiosity up now. I think I'll go out with the horses . . . what do you say if tomorrow you and I make sure your mother's all right, then saddle up Hertha and Kelpie and ride out to see Duncan together?"

Andrew nodded.

"Good idea, Dad. I'd like that."

His father turned and left the room. In another few seconds Andrew heard the front door open and close.

With his heart full, a tray of tea and oatcakes on the stand beside him, and the whole lazy afternoon ahead, this was the moment he had been waiting for.

Andrew opened the faded front board of the book and flipped the pages back to where lay his leather marker. He took a satisfying sip of tea, then began.

"It was a rugged, mountainous glen," he read, *"through which tumbled the small river for which it was named. . . ."*

Two hours later, Andrew Trentham still sat, the teapot long empty, a few crumbs of oatcake on his shirt, his mind miles and centuries away. . . .

Once they were through the snow to the safety of the cave, Ginevra quickly pulled off Brochan's boots, rubbed his feet with her hands, then wrapped them in the dry plaid of her clan, left for her by the son of Glencoe's new chief. Here they would rest, and she would do what she could to nurse the wounds of the man she loved.

Back in the glen of death, Major Duncanson did not arrive until seven. Lieutenant Colonel Hamilton, finding the Devil's Staircase impassable in the blizzard, did not get through until eleven.

By then the killing was nearly done.

The regiments under the major's and the lieutenant colonel's charge did little more than round up the rest of the cattle, loot what goods they cared to steal, and then set what remained of the glen's villages ablaze. A few halfhearted attempts to track the survivors into the surrounding snow-covered mountains followed, but without much result. Thirty or forty bodies were found but left where they lay, already frozen.

Both Duncanson and Hamilton were furious with Campbell of Glenlyon when they learned that both of Maclain's sons had escaped. He had entirely failed in the orders given him—less than a tenth of Glencoe's population was found dead.

Only some thirty-eight had actually been murdered by guns, bayonets, knives, swords, and fires before most escaped. Many more, however, had perished in the freezing storm, driven from their beds but half dressed and without provisions adequate to hide out for long in the hills.

The several escape parties, as well as some who had taken the soldiers' cryptic warnings to heart and made off into the hills the night before, managed to meet later in the glens of Appin. There did Ruadh Og again see his father, telling him what had happened . . . and to whom he owed his life. In Appin the remnant of clan Maclain settled. They would rise again from the ashes of devastation and spilled blood of that fateful winter's morning in the glen called Coe.

But the clan never returned to make Glencoe its home. The blood of Maclain stained the ground of the place for all time. Henceforth would Glencoe be a desolate shrine to the rape of a people and a promise of freedom unfulfilled.

Once she had her patient comfortably resting, Ginevra returned the next day to the glen that had been her home. Thankfully the bodies of her mother and younger brother had been buried with the rest of the dead.

In the rubble of a certain cottage of Achtriachtan, Ginevra discovered the charred harp of bard Ranald of the Shield. Half its strings had snapped, and its body was badly blackened. Yet the shape of oak and willow was intact, and the strength of its wood still firm. She carried it with her to Brochan's hideaway and sat by his side through the cold nights of winter, attempting to make what music she could, with harp and voice, to cheer him.

Neither of the two were ever seen again by the people of the glen.

Years later, high upon the slopes of Aonach Mor, a small deserted stone cottage was discovered that none in the region knew of. It had apparently not been in use for some time.

The only item in it of apparent interest was a very old and well-worn tartan blanket, which was carried back to the village in Appin, where dwelt a certain Ruadh Og Maclain, brother to the present chief of the small clan.

When he saw it, Ruadh smiled. Well he knew that this tartan was worn only by the family of the chief and had once, many years before, been his own.

In after years the only reminder of those previous times, faintly heard occasionally on the edge of a lonesome Highland wind, was the thin ghostly whine of the final lingering mournful tones, as of an aeolian harp, of the departed dead of Glencoe.

To some it sounded as if an invisible finger were plucking the melancholy strains of the dead bard's lament to the lassie with the spirit of the Highlands in her soul.

> *We gaze into yer eyes—only blue looks oot.*
> *We see only the twinkle o' stars, the pale o' dawn . . .*
> *A vast empty sky. Tell us gien ye can.*
> *Wha are ye, lass?*
> *Tell us gien ye can.*

EPILOGUE

✦

Six months later . . .

This is Patricia Rawlings reporting live from outside the Palace of Westminster. . . ."

The little-known American journalist had finally landed a scoop big enough to justify her being put on live camera before the nation. A cold winter drizzle stung her cheeks but could not dampen her spirits as she looked into the camera and began her report.

These were the most talked-about stories to break since Luddington's reporting of the Queen's abdication. And the fact that Rawlings herself had been instrumental in Scotland Yard's finally solving the two related cases meant that Pilkington had had little choice.

Suddenly the young woman who had awkwardly put her foot in her mouth at this same spot before her reportorial colleagues was, for a few days at least, the most famous journalist in London. Her daring sleuthing in both the matter of the Stone of Scone and the solving of a murder had made of her, if not exactly a hero, then certainly a newswoman who would have plenty of offers on the table by next week had her BBC producer not given her the air time she wanted. She was already being talked about as potentially the next Jill Dando.

All at once Rawlings' American accent had become a trump card rather than a liability.

So here Paddy was—while Luddington cooled his heels in the crowd—her heart pounding in fear lest some Yankee blooper pop out of her mouth, and doing her best to look calm and collected as she conveyed details to a listening world.

"After secret machinations behind these very walls," Paddy continued, "involving Liberal Democratic leader Andrew Trentham and parliamentary colleagues from several parties—"

As she spoke, Paddy could not prevent a momentary glance toward Andrew, where he stood among the crowd of notables present.

"—late yesterday afternoon, investigators at last broke wide open the case involving last year's murder of the Honorable Eagon Hamilton. As suspected, the murder was connected with the theft of the fabled Stone of Destiny, which was recovered early last summer from the Celtic Druidic Center in County Carlow, Ireland, and is now once again safely in the Crown Room of Edinburgh Castle."

Paddy drew in a steadying breath, gradually feeling more comfortable as the cameras rolled.

"All the United Kingdom," she went on, "indeed, the entire world, is now waiting to see how these events, and Mr. Trentham's involvement in them, will affect the growing debate over the future of Scotland. No statement from Mr. Trentham has yet been released, but sources close to the Cumbrian MP suggest that a momentous announcement may be forthcoming within a few days."

Another look followed in Andrew's direction. This time Paddy could not prevent the edges of her lips from curling in the hint of a smile at the veiled reference to herself in her own report. Andrew smiled, then chuckled lightly at her words, as most of the cameras broke from the reporter's to his face.

After a moment, Paddy continued.

"We will update you with more details as they become available," she said. "According to Scotland Yard spokesman Jack Hensley, three arrests have been made thus far, and more are expected. Scotland Yard will issue a full report within forty-eight hours, Hensley said. The House of Commons, shaken as it is by the implication of its own in these events, must now prepare for debate on what may prove to be one of its most historic decisions in centuries. . . ."

The epic drama of Scotland's land and people, Andrew Trentham's personal quest for roots, and the Scots' struggle for independence, will continue in book two of the Caledonia series. Watch for announcements of title and release date from your local bookstore, or check Bethany House Publishers' web page—www.bethanyhouse.com.

Early Ancestry of Andrew Gordon Trentham

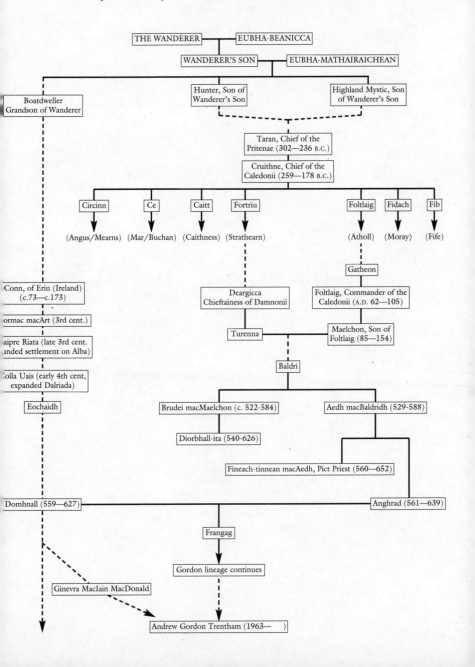

The British Parliamentary System,
Scottish Home Rule, and Devolution:
A Short Course for American Readers

The parliamentary system of government as practiced in the United Kingdom can be mysterious and baffling to those who have not grown up familiar with it. This *extremely* brief and simplified outline of a few basics related to issues in the story is merely intended to make *Caledonia* easier to understand for American readers, without attempting to provide a comprehensive explanation of the system.

Most of the significant legislative business of Parliament is conducted through the lower branch, the House of Commons, which at the time of this writing is comprised of 659 elected members of Parliament, or MPs. For centuries, membership in the upper House of Lords has been primarily hereditary—although moves were afoot at the end of the twentieth century to change this policy. In addition to the hereditary seats, Lords includes "life peers" appointed specifically for their lifetime. The role of the House of Lords is generally consultative, as is that of the monarchy (King or Queen.)

The role given to the party who holds a majority of seats in the House of Commons is far more significant in parliamentary affairs than is the case in the American system. In Washington, when a given bill comes before Congress for a vote, representatives and senators of both parties vote as they are inclined. Accordingly, bills either pass or are defeated no matter which party initiated the legislation or which party holds the majority of seats. Both parties are free to draw up bills and present them to Congress. Though the majority party certainly has a distinct advantage in the passage of its legislative program, the passage of its bills is not automatic. And once a bill *is* passed by Congress, the president may veto it, even in the face of a Congressional approval. The president is neither part of nor answerable to Congress. The distinct terms of office in the House of Representatives, the Senate, and the presidency (two, six, and four years respectively) underscore the independence in which they all stand with respect to one another.

The United Kingdom's legislative system is entirely different. Whereas in the United States the House, the Senate, and the president all contribute a substantially equal voice in the passage of legislation, in the UK *all* power toward that end essentially proceeds out of the House of Commons. Neither the House of Lords, the King or Queen, or the minority parties have any determinative power of influence.

The primiership is not a separate nonparliamentary office like the United States presidency, but is occupied by the highest-ranking MP in the Commons. He or she is not elected by the people *as* prime minister but as a member of Parliament from a certain constituency, along with all the other MPs. Each party votes within its membership for its own leadership, and the leader of the majority party thus becomes prime minister. Party leadership and even the office of prime minister may change *without* a general public election.

The majority party (in *Caledonia* the Labour party, or the Socialists, led by Prime Minister Richard Barraclough) is referred to as the *government.* The largest minority party (in *Caledonia* the Conservatives, or the Tories, led by Miles Ramsey) is called the *opposition.* As a point of historical interest, the centuries-old party known as the *Whigs* became the Liberal Party in 1828, shortly before the Tories became known as the Conservative Party. The Labour Party was formed in 1892 and formed its first (coalition) government in 1924. The Liberal Party held power in Britain for long periods late in the nineteenth and early years of the twentieth century, until a split in 1931. A merger between the Liberals and the Social Democratic Party in 1988 led to the title Social and Liberal Democrats. At present they are simply known as Liberal Democrats, or LibDems.

Perhaps the greatest difference between the two systems for the purposes of the story of *Caledonia* concerns the way legislation is passed.

In the House of Commons, the legislative agenda is *entirely* determined by the majority party. *Only* the majority party may introduce legislation. Thus, because voting is usually carried out *en bloc* rather than individually, passage of this legislation is virtually automatic. The minority parties occupy a role chiefly limited to adversarial debate—attempting to sway public opinion and sow seeds, both of discontent with the government's policies and support for its own, that may be harvested during the next general election—but without much actual power, insofar as daily affairs are concerned, on the floor of the House of Commons itself.

The legislative agenda of the majority party is generally determined in advance. The prime minister gathers his or her cabinet and party leaders toward the end of each summer's recess and into early fall in order to plan their legislative strategy for the following parliamentary session. This strategy is coalesced into a specific agenda, which is then given to the monarch.

Parliament is officially opened in late October or early November by the King or Queen, who reads a speech outlining what his or her "government" (the party in power) will seek to accomplish in the following session, as prescribed by the prime minister. The Commons "sits" for about 160 days a year, a period broken into various periods and lasting from the monarch's speech until late July or early August. The points of a given year's agenda, as given in the monarch's speech, thus provide the legislative program that, in the term that follows, the majority party will proceed to carry out, bringing bills before Parliament and passing them into law.

When one party holds more than fifty percent of the total number of MPs in the House of Commons, the task of passing its agenda is relatively straightforward. If such is not the case, however, a "minority" or "coalition government" must be formed. This involves creating a coalition of two or more parties to form an absolute majority, the prime minister being the leader of the largest of these. In such a case, the coalition must be held together at every vote, or else the government falls.

In the British parliamentary system, the ruling party or coalition and the prime minister as its leader *must* remain capable of passing its predetermined legislation. This is one of the significant differences between the American and British systems. In the United Kingdom, bills *must* pass.

If the opposition calls for a vote on a given bill and manages to defeat it (because of defection within the government or within one of the coalition parties), the prime minister's party loses the power and therefore the right to rule. The government is dissolved and elections are announced, to be held within thirty days. MPs return to their constituencies to campaign, the former prime minister included. Opponents from other parties may then enter these parliamentary races against them.

The significance of these elections lies in the total number of MPs seated by each party. Whichever party gains the majority of elected MPs from all the constituencies in the United Kingdom (based, as in the U.S. House of Representatives, on geographic distribution of population, with each member representing 60,000 or 70,000 voters) is formally invited by the monarch to "form a government." That winning party—which may be the same party that was in power before or a different one altogether—must then seek to establish a majority that will be capable of ruling and passing its legislation. This may entail a change in the majority party or require a coalition realignment, and may result in a new prime minister or a shift in the numerical configuration of the parties in Parliament—any or all of which may resolve whatever conflict prevented the pre-election government from being able to pass the bill and which forced the election.

A coalition government (as is the fictional case in this book) *may* be able to rule effectively. If such is not the case, the prime minister may choose to call for new elections if he or she thinks it likely that another vote will increase his party's plurality to a majority. Elections held in February of 1974 resulted in a Labour plurality of 301 seats, short of an outright majority in the 635-seat House of Commons. Labour was unable to form a coalition government from amongst the smaller parties and thus called for *new* elections in October of that same year. The second election supplied Labour with eighteen additional seats, bringing their total numbers to 319 and giving Labour an absolute majority. Labour was then able to rule for the entire five-year term.

A bill comes up for formal "reading" three times on the floor of the Commons. Since passage is a foregone conclusion in most cases, bills are only "voted" upon (after the second reading and debate) when called for by the opposition. A vote is called a *division*. When one is called, all members of Parliament rise and "divide," exiting the Commons chamber into the lobby through one of two doors. Exiting through the door on the prime minister's side of the aisle to his right (where the prime minister and government are seated, the prime minister and cabinet on the front bench and the rest of the majority party on the back benches behind them) signifies an *aye* vote. Exiting through the door on the opposition side (where the opposition leaders and shadow cabinet occupy the front bench) signifies a *no*.

A division usually takes about ten minutes, and there are on average one or two divisions daily. It is rare for an MP to cross the aisle and divide with the opposition. When this does occur, it may signal that a prime minister is losing the support of his own party and that his majority may be in danger.

Nationwide elections are held at least every five years, at a specific date chosen by the prime minister. He or she *must* call for an election at least every five years, which is the official elected "term" for MPs, though the prime minister *may* do so sooner, as explained above, if to do so suits his or her purpose.

The sitting prime minister may call for new elections (called "going to the country") at *any* time, even if a bill has not been defeated or if the five years have not yet elapsed. He or she may do so for various reasons. For instance, the mood of the country may have become even *more* supportive of the prime minister's party's objectives and priorities since the previous election. If going to the country for new elections will return his or her party an even *greater* majority and enable the government to rule all the more easily without opposition, the prime minister may call for elections.

On the other hand, the prime minister may feel that support for his party is slipping. To wait another two or three years for the next scheduled election could mean serious defeat and loss of power, while an election now might enable him to retain power for an additional five years. For this very different reason, therefore, the prime minister may choose to dissolve Parliament and call for new elections.

Prior to elections (however precipitated) each party must announce to the public a five-year *Manifesto*, or legislative program. These Manifestos, which are published in the first week of a campaign, set forth the priorities and policies of each party and form the basis of the legislation which the victorious party will later attempt to pass.

Manifestos resemble the "Contract with America" set forth by the Republican Party prior to the 1994 U.S. Congressional elections. Unlike traditional American party "platforms," which have always meant little or nothing, the prepublished manifestos in the United Kingdom largely determine the legislative agenda of the party that wins the elections and then establishes a government. Elections in Great Britain, therefore, can be more reflective of public sentiment than those in the United States, where image and money often weigh more heavily than specific political persuasion.

The prime minister and his cabinet, in the years following an election, will prioritize the issues, setting certain items for passage during each parliamentary session. These then form the substance of the party's agenda, which is given to the monarch and forms the basis of his or her speech at the opening of Parliament.

To be passed into law, therefore, any bill or issue or cause (such as devolution and Scottish independence) must go through a number of important stages, each taking it one step closer to actual debate on the Commons floor. It must first be included as a Manifesto item of the majority party prior to a general election. Then it must be brought to the front burner, so to speak, by being included in the monarch's speech for the present-session's legislative agenda.

Yet this is only the beginning. For then the prime minister must actually bring the issue before the House of Commons for reading, debate, and passage. The setting of the specific legislative schedule is entirely determined by the prime minister. At any of these junctures, he or she may opt to let the matter lay dormant and not actively pursue its passage. All bills not completed during a given session of Parliament lapse. Unless they are reintroduced as part of the agenda for the next session, they will be abandoned.

The issue of Scottish nationalism and the political push for home rule, as related in *Caledonia*, is one that regularly surfaces in the parliamentary debates of the United Kingdom. It has been an issue in British politics for centuries. There are at present three specifically Scottish parties, each reflecting differing views with respect to Scotland's future: the Scottish Conservative and Unionist Party, Scottish Liberal Democratic Party, and the Scottish National Party.

For many years after its union with England (The Act of Union, 1707) and the dissolution of Scotland's parliament, there was little or no discussion of Scottish independence. But thoughts of the ancient kingdom began gradually again to resurface. In 1853 was founded a National Association for the Vindication of Scottish Rights. In 1884 the Scottish Grand Committee was set up to consider Scottish bills, and two years later the Scottish Home Rule Association was established.

During the rule of Liberal governments in the early years of the twentieth century, frequent "government of Scotland" bills were put before Parliament. A new Home Rule Association was formed in 1917. When the Labour party rose to prominence, it gave lip service to the idea of home rule for Scotland but did nothing about its promises once it was in office.

A steady number of home rule bills were introduced through the 1920s, though without any chance of any becoming law. No others appeared thereafter until 1966. The Liberal Party was the only party to show significant interest in the Scottish home rule question, yet its influence in parliamentary affairs dwindled as the century progressed to near negligibility.

The National Party of Scotland was formed in 1928, advocating complete separation from the United Kingdom. A more moderate Scottish Party was founded in 1932. Neither made much of a showing in the general elections, however, and in 1934 they joined and became the Scottish National Party, or SNP, which has existed until the present day.

The SNP had little national impact until 1959, when it garnered over 21,000 votes, though without seating any MPs in the House of Commons. Sentiment grew quickly over the fifteen years that followed. The vote total in general elections mounted rapidly, reaching an astonishing peak, in the second election of 1974, of 839,617 total votes. That election sent eleven Scottish Nationalists to the House of Commons. SNP support dropped in the two general elections following 1974, but this downward trend proved temporary, gradually reversing itself over the course of the next three elections.

Support for the cause of Scottish nationalism has continued to rise since then as the world in general has witnessed a downward shift of power, or "devolution," from centralized and/or imperial governments toward regional administrations. Prime Minister John Major's return of the Stone of Scone to Edinburgh in 1996, on the seven hundredth anniversary of its removal to England, reflected this national shift of sentiment, as did the Devolution Referendum of 1997, which indicated a high level of popular support for local rule in Northern Ireland, Wales, and Scotland. Seventy-four percent of those Scots who turned out for the referendum voted in favor of devolution and the establishment of a Scottish parliament.

In accordance with the clear direction of public thought, Prime Minister Tony Blair's Labour government, elected in 1997, initiated a process of devolution that resulted in elected assemblies for Northern Ireland and Wales and an elected parliament for Scotland. These regional governing bodies have legislative power over all "devolved matters," though Scotland, Wales, and Northern Ireland continue to seat MPs in the national Parliament in Westminster. As this book went to press, however, the specifics of jurisdiction and representation between these various legislative bodies were still being hotly debated.

The first elections for the ministers in the new Scottish parliament took place in May of 1999. In general the new parliament is expected to have power in the areas of health, education, economic development, environment, law, and local government.

There are some, however, notably in Scotland, who are far from satisfied with devolution and who continue to call for full independence from the United Kingdom. Whether their voice will grow—and whether their nationalistic cause eventually comes to represent a majority of Scots—remains for history to determine.

Political Allignment in the Lower House of the British Parliament Following General Election (Fictional)

			Party Leader
Labour (Socialist) Party	285	Members of Parliament	Richard Barraclough
Conservative Party (Tories)	277	"	Miles Ramsey
Liberal Democrats (Lib Dem)	51	"	Eagon Hamilton/Andrew Trentham
Scottish Nationalist Party (SNP)	21	"	Dugald MacKinnon
Miscellaneous MPs and Speaker	25	"	Various
Total MPs in House of Commons	659	(Needed for Coalition and Majority Vote—330)	

Party Breakdown of MPs in House of Commons Since 1974

	1974 (Feb)	1974 (Oct)	1979	1983	1987	1992	1997	(Fictional)
Labour	301	319	268	209	229	270	418	285
Conservative	296	276	339	397	375	336	165	277
Liberal Democrat	—	—	—	—	—	20	46	51
Liberal	14	13	11	17	17	—	—	—
Scottish Nationalist	7	11	2	2	3	3	6	21
Social Democrat	1	—	—	6	5	—	—	—
Plaid Cymru	2	3	2	2	3	4	4	4
Democrat Unionist	—	—	3	3	3	3	2	2
SDLP	1	1	1	1	3	4	3	3
Sinn Fein	—	—	—	1	1	—	2	2
Ulster Popular Unionist	—	—	—	1	1	1	—	1
Ulster Unionist	11	10	6	10	9	9	10	10
UK Unionist	—	—	—	—	—	—	1	1
Independent	1	1	2	—	—	—	1	1
The Speaker	1	1	1	1	1	1	1	1
	635	635	635	650	650	651	659	659

It will be clear that Andrew Trentham's story, and Caledonia's, has only begun.

Though it has many of its own rewards, one of the frustrations with what is called "series fiction" is that those who read a particular book immediately or soon after its release are required to wait an interim period for the publication of whatever volume is to follow. The simple fact of the matter is that books take much longer to research and write, then to produce and publish, than they do to read. I began this present project ten years ago, and it is just now hitting the bookshelves.

The paradox of this frustration is that the *more* one enjoys a book, the more eager he or she is to continue and thus the *less* patient he or she is likely to be during this time lapse between volumes. I do hope you have enjoyed *Legend of the Celtic Stone*. At the same time I hope you will patiently await its continuation and will enjoy it no less as a result of the inevitable delay between "episodes." I do not anticipate a hiatus of ten years between books one and two in this series! You may be relieved to know that volume two is already well on its way to completion, and that many of the questions you probably have about "what happened about such-and-such!" have already been answered. In the meantime, a few notes concerning this present volume may be in order.

The further back in time one attempts to gaze, the more blurry becomes the line between fact and fiction, legend and history.

Historians typically try to eliminate the fuzz by adhering to facts, while novelists allow the blurry line to widen in order to feel the "story" to which their interpretation of the facts points.

Legend of the Celtic Stone is fiction. It thus should not be read as historical text, but as a story. Subject to the limitations of this genre of work, the history is accurate enough. But there *are* limitations when past events are imaginatively interpreted. Flexibility is necessary. Historical fiction is just that—fiction, an interpretive representation of what *may* have happened, woven through fictionalized events.

Having said that, however, for the layman I am attempting to tell something of a complete though abbreviated history of Scotland through fictional events. My training and study is more as historian than novelist, and I love history for history's sake. The original versions of the manuscript contained probably four times as much "pure history" as this final edition you have read! If my historian-self had its way, this book would be a thousand pages long!

The following comments and explanations may be helpful to those of you who are interested in knowing more specifically where that blurry line between story and history, fact and fiction, exists.

The Highland background of the Stone of Scone, which will continue in the next volume, is entirely fictional, though Irish stories and other legends surrounding its origin have circulated through the centuries as I have recounted them.

Andrew Trentham is fictional, as are all contemporary characters, political and otherwise. But if you haven't realized it by now, all these ancients whose stories are told are also Andrew's ancestors. It is his lineage we are tracing. This genealogy will continue in subsequent volumes, eventually establishing an unbroken line from the Wanderer to the present—a lineage reminiscent of that given in Matthew 1, with many offshoots, a lineage which tells in itself the colorful saga of Caledonia's history.

The story of the Jews recounted in the Bible, in many respects, parallels the history of mankind in general and bears similarities to the story of other races and countries. The Jewish account is unique, of course, in that it has been preserved, and in the fact that it bears God's divine hand upon it. It is my belief that the Hebrews were a people "chosen" to portray the human saga, and the Bible was supernaturally inspired to tell that drama. Yet in another way, the Hebrew story can be seen as a *type* of the stories of all peoples and races.

The saga of Caledonia, in the manner in which I am attempting to tell it, I view as the Celtic branch on that same tree which began with Genesis. It offers a tale told in Celtic lore to parallel the Hebrew story—with its own legends, prophecies, poetry, warfare, romance, treachery, and so on.

Thus can the volumes of this series be seen as a parable, so to speak, outlining not the lineage of him who would be the Savior of men, but the lineage of him who will become the savior of Caledonia's nationhood. But I get ahead of myself!

Ginevra and Brochan of Glencoe are fictional, though most of the other characters in their story, as well as the grisly facts of the Glencoe account, sad to say, are factually accurate.

The Wanderer and his son and grandsons are, of course, entirely my own creation.

Legends point to ancient tribesmen by the names of Cruithne, Fidach, and Foltlaig, though no details are known of their lives. An ancient Pict king by the name of Cruithne is mentioned. His sons are associated with Scotland's seven regions as their original "seven earls."

The ancient Picts provide a fascinating historical study that has intrigued and bewildered historians and archaeologists for centuries. Though they left no written language nor records, their artistic carved "standing stones" (of which there are more than two hundred examples *still* standing and visible) and "drystone" brochs and forts and home sites and tombs (of which there are numerous examples still in good repair throughout Scotland) tell of a rich and accomplished prehistoric culture. The stones of these Pictish constructions are remarkably well preserved, and the interested individual will find it fascinating to visit these two-thousand-year-old monuments. The many place names in Scotland beginning with the prefix *pit-* are contemporary reminders of this *Pict* heritage.

Known and documented history begins in Britain with the Roman occupation, for the simple reason that Cornelius Tacitus, one of Rome's greatest historians and most prolific writers, published various accounts of Roman policy in the first century, including a detailed account of Gnaeus Julius Agricola's travels in the north. Agricola also happened to be Tacitus' father-in-law, which added to the latter's motivation to document Rome's efforts in such a remote outpost of its empire. It was the Romans who first encountered the Celtic Picts (the painted or tattooed warriors whom they named accordingly) and other tribes, all of whom they considered a single ethnic group. They called them Caledonians and gave the region north of Hadrian's Wall the name *Caledonia*.

Galgacus was the name given by the Romans to the great Pict leader, whom I have called Gaelbhan, who led his people against the Romans in A.D. 84. That portion of his speech on the eve of the battle at Mons Graupius, whether factual or not, *is* reported in the Annals of Imperial Rome much as I have given it in chapter 9.

Roman forts in southern Scotland *were* indeed burned some time after A.D. 105 by, it is thought, a united effort of Pict tribes. Few details, however, are known.

The life of Columba is surrounded by as much uncertainty as it is legend and mystery, though the facts of his biography included herein are accurate. Nearly all the events here recounted in fictional form have at least some factual basis in Adamnan's *Life of Saint Columba*, written about a hundred years after Columba's death by one of his succeeding abbots at Iona. Adamnan's hagiographic account of the miracles that flowed from Columba's hand is almost wholly sentimental, distorted, and idealized. Yet from it and other contemporary sources, historians have pieced together a fragmentary biography of the saint's later life.

Columba's early life and background in Ireland is well documented. He sailed to Iona in A.D. 563. The verses quoted en route I have adapted from an Irish manuscript in the Burgundian Library in Brussels, attributed to Columba's hand and entitled "Columcille fecit." Within a year or two of his landing, Columba journeyed to the heart of the northern Pict empire to meet King Brudei macMaelchon. The encounter with Broichan the druid priest outside the king's residence was recorded sketchily by Adamnan, as was the incident of the white stone and the other miraculous manifestations. I have fictionalized my accounts using Adamnan's miraculous legends as framework for the story.

Brudei, king of the Picts, and the druid Broichan are historical characters, and Columba's interactions with them are reported to have actually occurred as I have recounted them, including the events of Columba's first day in Inbhir-Nis. Diorbhall-ita is entirely fictional. Aedh and his son Fintenn were indeed factual Pict individuals, though unrelated to the king. Both were converted to Christianity. The healing of Fintenn macAedh is recorded, as is the boy's eventual founding of the monastery at Kailli-an-Inde, whose location remains unknown.

The events of the day of Columba's death—recorded by Adamnan in detail—are, though I have translated them into fictional format, as historically accurate in their germinal form as is possible to ascertain. I have, of course, placed Diorbhall-ita into those events, in some cases occupying the role said to belong to Columba's servant Diormait. The occasionally ornate and perhaps overly dramatic style I employed in recounting some of the events of Columba's life results from my attempt to retain a little of the hagiographic (pertaining to idealized, worshipful renditions of the lives of the saints) feel of the original accounts upon which all we know of Columba's life is based.

Of the ensuing "conversion" of the Picts, little is known. Subsequent to Columba's visit to the king at Inverness, it is clear that Christian monasteries began springing up rapidly throughout Caledonia, which became "Christianized" within a relatively short time. Whatever may *not* be known, Columba's influence was certainly enormous, and it altered the direction of the history of the British Isles.

Domhnall, Fintenn's brother-in-law, is entirely fictional. His Irish ancestry, however, and the later names you will encounter as this line continues in Scotland *after* Domhnall, is configured entirely from historical individuals who form the roots of the Clan Donald, springing from Donald, grandson of Somerled, Lord of the Isles. Even the "purest" of Scots—if there is such a thing!—by tracing their descent back far enough, would find the intermingled blood of dozens of clans. Thus, we find Andrew Trentham's line infused with MacDonald and Gordon ancestry, combining Pict *and* Scot heritage, and later, as we shall see, with Norse and Norman blood.

The Gaelic verses in chapter 5 are from the poem *The Path of the Old Spells* by Donald Sinclair, those sung by Domnall in chapter 7 are two verses of the song "The Misty Dell" (*Coire-Cheathaich*), taken from *The Minstrelsy of the Scottish Highlands* (Arr. Alfred Moffat).

The druidic chant in the last chapter is adapted from a poetical incantation for the new Ireland attributed to Amairgen, the first druid of the Gaels in Ireland, whose name was taken by the fictional character of this story, Cooney Dwyer.

Most of the specific research for *Legend of the Celtic Stone*, besides what formal education in history is included in my biography, comes from travel and from books.

The first of these is difficult to chronicle. I have been to Scotland several times, most recently just months prior to publication. Much of *Legend of the Celtic Stone* was written in Scotland, Cumbria, and London, where I walked the streets, parks, and hillsides, so to speak, along with Andrew Trentham, asking myself the same questions he would ask about the land of his ancestry. I think I have been to nearly every place written about in the book—from Regent's Park to the slopes of the Skiddaw, from Iona to Glencoe. Such travels do not necessarily guarantee accuracy, but I hope it will give these pages a sense of authenticity.

Andrew Trentham's fictional home, Derwenthwaite Hall, is modeled after Armathwaite Hall, now a hotel in Cumbria, where I had a pleasant stay and where portions of Andrew's story were written. For fictional purposes, a few place names of the region have been slightly altered.

Caledonia, I have found, is truly a land which gets "into" you. Feelings, thoughts, chance conversations, impressions, long walks, landscapes, weather, and a host of seemingly insignificant situations and events all combine in a mysterious way as the mystique of Scotland penetrates into one's emotional marrow. Such "emotional research" is as intrinsic to the writing of any book as are the facts one uncovers and the literature one sifts through.

The second method of inquiry I will attempt to document as best I can by noting the following books that have been extremely helpful.

The Complete Book of London. Basingstoke, UK: AA, 1992

Parliament. London: Her Majesty's Stationery Office, 1991.

Parliamentary Elections. London: Her Majesty's Stationery Office, 1991.

The Complete Book of London. Basingstoke, UK: AA, 1992.

Westminster Abbey. Norwich: Jarrold Colour Publications, 1987.

Whitaker's Almanack, 1999. London: The Stationery Office, Ltd., 1999.

Adam, James. *Gaelic Wordbook*. Edinburgh: Chambers, 1992.

Adamnan. *The Life of Saint Columba*, written circa A.D. 700, translated by William Reeves, 1856. Dyfed: Llanerch Enterprises, 1988.

Barke, James, ed. *Poems and Songs of Robert Burns*. London: Fontana/Collins, London, 1955.

Bede. *A History of the English Church and People*, written A.D. 731, translated by Leo Sherley-Price, 1955. New York: Dorset Press, 1985.

Bidwell, Paul. *Roman Forts in Britain*. London: B.T. Batsford, Ltd., 1997.

Breeze, David and Graeme Munro. *The Stone of Destiny*. Historic Scotland, 1997.

Carruth, J.A. *Scotland the Brave*. Norwich: Jarrold & Sons, 1973.

Chadwick, Nora. *The Celts*. London: Penguin, 1971.

Crowl, Philip. *The Intelligent Traveller's Guide to Historic Scotland*. New York: Congdon & Weed, 1986.

Delaney, Frank. *The Celts*. Glasgow: HarperCollins, 1986.

Dickinson, William Croft. *Scotland from the Earliest Times to 1603*. Edinburgh: Thomas Nelson & Sons, Ltd., 1961.

Dunbar, John. *Iona*. Edinburgh: Her Majesty's Stationery Office.

Duncan, A.A.M. *Scotland: The Making of the Kingdom*. Edinburgh: Oliver & Boyd, 1975.

Ellis, Peter Berresford. *The Druids*. Grand Rapids, Michigan: Wm. B. Eerdmans, 1994.

Embleton, Ronald and Frank Graham. *Hadrian's Wall in the Days of the*

Romans. Newcastle upon Tyne: Frank Graham, 1984.

Fell, Bryan H. and K.R. Mackenzie. *The Houses of Parliament.* London: Her Majesty's Stationery Office, 1994.

Ferguson, William. *Scotland, 1689 to the Present.* Edinburgh: Oliver & Boyd, 1968.

Finlay, Ian. *Columba.* Edinburgh: W & R Chambers, Ltd., 1979.

Fisher, Andrew. *A Traveller's History of Scotland.* Gloucestershire, UK: Windrush Press, 1990.

Jackson, Anthony. *The Pictish Trail.* Orkney, Scotland: Orkney Press, 1989.

MacDonald, Donald J. of Castletone. *Clan Donald.* Loanhead, Scotland: MacDonald Publishers, 1978.

MacDonald, Micheil. *Scots Kith & Kin.* Glasgow: HarperCollins, 1953.

Maceachen, Evan. *Gaelic/English Dictionary,* reprint of 1842 edition. Inverness, Scotland: Highland Printers, 1970.

MacGowan, Douglas. "Stealing the Stone." *The Highlander.* Vol. 34, no. 2 (March/April 1996).

Mackechnie, John. *Gaelic Without Groans.* Edinburgh: Oliver & Boyd, 1934.

MacKintosh, John. *Scotland, from the Earliest Times to the Present Century,* first published 1890. Freeport, New York: Books for Libraries Press, 1972.

Maclean, Fitzroy. *A Concise History of Scotland.* London: Thames and Hudson, 1970.

Piggott, Stuart. *The Prehistoric Peoples of Scotland.* London: Routledge & Kegan Paul, 1962.

Prebble, John. *Glencoe.* Martin Secker & Warburg, Ltd., 1966.

Ritchie, Anna. *Picts.* Edinburgh: Her Majesty's Stationery Office, 1989.

Ritchie, Anna and David Breeze. *Invaders of Scotland.* Edinburgh: Her Majesty's Stationery Office.

———. *Scotland BC.* Edinburgh: Scottish Development Department, 1988.

Smout, T.C. *A History of the Scottish People 1560–1830.* London: William Collins and Sons, 1969.

Wainwright, F.T. *The Problem of the Picts.* Westport, Connecticut: Greenwood Press, 1954.

Several of the above authors require singular recognition.

First, Dr. Archie Duncan of the University of Glasgow, for his definitive work on Scotland's early centuries, which I used almost daily in the early stages of my work as my baseline historical reference point. This is not to say that I have not, as any novelist must, in places been fluid and "interpretive" in the manner in which I have written of events. Any inaccuracies I may have committed in the process are certainly my own, not Dr. Duncan's. But wherever possible I have used the archaeological and historical evidence he so thoroughly presents as my jumping-off point. I also am appreciative of Dr. Duncan's review of the manuscript.

Secondly, I would laud Ian Finlay for his magnificent interpretive study of Saint Columba which is noted above. Archie Duncan comments, "There is now a huge literature on Columba. . . . [Much of] it has abandoned the 'gentle dove' picture presented by Adamnan for something much fiercer— a prince of an Irish kindred who left Ireland for reasons of feud." In striking a balance between these two interpretations, I found Mr. Finlay helpful and, to my view, on the mark with so much of his insight into the Celtic world of the fifth, sixth, and seventh centuries that I almost felt compelled to footnote sections of the narrative where I found my thinking influenced by his insights, especially with regard to the intermingling influence of Celtic myth into the Christian mission of the sixth century. *Legend of the Celtic Stone* is fiction, however, not a scholarly paper, and thus this brief tribute to his groundbreaking work will have to suffice to acknowledge my debt. Those who wish to study Saint Columba's life in more detail will not do better than Mr. Finlay's excellent study.

My thanks likewise go to William Croft Dickinson for his extremely thorough, authoritative, and well-documented history of early Scotland, referenced above, about which I would make the same comments as I did earlier of Dr. Duncan.

Finally, I am indebted to John Prebble, author of many wonderfully readable history books, whose definitive work *Glencoe* was extremely helpful and gave me such an emotive sense of the "people behind the story" of those terrible events. Mr. Prebble writes with a feel for the wonderful "story" of history. His accounts are zestful and alive—the most interesting history you will find anywhere. As with the other writers mentioned, I found myself wanting to footnote Mr. Prebble's work on every page, but will have to satisfy myself with this acknowledgment. His work, too, I heartily commend to you.

In all these instances, I would not want my efforts in any way to detract from these men's more original nonfiction efforts, and I would strongly encourage readers to seek out these works for themselves.

Thank you, each one!

Books by Michael Phillips

Best Friends for Life (with Judy Phillips)
The Garden at the Edge of Beyond
George MacDonald: Scotland's Beloved Storyteller
A God to Call Father†
Good Things to Remember
Robbie Taggart: Highland Sailor*
A Rift In Time†

CALEDONIA

Legend of the Celtic Stone

THE JOURNALS OF CORRIE BELLE HOLLISTER

My Father's World*
Daughter of Grace*
On the Trail of the Truth
A Place in the Sun
Sea to Shining Sea

Into the Long Dark Night
Land of the Brave and the Free
A Home for the Heart
The Braxtons of Miracle Springs
A New Beginning

Grayfox (Zack's story)

MERCY AND EAGLEFLIGHT†

Mercy and Eagleflight

A Dangerous Love

THE RUSSIANS*

The Crown and the Crucible
A House Divided

Travail and Triumph

THE SECRET OF THE ROSE†

The Eleventh Hour
A Rose Remembered

Escape to Freedom
Dawn of Liberty

THE SECRETS OF HEATHERSLEIGH HALL

Wild Grows the Heather in Devon *Heathersleigh Homecoming*
Wayward Winds

THE STONEWYCKE TRILOGY* and LEGACY*

The Heather Hills of Stonewycke
Flight From Stonewycke
Lady of Stonewycke

Stranger at Stonewycke
Shadows Over Stonewycke
Treasure of Stonewycke

*with Judith Pella   †Tyndale House

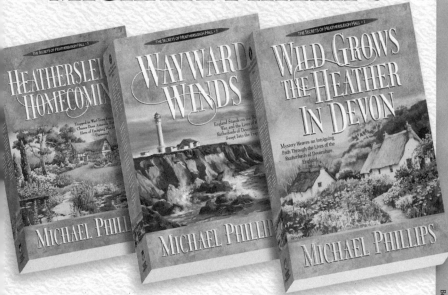